Business Ethics

Corporate Values and Society

Business Ethics
Corporate Values and Society

edited by
Milton Snoeyenbos
Robert Almeder
James Humber

 **Prometheus Books**

700 East Amherst St. Buffalo, New York 14215

Published 1983 by Prometheus Books
700 East Amherst Street, Buffalo, New York 14215

Library of Congress Card Number: 83-60252
ISBN: 0-87975-207-6

Printed in the United States of America

Contents

6. ETHICS AND THE ACCOUNTING PROFESSION

9. MULTINATIONAL CORPORATIONS

Preface

Many of the job related decisions corporate employees must make are moral in nature. Recognizing this fact, most institutions of higher learning now offer business ethics courses in an attempt to provide students with the tools necessary to make such decisions. As business ethics courses have proliferated, the number of texts designed for teaching such courses has increased as well. Unfortunately, however, many of these texts are flawed in one of two ways: (1) those that address issues of interest to business students are generally not philosophically sophisticated, and (2) philosophically sophisticated texts are often *too* sophisticated, concentrating on issues that appeal to philosophers rather than business students.

In designing this book a conscious attempt has been made to avoid both of these extremes. We began with the intuition that business ethics courses should be designed primarily for business students, and should therefore address the issues faced by businessmen and women in their professional lives. Furthermore, we felt that only "essential" elements of ethical theory need be considered; lengthy discourses on distributive justice, Kant's categorical imperative, metaethics, and similar topics would only bore students and leave them with the impression that moral philosophy is unintelligible to all but a few "eggheads," and totally irrelevant to "real life."

To achieve our goals we worked closely with the College of Business at Georgia State University in an effort to identify moral issues relevant to businessmen and women. We have taught a number of business ethics courses to students enrolled in the school of business, and, in the process, a wide variety of teaching materials have been evaluated. Sometimes the extant literature did not fill our needs; and where we found this to be the case we wrote essays ourselves or commissioned others to write them. All the essays included in this text have been chosen for their intelligibility and their potential to encourage classroom discussion. The essays are not intended to *solve* moral problems. Rather, they raise moral issues, and propose "bold hypotheses" which invite further discussion.

11

Business students who work through this text will learn some of the essentials of ethical theory, and will acquire the basic tools needed to deal with the types of moral problems they will face during their professional lives. On the other hand, philosophy students will learn a great deal about the business world and the problems confronting corporate employees. Both philosophy and business have much to gain by a closer alliance; and if that alliance is strengthened in any way by our text we will count it a success.

We wish to thank the faculty of the College of Business at Georgia State University for their advice and assistance in this project. Special thanks must also go to our wives, Peg Snoeyenbos, Virginia Almeder, and Helene Humber, whose patience and understanding make our work considerably easier than it might otherwise be.

It was our pleasure and good fortune to work with a highly skilled editor, Mr. Steven L. Mitchell of Prometheus Books. He brought not only diligence and editorial ability to his task, but philosophical acumen as well.

Milton Snoeyenbos
Robert Almeder
James Humber

Georgia State University

1

INTRODUCTION

This collection of essays is about ethical issues that arise within the context of business practices. As such, it does not describe actual business practices; its primary concern is not with detailing how businesspersons actually finance an enterprise, market products, or handle labor negotiations. Instead, its focus is on such issues as whether businesspersons should give preferential treatment to disadvantaged individuals, whether managers have moral and social obligations other than maximizing profits for their firm's shareholders, whether investment in South Africa is morally justifiable, and whether some advertising is deceptive or creates false wants and therefore should be restricted or banned. All of us have opinions on these issues, and the readings in this volume contain contrasting points of view; but in order to understand fully such controversies and to resolve them rationally some acquaintance with ethical theory is required. This introduction presents some of the fundamentals of ethical theory; it provides a framework for informed discussion of the specific ethical issues taken up in the rest of the book.

Ethics is a discipline involving inquiry into the moral judgments people make and the rules and principles upon which such judgments are based. All of us are able to recognize moral judgments; we know, for example, that the following sentences express moral judgments:

1. The drug companies' practice of selling infant formula to Third World mothers is harmful and ought to be banned.
2. The Lockheed payoffs to Japanese government officials to obtain sales of the TriStar were reprehensible and should not have been made.
3. Price fixing is wrong.

The following sentences, however, do not typically express moral judgments:

4. Several multinational drug companies sell infant formula to Third World mothers.
5. Lockheed officials made payments to Japanese government officials to obtain sales of the TriStar.
6. Price fixing occurred in the U.S. electrical equipment industry in the 1950s.

13

In examining these lists we can note that the sentences expressing moral judgments contain such *evaluative* terms as "good," "bad," "right," "wrong," "ought," and "should." The presence of these words frequently indicates that a moral judgment has been made. The presence of an evaluative word is not, however, sufficient for a judgment to be considered moral, for there are non-moral judgments that also contain evaluative terms. For example,

7. The Mona Lisa is a good painting.

makes an aesthetic, not a moral, judgment about the painting, and

8. If you want to get to Chicago in two hours, then you ought to take United flight 247.

makes a nonmoral, prudential claim; it tells you the best means to employ to achieve a practical goal. There is no connection with morality here whatsoever. Furthermore,

9. Most Americans believe price fixing is wrong.

does not express a moral judgment; it merely states a statistical fact about American opinion. It follows that we cannot simply say that a judgment containing an evaluative word is a moral judgment; nor is it the case that all moral judgments contain evaluative words, for there are contexts in which

10. Hooker Chemical polluted the Love Canal.

could be used to judge that Hooker's action was wrong. Although there do not seem to be hard and fast linguistic rules for marking off moral from nonmoral judgments, it is the case that the former typically contain an evaluative term. Furthermore, most of us have a firm enough intuitive grasp of the moral/nonmoral distinction so that we can recognize moral judgments when they are made, and this is enough for our present purposes.

Having said that ethics involves the systematic study of moral judgments and the rules and principles upon which such judgments are based, we should note that there are two major types of systematic inquiry regarding moral judgments: *descriptive ethics* and *normative ethics*. The former is concerned with facts about the moral judgments or moral beliefs of a person or a group of persons; for example:

11. John Jones believes Ford Motor ought to have installed a safer gas tank on the early models of the Pinto.
12. Most Americans believe that International Telephone and Telegraph (ITT) was wrong in trying to destabilize the Allende government in Chile.

These are factual claims, the truth or falsity of which is determinable by empirical investigation. Research regarding such issues is conducted by social scientists with the aim of finding out what moral beliefs people actually hold or what judgments they make. Thus, we can ask Jones whether he believes Ford should have installed a safer gas tank on the early Pinto and receive a yes or no answer, and if we poll a large, representative sample of the American people and find that most of the sample believe ITT was wrong in trying to destabilize the Allende government, then (12) can legitimately be inferred to be true.

Now as we have noted, there are differences between the factual claim made in (12), the truth of which is determinable by a poll, and the following moral judgment:

13. ITT was wrong in trying to destabilize the Allende government.

Some people allow that (12) is true, while claiming that ITT was morally right in trying to destabilize the Allende government. Descriptive ethics, however, is not primarily concerned with the correctness or adequacy of moral judgments such as (13); the scientist focuses on establishing what moral beliefs are held by an individual or group of persons.

Normative ethics is a second important branch of ethical inquiry. It is concerned primarily with two questions: (A) What kinds of things are good? (B) What kinds of acts are right and should be performed? The latter question is of primary interest in business ethics, and we shall return to it after a brief discussion of (A).

Since the time of the ancient Greeks normative ethical theorists have attempted to develop a defensible account of what kinds of things are good or valuable. In the course of their investigations they have sorted out three distinct senses of "value." In one sense, the *preference* sense, a person values something if he prefers, likes, or takes an interest in it; some people, for example, value their work while others value leisure time. In this sense, those who take an interest in smoking, or who like to smoke, can be said to value smoking. In another sense, something can be valuable to a person even though he does not take an interest in it. We say that a person's health is valuable to him even though he may neglect it, and, in this sense, smoking is not of value to a person even though he likes to smoke. In the first sense, then, what is valuable is what is liked or preferred, and in the second sense what is valuable is what serves as a means to some end independent of whether it is preferred. For example, milk is valuable as a means to a healthy body, irrespective of whether an individual likes milk. A thing valued because it serves as a means to some end independent of whether it is preferred is said to be *instrumentally valuable*. There are many things—such as money, food, and security—that would normally be considered of instrumental value for humans, but are there things that are good in and for themselves and not merely of instrumental value; that is, are there things that are good for their own sakes, or *intrinsically valuable,* without reference to a further end? Many normative theorists have argued that there are such instrinsically good things, but there is considerable disagreement as to what things possess this sort of value. Pleasure, happiness, good-will, freedom, honesty, knowledge, benevolence, and self-development have all been proposed as being intrinsically good, and one task of normative ethics is to assess these proposals. Can it be shown, for example, that one of the above-mentioned things is intrinsically valuable whereas the others are merely instrumentally valuable, or should we allow that several or all of them are intrinsically valuable?

Without resolving this issue, we can note the relevance of the instrumental/intrinsic value distinction to issues in business ethics. In a general sense the defenses of the capitalistic economic system rest on emphasizing either its instrumental or intrinsic value. Given that people have basic intrinsic wants, and that a modern society requires capital to satisfy those wants, the instrumental defense of capitalism rests on showing that it can accumulate and allocate capital more effectively than alternative economic systems, and therefore better satisfy those wants. The defender of capitalism may also stress its intrinsic values. Freedom, for example, is often regarded as having intrinsic value, and economic freedom, the freedom to buy, sell, and compete for profits, can be regarded as one aspect of that intrinsic good. The distinction between instrumental and intrinsic value is also important in discussing issues within the framework of capitalism. For example, if freedom of speech has intrinsic value, and justified uses of advertising involve an exercise of free speech, then advertising can be said to have intrinsic value. On the other hand, if promotion of the public good is regarded as intrinsically valuable, then advertising may or may not have instrumental value depending on whether it is regarded as a successful means toward realizing the public good. Furthermore, ethical problems may emerge within a firm if a manager and his employees stress different values. If a manager regards profit as the sole intrinsic value whereas a subordinate emphasizes family life, the latter may be pressured to acquiesce in an illegal or immoral business practice due to his family obligations and the fear that failure to cooperate could cost him his job. And the amount of work required of a subordinate for profit maximization may lead to a form of "corporate bigamy" leaving little time for the family. Similarly, a manager may value corporate loyalty while an employee believes that the public has a right to know about a potentially unsafe product. In such cases an awareness that the disputants are emphasizing different intrinsic values is an important first step in resolving the conflict.

Having noted three distinct uses of "good" or "value," and their relevance for business contexts, we should also note that when we morally assess a person's acts we generally speak of "right" and "wrong." The second major branch of normative ethics, the branch that is perhaps most relevant to business ethics, is concerned with establishing standards for assessing acts as right or wrong, that is, with the development of a theory of right conduct. For purposes of illustration, suppose that a struggling minority firm submits the second lowest bid to supply a large corporation with a machine part, and suppose the corporation's purchasing agent (P) rejects the minority firm's bid; then consider the following conversation P has with his corporation's affirmative action officer (A):

A_1: Rejecting that minority firm's bid was wrong; although there is no law governing this sort of purchase, the rule we should adopt is to help those who have been disadvantaged, whenever it does not put our own company in serious economic jeopardy. Since the bids are so close, we should award the contract to the minority firm.

P_2: I disagree. We have an obligation to our company, and my act was right because, as a rule, the best course of action in these cases, the right thing to do, is to accept the lowest bid.

A_3: Wait a minute. We should treat our suppliers fairly; that's just an instance of the Golden Rule: treat others as you wish them to treat you. But in order to be fair to minority firms we must take past discriminatory practices into account in order to give them a fair shake.

P_4: I still think I am right. I think it is the case that economic efficiency — and that means accepting the lowest bid — leads to the best consequences for everyone, black and white, in the long run.

For our present purposes we need not extend this argument to try to determine who is right. What is noteworthy about this exchange is how one usually goes about justifying moral judgments. Ordinarily, moral disagreements occur within a context of action, and what one judges are *acts* (in this case P's act of rejecting the minority firm's bid). Furthermore, when a person judges an act he usually appeals to some *moral rule* to justify his judgment: A_1 and P_2 both involve appeals to moral rules. But appeals of this type do not invariably settle a moral dispute, because, as A_1 and P_2 illustrate, moral rules may differ; and if two people accept different moral rules, their moral judgments may differ. To fully justify his moral judgments, then, a person must show why *his* moral rules are correct while his adversary's are not. To accomplish this a person appeals to a more general rule, a *moral principle* or standard. A_3 contains an appeal to the Golden Rule, while P_4 appeals to the principle that an act is right if and only if it has the best consequences for everyone.

Let us say that a set of moral rules justified by an appeal to a moral principle constitutes a *moral theory*. If a person has a moral theory, he makes moral judgments based on moral rules and he justifies his moral rules by appeal to a moral principle. When A judges P's act to be wrong he does so by appealing to the moral rule in A_1, and he justifies that rule in terms of the moral principle expressed in A_3. On the other hand, P justifies his act by appealing to the moral rule in P_2, and he justifies that rule by having recourse to the moral principle in P_4. Our example indicates that moral theories differ; distinct moral judgments may be based on different rules and principles. To adjudicate this dispute, then, A and P will have to assess the adequacy of the moral principles expressed in A_3 and P_4. Normative ethics involves the attempt to discover, formulate, and defend fundamental moral principles.

If the field of ethics has descriptive and normative domains, and if our primary concern in business ethics is with the normative domain, it would seem that our next task is to discuss and assess the various moral principles that normative ethical theorists have set forth. Before we can justifiably do so, however, we must take up two challenges that seem at the outset to undercut the relevance of the normative enterprise to the actions of businesspersons. First, it is often maintained that morals are relative. As we shall see, this claim can be interpreted in a variety of ways, but it is often taken to mean that, since all moral judgments, rules, and principles are relative to a particular cultural context, there can be no adequate universal normative theory, i.e., no normative moral theory that is binding on all people in all circumstances. It is claimed that if relativism is correct, there is simply no point in examining the various normative theories proposed as universal and hence asserted to be relevant within business contexts. Second, it is often claimed that the relation between morality and the law is such that, while businesspersons should obey the law, morality is in some fashion irrelevant in the context of business. If this view is defensible, there is surely no point in trying to formulate a normative ethical theory applicable within the business community. Let us examine these challenges in turn.

Many people believe that some form of moral relativism is acceptable — you have your moral rules and principle(s), I have mine, and that's that. In fact, however, there are different versions of relativism, and it is worthwhile to distinguish some of them to see whether they are acceptable and to note their relevance to issues in business ethics. In line with our previous discussion, let us focus on factual and normative versions of moral relativism.

It is often claimed that moral beliefs are in fact relative, that different people do make different moral judgments and advocate different moral rules and principles. Let us call this position *factual moral relativism* (FMR). As a factual matter, the truth of FMR can be decided by empirical investigation; the study of FMR falls within the domain of descriptive ethics. We can distinguish several specific claims within the domain of FMR; being factual claims, each is either true or false:

(R₁) *Individual moral belief relativism*: the moral beliefs of one individual may differ from those of another.

(R$_2$) *Societal moral belief relativism*: the moral beliefs widely accepted in one society may differ from the moral beliefs widely accepted in another society.

(R$_3$) *Societal moral rule relativism*: the moral rules widely accepted in one society may differ from the moral rules widely accepted in another society.

(R$_4$) *Societal moral principle relativism*: the moral principle(s) widely accepted in one society may differ from the moral principle(s) widely accepted in another society.

R$_1$ is true because one person may believe that Lockheed was morally right in making payoffs to Japanese officials to secure sales of its Tristar aircraft, while another person believes Lockheed's actions were wrong. R$_2$ and R$_3$ also seem to be true. In many areas of the Middle East, the Far East, and Africa, where a private sector market economy governed by competitive pricing does not exist, the exchange of goods is governed by a complex network of tribal, social, and family relations and obligations. In this context bribery is often regarded as a morally acceptable practice. In some cases it is governmentally sanctioned; civil servants' salaries, for example, may be kept low with the expectation that they will supplement their wages with bribe money. In America, on the other hand, bribery is widely acknowledged to be morally wrong. Lockheed's officials, for example, allowed that the bribes paid to Japanese officials were morally wrong; they defended the pay-offs only as necessary for commercial success. It seems clear, therefore, that the specific moral beliefs widely accepted in one society may differ from those in another society, and the rules used to justify such acts may differ as well; R$_2$ and R$_3$ are true.

The truth or falsity of R$_4$ is not as easily established as the other forms of FMR. Certainly the truth of R$_1$, R$_2$, and R$_3$ does not establish the truth of R$_4$. Suppose that in society S$_1$ the judgment that a specific act of bribery is morally right and the belief that bribery is morally right are both widely accepted, while in society S$_2$ it is widely held that the act is wrong and that in general bribery is reprehensible. R$_2$ and R$_3$ are then true. But suppose the members of S$_1$ justify their moral rule by claiming that the practice of bribery has the best consequences for everyone concerned, while the members of S$_2$ justify their moral rule by maintaining that bribery does not have the best consequences for everyone. Both societies would then have justified incompatible moral rules by appeal to the same moral principle. Therefore, the truth of R$_1$, R$_2$, and R$_3$ does not substantiate R$_4$. Of course, the truth or falsity of R$_4$ is, as previously noted, a factual matter determinable by scientific investigation. The problem is that at present the anthropological evidence is not conclusive; there is data both for and against the truth of R$_4$.

Let us assume, however, that all the versions of FMR are true, including

R_4, and proceed to raise the question of whether relativism's truth has any relevance for normative ethics. We have already noted that R_1, R_2, and R_3 do not necessarily conflict with the acceptance of one normative principle. Furthermore, even if R_4 is true, and societies do actually accept different normative moral principles, we still cannot conclusively infer that there is no single normative principle binding on all humans. If people in society S_1 accept moral principle P_1 while people in S_2 accept P_2, and P_1 and P_2 are incompatible, then the most we can infer is that one of the principles must be mistaken. In fact, both may be mistaken. But it does not follow that there is no true normative principle. Even if it could be shown that all the normative principles accepted by all societies to this point in time are, for one reason or another, inadequate, it would still not follow that there is no true normative principle; it may simply be the case that no person has discovered that principle. In short, the truth of the varieties of FMR does not preclude our finding a universally binding normative theory. The best that can be said for relativism is that if R_4 is, as a matter of fact, true, and if there is considerable disagreement on fundamental moral principles (a claim that anthropologists have yet to establish), then there is some inductive evidence for the claim that there is no such universal normative principle to be found.

Relativism is sometimes presented as a normative principle; *normative ethical relativism* (NER) is the claim that an act A in society S is right if and only if most people in S believe A is right. This is a universal normative principle insofar as it applies to any person in any society; it is relativistic insofar as it allows that an act that is right in one society may be wrong in another society. NER may be attractive to businesspersons, especially those doing business in the international arena. There is a democratic ring to NER, and it seems to capture the truth in the maxim "When in Rome do as the Romans do." Actually, there seem to be rather conclusive reasons for rejecting NER, and, in addition, the arguments commonly advanced to support it are weak.

One argument against NER is that it may have morally objectionable consequences. If the majority of people in a society believe that owning slaves is an acceptable business practice, then it is morally right to own slaves in that society. Many people claim that the very possibility of allowing and sanctioning such practices is morally indefensible, and they reject NER on this basis alone. A second objection to NER is that it entails the infallibility of the majority, for what the majority believes to be right *is* right. Surely, we want to say, there are at least some cases in which the majority is wrong. A third criticism of NER is that it precludes the possibility of intersocietal comparisons. Suppose society S_1 regards slavery as right while S_2 regards it as wrong. Other things being equal, we would want to say the members of S_2 are more moral than the members of S_1. But if NER is true, we cannot justifiably say this. For the members of S_1 are right in following the majority's beliefs in S_1, and the same holds for S_2; both are performing right acts. We cannot fault the members of S_1 for not following the wishes of the members of S_2, because, according to NER, the members of S_1 are acting morally when they follow the majority opinion in S_1. Since the NER is society-relative, there is no basis for condemning the members of S_1 for failing to adopt the majority opinion in S_2. Since we do want to make intersocietal moral comparisons, but NER precludes them, NER seems unacceptable.

In addition to these objections the arguments used to support NER are weak. First, it is sometimes claimed that the facts of factual moral relativism (FMR) provide evidence for NER. But even if it is true that individuals and societies have different moral beliefs, rules, and principles, as stated in R_1, R_2, R_3, and R_4, what people actually *believe* to be morally right cannot establish what *is* right, for, as we previously noted, some or even all of the individuals or groups may have mistaken beliefs. Hence, the facts of FMR seem irrelevant to the establishment of *any* normative principle, including NER. Second, it is argued that if we accept the principle of tolerance, namely, that we should not try to impose our moral beliefs on others, then we should accept NER because it is the only normative principle compatible with a commitment to tolerance. However, that conclusion does not follow. According to NER, if the majority believes in forcing a minority to accept some moral belief, then the act they are committing (an act of intolerance) is right. So NER need not foster tolerance. Furthermore, the denial of NER, and the acceptance of a nonrelativist normative principle, need not necessarily lead to intolerance, for the nonrelativist may accept the principle of tolerance as a moral rule. In general, then, the standard defenses of NER seem rather weak, and there do seem to be good arguments against its acceptance as a normative principle.

Let us now turn to the claim that although businesspersons should obey the law, if for none other than pragmatic reasons, ethical issues are in some sense irrelevant in the context of business, and hence, there is no point in attempting to formulate a normative theory that is applicable to business contexts.

One version of this position is that the jurisdictions of morality and the law are the same, so that the businessperson need not pay attention to moral rules or principles supposedly expressed independently of, or distinct from, the law—there are no such independent rules or principles. What is moral can be determined by simply examining the law. Furthermore, in following the law a businessperson is acting ethically; to act ethically is just to act in accordance with the law.

This view certainly simplifies moral matters; to check whether an act is morally wrong a businessperson need only check the legal statutes. But there are difficulties with this view of the relation between law and morality. First, if morality is synonymous with the law, then we cannot morally criticize the law. If act x is morally wrong only because it is considered illegal, then a person cannot legitimately claim that x is morally right even though it is illegal. So the view tends to entrench a form of societal conservatism; if slavery is legal in a society, and selling slaves an acceptable business practice, it cannot be legitimately claimed that the law should be changed because it is immoral. Furthermore, it should be noted that the law is coercive; enforcement is essential to the law, whereas, apart from societal pressures, our actions in the moral realm seem to be rooted in rational persuasion, conscience, and personal choice. These features of morality often serve as a basis for moral criticism of the law. The identification of law and morality, however, undercuts this voluntary or personal dimension and places considerable emphasis on enforcement. Individuals at odds with the public morality expressed in law are subjected to enforced penalties and at the same time are precluded from raising moral objections to the law, i.e., precluded from attempting to change the law by independent moral persuasion. In addition, on this view a change in law is a change in morality; so slavery is now illegal and immoral in America, yet in 1780 it was not only legal but also moral. Those who claim that slavery is always immoral must reject the identification of morality with the law.

A second version of the irrelevance of morality to business contexts rests on the claim that the law is totally independent of morality, and that although the law should be obeyed just because it is the law, moral considerations should not enter into the context of business.

This view seems partially correct insofar as it points out some differences between legality and morality. The law, as we noted, is coercive — it is connected with enforcement — whereas morality is not. Again, laws are made or enacted by humans, whereas it seems odd to say that moral rules or principles are *made* or *enacted*. But these differences do not entail a complete separation of law and morality. In fact, if we separate them completely, and claim that the law should be obeyed, then we once again seem to have no basis for failing to obey the law. If the law said slavery was legal, the question of its moral status would be irrelevant. On this view the law tends to be reduced to the domain of enforcement, and questions of the morality and justice of the law are simply set aside.

If moral rules are not synonymous with or reducible to positive law, and if legality is not totally independent of morality, it seems reasonable to say that legality rests, in some sense, on morality. Legal obligation is not the basis of moral obligation, for the law is not as ultimate as fundamental moral principles. Laws are made and then repealed, but a genuine moral obligation is categorical and not repealable. For example, we should treat people with respect not because of any legal considerations but because humans intrinsically ought to respect each other. And laws are often repealed on the basis of moral considerations. If a person argues that some laws are morally bad and ought to be changed, that the Constitution (morally) should be amended to preclude, say, abortion, or that a judge's decision ought to be reversed in the interest of justice, he is acknowledging the dependence of law on morality.

The upshot of our discussion is that normative ethics does seem relevant to the actions of businesspersons. We found that relativism does not undercut the attempt to find a universal normative theory, and we argued that the relation between law and morality is such that the former rests on the latter; and therefore it cannot be maintained that, although businesspersons should obey the law, morality is irrelevant in the business world. In light of our discussion, we can expand our notion of a moral theory to include legal rules or laws. Moral rules serve as the justification for legal enactments and moral rules, in turn, are justified on the basis of ultimate moral principles. This ordering of reasons reflects our claim that legality rests on morality.

If there were only one moral theory to which appeal could be made in making moral judgments, ethical disputes would be relatively easy to resolve. Unfortunately, things are not so simple in real life; and what we discover as we go about the process of living is that there are a number of competing moral theories from which we must choose. Although these theories can differ radically, some of them do have characteristics in common. The existence of these shared traits allows for the classification of moral theories into specific types. Traditionally, the broadest classification of moral theories is into one or the other of two classes: (1) teleological (or consequentialist) moral theories, and (2) deontological (or nonconsequentialist) theories. Teleological theories hold that the rightness or wrongness of an act is ultimately determined by the act's *consequences*; i.e., an act is said to be morally right if it produces good consequences, and wrong if it produces bad results. Deontologists reject this view and claim that ultimately an act is right or wrong because of some aspect of its character, form, or nature. In addition, most deontologists insist that an action cannot be judged morally unless one knows why the person who performed the action did what he did. In other words, deontologists tell us that a person's *motives* for acting are important, and that an action cannot be morally right unless the person (the agent) who performed it did what he did for the right reasons.

Many businessmen and economists accept a moral theory that attempts to combine elements of both teleology and deontology into one all-encompassing system. For reasons that will become apparent later, we have chosen to call this moral theory "restricted egoism." In what follows we shall examine restricted egoism in some detail. In addition, four other moral theories will be analyzed. Two of these theories (ethical egoism and utilitarianism) are teleological, and two (Kantianism and theologism) are deontological. Our purpose in introducing these theories is not simply to make the reader aware of certain "traditional" moral positions. Rather, our discussion is prompted by two considerations. First and foremost, we want the reader to have a clear understanding of what it is that restricted egoism asserts; and this is made most evident by considering the four theories listed above. Our second purpose is critical. Restricted egoism is not a "perfect" moral theory; and many of the problems one encounters in restricted egoism find their roots in ethical egoism and utilitarianism. Thus, analysis of these "traditional" theories will better enable us to evaluate the claims of restricted egoism.

TELEOLOGY: ETHICAL EGOISM, UTILITARIANISM AND RESTRICTED EGOISM

Ethical Egoism. Ethical egoists claim that an act is morally right if and only if it tends, more than any alternative act open to the agent at the time, to promote the interests of the agent. That is to say, what is right, or what one ought to do, is to act in accordance with one's own self-interest.

Ethical egoism should be distinguished from psychological egoism, which is the claim that people do, as a matter of fact, always act in their own perceived self-interest. Ethical egoism is an ethical theory that purports to tell us what people should do; psychological egoism, on the other hand, is a factual or empirical theory that makes a claim about what people actually do or what motivates them to act. Psychological egoism is sometimes used to support ethical egoism; the claim is that if people do invariably act in their own self-interest, then the only moral theory compatible with this fact is ethical egoism. If psychological egoism is true, though, ethics becomes pointless. This is so because a moral theory must tell us either that there are times when it is right to sacrifice our own self-interests or that we should always do what is in our own interests. If psychological egoism is true, it would make no sense to say that we *ought* to sacrifice our own interests (because we cannot, or as a matter of fact do not, do this), and it is pointless to enjoin us to maximize our self-interest (because we will do this anyway).

In discussing ethical egoism it is important to note that the theory advocates the long-term self-interest of the agent, and hence it is not a fair objection against ethical egoism to say that it favors short-term or immediate self-interest. In business, for example, an employee who is an ethical egoist may be very loyal and hard-working in the belief that these traits will promote the firm's interests, and that promotion of the firm's interests, e.g., profit maximization, is the best means to serve his own long-term self-interest. Similarly, an ethical egoist shareholder may advocate that the firm defer dividend payments and reinvest them in order to maximize capital gains, which he takes to be in his long-term self-interest. Acting in a self-sacrificing way is compatible with being an ethical egoist as long as the act leads to the long-term best interest of the agent. One advantage of ethical egoism in a business context, then, is that the egoist is obligated to act in the firm's interest so long as that interest is the best means to achieve his own long-term self-interest; in a large percentage of cases egoism is compatible with the firm's interests.

A second advantage of ethical egoism is that it provides a basis for the flexibility that seems to be needed in business decision-making. Normally a businessperson should keep his contracts, and the ethical egoist can explain why this is so; in most cases it is in his interest that contracts be kept. But the egoist claims that moral rules, e.g., "always keep your contracts," are not inviolate. In fact, the principle of ethical egoism makes no reference to moral rules, for the rightness of an act is solely determined by whether it maximizes self-interest, and in certain cases strict adherence to a moral rule will not maximize self-interest. The egoist claims that business decision-making is too complex to be bound by rules and that the principle of ethical egoism provides the moral basis for both breaking and adhering to such rules.

In spite of these advantages, egoism has several weaknesses as an ethical theory in business contexts. First, if a businessperson believes that profit maximization is in his self-interest, then any means that he can employ and "get away with" to maximize profit are regarded as morally right. Thus, if in certain cases a businessperson can maximize profit by dumping a harmful pollutant or marketing an unsafe product, and the chances of his getting caught are slim, then he ought to commit such acts. In such cases the flexibility afforded the businessperson by ethical egoism allows him to commit acts that intuitively seem wrong.

More generally, one can argue that the ethical egoists' definition of "right act" does not reflect the society's ordinary ways of speaking, and that, as a result, ethical egoists must be wrong when they say that we ought to pursue our own interests. Let us say, for instance, that we know a person, *P,* who acts only to further his own interests. Whenever *P* helps others he does so only because this ultimately serves his own ends. At the same time, he never allows anyone to "get in his way." Furthermore, if it will ultimately benefit *P* to lie about someone, or hurt someone, he will do so. Now would we ordinarily say that *P* was a moral person, or that he was acting in morally right ways? It seems clear that we would not. Consequently, it seems that ethical egoists' understanding of what is right to do is mistaken and that their moral theory must be rejected.

Few ethical egoists would be convinced by the above criticism of their position. It might well be the case, they would say, that by "right act" most people do not mean "action which serves one's self-interest." Nevertheless, they would claim, this is what people should mean, and if they hold a contrary view they are mistaken. At this point, however, there is a second criticism that can be brought against the ethical egoists' position; namely, that the position is inconsistent. After all, ethical egoists claim that everyone should act to further his own interests. But how can business *X* enjoin a competing firm *Y* to seek only what is in *Y*'s best interest when there certainly will be competitive situations in which those acts serving *Y*'s interest will be detrimental to *X*'s interests? And in such cases *X* seems to be telling *Y* that it is morally right for *Y* to work against *X*'s interests, that is, to do what *X* considers to be morally wrong.

In conclusion, then, insofar as the calculation of interests and consequences enters into moral decision-making, it seems that impartiality is required of the agent; i.e., he should attempt to impartially consider the interests of all affected parties when calculating the consequences of an action. Ethical egoism's failure to meet the test of impartiality is a basic weakness of the theory.

Utilitarianism. A consequentialist ethical theory that does attempt to take everyone into account is utilitarianism. There are a number of versions of utilitarianism, two of which we shall consider: act utilitarianism and rule utilitarianism.

According to the act utilitarian, an act is morally right if and only if it maximizes utility, i.e., if and only if the ratio of benefit to harm calculated by taking everyone affected by the act into consideration is greater than the ratio of benefit to harm resulting from any alternative act. In deciding to act, then, the act utilitarian will first set out the alternatives open to him. Second, he calculates the ratio of benefit to harm for each individual, including himself, affected by the alternative acts. Third, he adds up the ratios for each alternative act. Finally, he chooses the act that results in the greatest total ratio of benefit to harm. Assume, for example, that there are three alternative acts (A_1, A_2, A_3) open to person P_1, and that there are three people (P_1, P_2, P_3) affected by each alternative act. Assume, furthermore, that the ratio of benefit to harm for each person affected by each act can be expressed quantitatively, with a plus value indicating a benefit and a negative value indicating a harmful effect. Finally, assume a calculation yields the following result:

	P_1	P_2	P_3	Totals
A_1	+4	−5	+8	+7
A_2	+6	+2	−3	+5
A_3	−2	−5	+4	−3

In this situation the act utilitarian will choose act A_1 because it produces the greatest ratio of benefit to harm (+7) when everyone affected by the act is taken into consideration. Thus, the act utilitarian often recommends a course of action different from that recommended by the ethical egoist. In the above situation the ethical egoist as agent P_1 would choose A_2, for that act maximizes P_1's self-interest.

In setting up our example we assumed that benefit/harm (or benefit/cost) ratios can be measured and compared, but these are assumptions that have been questioned. First, it is not altogether clear in some cases what is to count as a benefit or harm. In locating a plant, for example, what some people regard as a benefit others may see as a cost. Second, in some cases it may be difficult to assign quantitative values; for example, how does one measure the value of aesthetically pleasant surroundings or the value of a human life? Analogously, can something like aesthetic value ever be meaningfully compared with the value of a life? Third, the act utilitarian is concerned with the long-term consequences of acts, and in such contexts it may be very difficult to delimit the alternative acts available and to obtain reliable predictions as to the long-term consequences of performable acts.

If such difficulties could be overcome, however, act utilitarianism would have several advantages as an ethical theory in business contexts. First, unlike ethical egoism, act utilitarianism is impartial in that it takes each person's interests into account, and requires that act which maximizes utility irrespective of who benefits. Thus, the businessperson who accepts act utilitarianism has a basis for claiming that he is acting in a socially responsible manner in the sense that he takes everyone's interests, including employees, consumers, suppliers, etc., into account in decision-making. Second, the theory is able to account for why we typically hold certain business practices, e.g., contract-breaking, to be immoral; in most cases such practices do not maximize utility. But the act utilitarian denies that there are any unbreakable moral rules, e.g., "always keep your contracts," for in certain contexts breaking such a rule may maximize utility. A third advantage for the businessperson employing act utilitarianism is that it does not force him to accept binding rules; it allows for the flexibility that some people believe is necessary in today's complex business environment. In contrast with the egoist, however, such flexibility is based on overall utility considerations and not solely on self-interest.

Act utilitarianism, however, is not free of problems. For example, let us assume that executive X in company A has worked for months in order to bring about a contractual agreement between his company and another company, B. Whether or not the agreement actually does take place is dependent, in large part, upon what X does, for negotiations are at a crucial stage. If the agreement is secured, both companies A and B will profit and many new jobs will be created. During the final negotiations the president of company A by chance discovers that X has embezzled $5,000 from the corporation. The company's books are scheduled to be audited in a day or two, and the president of A knows that the accountants will discover X's theft. The president of A confronts X and tells him what he has learned. X explains that he needed the money to pay for an operation for his wife, but that his wife has died and he never again will be pressed to steal money from the company. Also, X says that if his theft is made known the people he is negotiating with in company B will no longer trust him, and the agreement between companies A and B will fall through. Since X's theft will be detected by the impending audit, the president says there is very little he can do. As luck would have it, however, there is a low-level executive, Y, in company A who has had bad relations with all his supervisors and is about to be fired. X suggests that the president make it appear as though Y embezzled the $5,000.

When Y is fired, the company will not press charges, and X quietly will repay the money he stole. The question then is this: should the president of A frame Y for the embezzlement actually perpetrated by X? It appears as though an act utilitarian would have to say yes, but this violates our ordinary moral intuitions regarding justice and fair play. Furthermore, the following sort of utility calculation could be employed to justify an unjust act such as enslavement.

	P_1	P_2	P_3	Totals
A_1	+ 22	+ 22	− 25	+ 19
A_2	+ 6	+ 6	+ 6	+ 18

It is conceivable that enslavement of P_3 via act A_1 would produce slightly greater total utility than act A_2, the other act open to the agent, even though A_2 results in a more equitable distribution. In that case the morally right act, according to the act utilitarian, is A_1. In such a case, however, act utilitarianism seems to clearly violate our ordinary perceptions of what is right.

Many utilitarians believe it is possible to avoid criticisms of the sort we have brought against act utilitarianism by reformulating the theory so that it has a place for moral rules. So reformulated, the position is known as *rule* utilitarianism. According to rule utilitarians an act A in circumstance C is morally right if and only if the consequences of everyone acting on the rule "Do A in C" are better than the consequences of everyone acting on any alternative rule. The notion of "best consequences" here is specified in terms of utility maximization. Thus, an act is right if and only if it is in conformity with a particular moral rule, and that rule is chosen because, of all alternative rules, it maximizes utility. For example, a rule utilitarian might claim that "We must not hold a person accountable for a crime he has not committed" is a proper rule of conduct because if this rule were followed by everyone, it would maximize utility. Using this rule, the rule utilitarian could conclude that in our first counterexample to act utilitarianism it would be wrong for the president of company A to frame Y for the crime committed by X. Since this result seems to accord with our moral intuitions, the rule utilitarian contends that his theory represents an advance over act utilitarianism.

Critics of rule utilitarianism, however, point out that if rule utilitarians are committed to the moral rule that maximizes utility, then they will have to allow that the acceptable rule in any case is one that allows exceptions that maximize utility. Thus, instead of the rule "We must not hold a person accountable for a crime he has not committed," the rule utilitarian must adopt the rule "We must not hold a person accountable for a crime he has not committed, unless doing so maximizes utility." In that case, rule utilitarianism collapses into the equivalent of act utilitarianism, and the objections we raised against act utilitarianism resurface. Analogously, in the enslavement counterexample to act utilitarianism, the rule utilitarian might argue that the rule "never enslave" maximizes utility. But he would have to allow that there are at least conceivable exceptions that maximize utility, and hence the rule he advocates is "never enslave except when utility is maximized by doing so." The result is that under certain circumstances rule utilitarianism, like act utilitarianism, does appear to sanction intuitively immoral practices such as slavery.

Restricted Egoism. Ethical egoists advise us to act in our own self-interest whereas utilitarians advise us to maximize utility, and hence it might seem that these theories are incompatible. Interestingly, however, their incompatibility has been challenged by a number of economists and businesspersons (see, for example, the selections from Milton Friedman in this volume). Following Adam Smith, these people claim that the universal pursuit of self-interest is a process guided by an "invisible hand"—an invisible hand ultimately assuring that the public interest or total utility will be served. One qualification is needed here. Those who accept the invisible hand theory do not believe that it is morally right, in the pursuit of one's own self-interest, to break either the laws of the land or the established rules of competition. Thus, their moral theory is one that might be labeled "restricted egoism"; the theory is egoistic because it tells us that it is right to promote our own interests, yet this egoism is restricted by the demand that we obey certain laws and rules. On this view a corporation acts in a morally right manner if and only if it: (a) obeys the laws of the land as well as the accepted rules of competition, and (b) pursues its own self-interest, thereby automatically furthering the interests of society as a whole.

There are two major advantages with this theory. First, it commits businesspersons to conformity with the law, which can be looked up in the legal statutes. Second, it sanctions corporate self-interest, which typically means profit maximization, on the basis that pursuit of such self-interest in a competitive context will maximize utility, or further the overall interests of society. Whereas ethical egoism asserts that the pursuit of self-interest is moral, restricted egoism justifies the pursuit of self-interest in terms of utility.

In turning to criticisms of the theory, the first thing one notices about restricted egoism is that it is not clear why its proponents assert (a). Two possibilities present themselves: (1) restricted egoists might claim that it is right to obey society's laws and the rules of competition because such action serves self-interests (of course, since the invisible hand is at work, such action also will further society's interests), (2) restricted egoists could say that laws and rules must be obeyed because without a context of rule-governed behavior the competitive game itself is impossible. That is to say, if one corporation or business were to claim the right to be exempted from having to follow laws and rules, all businesses legitimately could claim that right. And in this situation—a situation in which any corporation could disregard any rule or law that it did not want to obey—business would be impossible.

Problems arise no matter which interpretation of restricted egoism one chooses to accept. If restricted egoists are interpreted as asserting (1), then why must corporations obey laws and rules in order to do what is morally right? For example, assume that the executives of a corporation know that they can break a law and not get caught. Furthermore, they know that breaking the law will benefit both the corporation and society. If the only justification for following laws and rules is that this ultimately conduces to the interests of business and society, why, in the absence of such a justification, should the corporation obey the law? Indeed, if any corporation refused to break the law when it was obvious that to do so would be in its own best long-term interests, as well as society's, would not that corporation be failing in its moral duty? Surely it would seem so. And if this is the case, restricted egoists should not tell us that businesses ought to obey certain rules and laws in order to do what is morally right, but rather that corporations have every right to break these laws and rules when it is clearly in their interests to do so.

If we interpret restricted egoists as using (2) rather than (1) to justify the inclusion of laws and rules within their moral theory, it now becomes impossible for any corporation to break the laws of society or the established rules of business practice without suffering moral condemnation. Still, on this view it is not necessarily true that a corporation acts morally when it obeys society's laws and the rules of good business practice. To be moral a corporation must follow rules *and* promote its own interests together with the interests of society. Both conditions are needed; and neither condition by itself is sufficient. That is to say, if a corporation is promoting its own interests and the interests of society, but breaks a law or rule in the process, then it is acting immorally. On the other hand, if it obeys society's laws and the accepted rules of competition but at the same time does not contribute to anyone's interest, then the corporation does not do what is morally right. It does not do anything wrong; but it does not do anything right either according to restricted egoism.

If restricted egoism is represented in the above manner, the theory suffers from at least two difficulties. First, justification could be given for virtually *any* set of rules and laws. (Rules prohibiting competition or corporate activity could not be justified, but almost any other set of rules could be accepted as unbreakable guidelines for corporate conduct.) This being the case, restricted egoists could argue for the morality of many acts that we would ordinarily call immoral. For example, if some corporation was doing business in a country where bribes and kickbacks were accepted as part of the "competitive game," restricted egoists should argue that the company is morally bound to follow this established rule. But surely such a position is questionable. Or again, assume that a racist government is in power in a foreign country. It passes a law requiring all businesses to charge blacks more for goods and services than other citizens pay. Presumably, restricted egoists would now have to claim that it would be wrong for any corporation to break this law. But this runs counter to our ordinary moral intuitions. How, after all, can a corporation have a moral duty to further the ends of racism?

If, as we now are assuming, restricted egoism holds that laws and rules are unbreakable, there is a second, even more severe problem with the theory. That is, what happens if there is a conflict between one or more of society's laws and the established rules of the "competitive game"? Should businesspersons obey the law or follow informal rules of competition? In other words, in cases of conflict, which set of rules has priority? And whatever the choice, how would businesspersons justify their decision? Both questions must be answered before restricted egoism can be considered a "complete" moral theory.

We have seen that restricted egoism can be interpreted in at least two different ways, and that each form has its problems. But things are really worse than we have made out, for there is another difficulty plaguing *any* form of restricted egoism. Regardless of how they justify the inclusion of laws and rules within their moral theory, all restricted egoists agree that a morally right act furthers both self-interest and the interests of society. Restricted egoists see no problem with this "dual consequence" theory, because they firmly believe in Adam Smith's invisible hand. That is to say, corporate executives need worry about nothing but maximizing the interests of their own corporations; for if they are successful in this enterprise, Smith's "invisible hand" will see to it that society's interests are also served. But is this true? Certainly in *some* cases societal and business interests are in accord; but it is not at all clear that this is true in every case. For example, prior to the advent of child labor laws it was in the interest of business to have children work 12 to 14 hours a day at low wages. Given the amount of human suffering involved, however, it is not apparent that this served the public interest. Indeed, the fact that laws were passed prohibiting such practices tends to indicate that our society did not see child labor as fostering its best interests. Thus the problem for the restricted egoist is this: what should a corporation do when some action it is contemplating would benefit society but not the corporation, or *vice-versa*? In circumstances such as these, restricted egoists are forced to choose between ethical egoism and utilitarianism. Neither choice is problem free.

Consider a case in which the corporation's interests and those of society do not mesh, and the corporation chooses to act egoistically. Now ordinarily ethical egoism makes no reference to moral rules, for the rightness of an act is solely determined by whether it maximizes self-interest. On the other hand, the restricted egoist who wants to accept ethical egoism will have to claim two things: (1) that a right act is one that maximizes self-interest, and (2) that a right act must conform to society's laws and the rules of competition.

It seems clear, however, that there will be times when (1) and (2) will conflict, e.g., times when it will be in a corporation's own interest to break a law. In cases such as these, restricted egoists seem to want to say that the corporation should obey the law. But why should (2) take precedence over (1)? Restricted egoists give us no clear answer. This is not to say that no answer can be given, only that such an answer must be forthcoming if restricted egoists are to present us with a fully worked-out moral theory. If in such cases the restricted egoist claims that (1) takes precedence over (2), then his position essentially reduces to ethical egoism, and we have already enumerated several difficulties with that theory.

Now consider a case in which the corporation's interests and those of society do not mesh, and the corporation acts on the basis of utilitarianism. First consider act utilitarianism. Because act utilitarianism is a theory that typically makes no reference to moral rules, the restricted egoist who opts for act utilitarianism faces a problem similar to that discussed in the previous paragraph. That is, how ought one to act when utility mandates action contrary to some law or rule? As we have noted, the businessperson's moral theory seems to hold that laws and rules are unbreakable. But how is this ordering of priorities justified? Why, in other words, should society's laws and the rules of competition take precedence over the demands of utility? On the other hand, if utility takes precedence over the laws and rules, then this version of restricted egoism reduces to pure act utilitarianism, several difficulties of which we have previously noted. Now consider rule utilitarianism. It would not be easy to combine rule utilitarianism with the rules and laws accepted by restricted egoists, for it is not clear that all these rules and laws could be justified by an appeal to utility. Or to put it another way, what would happen if, through application of the principle of utility, rule utilitarians were led to formulate a set of rules that differed significantly from the laws of our society and the rules of competition? Which rules would the businessperson accept? If he were to accept the utilitarian rules he would have to admit openly that he was not morally bound to follow either the laws of society or the accepted rules of competition. And this seems to be a conclusion that businesspersons are loath to accept. On the other hand, acceptance of the rule utilitarian's rules opens one up to the difficulties previously noted.

We have seen that there might well be circumstances in which corporate policy makers would be forced to choose between ethical egoism and utilitarianism, and that, regardless of the decision made, problems would arise. But what if we assume that Adam Smith's invisible hand is at work so that (incredibly) whatever conduces to a corporation's interests also operates to secure the best interests of society as a whole? Even in these circumstances we could not say that restricted egoism was a problem-free moral theory. Consider this example. A company manufactures aerosol spray containing chemicals that destroy ozone. This is the cheapest method of production, and if the company continues to use ozone destroying elements in its manufacturing process, profits will be maximized and stockholders will be paid the highest possible dividends. As stockholders are rewarded this creates greater demand in other sections of the economy, etc. In sum, the *short-term* consequences of using ozone destroying chemicals are beneficial both to the manufacturer and to society. If one looks to the *long-term* effects, however, things could be quite different. For instance, as the ozone layer is destroyed incidents of skin cancer could increase. And once people realize what is causing the destruction of the ozone layer they could refuse to buy any aerosol spray. Indeed, even if the manufacturer were to stop using destructive chemicals in its product, public distrust could be so great that the company might never recover its original market. Now, in these circumstances, what should the aerosol manufacturer do? Specifically, should the manufacturer take the short-term or the long-term consequences of its actions as determining moral rightness? Restricted egoists give us no answer to this question. We can also conceive of a situation in which enslavement of a small part of a society is legal, that it is in a corporation's interest to employ slaves, and that such a practice actually maximizes utility for society. In such a case all the conditions are satisfied for right action according to restricted egoism, but the use of slaves in a business is clearly immoral.

The criticisms of restricted egoism, ethical egoism, and utilitarianism are all limited in scope in that they call attention to specific problems within particular moral theories. We must, however, consider a much broader challenge to these moral theories. Some moral philosophers reject all forms of egoism and utilitarianism because these theories are teleological in nature. Moral theorists who reject teleology in ethics are called deontologists. Usually deontologists claim that the rightness or wrongness of an action is to be determined by two things: (1) the action's form or character, and (2) the motives of the agent, i.e., the motives of the person who performs the act. In what follows we shall examine two deontological moral theories, briefly enumerate some of the problems faced by those who advocate them, and then see how deontology constitutes a challenge to restricted egoism.

Deontology: Theologism and Kantianism

Theologism asserts that an act is right if, more than any alternative open to the agent at the time, it is the one most consistent with what God wills, either directly or indirectly. Usually, theologism provides us with a set of rules (e.g., the Ten Commandments) thought to express God's will. Whether or not an act is right or wrong, then, is determined *in part* by reference to these rules. We say that the rightness or wrongness of an action is *partially* determined by reference to moral rules because most theologians hold that an act may conform to the requirements specified by a legitimate rule of conduct and still not be morally proper. For example, let us say that a person accepts the Ten Commandments as specifying God's will, and refuses to steal when he has an opportunity to do so. In this case, then, he has followed one of God's commands. But if the individual refused to steal because he was afraid of being caught, or because he wanted to be rewarded in heaven for his good behavior, his action would not be truly right. The motives for action would be "impure," and this impurity would affect (perhaps "infect" is a better word) the moral character of his action. For his action to be truly right, God's command must be followed for the right reason, viz., stealing must be rejected, not out of concern for oneself, but rather out of love for God and fellow men. Given *this* motive, then, the action would be right and its subject truly would be deserving of reward in heaven. In short, most versions of theologism hold that God not only wants us to act in certain ways, but also to act in those ways for the right reasons.

Kantianism, named after the German philosopher Immanuel Kant (1724–1804), is similar to theologism in a number of ways. Like theologism, Kantianism holds that an action's rightness or wrongness is to be determined by: (1) the action's form or character (i.e., the action must be such that it conforms to certain rules of conduct), and (2) the motives or intentions of the agent. On the other hand, Kantianism differs from theologism in certain significant respects. For one thing, it might well be the case that Kant's moral rules and the rules of theologism differ. The reason this is so is that while theologism justifies its rules by an appeal to God as the moral lawgiver, Kant appeals to what he calls the *categorical imperative*. This principle is an imperative because it is a command. It is categorical because it is a command that holds without qualification. Unfortunately, Kant states the categorical imperative in a variety of different ways. In what follows we shall discuss the two best known formulations.

Sometimes Kant states the categorical imperative as follows: "One ought never to act except in such a way that one can also will that one's maxim should become a universal law." Using such a guideline, Kant claims that practices such as lying, killing, stealing, and cheating are all forbidden by the moral law. And the reason they are forbidden is that if these acts were universalized (i.e., if they were practiced by everyone) it no longer would make any sense to speak of such practices occurring. To put it another way, universalization of the practice would destroy the practice itself. For example, consider lying. Unless there is a general context of truth telling, the concept of lying makes no sense, for to lie is not to tell the truth. But if everyone always lied there would be no truth, i.e., nothing with which lying could be contrasted, and hence no way meaningfully to say that one was lying. On the other hand, the same considerations do not apply to truth telling. If everyone always told the truth it still would make sense to say that people were speaking truly. This is so because "truth" is not defined in terms of "lying," but rather in terms of other criteria, e.g., a statement is true if it

Using the universalization formulation of the categorical imperative Kant believes he can derive a set of moral rules that must *always* be obeyed. In other words, to break one of these rules is always to do something wrong, regardless of the particular circumstances in which one acts. On the other hand, simply to act in the ways specified by these rules is not to insure that one's actions are morally right. Like the theologian, Kant insists that an action cannot be counted as morally right unless the agent performs the action for the right reason. For Kant, however, one should not act from the motives specified by the theologian. Rather, one must obey moral rules *simply because this is the right thing to do.* In short, one's motive for action must be respect for the moral law. And when one obeys a rule for this reason, one is doing what is morally right.

Kant's second formulation of the categorical imperative is as follows: "Act so that you treat humanity, whether in your own person or that of another, always as an end and never as a means only." Kant's point here seems to be that all persons deserve respect simply because they are persons. If this principle is accepted everyone has a moral duty to treat others fairly and equitably, to refrain from "using" humans as means for the procurement of one's own or other's ends, etc. In effect, the second statement of the categorical imperative, like the first, leads one to formulate a set of moral rules that must be obeyed if one is to act in morally right ways.

Because Kantianism and theologism are similar, there are criticisms which apply equally to both moral theories. Perhaps the best known criticism applicable to both theories is that they provide us with moral rules that cannot be violated without doing something wrong. Take, for instance, the Kantian injunction against lying. For Kant, lying is *always* wrong; there are no exceptions to this rule. But surely there are some circumstances in which we ordinarily would say it was right to lie. Consider this case. You are a security guard for a large company that you know does secret work for the CIA. One day while making your rounds you discover an old friend of yours planting a bomb on the premises. He pulls a gun, holds it to your head and says that he is bombing the building and its occupants because he suspects the company does work for the CIA. At the same time he says that he trusts you, and that if you swear on everything you hold holy that the company does not work for the CIA he will take his bomb and leave. Surely we believe that in these circumstances it would be morally right to lie, for to tell the truth would have truly disastrous consequences. This being the case we must conclude that there is something wrong with any moral theory that tells us to wholly disregard consequences, and to concern ourselves only with obeying pre-established, unbreakable moral rules.

Although Kantianism and theologism are alike, they are also dissimilar in various ways. And because of these dissimilarities there are specific criticisms applicable to each theory. For example, we have seen that Kant states the categorical imperative in a variety of different ways. On the face of it, these various formulations do not appear to assert exactly the same things.

This being so it is quite likely that different moral rules could be justified, depending upon which formulation of the categorical imperative one happened to accept. But then, which moral rules ought to be accepted? All of them? At first glance this may sound fine; but what if some of the rules derived from one formulation of the categorical imperative should happen to conflict with rules derived from another formulation? Kantianism gives us no way to resolve a conflict of this sort.

Unlike Kantianism, theologism appeals only to one principle to justify its set of moral rules. Supposedly, the rules of theologism specify right action because these rules, and no others, express God's will. It is at this point, however, that a problem arises. Namely, do the theologians' moral rules express what is right because of God's command or not? If the theologian says that the rules express what is right because of God's command, two untoward consequences follow. First, it no longer makes any sense to say that God is good. (Since *anything* God wills is good, for God Himself there is no difference between good and evil; and when we say God is good we assert nothing.) And second, theologians have to admit that if God commanded murder, theft, or cruelty, these actions would be right and morally obligatory. But few people—theologians included—want to admit that actions of this sort ever could be morally right. On the other hand, if the theologians were to claim that their set of moral rules specified right action independently of God's command, then they would have to find a new justification for their moral rules. This is so because the theologians' present position would then be that *regardless* of what God commands, their set of moral rules specifies right action. And in these circumstances it simply would be contradictory for the theologians to assert that it is because of God's command that their moral rules delineate right conduct.

Although theologism and Kantianism have their problems, these theories nevertheless call attention to the fact that moral judgments are rarely if ever made on the basis of consequences alone. Ordinarily, moral rules play a part in our moral considerations; and any moral theory seeking widespread acceptance must take notice of this fact. Apparently, restricted egoists would agree with this assessment, for they try to make a place for rules in their moral theory. However, deontologists would not be satisfied with the rules of restricted egoism because neither the laws of society nor the rules of competition are *moral* rules. Indeed, Kantians and theologians would insist that restricted egoists have been far too hasty in their rule selection; for rather than taking the difficult road of attempting to justify rules of conduct by appealing to a moral principle, these individuals simply have accepted a "handy" set of rules. However, operating in this fashion ultimately leaves one open to the possibility that one will accept rules of conduct that mandate immoral action. And, deontologists would insist, this is exactly what has happened to restricted egoists. For instance, at one time southern states had laws requiring that blacks and whites be segregated. Rather than opposing these laws, companies located in the south (even large national and international corporations) obeyed them. Or again, some members of the business community argue that there are circumstances in which one businessperson may lie to another because lying is an accepted part of the "competitive game." Such a position is surely unacceptable to a Kantian. And theologians would be just as anxious to reject the businessperson's "game" theory. After all, the Mafia sees itself as being engaged in a competitive game too. In this game, however, killing as well as lying is an accepted rule. Are we then forced to conclude that a hired killer does not act immorally when he kills a Mafia official?

Even if restricted egoists were to justify their rules of conduct by appealing to a moral principle, it is unlikely that deontologists would be happy with the end product. This is so because restricted egoists do not seem to fully recognize that an agent's motives for acting are important in assessing the moral quality of his or her act. This is not to say that restricted egoists never speak of motives. However, when motives are mentioned by restricted egoists one gets the feeling that they believe humans always should be motivated by self-interest. Given our discussion of Kantianism and theologism we know that deontologists disagree concerning the proper motives for human conduct. Despite this disagreement, however, deontologists are unanimous in their rejection of self-interest as a morally proper motive for action. And here, the deontologists' position would seem to be in accord with our ordinary ways of thinking and speaking (see above, pp. 25–6). Furthermore, restricted egoists also seem to realize that there is some problem with claiming that humans ought always to be motivated by self-interest, for they invoke the "invisible hand" theory and thus imply (albeit tacitly) that self-interest is acceptable as a universal motive for human action because actions prompted by self-interest ultimately contribute to the interests of society. But the invisible hand theory is questionable at best; in fact, it is probably false. However, even if it were clear that self-interested actions always secured society's best interests, it is not likely that deontologists would be satisfied with restricted egoism. Deontologists would insist that in addition to a desire to further society's interests there also are other motives that contribute to right actions. This claim is certainly disputable, but it is undeniable that restricted egoists have not paid careful attention to the important role motives play in moral judgment.

In addition to the above, all deontologists would reject restricted egoism because it fails to take note of the fact that human beings are deserving of respect. Kant insists that we should be treated as "ends" and not as "means." Theologism claims that we are all equally "children of God." However the doctrine is stated, the point is that we have certain rights as human beings, and abrogation of these rights cannot be justified either by an appeal to self-interest or by an appeal to the interests of society as a whole. That businesses often treat persons as mere "means" seems undeniable; there are cases in which workers are considered simply as pieces of equipment in the production process. Whether such action is justifiable by appeal to finite goals is not an easy question to answer. What is true about the deontologists' charge is that restricted egoists must pay some attention to the issue. If businesspersons believe they sometimes are justified in treating people as "means" rather than as "ends," then they must be able to support this position. And at this point in time, no acceptable justification has been given.

Finally, deontologists would object to the restricted egoists' moral position by claiming that its concept of moral duty is too narrow. At first glance, at least, restricted egoism seems to impose only two moral duties upon us: (1) there is a duty to maximize self-interest, and (2) there is a duty to follow certain rules and laws. But deontologists claim that because human beings are "ends" rather than "means," they have certain rights. And where there are rights there are correlative duties. For example, if P promises his dog that he will feed him chicken livers tomorrow, P has no moral duty to keep that promise, for dogs are not intrinsically valuable ends-in-themselves. However, if P promises to pay Q for services the latter has performed, then Q has a right to expect payment and P has a moral duty to pay Q.

To be fair, restricted egoists do try to make a place for duties of the sort just mentioned, for they claim that employees must be regarded as having certain duties to their employer, e.g., employees have a duty to be loyal, a duty to follow orders, etc. Still, deontologists would argue that there are duties not recognized by restricted egoists, and that these duties are at least as important as those accepted by restricted egoists. For example, in addition to the duties employees have to their employers, they also have special duties to their families and friends, etc. Furthermore, there are duties that each person has to all other persons, e.g., we all have a duty to treat others fairly and justly. Now there are times when these duties conflict with the duties recognized by restricted egoism. Such cases arise most often in so-called "whistle-blowing" incidents. Generally, restricted egoists condemn whistle-blowing because they feel such action harms the company and violates the employee's duty to be loyal to his employer. But once a person admits that employees have duties to people outside the corporation, the morality of whistle-blowing is debatable. For instance, let us say that employee P knows that his company's head of personnel Q is a racist, and that Q always hires as few blacks as he can. In effect, P knows that Q does not treat blacks fairly. What is P to do? He has a duty to help others when they are in need of aid; and the blacks who are being mistreated are in need of aid. But P also has a duty to be loyal to his employer and not to do harm to his company's reputation. In these circumstances would it be right for P to blow the whistle on Q? Luckily, we need not decide the issue; for even if a person thinks that P should not blow the whistle, it seems unlikely that this is because he or she believes P has no duty to help other people. That is to say, if our example shows anything it is that we ordinarily do acknowledge employees as having duties that are not recognized by restricted egoists. And until restricted egoism makes some place for these duties in its moral theory, that theory cannot be considered fully adequate.

We have examined restricted egoism in some detail and have found the theory lacking. Whether or not the theory can be modified so as to overcome some or all of its shortcomings is another question entirely, one that each reader will have to decide for himself after examining the essays in this volume. If nothing else, an analysis of these readings will convince the reader of the enormity of the task facing the businessperson.

SELECTED BIBLIOGRAPHY

Barry, V. *Moral Issues in Business.* 2nd ed. Belmont, Cal.: Wadsworth, 1982.

Bartels, R., ed. *Ethics in Business.* Columbus: Ohio State University, 1963.

Beauchamp, T. *Philosophical Ethics.* New York: McGraw-Hill, 1982.

Beauchamp, T., and Bowie, N., eds. *Ethical Theory and Business.* Englewood Cliffs, N.J.: Prentice-Hall, 1979.

Bowie, N. *Business Ethics.* Englewood Cliffs, N.J.: Prentice-Hall, 1982.

DeGeorge, R. *Business Ethics.* New York: Macmillan, 1982.

DeGeorge, R., and Pichler, J., eds. *Ethics, Free Enterprise, and Public Policy.* New York: Oxford University Press, 1978.

Donaldson, T. *Corporations and Morality.* Englewood Cliffs, N.J.: Prentice-Hall, 1982.

Donaldson, T., and Werhane, P., eds. *Ethical Issues in Business.* Englewood Cliffs, N.J.: Prentice-Hall, 1979.

Frankena, W. *Ethics.* 2nd ed. Englewood Cliffs, N.J.: Prentice-Hall, 1973.

Garrett, T. *Business Ethics.* Englewood Cliffs, N.J.: Prentice-Hall, 1966.

LaCroix, W. *Principles for Ethics in Business.* Washington, D.C.: University Press of America, 1976.

Missner, M., ed. *Ethics of the Business System.* Sherman Oaks, Cal.: Alfred, 1980.

Velasquez, M. *Business Ethics.* Englewood Cliffs, N.J.: Prentice-Hall, 1982.

2

ETHICS AND ORGANIZATIONS

INTRODUCTION

The concept of responsibility introduces two issues that recur throughout this book. First, if we assume we are reasonably clear about what is involved in saying that people have moral and legal responsibilities, in what sense can corporations or organizations be said to be responsible? Second, if we assume that either corporations or the individuals in them can be said to have responsibilities, what sorts of responsibilities do they have, and, in particular, do they have responsibilities to society, i.e., social responsibilities extending beyond that of making as much money as is legally possible?

In "Morality and the Ideal of Rationality in Formal Organizations," John Ladd argues that corporations have goals such as profit maximization, that the rational act for the firm's agents is to employ the best means to achieve the corporation's goals, and that because of the firm's structure moral considerations cannot factor into rational decision-making in corporations. In their reply, C. Richard Long and Milton Snoeyenbos criticize several premises of Ladd's argument, which leaves open the possibility that corporations, as well as the individuals in such organizations, can be said to have moral and/or social responsibilities. The case study discusses the basis of organizational decision-making in Aero Products.

In his two articles, Milton Friedman argues that corporations have only one social obligation, namely, to maximize profits within the constraint of the law and ethical custom. Friedman offers two primary arguments, one based on property rights, the other on utility. The rights argument is that shareholders who own the firm typically want profits maximized; managers, as the agents of the owners should maximize profit. He also argues that if a manager acts other than to maximize profit, his act will probably have social disutility. Friedman sees institutions as having distinct functions; e.g., business should maximize profit and government should fulfill a separate set of social obligations. If businesses play a socially responsible role beyond that of profit maximization, they not only undercut shareholder rights and social utility, they actually encourage a blurring of institutional functions, which may lead to socialism. In response, Robert Almeder argues that Friedman's arguments are unsound. Furthermore, he claims that from a moral point of view there are certain acts a corporation should not perform even though those acts have utility and are not legally prohibited. Almeder goes on to argue that it is strict adherence to the Friedman position that will most likely lead to socialism; the only kind of capitalism that can survive in the long run is one that repudiates certain central tenets of Friedman's position. The case study in this section considers Ford Motor Company's rationale for placing the gas tank in its early Pinto model, and provides a specific context for discussing the Friedman-Almeder debate.

A discussion of ethics and organizations should take into account the ethical issues that managers themselves regard as central in corporate life. This is the focus of the article by Milton Snoeyenbos and Donald Jewell. They pay particular attention to industry-wide ethical issues and controversies that arise inside organizations due to their hierarchical structure. The ethical issues discussed generally in this paper are precisely those to be covered in more detail in the later chapters. The authors also suggest general strategies for improving ethical behavior in organizations.

Ethics within Organizations

Organizational Decision-making at Aero Products

Aero Products is the Aerospace division of XYZ Corporation, a U.S. capital goods conglomerate. Aero is a major producer of subassemblies for the aerospace industry, and in 1967 it placed the low bid for an order of brake assemblies for an Air Force aircraft under contract to PQR Corporation. Aero assigned responsibilities as follows:

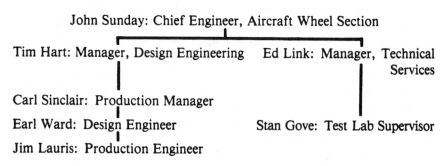

John Sunday: Chief Engineer, Aircraft Wheel Section

Tim Hart: Manager, Design Engineering   Ed Link: Manager, Technical Services

Carl Sinclair: Production Manager

Earl Ward: Design Engineer   Stan Gove: Test Lab Supervisor

Jim Lauris: Production Engineer

Ward designed the brake, called B-9. Ward was regarded as a brilliant design engineer; he had an excellent track record of product innovation. He also had a nasty temper, which flared when his work was questioned. No one questioned his preliminary design for B-9 when it was submitted. Ward selected Lauris for the task of producing the final production design. Lauris, 24, and one year out of Caltech, had shown great promise. This was his first major assignment; his task was to determine the best brake lining materials and make minor design adjustments in the brake. Lauris would work out the kinks prior to production and submit a brake assembly to the dynamometer tests required by the government. These tests, which simulate

43

the aircraft's weight and speed, must be passed prior to production. Lauris was told by Tim Hart, Design Manager, that PQR wanted to begin flight testing in mid-1968, hence Lauris had to work fast. Since Aero's suppliers had not delivered the housing and other parts, Lauris made a prototype using the disc brake Ward had designed and the suggested lining material.

In September 1967, Lauris tested the prototype for thermal build-up and wear. Normal aircraft brake lining temperatures run to 1000 degrees but the test showed the B-9 prototype reached 1500 degrees, and the linings disintegrated. After three more similar failures Lauris began to suspect the brake's design. He reworked the design computations, and it seemed to him that the brake was too small; five discs, he figured, should be used instead of four.

Lauris then took his test results and computations to Ward, who said that it was a borderline case between the two computations. He indicated that Lauris could improve results by testing more materials. The four disc brake, he noted, would be very cost effective, very light — which pleased the Air Force — and could help Aero land new contracts. He informed Lauris that brake subassemblies designed for the four disc assembly had begun arriving, that to redesign and reorder new subassemblies would be costly, and that flight testing was still scheduled for mid-1968. Ward was also aware, but did not inform Lauris, that his superior, Sinclair, had reported to PQR that initial tests of the B-9 were very successful. Sinclair had checked with Ward just prior to the second test, and asked how things were going. Ward said: "The kid has some problems, but he'll work them out. It will be okay." On that basis Sinclair sent his optimistic report to PQR.

Lauris ran two more tests in mid-November. Both failed government specifications, but he did reduce the temperature to 1300 degrees. Still unsatisfied, he decided to talk it over with Sinclair. As an MBA in industrial management, Sinclair was not an engineer. He said that he trusted Ward's experience and judgment, and noted that it would be a coup if the B-9 could be made to work. His advice was to retest. He pointed out that this was a big contract and that everyone was relying on Lauris to work out the bugs.

By this time the main housing had arrived, so Lauris built a production model. It was this model that had to pass formal qualifications tests for the military. Using a new lining, Lauris got the temperature down to 1150 degrees, but this was still 150 degrees too high and there was still some disintegration beyond normal wear. Lauris ran a dozen tests between January and March 1968, with similar results. He reported to Ward that he didn't think the B-9 could qualify. He was convinced a five disc brake was necessary.

Ward then met with Sinclair, who called in his boss, Tim Hart. Hart was aware of the problems, but said that John Sunday told him to "Get that brake qualified." Hart inquired as to the best strategy. Sinclair said they were close but needed more time. He suggested that Ward show Lauris how to run a controlled test and how to work up the data. Ward agreed.

Ward and Lauris retested. The brake had to stand up under fifty simulated stops. Fans were employed as a cooling device. Instead of maintaining pressure on the brake until the wheel stopped, the pressure was reduced when the wheel decelerated to 15 mph. This meant the wheel had to "coast to a stop." In some cases it rolled over 16,000 feet, whereas normal stopping distance was 3,000 feet. This data was deleted. After each stop the brake was disassembled and parts were machined to reduce friction. In this way the disintegration was reduced to a satisfactory level, but the temperature was still too high. Some of the data recording instruments were then recalibrated to read lower temperatures than were actually recorded. Ward assured Lauris that there was no problem, that standards were always set too high, and the brake would perform well in flight tests. He said: "Sinclair and the big boys know what's going on. They'll back us up." Lauris then turned the data over to Stan Gove, Test Lab Supervisor, who would prepare the qualification report for the military.

In checking the data, Gove caught several errors and discrepancies, and consulted with Lauris. The latter readily allowed that there were calibration errors, but said he thought they were minor. Gove then checked with Ed Link, Technical Services Manager. He told Link he could not sign a report that had errors. Link said he had talked with Sinclair and Hart; the two had indicated that testing was rushed because of the time factor, but that the data was basically alright and could be cleaned up. Link said that he would try to take Gove off the hook; if Gove would prepare the data, he would get someone upstairs to actually write the report. "After all," he said, "we're just filling in blanks and drawing curves, we're not responsible for it after it leaves here." Gove suggested that Link could discuss the issue with Sunday, but Link said: "Look, this is no big deal. Sunday probably already knows about it, but if he doesn't I'm not going to be the one to tell him." Gove asked Link if his conscience would bother him if the plane crashed on test flight landing. Link said: "I only worry about things I have control over. I have no control over this, neither do you, so why worry? Look, you've got five kids—worry about them and the wife. We'll take care of you, we'll get somebody to sign it."

Gove prepared the data and graphs. He was told by Ward to review the data and then deliver it to Sunday, who would assign someone in the engineering section to write the report and sign it. After his review, however, he was visisted by Hart, Link, and Lauris. Hart said that no one was available to write it, and that the job fell to Lauris and Gove. Lauris protested that it would violate his professional code as an engineer. Hart said, "Look, there is always some latitude in experimental design and data interpretation; professionals have to use judgment." Gove said that he knew there had been data manipulation and falsification—he could see it in the contradictory data he had been given. Link said: "You always have to rationalize the data when it comes in from a number of sources, that's part of engineering knowhow. Besides, the military has a fudge factor built in—nobody will ever know the difference. Sure you changed the data, but only to make it consistent with the big picture." Gove said he thought he should discuss the matter with Sunday. "Sunday won't touch this thing," said Hart. "Somebody's got to write and sign it, and you two are it. If the government checks us, well, Lauris did the tests and Gove drew the curves. You can defend it better than anyone. So you guys write it up and sign it, that's it. You'll get a big bonus for this, and we'll work out the kinks after the flight tests. We'll take care of you; write it up and sign it."

For Discussion

What course of action should Lauris and/or Gove pursue? Why? Do Gove and/or Lauris have obligations to: (1) their superiors, (2) XYZ Corporation, (3) society? If so, what obligations do they have, and how should they be fulfilled? Discuss the organizational context in which this problem arose. If you were brought in as Chief Engineer to replace John Sunday and this issue became known to you, what steps would you take in the present case? Why? What steps would you take to change future decision-making procedures in your section of the organization?

SOURCE

This case is based on Kermit Vandiver's "Why Should My Conscience Bother Me?" in *In the Name of Profit,* edited by Robert L. Heilbroner, et al. (New York: Doubleday, 1972), pp. 3-31.

John Ladd

Morality and the Ideal of Rationality in Formal Organizations

I. INTRODUCTORY

The purpose of this paper is to explore some of the moral problems that arise out of the interrelationships between individuals and formal organizations (or bureaucracies) in our society. In particular, I shall be concerned with the moral implications of the so-called ideal of rationality of formal organizations with regard to, on the one hand, the obligations of individuals both inside and outside an organization to that organization and, on the other hand, the moral responsibilities of organizations to individuals and to the public at large. I shall argue that certain facets of the organizational ideal are incompatible with the ordinary principles of morality and that the dilemma created by this incompatibility is one source of alienation in our contemporary, industrial society. The very conception of a formal organization or bureaucracy presents us with an ideological challenge that desperately needs to be met in some way or other.

The term "formal organization" will be used in a more or less technical sense to cover all sorts of bureaucracies, private and public. A distinctive mark of such organizations is that they make a clear-cut distinction between the acts and relationships of individuals in their official capacity within the organization and in their private capacity. Decisions of individual decision-makers in an organization are attributed to the organization and not to the individual. In that sense, they are impersonal. Individual office-holders are in principle replaceable by other individuals without affecting the continuity or identity of the organization. In this sense, it has sometimes been said that an organization is "immortal."

This kind of impersonality, in particular, the substitutability of individuals, is one way in which formal organizations differ from other kinds of

From *The Monist* Vol. 54, no. 4 (October, 1970). Reprinted by permission of the author and *The Monist*.

social systems, e.g. the family, the community or the nation, which are collectivities that are dependent for their existence on specific individuals or groups of specific individuals and that change when they change.

Under formal organizations I shall include not only all sorts of industrial, military and governmental bureaucracies but also formal organizations like large universities (multiversities), hospitals, labor unions, and political machines. For our purposes, we may even include illegal and undercover organizations like the Mafia, the Communist Party, the FBI, and the CIA. The general characteristics of all these organizations are that they are "planned units, deliberately structured for the purpose of attaining specific goals,"[1] and such that each formal organization is a "continuous organization of official functions bound by rules."[2] One of the distinctive features of formal organizations of the type we are interested in is that they are ordinarily hierarchical in structure; they not only have a "horizontal" division of labor but a "vertical" one as well—a "pyramid of authority."[3]

*   *   *

Social critics, e.g. W. H. Whyte, use phrases like the "smothering of the individual" to describe the contemporary situation created by organizations. It is not my purpose here to decry once more the unhappy condition of man occasioned by his submergence as an individual in the vast social, economic and political processes created by formal organizations. Instead, I shall try to show that the kind of alienation that we all feel and complain about is, at least in part, a logical necessity flowing from the concept of formal organizations itself, that is, it is a logical consequence of the particular language-game one is playing in organizational decision-making. My analysis is intended to be a logical analysis, but one that also has important ethical implications.

*   *   *

Here we may find the concept of a language-game, as advanced by Wittgenstein and others, a useful tool of analysis. The point about a language-game is that it emphasizes the way language and action are interwoven. . . . A particular language-game determines how the activities within it are to be conceptualized, prescribed, justified and evaluated. Take as an example what is meant by a "good" move in chess: we have to refer to the rules of chess to determine what a "move" is, how to make one, what its consequences will be, what its objective is and whether or not it is a good move in the light of this objective.[4] Finally, this system of rules performs the logical function of defining the game itself.

One advantage of the language-game model is, therefore, that it enables us to describe a kind of activity by reference to a set of rules that determine not only what should or should not be done, but also how what is done is to be rationally evaluated and defended. And it allows us to describe the activity without reference to moral rules (or norms). In other words, it provides us with a method of analyzing a rational activity without committing ourselves to whether or not it is also moral.

If we pursue the game-analogy one step further, we find that there may be even more striking similarities between the language-game of formal organizations and the language-game of other types of games. For instance, the rules and rationale obtaining in most typical games like chess and baseball tend to make the activity logically autonomous, i.e. the moves, defenses and evaluations are made independently of external considerations. In this sense they are self-contained. Furthermore, while playing a game it is thought to be "unfair" to challenge the rules. Sometimes it is even maintained that any questioning of the rules is unintelligible. In any case, there is a kind of sanctity attached to the rules of a game that renders them immune to criticism on the part of those engaged in playing the game. The resemblance of the autonomy of the activity and the immunity of the rules governing the game to the operations of bureaucracies can hardly be coincidental![5]

II. THE CONCEPTS OF SOCIAL DECISION AND SOCIAL ACTION

Let us take as our point of departure Herbert Simon's definition of a formal organization as a "decision-making structure."[6] The central concept with which we must deal is that of a decision (or action) that is attributable to the organization rather than to the individuals who are actually involved in the decisional process. The decision is regarded as the organization's decision even though it is made by certain individuals acting as its representatives. The latter make the decision only for and on behalf of the organization. Their role is, i.e. is supposed to be, impersonal. Such nonindividual decisions will be called *social decisions,* choices or actions. (I borrow the term "social choice" from Arrow, who uses it to refer to a choice made on behalf of a group as distinct from the aggregate of individual choices.)[7]

The officials of an organization are "envisaged as more or less ethically neutral . . . (and) the values to be taken as data are not those which would guide the individual if he were a private citizen. . . ."[8] When the official decides for the organization, his aim is (or should be) to implement the objectives of the organization *impersonally,* as it were. The decisions are made for the organization, with a view to its objectives and not on the basis of the personal interests or convictions of the individual official who makes the decision. This is the theory of organizational decision-making.

One might be tempted to call such organizational decisions "collective decisions," but that would be a misnomer if we take a collective decision to be a decision made by a collection of individuals. Social decisions are precisely decisions (or actions) that are to be *attributed* to the organizations themselves and not to collections of individuals. In practice, of course, the organizational decisions made by officials may actually be collective decisions. But in theory the two must be kept separate; for the "logic" of decisions attributed to organizations is critically different from the "logic" of collective decisions, i.e. those attributed to a collection of individuals.

Underlying the concept of social decisions (choices, actions) as outlined here is the notion that a person (or group of persons) can make decisions that are not his, i.e. are not attributable to him. He makes the decisions on behalf of someone else and with a view to the latter's interest, not his own. In such cases, we ordinarily consider the person (or group) that acts to be a representative or agent of the person or thing he is acting for.

*   *   *

The theory of social decision-making that we are considering becomes even clearer if we examine the theory of organizational authority with which it is conjoined. Formal organizations are hierarchical in structure, that is, they are organized along the principle that superiors issue commands to those below them. The superior exercises authority over the subordinates. . . .

In summary, then, the organizational order requires that its social decisions be attributed to the organization rather than to the individual decision-maker, the "decision is to be made nonpersonally from the point of view of its organization effect and its relation to the organizational purpose,"[9] and the officials, as its agents, are required to abdicate their choice in obedience to the impersonal organizational order.

We now turn to another essential facet of the organizational language-game, namely, that every formal organization must have a goal, or a set of goals. In fact, organizations are differentiated and defined by reference to their aims or goals, e.g. the aim of the Internal Revenue Service is to collect taxes. The goal of most business ventures is to maximize profits, etc. We may find it useful to distinguish between the real and stated goals of an organization. Thus, as Galbraith has pointed out, although the stated goal of large industrial organizations is the maximization of profits, that is a pure myth; their actual, operative goals are the securing of their own survival, autonomy and economic growth.[10] There may, indeed, be a struggle over the goals of an organization, e.g. a power play between officials.[11]

For our present purposes, we may consider the real goal of an organization to be that objective (or set of objectives) that is used as a basis for decision-making, i.e. for prescribing and justifying the actions and decisions of the organization itself, as distinct from the actions and decisions of individual persons within the organization. As such, then, the goal is an essential element in the language-game of a formal organization's activities in somewhat the same way as the goal of checkmating the king is an essential element in the game of chess. Indeed, formal organizations are often differentiated from other kinds of social organizations in that they are "deliberately constructed and reconstructed to seek specific goals."[12]

The logical function of the goal in the organizational language-game is to supply the value premises to be used in making decisions, justifying and evaluating them. "Decisions in private management, like decisions in public management, must take as their ethical premises the objectives that have been set for the organization."[13]

It follows that any considerations that are not related to the aims or goals of the organization are automatically excluded as irrelevant to the organizational decision-making process. This principle of the exclusion of the irrelevant is part of the language-game. It is a logical requirement of the process of prescribing, justifying and evaluating social decisions. Consequently, apart from purely legal considerations, decisions and actions of individual officers that are unrelated to the organization's aims or goals are construed, instead, as actions of those individuals rather than of the organization. If an individual official makes a mistake or does something that fails to satisfy this criterion of social decision, he will be said to have "exceeded his authority," and will probably be sacked or made a vice-president! Again, the point is a logical one, namely, that only those actions that are related to the goal of the organization are to be attributed to the organization; those actions that are inconsistent with it are attributed to the individual officers as individuals. The individual, rather than the organization, is then forced to take the blame for whatever evil results.

Thus, for example, a naval officer who runs his ship aground is court-martialed because what he did was inconsistent with the aims of the naval organization; the action is attributed to him rather than to the Navy. On the other hand, an officer who successfully bombards a village, killing all of its inhabitants, in accordance with the objectives of his organization, is performing a social action, an action that is attributable to the organization and not to him as an individual. Whether or not the organization should take responsibility in a particular case for the mistakes of its officials is a policy decision to be made in the light of the objectives of the organization.

In other words, the concept of a social decision or action is bound up logically with the notion of an organizational aim. The consequence of this co-implication of action and aim is that the notion of an action or decision taken by an organization that is not related to one of its aims makes no sense. It is an unintelligible notion within the language-game of formal organizations. Within that language-game such an action would be as difficult to understand as it would be to understand how a man's knocking over the pieces in a chess game can be part of playing chess.

We finally come to the concept of "rationality," the so-called "ideal of pure rationality."[14] From the preceding observations concerning the organizational language-game, it should be clear that the sole standard for the evaluation of an organization, its activities and its decisions, is its effectiveness in achieving its objectives—within the framework of existing conditions and available means. This kind of effectiveness is called "rationality." Thus, rationality is defined in terms of the category of means and ends.

"Behavior . . . is rational insofar as it selects alternatives which are conducive to the achievement of previously selected goals."[15] And "the rationality of decisions . . . is their appropriateness for the accomplishment of specified goals."[16]

"Rationality," so construed, is relative, that is, to be rational means to be efficient in pursuing a desired goal, whatever that might be. In the case of organizations, "a decision is 'organizationally' rational if it is oriented to the organization's goals."[17] Rationality is consequently neutral as to "what goals are to be attained."[18] Or to be more accurate, "rationality" is an incomplete term that requires reference to a goal before it is completely intelligible.

*   *   *

Let us return to the organizational language-game. It was observed that within that game the sole standard of evaluation of, e.g. a decision, is the "rational" one, namely, that it be effective in achieving the organization's goal. Hence, any considerations that are taken into account in deliberation about these social decisions and in the evaluation of them are relevant only if they are related to the attainment of the organization's objectives. Let us suppose that there are certain factual conditions that must be considered in arriving at a decision, e.g. the available means, costs, and conditions of feasibility. The determination of such conditions is presumably a matter of empirical knowledge and a subject for empirical investigation. Among these empirical conditions there is a special class that I shall call *limiting operating conditions*. These are conditions that set the upper limits to an organization's operations, e.g. the scarcity of resources, of equipment, of trained personnel, legal restrictions, factors involving employee morale. Such conditions must be taken into account as *data,* so to speak, in organizational decision-making and planning. In this respect information about them is on a par logically with other information utilized in decision-making, e.g. cost-benefit computations.

Now the only way that moral considerations could be relevant to the operations of a formal organization in the language-game that I have been describing is by becoming limiting operating conditions. Strictly speaking, they could not even be introduced as such, because morality is itself not a matter of empirical knowledge. Insofar as morality in the strict sense enters into practical reasoning it must do so as an "ethical" premise, not as an empirical one. Hence morality as such must be excluded as irrelevant in organizational decision-making — by the rules of the language-game. The situation is somewhat parallel to the language-game used in playing chess: moral considerations are not relevant to the decisions about what move to make there either.

Morality enters in only indirectly, namely, as moral opinion, what John Austin calls "positive morality."[19] Obviously the positive morality, laws and customs of the society in which the organization operates must be taken into account in decision-making and planning. The same thing goes for the religious beliefs and practices of the community. A decision-maker cannot ignore them, and it makes no difference whether he shares them or accepts them himself personally. But the determination of whether or not there are such limiting conditions set by positive morality, customs, laws, and religion is an empirical matter. Whether there are such limitations is simply a matter of fact and their relevance to the decision-making is entirely dependent upon how they affect the efficiency of the organization's operations.

Social decisions, then, are not and cannot be governed by the principles of morality, or, if one wishes, they are governed by a different set of moral principles from those governing the conduct of individuals as individuals. For, as Simon says: "Decisions in private management, like decisions in public management, must take as their ethical premises the objectives that have been set for the organization."[20] By implication, they cannot take their ethical premises from the principles of morality.

Thus, for logical reasons it is improper to expect organizational conduct to conform to the ordinary principles of morality. We cannot and must not expect formal organizations, or their representatives acting in their official capacities, to be honest, courageous, considerate, sympathetic, or to have any kind of moral integrity. Such concepts are not in the vocabulary, so to speak, of the organizational language-game. (We do not find them in the vocabulary of chess either!) Actions that are wrong by ordinary moral standards are not so for organizations; indeed, they may often be required. Secrecy, espionage and deception do not make organizational action wrong; rather they are right, proper and, indeed, *rational,* if they serve the objectives of the organization. They are no more or no less wrong than, say, bluffing is in poker. From the point of view of organizational decision-making they are "ethically neutral."

Of course, I do not want to deny that it may be in the best interests of a formal organization to pay lip service to popular morality (and religion). That is a matter of public relations. But public relations operations themselves are evaluated and justified on the same basis as the other operations of the organization. The official function of the public relations officer is to facilitate the operations of the organization, not to promote morality.

*   *   *

The upshot of our discussion so far is that actions are subject to two entirely different and, at times, incompatible standards: social decisions are subject to the standard of rational efficiency (utility) whereas the actions of individuals as such are subject to the ordinary standards of morality. An action that is right from the point of view of one of these standards may be wrong from the point of view of the other. Indeed, it is safe to say that our own experience attests to the fact that our actual expectations and social approvals are to a large extent based on a tacit acceptance of a double-standard — one for the individual when he is in his office working for the company and another for him when he is at home among friends and neighbors. Take as an example the matter of lying: nobody would think of condemning Joe X, a movie star, for lying on a TV commercial about what brand of cigarettes he smokes, for it is part of his job. On the other hand, if he were to do the same thing in private among friends, we should consider his action to be improper and immoral. Or again, an individual who, acting in his official capacity, refuses help to a needy suppliant, would be roundly condemned if he were to adopt the same course of action in his private life.

The pervasiveness of organizational activity throughout modern society makes the impact of this double-standard on the individual particularly unsettling. It produces a kind of moral schizophrenia which has affected us all. Furthermore, the dilemma in which we find ourselves cannot so easily be conjured away; for it has its logical ground as well as basis in the dynamics of social structure.

*   *   *

III. The Moral Relationship of Individuals to Organizations

It follows from what has already been said that the standard governing an individual's relationship to an organization is likely to be different from the one governing the converse relationship, i.e. of an organization to individuals. The individual, for his part, is supposed to conduct himself in his relationship to an organization according to the same standards that he would employ in his personal relationships, i.e. the standards of ordinary morality. Thus, he is expected to be honest, open, respectful, conscientious, and loyal towards the organization of which he is a member or with which he has dealings. The organization, represented by its officials, can, however, be none of these in return. "Officials are expected to assume an impersonal orientation. . . . Clients are to be treated as cases . . . and subordinates are to be treated in a similar fashion."[21]

The question I now want to explore is whether or not the individual is justified in applying the standard of individual morality to his relations with formal organizations. It will, of course, generally be in the interest of the formal organizations themselves to encourage him to do so, e.g. to be honest, although the organization as such cannot "reciprocate." But we must ask this question from the point of view of the individual or, if you wish, from the moral point of view: what good moral reasons can be given for an individual to assume a moral stance in his conduct and relations with formal organizations, in contradistinction, say, to his conduct and relations with individuals who happen to be employees of such an organization?

*   *   *

Can any moral reasons be given why individual subjects should comply with the decisions of organizations? Or, what amounts to the same thing, what is the basis of the authority of organizations by virtue of which we have an obligation to accept and obey their directives? And why, if at all, do we owe them loyalty and fidelity?

The most obvious answer, although perhaps not the most satisfactory one ethically, is that it is generally expedient for the individual to go along with what is required by formal organizations. If I want a new automobile, I have to comply with the financial requirements. If I want to avoid being harassed by an internal revenue agent, I make out my income tax form properly. If I want to be legally married, I comply with the regulations of the Department of Public Health. In other words, I comply from practical necessity, that is, I act under a hypothetical imperative.

Still, this sort of answer is just as unsatisfactory from the point of view of moral philosophy as the same kind of answer always has been with regard to political obligation, namely, it fails to meet the challenge of the conscientious objector.

*   *   *

The utilitarian answer to our question, like its ancestor the utilitarian theory of political obligation, maintains that somehow or other an individual act of compliance with the established order inevitably contributes to the stability of the whole system, whereas an individual act of defiance inevitably contributes to its instability. Thus Hume compares the social order of inflexible rules to a vault, where the "whole fabric is supported but by the mutual assistance and combination of its corresponding parts."[22] There is, it appears, no empirical evidence to support the contention that an individual act will strengthen or weaken the system. Nor is there any reason to suppose that the preserving of the status quo is either necessary or sufficient for promoting the public interest. In view of the complexity of the impact of modern social and political organizations on society, it is difficult, if not impossible, to accept a utilitarian argument as the basis of an individual's obligation towards formal organizations.

*   *   *

In the final analysis perhaps the most plausible basis of the authority of formal organizations, or at least within formal organizations, is the Platonic one, namely, that the commands of officials should be complied with because they have superior knowledge. The superiors, like the guardians in Plato's *Republic,* are experts; they have the expertise that the subordinates do not possess but need in order to act effectively. That much of the authority relationship within military and industrial organizations is founded on expert-know-how or alleged know-how is unquestionable. Many organizations, however, e.g. the public bureaucracies, make decisions that are not based upon superior knowledge, but involve the same kind of information and knowledge that is available to the general public, and in particular, to many individuals outside the organization. This is, of course, particularly true where issues of public (and foreign) policy are concerned.[23]

The breakdown of the argument from superior expertise is due, no doubt, to advances in technology, mass education and mass communication. More information of a higher quality is available to large numbers of people who are simply subjects and do not have command positions within the bureaucracies to which they are subject. It is too easy to see through the claims to superior knowledge when we also have some knowledge of our own about what is going on.

I have been able to touch only on some very limited aspects of the relationship of individuals to organizations. I hope, however, that it is now abundantly clear that some sort of crisis is taking place in our moral relationships, and in particular in our conceptions of authority, and that this crisis is due not only to complex historical, psychological and sociological factors, but also to an inherent *logical* paradox in the foundations of our social relations.

IV. THE MORAL RELATIONSHIP OF ORGANIZATIONS TO INDIVIDUALS

For logical reasons that have already been mentioned, formal organizations cannot assume a genuine moral posture towards individuals. Although the language-game of social decision permits actions to be attributed to organizations as such, rather than to the officials that actually make them, it does not contain concepts like "moral obligation," "moral responsibility," or "moral integrity." For the only relevant principles in rational decision-making are those relating to the objectives of the organization. Hence individual officers who make the decisions for and in the name of the organization, as its representatives, must decide solely by reference to the objectives of the organization.

According to the theory, then, the individuals who are officers of an organization, i.e. those who run it, operate simply as vehicles or instruments of the organization. The organization language-game requires that they be treated as such. That is why, in principle at least, any individual is dispensable and replaceable by another. An individual is selected for a position, retained in it, or fired from it solely on the grounds of efficiency, i.e. of what will best serve the interests of the organization. The interests and needs of the individuals concerned, as individuals, must be considered only insofar as they establish limiting operating conditions. Organizational rationality dictates that these interests and needs must not be considered in their own right or on their own merits. If we think of an organization as a machine, it is easy to see why we cannot reasonably expect it to have any moral obligations to people or for them to have any to it.

For precisely the same reason, the rights and interests of persons outside the organization and of the general public are *eo ipso* ruled out as logically irrelevant to rational organizational decision, except insofar as these rights and interests set limiting conditions to the effectiveness of the organization's operations or insofar as the promoting of such rights and interests constitutes part of the goal of the organization. Hence it is fatuous to expect an industrial organization to go out of its way to avoid polluting the atmosphere or to refrain from making napalm bombs or to desist from wiretapping on purely moral grounds. Such actions would be irrational.

It follows that the only way to make the rights and interests of individuals or of the people logically relevant to organizational decision-making is to convert them into pressures of one sort or another, e.g. to bring the pressure of the law or of public opinion to bear on the organizations. Such pressures would then be introduced into the rational decision-making as limiting operating conditions.

Since formal organizations cannot have moral obligations, they cannot have moral responsibilities in the sense of having obligations towards those affected by their actions or subject to their actions because of the power they possess. Organizations have tremendous power, but no responsibilities. . . .

Hence, as I have pointed out, the only way to influence such a rational organization is through coercion, legislative or otherwise. And the more rational it is, the more necessary it is that such external pressures be maintained.

Since, as I have argued in some detail, formal organizations are not moral persons, and have no moral responsibilities, they have no moral rights. In particular, they have no *moral* right to freedom or autonomy. There can be nothing morally wrong in exercising coercion against a formal organization as there would be in exercising it against an individual. Hence, the other side of the coin is that it would be irrational for us, as moral persons, to feel any moral scruples about what we do to organizations. (We should constantly bear in mind that the officials themselves, as individuals, must still be treated as moral persons with rights and responsibilities attached to them as individuals.)

*   *   *

V. UTILITARIANISM AND ALIENATION

It is abundantly evident that the use of a double standard for the evaluation of actions is not confined to the operations of formal organizations, as I have described them. The double standard for social morality is pervasive in our society. For almost all our social decisions, administrative, political and economic, are made and justified by reference to the "rational" standard, which amounts to the principle that the end justifies the means; and yet as individuals, in our personal relations with one another, we are bound by the ordinary principles of morality, i.e. the principles of obligation, responsibility and integrity.

*   *   *

A great deal more needs to be said about the effects of working from a double standard of morality. In our highly organized (and utilitarian) society, most of us, as individuals, are forced to live double lives, and in order to accommodate ourselves to two different and incompatible standards, we tend to compartmentalize our lives, as I have already pointed out. For the most part, however, the organizational (or utilitarian) standard tends to take over.

Accordingly, our actions as individuals are increasingly submerged into social actions, that is, we tend more and more to use the social standard as a basis for our decisions and to evaluate our actions. As a result, the individual's own decisions and actions become separated from himself as a person and become the decisions and actions of another, e.g. of an organization. They become social decisions, not decisions of the individual. And in becoming social decisions, they are, in Hobbes's terms, no longer "his," they are "owned" by another, e.g. an organization or society.

This is one way of rendering the Marxian concept of alienation. As his actions are turned into social decisions, the individual is alienated from them and is *eo ipso* alienated from other men and from morality. In adopting the administrator's point of view (or that of a utilitarian) and so losing his actions, the individual becomes dehumanized and demoralized. For morality is essentially a relation between men, as individuals, and in losing this relation, one loses morality itself.

VI. Closing Remarks on the Source of the Paradox

It is unnecessary to dwell on the intolerable character of the moral schizophrenia in which we find ourselves as the result of the double standard of conduct that has been pointed out. The question is: what can be done about it? The simplest and most obvious solution is to jettison one of the conflicting standards. But which one? The choice is difficult, if not impossible. If we give up the standard of "rationality," e.g. of organizational operations, then we surrender one of the chief conditions of civilized life and progress as well as the hope of ever solving mankind's perennial practical problems, e.g. the problems of hunger, disease, ignorance and overpopulation. On the other hand, if we give up the standard of ordinary moral conduct, then in effect we destroy ourselves as moral beings and reduce our relationships to each other to purely mechanical and materialistic ones. To find a third way out of the dilemma is not only a practical, political and sociological necessity, but a moral one as well.

* * *

NOTES

[The notes for this essay have been renumbered. —Eds.]

1. Amitai Etzioni, *Modern Organizations* (Englewood Cliffs, N.J.: Prentice-Hall, 1964), p. 4. Hereinafter cited as MO.

2. Max Weber, quoted in Etzioni, MO, p. 53.

3. Herbert A. Simon, *Administrative Behavior,* 2nd ed. (New York: Free Press, 1965), p. 9. Hereinafter cited as Simon, AB. For a useful survey of the subject of formal organizations, see Peter M. Blau and W. Richard Scott, *Formal Organizations* (San Francisco: Chandler Publishing Company, 1962). Hereinafter cited as Blau and Scott, FO. I am indebted to my friend Richard Taub for many helpful suggestions in writing this paper.

4. These rules are called "constitutive rules" by John Searle. See his *Speech Acts* (Cambridge: The University Press, 1969), Ch. 2, Sec. 5.

5. For further discussion of the game-model and this aspect of rules, see my "Moral and Legal Obligation," in J. Roland Pennock and John W. Chapman, editors, *Political and Legal Obligation, Nomos,* 12 (New York: Atherton Press, 1970).

6. See Simon, AB, *passim.* Also, Blau and Scott, FO, p. 36.

7. See Kenneth Arrow, *Social Choice and Individual Values* (New York: John Wiley, 1951), *passim.*

8. Quoted from A. Bergson by Kenneth Arrow in "Public and Private Values," in *Human Values and Economic Policy,* ed. S. Hook (New York: New York University Press, 1967), p. 14.

9. Quoted from Chester I. Barnard in Simon, AB, p. 203.

10. See John Kenneth Galbraith, *The New Industrial State* (Boston: Houghton Mifflin, 1967), pp. 171-78. Hereinafter cited as NIS.

11. See Etzioni, MO, pp. 7-9.

12. Etzioni, MO, p. 3. See also Blau and Scott, FO, p. 5. In a forthcoming article on "Community," I try to show that communities, as distinct from formal organizations, do not have specific goals. Indeed, the having of a specific goal may be what differentiates a *Gesellschaft* from a *Gemeinschaft* in Tönnies' sense. See Ferdinand Tönnies, *Community and Society,* trans. Charles P. Loomis (New York: Harper and Row, 1957), *passim.*

13. Simon, AB, p. 52.

14. "The ideal of pure rationality is basic to operations research and the modern management sciences." Yehezkel Dror, *Public Policymaking Reexamined* (San Francisco: Chandler Publishing Company, 1968), p. 336. Dror gives a useful bibliography of this subject on pp. 336-40.

15. Simon, AB, p. 5.

16. Simon, AB, p. 240.

17. Simon, AB, p. 77.

18. Simon, AB, p. 14.

19. "The name *morality,* when standing unqualified or alone, may signify the human laws which I style positive morality, without regard to their goodness or

badness. For example, such laws of the class as are peculiar to a given age, or such laws of the class as are peculiar to a given nation, we style the morality of that given age or nation, whether we think them good or bad, etc." John Austin, *Province of Jurisprudence Determined,* ed. H. L. A. Hart (New York: Noonday Press, 1954), p. 125. The study of positive moralities belongs to what I call "descriptive ethics." See my *Structure of a Moral Code* (Cambridge, Mass: Harvard University Press, 1957).

20. Simon, AB, p. 52.

21. Blau and Scott, FO, p. 34.

22. David Hume, *An Enquiry Concerning the Principles of Morals,* ed. L. A. Selby-Bigge (Oxford: Clarendon Press, 1902), p. 305.

23. It is easy to understand why officials often go to such extremes to monopolize information; for monopolizing information is one of the few remaining ways for them to protect an authority that is already wobbling.

C. Richard Long
Milton Snoeyenbos

Ladd on Morality
and Formal Organizations

In "Morality and the Ideal of Rationality in Formal Organizations," John Ladd argues as follows:

1. Corporate, military, and governmental organizations are formal organizations.
2. A formal organization is a decision-making structure characterized by:
   a. a goal or set of goals,
   b. the concept of an organizational (or "social") act or decision whereby an individual, as an agent for the organization, makes decisions for and on behalf of the organization.
   c. a hierarchical structure of authority for establishing and implementing organizational decisions, and,
   d. a standard of rationality according to which the rational organizational act is the one that best achieves the organization's goal(s).
3. The only way moral principles could enter into organizational decision-making is by either being organizational goals or limiting operating conditions.
4. All limiting operating conditions are factual conditions.
5. Moral principles are not factual conditions.
6. Moral principles are not organizational goals.
7. Therefore, organizational decisions cannot be based on moral principles.

If Ladd's argument is sound it has unsettling implications both for corporate behavior and for how ordinary citizens regard corporations. On the one hand, in fulfilling his organizational role the individual cannot legitimately appeal to moral principles. But, since people do have a moral dimension, which at times conflicts with decisions demanded by one's organizational role, individuals in organizations experience a moral schizophrenia or alienation that Ladd contends can be eliminated only by abandoning either the standard of organizational rationality or the standards of moral conduct. Since the former underpins the efficiency of organizational operations necessary for our complex society and the latter are the glue of social civility, this indeed is a dilemma. On the other hand, if, as Ladd suggests, corporations have no moral responsibilities or rights, it is not morally wrong to coerce them (p. 57). But, since this can be only realistically accomplished by governmental action, it pits one type of formal organization against another (neither of which has moral responsibilities), and, given the power of government, this threatens the private/public distinction.

If we accept (2), (3), and (5), this still leaves us with (1), (4), and (6) as controversial premises. Let us first consider (4). If limiting operating conditions (i.e., those factors that set limits to or place constraints on achievement of a firm's goals) *could* include moral principles, then there could be moral constraints on corporate decision-making. And if there were cases in which moral principles actually served as limiting operating conditions, then (4) would be false.

According to Ladd, moral principles cannot be introduced as limiting operating conditions, because the latter are factual whereas the former are evaluative and not factual. But Ladd simply *asserts* that limiting operating conditions are factual; no argument is offered for the assertion. He does distinguish moral principles from moral beliefs or opinions (pp. 52-3). And there is a difference between the moral claim "act x is morally right," and moral beliefs of the form "person P (or the members of society S) believe act x is morally right"; the former is evaluative, the latter is factual. Accordingly, Ladd allows that moral beliefs, "the positive morality, laws, and customs of the society . . . must be taken into account in decision-making" (pp. 52-3). The moral beliefs of a society, being factual, can, on Ladd's view, serve as limiting operating conditions. Again, however, this distinction does not entail that moral principles could not *also* be limiting operating conditions. Once one adopts a moral principle it is a fact that the principle has been adopted, but it does not cease to be a moral principle because one adopts, believes, or accepts it. So, Ladd simply asserts, but does not support, his claim that limiting operating conditions must be factual.

If we now consider *actual* corporate behavior, we must acknowledge that while we have numerous theoretical models of organizational decision-making, we have few concrete, empirical studies that would enable us to decide whether moral principles in fact do sometimes serve as limiting operating conditions. Perhaps the best we can do, then, is to examine corporate policy statements under the assumption that corporate behavior is sometimes in accord with such statements. Now, certainly, in some cases it appears that moral customs or beliefs are regarded as limiting operating conditions. General Mills, while acknowledging that its economic goals are primary, also recognizes an "obligation to conduct ourselves in a way that is consistent with social goals . . . compliance with these social goals is an important way of retaining an environment in which we can conduct our economic activity."[1] Exxon says that in addition to its economic functions it is "acutely aware that it must conduct its activities in a responsible and ethical manner. . . it is in the best interest of business to continue to meet public expectations." Exxon's Chairman, C. C. Garvin, recently elaborated on this, saying that ". . . business managers must begin by understanding the laws of the countries in which they operate—and, beyond this, develop a sensitivity to the spirit of the law. . . . Second, they must stay sensitive to shifts in public policy. . . . At Exxon we make frequent use of opinion research surveys to identify social concerns and to gauge their importance in the public mind."[2] While somewhat ambiguous, such statements have a prudential ring to them; consistent with Ladd's position, both could be interpreted as meaning that, although economic goals are primary, moral beliefs or customs, when adequately factored into organizational decision-making as constraints or limiting operating conditions, can better enable the firm to achieve its economic goals. But other corporations, while also acknowledging the primacy of economic goals, seem to allow that moral principles themselves can serve as limiting operating conditions. Alcoa lists traditional economic goals as "fundamental" corporate objectives, but states that in "achieving its fundamental objectives, Alcoa . . . pledges to conduct its business in a legal and ethical manner." Similarly, in achieving its economic "objectives," Bankers Life is "dedicated to conducting all its operations with high ethical and moral standards." On the face of it, these statements directly place evaluative constraints on the achievement of basic, economic corporate goals. In such cases, (4) seems false.

Our point, then, is that an argument rather than an assertion is required if Ladd is to establish that limiting operating conditions are factual and hence (assuming the truth of (5)) that moral principles are not (or cannot be) limiting operating conditions. For even if no firm has ever acted by using a moral principle as a limiting operating condition, this would not preclude the possibility or desirability of their so acting. And, as we noted, some corporate policy statements commit firms to regard moral principles as limiting operating conditions. If such firms act in accordance with their policy statements, then (4) is certainly false.

Premise (6) may also be questioned, because it is not obviously true that moral principles are not (in some cases) corporate goals. On the face of it, there seem to be no reasons why moral principles *could not* be corporate goals. While it may be true that many corporations do not include moral principles as explicitly stated goals, Ladd himself allows that corporations may have a multiplicity of goals (p. 50), that formal organizations are "deliberately constructed and reconstructed to seek specific goals" (p. 50), and that there may be a "struggle over the goals of an organization" (p. 50). Since corporations lacking moral principles and obligations as corporate goals could be "reconstructed" to include them, there appears to be nothing intrinsic to the notion of a formal organization that precludes incorporation of moral principles into a corporate goal structure.

If we consider actual corporate policy statements, we find that firms frequently specify a variety of objectives, and some include moral goals. In certain cases, e.g., Hewlett-Packard and IBM, a firm simply provides a non-ordered list of corporate aims that includes moral obligations to employees, customers, society, etc., in addition to profit and growth objectives. In other cases, firms order their goals, and, interestingly enough, some corporations list profit as a means to goals that could reasonably be said to be moral:

> *The Dow Chemical Co. Objectives:* To seek maximum long-term profit growth as the primary means to ensure the prosperity of our employees and stockholders, the well-being of our customers, and the improvement of people's lives everywhere. To attract and hire talented, competent people, and pay them well for their performance. To provide our employees with equal opportunity for career growth and personal fulfillment. To give our employees greater opportunity to participate in decision-making. To strengthen our commitment to individual freedom and self-renewal. To be scrupulously ethical in the means to our ends and in the ends themselves. To be responsible citizens of the different societies in which we operate. To grow through continuous innovation of our products and processes. To make price a measure of true market value for our products and services. To practice stewardship in the manufacture, marketing, use and disposal of our products. To share in the responsibility of all peoples for protection of the environment. To make wise and efficient use of the earth's energy and natural resources. To make this world a better place for our having been in business.

Dow is quite explicit in claiming that profit maximization is a means to moral and social ends:

> To seek maximum long-term profit growth . . . . This is our first and overriding concern, of course. It is totally consistent with our view of social responsibility and should come as no surprise. Some people might prefer to see us downplay our concern for profit in favor of doing great and good things for society. Somehow, they misunderstand the role of business. They have been lulled into thinking of profit as an end in itself. It is not. At Dow, we do not squirrel away our money in an old sock like some corporate Scrooge. We use profit as a tool, as the *means* to an end. That end, we feel, is very simple and very clear: . . . To ensure the prosperity of our employees and stockholders, the wellbeing of our customers, and the improvement of people's lives everywhere. This is our reason for being. It is a legitimate one. Profit is not a reward, but a way to achieve our objective. Indeed, our reward for continuing to provide the goods and services people want and need is to *stay* in business, to keep doing what we are very good at doing. Profit makes that possible.

Profit enables the firm to survive, but neither profit nor survival are the end of the firm; they are means to ends that embed moral and social principles. American Can Company has a similar policy statement:

The American Can Creed: American Can Company is a business enterprise dedicated to supplying goods and services of the highest quality to all of our customers worldwide, at the same time satisfying the needs of our shareowners and employees. Our fundamental goal is to provide a reasonable return on the investment made by our shareowners. By achieving this basic objective, we retain the strength and vigor needed to promote healthy competition and fulfill our social and moral responsibilities. We are committed to the highest standards of personal integrity in our daily work, and are pledged to respect both the letter and the spirit of the laws under which we operate. Through constant dedication to these principles, we will exemplify responsible leadership in the business community and ensure the continued confidence of the publics we serve.

The company acknowledges a number of goals, and then specifies a fundamental, *instrumental* goal ("a reasonable return on investment") that is a means of fulfilling the firm's "social and moral responsibilities."

Although there seem to be no reasons why firms cannot incorporate moral and social goals in their corporate goal structures, and although some firms explicitly *state* such goals as basic or central aims of the organization, Ladd differentiates stated from *actual* organizational goals (p. 50). For example, he claims, following John Kenneth Galbraith, that profit maximization is a "mythical" (although frequently stated) corporate goal, and that firms actually seek their own survival, autonomy, and growth. Is it the case, then, that stated moral goals such as those expressed in the policy statements of Dow Chemical and American Can are a form of window dressing that masks actual economic goals?

Only detailed empirical research that we do not now possess could adequately answer this question, but three points are worthy of note. First, Ladd's distinction between stated and actual goals cuts both ways; it may be that firms stating profit maximization, survival, etc., as goals also accept adherence to moral principles as an actual but unstated goal. If a firm implicitly expects moral behavior from its employees in relation to the organization, it may analogously expect such behavior in their organizational decisions. Second, not every stated and actual goal has to be set down in a written, formal company policy statement. A corporate president recently made this observation: "Over the years we have insisted that our employees have the highest possible ethical principles in doing business in all areas of our company. This philosophy is impressed upon the employees when they are hired and it is maintained through our various supervisors and department heads. The standard of ethics of this company is considered one of the highest in our industry and I believe that the word-of-mouth procedure has been effective over the years."[3] Presumably, these principles are actual goals, and they are orally stated, although they are not stated in the company's formal statement of objectives. Third, the increased incorporation of moral objectives in recent corporate policy statements is accompanied by an increased institutionalization of explicit ethical codes with attendant enforcement mechanisms. Since these codes typically cover employees' organizational decisions, they are *prima facie* evidence that moral principles are actually being incorporated as organizational goals.

The upshot is that premise (6) seems false. Ladd provides no evidence for the claim that moral principles cannot be part of a corporate goal structure. Even if there were no empirical evidence of the adoption of moral principles as corporate goals, nothing precludes the "reconstructing" of firms to incorporate such goals. In certain cases such principles are stated goals, and where they are not stated they may be actual goals. In fact, there is some evidence that such goals are actual, in which case (6) definitely is false.

Finally, given that (2) is a reasonable definition or characterization of a formal organization, is a corporation a formal organization, i.e., is (1) true? This can be determined by examining whether corporations satisfy (2a), (2b), (2c), and (2d). Although a comprehensive investigation is beyond the scope of this paper, we can offer some comments indicating that corporations are not fully formal.

As Ladd allows, corporations may have multiple goals; for example, Hewlett-Packard lists profit, customer and employee satisfaction, growth, and fulfillment of societal obligations as goals. Although such goals are not necessarily incompatible, they may at times conflict: profit maximization may, in certain circumstances, conflict with the fulfillment of social obligations and also with corporate growth. In such cases it will not do to say simply, as in (2a), that corporations pursue a *set* of goals; some weighting of goals will have to be made to preserve the rationality mentioned in (2d). The mathematical apparatus is available to preserve rationality in a context of multiple goals *if* stable weights can be assigned to goals; but, given the rather large number of goals corporations typically pursue and the complexity and unpredictability of environmental factors that would affect weighting in specific contexts, it is doubtful that corporations can or do follow the dictates of the formal model.

It should also be noted that Herbert Simon, to whom Ladd frequently refers in setting up his formal model, does not give a purely formal account of organizations.[4] Simon, and subsequent Carnegie theorists, provide a descriptive rather than a normative account, i.e., they attempt to tell us what organizations are like, not what they should be like. Their account is based on several observations about humans; they view humans as (1) intending to be rational but possessing limited and imperfect information processing capabilities; (2) exercising selective perception based on interests and preconceptions, which in organizations leads to coalitions or factions based on similar interests; and, consequently, (3) seeking "satisficing" solutions to problems, i.e., solutions that are "good enough" rather than the best or optimal, as in (2d). Rationality in organizations is, to use Simon's term, "bounded" or limited rationality. In addition, Amitai Etzioni, cited by Ladd as an organizational theorist who articulates the goal-oriented formal model, actually argues that the goal model is not the best way to examine and understand organizations. Instead, he advocates a systems approach that takes into account complicating factors beyond the simplified means-end formalist model.[5] If the end-oriented formalist model does not match what can reasonably be expected of humans (Simon), and it is not the best way to study and understand organizational behavior (Etzioni), then the two main sources of Ladd's conceptual analysis of organizations actually undercut his analysis if it is meant to apply to actual organizational behavior.

The work of James March and Herbert Simon casts doubt on the sharp distinction between organizational and personal decisions that underlies (2b) and (2d).[6] March and Simon claim that actions in organizations are affected by an individual's identification patterns, which typically are multiple and often are rooted in sources other than the organization and its goals. An employee may identify with his sub-group in an organization, and the sub-group's goals may vary from those of the organization or top management. The individual may have sources of identification outside the organization, e.g., one's family or profession, that affect his decision-making role in the organization. Even if one's primary identification is with the firm, it may be that overidentification with one's organizational role turns out to be dysfunctional for the firm. Robert K. Merton and Victor Thompson have documented how excessive organizational identification, particularly with respect to organizational means, can lead to inflexible behavior that may not benefit the firm.[7] In addition, the bureaucratic (or hierarchical) and rational dimensions of the formal model of organizations (2c and 2d) do not necessarily mesh. Stanley H. Udy, Jr.'s study found, for example, that these factors tend to be mutually inconsistent, and Richard H. Hall's study suggests that these dimensions have only weak or negative correlations.[8]

To summarize, then, we have suggested that, even if (2a–d) does adequately characterize a formal organization, there are some grounds to question whether (1) is true, i.e., whether corporations are formal organizations. Moreover, even if the truth of (1) is granted, we argued there is no reason to accept (4). Ladd asserts, but does not establish, that limiting operating conditions are factual. Even if we grant Ladd's distinction between moral beliefs and principles, we found no reason to suggest that the latter could not serve as limiting operating conditions; in fact, we cited corporate policy statements that do seem to place moral constraints on primary economic goals. Finally, we argued that moral principles certainly can be factored into a corporate goal structure. Indeed, if corporate behavior sometimes matches with corporate policy statements, we found evidence that some corporations do include moral principles as corporate goals. Hence, (6) seems false. If most firms neither include moral objectives in their goal structures nor construe moral principles as limiting operating conditions, we suggest that they consider doing so as one strategy for overcoming the alienation that Ladd mentions.

NOTES

1. This and subsequent citations of corporate policy statements are from: *A Study of Corporate Ethical Policy Statements,* The Foundation of the Southwestern Graduate School of Banking (Dallas, Texas: Southern Methodist University, 1980).

2. Address to shareholders at the 1981 Exxon annual meeting.

3. Sorrel M. Mathes and G. Clark Thompson, "Ensuring Ethical Conduct in Business," *The Conference Board Record,* vol. 1, no. 12 (December, 1964), pp. 17–18.

4. Herbert Simon, *Administrative Behavior* (New York: Free Press, 1957), 2nd edition, pp. 61–109.

5. Amitai Etzioni, *Modern Organizations* (Englewood Cliffs, N.J.: Prentice-Hall, 1964), pp. 16–19.

6. James March and Herbert Simon, *Organizations* (New York: Wiley, 1958), pp. 35–171.

7. Robert K. Merton, "Bureaucratic Structure and Personality," *Social Forces,* vol. 18, no. 4 (May, 1940), pp. 560–68; Victor Thompson, *Modern Organizations* (New York: Knopf, 1961), pp. 152–77.

8. Stanley H. Udy, Jr., " 'Bureaucracy' and 'Rationality' in Weber's Organization Theory," *American Sociological Review,* vol. 24, no. 6 (December, 1959), pp. 791–95; Richard H. Hall, "The Concept of Bureaucracy: An Empirical Assessment," *American Journal of Sociology,* vol. 69, no. 1 (July, 1963), pp. 32–40.

Business and Social Responsibility

Cost-Benefit Analysis and the Ford Pinto

In the late 1960s, American automakers were faced with serious competition from German and Japanese firms in the subcompact market. Some Detroit executives felt that they should concentrate on medium-size and large models and let foreign competitors with their lower costs have the small car market. Others argued that the subcompact market was potentially lucrative and should be pursued. Ford, whose market position had eroded, opted for the latter strategy, and in 1968 it decided to produce the Pinto.

Although production planning for a new model normally takes about three and one-half years, Ford decided to try to move from conception to production in two years; it wanted the Pinto ready for the 1971 model year. In the normal time frame, design changes and quality assurance standards are in place largely before production line tooling. But tooling requires about a year and a half, and hence, in the case of the Pinto, tooling and product development overlapped considerably.

Prior to production of the Pinto, Ford crash-tested 11 Pintos as part of its quality assurance program. The tests were conducted in part with an eye to Federal Motor Vehicle Safety Standard 301, which was proposed for adoption by the National Highway Traffic Safety Administration (NHTSA) in 1968. Standard 301 proposed that all autos be required to withstand a fixed-barrier impact of 20 mph without loss of fuel. Of Ford's 11 tests, conducted at an average impact speed of 31 mph, only three autos passed with unbroken fuel tanks. None of the eight standardly designed Pintos passed. In one successful test a plastic baffle was placed between the front of the gas tank and the differential housing. In a second successful test, a piece of steel was placed between the tank and rear bumper. The third successful test was of a Pinto with a rubber-lined gas tank.

Ford decided to go ahead with its gas tank design, and not alter the tank in light of its crash-tests. It did so for several reasons. First, cost-benefit analysis, as detailed in a Ford memorandum titled "Fatalities Associated with Crash-Induced Fuel Leakage and Fires," suggested that there were no advantages in upgrading the Pinto's fuel tank. In the early 1970s, NHTSA decided that cost-benefit analysis was an appropriate basis for safety design standards. To make such an analysis some specific value had to be placed on a human life, and NHTSA decided on a figure of $200,725 as the estimated cost to society every time a person is killed in an auto accident:

Future Productivity Losses	
Direct	$132,000
Indirect	41,300
Medical Costs	
Hospital	700
Other	425
Property Damage	1,500
Insurance Administration	4,700
Legal and Court	3,000
Employer Losses	1,000
Victim's Pain and Suffering	10,000
Funeral	900
Assets (Lost Consumption)	5,000
Miscellaneous Accident Cost	200
Total Per Fatality	$200,725

Using NHTSA's data, Ford calculated costs and benefits by considering the variables of lives saved by product redesign and the cost of the product. For example, a Ford internal memorandum gives the following calculation of an $11 gas tank improvement, which was estimated to save 180 lives:

BENEFITS

Savings: 180 burn deaths, 180 serious burn
injuries, 2,100 burned vehicles.

Unit Cost: $200,000 per death, $67,000 per
injury, $700 per vehicle.

Total Benefit: $180 \times (\$200,000) + 180 \times (\$67,000)$
$+ 2,100 \times (\$700) = \$49.5$ million.

COSTS

Sales: 11 million cars, 1.5 million light trucks

Unit Cost: $11 per car, $11 per truck
Total Cost: 12,500,000 × ($11) = $137 million.

Since the costs of the $11 safety improvement outweighed its benefits, Ford maintained they were not justified in making the improvement.

A second factor in Ford's decision was that the Pinto did meet all Federal Auto Safety Standards at the time. NHTSA Standard 301 was only a *proposed* rule. It was strenuously opposed by the auto industry, and was only adopted in 1977. Furthermore, Ford's Pinto tests were at an average speed of 31 mph—considerably over the 20 mph speed proposed in Standard 301.

A third factor was that Ford had to cut costs to be competitive. Ford wanted the Pinto to weigh less than 2,000 lbs. and cost less than $2,000. It felt that control of both variables was necessary to compete against Volkswagen and the Japanese imports. Within the scope of the law, it had to control both weight and cost.

A fourth factor in Ford's decision was a belief that Americans were not primarily interested in safety. As Lee Iacocca was fond of saying, "Safety doesn't sell."

A fifth factor was that Ford had experimented with other gas tank designs, but had ruled them out for various reasons. For example, the tank could be placed over the rear axle and differential housing, as in the Ford Capri. This design had been successful in over 50 crash tests at speeds of up to 60 mph. The problem with the Pinto, however, was that this sort of placement drastically reduced its already scanty trunk space. Variables such as trunk space, as well as safety, had to be taken into consideration.

A sixth factor was undoubtedly Ford's tight production schedule. When crash tests revealed the gas tank problem, production tooling was already underway. Redesign and retooling would have been expensive.

From 1968 until its adoption by NHTSA in 1977, Ford opposed Standard 301. Studies showed that 400,000 autos burned every year, that 3,000 people were burned to death in autos every year, and that 40 percent of auto burn deaths could be prevented by adoption of Standard 301. The Pinto now has a rupture-proof fuel tank that meets the standard.

Reactions to the Pinto case have been very divergent. An industry spokesman said: "We have to make cost-benefit analyses all the time. That's part of business. Everyone knows that some people will die in auto accidents, but people do accept risks and they do want us to hold down costs. We could build an absolutely safe car, but nobody could afford it." A Pinto critic said, "One wonders how long the Ford Motor Company would continue to market lethal cars were Henry Ford II and Lee Iacocca serving twenty-year terms in Leavenworth for consumer homicide."

For Discussion

In your opinion, is cost-benefit analysis the appropriate basis for safety design standards? Why or why not? If not, what other factors should be considered? Discuss NHTSA's figures regarding the estimated cost of an auto fatality. Analyze each factor in Ford's decision not to implement the $11 gas tank improvement. Do the reasons (individually or together) provide an adequate justification for Ford's decision? Discuss the moral basis of Ford's opposition to NHTSA Standard 301.

SOURCES

Ralph Drayton, "One Manufacturer's Approach to Automobile Safety Standards," *CLTA NEWS,* vol. VIII, no. 2 (Feb. 1968), pp. 11 ff; "Magazine Claims Ford Ignored Pinto Fire Peril," *Automotive News* (Aug. 15, 1977), p. 3; "Ford Rebuts Pinto Criticisms and Says Article Is Distorted," *The National Underwriter* (Prop. Ed.), vol. 81 (Sept. 9, 1977), p. 36; Mark Dowie, "How Ford Put Two Million Firetraps on Wheels," *Business and Social Review,* no. 23 (Fall, 1977), pp. 46–55; "Ford Fights Pinto Case: Jury Gives $128 Million," *Automotive News* (Feb. 13, 1978), pp. 3 ff; J. Gamlin, "Jury Slaps Massive Fine on Ford in 1972 Pinto Crash," *Business Insurance,* vol. 12 (Feb. 20, 1978), pp. 1 ff; "Ford Motor Is Indicted in Indiana Pinto Death," *Automotive News* (Sept. 18, 1978), p. 2; "After Pinto," *U.S. News and World Report,* vol. 88 (March 24, 1980), p. 11; "Ford's Pinto: Not Guilty," *Newsweek,* vol. 95 (March 24, 1980), p. 74.

Milton Friedman

The Social Responsibility of Business
Is to Increase Its Profits

When I hear businessmen speak eloquently about the "social responsibilities of business in a free-enterprise system," I am reminded of the wonderful line about the Frenchman who discovered at the age of 70 that he had been speaking prose all his life. The businessmen believe that they are defending free enterprise when they declaim that business is not concerned "merely" with profit but also with promoting desirable "social" ends; that business has a "social conscience" and takes seriously its responsibilities for providing employment, eliminating discrimination, avoiding pollution and whatever else may be the catchwords of the contemporary crop of reformers. In fact they are—or would be if they or anyone else took them seriously—preaching pure and unadulterated socialism. Businessmen who talk this way are unwitting puppets of the intellectual forces that have been undermining the basis of a free society these past decades.

The discussions of the "social responsibilities of business" are notable for their analytical looseness and lack of rigor. What does it mean to say that "business" has responsibilities? Only people can have responsibilities. A corporation is an artificial person and in this sense may have artificial responsibilities, but "business" as a whole cannot be said to have responsibilities, even in this vague sense. The first step toward clarity in examining the doctrine of the social responsibility of business is to ask precisely what it implies for whom.

Presumably, the individuals who are to be responsible are businessmen, which means individual proprietors or corporate executives. Most of the discussion of social responsibility is directed at corporations, so in what follows I shall mostly neglect the individual proprietor and speak of corporate executives.

*　　*　　*

The New York Times Magazine, September 13, 1970, pp. 33, 122–126. © 1970 by The New York Times Company. Reprinted by permission.

In a free enterprise, private-property system, a corporate executive is an employe of the owners of the business. He has direct responsibility to his employers. That responsibility is to conduct the business in accordance with their desires, which generally will be to make as much money as possible while conforming to the basic rules of the society, both those embodied in law and those embodied in ethical custom. Of course, in some cases his employers may have a different objective. A group of persons might establish a corporation for an eleemosynary purpose—for example, a hospital or a school. The manager of such a corporation will not have money profit as his objective but the rendering of certain services.

In either case, the key point is that, in his capacity as a corporate executive, the manager is the agent of the individuals who own the corporation or establish the eleemosynary institution, and his primary responsibility is to them.

Needless to say, this does not mean that it is easy to judge how well he is performing his task. But at least the criterion of performance is straightforward, and the persons among whom a voluntary contractual arrangement exists are clearly defined.

Of course, the corporate executive is also a person in his own right. As a person, he may have many other responsibilities that he recognizes or assumes voluntarily—to his family, his conscience, his feelings of charity, his church, his clubs, his city, his country. He may feel impelled by these responsibilities to devote part of his income to causes he regards as worthy, to refuse to work for particular corporations, even to leave his job, for example, to join his country's armed forces. If we wish, we may refer to some of these responsibilities as "social responsibilities." But in these respects he is acting as a principal, not an agent; he is spending his own money or time or energy, not the money of his employers or the time or energy he has contracted to devote to their purposes. If these are "social responsibilities," they are the social responsibilities of individuals, not of business.

What does it mean to say that the corporate executive has a "social responsibility" in his capacity as businessman? If this statement is not pure rhetoric, it must mean that he is to act in some way that is not in the interest of his employers. For example, that he is to refrain from increasing the price of the product in order to contribute to the social objective of preventing inflation, even though a price increase would be in the best interests of the corporation. Or that he is to make expenditures on reducing pollution beyond the amount that is in the best interests of the corporation or that is required by law in order to contribute to the social objective of improving the environment. Or that, at the expense of corporate profits, he is to hire "hard-core" unemployed instead of better-qualified available workmen to contribute to the social objective of reducing poverty.

In each of these cases, the corporate executive would be spending someone else's money for a general social interest. Insofar as his actions in accord with his "social responsibility" reduce returns to stockholders, he is spending their money. Insofar as his actions raise the price to customers, he is spending the customers' money. Insofar as his actions lower the wages of some employes, he is spending their money.

The stockholders or the customers or the employes could separately spend their own money on the particular action if they wished to do so. The executive is exercising a distinct "social responsibility," rather than serving as an agent of the stockholders or the customers or the employes, only if he spends the money in a different way than they would have spent it.

But if he does this, he is in effect imposing taxes, on the one hand, and deciding how the tax proceeds shall be spent, on the other.

This process raises political questions on two levels: principle and consequences. On the level of political principle, the imposition of taxes and the expenditure of tax proceeds are governmental functions. We have established elaborate constitutional, parliamentary and judicial provisions to control these functions, to assure that taxes are imposed so far as possible in accordance with the preferences and desires of the public – after all, "taxation without representation" was one of the battle cries of the American Revolution. We have a system of checks and balances to separate the legislative function of imposing taxes and enacting expenditures from the executive function of collecting taxes and administering expenditure programs and from the judicial function of mediating disputes and interpreting the law.

Here the businessman – self-selected or appointed directly or indirectly by stockholders – is to be simultaneously legislator, executive and jurist. He is to decide whom to tax by how much and for what purpose, and he is to spend the proceeds – all this guided only by general exhortations from on high to restrain inflation, improve the environment, fight poverty and so on and on.

The whole justification for permitting the corporate executive to be selected by the stockholders is that the executive is an agent serving the interests of his principal. This justification disappears when the corporate executive imposes taxes and spends the proceeds for "social" purposes. He becomes in effect a public employe, a civil servant, even though he remains in name an employe of a private enterprise. On grounds of political principle, it is intolerable that such civil servants – insofar as their actions in the name of social responsibility are real and not just window-dressing – should be selected as they are now. If they are to be civil servants, then they must be selected through a political process. If they are to impose taxes and make expenditures to foster "social objectives," then political machinery must be set up to guide the assessment of taxes and to determine through a political process the objectives to be served.

This is the basic reason why the doctrine of "social responsibility" involves the acceptance of the socialist view that political mechanisms, not market mechanisms, are the appropriate way to determine the allocation of scarce resources to alternative uses.

On the grounds of consequences, can the corporate executive in fact discharge his alleged "social responsibilities"? On the one hand, suppose he could get away with spending the stockholders' or customers' or employes' money. How is he to know how to spend it? He is told that he must contribute to fighting inflation. How is he to know what action of his will contribute to that end? He is presumably an expert in running his company—in producing a product or selling it or financing it. But nothing about his selection makes him an expert on inflation. Will his holding down the price of his product reduce inflationary pressure? Or, by leaving more spending power in the hands of his customers, simply divert it elsewhere? Or, by forcing him to produce less because of the low price, will it simply contribute to shortages? Even if he could answer these questions, how much cost is he justified in imposing on his stockholders, customers and employes for this social purpose? What is his appropriate share and what is the appropriate share of others?

And, whether he wants to or not, can he get away with spending his stockholders', customers' or employes' money? Will not the stockholders fire him? (Either the present ones or those who take over when his actions in the name of social responsibility have reduced the corporation's profits and the price of its stock.) His customers and his employes can desert him for other producers and employers less scrupulous in exercising their social responsibilities.

This facet of "social responsibility" doctrine is brought into sharp relief when the doctrine is used to justify wage restraint by trade unions. The conflict of interest is naked and clear when union officials are asked to subordinate the interest of their members to some more general social purpose. If the union officials try to enforce wage restraint, the consequence is likely to be wildcat strikes, rank-and-file revolts and the emergence of strong competitors for their jobs. We thus have the ironic phenomenon that union leaders—at least in the U.S.—have objected to Government interference with the market far more consistently and courageously than have business leaders.

The difficulty of exercising "social responsibility" illustrates, of course, the great virtue of private competitive enterprise—it forces people to be responsible for their own actions and makes it difficult for them to "exploit" other people for either selfish or unselfish purposes. They can do good—but only at their own expense.

Many a reader who has followed the argument this far may be tempted to remonstrate that it is all well and good to speak of Government's having the responsibility to impose taxes and determine expenditures for such "social" purposes as controlling pollution or training the hard-core unemployed, but that the problems are too urgent to wait on the slow course of political processes, that the exercise of social responsibility by businessmen is a quicker and surer way to solve pressing current problems.

Aside from the question of fact—I share Adam Smith's skepticism about the benefits that can be expected from "those who affected to trade for the public good"—this argument must be rejected on grounds of principle. What it amounts to is an assertion that those who favor the taxes and expenditures in question have failed to persuade a majority of their fellow citizens to be of like mind and that they are seeking to attain by undemocratic procedures what they cannot attain by democratic procedures. In a free society, it is hard for "good" people to do "good," but that is a small price to pay for making it hard for "evil" people to do "evil," especially since one man's good is another's evil.

I have, for simplicity, concentrated on the special case of the corporate executive, except only for the brief digression on trade unions. But precisely the same argument applies to the newer phenomenon of calling upon stockholders to require corporations to exercise social responsibility (the recent G.M. crusade, for example). In most of these cases, what is in effect involved is some stockholders trying to get other stockholders (or customers or employes) to contribute against their will to "social" causes favored by the activists. Insofar as they succeed, they are again imposing taxes and spending the proceeds.

The situation of the individual proprietor is somewhat different. If he acts to reduce the returns of his enterprise in order to exercise his "social responsibility," he is spending his own money, not someone else's. If he wishes to spend his money on such purposes, that is his right, and I cannot see that there is any objection to his doing so. In the process, he, too, may impose costs on employes and customers. However, because he is far less likely than a large corporation or union to have monopolistic power, any such side effects will tend to be minor.

Of course, in practice the doctrine of social responsibility is frequently a cloak for actions that are justified on other grounds rather than a reason for those actions.

To illustrate, it may well be in the long-run interest of a corporation that is a major employer in a small community to devote resources to providing amenities to that community or to improving its government. That may make it easier to attract desirable employes, it may reduce the wage bill or lessen losses from pilferage and sabotage or have other worthwhile effects. Or it may be that, given the laws about the deductibility of corporate charitable contributions, the stockholders can contribute more to charities they favor by having the corporation make the gift than by doing it themselves, since they can in that way contribute an amount that would otherwise have been paid as corporate taxes.

In each of these—and many similar—cases, there is a strong temptation to rationalize these actions as an exercise of "social responsibility." In the present climate of opinion, with its widespread aversion to "capitalism," "profits," the "soulless corporation" and so on, this is one way for a corporation to generate good will as a by-product of expenditures that are entirely justified in its own self-interest.

It would be inconsistent of me to call on corporate executives to refrain from this hypocritical window-dressing because it harms the foundations of a free society. That would be to call on them to exercise a "social responsibility"! If our institutions, and the attitudes of the public, make it in their self-interest to cloak their actions in this way, I cannot summon much indignation to denounce them. At the same time, I can express admiration for those individual proprietors or owners of closely held corporations or stockholders of more broadly held corporations who disdain such tactics as approaching fraud.

Whether blameworthy or not, the use of the cloak of social responsibility, and the nonsense spoken in its name by influential and prestigious businessmen, does clearly harm the foundations of a free society. I have been impressed time and again by the schizophrenic character of many businessmen. They are capable of being extremely far-sighted and clear-headed in matters that are internal to their businesses. They are incredibly short-sighted and muddle-headed in matters that are outside their businesses but affect the possible survival of business in general. This short-sightedness is strikingly exemplified in the calls from many businessmen for wage and price guidelines or controls or incomes policies. There is nothing that could do more in a brief period to destroy a market system and replace it by a centrally controlled system than effective governmental control of prices and wages.

The short-sightedness is also exemplified in speeches by businessmen on social responsibility. This may gain them kudos in the short run. But it helps to strengthen the already too prevalent view that the pursuit of profits is wicked and immoral and must be curbed and controlled by external forces. Once this view is adopted, the external forces that curb the market will not be the social consciences, however highly developed, of the pontificating executives; it will be the iron fist of Government bureaucrats. Here, as with price and wage controls, businessmen seem to me to reveal a suicidal impulse.

The political principle that underlies the market mechanism is unanimity. In an ideal free market resting on private property, no individual can coerce any other, all cooperation is voluntary, all parties to such cooperation benefit or they need not participate. There are no "social" values, no "social" responsibilities in any sense other than the shared values and responsibilities of individuals. Society is a collection of individuals and of the various groups they voluntarily form.

The political principle that underlies the political mechanism is conformity. The individual must serve a more general social interest — whether that be determined by a church or a dictator or a majority. The individual may have a vote and a say in what is to be done, but if he is overruled, he must conform. It is appropriate for some to require others to contribute to a general social purpose whether they wish to or not.

Unfortunately, unanimity is not always feasible. There are some respects in which conformity appears unavoidable, so I do not see how one can avoid the use of the political mechanism altogether.

But the doctrine of "social responsibility" taken seriously would extend the scope of the political mechanism to every human activity. It does not differ in philosophy from the most explicitly collectivist doctrine. It differs only by professing to believe that collectivist ends can be attained without collectivist means. That is why, in my book *Capitalism and Freedom*, I have called it a "fundamentally subversive doctrine" in a free society, and have said that in such a society, "there is one and only one social responsibility to business—to use its resources and engage in activities designed to increase its profits so long as it stays within the rules of the game, which is to say, engages in open and free competition without deception or fraud."

Milton Friedman Responds

*   *   *

McLaughry: The question of environmental pollution is very much on the public's mind. There are various ways to approach this question. One is the completely laissez-faire approach; another is to tax pollution; another is to give tax incentives or subsidies to companies to encourage them to stop polluting; a fourth is to use police power to make pollution illegal and impose penalties. What would you view as the best way to attack the pollution problem in a free enterprise society?

Friedman: Well, there is a great deal of misunderstanding about the pollution problem in our society. First, it is often in the private interest not to pollute. That being said, we mustn't suppose that there are no mechanisms within the free enterprise society which lead to the "right" amount of pollution.

Let me stop here for a minute. An ideal of zero pollution is one of the fallacies mouthed about the problem. That is absurd. As in all these cases, you must balance returns with costs. People's breathing is one source of pollution. We breathe in oxygen and breathe out carbon dioxide. If too much carbon dioxide is breathed out, there is a lot of pollution. Now we can simply stop breathing, but most of us would consider the cost of eliminating that pollution greater than the return. We must decide upon the "right" amount of pollution, that amount at which the cost of reducing pollution to all the people concerned would be greater than the gain from reducing the level.

In many cases, the private market provides precisely that incentive. For example, consider a town that has been cited as a horror—Gary, Indiana, where the U.S. Steel Company is the major source of pollution. Let's assume for a moment that contrary to fact, none of the pollution spreads into Chicago. Instead, it's all concentrated in Gary. Now, if

U.S. Steel pollutes heavily in Gary, the Gary environment becomes unattractive. People don't want to live and work there. U.S. Steel has to
pay higher wages to lure employees. You'll say to me that not all the
people in Gary work for U.S. Steel. Some people run stores and gas
stations. But exactly the same thing is true. If Gary is an unpleasant
environment, nobody will run a grocery store there unless he can earn
sufficiently more there than he can elsewhere to compensate for enduring the pollution. Consequently, food costs will be high and that again
will raise the wages U.S. Steel will have to pay to attract a labor force.
Under those circumstances, all the costs of pollution are borne by U.S.
Steel, meaning a collection of its stockholders and customers.

MCLAUGHRY: Doesn't your argument depend on an assumption of perfect
labor mobility?

FRIEDMAN: No, no. It depends on some labor mobility, but after all, there
is labor mobility. It isn't necessary that every person be mobile. Wages
are determined at the margin.

For example, the fact that 2 percent of the people are good shop-
pers makes it unnecessary for the other 98 percent to be good shoppers.
Why is it that the prices are roughly the same in different stores?
Doesn't that assume that every shopper is a good shopper? Not at all.
It's a fact that because some people do compare prices and select the
better buys, the rest of us don't have to pay such careful attention. The
same is true here. Some people in the labor force will move in and out.
The people in Gary will not live in Gary unless it offers better opportunity than they can get elsewhere. Maybe other things aren't very good;
maybe by your standards and my standards these people are not very
well off. But among the alternatives they have, that's best.

MCLAUGHRY: Don't the traditions and habits of people with lower income
and lower education levels combine to frustrate that easy mobility of
labor?

FRIEDMAN: On the contrary. There is enormous mobility of labor at the
very lowest levels—not only in this country, but all over. How were
Indians ever led from India to Africa, to Malaysia, to Indonesia, except
for the fact that they heard of better opportunities? How was the
United States settled? From the end of the Civil War to World War I, if
I remember correctly, a third of the people in the United States had
immigrated from abroad. The people who came here were not those
who earned high wages; they were not the "jet set." They were poor,
ignorant people who arrived with nothing but their hands. What
encouraged them to migrate? The fact that they had heard at distances
of five or six thousand miles that there were better jobs and better

conditions in the United States than where they were. So it's absurd to say that because people in Gary, Indiana are in the low-income bracket they can't migrate elsewhere. Look at the enormous migration to the West Coast. Look at the Okie migration. If you count the number of people in the low-income class who every year move back and forth, it is quite obvious that there is enormous mobility of labor.

McLaughry: How does your argument relate to another topic of current interest—safety?

Friedman: What's the "right" number of accidents for Consolidated Edison to have? Now that seems like a silly question. All accidents are bad. But let's suppose for a moment that Con Ed does have an accident. One of its trucks hits your car. You have a case against them and they will have to pay damages. Well, that's part of their operating expense, and it has to be recouped from their customers. Suppose it costs them less to avoid a certain number of accidents than it does to pay for damages in these accident suits. Well, that would reduce the price they have to charge their customers. Obviously it's in their interest—and their customer's as well—to avoid these accidents. On the other hand, suppose it costs Con Ed more to avoid additional accidents than it does to pay damages—and it well might. To avoid all accidents, they might have to do all their work at night, give instructions that their trucks should never go faster than 2 MPH, and so on. You can see by this that Consolidated Edison must have the "right" number of accidents, that number where the cost of avoiding an additional accident would be more than the damages paid the victim.

Well now, what is the difference between this situation and the pollution case? There's only one: In the pollution case, it is often impossible to identify the individual victims and to require person-by-person compensation. In Consolidated Edison's case you can identify the victims early. In the U.S. Steel case, you can identify the victims as a group, and *all* the costs fall back on U.S. Steel. Therefore, in a single-company town like Gary, U.S. Steel has a private interest in maintaining the right level of pollution, because an extra $100 spent to reduce pollution would add less than $100 to the welfare of all of the people in the city of Gary. Under the circumstances where you cannot identify the victim, however, it is highly desirable to take measures to see that costs are imposed on the consumer. There is only one person who can pay the costs, and that's the consumer. If the people whose shirts are dirtied by Consolidated Edison could bring suit, Con Ed would have to pay the cost of cleaning their shirts—which is to say, Con Ed's customers would. If it were cheaper to stop polluting than it was to pay those costs, Con Ed would do so.

In those cases where you can determine what costs are being imposed on people other than the customer, the least bad solution seems to me to be a tax. Let's consider an industrial enterprise which pollutes a river. If you can calculate roughly that by putting in the effluent, an industry is causing a certain amount of harm to people downstream, then the answer would seem to be to tax it, roughly equal to the amount of harm it has imposed. This provides the right incentive. If it's cheaper for the corporation to put the effluent in the water and pay the tax than it is not to pollute or to clean up the river, then that is what should be done.

*   *   *

Robert Almeder

Morality in the Marketplace

I. INTRODUCTION

In order to create a climate more favorable for corporate activity, International Telephone and Telegraph allegedly contributed large sums of money to "destabilize" the duly elected government of Chile. Even though advised by the scientific community that the practice is lethal, major chemical companies reportedly continue to dump large amounts of carcinogens into the water supply of various areas and, at the same time, lobby to prevent legislation against such practices. General Motors Corporation, other automobile manufacturers, and Firestone Tire and Rubber Corporation have frequently defended themselves against the charge that they knowingly and willingly marketed a product that, owing to defective design, had been reliably predicted to kill a certain percentage of its users and, moreover, refused to recall promptly the product even when government agencies documented the large incidence of death as a result of the defective product. Finally, people often say that numerous advertising companies happily accept, and earnestly solicit, accounts to advertise cigarettes knowing full well that as a direct result of their advertising activities a certain number of people will die considerably prematurely and painfully. We need not concern ourselves with whether these and other similar charges are true because our concern here is with what might count as a justification for such corporate conduct were it to occur. There can be no question that such behavior is frequently legal. The question is whether corporate behavior should be constrained by nonlegal or moral considerations. As things presently stand, it seems to be a dogma of contemporary capitalism that the sole responsibility of business is to make as much money as is legally possible. But the question is whether this view is rationally defensible.

This paper is a revised and expanded version of an earlier paper, "The Ethics of Profit: Reflections on Corporate Responsibility," *Business and Society* (Winter, 1980): 7-15.

Sometimes, although not very frequently, corporate executives will admit to the sort of behavior depicted above and then proceed proximately to justify such behavior in the name of their responsibility to the shareholders or owners (if the shareholders are not the owners) to make as much profit as is legally possible. Thereafter, less proximately and more generally, they will proceed to urge the more general utilitarian point that the increase in profit engendered by such corporate behavior begets such an unquestionable overall good for society that the behavior in question is morally acceptable if not quite praiseworthy. More specifically, the justification in question can, and usually does, take two forms.

The first and most common form of justification consists in urging that, as long as one's corporate behavior is not illegal, the behavior will be morally acceptable because the sole purpose of being in business is to make a profit; and the rules of the marketplace are somewhat different from those in other places and must be followed if one is to make a profit. Moreover, proponents of this view hasten to add that, as Adam Smith has claimed, the greatest good for society is achieved not by corporations seeking to act morally, or with a sense of social responsibility in their pursuit of profit, but rather by each corporation seeking to maximize its own profit, unregulated in that endeavor except by the laws of supply and demand along with whatever other laws are inherent to the competition process. Smith's view, that there is an invisible hand, as it were, directing an economy governed solely by the profit motive to the greatest good for society,[1] is still the dominant motivation and justification for those who would want an economy unregulated by any moral concern that would, or could, tend to decrease profits for some *alleged* social or moral good.

Milton Friedman, for example, has frequently asserted that the sole moral responsibility of business is to make as much profit as is legally possible; and by that he means to suggest that attempts to regulate or restrain the pursuit of profit in accordance with what some people believe to be socially desirable ends are in fact *subversive* of the common good since the greatest good for the greatest number is achieved by an economy maximally competitive and unregulated by moral rules in its pursuit of profit.[2] So, on Friedman's view, the greatest good for society is achieved by corporations acting legally, but with no further regard for what may be morally desirable; and this view begets the paradox that, *in business,* the greatest good for society can be achieved only by acting without regard for morality. Moreover, adoption of this position constitutes a fairly conscious commitment to the view that while one's personal life may well need governance by moral considerations, when pursuing profit, it is necessary that one's corporate behavior be unregulated by any moral concern other than that of making as much money as is legally possible; curiously enough, it is only in this way that society achieves the greatest good. So viewed, it is not difficult to see how a corporate executive could consistently adopt rigorous standards of morality in his or her personal life and yet feel quite comfortable in abandoning those standards in the pursuit of profit. Albert Carr, for example, likens the conduct of business to that of playing poker.[3] As Carr would have it, moral busybodies who insist on corporations acting morally might do just as well to censure a good bluffer in poker for being deceitful. Society, of course, lacking a perspective such as Friedman's and Carr's, is only too willing to view such behavior as strongly hypocritical and fostered by an unwholesome avarice.

The second way of justifying, or defending, corporate practices that may appear morally questionable consists in urging that even if corporations were to take seriously the idea of limiting profits because of a desire to be moral or more responsible to social needs, then corporations would be involved in the unwholesome business of selecting and implementing moral values that may not be shared by a large number of people. Besides, there is the overwhelming question of whether there can be any nonquestionable moral values or noncontroversial list of social priorities for corporations to adopt. After all, if ethical relativism is true, or if ethical nihilism is true (and philosophers can be counted upon to argue for both positions), then it would be fairly silly of corporations to limit profits for what may be a quite dubious reason, namely, for being moral, when there are no clear grounds for doing it, and when it is not too clear what would count for doing it. In short, business corporations could argue (as Friedman has done)[4] that corporate actions in behalf of society's interests would require of corporations an ability to clearly determine and rank in noncontroversial ways the major needs of society; and it would not appear that this could be done successfully.

Perhaps another, and somewhat easier, way of formulating this second argument consists in urging that because philosophers generally fail to agree on what are the proper moral rules (if any), as well as on whether we should be moral, it would be imprudent to sacrifice a clear profit for a dubious or controversial moral gain. To authorize such a sacrifice would be to abandon a clear responsibility for one that is unclear or questionable.

If there are any other basic ways of justifying the sort of corporate behavior noted at the outset, I cannot imagine what they might be. So, let us examine these two modes of justification. In doing this, I hope to show that neither argument is sound and, moreover, that corporate behavior of the sort in question is clearly immoral if anything is immoral — and if nothing is immoral, then such corporate behavior is clearly contrary to the long-term interest of a corporation. In the end, we will reflect on ways to prevent such behavior, and on what is philosophically implied by corporate willingness to act in clearly immoral ways.

II.

Essentially, the first argument is that the greatest good for the greatest number will be, and can only be, achieved by corporations acting legally but unregulated by any moral concern in the pursuit of profit. As we saw earlier, the evidence for this argument rests on a fairly classical and unquestioning acceptance of Adam Smith's view that society achieves a greater good when each person is allowed to pursue her or his own self-interested ends than when each person's pursuit of self-interested ends is regulated in some way or another by moral rules or concern. But I know of no evidence Smith ever offered for this latter claim, although it seems clear that those who adopt it generally do so out of respect for the perceived good that has emerged for various modern societies as a direct result of the free enterprise system and its ability to raise the overall standard of living of all those under it.

However, there is nothing inevitable about the greatest good occurring in an unregulated economy. Indeed, we have good inductive evidence from the age of the Robber Barons that unless the profit motive is regulated in various ways (by statute or otherwise) untold social evil can (and some say *will*) occur because of the natural tendency of the system to place ever-increasing sums of money in ever-decreasing numbers of hands. If all this is so, then so much the worse for all philosophical attempts to justify what would appear to be morally questionable corporate behavior on the grounds that corporate behavior, unregulated by moral concern, is necessarily or even probably productive of the greatest good for the greatest number. Moreover, a rule utilitarian would not be very hard pressed to show the many unsavory implications to society as a whole if society were to take seriously a rule to the effect that, provided only that one acts legally, it is morally permissible to do whatever one wants to do to achieve a profit. Some of those implications we shall discuss below before drawing a conclusion.

The second argument cited above asserts that even if we were to grant, for the sake of argument, that corporations have social responsibilities beyond that of making as much money as is legally possible for the shareholders, there would be no noncontroversial way for corporations to discover just what these responsibilities are in the order of their importance. Owing to the fact that even distinguished moral philosophers predictably disagree on what one's moral responsibilities are, if any, it would seem irresponsible to limit profits to satisfy dubious moral responsibilities.

For one thing, this argument unduly exaggerates our potential for moral disagreement. Admittedly, there might well be important disagreements among corporations (just as there could be among philosophers) as to a priority ranking of major social needs; but that does not mean that most of us could not, or would not, agree that certain things ought not be done in the name of profit even when there is no law prohibiting such acts. There will always be a few who would do anything for a profit; but that is hardly a good argument in favor of their having the moral right to do so rather than a good argument that they refuse to be moral. In sum, it is hard to see how this second argument favoring corporate moral nihilism is any better than the general argument for ethical nihilism based on the variability of ethical judgments or practices; and apart from the fact that it tacitly presupposes that morality is a matter of what we all in fact would, or should, accept, the argument is maximally counterintuitive (as I shall show) by way of suggesting that we cannot generally agree that corporations have certain clear social responsibilities to avoid certain practices. Accordingly, I would now like to argue that if anything is immoral, a certain kind of corporate behavior is quite immoral although it may not be illegal.

III.

Without caring to enter into the reasons for the belief, I assume we all believe that it is wrong to kill an innocent human being for no other reason than that doing so would be more financially rewarding for the killer than if he were to earn his livelihood in some other way. Nor, I assume, should our moral feelings on this matter change depending on the amount of money involved. Killing an innocent baby for fifteen million dollars would not seem to be any less objectionable than killing it for twenty cents. It is possible, however, that some self-professing utilitarian might be tempted to argue that the killing of an innocent baby for fifteen million dollars would not be objectionable if the money were to be given to the poor; under these circumstances, greater good would be achieved by the killing of the innocent baby. But, I submit, if anybody were to argue in this fashion, his argument would be quite deficient because he has not established what he needs to establish to make his argument sound. What he needs is a clear, convincing argument that raising the standard of living of an indefinite number of poor persons by the killing of an innocent person is a greater good for all those affected by the act than if the standard of living were not raised by the killing of an innocent person. This is needed because part of what we mean by having a basic right to life is that a person's life cannot be taken from him or her without a good reason. If our utilitarian cannot provide a convincing justification for his claim that a greater good is served by killing an innocent person in order to raise the standard of living for a large number of poor people, then it is hard to see how he can have the good reason he needs to deprive an innocent person of his or her life. Now, it seems clear that there will be anything but unanimity in the moral community on the question of whether there is a greater good achieved in raising the standard of living by killing an innocent baby than in leaving the standard of living alone and not killing an innocent baby. Moreover, even if everybody were to agree that the greater good is achieved by the killing of the innocent baby, how could that be shown to be true? How does one compare the moral value of a human life with the moral value of raising the standard of living by the taking of that life? Indeed, the more one thinks about it, the more difficult it is to see just what would count as objective evidence for the claim that the greater good is achieved by the killing of the innocent baby. Accordingly, I can see nothing that would justify the utilitarian who might be tempted to argue that if the sum is large enough, and if the sum were to be used for raising the standard of living for an indefinite number of poor people, then it would be morally acceptable to kill an innocent person for money.

These reflections should not be taken to imply, however, that no utilitarian argument could justify the killing of an innocent person for money. After all, if the sum were large enough to save the lives of a large number of people who would surely die if the innocent baby were not killed, then I think one would as a rule be justified in killing the innocent baby for the sum in question. But this situation is obviously quite different from the situation in which one would attempt to justify the killing of an innocent person in order to raise the standard of living for an indefinite number of poor people. It makes sense to kill one innocent person in order to save, say, twenty innocent persons; but it makes no sense at all to kill one innocent person to raise the standard of living of an indefinite number of people. In the latter case, but not in the former, a comparison is made between things that are incomparable.

Given these considerations, it is remarkable and somewhat perplexing that certain corporations should seek to defend practices that are in fact instances of killing innocent persons for profit. Take, for example, the corporate practice of dumping known carcinogens into rivers. On Milton Friedman's view, we should not regulate or prevent such companies from dumping their effluents into the environment. Rather we should, if we like, tax the company after the effluents are in the water and then have the tax money used to clean up the environment.[5] For Friedman, and others, the fact that so many people will die as a result of this practice seems to be just part of the cost of doing business and making a profit. If there is any moral difference between such corporate practices and murdering innocent human beings for money, it is hard to see what it is. It is even more difficult to see how anyone could justify the practice and see it as no more than a business practice not to be regulated by moral concern. And there are a host of other corporate activities that are morally equivalent to deliberate killing of innocent persons for money. Such practices number among them contributing funds to "destabilize" a foreign government, advertising cigarettes, knowingly to market children's clothing having a known cancer causing agent, and refusing to recall (for fear of financial loss) goods known to be sufficiently defective to directly maim or kill a certain percentage of their unsuspecting users because of the defect. On this latter item, we are all familiar, for example, with convincingly documented charges that certain prominent automobile and tire manufacturers will knowingly market equipment sufficiently defective to increase the likelihood of death as a direct result of the defect and yet refuse to recall the product because the cost of recalling and repairing would have a greater adverse impact on profit than if the product were not recalled and the company paid the projected number of predictably successful suits. Of course, if the projected cost of the predictably successful suits were to outweigh the cost of recall and repair, then the product would be recalled and repaired, but not otherwise. In cases of this sort, the companies involved may admit to having certain marketing problems or a design problem, and they may even admit to having made a mistake; but, interestingly enough, they do not view themselves as immoral or as murderers for keeping their product in the market place when they know people are dying from it, people who would not die if the defect were corrected.

The important point is not whether in fact these practices have occurred in the past, or occur even now; there can be no doubt that such practices have occurred and do occur. Rather the point is that when companies act in such ways as a matter of policy, they must either not know what they do is murder (i.e., unjustifiable killing of an innocent person), or knowing that it is murder, seek to justify it in terms of profit. And I have been arguing that it is difficult to see how any corporate manager could fail to see that these policies amount to murder for money, although there may be no civil statute against such corporate behavior. If so, then where such policies exist, we can only assume that they are designed and implemented by corporate managers who either see nothing wrong with murder for money (which is implausible) or recognize that what they do is wrong but simply refuse to act morally because it is more financially rewarding to act immorally.

Of course, it is possible that corporate executives would not recognize such acts as murder. They may, after all, view murder as a legal concept involving one noncorporate person or persons deliberately killing another noncorporate person or persons and prosecutable only under existing civil statute. If so, it is somewhat understandable how corporate executives might fail, at least psychologically, to see such corporate policies as murder rather than as, say, calculated risks, tradeoffs, or design errors. Still, for all that, the logic of the situation seems clear enough.

IV. CONCLUSION

In addition to the fact that the only two plausible arguments favoring the Friedman doctrine are unsatisfactory, a strong case can be made for the claim that corporations *do* have a clear and noncontroversial moral responsibility not to design or implement, for reasons of profit, policies that they know, or have good reason to believe, will kill or otherwise seriously injure innocent persons affected by those policies. Moreover, we have said nothing about wage discrimination, sexism, discrimination in hiring, price fixing, price gouging, questionable but not unlawful competition, or other similar practices that some will think businesses should avoid by virtue of responsibility to society. My main concern has been to show that since we all agree that murder for money is generally wrong, and since there is no discernible difference between that and certain corporate policies that are not in fact illegal, then these corporate practices are clearly immoral (that is, they ought not to be done) and incapable of being morally justified by appeal to the Friedman doctrine since that doctrine does not admit of adequate evidential support. In itself, it is sad that this argument needs to be made and, if it were not for what appears to be a fairly strong commitment within the business community to the Friedman doctrine in the name of the unquestionable success of the free enterprise system, the argument would not need to be stated.

The fact that such practices do exist — designed and implemented by corporate managers who, for all intents and purposes, appear to be upright members of the moral community — only heightens the need for effective social prevention. Presumably, of course, any company willing to put human lives into the profit and loss column is not likely to respond to moral censure. Accordingly, I submit that perhaps the most effective way to deal with the problem of preventing such corporate behavior would consist in structuring legislation such that senior corporate managers who knowingly concur in practices of the sort listed above can effectively be tried, at their own expense, for murder, rather than censured and fined a sum to be paid out of corporate profits. This may seem a somewhat extreme or unrealistic proposal. However, it seems more unrealistic to think that aggressively competitive corporations will respond to what is morally necessary if failure to do so could be very or even minimally profitable. In short, unless we take strong and appropriate steps to prevent such practices, society will be reinforcing a destructive mode of behavior that is maximally disrespectful of human life, just as society will be reinforcing a value system that so emphasizes monetary gain as a standard of human success that murder for profit could be a corporate policy if the penalty for being caught at it were not too dear.

In the long run, of course, corporate and individual willingness to do what is clearly immoral for the sake of monetary gain is a patent commitment to a certain view about the nature of human happiness and success, a view that needs to be placed in the balance with Aristotle's reasoned argument and reflections to the effect that money and all that it brings is a means to an end, and not the sort of end in itself that will justify acting immorally to attain it. What that beautiful end is and why being moral allows us to achieve it, may well be the most rewarding and profitable subject a human being can think about. Properly understood and placed in perspective, Aristotle's view on the nature and attainment of human happiness could go a long way toward alleviating the temptation to kill for money.

In the meantime, any ardent supporter of the capitalistic system will want to see the system thrive and flourish; and this it cannot do if it invites and demands government regulation in the name of the public interest. A *strong* ideological commitment to what I have described above as the Friedman doctrine is counterproductive and not in anyone's long-range interest because it is most likely to beget an ever-increasing regulatory climate. The only way to avoid such encroaching regulation is to find ways to move the business community into the long-term view of what is in its interest, and effect ways of both determining and responding to social needs before society moves to regulate business to that end. To so move the business community is to ask business to regulate its own modes of competition in ways that may seem very difficult to achieve. Indeed, if what I have been suggesting is correct, the only kind of enduring capitalism is humane capitalism, one that is at least as socially responsible as society needs. By the same token, contrary to what is sometimes felt in the business community, the Friedman doctrine, ardently adopted for the dubious reasons generally given, will most likely undermine capitalism and motivate an economic socialism by assuring an erosive regulatory climate in a society that expects the business community to be socially responsible in ways that go beyond just making legal profits.

In sum, being socially responsible in ways that go beyond legal profit-making is by no means a dubious luxury for the capitalist in today's world. It is a necessity if capitalism is to survive at all; and, presumably, we shall all profit with the survival of a vibrant capitalism. If anything, then, rigid adherence to the Friedman doctrine is not only philosophically unjustified, and unjustifiable, it is also unprofitable in the long run, and therefore, downright subversive of the long-term common good. Unfortunately, taking the long-run view is difficult for everyone. After all, for each of us, tomorrow may not come. But living for today only does not seem to make much sense either, if that deprives us of any reasonable and happy tomorrow. Living for the future may not be the healthiest thing to do; but do it we must, if we have good reason to think that we will have a future. The trick is to provide for the future without living in it, and that just requires being moral.[6]

NOTES

1. Adam Smith, *The Wealth of Nations,* ed. Edwin Canaan (Modern Library, N.Y., 1937), p. 423.

2. See Milton Friedman, "The Social Responsibility of Business Is to Increase Its Profits" in *The New York Times Magazine* (September 13, 1970), pp. 33, 122–126 and "Milton Friedman Responds" in *Business and Society Review* (Spring, 1972, No. 1), p. 5 ff.

3. Albert Z. Carr, "Is Business Bluffing Ethical?" *Harvard Business Review* (January–February 1968).

4. Milton Friedman in "Milton Friedman Responds" in *Business and Society Review* (Spring 1972, No. 1), p. 10.

5. Milton Friedman in "Milton Friedman Responds" in *Business and Society Review* (Spring 1972, No. 1), p. 10.

6. I would like to thank C. G. Luckhardt, J. Humber, R. L. Arrington, and M. Snoeyenbos for their comments and criticisms of an earlier draft.

Shortly after this paper was initially written, an Indiana superior court judge refused to dismiss a homicide indictment against the Ford Motor Company. The company was indicted on charges of reckless homicide stemming from a 1978 accident involving a 1973 Pinto in which three girls died when the car burst into flames after being slammed in the rear. This was the first case in which Ford, or any other automobile manufacturer, had been charged with a criminal offense.

The indictment went forward because the state of Indiana adopted in 1977 a criminal code provision permitting corporations to be charged with criminal acts. At the time, twenty-two other states allowed as much.

The judge, in refusing to set aside the indictment, agreed with the prosecutor's argument that the charge was based not on the Pinto design fault, but rather on the fact that Ford had permitted the car "to remain on Indiana highways knowing full well its defects."

The case went to trial, a jury trial, and Ford Motor Company was found innocent of the charges. Of course, the increasing number of states that allow corporations to fall under the criminal code is an example of social regulation that could have been avoided had corporations and corporate managers not followed so ardently the Friedman doctrine.

Corporate Policy Statements

Views on Corporate Responsibility: The state provides a corporation with the opportunity to earn a profit if it meets society's needs. It follows inevitably that reported profits are the primary scorecard that tells the world how well a corporation is meeting its basic responsibility to society. This is all pretty simple and pretty elementary and I am sure you all studied it years ago in school. However, in recent times critics of our business structure seem to be losing sight of the primary purposes of the corporation and some want to blame the corporation for all of society's ills — real and imaginary. I have no quarrel with the citizenry, the bureaucrats, the legislators or the educators who say that corporations have a responsibility to society beyond the obligation to generate a fair return or profit for the investor. The corporation — as I have said earlier — is a paper citizen, and every citizen has a responsibility to his fellow citizen. Democratic society is based on that fact. The corporation cannot ignore the truth any more than an individual human being can. However, I take real issue with the critics when they propose that corporations must put their other citizenship responsibilities ahead of their responsibility to earn a fair return for the owners. The only way in which corporations can carry their huge and increasing burden of obligations to society is for them to earn satisfactory profits. If we cannot earn a return on equity investment, which is more attractive than other forms of investment, we die. I am not aware of any bankrupt corporations which are making important social contributions.

. . . There are times when it is hard to define and quantify our responsibility. How much of our shareholder's money should the managers of the business give away in the interest of higher education, and to the United Way campaigns of our base communities? To the fostering of culture and the arts? How much should we spend in money and time attempting to persuade the public to adequately finance public schools, or to help reorganize local government? There is no charity for charity's sake in our handing out the Company's money or in our asking the Company's people to give of their time. Procter & Gamble's support of civic campaigns is now and always will be limited to what we believe represents the enlightened self-interest of the business. Here in the term self-interest we are back to the word "profit" again. Let's take our own home city of Cincinnati as an example. The future earnings of this Company rest first and foremost on our ability to attract and hold bright, capable, dedicated and concerned people as our employees. If one-quarter of those people are expected to spend their careers in Cincinnati, then it serves the interests of the stockholders for us to support soundly-conceived efforts to maintain and enhance this community as a good place to live and raise families.

Procter and Gamble Co.

Alcoa's Fundamental Objectives: Aluminum Company of America, as a broadly owned multinational company, is committed to four fundamental, interdependent objectives, all of which are essential to its long-term success. The ideas behind these words have been part of Alcoa's success for many years — as has the company's intention to excel in all these objectives: 1. Provide for shareholders a return superior to that available from other investments of equal risk, based on reliable long-term growth in earnings per share; 2. Provide employees a rewarding and challenging employment environment with opportunity for economic and personal growth; 3. Provide worldwide customers with products and services of quality; 4. Direct its skills and resources to help solve the major problems of the societies and communities of which it is a part, while providing these societies with the benefits of its other fundamental objectives. Supporting Principles — In achieving its fundamental objectives, Alcoa endorses these supporting principles and pledges to: Conduct its business in a legal and ethical manner; Provide leadership and support for the free market system through successfully achieving its corporate objectives, superiority in product development and production, integrity in its commercial dealings, active awareness of its role in society, and appropriate communication with all employees and with the public; Maintain a working environment that will assure each employee the opportunity for growth, for achievement of his or her personal goals, and for contributing to the achievement of the corporate goals; Without regard to race, color, national origin, handicap or sex, recruit, employ and develop individuals of competence and skills commensurate with job requirements; Make a positive contribution to the quality of life of the communities and societies in which it operates, always mindful of its economic obligations, as well as the environmental and economic impact of its activities in these communities; For the well-being of all employees at all locations, maintain safe and healthful working conditions, conducive to job satisfaction and high productivity.

Aluminum Co. of America

The Role of the Corporation in a Changing Era: At a recent meeting of senior management, discussion focused on TRW's responsibility to the constituents it serves: shareholders, customers, employees, government, plant communities and the general public. In answer to the question, 'How do you define the social impact of a corporation?' Dr. Ruben F. Mettler, president of TRW, expressed the corporate policy: A meaningful definition requires looking at the three levels at which TRW should have a positive impact on society. The first level concerns the basic performance of the company as an economic unit. How many jobs does it provide? Is its productivity increasing? Is it profitable enough to pay employees and shareholders fairly? What is the quality of its goods and services? Does it provide stability and growth in employment? What is its contribution to the economy of the countries in which it operates? Clearly, TRW's primary social impact lies in our success as an economic institution efficiently producing quality products to fill society's needs. The next level concerns the quality of the conduct of our internal affairs. For example, are we ensuring equal employment and advancement opportunity for all? Is there job satisfaction? Do we provide proper health protection and safety devices and adequate pollution control? Is our advertising truthful? The third level concerns the additional things we do in relating to our external environment. This includes charitable and cultural contribution programs, youth projects, urban action programs, assistance to educational institutions, employees' participation in community affairs and our good government program. TRW focuses its activities in these areas in communities where we have plants because we can have the most meaningful impact there. It would be a mistake to think that any one, or two, of these levels fully defines our corporate impact, and hence our responsibility. We must meet our responsibilities at all three levels. The corporate constituents that we're concerned about — shareholder, employee, customer, government, community, general public — have a particular interest at each level. For example, shareholders are not just interested in their return on investment — a part of the first level. They want to be sure that our activities at the second level and third level will not adversely affect that investment. Employees are interested in more than their paycheck. They want to be treated fairly and to enjoy equal rights and opportunities. They want to be proud of their company's outside activities and to participate in them. We are determined to meet the needs and expectations of each of our constituents at each of these three levels. That's how I believe TRW will be measured and judged on its impact and its responsibilities to society.

TRW

Morals, Management, and Codes

Milton Snoeyenbos
Donald Jewell

Morals and Management

A number of surveys on ethics in business have been conducted that not only provide us with data regarding the ethical issues businesspersons actually consider to be most troublesome, but also indicate that top and middle managers have different perspectives regarding the source and nature of business disputes containing an ethical component. This article discusses the data and offers some suggestions for resolving the ethical problems revealed.

In 1961, Raymond Baumhart surveyed a large sample of subscribers to the *Harvard Business Review,* and in 1977, Steven Brenner and Earl Molander reported the results of a survey that repeated some of Baumhart's questions.[1] These studies are not representative of businesspersons. Less than 30% of the readers queried actually replied, and it is known that subscribers are significantly above average in position, income, and education. In fact, 44% of the respondents were top managers, 35% were middle managers and 20% were either lower management or nonmanagement business personnel. Nevertheless, the large sample size (over 2,700 replies from 10,000 queried) gives us some indication of how businesspersons actually regard ethical issues and how their views have changed in the last twenty years.

Of those who responded to the Brenner-Molander survey 80% believe there are ethical absolutes and that ethical matters are not relative. Furthermore, in both surveys 98% agreed that "in the long run, sound ethics is good business." However, about half of the respondents in both surveys agree that "the American business executive tends not to apply the great ethical laws immediately to work. He is preoccupied chiefly with gain." Evidently, then, for the businessperson, as for most of us, there frequently is a gap between what the person knows or believes that he ought to do and what he actually does; behavior fails to match a professed standard.

One reason for this gap may be that the manager finds himself in a context in which there is pressure to follow generally accepted *industry* practices that he regards as unethical. In 1961, 80% of the respondents agreed that such practices existed, as compared with 67% in 1977. Although the decline is significant, and may indicate greater ethical awareness or legal enforcement, Brenner and Molander point out that it could also reflect a greater ability to conceal unethical practices, or an actual decline in ethical standards, i.e., what was formerly viewed as unethical may now be acceptable behavior. In both surveys respondents were asked to indicate which industry practices they would most like to see eliminated. The results, in order of importance, are:

	1961		*1977*
1.	Gifts, gratuities, bribes	1.	Gifts, gratuities, bribes
2.	Unfair pricing practices	2.	Unfair competitive practices
3.	Dishonest advertising	3.	Cheating customers
4.	Unfair competitive practices	4.	Unfairness to employees
5.	Cheating customers	5.	Unfair pricing practices
6.	Competitors' pricing collusion	6.	Dishonest advertising
7.	Contract dishonesty	7.	Competitors' pricing collusion
8.	Unfairness to employees	8.	Contract dishonesty

The decreased concern with unfair pricing practices and dishonest advertising probably reflects increased societal concern with these issues in the 1960s, subsequent legislation, and effective measures taken by businesspersons to combat the problems. Discriminatory employment practices emerged as a central issue in the late 1960s, with the recognition that disadvantaged minorities have a right to equal consideration. The 1964 Civil Rights Act and concerted action taken by businesspersons to correct such inequities have undeniably improved the situation. But a certain amount of political and legal equivocation and indecision, along with difficulties regarding how discriminatory employment practices are to be measured and alleviated, ensure that this will continue as a central ethical issue in the 1980s.

Aside from the question of unethical industry practices, both surveys asked managers whether they had ever *personally* experienced a role conflict between what was expected of them as efficient, profit-conscious managers and what was expected of them as ethical persons. In 1961, 75% reported such conflicts, compared with 59% in 1977. Again, while it may be that competitive pressures have lessened, so that there are fewer role conflicts today, it may also be the case that standards have fallen, so that practices formerly regarded as unethical are accepted today.

The types of role conflict most frequently experienced have changed:

1961	*1977*
1. Firings and layoffs	1. Honesty in communications
2. Honesty in communication	2. Gifts, entertainment, kickbacks
3. Price collusion	3. Fairness and discrimination
4. Gifts, entertainment, kickbacks	4. Contract honesty
	5. Firings and layoffs

Honesty in communication is a more significant problem now than in 1961, with a major increase in number manipulation in reports submitted to top management, governmental agencies, and clients. The decreased experience of role conflicts connected with firings and layoffs may indicate that such practices are becoming accepted as routine or that there is more equity built into firing decisions. The decreased experience of role conflicts with respect to price collusion probably reflects the passage of stricter laws, along with tighter enforcement.

As noted, both the Baumhart and Brenner-Molander surveys are weighted toward the opinion of top management. The 1965 Evans survey, focusing on middle managers, reveals that their most important moral conflicts are:

1. Complying with superior's requirements when they conflict with one's own ethical code,
2. Job demands infringing on home obligations,
3. Methods employed in competition for advancement,
4. Avoiding or hedging responsibility,
5. Maintaining integrity when it conflicts with being well-liked,
6. Impartial treatment of subordinates because of race, religion or personal prejudice,
7. Moral concern that your job does not fully utilize your capabilities.[2]

These data indicate that middle managers experience role conflicts primarily because of "pressure from the top," a conclusion reinforced by a recent survey by Archie Carroll.[3] In Carroll's survey, 64% of the managers surveyed agreed that "managers today feel under pressure to compromise personal standards to achieve company goals," but of those agreeing 50% of top managers, 65% of middle managers, and 84% of lower managers agreed with the statement. And of the 59% who agreed that "the junior members of Nixon's re-election committee who confessed that they went along with their bosses to show their loyalty is just what young managers would have done in business," only 37% of top managers agreed, but 61% of middle managers and 85% of lower managers agreed. Apparently, then, the lower one is in the managerial hierarchy the more one feels pressure to act unethically. Of course, pressure *per se* is not unethical; in a competitive, profit-oriented environment, pressure to produce is necessary for the efficiency that benefits both consumer and producer. But unethical pressure arises when top management sets a return on equity, sales quota, market share, etc., that cannot reasonably be achieved without a subordinate's engagement in unethical behavior. Unethical pressure may be either intentional or inadvertent. In other words, the manager may or may not be aware that he is pressuring a subordinate to the point that the latter is likely to commit an unethical or illegal act. Some unethical pressure is undoubtedly intentional. A manager may adopt a "produce or else" attitude toward subordinates, knowing it will probably result in unethical behavior, but believing that it will yield greater production or sales and that the subordinate can be held responsible for the unethical acts. A manager may require a subordinate to manipulate figures in a report that requires the latter's signature, believing that responsibility for wrongdoing will fall on the subordinate. Many people in business believe that advancement is open only to those individuals who are unethical, and a manager may intentionally encourage unethical behavior in intrafirm competition.[4] More generally, a manager who deliberately fails to provide a context in which ethical concerns can be voiced, and wrongdoing reported and corrected, may encourage unethical behavior.

On the other hand, some top managers are undoubtedly unaware that they are placing unethical pressure on their subordinates. This hypothesis is consistent with the results of Carroll's survey and the data from the 1961 and 1977 surveys. First, many of the industry-wide practices that top managers do not themselves condone and would most like to see eliminated (e.g., gratuities and bribes, unfair competitive and pricing practices, cheating customers, and contract dishonesty) may arise in large part because of inadvertent pressure from above. Second, the role conflicts actually experienced by managers, and prominently mentioned in both surveys (e.g., honesty in communication, gifts and kickbacks, fairness and discrimination, and contract honesty), may arise in part because of pressure superiors inadvertently place on subordinates. The 1961 and 1977 surveys indicate that the role conflicts and industry practices that managers most want to see eliminated are those they have personally experienced, and, although some managers may be familiar with unethical acts they believe they can pressure subordinates into committing, others may simply not be well enough acquainted with lower-level operational details to recognize the unreasonableness of particular demands they make of subordinates. This may be especially significant in large diversified firms in which a manager with training and experience in one department may be transferred to the upper levels of a department in which he has little or no lower-level experience. Third, this hypothesis could account for the fact that the top-level respondents to the 1961 and 1977 surveys profess to have absolute ethical standards but also claim both that their standards are higher than those of the average manager and that the average manager does not apply these standards. It seems reasonable to assume that the professed standards of top, middle, and lower managers are about the same. But inadvertent pressure from the top may force subordinates to act contrary to the standards both profess. In turn, the subordinate's actions may be interpreted by top managers as an indication that other managers actually have lower standards. The problem is compounded when general corporate policies or codes are not linked with a mechanism that permits ethical concerns to be relayed to top management, when top managers are unwilling to listen, or when no sanctions are fixed for transgressions and ethical behavior goes unrewarded.

What steps can be taken to improve ethical behavior in business? It seems clear from the surveys that there must be greater awareness on the part of top managers that their leadership is essential. In one sense, managers should already be aware of this, since it is a principle of management theory that top management sets the standards of behavior and subordinates imitate the behavior that is expected for success within the organization. The 1970 survey, however, indicates that 65% of managers believe that society, not business, has the primary responsibility for setting ethical standards. Certainly there is some basis for this opinion; individuals are members of society long before they enter business, and the manager should be able to assume that the person he or she hires are already ethical. Yet the surveys also reveal the importance of an organizational influence. Respondents to the 1961 survey ranked the following as factors that influence a person to make ethical decisions.

> An individual's personal code of behavior,
> Behavior of a person's superiors in the firm,
> Formal company policy,
> Ethical climate of the industry,
> Behavior of a person's equals in the company.

The following were ranked as factors influencing a person to make unethical decisions:

> The behavior of a person's superiors in the company,
> Ethical climate of the industry,
> The behavior of a person's equals in the company,
> Lack of company policy,
> Personal financial needs.

In the 1977 survey, the following factors were ranked as most influencing a person to make unethical decisions:

> Behavior of superiors,
> Formal policy or lack thereof,
> Industry ethical climate,
> Behavior of one's equals in the company,
> Society's moral climate,
> One's personal financial needs.

We have already noted Evans's survey result that middle managers experience role conflicts primarily because of organizational pressure. Furthermore, that survey indicates that when middle managers are pressured to comply with a superior's directive that is contrary to their personal code of behavior, they most often comply rather than resign or object and leave themselves open to dismissal, demotion or horizontal transfer. Similarly, the Carroll survey reveals that 61% of middle managers and 85% of lower managers would "go along with their bosses to show their loyalty" if asked to engage in behavior they personally believe to be unethical. Thus, the surveys unambiguously indicate that, although a person's socially acquired ethical beliefs may strongly influence his behavior, when faced with an ethical dilemma a person in a lower-level organizational position will typically seek guidance in his immediate organizational context and, in particular, will refer to his superiors' ethical behavior. Organizational factors are central both to a person's perception of an ethical dilemma and his subsequent behavior once a problem is recognized. And, since it is clear that pressure to commit unethical acts is in part traceable to the managerial hierarchy, it is unreasonable for a top manager to expect that a subordinate's decisions will be based solely or primarily on values acquired prior to and independent of his business experience. Unless top management sets the standards of behavior expected in the organization, the pressure to produce may well lead to unethical behavior of the sort revealed in the surveys. And top managers must not only exhibit leadership by professing high standards, they must clearly articulate them and see that they are enforced.

How can top management develop and enforce high ethical standards in business? We can begin to answer this question by addressing the trouble spots our surveys reveal. Since we have noted that a considerable amount of unethical behavior arises from questionable industry practices, one suggestion is that top managers take an active role in curbing such practices through the implementation of industry-wide ethical standards (or codes) that not only are clearly articulated but also have an adequate enforcement mechanism. Respondents to both the 1961 and 1977 surveys indicate that they favor industry-wide codes. In 1961, 71% favored codes, 19% were neutral, and 10% were opposed. In 1977, 55% were in favor, 20% neutral and 25% opposed. Respondents indicated the following as likely consequences of industry code adoption:

	1961 Percentages			1977 Percentages		
	Agree	Neutral	Disagree	Agree	Neutral	Disagree
1. Would raise the industry's ethical level	71	12	17	56	17	27
2. Would help executives define clearly the limit of acceptable conduct	81	7	12	67	11	21

	1961 Percentages			1977 Percentages		
	Agree	Neutral	Disagree	Agree	Neutral	Disagree
3. Managers would welcome as a useful aid when the wanted to refuse an unethical request impersonally	87	5	8	79	9	12
4. People would violate when they thought they could avoid detection	57	8	35	61	11	28
5. In situations of severe competition, it would reduce the use of underhanded practices	51	9	40	41	12	47
6. Would be easy to enforce	9	4	87	7	4	89

While respondents to the 1977 survey are less convinced of the merits of industry-wide codes, the majority in both surveys believe codes would help managers raise their industry's ethical level, define limits of acceptable behavior, and refuse unethical requests. Responses to 4 and 5, however, indicate that codes are not perceived as cure-alls, and enforcement is clearly seen as a major problem. Both surveys queried respondents regarding their choices of an enforcement body, with the following results:

	1961 Percentages	1977 Percentages
The management of each company (i.e., self-enforcement)	40	35
A combined group of industry executives or a trade association	28	29
A group composed of executives from the industry plus other members from the community	28	33
A governmental agency	4	3

There are advantages to self-enforcement: (a) it places the enforcer close to the source of the problem, since management has inside information and detection capability; (b) given management's power and legal authority, and assuming the commitment of top management, it can provide for the possibility of vigorous enforcement; and (c) given management's inside knowledge, it may be more sensitive to the actual context of the violation than outside enforcers, i.e., it may be fairer to violators. On the other hand, if superiors' pressure and the organizational framework are major factors in influencing an individual to act unethically, as our surveys reveal, then there can be disadvantages to self-enforcement of industry codes: (d) some managers may not be committed fully to the code and may ignore or suppress disclosure of violations; (e) conflict between profit and ethics may tend to be resolved in favor of the former; and (f) enforcement may vary from firm to firm within an industry.

It should be noted that, although managers themselves seem strongly opposed to governmental enforcement, the majority do favor an enforcement mechanism that is external to the firm. Enforcement by either a board of industry executives, or executives plus community members, can have certain drawbacks: (a) conflicts with the management of some firms may arise; (b) since a firm may "look good" simply by not reporting violations, there may be cases of under-reporting; (c) it may be difficult to obtain information about reported violations; (d) firms may be reluctant to grant the necessary authority to an outside enforcement agency; and hence, (e) some firms may simply not become members of the industry-wide association. However, assuming a context of industry-wide commitment to a code by top management, such enforcement procedures hold the promise of: (f) providing uniform and impartial treatment, (g) offering employees an independent basis for refusing unethical requests, and (h) improving an industry's public image. Several industries have such enforcement mechanisms; for example, the Rocky Mountain Jewelers Association, in conjunction with the Denver Area Better Business Bureau, has developed the following successful code and enforcement procedure:

CODE OF ETHICS

1. Serve the public with honest values.
2. Tell the truth about what is offered.
3. Tell the truth in a forthright manner so its significance may be understood by the trusting as well as the analytical.
4. Tell customers what they want to know—what they have a right to know and ought to know—about what is offered so that they may buy wisely and obtain the maximum satisfaction from their purchases.
5. Be prepared and willing to make good as promised without quibble on any guarantee offered.
6. Be sure that the normal use of merchandise or services offered will not be hazardous to public health or life.
7. Reveal material facts, the deceptive concealment of which might cause consumers to be misled.
8. Advertise and sell merchandise or service on its merits and refrain from attacking your competitors or reflecting unfairly upon their products, services, or methods of doing business.

9. If testimonials are used, use only those of competent witnesses who are sincere and honest in what they say about what you sell.
10. Avoid all tricky devices and schemes such as deceitful trade-in allowances, fictitious list prices, false and exaggerated comparative prices, bait advertising, misleading free offers, fake sales, and similar practices which prey upon human ignorance and gullibility.

ARBITRATION PROCEDURE

Consumer complaints, which cannot be resolved to the satisfaction of both consumer and participating firm, will be arbitrated before the Industry Arbitration Committee.

The Arbitration Committee shall consist of five members as follows: two jewelers, two consumers, and a Better Business Bureau representative. The BBB representative will act as Chairman and will vote only if there is a tie. Four members of the Committee shall constitute a quorum. Committee decisions will be based on a majority of those present.

Members of the Committee will not be given the name of the complainant nor the name of the merchant concerned. The facts in each case will be presented to the Committee by a representative of the Better Business Bureau. The Committee will then decide where the responsibility lies and what adjustment should be recommended. Participating firms will be so notified and expected to make adjustment on the basis recommended. In cases where others may be at fault, that firm will be advised accordingly and asked to make an adjustment. Participants agree to abide by the decision of the Arbitration Committee on all matters being arbitrated.[5]

Of course, codes have to be structured with an eye to the particular trouble spots faced by an industry: the retail jewelers' code addresses primarily consumer concerns. Other industries may be more concerned with antitrust violations, trade secrets, unfair competitive and pricing practices, and contract dishonesty.

The second major way that top management can improve the ethical climate of business is to institutionalize ethics in the corporation. Of course, in the small firm there may not be a need for an elaborate formal structure, but in the large corporation there is a need for articulated objectives, relatively formal procedures and rules, and communication and enforcement mechanisms. If people want their organizations to be ethical as well as productive, then in complex firms there is a need to articulate and communicate ethical standards that are both equitable and effectively enforced. To accomplish these ends, the standards of expected behavior should be institutionalized, i.e., they should become a relatively permanent aspect of the organization. To institutionalize ethics we suggest that the firm: (a) adopt a corporate ethical code, (b) designate an ethics committee at a relatively high level in the organization, and (c) make ethics training part of its management development program.

The first step in institutionalizing ethics is to articulate the firm's values or goals. Many corporations do have general objectives; 3M Corporation, for example, has goals relating to profits, customers, employees, and society. With respect to profit, it states, "3M management will endeavor to maintain optimum profit margins in all product lines in order to finance 3M's future growth and to provide an adequate return to stockholders." The corporation also states that in pursuing its goals the firm will adhere to "uncompromising honesty and integrity . . . manifested in the commitment to the highest standards of ethics throughout the organization and in all aspects of 3M's operations." So 3M's code, developed by top management, has committed the firm's employees to ethical behavior in the achievement of general corporate goals. However, since our surveys reveal that the pressure to achieve goals can and does override ethics, the emphasis should be on setting *reasonable* goals and sub-goals, i.e., goals should be set so that unethical pressure is not placed on subordinates. In addition to a general statement of goals and the means to implement them, a top management committed to ethics should: (a) extensively consult with personnel at all levels of the firm regarding goals and sub-goals; (b) see to it that reasonable, specific sub-goals are set; and (c) articulate a fine-grained ethical code that addresses ethical issues likely to arise at the level of sub-goals.

A code, then, should be relatively *specific*. In addition to general policy statements mentioning overall corporate objectives and means, it should spell out in some detail policy regarding ethical issues that are liable to arise in the conduct of a particular corporation's business. It should detail the individual's obligations to the organization in areas such as: confidential information, trade secrets, bribes, gratuities, gifts, conflicts of interest, expense accounts, honesty, etc. But it should also mention employer obligations in areas such as: hiring, affirmative action, promotion, layoffs, termination, privacy, dissent, grievances, communication, worker and product safety, contributions, employee development, and job quality. In addition, specificity can be enhanced by integrating a firm's ethical concerns with its legal requirements. In the areas of safety and health, for example, specific ethical policy could be integrated with the law in areas such as: equipment, apparel, handling and testing of materials, testing of employees, treatment, compensation, and employment of the handicapped.

If a code is to be more than window-dressing, it must be enforced, equitable, and effective; it must be a living document that organizational members are aware of, comprehend, and to which they are committed. If top management is genuine in its ethical commitment, there are a variety of ways to institutionalize a code; the "best" way will largely depend on the individual organizational context. In some cases, a board of directors' subcommittee comprised of inside and outside directors will be effective. In other cases, a committee comprised of managers and employees from different organizational strata will be successful. However it is constituted, the committee should have the authority and responsibility to: (1) communicate the code, pertinent changes, and decisions based on it to all members of the firm; (2) clarify the code and issues relating to its interpretation; (3) facilitate the code's use; (4) investigate grievances and possible code violations; (5) enforce the code by disciplining violators and rewarding those who comply with and uphold it; and (6) review, update, and upgrade the code.

In addition to an explicit ethical code and ethics committee, institutionalization can be aided by devoting part of the employee training program to ethics. Ideally this would embrace all employees, and could focus on the code, the ethics committee, and the responsibilities of employer and employee. In practice, only a few firms, such as IBM and Allied Chemical, currently have such programs and these are restricted to employee development programs for managers. Allied's program for top and upper-middle managers spans three days and is conducted by a corporate personnel manager and an external individual with training in ethics. To ensure relevance, each participant presents a case from personal experience for group discussion.

This sort of program has several merits. The case study approach fosters awareness of actual dilemmas managers face, and the range of people involved in such a program exposes managers to a diversity of ethical problems. The presence of a trained ethicist should help to focus the discussion and elucidate models of ethical decision-making. But this sort of approach, as the *sole* method of institutionalizing ethics, also has several drawbacks. The brevity of the typical program, combined with the complexity of ethical issues may lead to bewilderment rather than clarity. Then, too, restriction of such a program to top and upper-middle management may skew the discussion; we noted, for example, the centrality of the problem of inadvertent pressure placed on subordinates by top and upper-middle management. Finally, a training program itself cannot fully institutionalize ethics, since it does not provide an institutional or corporate procedure for handling actual ethical issues that arise. Accordingly, incorporation of an ethics module in a management development program is best regarded as one component of a more comprehensive strategy to institutionalize ethical behavior.

Within the firm, then, top management can create an ethical environment by: (1) articulating goals for the firm, and, in particular, by developing a two-way communicative process that sets realistic sub-goals, such as sales quotas, for employees; (2) encouraging the development of an ethical code applicable to all members of the firm; (3) instituting an ethics committee to oversee, enforce, and develop the code; and (4) incorporating ethics training in the employee development program. Establishment of such internal programs, in the context of developing industry-wide codes of ethics to deal with issues that transcend a particular firm, would be a significant step in establishing an ethical climate in business.

NOTES

1. Raymond C. Baumhart, "How Ethical Are Businessmen?" *Harvard Business Review,* vol. 39, no. 4 (July–August, 1961), pp. 6 ff; *Ethics in Business* (New York: Holt, Rinehart and Winston, 1968); Steven N. Brenner and Earl A. Molander, "Is the Ethics of Business Changing?" *Harvard Business Review,* vol. 55, no. 1 (Jan.–Feb., 1977), pp. 57–71.

2. Appendix B to Thomas F. McMahon's "Moral Problems of Middle Management," in *Proceedings of the Catholic Theological Society of America,* vol. 20 (1965), pp. 23–49.

3. Archie B. Carroll, "Managerial Ethics: A Post-Watergate View," *Business Horizons,* vol. 18, no. 2 (April, 1975), pp. 75–80.

4. Harrison Johnson, "How to Get the Boss's Job," *Modern Office Procedure,* vol. 6, no. 5 (1961), pp. 15–18.

5. Cited in *Ethics and Standards in American Business,* edited by Joseph W. Towle (Boston: Houghton-Mifflin Co., 1964), pp. 281–2.

Corporate Policy Statements

The John Deere organization has met and overcome many changes since its beginnings in 1837. It has learned that change is to be expected. Change is one of the few things to be counted on with certainty and it is good business always to be ready for the ones that surely lie ahead. A great part of our ability to make changes successfully lies in the flexibility of our organization. That flexibility makes it all the more necessary that we never lose sight of our basic concepts of the way John Deere management works. A key factor in John Deere management is participation in the development and establishment of policy by those who are directly responsible for putting policy into action. The senior officers of Deere & Company participate in the development and establishment of over-all, company-wide policies. Factory, sales branch and region managers participate in the development of policies concerning manufacturing and marketing. Factory sales branch and region department heads participate in the development of policies in their specific areas of functional responsibility. Department heads and supervisors in each unit should participate in the development of the local policies of their units. This system is a tremendous source of strength for the John Deere organization as a whole and for its management people individually. It taps the experience and judgment of responsible managers as no other means can. It is the best insurance that the policies developed by this means will be understood and energetically applied. It also helps significantly to develop individuals as effective managers and supervisors. Such a system requires strong leaders who make the basic decisions appropriate to their positions and functions. Nevertheless, those decisions should not be unilateral. Instead, effective leaders encourage participation by their associates and subordinates. This they should do somewhat as follows: a) By making major decisions only after conferring with associates and subordinates; b) By establishing mutually agreed upon goals and objectives for subordinates. Such goals and objectives should be few in number, consistent with each other, and preferably measurable; c) By explaining conditions and priorities, helping to plan and to organize and schedule the steps to be taken to reach those goals and objectives; d) By actively seeking participation of associates and subordinates in developing the policies to be followed and the methods to be used to reach the goals and objectives; e) By periodically assessing progress toward the goals and objectives; f) By evaluating end results in terms of the degree to which goals are reached and objectives are gained; g) By seeing to it that the rewards to subordinates are commensurate with the actual contributions of each of them. Any manager or supervisor is greatly dependent on his associates and subordinates for his success. The John Deere system of participative management is a tested means to such success. It is based upon a confidence in the inherent worth and abilities of each individual. Results show that this trust is not often misplaced. Successful as this procedure can be when properly used, there is a danger in it which managers should recognize and guard themselves against. It must not be abused by a manager abdicating the responsibility for making the decisions which are clearly his to make. A manager should seek facts, opinions and recommendations from his associates and subordinates, but in the last analysis only he should make the decisions which it is his duty to make and for which he is held responsible. He should be neither autocratic nor subservient.

Deere & Co.

1. Any employee of the Company having information or knowledge of any actual or contemplated transaction which appears to violate this Code shall promptly report the matter in writing to the Controller and to the Legal Department; 2. The Internal Audit Department, as part of its regular procedures, shall assess compliance with this Code. Any matters discovered by the Internal Audit Department which appear to violate this Code shall be reported in writing to the Controller and to the Legal Department; 3. The Company's outside independent auditors shall be requested to report in writing to the Controller and to the Legal Department any matter discovered in the course of their examination of the Company's financial statements which appears to violate this Code, to review periodically the procedures and controls instituted by the Company and to recommend any additional procedures or controls they believe may be necessary or appropriate; 4. Each officer or Regional Manager of the Company with direct responsibility for a function which has obligated the Company to a consultant for fees and/or reimbursement of expenses for a period continuing one year or more, either initially or as a result of separate referrals, shall, at least once during each twelve months period, review the services performed by such consultant as well as the fee paid and/or expenses reimbursed by the Company and, if it is determined to continue such arrangement, provide a written report to the Legal Department including a statement that the value of the services rendered is commensurate with its cost; 5. Officers and appropriate other

employees or representatives of the Company, as selected by the Legal Department or requested by management, shall be required at least annually to confirm, to the best of their knowledge, that they have complied with this Code and have no knowledge of any violation not reported; 6. The Legal Department shall report periodically to management and to the Audit Committee each confirmed violation, if any, of this Code and any approvals granted under or reports provided pursuant to this Code of which it has knowledge; 7. Failure of any employee of the Company to comply with this Code will result in disciplinary action which, depending on the seriousness of the matter, may include reprimand, probation, suspension, demotion or dismissal. Disciplinary measures will apply to superiors and senior executives who condone questionable, improper or illegal conduct by those reporting to them or who fail to take appropriate corrective action when such matters are brought to their attention.

The Southland Corp.

SELECTED BIBLIOGRAPHY

Anshen, M., ed. *Managing the Socially Responsible Corporation*. New York: Macmillan, 1974.

Baumhart, R. *Ethics in Business*. New York: Holt, Rinehart and Winston, 1968.

Carroll, A., ed. *Managing Corporate Social Responsibility*. Boston: Little, Brown and Co., 1977.

————. *Business and Society*. Boston: Little, Brown and Co., 1981.

Chamberlain, N. *The Limits of Corporate Responsibility*. New York: Basic Books, 1973.

Donaldson, T. *Corporations and Morality*. Englewood Cliffs, N.J.: Prentice-Hall, 1982, Chs. 2-6.

Flew, A. "The Profit Motive." *Ethics,* 86 (July, 1976), 312-21.

French, P. "The Corporation as a Moral Person." *American Philosophical Quarterly,* 16 (July, 1979), 207-15.

Friedman, M. *Capitalism and Freedom*. Chicago: University of Chicago Press, 1962.

————. *Free to Choose*. New York: Harcourt Brace Jovanovich, 1980.

Hoffman, M., ed. *Proceedings of the Second National Conference on Business Ethics*. Washington, D.C.: University Press of America, 1979. Contains articles by T. Donaldson and K. Goodpaster on Ladd, and a response by Ladd, 81-115.

Humber, J. "Milton Friedman and the Corporate Executive's Conscience." *Philosophy in Context,* 10 (1980), 71-80.

Ozar, D. "The Moral Responsibility of Corporations," in *Ethical Issues in Business*. Donaldson, T., and Werhane, P., eds. Englewood Cliffs, N.J.: Prentice-Hall, 1979, pp. 294-300.

Steiner, G. *Issues in Business and Society*. 2nd ed. New York: Random House, 1977.

Stone, C. *Where the Law Ends: The Social Control of Corporate Behavior*. New York: Harper and Row, 1975.

Sturdivant, F. *Business and Society*. Homewood, Ill.: Richard D. Irwin, 1977.

3

EMPLOYEE OBLIGATIONS

INTRODUCTION

The work contract establishes employee obligations to the employer; in return for his wage the employee is expected to utilize his knowledge and skills for the benefit of the organization. Employees have clear, specific, and extensive legal obligations to their employers, and these are spelled out in C. G. Luckhardt's article "Duties of Agent to Principal." The rest of this chapter discusses employee obligations in the areas of conflict of interest, gifts, payoffs, trade secrets, and honesty in organizational communication.

If employees have an obligation to adhere to their work contracts, the firm also has an obligation to be relatively specific about the details of the work contract. This point is clearly made in Robert E. Frederick's discussion of conflicts of interest. Although firms have a right to preclude conflicts of interest, Frederick's discussion of Inorganic Chemical's policy points up the fact that corporate policies are often excessively general and biased in favor of the organization. The need for specificity in corporate policy statements is echoed in Robert Almeder's discussion of bribes and gifts.

Although bribes and kickbacks are illegal and considered immoral in the U.S., similar practices are commonplace in some foreign countries, particularly in those lacking a vigorous free market. The case study on Lockheed's selling of the Tristar in Japan provides insight into the reasons used by the executives of one corporation to justify making payoffs to foreign government officials in order to make a sale, and raises the question of what ethical principles or values American firms should adopt in such contexts. Patricia Werhane argues that defenses of foreign payoffs are often inconsistent; she then discusses some of the ethical variables companies need to consider when operating transnationally. Mark Pastin and Michael Hooker argue that the 1977 Foreign Corrupt Practices Act, which bans corporate payoffs to foreign government officials for the purpose of securing or retaining business, has no moral basis and hence should be repealed.

We commonly regard knowledge as a social good and value its dissemination, which raises the question of whether we should allow corporations to protect the information they generate. Robert E. Frederick and Milton Snoeyenbos argue that there is a moral basis for allowing patents and trade secrets, but they also argue that an individual has a right to use *his* skills and knowledge to better himself, and hence the firm has an obligation to make sure that its secrets are legitimate trade secrets. The case study in this section points up the conflict between corporate and individual rights within the context of trade secrets.

Surveys reveal that honesty in communication is a major problem in organizations, and the Von Products case study illustrates communication dilemmas that can arise. James M. Humber argues that employees have a *prima facie* responsibility to tell the truth, and he points out that it is very difficult to justify lying in corporate communications. Humber also discusses conditions under which the liar would legitimately be excused from responsibility for his act. H. B. Fuller's corporate policy statement details specific methods a firm can adopt to keep lines of communication open.

Agents' Duties

C. G. Luckhardt

Duties of Agent to Principal

Agency is defined as "the fiduciary relation which results from the manifestation of consent by one person to another that the other shall act on his behalf and subject to his control, and consent by the other so to act."[1] The person for whom action is taken is called the principal, and the person who takes the action is called the agent. In order to understand the extent of and rationale for the various duties agents have with regard to their principals, it is important to distinguish and understand four elements of this definition of agency. The first is the concept of acting on behalf of, or for, another. "Acting for another" implies that the agent is a kind of stand-in for the principal, for *were* the principal able to act, there would be no need for him to employ an agent. But since the principal is unable to act, perhaps because of constraints of time or ability, he deputizes another person to act in his place. This suggests that the agent is, in effect, a "mini"-principal, i.e., a person whose own identity is submerged, and who takes on the identity of the principal. Ideally, the agent would be identical with the principal, but obviously this is impossible in practice. As your agent, I cannot have *exactly* the same intentions, thoughts, desires, abilities you have; nor can I make the same decisions as you. But one of the guiding thoughts behind the law of agency is the idea that I should resemble you in as many ways as is relevantly possible. As we shall see, the ramifications of this idea for the duties of agents are vast, and the questions it raises legion. Must the agent, for example, have all of the interests of the principal at heart when he represents him? If not, then what kinds and how many? And if so, does that mean that he must have none of his own? And if he may have his own interests, may these conflict with those of the principal?

A second important element of the definition of agency given above is that of consent. The principal must consent to the agent's acting on his behalf, and the agent must consent to work for the principal. Intuitively, this requirement of an agency relationship is understandable: I can represent your interests only if you want me to, and you can't force me to represent your interests if I don't want to. But plausible though it may be, this requirement is fraught with many legal difficulties. What constitutes consent, for example? How may the principal and the agent manifest their respective consents? Can either consent tacitly, or implicitly? And how may either revoke his consent? The general rule is that failure of the agent to perform his duties will constitute adequate grounds for the principal to revoke his consent, and so the requirement of consent is closely linked with the duties that the agent is determined to have.

A third aspect of this definition of agency is the notion of control. This element gives the principal the right to direct and control the agent's activities. But this means that the agent must be subject to that control, i.e., that he must obey the instructions and directions of the principal. The duty of obedience is, as we shall see, one of the most strictly enforced of all the duties agents bear.

The fourth important aspect of the definition of agency given above is that of a fiduciary relationship. For purposes of understanding the duties agents bear to principals, this is perhaps the most important aspect of agency. In general, a fiduciary relationship is one based on trust, or faith (from the Latin *fidere*), and in the case of agency the legal requirements stemming from this concept extend beyond mere obedience to those of care and loyalty. Even though we may have mutually consented for me to be your agent, the idea here is that you must be able to trust me in order for the relationship to persist. Therefore, if I show through my lack of care or loyalty that I cannot be trusted, you may unilaterally terminate my employment as your agent. In addition you may have further causes of action against me for violating this requirement of trust.

Care, loyalty, and obedience are the three major elements constituting the agent's duties towards his principal. But in the minds of the courts, they have far-reaching connotations and sometimes surprising applications. In what follows we shall examine how these requirements are commonly interpreted and applied.

Duties of Care and Skill. The duties of care and skill arise from the courts' understanding that an agent who is paid for his services is required to act "with standard care and with the skill which is standard in the locality for the kind of work which he is employed to perform."[2] When the agent contracts with the principal, the former is ordinarily presumed to possess the skills standardly required for carrying out his agency. There are two exceptions to this, however. If the agent represents himself as possessing more than standard skills, he can be held liable if he does not possess them. And if the principal knows that the agent does not possess the standard skills, then he may not hold the agent liable for not possessing them. Suppose *P* employs *A* as his attorney to sue *T*. Ordinarily *A* can be held liable only if he does not possess the skills and exercise the care of other attorneys in the locality in which he is employed. But if *A* holds himself out as being a specialist in tax law, for example, then *P* may reasonably expect him to possess the skills and exercise the care of a tax specialist. (These do not, of course, amount to his being expected to win every case he represents.) Conversely, if *P* knows that *A* is not a tax specialist when the latter is hired, he may not expect that *A* should exercise the skills or care of a specialist. An interesting question arises when the agent possesses special skills not known to the principal, but fails to exercise them. Technically speaking, the principal cannot expect the agent to exercise them. Nevertheless, most holdings suggest that the agent may nevertheless be held liable for not exercising such special skills.

Furthermore, agents are under a general obligation to exercise a standard degree of care in their transactions and behavior. In other words, they should not act negligently. If an agent *A* is hired to buy milk-cows for *P* from *T,* and he discovers at the time of delivery that the cows are on the verge of death, normal discretion and care would dictate that he not go through with the purchase. Failure to exercise such discretion would constitute a violation of his duties.

Nor would a person exercising a standard degree of care attempt to do the impossible or the impracticable. If the agent discovers that he cannot do what he has been told to do, or that it is impracticable to do so, it is his duty not to waste his time and effort (and possibly the principal's money) attempting to do so. Thus if just before he sets out to buy *T*'s milk-cows, *A* discovers that they are dead, he is not only not under a duty to purchase them, but he also has a duty not to continue in his efforts, such as going to *T*'s place of business. The standard that is commonly used in determining whether he should continue his efforts is whether the agent could reasonably expect that the principal would want him to do so. That is, he is to put himself in what he reasonably views as the principal's shoes. Of course, if he has been able to determine the principal's desires directly, then the agent is under a duty to do just that, even if this means that he continue his best efforts to attain what he, the agent, might regard as impracticable goals.

Duty to Give Information. Closely related to the duty of care is the duty to give information. If the agent receives information bearing on the principal's interests, he has a duty to communicate this information to the principal. If *P* instructs *A,* his agent, to sell some of his real estate to *T,* and *A* meantime acquires the information that *F* would be willing to pay more for the property than *T,* he is obliged to tell this to *P.* Or if the agent is unable to carry out the directions of his principal, because events make it impossible, impracticable or illegal for him to do so, he should make that known to his principal. In the milk-cow examples above, the agent is also under an obligation to tell the principal that he has not bought the nearly dead or dead cows. Or again, an agent unable to obtain fire insurance for a principal must tell the principal that he has not been able to do so. Otherwise, in addition to being lawfully fired, he may be held liable for the amount of the insurance settlement that the principal might have received for his uninsured goods. The exceptions to this duty occur in cases where the agent has a superior duty to a person other than the principal. Thus, an attorney who acquires confidential information from one client is under no obligation to disclose it to another client whose interests it might affect.

Duty of Good Conduct. The requirements of skill, care, and the giving of information on the part of the agent are all related to actions for which the agent is employed. But the agent may also be held liable for some actions that are clearly outside the ambit of his employment. Thus, the duty of good conduct is usually understood as part of the agent's duty to care for the principal's interests. Actions that bring disrepute upon the principal, although not within the scope of the agent's employment, may be grounds for dismissal. Thus in a famous McCarthy-era case, a Hollywood screenwriter was found to have been legitimately dismissed from his job when he was convicted of contempt of Congress for refusing to answer whether he was a communist.[3] Furthermore, the duty of good conduct requires that the agent not act towards the principal in such a way as to "make continued friendly relations" with him impossible.[4] Insubordination, either in speech or by other means which jeopardize the "friendly relations," may subject an agent to lawful dismissal.

Duty to Obey. All agents have a duty to refrain from knowingly violating the reasonable directions of the principal. This is an essential element of agency, stemming from the requirement of control. If the agent does violate the reasonable instructions of the principal, either as to acts to be performed, or the manner of performing them, he may lose his job and incur liability for any loss his violation has caused the principal. If, however, the principal's directions were unreasonable, then the agent may disobey, and may even have a valid claim against the principal for breach of his employment contract. Unreasonable directions include: a) those which are illegal, unethical, or (according to a few holdings) contrary to public policy; b) those which threaten the physical condition of the agent; c) those which violate the ordinary customs of business with regard to such agency; d) those which are impossible or impracticable for the agent to carry out; and e) those which conflict with interests the agent is otherwise privileged to protect, whether such interests be his own or those of a third party. It is not proper for an agent to refuse to carry out orders solely on the grounds that doing so will harm the principal's interests. However, the agent may refuse to obey instructions if he stands directly to lose by doing so. Thus, if A is on salary, he may not refuse to sell P's goods at the price P demands, even if the price is so low that *A* knows that *P* will lose money selling them at that rate. If, however, *A* is working on commission, and knows that such a price will adversely affect his own income, he may refuse to sell at that price. Or, alternatively, if he knows that following the principal's directions will damage his own business reputation, he may refuse to follow them.

In the absence of instructions to the contrary the agent is ordinarily free to carry out the principal's orders in a manner customary to such undertakings. Thus real estate agents are free to advertise their clients' property in newspapers, unless the clients instruct them otherwise. If the principal's instructions are ambiguous and the agent is unable to receive clarification from the principal before the time to act, then his obligation is to act reasonably, in light of the facts of which he is aware.

Duty to Act Only as Authorized. The duty to obey requires that the agent do what the principal tells him to do. The duty to act only as authorized is the other side of that coin, insofar as it requires the agent not to do what he has been told or should infer that he is not to do, except when he is privileged to protect his own or another's interests. The usual standard that is applied here is that the agent act in accordance with "reasonable customs or, if there are no customs, that he is to use good faith and discretion."[5] Ordinarily, if his actions are based on a misinterpretation of the principal's unambiguous instructions, the agent can be held liable for the costs of his actions. Thus, if *A* is instructed to buy *T*'s milk-cows, and he buys a bull as well, he may then be held liable to *P* for its value. Furthermore, the agent may be liable to the principal where he makes a mistake concerning the facts upon which his instructions depend. If *P* directs *A* to deliver some goods to *T*, then *A* may be liable for the cost of recovery of goods, or for the cost of the goods themselves, if they are delivered to *F* and cannot be recovered. Factors determining whether an agent is liable for acting mistakenly include "the subject matter of the authorization, the language used in conferring it, the type of agent, and the kind of business done by him."[6]

Duty of Loyalty. The duty to obey is predicated on the view that the agent should not do anything the principal directs him not to do. The duty of loyalty extends beyond the doing of intentionally forbidden acts. It states that the agent has a duty to act solely for the interests of the principal. In its narrowest sense, the duty of loyalty requires that an agent not "act or speak disloyally in matters which are connected with his employment."[7] Outside his employment, however, the agent is not prevented from acting in good faith in a way that might injure his principal's business. Thus the agent for a soft drink company may not use his title as employee of that company, nor the special information he has acquired as an employee of the company, to advocate legislation banning the use of saccharine in soft drinks, when such legislation could harm his company's interests. However, as a citizen he may advocate such legislation, so long as he does not use the information he has acquired as an employee of the company. One important upshot of this rule is that employees are under a duty not to advise the public to buy elsewhere than from their employers, nor are they to suggest that their employers' products are inferior to those of a competitor.

Duty Not to Acquire an Adverse Interest. Closely related to the duty of loyalty (and often construed as one element of it) is the duty not to acquire an adverse interest. This requires that an agent not acquire any interest adverse to that of the principal unless the latter agrees that the agent may do so. Thus a buyer for a department store may not acquire an interest in a manufacturing business from which he purchases goods for the store, either directly or through a "straw." Neither may a seller purchase the principal's goods for himself, either directly or through a "straw." To act in either of these ways would put the agent in a position in which he would have an adverse interest: to buy for less insofar as he represents the principal, while at the same time buying for more in terms of self-interest, or selling for more in terms of the principal's interest, while selling for less in terms of his own interest. Such divided interest means that the agent is not being completely loyal to the principal, as the law requires, and it subjects the agent to liability, to discharge from his employment, breach of contract, loss of compensation, as well as tort liability for losses caused and for profits made. If the agent makes his potential adverse interests known to the principal, however, and takes no unfair advantage of him, then the agent is not liable if the principal agrees that he may act in this way.

Duty Not to Compete. In addition to acquiring an adverse interest, agents are also required not to compete with their principals, unless the principals consent to it. A real estate agent who represents a seller may not also show his own property to prospective buyers, in competition with that of the seller whom he represents. Nor may he buy property for himself which had originally been sought by the principal. Both of these actions would constitute a breach of duty during the time of the agent's employment. But during this time the agent is free to make plans to compete with the principal at the end of such employment, so long as he does not use confidential information in order to do so. After his employment has ended he may even hire the principal's employees for himself, as well as solicit customers for his competing business.

Duty to Account for Profits. The duty to account for profits requires that the agent account for the value of goods received from third parties. Thus, bribes, kickbacks, and gifts to the agent, regardless of whether they are received corruptly, must be forfeited to the principal, even if he incurs no loss by the agent's receiving them. In addition, the principal may hold the agent liable for any harm that may arise because of the bribe or kickback, as well as breach of contract and actions based in tort. The general rule with regard to such matters is that "an agent who, without the knowledge of the principal, receives something in connection with, or because of, a transaction conducted for the principal, has a duty to pay this to the principal."[8] The burden of proving that the value received was not "in connection with, or because of, a transaction conducted for the principal" lies strictly with the agent. This duty has been interpreted to extend even to opportunities for gain which an agent's employment has made possible, such as information acquired in the course of his employment which benefits the agent, even though it causes no harm to the principal.

Duty of Confidentiality. The duty of confidentiality requires that an agent not use or communicate confidential information for anyone's benefit other than that of the principal. The use of such information, acquired as a result of a person's agency, is prohibited both for the agent's own benefit, as well as for the benefit of third parties, even though the information does not relate to the subject of his agency. Thus a dairy worker who overhears the owner discussing plans to buy adjacent land may not use this information for his own advantage, nor may he disclose it to others for their advantage. Included within this restriction are such matters as "unique business methods of the employer, trade secrets, lists of names, and all other matters which are peculiarly known in the employer's business."[9] After the termination of his employment the agent has a continuing duty not to reveal such information, with the exception of "the names and customers retained in his memory as the result of his work for the principal and also methods of doing business and processes which are but skillful variations of general processes known to the particular trade."[10]

NOTES

1. *Restatement, Second, Agency* § 1.
2. Ibid., § 379.
3. Twentieth-Century Fox Film Corp. v. Lardner, 216 F. 2d 844.
4. *Restatement,* § 380.
5. Ibid., § 383, a.
6. Ibid., § 383, c.
7. Ibid., § 387.
8. Ibid., § 388, a.
9. Ibid., § 395, b.
10. Ibid., § 396, b.

Conflict of Interest

Sorrel M. Mathes
G. Clark Thompson

Inorganic Chemicals Company's Conflict of Interest Policy

General Statement of Policy

The company expects and requires directors, officers and employees (herein "employees") to be and remain free of interests or relationships and to refrain from acting in ways which are actually or potentially inimical or detrimental to the Company's best interests.

Application of Policy

1. *"Conflicts of Interests" Defined*

A conflict of interest exists where an employee

(a) has an outside interest which materially encroaches on time or attention which should be devoted to the Company's affairs or so affects the employee's energies as to prevent his devoting his full abilities to the performance of his duties.

(b) has a direct or indirect interest in or relationship with an outsider such as a supplier (whether of goods or services), jobber, agent, customer or competitor, or with a person in a position to influence the actions of such outsider, which is inherently unethical or which might be implied or construed to

---

From Sorrel M. Mathes and G. Clark Thompson, "Ensuring Ethical Conduct in Business," in *The Conference Board Record,* vol. 1, no. 12 (December, 1964), p. 22. Reprinted by permission of The Conference Board.

i. make possible personal gain or favor to the employee involved, his family or persons having special times to him, due to the employee's actual or potential power to influence dealings between the Company and the outsider,

ii. render the employee partial toward the outsider for personal reasons, or otherwise inhibit the impartiality of the employee's business judgment or his desire to serve only the Company's best interests in the performance of his functions as an employee,

iii. place the employee or the Company in an equivocal, embarrassing or ethically questionable pcsition in the eyes of the public, or

iv. reflect on the integrity of the employee or the Company.

Practically, conflicts of interests of the types just mentioned are reprehensible to the degree that the authority of the employee's position makes it possible for him to influence the Company's dealings with the outsider; thus, for example, the situation of those who buy or sell for the Company, or who can influence buying or selling, is particularly sensitive.

(c) has any direct or indirect interest or relationship or acts in a way which is actually or potentially inimical or detrimental to the Company's best interests.

2. *Examples of Improper Conflicts*

There follows a few obvious examples of relationships which probably would run afoul of the foregoing definition, but any relationship covered by the definition is subject to this policy:

(a) Holding an outside position which affects the performance of the employee's work for the Company.

(b) Relatively substantial (whether with reference to the enterprise invested in or to the employee's net worth) equity or other investment by the employee or members of his immediate family in a supplier, jobber, agent, customer or competitor. Under normal circumstances, however, ownership of securities of a publicly held corporation is not likely to create a conflict of interests unless the ownership is so substantial as to give the employee a motive to promote the welfare of that corporation and unless the employee, through his position with the Company or otherwise, is able to promote such welfare.

(c) The acquisition of an interest in a firm with which, to the employee's knowledge, the Company is carrying on or contemplating negotiations for merger or purchase. In some cases, such an interest may create a conflict even though the interest was acquired prior to the time the Company evinced any interest in merger or purchase. Similar considerations are applicable to real estate in which the Company contemplates acquiring an interest.

(d) The receipt of remuneration as an employee or consultant of, or the acceptance of loans from, a supplier, jobber, agent, customer or competitor of the Company.

(e) The acceptance by the employee or members of his family from persons or firms having or seeking to have dealings with the Company of any cash gifts, or of gifts or entertainment which go beyond common courtesies extended in accordance with accepted business practice or which are of such value as to raise any implication whatsoever of an obligation on the part of the recipient.

(f) Speculative dealing in the Company's stock on the basis of information gained in the performance of the employee's duties and not available to the public, or other misuse of information available to or gained by the employee by reason of his employment.

Robert E. Frederick

Conflict of Interest

The employee has legal obligations to the organization he works for via the law of agency. For example, an agent has a "duty to his principal to act solely for the benefit of the principal in all matters concerned with his agency" (*Restatement,* Sec. 385).[1] Again, the agent is barred from acting for individuals whose "interests conflict with those of the principal in matters in which the agent is employed" (*Restatement,* Sec. 394). However, the agent's interests may conflict with those of his principal. Perhaps only the total "organization man" completely identifies his interests with those of his employer, but that individual is a caricature not found in reality. These differing interests can lead to conflicts unless the broad and nonspecific language of the law of agency is clarified by an explicit and detailed work contract between employer and employee.

A conflict of interests in the corporate setting arises when an agent has an interest that influences his judgment in his own behalf or in behalf of a third party, and which is contrary to the principal's interest. The moral and legal basis of conflicts of interest is relatively clear. Via the work contract the agent agrees to further the principal's interest. If the agent acts for himself or a third party in a manner contrary to the principal's interest, he breaks his contract with the principal. Contract breaking is unfair to the principal, and, if generally practiced, would undermine the institution of business, with attendant social disutility. Given the asymmetry in the law of agency, however, which places obligations of loyalty, obedience, and confidentiality on the agent, and given that the employer typically sets the majority of the provisions in the work contract, it seems morally, if not legally, incumbent on the employer to clearly specify in the contract what constitutes a conflict of interest.

In many cases there is little in the way of such specification. An example is (1a) of Inorganic Chemicals' policy, which says that a conflict of interest occurs when an employee "has an outside interest which materially encroaches on time or attention which should be devoted to the Company's affairs or so affects the employee's energies as to prevent his devoting his

125

full abilities to the performance of his duties." As it stands, this is rather vague, particularly for the at-will employee whose work contract may not contain an explicit job description and clauses proscribing certain sorts of management directives. Thus, a sales manager might find that his "duty" is to maximize sales—a rather open-ended task. But that manager may have "outside interests," such as family interests and obligations, which may "prevent his devoting his full abilities to the performance of his duties."

We can begin to devise more specific guidelines by dividing employees' outside interests into the broad categories of those that the employer believes do not conflict with his interests, and those the employer believes do conflict with his interests. The latter category is divided into those interests of the employee that the employer *mistakenly* believes are in conflict with his interests, and interests of the employee that the employer *correctly* believes conflict with his. This last category is in turn divided into those areas in which the employer has a *legitimate* claim that the employee modify his activities, and those in which he does *not* have a legitimate claim. Our schema, then, looks like this:

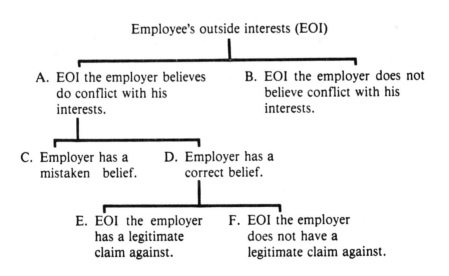

Let us say that Jones is Smith's employee. Then we can give the following examples of the various categories:

B. Jones collects stamps and Smith does not believe Jones's hobby conflicts with his interests. Nevertheless, Smith, in his capacity as Jones's employer, demands that Jones stop collecting stamps.

C. Jones collects stamps, and, for reasons we need not speculate on, Smith mistakenly believes this conflicts with his interests, and demands that Jones stop collecting stamps.

E. Jones is a government civil rights lawyer and in his spare time is an organizer for the local Ku Klux Klan. Smith demands that Jones cease this activity.

F. Jones works for XYZ Publishing Company and in his spare time writes successful novels. Company rules prohibit Jones from publishing at XYZ. Smith correctly believes that Jones's novels detract from XYZ's sales and demands that Jones stop writing novels.

Each of the above examples follows the same pattern: the employee engages in certain outside activities that the employer attempts to interfere with or prevent. Typically, clauses in the work contract, e.g., Inorganic's (1a), give the employer the right to interfere, in some cases, with the employee's outside activities. However, such clauses should not give the employer the right to interfere in all of the employee's outside activities since the employee has legitimate outside interests that are protected by his right to privacy and freedom of action. For instance, example B is a clear case where Jones's rights to privacy and free action are violated by Smith. In order to prevent this sort of abuse the work contract should unequivocally state that employees have legitimate outside interests and that the employer has no right to regulate those interests either by design or suggestion. Another example is employees' interests in and duties to their families. We all know of firms that place undue burdens on employees to the detriment of family life. However, employees are properly interested in their families and have a right to act so as to satisfy those interests. Hence the work contract should not be such that it can be construed as giving the employer the right to interfere in all of the employee's outside activities.

But there are many cases where the interests of the employer and the employee genuinely conflict. And since each has a right, within legal limits, to serve those interests, the work contract should provide some mechanism for determining whose rights prevail in particular instances. Example C is a situation in which Jones's rights to privacy and free action prevail since Smith has no interests that are at stake, although he incorrectly believes he has. Example E is more difficult. In a free society such as ours, individuals have great latitude when engaging in activities that satisfy their interests. Indeed, many people would say that individuals have a right, providing they do not violate the law, to engage in any activity they please as long as it does not result in significant harm to others. Now, Jones has a legal right to organize for the Klan, but even if his outside activity does not impair his job performance, it is highly likely that his activities will severely damage the credibility of the organization for which he works. Thus Smith can legitimately demand that Jones cease this sort of activity. Similar considerations apply to example F, but it seems that in the circumstances in question Jones's rights should prevail rather than Smith's.

The issue of outside interests, then, is relatively clear. In E and F both the employer and the employee have interests that are protected by rights. Each can justify his position by appeal to those rights, but there has to be some determination of whose rights are overriding. There are two ways that work contracts can apply in such cases. First, if the contract specifically prohibits a certain activity, e.g., organizing for the Klan, then by entering into the contract the employee forfeits his right to engage in that activity. If he does so anyway, he breaks the contract and is thereby subject to the appropriate penalty. Second, since the contract cannot possibly deal specifically with all potential conflicts, it should provide a means for settling disputes. I will discuss both of these points more fully in a moment, but first there are some other difficulties with Inorganic's policy that should be noted.

Thus far I have not considered conflicts of interest that occur in the actual work setting. Most of these conflicts should be specifically dealt with by the work contract. But note that 1(c) of Inorganic's policy defines a conflict as any act that is "actually or potentially inimical or detrimental to the company's best interests." If we suppose the company's "best interest" is profit maximization, then in every situation there is only one proper act, and an indefinite number of acts which are, perhaps unbeknown to the agent, "potentially inimical or detrimental" to maximizing profit. If an employee performs an act that does not maximize profit, then, even though he is interested in maximizing profit and believes his act to be in the company's best interest, according to 1(c) there is a conflict of interest. However, it seems more reasonable to describe his act as a performance shortcoming rather than a conflict of interest, since the employee acted in what he believed was the company's interest. If the employee's performance continually exhibits such shortcomings, management has the right to take appropriate measures to correct it, but they cannot justify such measures by an appeal to conflict of interest. Thus, since Inorganic's policy applies to performance shortcomings as well as genuine conflicts of interests, it is too broad to serve as a useful guideline for identifying cases of conflict of interest.

Furthermore, Inorganic's 1(c) states that a conflict arises when an agent has an interest that is "potentially inimical or detrimental to the company's best interests." If an actual conflict arises when an agent's self-interest influences his act contrary to a principal's interest, then a potential conflict arises when an agent has not acted but does have a self-interest or motive contrary to the principal's interest. Now the *Restatement* (Sec. 385) says that an agent has a "duty to his principal to *act* solely for the benefit of the principal," not that he must have no self-interests. Some individuals, after all, are able to place self-interests aside; they do not act on them. So, a potential conflict of interest is not inherently unethical. The issue rests on how the agent acts.

Since the Inorganic policy is typical of corporate policy statements, the foregoing suggests that such policies are often too general and tend to be biased in favor of the organization, particularly where factors such as performance shortcomings can be regarded as conflicts of interest. The remedy would seem to be a list of more specific guidelines covering particular areas where conflicts arise. The hazard with this approach is that the scope of such conflicts is difficult to circumscribe solely with specific guidelines. There will always be exceptions or borderline cases.

This suggests the following strategy: (1) the firm should have a brief, general, but accurate conflict of interest policy statement; (2) it should establish specific guidelines to cover clear-cut interests; (3) it should establish a committee, officer, or procedure to: (a) handle borderline cases, and (b) set policy in new areas by articulating and developing specific guidelines; (4) new policies should be disseminated to employees; (5) employees should be required to consult with the conflict of interest body prior to acting in borderline or new but questionable areas; and (6) the firm should make clear the penalties for violation of corporate policy in conflicts cases.

The following should suffice as a general policy statement covering all conflict of interest cases:

> The law states that employees have a legal obligation to use their best judgment to act solely for the benefit of the company in all job related matters. The law also prohibits employees from acting for individuals (including themselves) and parties whose interests conflict with the firm's interests in matters related to the employee's employment. The company has established guidelines to cover company policy regarding situations in which conflicts of interest frequently arise. Managers have the responsibility to see that their employees understand these guidelines. The company has a Conflict of Interest Board that handles situations not clearly covered by the guidelines. If an employee is in doubt as to whether an act constitutes a conflict, he should consult with the Board before he engages in the act. If at any time the company determines that an employee has acted in a way such that he has an interest in his act that influences his judgment in his own behalf or in the behalf of a third party, and which is contrary to the company's interest as spelled out in the following guidelines, the employee will be disciplined as deemed appropriate to the act(s) involved.

Now the key is the list of specifics delineating this policy statement. Fortunately, such specifics can be articulated in the four major areas in which most conflict of interest cases arise: bribes, gifts, external affiliations, and insider information.

Bribes, kickbacks, payoffs, etc., in a competitive context, are immoral for two reasons: (1) Kantian universalization of maxims allowing bribery would undermine the institution of business, which rests on competitive bidding based on price, and (2) although bribes may be advantageous to the few persons involved, they generally have disutility for the vast majority of society's members, and hence rule utilitarian considerations weigh against bribery. Since such practices are also illegal, a firm's conflict of interest policy should be very straightforward:

> Bribes, kickbacks, payoffs, etc., are illegal and immoral; any employee who engages in or encourages others to engage in such acts will be summarily fired and his acts will be reported to the appropriate legal authorities.

Specific, clear-cut policy statements can also be developed regarding gifts and entertainment. In some firms individuals cannot give any gift to, or receive any gift from, another party. Where specific sanctions are listed for violations, one has a clear-cut policy. If gifts are allowed, morally relevant variables can be specified, e.g., data on the value of the gift, the context in which it was given or received, the intent behind giving the gift, and the position of the giver or receiver in the organization. Borderline cases will invariably arise, but these can be handled by (3), (4), (5), and (6) of our suggested strategy for dealing with conflicts. That is, all gifts should be reported to the conflict of interest body in the firm. Consultation with the body should be required before a borderline case or a new but questionable case is acted upon by the gift giver or recipient in the firm. Finally, new guidelines should be disseminated to employees.

A similar strategy applies to external affiliations. Conflicts of interest frequently arise when an employee has a financial interest in another organization with which the firm does business. Such conflicts can be precluded by explicitly forbidding employees to invest in suppliers, distributors, or customers associated with their employer. If investments are allowed they may be limited in a variety of ways (e.g., percentage of stock limits), and the firm may also require disclosure of outside interests. Borderline cases can be handled by the firm's conflict of interest body.

A corporate policy on insider information can also be spelled out more completely than Inorganic's policy. Saying, with 1(c), that a conflict occurs when an employee "has any direct or indirect interest or relationship or acts in a way which is actually or potentially inimical or detrimental to the company's best interests" is simply too general. Employees should know that the law states that insider information must be disclosed to the public before anyone possessing it can trade in or recommend the purchase or sale of the securities involved. Disclosure of insider information should be done in strict accordance with company policy. Insider information is material, nonpublic information; the test of materiality being that the information itself would affect investment decisions of investors and, if generally known, affect the price of the security. The following have been held by the courts to involve insider information based investment decisions: (a) dividend change, (b) indication of a new discovery or product, (c) corporate projections indicating a change in rate of earnings, (d) a sharp drop in earnings, (e) a sharply downward revised projection of earnings, and (f) significant unexpected losses. Finally, if there is any question about whether an item is insider information, the company's Conflict of Interest Board should be consulted prior to acting on the information.

It should be stressed that each firm will have to articulate its own specific guidelines. For example, a privately held firm may not need a policy on insider information, and a bank may want to have very specific guidelines regarding lending officers who might have a personal financial interest in a business that makes loans with the bank. All in all, however, the strategy I have developed promises to diminish the conflict of interest problem if a firm is serious about its implementation.

Robert Almeder

Morality and Gift-Giving

A bribe is the offering of some good, service, or money to an appropriate person for the purpose of securing a privileged and favorable consideration (or purchase) of one's product or corporate project. Typically, but not necessarily, the person offering the bribe does so in secret and only when the person receiving the bribe antecedently agrees (either explicitly or implicitly) to accept the bribe under the conditions indicated by the briber. Understandably, the briber's business posture is enhanced by the successful bribe and it would not be otherwise enhanced, because, presumably, without the bribe the briber's product or project would not merit any special consideration as against the product or projects of the briber's competitors.[1]

For various reasons, few people in the business community are willing to defend the morality of the practice of bribery. Most people in the business community see the practice of bribery as one that, if adopted on a wide-scale basis, tends to undermine a free, competitive, and open economy by encouraging a lack of real competition for quality products. After all, where bribery is an acceptable practice, the briber (or the company with the biggest bribe) gains unfair advantage because the briber's product secures preferential treatment not based upon the merits or price of the product. Even at its best, the practice of bribery, *as a rule,* tends to undermine open competition along with the usual efficiencies and quality of goods characteristic of the open economy. Thus, what is basically wrong with bribery is that, *as a rule,* it strikes at the heart of capitalism by undermining a free and strenuously competitive economy. If capitalism is to survive as the best of

I would like to thank James Humber for his comments on an earlier draft of this paper.

economic systems, it can do so only where there is earnest and open competition.

The practice of bribery can also be faulted for the reason that the briber violates the golden rule because the briber, presumably, would not want his product discriminated against for reasons that had nothing to do with the quality of his product.

But what about the practice of giving gifts to persons with whom one is doing business? Is gift-giving of this sort a clear case of bribery? If it is, then for the reasons just mentioned it, like bribery, should be considered immoral. In other words, if one gives a gift in order to secure a business advantage that would not otherwise occur, and if in the typical case the person receiving the gift accepts it under the conditions indicated by the giver, then this act of gift-giving is in fact a bribe and should be considered a bribe. Many businessmen, however, do not see *all* gift-giving to one's clients as a clear case of bribery. They see nothing wrong with the practice of gift-giving if it is done under certain circumstances.

Those who favor some form of gift-giving in the marketplace do so because they think such a practice, unlike bribery, need not be an instance of deliberately intending to secure a decision that enhances one's business posture. A salesman, for example, may or may not intend his gift as a bribe. He may give a gift not for any special treatment, but only for fair treatment, or to insure equal treatment. He may even give the gift simply because in the years of doing business with someone he has become genuinely friendly with the person who just happens to be able to enhance the salesman's business posture and profit.

In response to this last line of reasoning, however, others are quick to note that what is wrong with bribery is not simply that those who offer bribes do so with the *intent* of securing special treatment, although certainly they do so. Rather, what is essentially wrong with bribery is that the practice has the effect of influencing the judgments of the bribed to provide special treatment not based on the merits or price of the product. This same effect can occur even when one merely offers a gift, that is, provides a service without intending or wishing that that service secure special treatment for the gift-giver. The person who receives the gift may, consciously or otherwise, be disposed predictably to favor the interests of the gift-giver. All that is needed to move a gift into the category of a bribe is that (a) the person receiving the gift be in a position to make a decision that enhances the assets of the giver and (b) the gift be of such a nontoken nature that it is reasonable to think that it may put the interests of the giver in a privileged status even when all else is equal.

As a result of these last considerations some corporations have in the past allowed gift-giving to their clients, or potential clients, only under the conditions that (a) the gift is not substantial enough to put the receiver into a conflict of interest position, and (b) the gift is given publicly and is not in any way a secret offering. Although these conditions seem sound in light of the reflections noted above, still we need to answer the question "Under what circumstances, if any, does an employee have a proportionate reason for running the risks involved in accepting gifts?" In answering this last question, Thomas Garrett urges that the basic question to be asked with regard to the practice of gift-giving is this: "Will this gift, entertainment or service cause any reasonable person to suspect my independence of judgment?"[2] Garrett goes on to urge that it should

> be clear that infrequent gifts of only a nominal cost, ten dollars or less, and small advertisement gifts will be acceptable by policy or law. On the other hand, practically any cash gift is liable to raise eyebrows and create a suspicion of bias.[3]

These same considerations would, presumably, apply with respect to entertainment. In other words, if the cost of entertainment is nominal, public, customary, and infrequent, there would be nothing morally wrong with the practice if it could not hamper the independence of the judgment of the person gifted or entertained. So, then, as Garrett would have it, if the gift is nominal, publicly given, and not intended to secure any special advantage, the practice of gift-giving would seem to be acceptable.

In spite of the sweet reasonableness of Garrett's conclusion, however, some people still think that even a nominal gift could, all else being equal, secure an advantage not merited in terms of quality or price of product. Even an annual gift of $10 (or its equivalent in goods or services) has the *potential* for securing an advantage for the giver, an advantage not merited by the quality or price of the product. Accordingly, even though Garrett's proposal seems quite sensible, any gift, depending on the nature of the receiver and the circumstances involved *could* have the effect of a bribe, even when the gift is nominal and public.

Given these last reasons, it would appear that the only safe moral position to adopt is the one that prohibits *all* gift-giving between corporate representatives and those with whom they would do business. In this latter regard, it is interesting to note that in a survey conducted by the Conference Board in 1964, most of the corporations surveyed were moving strongly in the direction of adopting policy statements prohibiting *all* gift-giving, even of the most nominal kind.[4] Only a few companies allowed, *officially,* small gifts provided the cost did not exceed $25 and did not occur more than three times annually. And, of course, some companies (perhaps too many) had perfectly ambiguous policy statements that provided no clear direction except to indicate that one should be "reasonable" and not do anything such that were it publicly disclosed it would embarrass the company.

In the end, the wisest policy to adopt would seem to be one of complete prohibition of any gift-giving between companies (and their representatives) and persons with whom companies do (or wish to do) business either directly or indirectly.

NOTES

1. Usually, but not necessarily, people are bribed not to do their job. We seldom talk about bribing someone to do his or her job rather than bribing them not to do their job. Still, it is possible to bribe somebody to do his or her job *faster* (thereby securing the briber a special advantage) than he might otherwise do it.

2. Thomas Garrett, *Business Ethics,* Appleton-Century Crofts, N.Y.: 1966, p. 78.

3. Ibid., p. 79.

4. *The Conference Board Record,* vol. 1, no. 12 (Dec. 1964), pp. 17–27.

Corporate Policy Statements

No company employee shall *ask for* or *accept* (directly or indirectly) payments, gifts, favors or meals and entertainment (except as customary in the trade) from a . . . government official, government employee or any other person in consideration for assistance or influence, or upon the representation that such assistance or influence has been or will be rendered, in connection with a purchase or any other transaction affecting the Company. No company employee shall *offer* or *give* (directly or indirectly) payments, gifts, or favors (except as customary in the trade) to . . . a government official, government employee or any other person in consideration for assistance or influence, or upon the representation that such assistance or influence has been or will be rendered, in connection with a sale or any other transaction affecting the Company. Acceptance or giving of gifts must be limited to incidentals which are obviously a custom of the trade, are acceptable as items of insignificant value, or in no way would cause the Company to be embarrassed or obligated. Gifts which do not fit in these categories must be returned. If return of a gift is not practicable because of its nature, it may be given to a charitable institution and the supplier informed of its disposition.

Honeywell

Gifts, favors and entertainment may be given to others at Company expense only if they meet *all* of the following criteria: (a) they are consistent with accepted business practices, (b) they are of sufficiently limited value, and in a form that will not be construed as a bribe or payoff, (c) they are not in contravention of applicable law and generally accepted ethical standards, and (d) public disclosure of the facts will not embarrass the Company. Secret commissions or other compensation to employees of customers (or their family members or associates) are contrary to company policy.

E. I. DuPont de Nemours & Co.

135

No IBM employee, or any member of his or her immediate family, can accept gratuities or gifts of money from a supplier, customer or anyone in a business relationship. Nor can they accept a gift or consideration that could be perceived as having been offered because of the business relationship. "Perceived" simply means this: If you read about it in your local newspaper, would you wonder whether the gift just might have something to do with a business relationship? No IBM employee can give money or a gift of significant value to a supplier if it could reasonably be viewed as being done to gain a business advantage. If you are offered money or a gift of some value by a supplier or if one arrives at your home or office, let your manager know immediately. If the gift is perishable, your manager will arrange to donate it to a local charitable organization. Otherwise, it should be returned to the supplier. Whatever the circumstances, you or your manager should write the supplier a letter, explaining IBM's guidelines on the subject of gifts and gratuities. Of course, it is an accepted practice to talk business over a meal. So it is perfectly all right to occasionally allow a supplier or customer to pick up the check. Similarly, it frequently is necessary for a supplier, including IBM, to provide education and executive briefings for customers. It's all right to accept or provide some services in connection with this kind of activity—services such as transportation, food or lodging. For instance, transportation in IBM or supplier planes to and from company locations, and lodging and food at company facilities are all right.

IBM

Gifts: Federal law restricts the extent of the deductibility of gifts to non-government clients, prospects or suppliers to an amount not exceeding $25 per year to any individual. ARA strongly discourages gifts in excess of $25 per year to any individual, but in the event a gift is proposed to be made in excess of $25, approval must be secured in advance from both the General Counsel and the most senior Management Committee member to whom the operating component involved ultimately reports. Any gifts given must meet the following criteria: (a) Gifts in the form of cash, stocks, bonds (or similar types of items) shall not be given regardless of amount; (b) Gifts are in accord with normally accepted business practices, and comply with the policies of the organization employing the recipient; (c) Such a practice would be considered legal and in accord with generally acceptable ethical practices in all governing jurisdictions; (d) Subsequent public disclosure of all facts would not be embarrassing to ARA. *Entertainment*: Where entertainment of a non-government client, prospect or supplier is involved, lavish expenditures are to be avoided. The cost and nature of the entertainment should be planned and carried out in a way which appropriately and reasonably furthers the conduct of the business of ARA. This, of course, does not mean that employees of prospective non-government clients may not be transported to, shown, and served at comparable service installations as part of the normal sales effort, at ARA expense.

ARA Services

Selling the Lockheed TriStar

In 1966, Lockheed Corporation earned $5.29 per share, had a net worth of $320 million, and had $140 million in debt. Its stock sold at a high of $74 per share. Earnings then declined for four years, and in 1970 the firm lost $7.60 per share, saw its net worth reduced to $266 million, its debt increase to $761 million, and its stock reach a low of $7 per share. By mid-1971, Lockheed was near backruptcy. The crisis was primarily caused by cost overruns on major defense projects, which cost the firm $480 million. In addition, in early 1969 a test model of Lockheed's armed helicopter, the Cheyenne, crashed during a test flight, and shortly thereafter the government cancelled the Cheyenne contract, charging default. Lockheed had to write off $132 million in development costs. In late 1969, Congress and the press began objecting to Lockheed's development costs for the C5A Galaxy transport, and the Air Force reduced its order from 115 units to 81.

Lockheed was also having difficulties on the nongovernmental side of its business. The company began developing the L-1011, or "TriStar," in 1967 to compete with Boeing's 747 and McDonnell-Douglas's DC-10. Since the DC-10 was based on earlier models, and the TriStar was a new plane, McDonnell-Douglas completed its development work earlier, and thereby gained the initial advantage in securing orders. Lockheed did secure early 1968 orders from TWA, Delta, and Eastern Airlines, but was hindered by the financial difficulties of its engine maker, Rolls-Royce, which itself was on the verge of bankruptcy throughout 1969-70. Early in 1971, Rolls-Royce went into receivership and announced that it would be unable to produce engines for the TriStar. After two months of negotiations the British government decided to continue production of Rolls-Royce engines for the TriStar, but at a sharply escalated price. It also demanded that the U.S. government provide some guarantee of Lockheed's financial viability. President Nixon then proposed a U.S. government loan guarantee of $250 million for Lockheed. The bill passed the U.S. House by three votes and the Senate by one vote in mid-1971.

By mid-1972, McDonnell-Douglas had 168 firm orders for the DC-10 and had delivered 43 planes. Lockheed had delivered 7 planes and had 100 firm orders. Lockheed claimed it could recoup development costs by selling 275 planes, but knowledgeable industry sources put the figure at 370. The variation was due to the fact that Lockheed did not break out development costs. Outside analysts concurred that Lockheed's inventory account included over $400 million in capitalized development costs for the TriStar, i.e., not really assets, but $400 million in deferred costs. If these figures were correct, and Lockheed had to write off its deferred development costs, the firm would have had negative net worth. In that case, the betting was that Lockheed would be forced into receivership in spite of its U.S. government loan guarantee. Lockheed's problems were compounded by the fact that by mid-1972 most of the U.S. market had been sold on either the TriStar or the DC-10, and furthermore, the DC-10 had already captured most of the European market. These facts dictated an all-out drive to secure sales in the largest market then untapped—Japan.

Lockheed recognized the importance of the Japanese market early on; in fact, in 1970, Lockheed's President, A. Carl Kotchian, said, "There is no way left but to win in the biggest market, Japan." Kotchian himself had experience in serving Lockheed in Japan. He had been there in 1961, shortly after Lockheed sold its F-104 fighter to the Japanese government. Kotchian returned in 1968 to scout prospects for selling the TriStar. Between 1968 and 1972 he returned ten times to work for sales of the TriStar. In Japan, Lockheed was officially represented by Marubeni Corporation, which handled most of the contacts with Japan's airline officials and Japanese politicians. Lockheed also had a secret agent, Yoshio Kodama, who had worked for the company since the late 1950s, and who had been helpful in obtaining the F-104 contract for Lockheed in 1960. Kodama was an ultranationalist who had been sentenced to jail both before World War II and during the American occupation, but who amassed a fortune during the war. Upon nis release from prison in 1948, he was probably the wealthiest man in Japan. Kodama helped finance the birth of Japan's dominant Liberal Party, and was a close, active supporter of most of Japan's post-war prime ministers.

On August 19, 1972, Kotchian flew to Tokyo to "devote all my energy and time to the sales campaign in Japan." On August 22, Toshiharu Okubu, a Marubeni representative, informed Kotchian that, at the latter's request, Marubeni officials would be meeting with Japanese Prime Minister Kakuei Tanaka on the next day. Okubu suggested that Kotchian make a pledge to pay $1.7 million for the favor. Kotchian said later that although the request did not "appall and outrage" him, it did "astonish" him that the political connection was so explicit. For, in response to the question of how the money was to be delivered by Marubeni, Okubu said a Marubeni representative was "very close to Mr. Enomoto, the prime minister's secretary." Kotchian said the exchange left him with "no doubt that the money was going to the office of Japan's prime minister." Later, on the same day, Kotchian consulted with Kodama about enlisting the aid of another important intimate of Tanaka, and Kodama said, "In order to include Mr. Osano, we need an extra $1.7 million." This amount was in addition to the $1.7 million that allegedly went to Tanaka, and the $1.8 that had already been pledged to Kodama.

On August 23, Hiro Hiyama, president of Marubeni, and Okubu met with Tanaka. Hiyama is alleged to have said that if Tanaka would help Lockheed he would be given $1.6 million. Tanaka replied, "O.K., O.K." On August 29, Tanaka called the president of All Nippon Airways (ANA) and asked him if he had decided to buy the TriStar. To the somewhat vague response, Tanaka said, "It will be convenient if you decide."

On August 31, Tanaka met with President Nixon in Hawaii. Tanaka had only been in office for two months, so the meeting was exploratory. But the subject of aircraft was discussed. At Nixon's request Tanaka agreed to purchase $720 million of products to reduce America's trade imbalance with Japan, and that was to include $320 million worth of commercial aircraft. Whether Lockheed was explicitly discussed is unknown, but Tanaka, on his return to Japan, claimed that Nixon spoke in favor of Lockheed. And Kotchian allowed that he encouraged the "idea of the Lockheed company being closely supported by the Nixon administration." In mid-September British Prime Minister Edward Heath met with Tanaka, and the subject included support for Rolls-Royce on the basis of Britain's trade imbalance with Japan.

During September and October, Kotchian, Kodama, and Marubeni's officials held a series of meetings with Japanese government officials and top managers of Japanese airlines to solidify Lockheed's case. On October 29, Kotchian received a call from Okubu, the Marubeni representative, suggesting that if Lockheed, through Marubeni, paid $300 thousand to the president of All Nippon Airways and a total of $100 thousand to six politicians, the airline would purchase the TriStar. Later, Kotchian said:

> If some third party had heard this conversation, he could ask why I responded to this request for secret payments. However, I must admit that it was extremely persuasive and attractive at that time to have someone come up to me and confidently tell me, "If you do this, you will surely get ANA's order in twenty-four hours." What businessman who is dealing with commercial and trade matters could decline a request for certain amounts of money when that money would enable him to get the contract? For someone like myself, who had been struggling against plots and severe competition for over two months, it was almost impossible to dismiss this opportunity.

On October 30, the payments were made and that same afternoon it was announced that All Nippon Airways would purchase six TriStars and take an option on more.

When the Watergate scandal engulfed the Nixon administration, many corporations were discovered to have made illegal contributions to Nixon's campaign. Although Lockheed did not make such contributions, its foreign payoffs were revealed in the subsequent investigation. In April, 1976, Lockheed consented, without acknowledging or denying, to a Securities and Exchange Commission (SEC) complaint that it made at least $25 million in secret payments to foreign government officials since 1968. It also admitted to payments in excess of $200 million since 1970 to "various consultants, commission agents and others." The SEC also charged that Lockheed kept secret funds not recorded on the books and records of Lockheed, and that the monies were disbursed "without adequate records and controls . . . and a portion of these funds were used for payments to certain foreign government officials." It was revealed that Lockheed's payments in Japan totaled $12.6 million. Kotchian estimated that $2.8 million went to high-ranking Japanese government officials. Kodama was reported to have received $7 million for his own use and disbursement to government officials.

In defense of the payments, Kotchian offered several arguments:

> The *first* is that the Lockheed payments in Japan, totaling about $12 million, were worthwhile from Lockheed's standpoint, since they amounted to less than 3 percent of the expected sum of about $430 million that we would receive from ANA for 21 TriStars. Further, as I've noted, such disbursements *did not violate American laws.* I should also like to stress that my decision to make such payments stemmed from my judgment that the TriStar payments to ANA would provide Lockheed workers with jobs and thus redound to the benefit of their communities, and stockholders of the corporation.

> *Secondly,* I should like to emphasize that the payments to the so-called "high Japanese government officials" were all requested by Okubu and *were not brought up from my side.* When he told me "five hundred million yen is necessary for such sales," from a purely ethical and moral standpoint I would have declined such a request. However, in that case, I would *most certainly* have sacrificed commercial success.

> *Finally,* I want to make it clear that I never discussed money matters with Japanese politicians, government officials, or airline officials.

> . . . Much has been made in press accounts in both Japan and the United States of secret agents and secret channels for sales efforts. Of course these consultations with advisers were secret: competitors do not tell each other their strategy or even their sales targets.

> And if Lockheed had not remained competitive by the rules of the game as then played, we would not have sold the TriStar and would not have provided work for tens of thousands of our employees or contributed to the future of the corporation. Nor would ANA have had the services of this excellent airplane.

> From my experience in international sales, I knew that if we wanted our product to have a chance to win on its own merits, we had to follow the functioning

system. If we wanted our product to have a chance, we understood that we would have to pay, or pledge to pay, substantial sums of money in addition to the contractual sales commissions. We never *sought* to make these extra payments. We would have preferred not to have the additional expenses for the sale. But, always, they were recommended by those whose experience and judgment we trusted and whose recommendations we therefore followed.

In Senate hearings Lockheed was not apologetic. It claimed the payments "were made with the knowledge of management and management believes they were necessary . . . and consistent with practices engaged in by numerous other companies abroad, including many of its competitors." The company also argued that its practices were consistent with business customs in many countries. When questioned as to whether such payments really were necessary, Lockheed's Chairman, Daniel Haughton, said, "If payments are made and you get the contract, it is good evidence that you needed to make the payments." Other American aerospace experts disagreed; one said, "They overpaid. . . . They could have gotten by for maybe $100 thousand. There was no need to pay a million bucks to anyone. It reflects their lack of expertise."

Haughton also refused to classify the payments as bribes, preferring instead to call them "kickbacks," presumably because bribes to government officials are illegal in most countries, whereas the legal status of kickbacks is less clear. At the time of the Japanese payments, however, the bribery of a foreign government official by a U.S. business was not illegal in the U.S. When it was revealed that Lockheed paid $1 million to a "high Dutch official" (later identified as Prince Bernhard, husband of Queen Juliana), Kotchian allowed that he knew "absolutely" that Bernhard received the money, but said it was a gift, not a bribe. Kotchian said the gift was made to assist in the sale of aircraft, but was paid after an initial idea of presenting Bernhard with the gift of a private aircraft was dropped because of difficulties in transferring title. When pressed by Senator Church as to whether the payoff really was a bribe, Kotchian said, "it brought a climate of goodwill. I consider it more as a gift, but I don't want to quibble."

Some support for Lockheed's position is based on a 1976 Italian court case in which government officials were charged with extorting money from Lockheed. The charges alleged that the Italian Air Force Chief of Staff "abused his position . . . and with others induced the Lockheed company to pay sums of money not less than one billion lire." Several observers saw this as placing Lockheed in the position of a victim rather than a willing participant in corruption.

Reaction to the Lockheed disclosures was mixed. Edwin Reischauer, former U.S. ambassador to Japan (1961–66), said: "We should devise legislation to prevent bribery of government officials abroad. In the Lockheed case the stupidities committed have been almost beyond belief. In a country not given to official bribery, in competition with American, not foreign, companies, Lockheed officials allegedly paid exorbitant bribes through Yoshio Kodama, a somewhat disreputable right-wing extremist, whose involvement in any cause is likely to do more harm than good." John Bierwirth, Grumman's chairman, argued that the prosecution of bribery abroad should be left to the country where the bribe occurred: "Most foreign governments don't want the U.S. to enact laws that define what is a crime in their countries. The thing that makes a bribe so bad is that it's a payment to get someone to take a less desirable product, and the people who are penalized are the people who use the less desirable product." A poll by the prestigious Conference Board showed that half of 73 business leaders surveyed said that they owed it to their companies to make payoffs in countries where such practices were accepted. Kenneth Keys, consultant to multinational firms, said: "Competition doesn't wholly explain the situation. In many areas of the world a market system doesn't exist; commerce is conducted by social connections that are lubricated by tribute. Even in Japan there are a variety of arrangements, such as, *On,* which requires that all favors be repaid, often in cash. Such payments are part of social convention, and failure to make them means loss of face." Senator Church said, "Lockheed's assertion that what it did is the industry norm and that there is nothing wrong with its actions underscores the need for congressional action to end these practices by American multinationals, especially those in the arms industry." Melvin Ness, corporate consultant, said: "You can pass a law banning bribes. But you have to deal with agents in many countries to do any business. The agent's fee is a legitimate tax-deductible business expense. How are you going to know whether part of that fee is passed on as a bribe? You can put a cap on an agent's fee, but the British, French, and Japanese won't do it, so U.S. firms won't be doing much business abroad."

The ramifications of the Lockheed case were widespread. In early 1976, Kotchian and Haughton were forced to resign. Tanaka was forced to resign and was arrested, along with several other Japanese officials, in 1974. In 1977, the U.S. passed the Foreign Corrupt Practices Act, which makes it a crime for U.S. corporations to offer or provide payments to foreign government officials for the purpose of securing or retaining business. Finally, in 1979, Lockheed pleaded guilty to hiding the Japanese payments from the U.S. government by falsely charging them off as marketing costs. The case was based on section 162C of the IRS Code stating that a deduction is impermissible for "any payment made, directly or indirectly, to any official or employee of any government if the payment constitutes an illegal bribe or kickback." Lockheed was found guilty of four counts of fraud and four counts of making misleading statements to the U.S. government. Kotchian, Haughton, and other Lockheed officials, were not indicted.

For Discussion

Carefully explain the differences between bribery, kickbacks, and extortion.

In your opinion was Lockheed's activity in Japan best classified as involving bribery, kickbacks, or extortion? Why? Do you believe Lockheed's payments in selling the TriStar were morally justified? Why or why not?

SOURCES

"Lockheed Digs Itself Out of a Hole," *Business Week,* Jan. 29, 1972, pp. 72–4; "Lockheed Wins an L-1011 Lift," *Business Week,* Nov. 4, 1972, pp. 24–5; "Who Will Save Lockheed?" *Forbes,* July 1, 1973, pp. 15–6; "Lockheed's Defiance: A Right to Bribe?" *Time,* Aug. 18, 1975, pp. 66–7; "Show and Tell Time," *Newsweek,* Aug. 18, 1975, p. 63; "I Prefer Not to Answer," *Newsweek,* Sept. 8, 1975, p. 54; "Rules for Lockheed," *Time,* Sept. 8, 1975, p. 60; "The Big Payoff," *Time,* Feb. 23, 1976, pp. 28–36; "Payoffs: The Growing Scandal," *Newsweek,* Feb. 23, 1976, pp. 26–33; "Extortion Alleged in Italy Lockheed Case," *Aviation Week and Space Technology,* March 29, 1976, pp. 14–15; "The Unfolding of a Torturous Affair," *Fortune,* March, 1976, pp. 27–8; "Secret Payment Complaint Consented to by Lockheed," *Aviation Week and Space Technology,* April 19, 1976, p. 21; Edwin Reischauer, "The Lessons of the Lockheed Scandal," *Newsweek,* May 10, 1976, pp. 20–1; A. Carl Kotchian, "The Payoff," *Saturday Review,* vol. 4, no. 20 (July 9, 1977), pp. 7–12; Robert Shaplen, "Annals of Crime: The Lockheed Incident," *New Yorker,* vol. 53 (Jan. 23, 1978), pp. 48–80 (January 30, 1978), pp. 74–91; "Lockheed Pleads Guilty to Making Secret Payoffs," *San Francisco Chronicle,* June 2, 1979.

Patricia H. Werhane

Ethical Relativism and Multinational Corporations

It was recently revealed that Lockheed Aircraft Corporation made a number of "sensitive payments" to high officials in the Japanese government in order to receive contracts for the TriStar and other airplanes from Japan. Some people are inclined to call such payments "bribes." But Lockheed management defended this practice.

> The payments, it is said, "were made with the knowledge of management and management believes they were necessary. . . . The company also believes that such payments are consistent with practices engaged in by numerous other companies abroad, including many of its competitors."[1]

Multinational corporations (MNCs) such as Lockheed often justify these questionable practices in their foreign operations with the following kinds of arguments:

(1) When operating in another country, one must adapt to the cultural and ethical mores of that country. One cannot apply one's own values in another socio-cultural context without morally offending the host country. Moreover, one cannot do business profitably in another country without adjusting to the value scheme and particular business practices of that country.

(2) American Corporations provide technology and economic services abroad, thus raising the standard of living for citizens in other countries. These services represent opportunities which would not be available to these countries otherwise.[2] The means an MNC may have to employ to make these goods and services available, e.g., sensitive payments, are thus justified by long-range economic results.

(3) If American corporations do not provide goods and services multinationally, other foreign corporations will do so, and they will do so through

Adapted from "Ethical Relativism and Multinational Corporate Conduct," *Proceedings of the Second National Conference on Business Ethics* (UPA, 1979): pp. 28-32.

the same means, e.g., sensitive payments. The only way to operate competitively and successfully on a multinational level is by engaging in transactions which are sometimes labeled as illegal or immoral by Americans; but these are transactions which are acceptable in other countries and to other non-American MNCs.

Let us examine each of these arguments. The first justification of questionable MNC conduct abroad appeals to the principle of ethical relativism. An ethical relativist is a person who argues, in brief, that values develop out of particular environmental and cultural situations. Therefore values, value judgments, moral judgments, and moral decisions are context-bound, relevant only to the particular socio-cultural context out of which they arose. There are no ethical principles which hold for everyone universally. Thus in justifying actions which might be questionable by American value standards the MNC is appealing to the principle that ethical values are culturally relative, and the MNC is arguing that one should respect this principle of ethical relativism in judging MNC actions in foreign countries where values and customs are different from our own.

The second justification is based on the principle of ethical absolutism. An ethical absolutist argues that there are at least some moral principles which apply universally to all people in any situation, regardless of cultural differences existing between human beings. Examples of principles which might apply to everyone are the right to life, freedom, and the right to equal opportunity, and there are others. Applying this concept of ethical absolutism to MNCs, when corporations defend their activities abroad by referring to the economic and technological advantages for foreign countries in which they operate, are they not assuming that economic advancement and technological development are in some sense universal values which are held, or should be held, by everyone?[3] It might be suggested, then, that MNCs are actually taking an absolutist position by assuming that economic growth and technological advancement are universal values to be applied to all cultures.

Justifications (1) and (2) thus contradict each other. For it cannot be argued both that one should operate within cultural and ethical mores of a particular country *and* claim at the same time that we should introduce that country to our own economic values because these are "better" or more advanced. If values are culturally relative we cannot assume, for example, that economic advances are universal ideals which will actually enhance all ways of life.

The third justification of questionable MNC conduct abroad is based on two arguments. First, it is being claimed that actions which are questionable in our value system are necessary for doing business successfully abroad. However, this argument cannot be pragmatically justified, since many corporations within and without the United States appear to operate profitably without making sensitive payments of any kind to anyone.

Second, it is being claimed that if some act is an accepted practice in a particular country, that act is also thought to be right or morally acceptable in that country. This misidentification of acceptability and rightness in foreign operations is a confusion to which one would never fall prey in one's own country. To give an example, pay-offs for building permits are a practice commonly accepted in most large cities. But these pay-offs are both illegal and considered morally wrong in this country. In the Lockheed case previously cited, the fact that high government officials in Japan, probably including the prime minister, accepted sensitive payments (and that this might have been a "commonly accepted practice" in Japan) did not make these actions right according to the Japanese. After this incident became public a number of Japanese officials including the prime minister were dismissed from office.

The difficulty with most justifications for questionable MNC conduct is that the arguments which supposedly support this kind of action are too simplistic. These arguments often misapply the concept of ethical relativism. They do not take into account the possible conflict between *accepted* business practices and morally *acceptable* principles in certain cultures. And MNCs often, at least unconsciously, apply the principle of ethical absolutism in transnational operations by assuming the universal value of economic progress.

A less simplistic view of ethical relativism and ethical absolutism might form a more suitable ground for justifying MNC actions abroad, and might form a basis for more ethically appropriate performances by these corporations in countries whose principles and practices are alien to their own. This view could develop as follows: It is likely that values, ethical principles, and the moral decisions which arise from them by and large develop in particular environmental, socio-cultural situations. Therefore, any moral judgment one makes about actions of oneself or others must first be placed in the context in which the ethical issue arose, and one cannot simply apply one's own moral principles *ad hoc* to other persons in other societies. For example, one cannot judge the ancient Eskimo more of letting the aged and feeble freeze to death without first understanding the extreme living conditions which the Eskimos endured. The moral judgment then, in the first instance, must be grounded on the culturally relative context in which the original problem occurred. This claim, however, neither supports nor contradicts the principle of ethical relativism. For it could be argued that *all* moral judgments should be context-grounded, even in our own society. I cannot morally judge the actions of a mother on welfare who steals food for her children, for example, until I have some inkling and understanding of the situation which was part of the impetus for the stealing.

Second, even if it is the case that moral judgments must be situational as we have suggested, it is still not impossible to hold a modified ethical absolutist point of view. Taking our Eskimo example, after relating our moral judgment to its ethical situation (i.e., snow, cold, shortage of food, etc.), one might still decide that the Eskimo custom was "wrong." The justification for this decision could be one of the following. One might defend the view that simply because values originate in culturally relative situations there is no reason to conclude that values are merely culturally espoused.[4] For example, it might turn out that many Eskimos thought their own treatment of their aged was wrong, even if hardship conditions seemed to necessitate these actions. And the Eskimo's evaluation of the rightness or wrongness of this custom would have to be an appeal to some ideal or principle which was not within the scope of particular Eskimo mores. Judgments of a value system are ordinarily appeals to principles which are not within that value system.

Or, one might analyze this problem by asking how would I, or should I, act, or expect myself to act if I were an Eskimo in this situation, and how might I expect anyone else to act in this particular situation? And it might turn out that one would judge the Eskimo custom to be wrong in the sense that universally in *that specific kind of situation* one expected that no one should allow the aged to die by freezing. This kind of judgment would be a value judgment applying to everyone in the specific context of an Eskimo-type situation, a universal ethical judgment based on the value of this kind of conduct in its culturally relative, particular context. The point is that we can agree that most values and most ethical judgments are culturally relative and still argue that there are one or some universal principles to which one appeals in judging the value of a custom or an ethical principle as it applies within a particular context in a specific ethical situation.

Returning to MNCs, it would be morally offensive and bad business advice to suggest that MNCs export their ethical mores to foreign, host countries. But, by the same justification, it is also offensive for MNCs to export their own economic and technological values and apply these to another culture without judging first the economic and technological values of that society. Moreover, what is accepted practice in any society is not always what is considered morally right by that society. And sometimes what is considered right in a particular culture is based on some principle or value which is universally held, or at least cross-cuts the cultural mores of that society. If an MNC is to operate seriously within a foreign cultural context it needs to be informed as to the ideals to which that society espouses as well as its every-day practices. To operate transnationally an MNC needs to know to which ideals a particular society appeals in justifying its own ethically relative principles. If MNCs were so informed and if MNCs operated according to this kind of information, I suspect that many issues of questionable behavior, sensitive payments, and the like would not arise.[5]

NOTES

1. *Newsweek,* August 18, 1975, p. 63. See also, A. Carl Kotchian, "The Pay-Off," *Saturday Review,* July 9, 1977, pp. 7–12.

2. For example, a vice-president of a large American multinational bank recently told me that American bankers introduced the concept of household credit to Italy,

a concept heretofore unknown in that country. The banker implied that this kind of credit is good, good for the Italians, and actually enhanced the Italian way of life.

3. It would also appear that at least some MNCs believe that the political values of their own nation are best for all people. For example, U.S. corporations often defend the American way of life and American democracy abroad.

4. See Carl Wellman, "The Ethical Implications of Cultural Relativity," *Journal of Philosophy,* LX (1963).

5. This paper originated as part of the Introduction to Part I of *Ethical Issues in Business: A Philosophical Approach,* an anthology in business ethics I am co-authoring with Thomas Donaldson of Loyola University, forthcoming by Prentice-Hall, Inc. I am deeply indebted to Professor Donaldson's suggestions, revisions and development of many of the ideas.

Mark Pastin
Michael Hooker

Ethics and the Foreign Corrupt Practices Act

Not long ago it was feared that as a fallout of Watergate, government officials would be hamstrung by artificially inflated moral standards. Recent events, however, suggest that the scapegoat of post-Watergate morality may have become American business rather than government officials.

One aspect of the recent attention paid to corporate morality is the controversy surrounding payments made by American corporations to foreign officials for the purpose of securing business abroad. Like any law or system of laws, the Foreign Corrupt Practices Act (FCPA), designed to control or eliminate such payments, should be grounded in morality, and should therefore be judged from an ethical perspective. Unfortunately, neither the law nor the question of its repeal has been adequately addressed from that perspective.

HISTORY OF THE FCPA

On December 20, 1977, President Carter signed into law S.305, the Foreign Corrupt Practices Act (FCPA), which makes it a crime for American corporations to offer or provide payments to officials of foreign governments for the purpose of obtaining or retaining business. The FCPA also establishes record keeping requirements for publicly held corporations to make it difficult to conceal political payments proscribed by the Act. Violators of the FCPA, both corporations and managers, face severe penalties. A company may be fined up to $1 million, while its officers who directly participated in violations of the Act or had reason to know of such violations, face up to five years in prison and/or $10,000 in fines. The Act also prohibits corporations from indemnifying fines imposed on their directors, officers, employees, or agents. The Act does not prohibit "grease" payments to foreign government

From *Business Horizons* vol. 23, no. 6 (December, 1980): 43–47. Copyright, 1980, by the Foundation for the School of Business at Indiana University. Reprinted by permission.

employees whose duties are primarily ministerial or clerical, since such payments are sometimes required to persuade the recipients to perform their normal duties.

At the time of this writing, the precise consequences of the FCPA for American business are unclear, mainly because of confusion surrounding the government's enforcement intentions. Vigorous objections have been raised against the Act by corporate attorneys and recently by a few government officials. Among the latter is Frank A. Weil, former Assistant Secretary of Commerce, who has stated, "The questionable payments problem may turn out to be one of the most serious impediments to doing business in the rest of the world."[1]

The potentially severe economic impact of the FCPA was highlighted by the fall 1978 report of the Export Disincentives Task Force, which was created by the White House to recommend ways of improving our balance of trade. The Task Force identified the FCPA as contributing significantly to economic and political losses in the United States. Economic losses come from constricting the ability of American corporations to do business abroad, and political losses come from the creation of a holier-than-thou image.

The Task Force made three recommendations in regard to the FCPA:

• The Justice Department should issue guidelines on its enforcement policies and establish procedures by which corporations could get advance government reaction to anticipated payments to foreign officials.

• The FCPA should be amended to remove enforcement from the SEC, which now shares enforcement responsibility with the Department of Justice.

• The administration should periodically report to Congress and the public on export losses caused by the FCPA.

In response to the Task Force's report, the Justice Department, over SEC objections, drew up guidelines to enable corporations to check any proposed action possibly in violation of the FCPA. In response to such an inquiry, the Justice Department would inform the corporation of its enforcement intentions. The purpose of such an arrangement is in part to circumvent the intent of the law. As of this writing, the SEC appears to have been successful in blocking publication of the guidelines, although Justice recently reaffirmed its intention to publish guidelines. Being more responsive to political winds, Justice may be less inclined than the SEC to rigidly enforce the Act.

Particular concern has been expressed about the way in which bookkeeping requirements of the Act will be enforced by the SEC. The Act requires that company records will "accurately and fairly reflect the transactions and dispositions of the assets of the issuer." What is at question is the interpretation the SEC will give to the requirement and the degree of accuracy and detail it will demand. The SEC's post-Watergate behavior suggests that it will be rigid in requiring the disclosure of all information that bears on financial relationships between the company and any foreign or domestic public official. This level of accountability in record keeping, to which auditors and corporate attorneys have strongly objected, goes far beyond previous SEC requirements that records display only facts material to the financial position of the company.

Since the potential consequences of the FCPA for American businesses and business managers are very serious, it is important that the Act have a rationale capable of bearing close scrutiny. In looking at the foundation of the FCPA, it should be noted that its passage followed in the wake of intense newspaper coverage of the financial dealings of corporations. Such media attention was engendered by the dramatic disclosure of corporate slush funds during the Watergate hearings and by a voluntary disclosure program established shortly thereafter by the SEC. As a result of the SEC program, more than 400 corporations, including 117 of the Fortune 500, admitted to making more than $300 million in foreign political payments in less than ten years.

Throughout the period of media coverage leading up to passage of the FCPA, and especially during the hearings on the Act, there was in all public discussions of the issue a tone of righteous moral indignation at the idea of American companies making foreign political payments. Such payments were ubiquitously termed "bribes," although many of these could more accurately be called extortions, while others were more akin to brokers' fees or sales commissions.

American business can be faulted for its reluctance during this period to bring to public attention the fact that in a very large number of countries, payments to foreign officials are virtually required for doing business. Part of that reluctance, no doubt, comes from the awkwardly difficult position of attempting to excuse bribery or something closely resembling it. There is a popular abhorrence in this country of bribery directed at domestic government officials, and that abhorrence transfers itself to payments directed toward foreign officials as well.

Since its passage, the FCPA has been subjected to considerable critical analysis, and many practical arguments have been advanced in favor of its repeal.[2] However, there is always lurking in back of such analyses the uneasy feeling that no matter how strongly considerations of practicality and economics may count against this law, the fact remains that the law protects morality in forbidding bribery. For example, Gerald McLaughlin, professor of law at Fordham, has shown persuasively that where the legal system of a foreign country affords inadequate protection against the arbitrary exercise of power to the disadvantage of American corporations, payments to foreign officials may be required to provide a compensating mechanism against the use of such arbitrary power. McLaughlin observes, however, that "this does not mean that taking advantage of the compensating mechanism would necessarily make the payment moral."[3]

The FCPA, and questions regarding its enforcement or repeal, will not be addressed adequately until an effort has been made to come to terms with the Act's foundation in morality. While it may be very difficult, or even impossible, to legislate morality (that is, to change the moral character and sentiments of people by passing laws that regulate their behavior), the existing laws undoubtedly still reflect the moral beliefs we hold. Passage of the FCPA in Congress was eased by the simple connection most Congressmen made between bribery, seen as morally repugnant, and the Act, which is designed to prevent bribery.

Given the importance of the FCPA to American business and labor, it is imperative that attention be given to the question of whether there is adequate moral justification for the law.

ETHICAL ANALYSIS OF THE FCPA

The question we will address is not whether each payment prohibited by the FCPA is moral or immoral, but rather whether the FCPA, given all its consequences and ramifications, is itself moral. It is well known that morally sound laws and institutions may tolerate such immoral acts. The First Amendment's guarantee of freedom of speech allows individuals to utter racial slurs. And immoral laws and institutions may have some beneficial consequences, for example, segregationist legislation bringing deep-seated racism into the national limelight. But our concern is with the overall morality of the FCPA.

The ethical tradition has two distinct ways of assessing social institutions, including laws: *End-Point Assessment* and *Rule Assessment.* Since there is no consensus as to which approach is correct, we will apply both types of assessment to the FCPA.

The End-Point approach assesses a law in terms of its contribution to general social well-being. The ethical theory underlying End-Point Assessment is utilitarianism. According to utilitarianism, a law is morally sound if and only if the law promotes the well-being of those affected by the law to the greatest extent practically achievable. To satisfy the utilitarian principle, a law must promote the well-being of those affected by it at least as well as any alternative law that we might propose, and better than no law at all. A conclusive End-Point Assessment of a law requires specification of what constitutes the welfare of those affected by the law, which the liberal tradition generally sidesteps by identifying an individual's welfare with what he takes to be in his interests.

Considerations raised earlier in the paper suggest that the FCPA does not pass the End-Point test. The argument is not the too facile one that we could propose a better law. (Amendments to the FCPA are now being considered.[4]) The argument is that it may be better to have *no* such law than to have the FCPA. The main domestic consequences of the FCPA seem to include an adverse effect on the balance of payments, a loss of business and jobs, and another opportunity for the SEC and the Justice Department to compete. These negative effects must be weighed against possible gains in the conduct of American business within the United States. From the perspective of foreign countries in which American firms do business, the main consequence of the FCPA seems to be that certain officials now accept bribes and influence from non-American businesses. It is hard to see that who pays the bribes makes much difference to these nations.

Rule Assessment of the morality of laws is often favored by those who find that End-Point Assessment is too lax in supporting their moral codes. According to the Rule Assessment approach: A law is morally sound if and only if the law accords with a code embodying correct ethical rules. This approach has no content until the rules are stated, and different rules will lead to different ethical assessments. Fortunately, what we have to say about Rule Assessment of the FCPA does not depend on the details of a particular ethical code.

Those who regard the FCPA as a worthwhile expression of morality, despite the adverse effects on American business and labor, clearly subscribe to a rule stating that it is unethical to bribe. Even if it is conceded that the payments proscribed by the FCPA warrant classification as bribes, citing a rule prohibiting bribery does not suffice to justify the FCPA.

Most of the rules in an ethical code are not *categorical* rules; they are *prima facie* rules. A categorical rule does not allow exceptions, whereas a prima facie rule does. The ethical rule that a person ought to keep promises is an example of a prima facie rule. If I promise to loan you a book on nuclear energy and later find out that you are a terrorist building a private atomic bomb, I am ethically obligated not to keep my promise. The rule that one ought to keep promises is "overridden" by the rule that one ought to prevent harm to others.

A rule prohibiting bribery is a prima facie rule. There are cases in which morality requires that a bribe be paid. If the only way to get essential medical care for a dying child is to bribe a doctor, morality requires one to bribe the doctor. So adopting an ethical code which includes a rule prohibiting the payment of bribes does not guarantee that a Rule Assessment of the FCPA will be favorable to it.

The fact that the FCPA imposes a cost on American business and labor weighs against the prima facie obligation not to bribe. If we suppose that American corporations have obligations, tantamount to promises, to promote the job security of their employees and the investments of shareholders, these obligations will also weigh against the obligation not to bribe. Again, if government legislative and enforcement bodies have an obligation to secure the welfare of American business and workers, the FCPA may force them to violate their public obligations.

The FCPA's moral status appears even more dubious if we note that many of the payments prohibited by the Act are neither bribes nor share features that make bribes morally reprehensible. Bribes are generally held to be malefic if they persuade one to act against his good judgment, and consequently purchase an inferior product. But the payments at issue in the FCPA are usually extorted *from the seller*. Further it is arguable that not paying the bribe is more likely to lead to purchase of an inferior product than paying the bribe. Finally, bribes paid to foreign officials may not involve deception when they accord with recognized local practices.

In conclusion, neither End-Point nor Rule Assessment uncovers a sound moral basis for the FCPA. It is shocking to find that a law prohibiting bribery has no clear moral basis, and may even be an immoral law. However, this is precisely what examination of the FCPA from a moral perspective reveals. This is symptomatic of the fact that moral conceptions which were appropriate to a simpler world are not adequate to the complex world in which contemporary business functions. Failure to appreciate this point often leads to righteous condemnation of business, when it should lead to careful reflection on one's own moral preconceptions.

NOTES

1. *National Journal,* June 3, 1978: 880.

2. David C. Gustman, "The Foreign Corrupt Practices Act of 1977," *The Journal of International Law and Economics,* Vol. 13, 1979: 367–401, and Walter S. Surrey, "The Foreign Corrupt Practices Act: Let the Punishment Fit the Crime," *Harvard International Law Journal,* Spring 1979: 203–303.

3. Gerald T. McLaughlin, "The Criminalization of Questionable Foreign Payments by Corporations," *Fordham Law Review,* Vol. 46: 1095.

4. "Foreign Bribery Law Amendments Drafted," *American Bar Association Journal,* February 1980: 135.

Corporate Policy Statements

It is the policy of Occidental and its subsidiaries NOT to make any of the following types of payments. . . Payments to Employees of Foreign Governments — Any payment to or for the benefit of any official or employee of a foreign government or of a corporation wholly or partly owned by a foreign government, as compensation for services specially rendered to Occidental; except that, Occidental may employ an official or employee of a foreign government provided that such employment is lawful under the laws of the country concerned, that either the Board of Directors or its Executive Committee and the employee have determined that the services rendered to Occidental do not conflict in any manner with the governmental duties of such persons, and that the employment does not violate the Foreign Corrupt Practices Act of 1977. Notice is taken of the fact that in many countries it is both customary and necessary to make facilitating payments or gratuities in various forms in the ordinary course of business to persons, some of whom may hold lower-echelon government employment, to expedite or advance the routine performance of their duties. Such customary gratuities for the purpose of facilitating the conduct of the Company's business are not prohibited, provided that they are not in significant amounts, do not constitute a material factor in the Company's business, and are accurately disclosed and properly recorded on the books of Occidental. Any officer or employee of Occidental found to have willfully violated these policies shall be subject to dismissal.

Occidental Petroleum Corp.

Facilitating payments or tips in nominal amounts to low level foreign government employees may be made to obtain or expedite the performance of ministerial or legitimate customary duties such as mail delivery, security, customs clearance and the like, where the practice is usual or customary in

156

the foreign country. Before such payments are made, a corporate officer shall have determined that: (1) the governmental action or assistance sought is proper for the Company to receive, (2) the payments are customary in the foreign country in which they are to be made, and (3) there is no reasonable alternative to making such payments. All such payments shall be reported to the Corporate Controller's office, quarterly.

Allied Chemical Corp.

In overseas jurisdictions where corporate political contributions may be legal, no majority owned or controlled unit of Wells Fargo shall make any contribution or expenditure whatever for political purposes without the approval of the Executive Office . . . .

Employees in foreign countries are not to accept or to offer any gift, rebate, hidden commission or other form of illegal payment or commercial bribery in connection with any business transaction, whether or not such a payment is customary in the particular locality. Any payment made in the form of a gratuity to expedite consideration of matters affecting the Company will be fully disclosed on our Company records. Similarly, payments made relative to the security of employees will be fully disclosed.

Wells Fargo Bank

Trade Secrets and Patents

Case Study

Trade Secrets at Atlas Chemical Corp.

Rudy Kern joined Atlas Chemical just after obtaining his master's degree in chemical engineering from Indiana University in 1961. His thesis was on heavy metal-chlorine reactions, and he was hired by Atlas to work on a chloride process for the production of titanium dioxide, TiO_2, an important ingredient in paints and paper. Initially, Kern believed his job would lead to a management slot; as Atlas moved from pilot plant to production, some of the technical staff would pick up management positions. Atlas, however, encountered major problems in scaling up its process. It had begun experimental work in 1956, but did not get its first small plant into production until 1971, and it wasn't until 1974 that the company broke even. That year was Kern's thirteenth at Atlas and, although he had been promoted twice and was now a senior engineer, at 39 he began to believe he would never join management's ranks. He began to read engineering publications with an eye on the help-wanted ads.

Finding a position with another firm was more difficult than Kern initially envisaged. He was narrowly specialized in a particular field of chloride chemistry, and furthermore, Atlas was the only firm using a chloride process to produce TiO_2; other firms used a sulfate process. This made it very difficult for Kern to utilize his skills for another TiO_2 producer. The fact that his expertise was narrowly based and highly technical seemed to preclude him from finding a management position.

In early 1975, however, Kern noticed the following ad:

> Major, innovative, chemical firm seeks experienced TiO_2 process engineer. Excellent opportunity for a person presently at the senior process engineering or plant production foreman

level. Must have extensive TiO_2 production process experience. Salary open. Title: Plant Manager, Technical Services. Equal Opportunity Employer.

Kern applied, and soon was contacted by Vulcan Chemical Corporation, which informed him that it was interested in interviewing him, since it was planning to use a chloride process to produce TiO_2. Prior to the interview, however, and prior to contact with any Vulcan representatives, Vulcan asked Kern to sign and mail an agreement pledging that he would "not disclose to Vulcan Chemical Corp., either during pre-employment contacts or in the course of any subsequent employment with Vulcan, any information that I know to be the proprietary information, data, or trade secrets of any third party." Once Kern complied with the request, he was interviewed by Vulcan and got the job. He received a 25% salary boost, but, more important to Kern was his promotion to manager.

When Atlas learned of Kern's plan to join Vulcan, it already knew of Vulcan's strategy to develop a TiO_2-chloride process. It immediately went to the State Court in New Jersey and obtained a restraining order blocking Kern from working for Vulcan in the TiO_2 position.

In subsequent court proceedings, Atlas allowed that there was nothing mysterious or secret about TiO_2 itself; any physical chemist could accurately enumerate its characteristics. Basically it is a white powder that has a high capacity for scattering light, and is hence opaque. This accounts for its ability to impart whiteness (or opacity) to paint, paper, rubber, etc.

About 92% of world TiO_2 production of roughly 3 million tons is produced by the sulfate process, which begins by dissolving titanium ore in sulfuric acid. The process is relatively uncomplicated, but it does use a lot of sulfuric acid, and it contaminates the acid to the extent that much of it cannot be recycled readily. The sulfate process leaves the producer with a disposal problem. The chlorine process is chemically simple but technologically complex. Any chemist would understand the basic chemistry, in which titanium ore is reacted with chlorine to produce titanium tetrachloride, which is then oxidized to produce TiO_2 and chlorine. The advantage of the chlorine process is that chlorine, one of the initial reactants, can be recovered in relatively pure form. The technical problem is that the oxidation of titanium tetrachloride must be accomplished at 2,200° F, at which temperature the tetrachloride is very, very corrosive.

Atlas is at present the only producer of TiO_2 via the chloride process. It produces 8% of TiO_2 worldwide. It started work on the process in 1956, along with three other firms, but Atlas was the only firm to move beyond the pilot plant to production. It began producing TiO_2 commercially via the process in 1971, encountered numerous problems, and only started to realize a profit on the process in 1974. Atlas calculates its research and development expenses for the process to be $42 million over 18 years. The process is reliably estimated to have a lower operating cost than the sulfate process.

In court proceedings, Atlas stated that its TiO_2 process was based on trade secrets, that Kern knew more about the secrets than anyone else at Atlas, that he had been informed of their confidential nature, and that it would be impossible for Kern, as plant manager of Vulcan's TiO_2 project, to serve without making use of his knowledge of Atlas's trade secrets. Atlas also pointed to its heavy research and development expense over many years, and the fact that two years of profitable production had not even enabled it to cover these costs. Atlas admitted that the basic chemistry of its process was uncomplicated, and that sooner or later someone else would solve the production problems and use the chloride process to make TiO_2. But, having spent $42 million to develop its process, Atlas argued that it should be allowed to keep any competitor from solving the difficult engineering problems by illegitimately securing Atlas's trade secrets.

In its memorandum to the court, Vulcan declared that it had invented its own chloride process and now wanted to move to the pilot plant stage and then to production. Its new process, it asserted, was a trade secret. It added that it in no way was seeking, and would not seek, Atlas's trade secrets. Atlas responded by saying the basic chemistry has to be essentially the same, hence, Kern would almost of necessity encounter the same or very similar scale-up problems he had already encountered and solved at Atlas.

In Kern's memorandum to the court, he acknowledged that Atlas had legitimate trade secrets in the TiO_2 area and that he knew the secrets, but he claimed he would not disclose or use such information. Vulcan, he stated, had not asked him to reveal Atlas's secrets, and he fully intended to abide by the document Vulcan asked him to sign saying he would safeguard Atlas's secrets. He noted that he had never signed a covenant with Atlas not to work with a competitor if he left Atlas. He asked the court to remember that Atlas was not alleging that he used Atlas's secrets, or that he took or copied Atlas's documents, or in any way actually violated Atlas's confidentiality. He reminded the court of his narrow background in TiO_2 chemistry, noted that Atlas and Vulcan were the only two firms currently experimenting with the chloride process, and argued that he had a legitimate right to change jobs and attempt to better himself as long as he did not violate his confidentiality pledge to Atlas.

In response, Atlas claimed the issue was not whether Kern intended to disclose or use Atlas's trade secrets, but, rather, whether he could avoid doing so. Atlas claimed that even if Kern had the best of intentions, the processes would be so similar that it would strain credulity to believe that Kern would: (1) not indicate to his employees when they were going into a blind alley, (2) fail to in fact point his employees down the trail that Atlas had successfully pursued, and hence (3) reveal Atlas's trade secrets. As project manager for Vulcan, Kern's task is to maximize production efficiency. Since Kern had already attained that end for Atlas via its trade secrets, Atlas asked how Kern could do the same for Vulcan without violating Atlas's trade secrets.

For Discussion

In your opinion is Atlas legally entitled to bar Kern from working as TiO_2 project manager for Vulcan? Why or why not? Is Kern morally justified in accepting the position at Vulcan? Why or why not? Is Vulcan morally justified in attempting to hire Kern? Why or why not?

Robert E. Frederick
Milton Snoeyenbos

Trade Secrets, Patents, and Morality

Suppose that company M develops a super-computer that gives it a competitive advantage, but decides that, rather than marketing it, it will use the computer to provide services to users. In doing so, it keeps its technical information secret. If another company, N, were to steal the computer, N would be subject to moral blame as well as legal penalty. But suppose that, without M's consent, N obtained M's technical information, which thereby enabled N to copy M's computer. Should N then be subject to moral blame and legal penalty?

At first glance it seems that N should be held morally and legally accountable; but N has a line of defense which supports its position. Information, or knowledge, unlike a physical asset, can be possessed by more than one individual or firm at any one time. Thus, in obtaining M's information N did not diminish M's information; since M possesses exactly the same information it had before, N cannot be said to have stolen it. Furthermore, everyone regards the dissemination of knowledge as a good thing; it has obvious social utility. M's competitive advantage, moreover, was not a good thing, since it could have enabled M to drive other firms out of the computer service business; M might have established a monopoly. Thus, M has no right to keep the information to itself, and, in the interests of social utility, N had a right to obtain M's information. Hence, N should be praised rather than blamed for its act.

This defense of N raises the general question of whether a firm's use of trade secrets or patents to protect information is justifiable. If it is not, then N may at least be morally justified in using clandestine means to obtain M's information. If there is a justification for allowing trade secrets and patents, then, not only is N's act unjustifiable, but we also have a basis for saying that the release of certain information in certain contexts to N by an employee of M is unjustifiable. In this paper we argue that there are both consequentialist and nonconsequentialist reasons for allowing firms to protect *their* proprietary information via patents and trade secrets. On the other hand, an individual has a right to liberty and a right to use *his* knowledge and skills to better himself. These rights place certain constraints on what can qualify as a trade secret or patentable item of information. We begin with a discussion of present patent and trade secret law.

Patents differ significantly from trade secrets. A patent provides a legal safeguard of certain information itself, but the information must be novel. Some internal information generated by a firm may not meet the U.S. Patent Office's standards of inventiveness. Then, too, even if an item is patentable, there may be disadvantages to the firm in seeking and securing a patent on it and/or advantages to the firm in just trying to keep the information secret. There are legal costs in securing a patent, and patents have to be secured in every country in which one wishes to protect the information. In the U.S. a patent expires in 17 years, and, since it is not renewable, the information then becomes public domain. Furthermore, since a patent is a public document, it both reveals research directions and encourages competitors to invent related products that are just dissimilar enough to avoid a patent infringement suit. So there are ample reasons for a firm to keep information secret and not attempt to secure a patent. If a firm can keep the information secret, it may have a long-term advantage over competitors. The disadvantage is that, unlike a patented device or information, the law provides no protection for a trade secret itself. A competitor can analyze an unpatented product in any way, and, if it discovers the trade secret, it is free to use that information or product. For example, if a firm analyzes Coca-Cola and uncovers the secret formula, it can market a product chemically identical to it, although, of course, it cannot use the name "Coca-Cola," since that is protected by trademark law.

It is, however, unlawful to employ "improper means" to secure another's trade secret. Legal protection of trade secrets is based on the agent's duty of confidentiality. Section 395 of the *Restatement of Agency* imposes a duty on the agent "not to use or communicate information confidentially given to him by the principal or acquired by him during the course of or on account of his agency . . . to the injury of the principal, on his own account or on behalf of another . . . unless the information is a matter of general knowledge." This duty extends beyond the length of the work contract; if the employee moves to a new job with another firm, his obligation to not disclose his previous principal's trade secrets is still in effect.

Since patents are granted by the U.S. Patent Office in accordance with the U.S. Patent Code, patent law cases are federal cases, whereas trade secrets cases are handled by state courts in accordance with state laws. Although there is no definition of "trade secret" adopted by every state, most follow the definition in Section 757 of the *Restatement of Torts,* according to which a trade secret consists of a pattern, device, formula or compilation of information used in business and designed to give the employer an opportunity to obtain an advantage over his competitors who neither know nor use the information. On this definition virtually anything an employer prefers to keep confidential could count as a trade secret.

In practice, however, the *Restatement* specifies several factors it suggests that courts should consider in deciding whether information is legally protectable: (1) the extent to which the information is known outside the business, (2) the extent to which it is known to employees in the firm, (3) the extent to which the firm used measures to guard secrecy of the information, (4) the value of the information to the firm and to its competitors, (5) the amount of money the firm spent to develop the information, and (6) how easily the information may be developed or properly duplicated.

According to (1), (2), (4), (5), and (6), not all internally generated information will count legally as a trade secret. And, via (3), the firm must take measures to guard its secrets: ". . . a person entitled to a trade secret . . . must not fail to take all proper and reasonable steps to keep it secret. He cannot lie back and do nothing to preserve its essential secret quality, particularly when the subject matter of the process becomes known to a number of individuals involved in its use or is observed in the course of manufacturing in the plain view of others" (*Gallowhur Chemical Corp. v. Schwerdle,* 37 N. J. Super. 385, 397, 117 A2d 416, 423; *J. T Healy & Son, Inc., v. James Murphy & Son, Inc.,* 1970 Mass. Adv. Sheets 1051, 260 NE2d 723 (Ill. App. 1959)). In addition to attempting to keep its information secret, the firm must inform its employees as to what data are regarded as secret: there "must be a strong showing that the knowledge was gained in confidence," (*Wheelabrator Corp. v. Fogle,* 317 F. Supp. 633 (D. C. La. 1970)), and employees must be warned that certain information is regarded as a trade secret (*Gallo v. Norris Dispensers, Inc.,* 315 F. Supp. 38 (D. C. Mo. 1970)). Most firms have their employees sign a document that (a) specifies what its trade secrets or types of trade secrets are, and (b) informs them that improper use of the trade secrets violates confidentiality and subjects them to litigation.

If a firm has information that really is a legitimate trade secret, if it informs its employees that this information is regarded as secret, and informs them that improper use violates confidentiality, then it may be able to establish its case in court, in which case it is entitled to injunctive relief and damages. But the courts also typically examine how the defendant in a trade secret case obtained the information. For example, if an employee transfers from company M to company N, taking M's documents with him to N, then there is clear evidence of a breach of confidentiality (or "bad faith") if the evidence can be produced by M. But trade secret law is equity law, a basic principle of which is that bad faith cannot be presumed. In equity law the maxim "Every dog has one free bite" obtains, i.e., a dog cannot be presumed to be vicious until he bites someone. Thus, if the employee took no producible hard evidence in the form of objects or documents, but instead took what was "in his head" or what he could memorize, then M may have to wait for its former employee to overtly act. By then it may be very difficult to produce convincing evidence that would establish a breach of confidentiality.

In considering possible justifications of patents and trade secrets, we have to take into consideration the public good or social utility, the firm's rights and interests, and the individual's rights and interests. Our aim should be to maximize utility while safeguarding legitimate rights.

As Michael Baram has noted, "A major concern of our society is progress through the promotion and utilization of new technology. To sustain and enhance this form of progress, it is necessary to optimize the flow of information and innovation all the way from conception to public use."[1] Given the assumption that technological progress is conducive to social utility, and that the dissemination of technological information is a major means to progress, the key issue is how to maximize information generation and dissemination.

One answer is to require public disclosure of all important generated information, and allow unrestricted use of that information. In some cases this is appropriate, e.g., government sponsored research conducted by a private firm is disclosed and can be used by other firms. Within a capitalistic context, however, it is doubtful that a general disclosure requirement would maximize social utility. The innovative firm would develop information leading to a new product only to see that product manufactured and marketed by another firm at a lower price because the latter firm did not incur research costs. The proposal probably would also result in less competition; only firms with strong financial and marketing structures would survive. Small, innovative firms would not have the protection of their technological advantages necessary to establish a competitive position against industry giants. If both research effort and competition were diminished by this proposal, then the "progress" Baram mentions would not be maximized — at least not in the area of marketable products.

In a market economy, then, there are reasons grounded in social utility for allowing firms to have some proprietary information. The laws based on such a justification should, in part, be structured with an eye to overall utility, and in fact they are so structured. Patents, for example, expire in 17 years. While the patent is in force it allows the firm to recoup research expenses and generate a profit by charging monopolistic prices. Patent protection also encourages the generation of new knowledge. The firm holding the patent, and realizing profits because of it, is encouraged to channel some of those profits to research, since its patent is of limited duration. Given that its patent will expire, the firm needs to generate new, patentable information to maximize profits. Competitors are encouraged to develop competing products that are based on new, patentable information.

Patent protection should not, however, extend indefinitely; it would not only extend indefinitely the higher costs that consumers admittedly bear while a patent is in force, but in certain cases, it could also stifle innovation. A firm holding a basic patent might either "sit on" it or strengthen its monopoly position. A company like Xerox, for example, with the basic xerography patent, might use its profits to fund research until it had built up an impenetrable patent network, but then cut reproductive graphics research drastically and rest relatively secure in the knowledge that its competitors were frozen out of the market. Patents allow monopoly profits for a limited period of time, but patent law should not be structured to forever legitimatize a monopoly.

Richard De George has recently offered another argument to the conclusion that the right to proprietary information is a limited right:

> Knowledge is not an object which one can keep locked up as long as one likes. . . . Whatever knowledge a company produces is always an increment to the knowledge developed by society or by previous people in society and passed from one generation to another. Any new invention is made by people who learned a great deal from the general store of knowledge before they could bring what they knew to bear on a particular problem. Though we can attribute them to particular efforts of individuals or teams, therefore, inventions and discoveries also are the result of those people who developed them and passed on their knowledge to others. In this way every advance in knowledge is social and belongs ultimately to society, even though for practical purposes we can assign it temporarily to a given individual or firm.[2]

Allowing the firm to use proprietary information has utility, but the right to such information is limited. In point of fact, although we have stressed the utility of allowing use of proprietary information, U.S. patent and copyright laws were enacted during the industrial revolution to reduce secrecy. Patent laws allow limited monopolies in return for public disclosure of the information on which the patent is based. Thus, patent laws provide information to competitors and encourage them to develop their own patentable information that not only generates new products, but also adds to the store of available knowledge.

If allowing limited use of proprietary information has utility, it is still an open question as to the proper limits of such use. Does the present 17 year patent limit maximize utility? This is an empirical question that we will not attempt to answer. Although most experts and industry representatives believe the present limit is about right, U.S. drug firms have recently argued that research and development time and Federal Drug Administration (FDA) testing and licensing requirements are so extensive that social disutility results, as well as disutility for innovative firms.

Although patents expire and the information protected can then be used by anyone, trade secrets can extend indefinitely according to present law. In 1623, the Zildjian family in Turkey developed a metallurgical process for making excellent cymbals. Now centered in Massachusetts, the family has maintained their secret to the present day, and they still produce excellent cymbals. Preservation of such secrets may well have utility for firms holding the secrets, but does it have social utility? Not necessarily, as the following case illustrates. Suppose that Jones, a shadetree mechanic, develops a number of small unpatentable improvements in the internal combustion engine's basic design. The result is an engine that is cheap, reliable, and gets 120 miles per gallon. With no resources to mass produce and market his engine, Jones decides to sell to the highest bidder. XYZ oil company, with immense oil reserves, buys the information. To protect its oil interests, it keeps the information secret. Now suppose it is in fact against XYZ's interests to divulge the information. Then, to calculate overall utility we have to weigh the social disutility of keeping the information secret against the social utility of keeping the existing oil industry intact. Although utility calculations are difficult, it seems clear that disutility would arise from allowing the information to be kept secret.

If the preservation of *some* secrets has social disutility, it also seems clear that requiring immediate disclosure of *all* trade secrets in a capitalistic context would have disutility as well. The arguments here parallel those we developed in discussing patents. Again, specification of the appropriate duration of a trade secret is a utility calculation. The calculation will, however, have to take into consideration the fact that the law provides no protection for the secret itself. The firm with a significant investment in a trade secret always runs the risk that a competitor may legitimately uncover and use the secret.

Allowing patents and trade secrets has obvious utility for the firm that possesses them, but the firm also has a *right* to at least the limited protection of its information. It has a *legal* right to expect that its employees will live up to their work contracts, and employees have a correlative duty to abide by their contracts. The work contract is entered into voluntarily by employer and employee; if a prospective employee does not like the terms of a (legitimate) trade secret provision of a contract, he does not have to take the job. The normal employment contract specifies that the firm owns all employee-generated information. Even if the employee transfers from firm M to firm N, M still owns the information produced when he was employed there, and the employee is obligated not to reveal that information.

The moral basis of contract enforceability, including contractual provisions for the protection of proprietary information, is twofold. First, as argued, allowing trade secrets has social utility in addition to utility for the firm. The institution of contract compliance is necessary for the systematic and orderly functioning of business, and a sound business environment is essential to general social utility. However, if only a few people broke their contracts, business would continue to survive. This leads to the second moral basis for adhering to the provisions of one's contract.

If an individual breaks his contract, then he must either regard himself as an exception to the rule banning contract-breaking, or he must believe, in Kant's terms, that a maxim concerning contract-breaking is universalizable. But if we agree that in moral matters everyone ought to adopt the moral point of view, and that point of view requires that one not make himself an exception to the rule, it follows that the person in question is not justified in breaking the rule. On the other hand, if he claims that breaking the contract is in accordance with a maxim, then we can properly demand to have the maxim specified. Clearly the maxim cannot be something like: "I will keep my promises, except on those occasions where it is not to my advantage to keep the promises." For if everyone followed this maxim, there would be no institution of promising or promise-keeping. Since the maxim is not universalizable, it cannot legitimately be appealed to as a sanction for action. Of course, other maxims are available, and the contract-breaker may claim that his act is in accordance with one of these maxims. But note that this reply at least tacitly commits the person to the moral point of view; he is agreeing that everyone ought to act only on universalizable maxims. The only dispute, then, is whether his maxim is in fact universalizable. If we can show him that it is not, he is bound to admit that he is not morally justified in breaking the contract. As a standard, then, contracts should be kept, and where an individual breaks, or contemplates breaking, a contract, the burden is on him to produce a universalizable maxim for his action.

Our analysis does not, however, imply that a person is morally obligated to abide by all contracts; some contracts, or provisions of certain contracts, may be morally and/or legally unacceptable. A person does have a right to liberty and a right to use his knowledge and skills to earn a living. Thus, firm M cannot legitimately specify that *all* knowledge an employee gains while at M is proprietary. This would prohibit the person from obtaining employment at another firm; in effect the work contract would amount to a master-slave relationship. As the *Restatement of Torts* appropriately specifies, only certain information qualifies as a legitimate trade secret. Furthermore, the employee brings to his job certain knowledge and skills that typically are matters of public domain, and, on the job, the good employee develops his capacities. As the court noted in *Donahue v. Permacil Tape Corporation*: an ex-employee's general knowledge and capabilities "belong to him as an individual for the transaction of any business in which he may engage, just the same as any part of the skill, knowledge, information or education which was received by him before entering the employment. . . . On terminating his employment, he has a right to take them with him."[3]

Given that an individual's rights to liberty and to use his knowledge and skills to better himself are primary rights, and hence cannot be overriden by utility considerations, the burden clearly is on the firm to: (1) specify to employees what it regards as its trade secrets, and (2) make sure the secrets are legitimate trade secrets. In addition, a company can employ certain pragmatic tactics to protect its trade secrets. It can fragment research activities so that only a few employees know all the secrets. It can restrict access to research data and operational areas. It can develop pension and consulting policies for ex-employees that motivate them not to join competitors for a period of time. More importantly, it can develop a corporate atmosphere that motivates the individual to remain with the firm.

We began by sketching an argument that company N was justified in obtaining information about company M's computer without M's consent.

Our conclusion is that N's argument is specious. Utility considerations justify allowing M to keep its information secret for a period of time, and any employee of M who divulges M's secret information to N is morally blameworthy because he violates his contractual obligations to M.

NOTES

1. Michael Baram, "Trade Secrets: What Price Loyalty," *Harvard Business Review,* vol. 46, No. 6 (Nov.–Dec., 1968), pp. 66–74.

2. Richard T. DeGeorge, *Business Ethics* (New York: Macmillan, 1982), p. 207.

3. Cited in Baram, p. 71.

Corporate Policy Statement

"TI's trade secrets, proprietary information and much other internal information are valuable assets. Protection of this information plays a vital role in TI's continued growth and in our ability to compete. Under the law of most countries, a trade secret is treated as property, usually in the form of information, knowledge or know how, the possession of which gives the owner some advantage over competitors who do not possess the 'secret.' A trade secret must be secret, that is, not generally or publicly known; but it need not be patentable subject matter to qualify as a trade secret. Our obligations with respect to proprietary and trade secret information of TI are: Not to disclose this information to persons outside of TI, for example, by conversations with visitors, suppliers, family, etc.; Not to use this information for our own benefit or for the profit or benefit of persons outside of TI, and; Not to disclose this information to other TIers except on a 'need to know' basis, and then only with a positive statement that the information is a TI trade secret. TIers who have the 'need to know' are those who can do their jobs properly only with knowledge of the proprietary or trade secret information. TI's trade secret and proprietary information is not always of a technical nature. Typical of such important information are TI business, research and new product plans; Objectives, Strategies and Tactical Action Programs; divisional and department sales, profits and any unpublished financial or pricing information; yields, designs, efficiencies, and capacities of TI's production facilities, methods and systems; salary, wage, and benefit data; employment levels for sites or organizations; employee, customer and vendor lists, and detailed information regarding customer requirements, preferences, business habits and plans except where such information is publicly available. This list, while not complete, suggests the wide scope and variety of TI proprietary information that must be safeguarded. Special safeguards should be observed for TI information classified 'TI Strictly Private' or 'TI Internal Data.' Each of these classifications imposes restrictions of a need to know within TI. But even without these classifications, most of what we know about our own jobs and the jobs of others should remain in the plant or office when we finish the day's work. If we leave TI, our legal obligation is to protect TI's trade secret and proprietary information until the information becomes publicly available or TI no longer considers it trade secret or proprietary. We should remember also that correspondence, printed matter, documents, or records of any kind, specific process knowledge, procedures, special TI ways of doing things — whether classified or not — are all the property of and must remain at TI."

Texas Instruments

Honesty in Communication

Case Study

A Communication Decision at Von Products, Inc.

Gerald Fowler inherited some money in 1949 and he used it to found Von Products, a company that manufactured air driers for use in refrigeration and air conditioning equipment. In 1949, Fowler was convinced that air conditioning was the new wave of the future. Fowler was right, and Von Products prospered. In 1963 and 1972, Fowler expanded his operations, each time selling stock in the corporation. In 1981, Von Products employed 406 people, with Fowler retaining ownership of 67% of the corporation's stock. The organization of Von Products' top-level management was as follows:

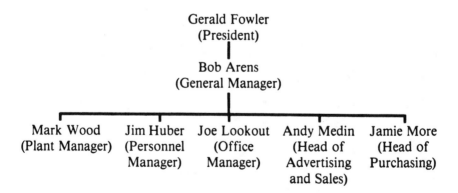

Gerald Fowler
(President)

Bob Arens
(General Manager)

| Mark Wood (Plant Manager) | Jim Huber (Personnel Manager) | Joe Lookout (Office Manager) | Andy Medin (Head of Advertising and Sales) | Jamie More (Head of Purchasing) |

Fowler felt that Von Products was "his baby," and he strictly reviewed most management decisions in the corporation. One of the things Fowler insisted upon was that he personally make all management-level appointments and promotions. Below the level of management, the personnel manager was empowered to make all decisions regarding hiring, firing, and promotion. When management positions were to be filled, however, Bob Arens, the general manager, made recommendations to Fowler, who then made the ultimate decision.

On November 10, 1981, Jim Huber was called into Fowler's office. Fowler told him that Andy Medin was leaving the corporation, and that he, Fowler, was going to appoint a new head of advertising and sales. At present no one except Medin, Fowler, Arens, and Huber knew of Medin's upcoming resignation, and Fowler said that he wanted the information to be kept confidential. Fowler further told Huber that the list of candidates for promotion to Medin's position had been narrowed to two: Milt Snobiski, currently manager of the advertising department, and Bob Allen, sales manager. Fowler asked Huber to go over the files of both men and make a recommendation for promotion. The request was unusual; however, Fowler explained that Arens had strongly recommended one person for promotion, while he favored the other. Before he made his final decision, then, Fowler wanted a third opinion. And since Huber was personnel manager, he was selected for the task. Fowler refused to tell Huber whom Arens had recommended or whom he, Fowler, favored, because he did not want to prejudice Huber's judgment.

From the outset Huber felt uneasy about making the decision requested of him. He knew both Snobiski and Allen well, for all three men had grown up together and had gone to the same high school. Still, Huber was not familiar with the dossiers of either man. Huber had joined Von Products only two years ago; and both Allen and Snobiski had been hired over 12 years ago by Huber's predecessor, a man who recently had died of a heart attack.

Even before he looked at the résumés of the two men, Huber knew whom he favored for promotion. Huber felt that Snobiski was hard working, loyal, and competent. Furthermore, Huber and Snobiski were good friends. On the other hand, Huber knew that Allen had been made sales manager by Fowler on the recommendation of Arens, even though Andy Medin, a competent department head, had not favored the decision. In Huber's opinion, Allen had risen high in the corporation only because he constantly "buttered up" Arens. Furthermore, Huber knew that Allen had assumed Andy Medin's duties for two months in 1980 while Medin was sick, and that during that time advertising and sales suffered.

When Huber examined Allen's file he found that the subject had a slightly better than average record. At the same time, there was nothing outstanding about it. Snobiski's file, on the other hand, was, with one exception, truly impressive. Great leaps in sales were recorded in 1973, 1975, and 1979, and all were traceable to aggressive advertising campaigns masterminded by Snobiski. Furthermore, the file was replete with complimentary evaluations by Medin. Yet there was a problem with Snobiski's record. When Huber examined data concerning Snobiski's educational background, he found that Snobiski claimed to have an associate's degree in business from Ohio State and a master's in business administration from Xavier University. The dates of the degrees accorded with times when Huber felt sure Snobiski was serving in the navy. To check, Huber called both Ohio State and Xavier and found that his friend had no degree from either university.

Huber knew Fowler very well. If Fowler found out that Snobiski had falsified his employment application, not only would Snobiski be fired, Fowler would do his best to see that he was not hired anywhere else. Furthermore, Fowler almost certainly would make Allen head of advertising and sales, a move that Huber honestly felt would be disastrous for the corporation. With this in mind, Huber considered the various options that he felt were open to him:

(1) He could tell Fowler all that he had found, and argue for Snobiski's promotion. But Huber knew that Fowler felt that falsification of records was among the worst of all evils. Thus, choice of this course of action probably would do little more than cause Fowler to doubt Huber's trustworthiness. Furthermore, Huber's report would cause Snobiski to be fired, and a truly productive person would be lost to Von Products.

(2) He could tell Fowler that he favored Allen, justify the recommendation by some strained arguments, and omit any mention of Snobiski's educational record.

(3) He could argue for Snobiski's promotion, withholding all information concerning Snobiski's educational background.

(4) He could give all the information at his disposal to Fowler, and then argue against the promotion of either man. Once again, however, Snobiski would be fired. Further, Huber felt sure that if Snobiski was removed from consideration, Allen would be promoted regardless of what he had to say in opposition to the appointment.

As Huber considered the various alternatives available to him, he felt caught between a rock and a hard place. To tell all he knew would bring about dismissal of a valuable employee and a good friend, and almost certainly put Allen in a position Huber felt he did not deserve. However, the alternative was to withhold information, and this made Huber feel uncomfortable.

For Discussion

If you were Jim Huber, which of the above alternatives would you find most appealing, and why? Can you think of any other course of action Huber might have pursued?

James M. Humber

Honesty in Organizational Communication

Top corporate executives consistently complain of problems involving communications within the organization.[1] In one study of 100 businesses and industries it was found that only 20% of the information downward from the level of the board of directors was understood at the worker level.[2] And if anything, problems with upward communications are even more severe than those encountered in downward transmissions of information.[3]

There are a variety of reasons to explain why communication problems arise within corporate structures. Upward communication is hampered by the very structure of the corporation itself. Top men insulate themselves from all but a few key employees to avoid undue interruptions and embarrassing encounters. Pressures of time and the routine demands of jobs also hinder the upward flow of information. The chain of command in most companies makes it impossible for employees to talk to decision makers in their organizations without first presenting their messages to each higher management echelon. Then too, some workers are not able to communicate clearly, either orally or in writing; and those who receive information sometimes misinterpret. In addition, subordinates are reluctant to pass on "bad" information to their superiors; and employees claim to feel pressures (sometimes real, sometimes imagined) to tell their bosses "only what they want to hear." With all of these impediments to upward communication, it is amazing that any undistorted information gets to the top.

There are at least as many factors operating to distort downward communication in corporations as there are factors working to hamper the upward flow of information. For example, some executives withhold bad news from their employees for fear of upsetting morale. In a large international or multinational corporation, top management and local management rarely come into contact. Furthermore, it is sometimes difficult, in a very large company, to identify the person or persons to whom information should be sent. Then too, managers, like their subordinates, are often burdened by routine tasks. Sometimes persons in executive positions are incapable of communicating clearly; and oftentimes those below top-level management misunderstand the messages they receive. Overarching all of this, of course, is the problem of the "authoritarian" executive. A person of this sort does not feel that company information is any of the worker's business. And naturally, in these circumstances very little information is communicated downward.

There are a host of books and studies in management theory that attempt to provide employers with the means for improving internal corporate communications. My purpose in this essay is not to add to that body of literature, but rather to assess the moral quality of certain kinds of intentional distortions in the flow of information within business and industry. The following three cases will help to illustrate the kinds of communicative distortions I want to examine.

Case #1. Joe Doe and Jim Roe are co-workers competing for a promotion. Doe purposely passes on false information to Roe. As Doe expects, Roe acts on the false information and so "looks bad" in the eyes of his superiors.

Case #2. A department manager (DM) must write a report evaluating the work of four employees in his department. The first three employees are good friends of his, but he does not like the fourth employee. In writing his report DM does not omit any pertinent information, but goes out of his way to stress his friends' strengths while emphasizing the weaknesses of the employee he does not like.

Case #3. A regional manager (RM) must report to top level executives concerning the operations of the various districts for which he has responsibility within the organization. RM instructs an assistant, *A,* to collect data and prepare a report, telling *A* in the process that it is very important for his region to "look good" to the bosses. *A* prepares a report that makes no mention of the problems plaguing various districts in RM's region.

In case #1 above, one employee straightforwardly tells another something that he knows to be false. In case #2, the truthfulness of communication is distorted by emphasis or "coloring." And in the final example, important information is withheld. What all three cases have in common, of course, is that in each instance an intentional deception or lie has been perpetrated.[4] Distortions of all three sorts occur in all organizations with varying degrees of frequency. But are such deceptions morally wrong? And if they are morally wrong, are the deceivers morally blameworthy? These are the questions that will serve as the focus of this essay. Before we can attempt to answer these questions, however, we first must decide whether employees in business and industry have any moral obligation to tell the truth in their corporate communications.

Ethicists and moral philosophers differ widely in their views concerning whether there is a moral duty to tell the truth. At one extreme we find people like Kant and St. Augustine claiming that there is an absolute, unconditional, or unbreakable moral obligation to tell the truth. Since an unbreakable moral duty is one that holds in all circumstances without exception, acceptance of this view would force the conclusion that *all* lies are morally wrong. But there are good reasons to believe that this theory, which we could call deontological extremism, is not correct.[5] For example, deontological extremists claim that there are other inviolable moral duties in addition to absolute moral obligation to tell the truth. How is one to act if two or more of these unbreakable moral duties conflict? Kant took note of the problem; but in the end claimed that there was no real difficulty because "a conflict of duties and obligations is inconceivable."[6] This "solution," however, is far too facile. For instance, let us assume that we have only two absolute moral duties—one is to keep our promises, and the other is to tell the truth. Let us say further that S is a soldier who promises faithfully to do all in his power to confuse the enemy and protect his comrades. During one battle S is captured, imprisoned, and repeatedly interrogated regarding troop placements. Though S is tortured, he gives the enemy no information. One day, however, S learns that the enemy is planning to attack his army's headquarters. S knows that he is due to be questioned the next day, and that if he pretends to "break" under pressure, he may lie convincingly concerning the location of his army's headquarters and so cause the enemy's attack to be misdirected. What should S do? If he deceives his captors, he breaks his absolute moral duty to tell the truth. If he does not lie, he fails to keep his unbreakable promise to protect his comrades and confuse the enemy. In this case, at least, absolute moral duties do seem to conflict, and deontological extremism would appear to make it impossible for S to act in a morally right way.

Another problem with deontological extremism is that we ordinarily believe moral duties may be broken when the consequences of not violating those duties would be disastrous. For example, assume that the captain of a fishing boat is smuggling innocent political prisoners out of a country ruled by a corrupt dictator. Just before the captain is about to leave port with his surreptitious cargo, his vessel is boarded by the police. The police chief is a good friend of the captain, and will believe whatever the captain tells him. Thus, if the captain lies about the location of the prisoners he will save all of their lives. On the other hand, if the captain tells the truth or refuses to say anything, the boat will be searched and all the innocent prisoners killed. Now if the captain were to lie in these circumstances would he really do something wrong? Kant and St. Augustine would have to answer affirmatively; but a judgment of this sort violates our most basic moral intuitions.

Although the above two criticisms of deontological extremism proceed along different lines, they make essentially the same point, i.e., even if we believe there is a moral duty to tell the truth, we ordinarily do not think that this obligation must *always* be obeyed if we are to act in morally right ways. Indeed, this belief is held so strongly by the vast majority of mankind that, historically, deontological extremism proved unworkable. For example, discontent with St. Augustine's absolute rejection of all lies gave birth to a theory known as the doctrine of mental reservations.[7] In its most extreme form this doctrine holds that it is not wrong for one person to say something misleading to another, just so long as the speaker is careful to add a qualification to the statement in his or her mind so as to make the verbal statement true. For instance, let us say that I am at Dick's house and that I pocket a $5.00 bill which I find on the floor. Dick enters the room and asks me if I have seen $5.00. According to the doctrine of mental reservations I would not be lying if I said, "I did not see $5.00," and then silently completed the statement by saying something to myself like "yesterday" or "on the table."

Although those who accept the doctrine of mental reservations insist that we have an absolute moral duty to tell the truth, they allow us to "mentally qualify" any false statement so as to make it true. Hence the actual effect of the doctrine is to deny that we have any moral duty at all to communicate truthfully. The reason this is so is that there can be no such thing as a private language. That is to say, if I tell Dick (x) 'I did not see $5.00,' what I communicate to Dick is nothing more or less than the meaning of (x), for the "mental addition" to (x), which I make in my mind, is no communication at all. In reality, then, when I assert (x) — albeit a "mentally qualified" (x) — I lie to Dick; for what I have actually communicated (viz., the meaning of (x)), is something that I know to be false. And if the doctrine of mental reservations allows me to do this with any statement, at any time, without fear of doing something wrong, it effectively denies that there is any moral duty to tell the truth.

Those who accept the doctrine of mental reservations leap from dissatisfaction with St. Augustine's absolute injunction against lying to a position that denies there is any moral duty at all to tell the truth. Proponents of the mental reservations doctrine make no attempt to justify this "leap," because they do not understand the true nature of their own position. That is, they believe there is an absolute duty of veracity, but that they do not violate this duty when they assert mentally qualified statements because all such statements are true. We now know that this view of things is wrong. But this still leaves one question unanswered; specifically, is it possible to justify the mental reservationists' true position? Or to put it another way, can we construct an argument showing that there is no moral duty to tell the truth? Perhaps the best known attempt to provide such a justification has been made by a group of moral philosophers whom we may call teleological extremists.[8] Teleological extremists believe that we have one and only one moral duty, and that is to maximize good consequences. Thus stealing, lying, killing, etc. cannot be said to be wrong because they violate moral injunctions against such actions. If actions of this sort are wrong, they are wrong only because they produce bad consequences. And of course, teleological extremists insist that there may be cases where it would be morally right to steal, lie, or kill. Specifically, it would be right whenever such action maximized good consequences. For example, teleological extremists might well claim that it would be right for the fishing boat captain to lie to the police chief in our earlier example because lying in this instance would save many innocent lives.

Insofar as teleological extremists claim that it sometimes may be morally permissible to lie, cheat, steal, etc., they no doubt are correct. On the other hand, there seems to be no reason to agree that we have no moral duties other than the duty to maximize good consequences. If this truly were the case, we would feel no moral qualms whatsoever about a person lying, stealing, cheating, etc., whenever it was clear that good consequences were produced by such action. But in fact, we often do feel morally troubled when such actions are performed and justified by an appeal to good consequences. For example, if I steal $50,000 from a millionaire who will never miss the money, and then give that money to charity, have I done something morally right? Or again, if I tell a dying friend on his deathbed that I will use his fortune to care for his pet cats, but after his death use his money to relieve human misery, is my lie justified? In cases such as these we do not feel that the moral issues are as clear-cut and simple as teleological extremists would have us believe. And we feel this way because we think there are many moral duties, and not just one as teleological extremists would have us believe.

We have rejected deontological extremism because it imposes *absolute* moral obligations upon us. On the other hand, teleological extremism goes too far in the opposite direction when it asserts that there are no moral obligations other than the duty to maximize good consequences. In the end, then, the truth would seem to lie somewhere between these extremes. And indeed, if the examples given throughout the text of this essay indicate anything, it is that we ordinarily acknowledge the existence of many moral duties (including the duty to tell the truth), but that we do not hold these duties to be absolute or unbreakable. Duties that are not absolute are called *prima facie* moral duties. *Prima facie* moral duties are so-called because violating them constitutes *prima facie* evidence of moral wrongdoing. That is to say, unless the person violating a *prima facie* duty can *justify* his or her violation, the person performing the action will be said to have done something morally wrong. Of course, what counts as an adequate justification for breaking a *prima facie* moral duty is the subject of much dispute; and more will be said of this later. For now, however, we need only note that our inquiries thus far would seem to require that we acknowledge the existence of a *prima facie* moral duty to tell the truth.

Having determined that there is a *prima facie* moral duty to tell the truth, it might appear that we now should try to specify those conditions under which violation of that duty would be justified. Before we can approach this task, however, there is another issue to be faced. There are some who allow that we ordinarily have a *prima facie* duty of veracity, but they go on to argue that the actions of employees in business and industry must be judged by a special moral theory. If this claim is true, and if this "special" moral theory imposes no duty on employees to tell the truth with respect to their internal corporate communications, we need not worry about seeking a justification for deceptive corporate communiques. Before we proceed further, then, we need to examine the major tenets of this "special" moral theory.

Milton Friedman is the propounder and chief advocate of a special moral theory that he feels must be used to judge the actions of employees in business and industry.[9] Admittedly, Friedman says, all persons have ordinary moral responsibilities. However, when individuals become employees of a company, they assume two duties that supersede their ordinary moral obligations. For Friedman, all employees must: (1) do their best to maximize profits for the corporation, and (2) obey the law and follow the rules of ethical custom.

Friedman's theory has been criticized from a number of quarters. Elsewhere, for example, I have argued that Friedman's theory is so beset by theoretical and conceptual difficulties that it must be rejected out of hand.[10] Also, Alan Goldman rejects the view that, as a general rule, professional obligations override or supersede ordinary moral obligations.[11] For the purposes of this paper, however, we may ignore these challenges to Friedman's position; even if we accept Friedman's theory we still must admit that employees in business and industry have a *prima facie* duty to communicate truthfully. There are two reasons for saying this. First, if our earlier reasonings are accepted, the *prima facie* moral duty to tell the truth is one of our society's "ordinary rules of ethical custom." Thus, insofar as Friedman imposes a moral duty upon employees to follow these rules, he also enjoins them to tell the truth. And second, virtually no one would dispute the claim that, generally, truthfulness in internal corporate communications is an aid to maximizing corporate profits. Indeed, recognition of this fact has spawned the many books, articles, and studies intended to provide employers with the means for improving the quality of information flow within their companies. If we accept Friedman's theory, then, we can say that corporate employees have a moral duty to be truthful in their communications because this helps to maximize company profits. On the other hand, this duty cannot be absolute, because we can imagine situations in which deception might be required for maximization of profits. For instance, one employee may have to lie in order to catch another who is stealing trade secrets.

No matter which way we turn it seems we must admit that company employees have a *prima facie* moral obligation not to distort the truth in their corporate communications. But if the duty to tell the truth is only *prima facie,* under what conditions would it be morally permissible for an employee to lie? Or, to put it another way, how could an employee morally justify lying in a corporate communication? In an essay of this length we cannot hope to take individual note of all the various cases in which lying might be justified. Nevertheless, we can say something in general about the process of justification, and so provide a means for testing the acceptability of moral justifications as they arise in actual practice. If nothing else, this examination should illustrate how very difficult it is to justify distorting the truth in corporate communications.

First, there seems to be agreement among many philosophers that a justification, if it is to be adequate, must be capable of being made public.[12] That is to say, appeals to personal conscience, secret moral knowledge, intuitions not shared by mankind in general, etc., will not do. Thus, if a moral view is to be adequately justified, the person doing the justifying must be able to present reasons and arguments capable of supporting the reasonableness of his or her position.

Second, because justifications must be capable of being made public, we would seem to have no alternative but to appeal to *consequences* in our justifications. For example, if an employee, *E,* were to lie in a corporate communication and then attempt to justify that lie by telling us that his lie was necessary to increase corporate profits, *E*'s "justification" could not be accepted; as it stands it tells us nothing more than that, in this particular instance, *E* feels that his duty to maximize profits supersedes his duty to tell the truth. But why should we accept this belief? It is hardly self-evident. To fully justify his position, *E* must appeal to some publicly accessible facts supporting his contention that the duty of veracity is outweighed by the duty to increase profits. And the only facts that would appear to be publicly accessible are the probable consequences of the two alternative courses of action. That is to say, if *E* is to justify his contention that he did not act wrongly when he lied, he must at the very least show that lying probably produced a greater balance of benefits over harms than not lying. If *E* cannot produce such factual support for his position, he cannot be said to have justified his belief that the duty to maximize profits outweighed his duty to tell the truth. And so long as this state of affairs remains, *E*'s action must be counted as morally wrong.

We have seen that we must appeal to the consequences of our actions whenever we attempt to justify lying in corporate communications. And this fact makes it so very difficult to justify deceptive communications in business and industry. The collective experience of mankind testifies to the fact that lying usually, if not always, produces harmful consequences. The individual who lies must worry about getting caught. If he is caught, his reputation suffers. If he is not caught, he oftentimes must continue to lie in order to conceal the original deception. Furthermore, trust is essential for the success of any cooperative venture; and lying, if it occurs frequently, undermines trust. In the corporate context an atmosphere of mistrust can have especially deleterious consequences: for if lying is continually expected, employees will tend to act on their own, oftentimes at cross purposes. In addition, when false information is passed on, decisions at various levels in the organization are made on the basis of incorrect data. And in these circumstances it is highly unlikely that decisions will be correct. Finally, if lying in internal corporate communications hurts business and industry, it also hurts society as a whole; for the more efficient and economically viable are our corporations, the stronger our economy.

Lying in corporate communications usually has harmful consequences for the liar, the corporation, and society. From past experience we *know* these effects customarily attend deceit; and it is from these negative consequences that this *prima facie* obligation not to lie in corporate communications derives its force. And this force is considerable. Of course, it is conceivable that an employee could show that some competing moral obligation superseded his duty not to lie; but this is quite unlikely. The reason this is so is that an employee who contemplates passing on false information is seldom in possession of the facts necessary to justify a deceptive communication. Even top-level executives do not have a complete and true picture of the organization's operations. As a result, they cannot predict the ultimate consequences of their actions with a high degree of certainty. On the other hand, they know perfectly well that lying will most likely produce the negative results noted previously. If it is difficult for persons at this level in the organization to justify deception, how much more so for individuals in middle-level management and below.[13]

We have seen that deceiving fellow employees in corporate communications is, in virtually all instances, morally wrong. But one question remains: are all those who lie in corporate communications morally blameworthy? Or, to put it another way, are there any conditions that would excuse a liar from responsibility for a wrongful act? In an essay of this length we cannot consider all possible excusing conditions. Nevertheless, we can consider the three most often appealed to, and see whether any succeeds in relieving the liar of responsibility.

First, we do not hold persons responsible for their actions when those actions are compulsory. For example, if we believe a murderer is mentally ill and unable to control his or her actions, we do not think the crime warrants punishment. Similarly, an employee could be a compulsive liar, and so not morally blameworthy if he or she were to lie. Cases such as this will be very rare, however; and if such an individual were discovered in an organization, he or she should be relieved of all responsibilities, at least until the illness has been corrected by proper medical attention.

Second, persons who act wrongfully out of ignorance are usually excused for their wrongdoing. I say "usually," because mere appeal to ignorance will not suffice to relieve one of responsibility. For instance, if an employee, *E*, purposely withholds information because of a mistaken belief that information is privileged, *E* is *not* excused if any reasonable person in the same position would have known that the information was not privileged. In every instance, the test is that of the "reasonable person," i.e., would a reasonable person have known what the person who passes on misinformation claims not to have known? If we believe a reasonable person would have known, we hold the employee who passes on distorted data responsible for his or her action. If we hold the contrary view, we do not blame. The difficulty, of course, is that the "reasonable person" test is very vague, and so difficult to apply in particular instances of wrongdoing. (How, after all, can we be sure what a reasonable person would have known in any given set of circumstances?) Thus, if an employee errs once or twice and then attempts to excuse his or her action by appealing to ignorance, it may be best to give the employee the benefit of the doubt. On the other hand, if an employee repeatedly passes on incorrect information, continued appeals to the excuse of ignorance cannot persist without placing the employee in a "no win" situation. Reasonable persons do not make the same mistake over and over again. Hence, if E continually misinforms co-workers, and then attempts to excuse these actions by appealing to ignorance, we must conclude: (a) that E is a reasonable person who is lying about being ignorant (in which case E is a liar), or (b) that E is a reasonable person who is purposely remaining ignorant (in which case E is responsible for his or her false communications), or (c) that E is not a reasonable person (in which case E is incompetent).

Finally, Aristotle long ago realized that all persons have a breaking point, and that when this point is reached wrongdoers are not held responsible for their actions. For instance, a prisoner of war (POW) may "break" under torture and divulge information leading to the death of many of his comrades. In this case we would ordinarily say that the POW has done something wrong (after all, his action has caused the deaths of many fellow soldiers); at the same time, we would not blame the POW for breaking under torture. Similarly, employee, E, may be subjected to great pressures by his or her superior to "color" reports, cover up damaging information, etc. If E is caught in such a situation, if the pressures are severe (e.g., loss of job, permanently damaged reputation, etc.), and if there is no way for E to escape the situation by appealing to authorities in the organization above the level of his or her immediate superior, then E may well have an excuse for forwarding deceptive information. Indeed, the person immediately responsible for E's wrongful action would appear to be E's superior. At the same time, one well might want to ask why responsibility for E's wrongful act should not extend further up in the organization. That is to say, one could claim that top-level executives have a duty to do their best to ensure truthful communications within their organizations, and that as a result, these individuals have an obligation to provide means for persons such as E to take action against superiors who pressure them to distort company communications. If these claims are true, and if an organization does not take steps to provide protection for employees who are pressured to deceive, does this mean that top-level management must assume some (or all) of the responsibility for lies prompted by pressure from above? The question is an interesting one; and it is one I will, quite happily, allow readers the freedom to answer for themselves.

NOTES

1. Throughout, I will be using 'communications' to refer to all messages internal to the organization which are relevant to the occupations of the organization. For example, all employees' oral, written, formal, and informal comments concerning business will be covered, while discussions among workers concerning football games or parties will not be counted as communications. Also excluded will be communications of all sorts between and among different corporations.

2. R. P. Cort, *Communicating With Employees* (Prentice-Hall: 1963), p. 10.

3. R. M. D'Aprix, *How's That Again?* (Dow Jones-Irwin: 1971), p. 10.

4. The term 'lie' has a variety of different uses in our language. In one use, 'lie' and 'deception' are synonymous. On the other hand, there are some philosophers who believe it is important to distinguish between lying and deception (see, for example, J. Ellin, "The Solution to a Dilemma in Medical Ethics," *Westminster Institute Review,* Vol. 1 (1980), pp. 3ff.). I do not wish to become embroiled in this conflict; and throughout, I will use 'lie' to mean 'intentionally deceptive statement'. For all intents and purposes, this is the definition accepted by Sissela Bok in her classic work on lying. (See S. Bok, *Lying* (Vintage Books: 1979), p. 14.)

5. Proponents of this extreme view almost always accept some version of deontology; hence the name 'deontological extremism'. For a discussion of deontology in ethics see the introduction to this text.

6. I. Kant, *The Doctrine of Virtue,* trans. M. J. Gregor (Harper & Row: 1964), p. 23.

7. For an excellent discussion of this doctrine see Bok, op. cit., pp. 37ff.

8. For a detailed discussion of teleology in ethics see the introduction to this text.

9. For a statement of Friedman's views see M. Friedman, "The Social Responsibility of Business Is to Increase Its Profits," *The New York Times Magazine,* Sept. 13, 1970, pp. 33, 122-126, and "Milton Friedman Responds," *Business and Society Review* (Spring, 1972), pp. 5-16.

10. J. Humber, "Milton Friedman and the Corporate Executive's Conscience," *Philosophy in Context,* Vol. 10 (1980), pp. 71-80.

11. A. H. Goldman, *The Moral Foundations of Professional Ethics* (Littlefield, Adams and Co.: 1980).

12. This view is accepted by philosophers who disagree about almost everything else. For example, Bok notes that Hume, Wittgenstein, and Rawls all agree that moral justification needs to have the capability of being made public. (See Bok, op. cit., p. 97.)

13. There are numerous studies which show, as R. Cort says, that "the divergence between what the employee thinks and what the supervisor *thinks* he thinks is nothing less than astounding." (See Cort, op. cit., p. 11.) If misunderstanding in the corporation is this widespread, how can anyone predict, with any degree of certainty, the beneficial effects which a deceptive communication will have?

Corporate Policy Statement

Within H. B. Fuller the ability to communicate with each other takes on added dimensions as we continue to grow as a company and as society becomes more complex. We must communicate purposefully, clearly, openly, and with understanding. Our responsibilities are:

(1) The manager will inform you of the goals and objectives of your department and how this relates to the company's total business, and maximize the flow of information to all employees with regard to company plans and decisions. We must maintain an atmosphere where all employees can openly discuss their views and the views of management. This will be accomplished through the following methods: (a) individual and group meetings, (b) internal publications, (c) budget reports, (d) productivity and/or sales reports, (e) written or verbal explanation of management's views on a particular subject.

(2) Your ideas and suggestions will be listened to and evaluated by your supervisor and an answer provided. This will be accomplished through the following methods: (a) verbal suggestion acknowledged in the discussion, (b) written suggestion will be acknowledged in writing by the manager.

(3) The company will let you know what is expected of you in the performance of your job by the following methods: (a) instructions and directions from your supervisor, (b) job description, (c) formal performance appraisal on request.

(4) The company will communicate a description and explanation of all fringe benefits and facilitate the utilization of all benefit programs by providing easily accessible assistance and interpretations. This will be accomplished by (a) Personnel Handbook, (b) Employee Benefit Statement, (c) your calling the Human Resources Department, 800-328-6816.

(5) The company will periodically determine the attitudes of employees on a variety of subjects as a basis for continued development of our employee relations function. The results will be reported to the employees.

(6) At our periodic meetings, managers and executives combined will

work to develop continuing understanding of corporate philosophy and programs.

(7) The company will implement a system of periodic employee/management communications meetings at all organizational levels with appropriate feedback systems to assure communications to employees and from employees to management. At each location a committee will meet quarterly to discuss: (a) current operations, (b) corporate goals and performance, (c) local operational goals, (d) new or existing programs, (e) employee suggestions or requests. The committee will consist of the local manager and an employee representative, appointed by the local manager from each job category. A report of each meeting will be submitted to all employees at the local operation, plus copies of the report will be submitted to all line management not in attendance at the meeting, the company's president, and the Human Resources Department. Any member of the committee has the option of calling a special meeting if circumstances warrant.

H. B. Fuller Company

Selected Bibliography

Barry, V. *Moral Issues in Business.* 2nd ed. Belmont, Cal.: Wadsworth, 1982, ch. 7.

Blumberg, P. "Corporate Responsibility and the Employee's Duty of Loyalty and Obedience: A Preliminary Inquiry," in *The Corporate Dilemma.* Votaw, D., and Sethi, S., eds. Englewood Cliffs, N.J.: Prentice-Hall, 1973, pp. 82–113.

Boulton, D. *The Grease Machine.* New York: Harper and Row, 1978.

Garrett, T. *Business Ethics.* Englewood Cliffs, N.J.: Prentice-Hall, 1966, ch. III.

Huseman, R., Logue, C., and Freshley, D., eds. *Readings in Interpersonal and Organizational Communication.* 2nd ed. Boston: Holbrook, 1973.

Jacobs, L. "Business Ethics and the Law: Obligations of a Corporate Executive." *The Business Lawyer,* 28 (July, 1973), 1063–88.

Jacoby, N., Nehemkis, P., and Eells, R. *Bribery and Extortion in World Business.* London: Collier Macmillan, 1977.

Kintner, E., and Lahr, J., eds. *Intellectual Property Law Primer: A Survey of the Law of Patents, Trade Secrets, Trademarks, Franchises, Copyrights, Personality, and Entertainment Rights.* New York: Macmillan, 1974.

Lieberstein, S. *Who Owns What Is in Your Head?: Trade Secrets and the Mobile Employee.* New York: Hawthorne Books, 1979.

Margolis, J. "Conflict of Interest and Conflicting Interests," in *Ethical Theory and Business.* Beauchamp, T., and Bowie, N., eds. Englewood Cliffs, N.J.: Prentice-Hall, 1979, pp. 361–72.

McGuire, J. "Conflict of Interest: Whose Interest? And What Conflict?" in *Ethics, Free Enterprise, and Public Policy.* DeGeorge, R., and Pichler, J., eds. New York: Oxford University Press, 1978, pp. 214–31.

Michalos, A. "The Loyal Agent's Argument," in *Ethical Theory and Business.* Beauchamp, T., and Bowie, N., eds. Englewood Cliffs, N.J.: Prentice-Hall, 1979, pp. 338–48.

Seavey, W. *Agency.* St. Paul, Minn.: West Publishing Co., 1964.

Thayer, L. *Communication and Communication Systems.* Homewood, Ill.: Richard D. Irwin, 1968.

4

HIRING AND DISCHARGE

INTRODUCTION

Selection procedures regarding hiring and discharge are of central concern to employees, employers, and society at large. Aside from salary considerations, they are undoubtedly a top priority among employees, who, from an ethical perspective, want fair procedures. Society has a similar interest, and the 1964 Civil Rights Act bans employment selection procedures that discriminate on the basis of race, sex, color, religion or national origin. Employers generally wish to structure selection procedures so they have utility for the firm. A key question, then, is whether criteria for selection procedures can be stated that are both fair to employees and have utility for the firm and society as a whole.

In their article on hiring practices, Snoeyenbos and Almeder argue that the 1964 Civil Rights Act is consistent with and reinforces a private enterprise, free market conception of the economy. They go on to offer what they believe to be fair suggestions having utility across the scope of the hiring procedure: job analysis, job description, job specification, recruitment, testing, and interviewing. The ethical basis of recent court cases regarding hiring practices is also explored. The case study in this section provides a specific context for discussing hiring practices.

Although there is no doubt that women, blacks, and members of certain other minority groups have been discriminated against in business practices in our society, there is considerable disagreement as to whether they are entitled to preferential employment treatment. Ernest van den Haag argues that reverse discrimination is both unfair and has disutility. In response, Humber develops a specific proposal for preferential treatment of disadvantaged individuals, which he claims not only has overall utility but is fair to all. These articles are prefaced by contrasting judicial comments regarding the recent Weber case, in which white craft workers at Kaiser Aluminum charge that their firm's affirmative action program violates the Civil Rights Act of 1964 by discriminating against white employees in favor of blacks.

The trauma of being fired has been compared to that attending divorce or the death of a loved one. Snoeyenbos and Roberts examine the legal basis of termination policy and provide an ethical rationale for altering present law. Criteria for a just cause dismissal are offered, along with a policy for due process within the firm, and an argument that the harmful effects of termination should be mitigated even if the firing is based on just cause and the employee has received due process. The case study invites discussion regarding a specific discharge and the way it is handled.

Hiring

Hiring Procedures at World Imports Inc.

World Imports Inc. purchases a variety of unassembled chandeliers and lamps from foreign producers for assembly at its manufacturing facility in Philadelphia and for sale through ten local outlets. The company also manufactures a variety of electrical items: fixtures, wall receptacles, plugs, switches, etc., for use in its own products and for sale to other assemblers of more complex electrical equipment. The company, privately owned and employer of 380 people, has the following organizational structure:

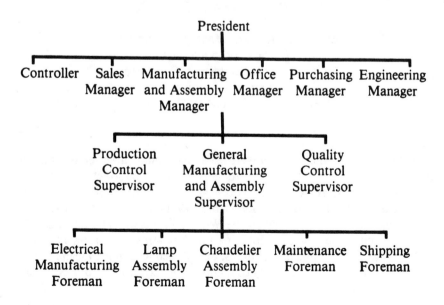

In the past, World Imports' personnel relations were handled by the manager of the office staff, but this manager had no formal training in personnel management and little experience with, or knowledge of, manufacturing or assembly work. The president, noting that his firm had a high personnel turnover ratio, significant personnel problems, and a high quality control rejection ratio, decided to create a personnel department at the manager level. He knew just who he wanted to hire as manager — Jim Miller, the son of his controller, a recent graduate in management, and a part-time maintenance worker at the firm for several years. Shortly after Jim graduated he was offered the job and accepted it.

Jim immediately set out to analyze and resolve the firm's personnel problems. He was a bit uneasy about the way in which he had been hired, and decided to focus initially on selection procedures, particularly in the manufacturing and assembly division, where most of the problems had occurred. He first checked for compliance with Equal Employment Opportunity Commission (EEOC) guidelines, and found that the firm was well within the 80% selection ratio guidelines for blacks and women, although he did find most minority group members holding low-level assembly jobs. He noted that no job analysis data were available for positions in the manufacturing and assembly division. When a position opened up, the foreman, the general supervisor, the division manager, and the office manager discussed the issue; the latter wrote up a brief job description and specification, which also served as an advertisement in the local newspapers. A current ad ran as follows:

ELECTRICIAN-ASSEMBLER

Electrician for mfgr., assembly and testing of electrical products. Responsible
for equipment maintenance. Supervises 2
helpers. Experience preferred. Good
benefits. Day shift. 634-0297.

Candidates for the position were asked to submit three references, and the office manager selected one to be queried about facts of previous employment. To facilitate the process, an informal telephone reference check was conducted. After undesirable candidates were eliminated, the remaining candidates were given the Wonderlic Personnel Test. This is a general intelligence test that contains items relating to verbal, arithmetical, clerical, and judgmental abilities, and is used as a quick means of estimating the general mental ability of adults in industrial situations. Standard questions are:

1. The eleventh month of the year is _____.
2. SEVERE is the opposite of: 1) harsh 2) stern 3) tender 4) rigid 5) unyielding _____.
3. Which word is different from the other?
   1) certainty   2) dubiousness   3) assuredness   4) confidence 5) 5) sureness _____.
4. Answer yes or no. Does B.C. mean "before Christ?" _____.

In order to be considered for hiring, a candidate's scores must exceed the norm on this test. The remaining candidates are interviewed by a group consisting of the division manager, the general supervisor, and the foreman. The interview is unstructured, but the following items are to be considered and subsequently discussed: appearance and mannerisms, home and family background, education, motivation, work history, personality, and health.

After the interviews are complete, the foreman, the general supervisor, the division manager, and the office manager review reference checks, test results and interviews, and then make a joint selection.

For Discussion

If you had Jim Miller's job as World Imports' personnel manager, what steps would you take to see that the firm's selection procedures were made both fairer to the candidates considered and of greater utility to the firm?

Milton Snoeyenbos
Robert Almeder

Ethical Hiring Practices

Whether one owns a firm, manages it, invests in it, works for it, purchases its products or relies on others who purchase its products, in some way we all have an important stake in a company's hiring practices. The firm seeks to hire those individuals who will contribute to its goals of efficiency and profitability. The individual seeks a position that is commensurate with his skills and will reward his efforts. Consumers want a quality product at the lowest possible cost, and this is, in part, a function of the quality of labor hired. In addition, our society also has an interest in hiring practices; since passage of the 1964 Civil Rights Act, we have attempted to ensure that candidates will be considered on the basis of merit rather than race, color, religion, sex, or national origin. An important question, then, is whether the stated interests of the firm, the prospective employee, and the larger society can all be met successfully and simultaneously within a private enterprise, free market economy.

In this article we argue for an affirmative answer to this question. In particular, we argue that the Civil Rights Act is consistent with and reinforces the private enterprise, free market economic framework. Thus, in addition to the interests of employer and prospective employee, the interests of society, as expressed in the Civil Rights Act, must be taken into consideration in developing an ethics of hiring. Keeping these interests in balanced perspective, we then discuss ethical dimensions of the employee selection procedure: job analysis, job description, job specification, recruitment, testing, and interviewing.

I. THE FREE MARKET AND THE MORALITY
OF THE CIVIL RIGHTS ACT

Although a private enterprise, free market based economy may be characterized in a variety of ways, the following features are commonly regarded as central:

1. A system of property in which private individuals are the primary owners.
2. A method of enforcing contracts between individuals and also between the economic units individuals construct.
3. An open, competitive market structure in which:
   a. Individuals have free access to the market as producers and consumers.
   b. Resources and products can be moved freely among firms and geographic locations.
   c. Prices and wages are set voluntarily without governmental interference.
   d. Producers and consumers have reasonably complete information about market transactions, prices, and wages.
   e. Each producer has a small enough share of a particular product that it cannot significantly affect market price.

Like the frictionless wheel, this idealized conception is an abstraction only more or less approximated, while never fully realized. For example, in many cases consumers do not actually have relatively complete market information, and in a number of our industries today a small group of firms have oligopolistic power that clearly affects market prices. On the whole, however, with the exception of legislation sanctioning monopolistic utilities and labor legislation such as the Clayton and Wagner Acts granting anti-trust exemption to unions, American society has basically supported this type of economic structure. We see this, for example, in the Sherman Act, which encourages competition by precluding restraints of trade and monopoly; in the Pure Food and Drug Act, which requires accurate labeling of products and thereby helps consumers realize (3d); and, more to the point of this article, the 1964 Civil Rights Act.

Although the United States has long had a significant amount of legislation on the statute books banning discrimination (in particular, the Fifth, Thirteenth, and Fourteenth Amendments to the Constitution), specific legislation regarding discrimination in employment was not enacted until 1964. Title VII of the 1964 Civil Rights Act (as amended by the Equal Employment Opportunity Act of 1972) mandates that employers cannot discriminate on the basis of race, color, religion, sex, or national origin; specifically, it is illegal for an employer to:

A. Fail or refuse to hire or to discharge an individual or otherwise to discriminate against any individual with respect to his compensation, terms, conditions, or privileges of employment, because of such individual's race, color, religion, sex, or national origin.

B. Limit, segregate, or classify his employees or applicants for employment in any way that would deprive or tend to deprive any individual of employment opportunities or otherwise adversely affect his status as an employee, because of such individual's race, color, religion, sex, or national origin.[1]

There is no doubt that this legislation restricts an employer's right to freely establish contractual agreements with employees; if an employer hires only white males, and openly discriminates against other classes of people, his act is simply illegal. In a sense, then, it limits the contractual rights of individuals presupposed by (2) above, and represents a governmental intrusion in the market. On the other hand, the act enhances (3a), for, if discrimination occurs, individuals are denied access to the market. In this sense, the Civil Rights Act is like the Sherman Act. In limiting contractual agreements that restrain trade or lead to the formation of monopolies, the Sherman Act enhances competition by encouraging the existence of competing firms in an industry. Similarly, by banning discriminatory employment agreements, the Civil Rights Act enhances market competition by ensuring that all individuals have fair access to the market, and that hiring, compensation, and promotion decisions are based on merit or job performance, not on characteristics that are unrelated to job success.

The ethical justification for the Civil Rights Act rests on both consequentialist and nonconsequentialist grounds. From management's standpoint, hiring, compensation, and promotion decisions should be based on merit and job performance-related factors rather than race, sex, etc., because the efficient, productive employee maximizes profit. Since such a worker also enhances product quality and lowers product price, he also benefits the consumer. Thus, it is simply bad business to hire, compensate, and promote on the basis of factors unrelated to merit and job performance. Moreover, even if a firm could successfully compete with a product manufactured by persons hired under policies that violate the principle embedded in the Civil Rights Act, such policies tend, as a rule, to limit access to and participation in the market. Depending on the size of the discriminated group, such policies may have serious social consequences. If the group in question is large, the result may be massive social upheaval. In such cases, utility points in the direction of adoption of a nondiscriminatory employment principle. If the group is small, however, the consequences of discrimination may also be relatively small, and utility may be difficult to calculate. Nonetheless, many utilitarians argue that unjust policies generally produce bad social consequences over the long term. Nonconsequentialist factors must also be considered. Discrimination in hiring is wrong because the person discriminating would never want to be treated in the manner that he is treating the prospective employee. On the whole then, the Civil Rights Act is morally justified on both consequentialist and nonconsequentialist grounds. Furthermore, insofar as it enhances market access, it is consistent with and reinforces the private enterprise, free market economic model that most Americans advocate. Keeping the interests of the firm, prospective employee, and society in balanced perspective, let us now focus on the ethics of hiring practices.

II. Hiring Practices

In the initial stages of the hiring process, a job opening is identified and the personnel manager performs a *job analysis*. Relevant information is collected and written up as a *job description* that details the job's main features and activities necessary for effective performance; it lists what the worker does and how he is to do it. In turn, the job description is used to develop a *job specification* which lists the necessary qualifications, i.e., knowledge, abilities, and experience needed to successfully perform the job. The organization then develops a pool of candidates by *recruiting,* and selects a person, primarily on the basis of *tests, interviews,* and reference checks. Although there can be other dimensions to the hiring process, the aspects denoted by the italicized terms above are the most important and the most commonly used, and on them our discussion will focus.

Job Analysis. From an ethical and practical standpoint, it is important for the personnel manager to conduct an accurate and thorough job analysis. The firm is interested in effective and efficient job performance that will enable it to maximize its goals. An accurate job description and job specification rest on having a detailed analysis of the position to be filled, and testing and interviewing should focus on those factors mentioned in the job description and specification, i.e., factors relevant to job performance. Utility for the firm thus requires a thorough analysis of the position to be filled. Fairness to the prospective employee also entails a thorough, accurate job analysis. The applicant should seek placement in a position where he can be rewarded commensurate with his ability, motivation, and output. If a job far exceeds or falls far short of a person's potential, these aims will not be realized. Since an individual typically seeks a position on the basis of a job description and job specification, and these rest on a job analysis, a person cannot seek a position commensurate with what he has to offer unless the employer conducts an accurate, thorough job analysis. Job analysis is also important in securing compliance with society's equal employment legislation. As we shall see, the law and federal guidelines require that personnel selection procedures must have validity, i.e., such procedures must represent actual, relevant aspects of job behavior. Since an accurate account of such behavior is typically developed in a job analysis, the law mandates that an employer conduct a thorough job analysis.

Let us now focus on the specifics of job analysis. If we assume we are dealing with an existing position to be filled, the personnel manager should not merely rely on the existing job description and job specification. A thorough job analysis requires a detailed understanding of the position as seen by its present jobholder and his supervisors. To acquire this understanding, the personnel manager can conduct interviews, observe the present employee on the job, or utilize questionnaires.

Questionnaires are frequently used to analyze a job. The employee is given a list of questions relating to various tasks and is asked to check whether he performs them and, if so, how long it takes. Other questions may be more open-ended, and simply ask the person to describe in writing the nature of some aspect of the job. But it is doubtful that a questionnaire can itself provide a thorough job analysis, since it places emphasis on the jobholder's ability to report accurately on his job functions. In practice this ability is often lacking, and hence information secured by a questionnaire is often incomplete or inconsistent. Questionnaires can, however, provide background information for a more thorough interview.

Observation of the incumbent jobholder can provide relevant information if the job involves routine or repetitive physical skills, but it is hardly sufficient for jobs requiring the exercise of judgment (e.g., paramedic) or those requiring a considerable amount of unquantifiable mental activity (e.g., draftsman). In these cases, observation must be coupled with an interview to obtain a thorough job analysis.

Interviews with the job incumbent and his supervisors are perhaps the most common way of conducting a job analysis. In many cases the utility of an interview is strengthened if it is used in conjunction with a questionnaire and direct observation of the incumbent jobholder. The interview can reveal information not obtainable by observation and can be used to confirm and clarify data gathered by both observation and the questionnaire. Since job incumbents frequently view the job analysis interview as an evaluation procedure, the most serious problem with such interviews is that the information received may be distorted. Edwin Flippo offers the following practical advice to avoid misunderstandings and to secure accurate information:

1. Prepare for the interview; rapport is facilitated if the worker feels he is not talking to a person totally ignorant of his job.
2. Introduce yourself so the worker and supervisor know who you are and why you are there.
3. Show a sincere interest in the worker and the job being analyzed.
4. Do not try to tell the employee how to do his job; your task is to obtain and organize information.
5. Verify the information obtained.[2]

Job Description. Assuming the personnel manager has a thorough, accurate job analysis, the next step is to write up a job description. This typically includes: (1) a job identification, which lists items such as the job title, department, division, plant location, and pay range; (2) a job summary detailing the position's procedures and responsibilities; it describes the duties performed, how they are to be performed, and the purpose of each duty, and (3) an account of working conditions.

A controversy has arisen recently concerning the degree of specificity necessary or desirable for job descriptions. Some management theorists argue for a detailed account of tasks, duties, and working conditions, whereas others favor a more unstructured or general job description. It is difficult to resolve this issue in a comprehensive manner because the nature of the job plays an important part in selecting the proper approach, e.g., managerial positions will typically require a more general description than a job on a factory line. In most cases, however, we favor a relatively specific job description. Arguments against a detailed job description are that it: (1) limits the jobholders initiative and creativity, (2) is easily dated with job changes, and (3) can be used by the employee to avoid additional duties. But (3) is a motivational issue; the unmotivated employee could also seek to avoid additional duties by appeal to the vagueness of a nonspecific job description, in which case changes as mentioned in (2) would also have to be addressed and the job description made more specific. And, against (1), the employee with initiative might be able to develop responsibilities in addition to those already specified in some detail, which might lead to a job description revision that increases the productivity of other employees holding the same type of job. An additional factor related directly to hiring is that if the job description is used to help train new workers how to perform their jobs, it should contain specifics.

There are two major reasons favoring a specific, complete job description. The pragmatic reason is that the law now requires it. In the case of hiring, selection tests are based on the job description; one tests for the ability to perform tasks specified in the job description. In *Griggs v. Duke Power Co.* (1971), the Supreme Court held that selection tests must have validity, i.e., they must accurately represent actual on-the-job activities. In *Albemarle Paper v. Moody* (1975), the Supreme Court held that if tests are used to screen candidates for a job, then the duties and responsibilities of that job must be carefully analyzed and described prior to testing. More fundamentally, utility for the firm and fairness to the prospective employee are enhanced when the employee knows what is expected of him. Turnover costs relating to mismatched employees who resign, and the long range consequences of retaining mismatched employees, favor having the employer provide a relatively specific and complete job description.

Job Specification. A job specification lists qualifications needed to perform the job. In some cases this may seem straightforward, as in law or accounting, where specific training is required and professional standards are well articulated. Where the firm intends to hire an untrained person and train him for a job, careful consideration must be given to developing a set of qualifications. In either case, however, morality and legality require that the employer use only those qualifying criteria that relate directly to success on the job.

The legality of this principle was established in the case of *Griggs v. Duke Power Co.* (1971). From 1955 on Duke Power required a high school education for all positions in its Dan River power plant except the lowest level janitorial jobs. In 1966, Willie Griggs brought suit against Duke, claiming the educational requirement for the position of coal handler was discriminatory because it was not valid, i.e., not related to success on the job. Coal handlers unload, weigh, and transport coal via the use of heavy equipment. Duke argued that, as its business became more technologically oriented, it needed the education requirement, that, for example, a coal handler must have language facility in order to read manuals relating to the use of machines and equipment he operates. Duke also argued that the educational requirement provided some basis for believing that its employees would be able to advance to supervisory positions. But Duke allowed that no studies had been conducted to that time to establish that the educational requirement was related to job performance and success.

Although lower courts had decided the case basically in favor of Duke, the U.S. Supreme Court heard the case in part to resolve the question of whether an employer is prevented by the 1964 Civil Rights Act from requiring a high school education as a condition of employment when such education has not been shown to be significantly related to successful job performance and when it disqualifies a disproportionally high number of minority applicants. The Court found that "Congress has placed on the employer the burden of showing that any given requirement must have a manifest relationship to the employment in question."[3] In an 8-0 ruling, the Court decided against Duke because the educational requirement was not shown to be related to successful job performance. In fact, it was pointed out that white employees without a high school education (who had become coal handlers before the educational requirement was instituted) performed the job satisfactorily.

The morality of employing only qualifying criteria that relate to job success rests on both consequentialist and nonconsequentialist grounds. If job qualifications are set too high for the actual job, the individual hired may not be able to work to potential; and if they are set too low, the individual hired may not be able to perform successfully. In either case, job satisfaction is not liable to be achieved and the firm's efficiency and profitability are liable to be impaired, with consequent disutility to the firm and society. In addition, those individuals not hired have been denied fair access to the market.

Recruitment. In recruiting candidates a firm typically attempts to obtain a large selection ratio, i.e., a large number of applicants relative to the positions open. In this way the company has a better chance of selecting the best person for the job. However, fairness to the job seeker and utility for the firm both require that the personnel manager seek to attract only relevant candidates. Interviewing and testing are expensive activities for the firm, and a considerable amount of applicants' time and money can be wasted if an overzealous recruiter, intent on maximizing his selection ratio, fails to recruit only relevant candidates who can fill the job description and specification. Also, we should not overlook the psychological damage to an otherwise qualified applicant who is rejected in the early stages of the screening process (perhaps with no subsequent explanation) because of a recruiting mismatch.

A recruiting device, such as an advertisement, should therefore be relatively complete. It should contain items such as the job title, duties, qualifications and experience required, working conditions, salary, and fringe benefits. It should also be somewhat detailed, if that is possible; relevant portions of the job description and specification could in certain cases be included. Of course, the amount of information included must be balanced with the cost of the advertisement. In addition, fairness requires that the employer reveal his identity if he expects the job seeker to provide detailed biographical data. It also requires that the advertisement portray the firm in a realistic manner. Hiring is only one aspect of personnel management; retaining good employees is another important function. Job satisfaction is a key element in attaining a high retention ratio, and a considerable amount of job dissatisfaction is traceable to unrealistic recruitment efforts that attempt to make a firm "look good" to applicants. Thus, utility to the firm and fairness to the applicant necessitate realistic recruiting techniques.

Testing. The hiring process through the recruitment stage involves gathering applicants. Subsequent steps involve the rejection of candidates until available positions are filled. While the actual selection process may involve many stages, including application blanks and reference checks, we will discuss only the testing and interviewing steps.

Psychological testing became an important tool in the hiring process in the 1920s. It held the promise of bringing scientific objectivity to selection procedures, and this promise has certainly been partially realized. The psychologists' intelligence, physical, achievement, aptitude, and personality tests have enabled many people to make better career selections and have helped firms to better match employees and available job, both of which lead to increased employee job satisfaction, productivity, and profitability. During the 1960s, however, with increased concern over civil rights, scientists were led to restudy tests because of the fact that a high percentage of minorities were failing them. For example, one study showed that only 6% of blacks could pass a battery of standardized tests, compared with 58% of whites.[4] Critics of such tests pointed out that they were culture bound, and reflected the majority culture. Also, the predictive ability of such tests was questioned; one study found that most industrial occupations tests had little validity.[5] Other studies indicated that many workers who could not pass commonly used tests could, nevertheless, perform tasks the tests were designed to measure as well as individuals who did pass.[6]

The 1964 Civil Rights Act banned tests that were designed or used to discriminate, but it did not ban all tests:

> . . . nor shall it be an unlawful employment practice for an employer to give and to act upon the results of any professionally developed ability test provided that such test, its administration or action upon the results is not designed, intended or used to discriminate because of race, color, religion, sex, or national origin.[7]

The Equal Employment Opportunity Commission, established to enforce employment antidiscrimination laws, interpreted "professionally developed ability test" to mean a test that:

> fairly measures the knowledge or skills required by the particular job or class of jobs which the applicant seeks, or which fairly affords the employer a chance to measure the applicant's ability to perform a particular job or class of jobs. The fact that a test was prepared by an individual or organization claiming expertise in test preparation does not, without more, justify its use.[8]

Now, in addition to addressing the issue of educational requirements, the *Griggs v. Duke Power* case also addressed testing. Griggs argued that there were no scientific studies establishing Duke's tests as job related and that they did not "fairly measure the knowledge or skills required by the particular job" sought. The plaintiff also claimed that Duke's tests discriminated against blacks. Duke argued that, although there were no formal studies validating its tests for the particular jobs available in its power plants, nevertheless some *general* measure of intelligence and aptitude was required for hiring people to work in its complex plants and for ensuring their capability of advancement to supervisory levels. The company also argued that its tests should be acceptable because they were "professionally developed" as required by law, and served a legitimate business purpose.

In its 8-0 decision, the U.S. Supreme Court rejected Duke's claim that its general intelligence and ability tests were permitted by the 1964 Civil Rights Act. The Court held that employment tests must be *validated,* i.e., they must demonstrably measure what they purpose to measure, which, in the case of a selection test, means the test must bear a predictive relationship to *actual* job performance regarding a particular job or type of work. Since Duke's general intelligence and ability tests were not validated, they could not be used:

> Congress has placed on the employer the burden of showing that any given requirement must have a manifest relationship to the employment in question . . .

nothing in the (Civil Rights) Act precludes the use of testing or measuring procedures; obviously they are useful. What Congress has forbidden is giving these devices and mechanisms controlling force unless they are demonstrably a reasonable measure of job performance.[9]

There are both consequentialist and nonconsequentialist grounds for the Supreme Court's decision. The firm's aim is to staff positions with people who can best enable it to attain its goals, and the Court's decision forces the employer to show that his test is actually related to job performance. This should lead to greater efficiency and profitability for the company. The consequences for the jobholder, in terms of success and satisfaction, should be better for the person whose qualifications fit the position than for a person who is mismatched with a job via an invalid test. Also, society not only benefits from the avoidance of mismatches, but also from the lessening of social unrest resulting from awareness that selection tests must be based on merit rather than factors unrelated to job performance. On the nonconsequentialist side, a test that is not valid can hardly be fair to an otherwise qualified candidate who is rejected via the test. And not only does the decision help ensure fairness in selection, it also reinforces the private enterprise, free market conception of the economy by helping to provide equal employment opportunity and fair access to the market. Hence, the decision promotes both social justice and economic efficiency.

Special care must be taken to ensure the validity of certain sorts of tests that may be used in screening candidates. Some firms use polygraphs to screen, and carefully fashioned tests of this sort can have validity. But the nature of the device is such that the questioner typically follows up on a response, and this can easily lead into non-job related areas of investigation that may represent a serious invasion of privacy. Similarly, personality tests, used to measure stability, motivation and other aspects of character, are frequently problematic. They may invade privacy and are difficult to evaluate properly. In many cases the relationship between personality traits and job success is tenuous. Where such a relationship can be established, however, it can both help the employee to better himself and his placement in the organization, and also enable the employer to provide the applicant more adequate placement. The American Psychological Association has ethical standards that, together with the requirement of test validity, would protect significantly the rights of test takers:

1. The individual test taker has the right to the confidentiality of the test results and the right to informed consent regarding the use of those test results.
2. The individual has the right to expect that only people qualified to interpret the scores will have access to those scores, or that sufficient information will accompany the test scores to ensure their appropriate interpretation.

3. The individual has the right to expect that the test is equally fair to all test takers in the sense of being equally familiar or unfamiliar, so that the test results reflect the test taker's true abilities. [10]

Interviewing. Tests are infrequently used as the only selection technique; most often they are used in conjunction with interviews. In fact, after passage of the Civil Rights Act, when it was found that some of the standard tests were invalid, many personnel managers dropped testing altogether and based their selection decisions primarily on interviews. But there are two major problems with this approach to hiring. On the one hand, as Robert Dipboye, Richard Arvey and David Terpstra have pointed out, there are problems with the interview itself. Interviewers frequently:

1. Issue judgments that are less reliable than objective tests; they frequently disagree in their assessments of a job candidate.
2. Miss or suppress information, and weigh negative data more than positive data.
3. Judge candidates via an ideal stereotype, e.g., white caucasian interviewers have the ideal of a young, white male.
4. Allow initial impressions to influence subsequent decisions.
5. Judge candidates on the basis of superficial traits such as physical attractiveness or manner of dress. [11]

Thus the interview method is often unreliable and invalid; it yields inconsistent results and fails to accurately predict job success. On the other hand, the courts have extended the validity requirement from tests to *any* selection procedure. In *Rowe v. General Motors* (1972), the Fifth Circuit Court of Appeals ruled against General Motors's practice of relying on its foremen to recommend employees for promotion; the Courts stated, "The foremen base their recommendations on subjective and vague standards, there are no safeguards designed to avert discriminatory practices and a disproportionately small percentage of Negro hourly employees have been promoted or transferred to salaried positions." [12] A 1971 Equal Employment Opportunity Commission decision regarding interviewing, held that "It is essential that the system be objective in nature and be such as to permit review." [13]

The ethical basis of the Court's decisions requiring interviewing validity is the same as we sketched in our discussion of testing. Fairness and utility regarding the person hired, the firm, and members of society require that interviews, and indeed any selection procedure, have validity. Gary Dessler offers some practical suggestions for structuring the interview process in a way that complies with the law and enables the firm to select the best candidate:

1. Select interviewers carefully and train them properly.
2. Know the requirements of the job via a fully developed job analysis, description, and specification.
3. Use a structured guide so that job related questions are asked.
4. Structure the process so that a decision is not premature.
5. Avoid a total reliance on interviews; balance them with tests, reference checks, etc.
6. Validate interviewer decisions as predictors of job success.[14]

Apart from its place in the hiring process, interviews also are used to give job candidates a preview of life in the firm. In many cases a preview is used to make the firm "look good" and "sell" it to the candidate. But there are reasons why a preview should be realistic, i.e., why it should balance the positive and negative aspects of the job and organization. If the candidate has unrealistic expectations, he may become dissatisfied and resign, with attendant turnover costs to the firm and himself; or he may stay on as a dissatisfied employee who affects the firm's productivity and other worker's morale. A recent study indicates that job longevity and satisfaction are increased if a job preview is realistic.[15]

III. Recent Developments

The underlying principle of the *Griggs v. Duke Power* case is this: employer practices that adversely impact on minorities *and* are not validated are illegal. Put another way, if a selection procedure is to be legal then it either has no adverse impact, or if it does have an adverse impact, then the procedure has to be validated. Congress confirmed this principle in the 1972 amendments to Title VII of the 1964 Civil Rights Act. By 1976, however, two different sets of compliance guidelines were being employed by the Equal Employment Opportunity Commission and other federal agencies (Justice, Labor and Civil Service). In 1978, a new, uniform set of compliance guidelines were issued stating, in part, that:

A procedure having adverse impact constitutes discrimination unless justified . . . unless the procedure has been validated.[15]

Although this is equivalent to the *Griggs* principle, the guideline is interpreted to mean that:

A selection procedure which has no adverse impact generally does not violate Title VII. . . . This means that an employer may usually avoid the application of the guidelines by use of procedures which have no adverse impact. If adverse impact exists, it must be justified on grounds of business necessity. Normally this means by validation which demonstrates the relation between the selection procedure and performance on the job.[16]

In other words, on this interpretation if a selection procedure has no adverse impact, then it is legal; *but* if a selection procedure has an adverse impact and is not validated, then it is illegal. An "adverse impact" is vaguely defined as "a substantially different rate of selection in hiring, promotion, or other employment decisions which works to the disadvantage of members of a race, sex, or ethnic group."[17] In practice, however, the guidelines spell out "adverse impact" in terms of selection ratios, i.e., the number of applicants hired divided by the total number of applicants. A selection ratio for any minority group that is less than 80% of the ratio for the group with the highest ratio is generally regarded as evidence of adverse impact.[18]

Now, from both the *Griggs* principle and the above interpretation of the new guidelines we can infer that a legal selection procedure that has adverse impact, must be validated. However, from the *Griggs* principle we cannot infer that if an invalidated selection procedure has no adverse impact, then it is legal; whereas we can infer this from the above interpretation of the new guidelines. Furthermore, the *Griggs* principle cannot be interpreted to imply that if a validated selection procedure has no adverse impact, then it is legal; but we can infer this from the new guidelines. Hence, although we cannot infer from the *Griggs* principle that if a selection procedure has no adverse impact (whether or not it is validated), then it is legal, we can infer this from the new guidelines. Accordingly, under the new guidelines a firm would only have to hire in accordance with the 80% selection ratio rule to be in compliance with the law. This raises the difficult question of the morality of hiring in terms of "quotas" or via affirmative action programs, a topic to which the next section is devoted.

NOTES

1. Civil Rights Act of 1964, Title VII, Section 703 (a).

2. Edwin B. Flippo, *Principles of Personnel Management* (New York: McGraw-Hill, 1966) 2nd ed., pp. 117–9.

3. *Griggs v Duke Power Co.,* 401 US 424, p. 432.

4. *Griggs v Duke Power Co.,* 420 F. 2d., p. 1239.

5. E. E. Ghisselli, *The Validity of Occupational Aptitude Tests* (New York: J. Wiley & Sons, 1966), p. 127.

6. T. A. Fermen, *The Negro and Equal Employment Opportunities* (New York: Frederick A. Praeger, 1968), p. 47.

7. Civil Rights Act of 1964, Title VII, Section 703 (h).

8. *Griggs,* 915 Ct., p. 855.

9. *Griggs*, 401 US 424, pp. 432, 436.

10. Based on Marilyn K. Quantance, "Test Security: Foundation of Public Merit Systems," *Personnel Psychology*, vol. 33, no. 1 (Spring, 1980), pp. 25–32.

11. Robert L. Dipboye, Richard D. Arvey, and David E. Terpstra, "Equal Employment and the Interview," *Personnel Journal*, vol. 55, no. 10 (October, 1976), pp. 520–4.

12. *Rowe vs. General Motors Corp.*, U.S. Court of Appeals, Fifth Circuit (New Orleans), no. 28959, March 2, 1972 (Summarized in the *Bureau of National Affairs Fair Employment Practices Cases*, vol. 4, pp. 445–454).

13. Equal Employment Opportunity Commission Decision no. 72-0703, December 27, 1971 (Summarized in the *Bureau of National Affairs Fair Employment Practice Cases*, vol. 4, pp. 435–437).

14. Gary Dessler, *Personnel Management* (Reston: Reston Publishing, 1981), 2nd ed., pp. 136–142.

15. "Uniform Guidelines on Employee Selection Procedures," *Federal Register*, vol. 43, no. 166 (August 25, 1978), p. 38297.

16. Ibid., pp. 38290–1.

17. Ibid., p. 38307.

18. Ibid., pp. 38291, 38297–8.

Corporate Policy Statements

It is the policy of the Republic National Bank of Dallas to extend equal opportunities to all qualified applicants for employment or staff without regard to race, creed, color, sex, age, or national origin. This policy encompasses all personnel practices including: hiring, placement, upgrading, promotion, transfer, or demotion; recruitment, advertising, or solicitation for employment; treatment during employment, rates of pay or other forms of compensation; selection for training; lay-off or termination. The objective of the bank is to recruit, develop and retain individuals qualified or trainable for positions by virtue of job related standards of education, training, experience, and personal qualifications.

Republic National Bank of Dallas

We believe in equal opportunity for all our employees. Of course, that is the law and we are bound to observe it. But it was a principle with Dow long before it became law. We do not believe that a person's sex, skin color, or national origin, is any basis for discrimination in a worldwide business such as ours. That is not to say we don't discriminate. We do. We hire only the brightest, most creative, most energetic people we can find.

Dow Chemical Co.

Reverse Discrimination

Case Study

United Steelworkers v. Weber

[*What follows are portions of the majority opinion by Justice Brennan, together with selected passages from the dissenting opinion of Justice Rehnquist. Some footnotes have been dropped, with those remaining having been renumbered.* —Eds.]

Mr. Justice Brennan delivered the opinion of the Court.

In 1974 petitioner United Steelworkers of America (USWA) and petitioner Kaiser Aluminum & Chemical Corporation (Kaiser) entered into a master collective-bargaining agreement covering terms and conditions of employment at 15 Kaiser plants. The agreement contained, *inter alia,* an affirmative action plan designed to eliminate conspicuous racial imbalances in Kaiser's then almost exclusively white craft work forces. Black craft hiring goals were set for each Kaiser plant equal to the percentage of blacks in the respective local labor forces. To enable plants to meet these goals, on-the-job training programs were established to teach unskilled production workers — black and white — the skills necessary to become craft workers. The plan reserved for black employees 50% of the openings in these newly created in-plant training programs.

This case arose from the operation of the plan at Kaiser's plant in Gramercy, Louisiana. Until 1974 Kaiser hired as craft workers for that plant only persons who had had prior craft experience. Because blacks had long been excluded from craft unions, few were able to present such credentials. As a

From *United Steelworkers, Etc. v. Weber* 443 U.S. 193, S.Ct. 2721 (1979).

consequence, prior to 1974 only 1.88% (five out of 273) of the skilled craft workers at the Gramercy plant were black, even though the work force in the Gramercy area was approximately 39% black.

Pursuant to the national agreement Kaiser altered its craft hiring practice in the Gramercy plant. Rather than hiring already trained outsiders, Kaiser established a training program to train its production workers to fill craft openings. Selection of craft trainees was made on the basis of seniority, with the proviso that at least 50% of the new trainees were to be black until the percentage of black skilled craft workers in the Gramercy plant approximated the percentage of blacks in the local labor force.

During 1974, the first year of the operation of the Kaiser-USWA affirmative action plan, 13 craft trainees were selected from Gramercy's production work force. Of these, 7 were black and 6 white. The most junior black selected into the program had less seniority than several white production workers whose bids for admission were rejected. Thereafter one of those white production workers, respondent Brian Weber, instituted this class action in the United States District Court for the Eastern District of Louisiana.

The complaint alleged that the filling of craft trainee positions at the Gramercy plant pursuant to the affirmative action program had resulted in junior black employees receiving training in preference to more senior white employees, thus discriminating against respondent and other similarly situated white employees in violation of §§ 703 (a)[1] and (d)[2] of Title VII (of the Civil Rights Act of 1964). The District Court held that the plan violated Title VII, entered a judgment in favor of the plaintiff class, and granted a permanent injunction prohibiting Kaiser and the USWA "from denying plaintiffs, Brian F. Weber and all other members of the class, access to on-the-job training programs on the basis of race." . . . A divided panel of the Court of Appeals for the Fifth Circuit affirmed. . . . We reverse.

We emphasize at the outset the narrowness of our inquiry. Since the Kaiser-USWA plan does not involve state action, this case does not present an alleged violation of the Equal Protection Clause of the Constitution. Further, since the Kaiser-USWA plan was adopted voluntarily, we are not concerned with what Title VII requires or with what a court might order to remedy a past proven violation of the Act. The only question before us is the narrow statutory issue of whether Title VII *forbids* private employers and unions from voluntarily agreeing upon bona fide affirmative action plans that accord racial preferences in the manner and for the purpose provided in the Kaiser-USWA plan. That question was expressly left open in *McDonald v. Santa Fe Trail Trans. Co.*, 427 U.S. 273 (1976) . . . which held, in a case not involving affirmative action, that Title VII protects whites as well as blacks from certain forms of racial discrimination.

Respondent argues that Congress intended in Title VII to prohibit all race-conscious affirmative action plans. Respondent's argument rests upon a literal interpretation of §§ 703 (a) and (d) of the Act. Those sections make it unlawful to "discriminate . . . because of . . . race" in hiring and in the selection of apprentices for training programs. Since, the argument runs, *McDonald v. Santa Fe. Trail Trans. Co.,* settled that Title VII forbids discrimination against whites as well as blacks, and since the Kaiser-USWA affirmative action plan operates to discriminate against white employees solely because they are white, it follows that the Kaiser-USWA plan violates Title VII.

Respondent's argument is not without force. But it overlooks the significance of the fact that the Kaiser-USWA plan is an affirmative action plan voluntarily adopted by private parties to eliminate traditional patterns of racial segregation. In this context respondent's reliance upon a literal construction of §§ 703 (a) and (d) and upon *McDonald* is misplaced. . . . It is a "familiar rule that a thing may be within the letter of the statute and yet not within the statute, because not within its spirit nor within the intention of its makers." *Holy Trinity Church v. United States,* 143 U.S. 457. . . . The prohibition against racial discrimination in §§ 703 (a) and (d) of Title VII must therefore be read against the background of the legislative history of Title VII and the historical context from which the Act arose. . . . Examination of those sources makes clear that an interpretation of the sections that forbade all race-conscious affirmative action would "bring about an end completely at variance with the purpose of the statute" and must be rejected. . . .

Congress' primary concern in enacting the prohibition against racial discrimination in Title VII of the Civil Rights Act of 1964 was with "the plight of the Negro in our economy." 110 Cong. Rec. 6548 (remarks of Sen. Humphrey). Before 1964, blacks were largely relegated to "unskilled and semiskilled jobs." *Id.,* at 6548. . . . Because of automation the number of such jobs was rapidly decreasing. . . . As a consequence "the relative position of the Negro worker (was) steadily worsening. In 1947 the non-white unemployment rate was only 64% higher than the white rate; in 1962 it was 124% higher." *Id.,* at 6547. . . . Congress considered this a serious social problem. As Senator Clark told the Senate:

> The rate of Negro unemployment has gone up consistently as compared with white unemployment for the past 15 years. This is a social malaise and a social situation which we should not tolerate. That is one of the principal reasons why this bill should pass. *Id.,* at 7220.

Congress feared that the goals of the Civil Rights Act — the integration of blacks into the mainstream of American society — could not be achieved unless this trend were reversed. And Congress recognized that that would not be possible unless blacks were able to secure jobs "which have a future." . . . As Senator Humphrey explained to the Senate:

> What good does it do a Negro to be able to eat in a fine restaurant if he cannot afford to pay the bill? What good does it do him to be accepted in a hotel that

is too expensive for his modest income? How can a Negro child be motivated to take full advantage of integrated educational facilities if he has no hope of getting a job where he can use that education? *Id.,* at 6547.

Accordingly, it was clear to Congress that "the crux of the problem (was) to open employment opportunities for Negroes in occupations which have been traditionally closed to them," *Id.,* at 6548 . . . , and it was to this problem that Title VII's prohibition against racial discrimination in employment was primarily addressed.

It plainly appears from the House Report accompanying the Civil Rights Act that Congress did not intend wholly to prohibit private and voluntary affirmative action efforts as one method of solving this problem. The Report provides:

> No bill can or should lay claim to eliminating all of the causes and consequences of racial and other types of discrimination against minorities. There is reason to believe, however, that national leadership provided by the enactment of Federal legislation dealing with the most troublesome problems *will create an atmosphere conducive to voluntary or local resolution of other forms of discrimination.* H.R. Rep. No. 914, 88th Cong., 1st Sess. (1963), at 18. (Emphasis supplied.)

Given this legislative history, we cannot agree with respondent that Congress intended to prohibit the private sector from taking effective steps to accomplish the goal that Congress designated Title VII to achieve. The very statutory words intended as a spur or catalyst to cause "employers and unions to self-examine and to self-evaluate their employment practices and to endeavor to eliminate, so far as possible, the last vestiges of an unfortunate and ignominious page in this country's history," *Albemarle v. Moody,* 422 U.S. 405 . . . , cannot be interpreted as an absolute prohibition against all private, voluntary, race-conscious affirmative action efforts to hasten the elimination of such vestiges.[3] It would be ironic indeed if a law triggered by a Nation's concern over centuries of racial injustice and intended to improve the lot of those who had "been excluded from the American dream for so long," 110 Cong. Rec., at 6552, constituted the first legislative prohibition of all voluntary, private, race-conscious efforts to abolish traditional patterns of racial segregation and hierarchy.

Our conclusion is further reinforced by examination of the language and legislative history of § 703 (j) of Title VII.[4] Opponents of Title VII raised two related arguments against the bill. First, they argued that the Act would be interpreted to *require* employers with racially imbalanced work forces to grant preferential treatment to racial minorities in order to integrate. Second, they argued that employers with racially imbalanced work forces would grant preferential treatment to racial minorities, even if not required to do so by the Act. Had Congress meant to prohibit all race-conscious affirmative action, as respondent urges, it easily could have answered both objections by providing that Title VII would not require or *permit* racially preferential integration efforts. But Congress did not choose such a course. Rather Congress added § 703 (j) which addresses only the first objection. . . . The section does *not* state that "nothing in Title VII shall be interpreted to *permit*" voluntary affirmative efforts to correct racial imbalances. The natural inference is that Congress chose not to forbid all voluntary race-conscious affirmative action.

The reasons for this choice are evident from the legislative record. Title VII could not have been enacted into law without substantial support from legislators in both Houses who traditionally resisted federal regulation of private business. Those legislators demanded as a price for their support that "management prerogatives and union freedoms . . . be left undisturbed to the greatest extent possible." . . . Section 703 (j) was proposed . . . to prevent § 703 of Title VII from being interpreted in such a way as to lead to undue "Federal Government interference with private businesses because of some Federal employee's ideas about racial balance or imbalance." 110 Cong. Rec., at 14314. Clearly, a prohibition against all voluntary, race-conscious, affirmative action efforts would disserve these ends. Such a prohibition would augment the powers of the Federal Government and diminish traditional management prerogatives while at the same time impeding attainment of the ultimate statutory goals. . . .

We need not today define in detail the line of demarcation between permissible and impermissible affirmative action plans. It suffices to hold that the challenged Kaiser-USWA affirmative action plan falls on the permissible side of the line.

(T)he plan does not unnecessarily trammel the interests of the white employees. The plan does not require the discharge of white workers and their replacement with new black hires. . . . Nor does the plan create an absolute bar to the advancement of white employees; half of those trained in the program will be white. Moreover, the plan is a temporary measure; it is not intended to maintain racial balance, but simply to eliminate a manifest racial imbalance. Preferential selection of craft trainees at the Gramercy plant will end as soon as the percentage of black skilled craft workers in the Gramercy plant approximates the percentage of blacks in the local labor force.

We conclude, therefore, that the adoption of the Kaiser-USWA plan for the Gramercy plant falls within the area of discretion left by Title VII to the private sector voluntarily to adopt affirmative action plans designed to eliminate conspicuous racial imbalance in traditionally segregated job categories. Accordingly, the judgment of the Court of Appeals for the Fifth Circuit is *Reversed.*

Mr. Justice Rehnquist, with whom the Chief Justice joins, dissenting.

In a very real sense, the Court's opinion is ahead of its time: it could more appropriately have been handed down five years from now, in 1984, a year coinciding with the title of a book from which the Court's opinion borrows, perhaps subconsciously, at least one idea. Orwell describes in his book a governmental official of Oceania, one of the three great world powers, denouncing the current enemy, Eurasia, to an assembled crowd:

> It was almost impossible to listen to him without being first convinced and then maddened. . . . The speech had been proceeding for perhaps twenty minutes when a messenger hurried onto the platform and a scrap of paper was slipped into the speaker's hand. He unrolled and read it without pausing in his speech. Nothing altered in his voice or manner, or in the content of what he was saying, but suddenly the names were different. Without words said, a wave of understanding rippled through the crowd. Oceania was at war with Eastasia! . . . The banners and posters with which the square was decorated were all wrong!

> (T)he speaker had switched from one line to the other actually in mid-sentence, not only without pause, but without even breaking the syntax. G. Orwell, *Nineteen Eighty-Four,* 182-3 (1949).

Today's decision represents an equally dramatic and equally unremarked switch in the Court's interpretation of Title VII.

The operative sections of Title VII prohibit racial discrimination in employment *simpliciter.* Taken in its normal meaning and as understood by all Members of Congress who spoke to the issue during the legislative debates, this language prohibits a covered employer from considering race when making an employment decision, whether the race be black or white. Several years ago, however, a United States District Court held that "the dismissal of white employees charged with misappropriating company property while not dismissing a similarly charged Negro employee does not raise a claim upon which Title VII relief may be granted." *McDonald v. Santa Fe Trail Transp. Co.,* 427 U.S. 273, 278. This Court unanimously reversed, concluding from the "uncontradicted legislative history" that Title VII prohibits racial discrimination against the white petitioners in this case upon the same standards as would be applicable were they Negroes. . . ." 427 U.S., at 280.

We have never wavered in our understanding that Title VII "prohibits *all* racial discrimination in employment, without exception for any particular employees." *Id.,* at 283. . . . In our most recent discussion of the issue, we uttered words seemingly dispositive of this case: "It is clear beyond cavil that the obligation imposed by Title VII is to provide an equal opportunity for each applicant regardless of race, without regard to whether members of the applicant's race are already proportionately represented in the work force." *Furnco Construction Corp. v. Waters,* 438 U.S. 567,569 (1978).[5]

Today, however, the Court behaves much like the Orwellian speaker earlier described, as if it had been handed a note indicating that Title VII would lead to a result unacceptable to the Court if interpreted here as it was in our prior decisions. Accordingly, without even a break in syntax, the Court rejects "a literal construction of § 703 (a)" in favor of newly discovered "legislative history," which leads it to a conclusion directly contrary to that compelled by the "uncontradicted legislative history" unearthed in *McDonald* and our other prior decisions. Now we are told that the legislative history of Title VII shows that employers are free to discriminate on the basis of race. . . . Our earlier interpretations of Title VII, like the banners and posters decorating the square in Oceania, were all wrong.

As if this were not enough to make a reasonable observer question the Court's adherence to the oft-stated principle that our duty is to construe rather than rewrite legislation, . . . the Court also seizes upon § 703 (j) of Title VII as an independent, or at least partially independent, basis for its holding. Totally ignoring the wording of that section, which is obviously addressed to those charged with the responsibility of interpreting the law rather than those who are subject to its proscriptions, and totally ignoring the months of legislative debates preceding the section's introduction and passage, which demonstrate clearly that it was enacted to prevent precisely what occurred in this case, the Court infers from § 703 (j) that "Congress chose not to forbid all voluntary race-conscious affirmative action."

Thus, by a *tour de force* reminiscent not of jurists such as Hale, Holmes, and Hughes, but of escape artists such as Houdini, the Court eludes clear statutory language, "uncontradicted" legislative history and uniform precedent in concluding that employers are, after all, permitted to consider race in making employment decisions. . . .

Were Congress to act today specifically to prohibit the type of racial discrimination suffered by Weber, it would be hard pressed to draft language better tailored to the task than that found in § 703 (d) of Title VII. . . . Equally suited to the task would be § 703 (a) (2), which makes it unlawful for an employer to classify his employees "in any way which would deprive or tend to deprive any individual of employment opportunities or otherwise adversely affect his status as an employee, because of such individual's race, color, religion, sex, or national origin."

Entirely consistent with these two express prohibitions is the language of § 703 (j) of Title VII, which provides that the Act is not to be interpreted "to require any employer . . . to grant preferential treatment to any individual or to any group because of race. . . ." Seizing on the word "require," the Court infers that Congress must have intended to "permit" this type of racial discrimination. Not only is this reading of § 703 (j) outlandish in the light of flat prohibitions of §§ 703 (a) and (d), but it is totally belied by the Act's legislative history.

Quite simply, Kaiser's racially discriminatory admission quota is flatly prohibited by the plain language of Title VII. This normally dispositive fact,[6] however, gives the Court only momentary pause. An "interpretation" of the statute upholding Weber's claim would, according to the Court, "bring about an end completely at variance with the purpose of the statute." To support this conclusion, the Court calls upon the "spirit" of the Act, which it divines from passages in Title VII's legislative history indicating that enactment of the statute was prompted by Congress' desire "to open employment opportunities for Negroes in occupations which (had) been traditionally closed to them." But the legislative history invoked by the Court to avoid the plain language of §§ 703 (a) and (d) simply misses the point. To be sure, the reality of employment discrimination against Negroes provided the primary impetus for passage of Title VII. But this fact by no means supports the proposition that Congress intended to leave employers free to discriminate against white persons. In most cases, legislative history . . . is more vague than the statute we are called upon to interpret. Here, however, the legislative history of Title VII is as clear as the language of §§ 703 (a) and (d), and it irrefutably demonstrates that Congress meant precisely what it said in §§ 703 (a) and (d) — that *no* racial discrimination in employment is permissible under Title VII, not even preferential treatment of minorities to correct racial imbalance.

Introduced on the floor of the House of Representatives on June 20, 1963, the bill — H.R. 7152 — that ultimately became the Civil Rights Act of 1964 contained no compulsory provisions directed at private discrimination in employment. The bill was promptly referred to the Committee on the Judiciary, where it was amended to include Title VII.

After noting that "(t)he purpose of (Title VII) is to eliminate . . . discrimination in employment based on race, color, religion, or national origin," the Judiciary Committee's report simply paraphrased the provisions of Title VII without elaboration. In a separate Minority Report, however, opponents of the measure on the Committee advanced a line of attack which was reiterated throughout the debates in both the House and Senate and which ultimately led to passage of § 703 (j). Noting that the word "discrimination" was nowhere defined in H.R. 7152, the Minority Report posited a number of hypothetical employment situations, concluding in each example that the employer *"may be forced to hire according to race,* to 'racially balance' those who work for him *in every job classification* or be in violation of Federal law."

When H.R. 7152 reached the House floor, the opening speech in support of its passage was delivered by Representative Celler, Chairman of the House Judiciary Committee. . . . A portion of that speech responded to criticism "seriously misrepresent(ing) what the bill would do and grossly distort(ing) its effects":

(T)he charge has been made that the Equal Employment Opportunity Commission to be established by Title VII of the bill would have the power to prevent a business from employing and promoting the people it wished, and that a "Federal Inspector" could then order the hiring and promotion only of employees of certain races or religious groups. This description of the bill is entirely wrong. . . .

Even (a) court could not order that any preference be given to any particular race, religion or other group, but would be limited to ordering an end of discrimination. The statement that a Federal inspector could order the employment and promotion only of members of a specific racial or religious group is therefore patently erroneous.

. . . (T)he bill would do no more than prevent . . . employers from discriminating against *or in favor of* workers because of their race, religion, or national origin. 110 Cong. Rec. 1518 (1964) (emphasis added).

Representative Celler's construction of Title VII was repeated by several other supporters during the House debate.

The Senate debate was broken into three phases: the debate on sending the bill to Committee, the general debate on the bill prior to invocation of cloture, and the debate following cloture. (1). When debate on the motion to refer the bill to Committee opened, . . . Senator Humphrey . . . was the first to state the proponents' understanding of Title VII. Responding to a political advertisement charging that federal agencies were at liberty to interpret the word "discrimination" in Title VII to require racial balance, Senator Humphrey stated: "(T)he meaning of racial or religious discrimination is perfectly clear. . . . (I)t means a distinction and treatment given to different individuals because of their different race, religion, or national origin." Stressing that Title VII "does not limit the employer's freedom to hire, fire, promote, or demote for any reasons—or no reasons—so long as his action is not based on race," Senator Humphrey further stated that "nothing in the bill would permit any official or court to require any employer or any labor union to give preferential treatment to any minority group." (2). In the opening speech of the formal Senate debate on the bill, Senator Humphrey addressed the main concern of Title VII's opponents, advising that not only does Title VII not require use of racial quotas, *it does not permit* their use. "The truth," stated the floor leader of the bill, "is that this title forbids discriminating against anyone on account of race. This is the simple and complete truth about Title VII." 110 Cong. Rec. 6549 (1964).

At the close of his speech, Senator Humphrey returned briefly to the subject of employment quotas: "It is claimed that the bill would require racial quotas for all hiring, when in fact it provides that race shall not be a basis for making personnel decisions." *Id.,* at 6553.

Senator Kuchel delivered the second major speech in support of H.R. 7152. Senator Kuchel emphasized that seniority rights would in no way be affected by Title VII: "Employers and labor organizations could not discriminate *in favor of or against* a person because of his race, his religion, or his national origin. . . ." *Id.,* at 6564 (emphasis added).

A few days later the Senate's attention focused exclusively on Title VII, as Senator Clark and Case rose to discuss the title of H.R. 7152 on which they shared floor "captain" responsibilities. . . . Of particular relevance to the instant case were their observations regarding seniority rights. As if directing their comments at Brian Weber, the Senators said:

> Title VII would have no effect on established seniority rights. Its effect is prospective and not retrospective. Thus, for example, if a business has been discriminating in the past and as a result has an all-white working force, when the title comes into effect the employer's obligation would be simply to fill future vacancies on a nondiscriminatory basis. He would not be obliged—*or indeed permitted*—to fire whites in order to hire Negroes, *or to prefer Negroes for future vacancies, or, once Negroes are hired, to give them special seniority rights at the expense of the white workers hired earlier. Ibid.* (emphasis added).

Thus with virtual clairvoyance the Senate's leading supporters of Title VII anticipated precisely the circumstances of this case and advised their colleagues that the type of minority preference employed by Kaiser would violate Title VII's ban on racial discrimination. . . .

While the debate in the Senate raged, a bipartisan coalition . . . was working with House leaders . . . on a number of amendments to H.R. 7152 designed to enhance its prospects of passage. . . . One of those clarifying amendments (was) § 703 (j). . . .

The Court draws from the language of § 703 (j) primary support for its conclusion that Title VII's blanket prohibition on racial discrimination in employment does not prohibit preferential treatment of blacks to correct racial imbalance. . . .

Contrary to the Court's analysis, the language of § 703 (j) is precisely tailored to the objection voiced time and again by Title VII's opponents. Not once during the 83 days of debate in the Senate did a speaker, proponent or opponent, suggest that the bill would allow employers *voluntarily* to prefer racial minorities over white persons. In light of Title VII's flat prohibition on discrimination "against any individual . . . because of such individual's race," such a contention would have been, in any event, too preposterous to warrant response. Indeed, speakers on both sides of the issue, as the legislative history makes clear, recognized that Title VII would tolerate no *voluntary* racial preference, whether in favor of blacks or whites. The complaint consistently voiced by the opponents was that Title VII, particularly the word "discrimination," would be *interpreted* by Federal agencies such as the Equal Employment Opportunity Commission to *require* the correction of racial imbalance through the granting of preferential treatment to minorities. Verbal assurances that Title VII would not require—indeed, would not permit—preferential treatment of blacks having failed, supporters of H.R. 7152 responded by proposing an amendment carefully worded to meet, and put to rest, the opposition's charge. Indeed, unlike §§ 703 (a) and (d), which are by their terms directed at entities — e.g., employers, labor unions — whose actions are restricted by Title VII's prohibitions, the language of § 703 (j) is specifically directed at entities — federal agencies and courts — charged with the responsibility of interpreting Title VII's provisions.

In light of the background and purpose of § 703 (j), the irony of invoking the section to justify the result in this case is obvious. The Court's frequent references to the "voluntary" nature of Kaiser's racially discriminatory admission quota bear no relationship to the facts of this case. Kaiser and the Steelworkers acted under pressure from an agency of the Federal Government, the Office of Federal Contract Compliance, which found that minorities were being "underutilized" at Kaiser's plants. That is, Kaiser's work force was racially imbalanced. Bowing to that pressure, Kaiser instituted an admissions quota preferring blacks over whites, thus confirming that the fears of Title VII's opponents were well founded. Today § 703 (j), adopted to allay those fears, is invoked by the Court to uphold imposition of a racial quota under the very circumstances that the section was intended to prevent. . . .

(After introduction of § 703 (j)), the Senate turned its attention to an amendment proposed by Senator Cotton to limit application of Title VII to employers of at least 100 employees. During the course of the Senate's deliberations on the amendment, Senator Cotton had a revealing discussion with Senator Curtis. . . . Both men expressed dismay that Title VII would prohibit preferential hiring of "members of a minority race in order to enhance their opportunity. . . ." 110 Cong. Rec. 13086 (1964). Thus in the only exchange on the Senate floor raising the possibility that an employer might wish to reserve jobs for minorities in order to assist them in overcoming their employment disadvantage, both speakers concluded that Title VII prohibits such, in the words of the Court, "voluntary, private, race-conscious efforts to abolish traditional patterns of racial segregation and hierarchy. . . ." (3). (In) the limited debate that followed (cloture), Senator Moss . . . had this to say about quotas:

> The bill does not accord to any citizen advantage or preference — it does not fix quotas of employment or school population — it does not force personal association. What it does is to prohibit public officials and those who invite the public generally to patronize their businesses or to apply for employment, to utilize the offensive, humiliating, and cruel practice of discrimination on the basis of race. In short, the bill does not accord special consideration. It establishes *equality*. *Id.,* at 14484 (emphasis added).

Reading the language of Title VII, as the Court purports to do, "against the background of (its) legislative history . . . and the historical context from which the Act arose, ". . . one is led inescapably to the conclusion that Congress fully understood what it was saying and meant precisely what it said. Opponents of the civil rights bill did not argue that employers would be permitted under Title VII voluntarily to grant preferential treatment to minorities to correct racial imbalance. The plain language of the statute too clearly prohibited such racial discrimination to admit of any doubt. . . .

Our task in this case, like any other case involving the construction of a statute, is to give effect to the intent of Congress. To divine that intent, we traditionally look first to the words of the statute and, if they are unclear, then to the statute's legislative history. Finding the desired result hopelessly foreclosed by these conventional sources, the Court turns to a third source — the "spirit" of the Act. But close examination of what the Court proffers as the spirit of the Act reveals it as the spirit animating the present majority, not the Eighty-eighth Congress. For if the spirit of the Act eludes the cold words of the statute itself, it rings out with unmistakable clarity in the words of the elected representatives who made the law. It is *equality*. . . .

In passing Title VII Congress outlawed *all* racial discrimination, recognizing that no discrimination based on race is benign, that no action disadvantaging a person because of his color is affirmative. With today's holding, the Court introduces into Title VII a tolerance for the very evil that the law was intended to eradicate, without offering even a clue as to what the limits on that tolerance may be. We are told simply that Kaiser's racially discriminatory admission quota "falls on the permissible side of the line." By going not merely *beyond* but directly *against* Title VII's language and legislative history, the Court has sown the wind. Later courts will face the impossible task of reaping the whirlwind.

NOTES

1. Section 703 (a), 42 U.S.C. ' 2000e-2(a), provides: (a) It shall be an unlawful employment practice for an employer —

(1) to fail or refuse to hire or to discharge any individual, or otherwise to discriminate against any individual with respect to his compensation, terms, conditions, or privileges of employment, because of such individual's race, color, religion, sex, or national origin; or

(2) to limit, segregate, or classify his employees or applicants for employment in any way which would deprive or tend to deprive any individual of employment opportunities or otherwise adversely affect his status as an employee, because of such individual's race, color, religion, sex, or national origin.

2. Section 703 (d), 42 U.S.C. § 2000e-2(d), provides: It shall be an unlawful employment practice for any employer, labor organization, or joint labor-management committee controlling apprenticeship or other training or retraining, including on-the-job training programs, to discriminate against any individual because of his race, color, religion, sex, or national origin in admission to, or employment in, any program established to provide apprenticeship or other training.

3. The problem that Congress addressed in 1964 remains with us. In 1962 the nonwhite unemployment rate was 124% higher than the white rate. . . . In 1978 the black unemployment rate was 129% higher. See Monthly Labor Review, U.S. Department of Labor Bureau of Labor Statistics 78 (Mar. 1979).

4. Section 703 (j) of Title VII, 42 U.S.C. § 2000e-2(j), provides: Nothing contained in this subchapter shall be interpreted to require any employer, employment agency, labor organization, or joint labor-management committee subject to this subchapter to grant preferential treatment to any individual or to any group because of the race, color, religion, sex, or national origin of such individual or group on account of an imbalance which may exist with respect to the total number or percentage of persons of any race, color, religion, sex, or national origin employed by any employer, referred or classified for employment by any employment agency or labor organization, admitted to membership or classified by any labor organization, or admitted to, or employed in, any apprenticeship or other training program, in comparison with the total number or percentage or persons of such race, color, religion, sex, or national origin in any community, State, section, or other area, or in the available work force in any community, State, section, or other area. . . .

5. Our statement in . . . *Furnco Construction* (which is) patently inconsistent with today's holding, (is) not even mentioned, much less distinguished, by the Court.

6. "If the words are plain, they give meaning to the act, and it is neither the duty nor the privilege of the courts to enter speculative fields in search of a different meaning."

". . . (W)hen words are free from doubt they must be taken as the final expression of the legislative intent, and are not to be added to or subtracted from by considerations drawn . . . from any extraneous source." *Caminetti v. United States,* 242 U.S. 470, 490, 37 S.Ct. 192, 196 (1917).

Ernest van den Haag

Reverse Discrimination: A Brief Against It

"How am I, as Secretary of HEW, ever going to find first-class black doctors, first-class black lawyers, first-class black scientists, first-class women scientists, if these people don't have the chance to get into the best [schools] in the country?"—Joseph A. Califano Jr., *New York Times,* March 18, 1977.

I

On April Fool's Day Mr. Califano wisely fudged these words he had spoken two weeks earlier. However, he still does not understand that reversing discrimination is inconsistent with enforcing equality of opportunity. Preferential admissions to colleges and professional schools are now widely practiced. So is "affirmative action," which is basically analogous to preferential admissions: it applies to hiring, promotion, and employment in general. Persons belonging to selected minorities or under-represented groups (such as women, or blacks) are admitted or hired if they meet scholastic standards which are specially lowered for them. Or, they are given preference over others who have performed as well or better in meeting requirements. This practice, which Secretary Califano endorses, discriminates, in effect, against those who are being displaced in favor of those who displace them. Its legality has been attacked with respect to state institutions. But the Supreme Court, although it heard the DeFunis case (*DeFunis v. Odegaard,* 1974), avoided deciding it because DeFunis, who had sued the university, had by that time been admitted and graduated.

From *National Review,* Vol. XXIX, No. 16 (April, 1977). Reprinted by permission of the author.

Both preferential admissions and affirmative action are meant to discriminate against discrimination, to reduce discrimination by favoring those discriminated against in the past, or elsewhere. Is this reversal morally justifiable? Can it be effective in achieving its purpose?

In the past Oxford and Cambridge gave preference to the sons of great English families even when their qualifications did not justify it. They were preferred because they would exercise power and influence whether admitted or not. It was thought that society would benefit more by educating these students than by educating others who, even if more meritorious, would be likely to exercise less influence on the course of social affairs. The advantage to the universities was expected to be greater as well—a matter that probably did not escape the attention of the admitting authorities. For similar reasons, American universities in the past gave preference to students likely to inherit great wealth. Is a reversal of this pattern required by justice, or is it socially useful, as the old pattern was thought to be? Let me consider the social usefulness before turning to the justice of reversal.

Could society benefit from the preferential admission of the disadvantaged as it might have benefited from the preferential admission of the privileged? Scarcely. There is no reason to believe that members of groups previously discriminated against will exercise disproportionate social power or influence, regardless of higher education denied or received. Hence their preferential admission cannot be justified by reasoning that their education deserves preference because it would be socially more useful than that of the more meritorious.

Preferential admissions might be useful in other respects. If one assumes that society consists of separate communities, each wanting indigenous leaders, preferential admissions (even quotas) might help provide higher education for the requisite number of members of each group. (This was the justification English universities advanced for giving some preference to potential Indian and African leaders.) But women, or even blacks, do not form segregated political or cultural communities. Where they do, our present policy is to integrate or at least to desegregate them. Although the "melting pot" image of America simplifies and exaggerates, the Swiss paradigm of full geographical and cultural separation is neither feasible nor desirable in the United States. (Anyway, those who desire it can avail themselves of the private colleges exclusively attended by the groups of their choice.) Preferential admission of the previously disadvantaged cannot rest, then, on the social benefit to be gained by educating the independently powerful, or on the need for indigenous leadership.

Another argument for preferential admissions conceives of institutions of higher learning and of other non-political institutions as representative bodies, in which all classes, races, sexes, and religions—however well integrated—ought to be represented in proportion to their share of the population, even if admission standards have to differ for each group to secure its proportional representation. Yet educational or business, unlike political, institutions are not meant to be representative. In politics, representativeness, rightly or wrongly, plays a major role, although it is often hard to see who, and what, is represented: the occupational, class, age, and sex ratios of our representative bodies scarcely reflect those of the population. Still, it would be hard for a white man to be elected in Harlem; and political tickets wisely tend to represent important ethnic, religious, or geographical groupings of voters.

However, institutions of higher learning are not political bodies and cannot represent the voters without defeating their function, which is to teach and do research, not to make political decisions. So too with business enterprises: to require representativeness in faculties, or student bodies, is no more justified than to require representativeness in Chinese restaurants, prisons, hospitals, or opera houses. These institutions have non-representative functions which require admission (or confinement) criteria relevant to those functions, regardless of representativeness. So too with graduate or professional schools. We want the most able and gifted to be prepared for the tasks at hand by the most able and gifted, regardless of sex or race. To demand representativeness would be contrary to the social interest which requires the best surgeon, or the best singer, to be educated for his task, not the racially or sexually most representative.

I can find no utilitarian justification, then, for preferential admission of previously under-represented national, racial, or sexual groups. On the contrary, it would be dysfunctional, favoring persons less able to learn and teach than those rejected, and thus causing society to be served by the less able in the professions education prepares for. *Mutatis mutandis,* this applies to non-educational institutions as well. Let me turn now to non-utilitarian justifications.

II

Should the preference given the powerful in the past be reversed for the sake of justice? Surely, to do so would shift rather than repair injustice. Injustice would not be reduced, but merely inflicted on a different group. If the preference given the powerful was wrong because it violated equality of individual opportunity and the rule of admission by relevant qualification only, then violation of that rule in favor of a different group, the powerless, would be no less wrong, however generous the reparative intent.

Individual reparations can be justified if the victim of discrimination and the victimizer are individually identifiable. Thus, qualified persons who were not hired because they were discriminated against may be compensated for their loss. There is a case even for collective compensation, if losses are tangible (e.g., racial firings, confiscations, or de-licensings as in Nazi Germany), and if victimizers and victims, though not individually identifiable, are roughly contemporary as groups. Matters become murky, however, if one considers granting compensation to persons not allowed to acquire the qualifications they might have acquired had they been admitted and which might have led to higher incomes than they actually did earn. Unjust losses certainly were suffered, but we cannot know their incidence and size.

Matters become even more murky if the discriminatory rules were imposed over a long period in the distant past. The incidence of the unjustly achieved advantages and of the unjustly imposed disadvantages becomes diffuse and uncertain, as does the liability for both. Moreover, current generations can bear no responsibility for discrimination imposed by generations past, other than to discontinue it. Can today's Italians be held liable for Caesar's invasion of Gaul, or today's Frenchmen for Napoleon's invasion of Germany? Can Polish or Italian workers be held liable for the fate inflicted on American Indians by the colonists? or Jewish teachers and students for disabilities imposed on blacks in the past? or contemporary males for past discrimination against women? We are told (Deuteronomy 24:16): "The fathers shall not be put to death for the children, neither shall the children be put to death for the fathers: every man shall be put to death for his own sin." It is a good rule. Those not responsible for it cannot be asked to compensate for the damage. They can only be restrained from causing further losses.

Justice, then, requires the cessation of discriminatory activities, including discrimination in admissions or hiring, but no reversal. Preferential admissions to repair past injustice might "discriminate for" persons who themselves suffered no "discrimination against" at the expense of persons not responsible for past "discrimination against."

The problem of compensation for the present consequences of past injustice cannot be met, then, by preferential admissions. Still, efforts to solve it are demanded by generosity, if not by justice. Some members of the formerly "discriminated against" groups have native abilities which would justify admission to the schools or hiring by the enterprises to which they have applied, had these abilities not remained undeveloped because of unfavorable circumstances co-produced by past discrimination. Colleges and universities may play a role in helping such applicants to overcome hardships, in order to prepare them for (non-preferential) admission. Pre-admission tutoring may be a reasonable effort to offset the present effects of past injustices in which colleges participated, and thus to make amends.

III

Occasionally it is argued that preferential admissions are needed to offset unfairness inherent in the tests which universities and professional schools use to decide on admissions. These tests are thought to discriminate against qualified persons who belong to disadvantaged groups. Actually, they are quite reliable in predicting the likely degree of success in the professional and graduate schools which use them. They measure relevant abilities, regardless of sex or race. Their value is limited: the tests do not measure non-academic abilities or human characteristics, nor predict the degree of success in activities for which they are not designed. However, though less than perfect, the tests serve well the limited purpose for which they are used. Preferential admissions, far from offsetting unfairness, instead would introduce it by setting aside the objective measurement the tests permit, in favor of racial or sexual privileges.

IV

Sexes and races are not proportionally represented among students admitted to professional and graduate schools, nor among faculties, nor in the ranks of corporations. This has been regarded as evidence of discrimination against the under-represented. Radicals insist that disproportionate representation is unfair even when it does reflect actual differences in abilities, qualifications, or motivations. Others, philosophically more moderate, believe that equal treatment necessarily would lead to proportional representation of all groups. Thus, disproportionate representation *eo ipso* demonstrates "discrimination against" the under-represented, even if it cannot be verified independently, and preferential admission may become an appropriate remedy.

If one assumes that all relevant aptitudes, talents, and motivations are equally distributed among classes, sexes, nationalities, and races, then over- or under-representation of any one group in desirable activities necessarily indicates unequal treatment. Such an assumption has never been shown to be true. Widespread abilities, e.g., the ability to be a farmer, a janitor, or a clerk, seem to be distributed fairly equally among groups. But the ability to study mathematics or teach it, or to run a major enterprise, is not that widespread. Universities and corporations cannot draw on a number of talented people in each group proportional to the size of the group. And if the members of different groups are not necessarily equally qualified *ab initio,* objective tests need not lead to proportional representation. Over- or under-representation does not indicate bias any more than proportional representation of groups among admitted candidates indicates unbiased admissions standards. Racist theories notwithstanding, the over-representation of Jews in important professions in Germany, and the consequent under-representation of non-Jewish Germans, did not indicate a discriminatory policy to place the latter at a disadvantage in favor of the former.

V

Is preferential admission of students, or affirmative action in hiring faculty or executives, a suitable remedy for actual or suspected discrimination? Both policies set numerical goals which, when achieved, would make faculties and student bodies, or executive units, reflect the proportions in which women or various racial groups occur, either in the general population, or among candidates with appropriate prior degrees and specializations.

Outside academic institutions, the advantages of using affirmative action to establish equality of opportunity may at times outweigh the disadvantages, when a licensing or admissions board, or an employer, currently discriminates against a group. There is a *prima facie* indication of discrimination if all those admitted, employed, or licensed are white, or male, even though others wish to be, and if 1) no distinctive qualifications are needed for the job or license; or 2) the distinctive qualifications needed can be shown to be possessed by the rejected candidates in substantially the same degree as by the accepted ones; or 3) the relevant qualifications can be tested, yet no suitable tests are used (or the tests used discriminate irrelevantly). In such cases numerical goals help to attain equality of opportunity. Yet they should be abandoned as soon as improper discriminatory practices cease, for numerical goals necessarily reduce the appropriate discriminations in hiring, promotion, firing, or licensing in terms of actual skill, reliability, diligence, etc.

Numerical goals *ipso facto* disregard the distinctive individual qualifications of candidates, or reduce the decisive weight they should have in most cases. They certainly cannot be appropriate for educational institutions, where these distinctive qualifications must be paramount. Further, academic institutions can (and do) properly test individual qualifications for admission. Therefore, numerical goals, far from reducing irrelevant discrimination, perpetuate or introduce it into academic institutions by placing more qualified persons at a disadvantage relative to less qualified or equally qualified ones who belong to an under-represented race or sex. (Where individual qualifications, although of decisive importance, are not always objectively testable—e.g., in hiring or promotions—universities and professional schools usually are willing to submit disputes to arbitrators.)

VI

Consider now the effect on persons, rather than institutions. The effect of academic affirmative action, or of preferential admissions, on those discriminated for is likely to be unhelpful. There are three possibilities. First, there is the unqualified law student who was preferentially admitted. He will drop out because of low grades which were predictable from his entrance test. He may be worse off than before.

Second, some preferentially admitted students graduate by dint of preferential grading or undemanding curricula specially fashioned for them. They profit from the credentials obtained. But the group which was to be favored pays a high price: the black college graduate, PhD, or lawyer who graduated because lower standards were applied to him than to his white counterparts is not as competent as they are and will reinforce the prejudice which maintains that blacks are necessarily less competent than whites.

Third, there is the preferentially admitted black student who, despite low entrance scores, actually catches up and does well without preferential grading. Yet he may never know whether he graduated because he was black or because he deserved to. If he does know, others will not: he will suffer from the image perpetuated by his fellow student whose preferential admission was complemented by preferential grading. Similarly, female or black professors hired or promoted because of affirmative action will not know whether they were hired because they were qualified or because they were female or black; nor will others. Those hired because they belong to an under-represented group though they are not the most qualified persons also will perpetuate the image of low competence of the under-represented group — the image that contributed to discrimination against it in the first place.

The persons excluded because of preferential admissions or affirmative action naturally are no less bitter than those who in the past were excluded by discrimination. Since "discrimination for" merely reverses "discrimination against," it cannot but perpetuate the group hostilities of the past. This applies as well to all enterprises which practice reverse discrimination.

There is also an unattractive arbitrariness about the whole procedure. Unless inclusion into the groups discriminated for is determined by sex, it often must be capricious. Puerto Ricans, Spaniards, Argentinians, and Mexicans are all "Spanish surnamed." It is hard to see what else they have in common, or why they should receive different treatment than Portuguese, Brazilians, or Arabs. And it is not obvious that various white "ethnics" suffered less from discrimination than females did. Yet they are not preferentially admitted, or hired, by affirmative action. These remedies, then, are not only counterproductive and unjust most of the time, but also arbitrarily selective. Perhaps this is a minor defect compared to those already mentioned: if an idea is bad, arbitrary application does not make it much worse. Nonetheless the inherent capriciousness of the scheme and the unavoidable arbitrariness in execution are psychologically repulsive.

VII

Affirmative action and preferential admissions were aided and abetted by persons who felt guilty enough about past discrimination to make amends, even at the expense of innocent third persons. Groups which, rightly or wrongly, felt discriminated against in the past also have supported affirmative action and preferential admissions. But in the main these are creatures of the federal bureaucracy and judiciary. The bureaucracy actually gave birth to the illegitimate child; the judiciary adopted and legalized it.

Fears that a bureaucratic monstrosity would be foisted on the country were voiced in Congress during the debate on the Civil Rights Act of 1964. Such fears were laid to rest when the managers of the bill, Senators Joseph Clark and Clifford Case, submitted a memorandum stating:

> There is no requirement in Title VII that an employer maintain a racial balance in his work force. On the contrary, any deliberate attempt to maintain a racial

balance, whatever such balance may be, would involve a violation of Title VII because maintaining such a balance would require an employer to hire or refuse to hire on the basis of race. It must be emphasized that discrimination is prohibited as to any individual . . . the question in each case would be whether that individual was discriminated against. [110 *Congressional Record* 7213, April 8, 1964.]

Further, at the behest of the bill's sponsors, the Department of Justice submitted a memorandum stating:

Finally, it has been asserted that Title VII would impose a requirement for "racial balance." This is incorrect. There is no provision, either in Title VII or in any part of this bill, that requires or authorizes any federal agency or federal court to require preferential treatment for any individual group for the purpose of achieving racial balance.

No employer is required to hire an individual because that individual is Negro. No employer is required to maintain any ratio of Negroes to whites, Jews to gentiles, Italians to English, or women to men. [110 *Congressional Record* 7207, April 8, 1964.]

Despite the clear language of these memoranda, the bureaucracy has perverted the intent of the legislation. Racial balance and the group preferences needed to attain it are prescribed and enforced. The courts have found constitutional arguments to help administrative agencies override the intent of Congress. Bureaucracy has replaced both democracy and common sense. They can be reinstated only when the citizens push Congress and the courts into disciplining and limiting the bureaucracy.

James M. Humber

Reversing the Arguments Against Reverse Discrimination

I

Generally, those who seek to defend reverse discrimination do so by appealing to some variation of either of the following arguments.[1]

(1) Women and members of certain minority groups have been consistently discriminated against. Justice demands that members of these groups be given compensation for their injuries; and compensation is best secured by practicing reverse discrimination.

(2) In our society equality of opportunity is recognized as a good. At present, women and minority group members do not have true equality of opportunity because they have been "conditioned" to think of themselves as inferior, or at least as unsuited for certain tasks. To remove these psychological constraints (and so to ensure genuine equality of opportunity), women and Blacks need "role models," i.e., individuals from "disadvantaged" groups who are successful in positions of importance. And to guarantee that there are persons serving as role models, it is necessary to practice reverse discrimination.

The arguments in favor of reverse discrimination have been attacked in various ways.[2] In opposition to the second argument, critics respond as follows:

(i) If equality of opportunity is a good to be realized in our society, it cannot be achieved by means of reverse discrimination. This is so because reversing discrimination is inconsistent with equalizing opportunity. After

---

Comments by Milton Snoeyenbos were helpful to me in the formulation of my ideas.

all, to favor Blacks and women in hiring and school admission is simply to discriminate against (and hence to deny equal opportunity to) white males.

(ii) Although equality of opportunity is recognized as a desirable end in our society, it is not the only desirable end. And to give preference to some simply because of their race or sex could well hamper achievement of another recognized "good" in our society, namely, that of putting the most qualified people in responsible positions. The reason this is so is that race and sex as properties are irrelevant qualifications for either hiring or school admission. Business serves society by making a profit while turning out a quality product. Institutions of higher learning, on the other hand, exist to foster research and to disseminate knowledge. This being the case, race and sex do not qualify one either to be a scholar or a businessperson. Thus, if an employer gives preference to one job candidate over another simply because of a candidate's race or sex, the person hired might well have fewer properties relevant to success than the person who was not hired. And if this were to happen, society as a whole would suffer because it would be served by the less able.

(iii) Finally, even if preference in hiring and school admission did not cause society to be served by the less able it could: (a) have deleterious effects for those hired under affirmative action programs, and (b) have an undesirable effect upon other minority group members. Both effects would follow because everyone (including the persons hired or admitted to school) would know that they were given preferential treatment. And in these circumstances the persons given such "special" treatment would never know whether they were truly competent or merely "kept on" by their employers to demonstrate that their companies hired without regard to race, sex, or creed. Furthermore, other Blacks and women might soon become aware of the advantages of being disadvantaged. After all, their "role models" had been hired because they were members of disadvantaged groups. Why, then, should they struggle to succeed? Would it not be far easier simply to complain of their disadvantaged status? Rather than inspiring, then, women and Blacks who were preferentially hired as role models could influence behavior in nonbeneficial ways.

As against the claim that reverse discrimination is required by the demands of justice, critics offer the following three counter-arguments.

(A) First, it is said, practicing reverse discrimination may not serve the interests of justice, because there is no way to identify either those discriminated against or those responsible for discrimination. For example, let us say that person P carelessly drives his car into person Q. In this case we can identify the injury, find the individual responsible for that harm, and determine what is needed as just compensation for Q's injuries. And given this knowledge we can serve the ends of justice. (In the case at hand, for instance, we can take just compensation for Q's injuries from P and give that compensation to Q.) However, when we use reverse discrimination in an attempt to rectify the wrongs done by discrimination we do not have the sort of knowledge illustrated in our *P/Q* example. To be sure, we know that Blacks and women have been discriminated against, principally at the hands of white males. To know this, though, is just to know that one *group* has wronged other *groups*. We do not know which *individuals* within these groups have suffered or practiced discrimination; and because we lack this information, reversing discrimination could well produce more injustice than justice. For example, imagine that a white male (*WM*) and a black woman (*BW*) are competing for a job. *WM* is slightly better qualified for the position than *BW* but the employer (*E*) practices reverse discrimination and hires *BW*. Has *E* done something to compensate Blacks and women for the debilitating effects of discrimination? Not necessarily, for *BW* may never have been a victim of discrimination, and *WM* may never have discriminated against anyone. And if this were the case *E* would have done nothing more than discriminate against *WM*, thus perpetrating rather than rectifying an injustice. Furthermore, if reverse discrimination were practiced widely in the United States there is no telling how often this scenario would be repeated. In the end, then, reverse discrimination should be rejected because it might produce more instances of injustice than justice.

(B) Unlike argument (A), which only tries to show that reversing discrimination *could* produce more injustice than justice, argument (B) attempts to show that reverse discrimination *is likely to* produce more injustice than it rectifies. Who, it is asked, would be the most likely beneficiaries of reverse discrimination? Would it not be the best educated, most sophisticated Blacks and women? Surely it would seem so; for if employers were required to practice reverse discrimination they would give preference to these individuals, hiring them first, before their "lower ranking" counterparts. But the best educated, most highly sophisticated members of any disadvantaged group are the very ones who, in all likelihood, have suffered the least discrimination within that group. Thus, the objection goes, reversing discrimination *probably* would produce more injustice than justice; it would deny employment to those who, in all probability had suffered the most from discrimination, while at the same time "compensating" those within disadvantaged groups who least deserved compensation.

(C) If argument (C) were sound it would be the strongest of all the arguments for the injustice of reverse discrimination, for this argument, unlike either (A) or (B), attempts to show that reversing discrimination *would* produce a greater amount of injustice than justice. As usually presented the argument proceeds as follows: First, it is said, discrimination against women and Blacks was most severe in the past, for it was then that Blacks were enslaved and women denied suffrage. The effects of such discriminatory actions may linger in the present but it would be wrong to attempt to rectify this unfortunate situation by practicing reverse discrimination. This is so because today's white males are not responsible for the actions of their forefathers. Consequently, to hold today's white males accountable (by taking jobs from them and giving them to Blacks and women), is to treat these white males in ways that are manifestly unjust. Of course, this is not to deny that women, Blacks, and members of other minority groups need to be recompensed for past wrongs. It is just to say that reverse discrimination is not the proper means for achieving that end.

Given the debate as presented above, I believe the arguments against reverse discrimination are far more persuasive than those offered in support of the practice. Still, I think there is more that can be said on the matter; and in what follows I intend to show that the arguments in favor of reverse discrimination can be modified so as to undercut all of the above-noted objections. Indeed, I want to go further and argue that reverse discrimination is justified, not only by the principle of justice, but also by the principle of utility. I will begin by reconsidering argument (C) for the injustice of reverse discrimination.

II

The Demands of Justice

Critics charge that reverse discrimination must be unjust because it denies jobs to today's white males, thus holding these individuals responsible for the sins of their forefathers. For this objection to have force, however, one must be willing to assume that discrimination is not being practiced in our society today; and there are two reasons why this assumption is false. The first reason may be made evident by means of an analogy.

Let us say we have two fighters, X and Y. Two months prior to their meeting in the ring X is given the best exercise, training, advice, food, etc., by the Fighting Commission. On the other hand, the Fighting Commission does not allow Y to sleep, forces him to live on a subsistence diet, and does not permit him to train. Now, if on the day of the fight the rules of the game were enforced "impartially" by the Fighting Commission, would we say that the fight was fair? I think not. Indeed, I believe we would say, not merely that Y *had been* discriminated against, but that he *was* being discriminated against because he was being forced to fight under rules favoring X. To make the fight fair, and so not to discriminate against Y, X needs to be handicapped in some way (e.g., he could be made to wear oversized gloves and a heavy weight belt). Today, women and Blacks are in a situation similar to that of our starved fighter, for these individuals often are forced to compete in the marketplace under rules which, if enforced "impartially," favor white males. And to end this sort of discrimination, white males need to be handicapped.

Actually, our fighter example only tells one-half of the story, for in today's society it simply is not true that the rules of the game are being enforced "impartially." What Irving Thalberg calls "visceral racism" still exists.[3] Many of the important "extras" that spell success in business (e.g., exclusive club memberships, housing in upper class neighborhoods, etc.) are denied to Blacks. And for the most part, women with intelligence and ambition are looked upon with suspicion. Furthermore, even though feminist and liberation movements have made great strides, the vast majority of women are "conditioned" from birth to seek only marriage and motherhood. To be sure, we have come a long way from the days of slavery and the denial of women's voting rights. But anyone who claims that women and minority group members today have no special obstacles to overcome in order to successfully compete is simply living in a dream world.

If our reasoning thus far is correct, we can say that discrimination is being practiced in our society today, not only because the "rules of the game" are unfair when enforced "impartially," but also because these rules are not truly being enforced impartially. Thus, if we were to engage in reverse discrimination we would not necessarily be punishing the sons for the sins of their fathers. Having shown this, however, we have not demonstrated that reverse discrimination is a just procedure. To do this we must show that reversing discrimination will compensate those who have suffered injury without harming those who have failed to practice discrimination.

The problem seems simple enough: We know that members of some groups are being discriminated against by members of another group. But reverse discrimination operates on an individual level; and if the critics of reverse discrimination are to be believed it is quite likely that reversing discrimination would produce more instances of injustice than justice. Are the opponents of reverse discrimination correct? I think not. Indeed, if a program of reverse discrimination were properly administered, I believe the facts would be quite otherwise than the critics assert. In order to see why this is the case it will be helpful to consider another example.

Let us say that two people are being considered for a job—a black woman, *BW,* who has been discriminated against, and a white male, *WM,* who knows *BW* has been the victim of discrimination. *WM* has a more impressive dossier than *BW* and so insists that he be hired. What should be our reaction? Remember our earlier example of the fighters. What would we think if fighter *X* were to balk at having to wear a weight belt and extra-large gloves, even though he knew how *Y* had been treated before the fight? Would we not say that he was seeking an unfair advantage? Similarly, if *WM* knew *BW* had been the subject of discrimination but insisted nevertheless that he be hired because his qualifications were superior to her's would he not be endorsing the past discrimination against *BW* by seeking to perpetuate it? It does not matter that *WM* had not himself discriminated against *BW* in the past. Fighter *X* did not starve fighter *Y* or refuse to allow him to sleep either; but if *X* refuses to handicap himself in his fight with *Y,* he is approving of those past practices and attempting to take unfair advantage of *Y.* In the same way, if *WM* knows that *BW* has been the victim of discrimination, and yet insists that he rather than *BW* deserves the job they both seek, *WM* is condoning the earlier discrimination against *BW* and trying his best to treat her unfairly. And in this case it would be in the interest of justice to employ BW rather than $WM,$ for this action would compensate a victim of discrimination and penalize one whom we knew condoned discriminatory practices.

At this point our argument may seem subject to a criticism. Throughout our WM/BW example we assumed that WM knew BW had been the victim of past discrimination. The assumption is important; for if WM had no reason to believe that BW had been discriminated against, it would be proper for him to demand that he rather than BW be given the sought-after job. And, our critics will insist, this is precisely the point: it is impossible for white males to know that *individual* minority group members with whom they are competing for jobs have been the victims of past discrimination. But is this true? Surely it is so if by "to know" we mean "to be absolutely certain," for we cannot be absolutely certain about any matter of fact. But do we not have evidence that most Blacks and women have been subject to discrimination? Surely we do. I suggest then, that whenever a woman or minority group member applies for employment or school admission, the initial assumption ought to be that this individual has been discriminated against. Furthermore, I do not think it would take much effort for an employer or school admissions officer to find evidence tending to support or disconfirm this initial assumption. Indeed, such an employer or admissions officer would only need information of the following two sorts: (1) relevant autobiographical information concerning the job candidate or school applicant (e.g., where the applicant lived between the ages of one and eighteen, what the candidate's family income had been during his formative years, what level of education the applicant's parents had attained, etc.), and (2) brief psychological profiles of all applicants for employment or school admission. If information of these sorts were appended to all applications for jobs and school admission, employers and admissions officers could determine, with a high degree of probability, whether or not a particular applicant had been the subject of discrimination. For example, consider the following two cases:[4]

Case #1. Three persons are applying for a job—a white male (WM), and two white women ($WW1$ and $WW2$). All three candidates meet the minimum requirements for employment, but according to all "objective" criteria, WM is best qualified for the job, $WW1$ next best qualified, and $WW2$ least qualified. The fact that $WW2$ seems least qualified to compete in a "man's domain" gives some evidence of her having been subject to the psychological "conditioning forces" so often brought to bear upon women in our society. It is hardly overwhelming evidence; but what if we assume that it is supplemented by psychological data indicating that $WW2$, unlike $WW1$ and WM, lacks aggressiveness and assertiveness, and is somewhat unsure of herself in her role as a businessperson? Further, $WW2$ (again unlike $WW1$ and WM) scores much higher on her verbal tests than on her mathematical examinations. All else being equal, I believe the employer then could say that it was highly probable that *WW*2 had been subjected to stronger "conditioning" forces than either *WM* or *WW*1. At this point it would not be improper for the employer to tell *WM* and *WW*1 that although *WW*2 did not score as high as they did on "objective" tests, she was being hired because she was qualified and most likely the subject of discriminatory pressures far more severe than those experienced by either of them. If either *WM* or *WW*1 protested, they would be advocating continued discrimination against *WW*2 and so justly denied employment. If neither protested, both would recognize what was in fact the case, namely, that they had competed fairly with *WW*2 for a position of employment and had lost.

Case #2. A white male (*WM*) and a black male (*BM*) are applying for admission to a school with one remaining opening. Although *BM* scores lower than *WM* on all examinations he nevertheless meets all the minimum requirements for admission. Furthermore, while the autobiographical history of *WM* shows that he comes from a solid middle class background, *BM*'s history indicates that he grew up in a ghetto, did not know his father, etc. Given these facts, it would be proper for the admissions officer to reason that in all probability, one of the principal reasons *BM* suffered as he did in his early life was that he and his family, being black, were victims of discrimination. And at this juncture *BM* could be admitted to school, and *WM* told why he was being rejected. Specifically, *WM* would be told that although his examination scores were better than *BM*'s, he was judged not to be as qualified an admissions candidate as *BM* in a fair competition, i.e., in a competition in which *BM* was given an advantage so as to offset the debilitating effects of probable past discrimination. And at this stage *WM* could react in either of two ways. He could accept the admissions officer's judgment, admit that he had lost in fair competition with *BM*, and so acknowledge that no injustice had been done. Or, he could claim that he should not be handicapped in his competition with *BM* even though *BM* probably had been the victim of discrimination. In the latter case, however, *WM* would be demanding that the past discrimination of *BM* be perpetuated. And in this circumstance it would be proper to tell *WM* that it was in the interest of justice to admit *BM* because this action compensated a victim of discrimination by taking away from one who condoned discriminatory practices.

At this point one might wish to object to both of our examples. What we have failed to notice, the critic could say, is that there is a third option open to those who believe they have been victimized by reverse discrimination. Namely (to use case #2 as an example) *WM* could object to the admissions officer's decision by claiming that he had been handicapped *too severely* in his competition with *BM*. And if this were the basis for *WM*'s protest he would *not* be condoning the past discrimination against *BM*. Indeed, *WM*'s point simply would be that his competition with *BM* had not been fair because of the degree of handicap. But what gives *WM* the authority to make such a judgment? Consider, once again, our earlier example of the fighters. Fighter *X* is handicapped in his bout with *Y*; the fight goes the distance and Y is declared the winner. What would we think if X objected to the decision, claiming that he had been overly penalized, e.g., his weight belt should have been ten pounds instead of twenty? Would we say, "Yes, X is right, the fighter who is being handicapped should be the one to determine the type and degree of handicap"? Surely this would be absurd. Rather, we would tell X that he was a sore loser, and that the best means we have been able to devise for guaranteeing fair fights is to let an impartial panel of judges determine handicaps and make judgments concerning victory. And the same rules should apply in the marketplace. *WM* cannot be allowed to determine the degree to which he should be handicapped in his competition with *BM*—indeed, to let him do so would virtually assure an *unfair* competition.

We have considered the major arguments for the injustice of reverse discrimination and concluded that none carries the day. Many of today's white males *are* responsible for discrimination. Thus, if we were to practice reverse discrimination we would not necessarily be "punishing the sons for the sins of their fathers." Furthermore, if the right information were made available to employers and admissions officers, victims of discrimination could be identified with a high degree of probability. And in these circumstances, reverse discrimination could be used to rectify many of the injustices of discrimination without harming anyone.

Before discussing the utilitarian claim that it would be harmful to society to practice reverse discrimination, I would like to say a few words about how programs of preferential treatment might actually function in practice. If we assume that all applicants for employment and school admission were required to file autobiographies and take psychological tests, there are five general rules or guidelines which, if followed, might go a long way towards assuring justice in hiring and admissions.

First, whenever two or more *equally qualified* individuals[5] apply for a job or school admission, and only one of these candidates (say candidate C) is a member of a disadvantaged class, preference ought to be given to C. And this holds true regardless of whether or not C has been the victim of discrimination. If C has suffered discrimination, he or she deserves to be preferentially treated as compensation for past injuries. If, on the other hand, C has not been a discrimination victim, he or she should be preferred because (as we shall see in the next section) such action would benefit society.

Second, an employer who practices reverse discrimination ought to consider only those candidates judged to be minimally qualified when evaluated according to "ordinary" standards (e.g., examinations, school grades, on-the-job experience, etc.). This is because nonqualified candidates probably would fail in their endeavors and, as critics of reverse discrimination quite rightly point out, such failures would be detrimental both to society as a whole and to the persons who failed.

Third, employers and school admissions officers (like impartial fight judges) should determine the degree of handicap in any competition for jobs and school admission. Furthermore, the handicap should increase as does the evidence of discrimination. Under this rule, of course, white males need not always "lose out" in competitions with individuals who have been victimized by discrimination. It is quite possible, for instance, that a white male's qualifications could be so outstanding that he would be selected over all candidates who had been given a preferential advantage due to past discrimination.

Fourth, in order to ensure that employers and school admissions officers do their best to practice reverse discrimination fairly, their applications for admission and employment should be reviewed periodically by officials of the government. And where differences of opinion arise, employers and admissions officers should be required to *justify* their decisions. If they could not justify their decisions, they should be required to make amends to the wronged parties.

Finally, critics of reverse discrimination often point out that reversing discrimination would be unfair to disadvantaged group members themselves because the most likely beneficiaries of such a practice would be the best qualified (and hence least discriminated against) minority group members. The assumption upon which this argument depends, namely, that the least qualified individuals will, in general, be those who have suffered the most from discrimination, seems plausible if not probable. Thus we are led to formulate a fifth "guideline": whenever an employer or admissions officer is deciding between two or more disadvantaged group members, he should select the least qualified person unless the autobiographies and/or psychological test *clearly indicate* that a better qualified individual has suffered more from discrimination.

I do not want to claim that the above five guidelines for practicing reverse discrimination are exhaustive. Nor am I so idealistic as to believe that it would be easy for employers and admissions officers to make judgments of merit using these guidelines. Injustices would be done, and honest mistakes would be made. However, if reverse discrimination were practiced in the manner broadly specified above it seems highly probable that more instances of injustice would be corrected than would be produced. And this is all the supporter of reverse discrimination need show in order to make the case that reverse discrimination is a just procedure. Indeed, it would be illegitimate to demand that the advocate of reverse discrimination show more than this, for there can be no such thing as certainty in the practical affairs of human life.

III

THE DEMANDS OF UTILITY

In order to fully defend reverse discrimination it is necessary to show not only that this practice serves the interests of justice, but also that it benefits the entire society. As a first step towards achieving this goal I will show why we must reject the major arguments in support of the view that reverse discrimination produces more harm than good.

(i) The first utilitarian objection to reverse discrimination recognizes that equality of opportunity is a good to be achieved in our society, but then claims that reversing discrimination is inconsistent with that goal. Given our earlier example of the fighters we can now see that this argument is plainly wrong. A boxer who has been starved and kept awake can have an equal opportunity to win a fight against one who has been well-fed and trained, only if the healthy fighter is handicapped in some way. Similarly, in order to give individuals who have been discriminated against a truly equal opportunity, those who have not been discriminated against must be handicapped.[6] Far from inhibiting equality of opportunity, then, reverse discrimination actually fosters that goal.

(ii) The second argument against reverse discrimination is that this procedure may well harm society by causing it to be served by the less able. Because I advocate hiring the least qualified individuals in some circumstances, it may seem that my defense of reverse discrimination is particularly susceptible to this criticism. But this is not so. On my view, every individual hired (or accepted in school) would be qualified. And to ensure that the persons who are given employment or accepted in school do a good job, we need only insist that it be made easy to dismiss those who fail to perform their tasks properly. Cases of incompetence could be documented, I think, with relative ease. And if incompetents could be dismissed without undue encumbrance, society would not suffer in the least.

(iii) The third objection to practicing reverse discrimination is that this procedure: (a) could have deleterious effects for those hired, and (b) could affect other minority group members in undesirable ways. But these arguments also miss the mark. Under the system as I have outlined it those hired or accepted in school would know that they were qualified. And if they were not dismissed they would know that they were performing their tasks well. Thus, they could take pride in their achievements. And similar considerations also apply to minority group members seeking employment or school admission. These individuals would know that in order to be considered for a job or an opening in school, they would have to achieve at a certain level. But, the critic will assert, might not members of disadvantaged groups see the advantages of being disadvantaged and so do their utmost to appear "disadvantaged" and "minimally qualified" in order to obtain employment? I think not. After all, how does one prepare to be "disadvantaged" and "minimally qualified"? And even if this were possible, what difference would it make? Those hired or admitted to school would be qualified. And to keep their positions, these qualified individuals would have to perform adequately. In the end, absolutely no one would suffer.

Given our brief examination of the utilitarian arguments against reverse discrimination certain conclusions seem mandated. First, rather than being at odds with equality of opportunity reverse discrimination is really a means for achieving that goal. Second, so long as it is relatively easy to dismiss incompetents hired under reverse discrimination programs, society will not suffer. And third, practicing reverse discrimination will give those who perform well a sense of pride, while at the same time providing other minority group members with truly inspiring "role models." To this we can add two further benefits. First, we have seen that practicing reverse discrimination will further the interests of justice. And although the demands of justice and the demands of utility may not always be in accord, in this instance, at least, they appear to be. Finally, once minority group members understand that they really are being given an equal opportunity to succeed in our society a giant step will have been taken towards achieving true harmony in our relations with one another. I am aware that there are those who would disagree with this assessment, and insist that reversing discrimination will do nothing but incite a white-male "backlash," thus ultimately making things worse. Of course, these pessimists may be right. For my own part, however, I much prefer the counsel of Hume, who tells us that men are motivated not only by self-interest, but also by humanity, fellow-feeling, and a desire for justice.

NOTES

1. For arguments in support of reverse discrimination see: J. J. Thomson, "Preferential Hiring," *Philosophy and Public Affairs* (Winter, 1975); Bernard Boxhill, "The Morality of Reparations," *Social Theory and Practice* (Volume 2, no. 1); Paul Taylor, "Reverse Discrimination and Compensatory Justice," *Analysis* (June, 1973); M. G. Fried, "In Defense of Preferential Hiring," *Philosophical Forum* (Volume 5, 1973-1974).

2. For arguments in opposition to reverse discrimination see: Alan Goldman, "Limits to the Justification of Reverse Discrimination," *Social Theory and Practice* (Volume 3, no. 3) and "Reparations to Individuals or Groups?" *Analysis* (Volume 33 no. 5); E. van den Haag, "Reverse Discrimination: A Brief Against It," *National Review* (April, 1977); and W. Blackstone, "Reverse Discrimination and Compensatory Justice," *Social Theory and Practice* (Spring, 1975).

3. Irving, Thalberg, "Visceral Racism," *The Monist* (Volume 56, 1972), pp. 43-65.

4. Case #1 illustrates how psychological tests could be used to determine a person's "discrimination status"; case #2 makes the same point with regard to autobiograhical data.

5. When I say "equally qualified" here I mean equally qualified *before* the imposition of any handicap to offset the debilitating effects of past discrimination.

6. Sometimes critics of reverse discrimination attack the practice by claiming that it "changes the rules" in the middle of the game. Put most simply, the claim is that employers practicing reverse discrimination will hire members of disadvantaged groups, and in many cases these individuals will not be as highly qualified as the white males who were denied employment. But this changes the rules of the game,

because we have all been led to believe that the person who is best qualified for a job should be the one hired. Given what I have said above, it should be clear that I do not think this criticism is sound. I agree that today in our society we believe that highly qualified persons deserve to be employed before those who are not as well qualified. But we accept this "informal rule" only because we tacitly assume that all individuals competing for a job or admission to school have been given an equal opportunity to develop their talents. More accurately, then, the "informal rule" accepted in our society today is: *"where equality of opportunity obtains,* the best qualified individual ought to be selected for employment or school admission." This being so, employers or school admissions officers who practice reverse discrimination do not change the rules in the middle of the game. In fact, they abide by them; for what they do is handicap white males in their competition with disadvantaged group members so as to assure equality of opportunity, and then, given this adjustment, hire or admit the individual whom they consider to be best qualified.

Corporate Policy Statements

Why an Affirmative Action Program? Because minorities and women have been discriminated against. In addition to the necessity of complying with the law, our Affirmative Action Program predicates on three basic beliefs: First: We believe equality of opportunity to be a fundamental principle and a moral imperative. Second: We believe that the preservation and continuity of our company within this free society requires equal opportunity for all members of society. Third: We believe that equal opportunity will enlarge our talent pool and enable us, with imaginative and effective management, to have a more competent and productive work force.

Beyond legalistic concerns, we have become increasingly aware that we must respect and protect the individual rights of every human being to exercise the full range of options with regard to what purpose each particular life is to serve. Each of us must have the opportunity to be all we can be — to maximize our human potential and to become a fulfilled person, possessing a sense of identity, self-esteem and individual worth. Equal opportunity does not exist when just an exceptional "star" is promoted to the better, higher-level jobs. Equal Opportunity comes when the woman or minority person of average ability is just as likely to be promoted as the average non-minority man, and just as likely, in the long run, to advance as far. . . . It has been traditional to think of Affirmative Action as being confined to a concern for equal employment opportunity. We now believe that this definition should be enlarged to encompass four components: I. *Equal Employment* — This is Affirmative Action that seeks to provide opportunity for equal access to jobs at all levels based upon qualifications (regardless of sex, race, color, ethnic origin, age, or handicap) for all. II. *Entrepreneurial Development* — This is Affirmative Action aimed at increasing business ownership by women, minorities, and the physically handicapped. III. *Social-Priority Investment* — This is Affirmative Action aimed at deployment of capital where needed to meet societal goals and requirements essential to continuity of a whole and wholesome society. IV. *Corporate Support* — This is an opportunity to advance the achievement of societal goals through financial backing of selected non-profit institutions and organizations whose work makes substantial contribution to the quality of life for all.

This four-part concept of Affirmative Action seems particularly fitting as we intensify efforts for "coming right with people" to assure a socio-economic environment that is conducive to our corporate growth, progress and survival. . . . Our Affirmative Action policy for the Handicapped seeks to assure equality of opportunity through a barrier free employment and advancement process. This policy applies to the handicapped no less than to minorities and women. Each Operations Area is responsible for implementing the policy with the counsel of the Employee Health Services Department. Specifically, Area personnel with hiring responsibilities are charged with seeking out and being responsive to those agencies which refer the employable handicapped. The Equal Opportunity Division has the responsibility for coordinating and monitoring the program in close coop-eration with the Employee Health Services Department and will help area personnel in identifying potential sources of handicapped referrals. . . . It is Equitable's policy to avoid any appearance of sex discrimination or invasion of privacy. Therefore in written materials and oral references: Avoid *unnecessary* reference to the marital status of the individual in rec-ords and documents. Avoid the titles Miss or Mrs. (With recognizable exceptions, a woman's marital status is not of business interest). Ms. is an acceptable business form, as the counterpart to Mr. Avoid the erroneous infer-ence that all Agents, Managers, Directors, Officers, physicians, clients, etc., are male; that all beneficiaries, spouses, and secretaries are female. In other words, check inadvertent inference of sex—male or female. As a way of avoiding such male-oriented usages as, the employer . . . he, use both male and female pronouns after a singular subject (he/she, his/hers, him/her). Or, as an alternative to tediously repeating these pairs of pronouns, don't use any pronoun with a singular subject or use the all-inclusive plural con-struction (employers . . . they or their). Common sense must govern. Avoid use of the word girls, ladies, gals, etc., relying on the more acceptable generic term: women.

Equitable Life Assurance Society

We will not discriminate against any minority groups nor will we discriminate against majority groups to facilitate minorities.

Fox & Jacobs

DISCHARGE

Discharge Policy at Pacemakers Inc.

When he took the job as manager of the circuit department in the technology division of Pacemakers Inc. three years ago, Jack Rice knew he was on a hot seat. Pacemakers, in business just twelve years, had achieved second place in sales in the industry in the short span of seven years. Then, a two-year series of product recalls based on circuit failures severely damaged the company's reputation and earnings. Sales slipped to fourth place in the industry and there were rumors that Pacemakers was a stockmarket take-over candidate. Top management, convinced there would be only two or three ultimate survivors in this business, and determined to be among them while also remaining independent, decided to clean house in the circuit department. To head the department they brought in Jack, largely because Stan Drew wanted him. Stan, manager of the technology division, had been Jack's old boss when they worked at Circuit Technology Inc., the leading U.S. firm in integrated circuits. Although he had never had management responsibilities, Jack had a reputation as an excellent new product man and he was hired to lead the development of a new series of pacemakers based on the latest work in integrated circuits.

Jack looked on the position as a real challenge. He was responsible for one of the three basic technological ingredients in a pacemaker: circuitry, battery, and pacing leads to the heart. And technology is the key to this business; doctors want the best pacemaker for their patients, and quality, not cost, is the primary factor. This was the challenge Jack desired; he'd had enough of designing circuits for products like electronic games, where cost factors dominated. Jack also got along well with his boss; he believed that Stan Drew knew what applied science was all about—hire creative people, increase the research and development budget, and quality products will emerge.

At first it was rough; Jack had to upgrade his staff—hire several new scientists, reorient others, and discharge a few. He also had to acquaint himself with battery technology, the basic aspects of biophysics, and his competitor's products. It took him a year and a half to see clearly what sort of a product he wanted. And then he had to motivate his staff to pull with him, often by spending long hours with them working on design and materials problems.

About that time Jack's boss, Stan Drew, was fired. Stan said little about his dismissal except that he had taken the long range view and both sales and earnings were still unimpressive and erratic. Stan was replaced by Mark Burns, who had a finance background. There was some grumbling about this among members of the circuit department, but top management explained that the firm's condition was still precarious and attention had to be focused on the present bottom line as well as the long range.

Jack did not get along well with Mark Burns from the start. Mark talked of management by objective and cost-benefit analysis, whereas Jack had always talked with Stan Drew as one inventor to another; Jack felt he did not share a common language with Mark. Jack also did not like the extended business lunches and lengthy departmental meetings that Mark favored; they seemed to be personnel relations ploys and unrelated to the job. Then, too, Jack felt that although Mark talked long-term he really had his eyes trained on the company's quarterly earnings report. Technology, Jack thought, takes time. But Jack also knew that the company was now tracked on his product and he was confident that in time it, or a successor based upon it, would be a winner.

Two and a half years into his job, a pacemaker with Jack's circuits hit the market. It had a good reception in tests, but market acceptance was mixed. Jack believed that this was largely due to the company's tarnished reputation, but he allowed that competitors had not stood still and that their recent products were still a bit ahead of Pacemaker's. As he entered the office of Bill Smith, executive vice president for manufacturing, to attend the monthly meeting, Jack felt secure in the knowledge that Pacemakers was at least competitive and that they could gain the edge with the next generation of pacemakers he had on the drawing board.

Bill Smith informed Jack that recent sales figures were disappointing and that it did not seem to him that a turnaround was near. He added that top management had been disappointed with Jack's performance for some time and that he was being terminated effective at the end of the day. Jack was stunned. He protested that he clearly had turned *his* department around and asked Bill to bring in Jack's immediate boss, Mark Burns, to discuss the issue. Bill said the decision was his, not Mark's, and that it was final. Jack asked for some reasons. Bill said they were in the sales figures. He added that a new circuit department manager had already been hired from outside the firm, and he would be reporting in two days. Allowing that the termination was abrupt, Bill offered Jack two months severance pay and told him he would provide him with a good recommendation.

A few days later, in discussing Jack with the firm's personnel manager, Bill Smith said:

> Jack Rice and Mark Burns just didn't see eye to eye. There was some personality conflict that I could not put my finger on. Maybe I should have canned Mark; he couldn't explain the problem to Jack, and Jack wasn't really aware of it — he was too concerned with his tinkering in the lab. But I couldn't fire Mark; he's ticketed for a top level managerial slot. And I couldn't transfer Jack — there's no other slot in the organization where he would fit. Instead of demoting him in his own department, I thought it was best to just let him go. He'll catch on as a new product man somewhere, but I won't recommend him for a managerial position.

Mark Burns said, in commenting privately on Jack's dimissal:

> Jack was not on top of things; he was too unorganized. He was a brilliant Lone Ranger from Silicon Valley with a narrow, inventor's mentality, who was always jumping ahead of his staff to the next, vaguely thought out project. He had to do everything himself on the technical side of things, but he could not delegate or understand other aspects of the business. His product is okay, it'll help us survive. But as we grow we need more coordination and long-term planning, and Jack was uncomfortable with that approach. He thought it inhibited him. And he never understood that top management wanted at least a show of social responsibility. I found out that he did not even pass out the United Fund cards, and, as for affirmative action, Jack refused to hire on the basis of anything but merit; he'd just laugh and say, "Put 'em in your steno pool." He just did not have a feel for the human side of things. I talked with him about these matters, but it did not seem to have an impact. When I told Bill Smith that I thought we should dump Jack, I offered to do it and give reasons, but Bill said that he would take care of it. Sales, he said, were not that good, which was sufficient.

One of the supervisors formerly under Jack made these observations three months after Jack's termination:

> Things have changed some around here; we are not quite as free-wheeling as we used to be under Jack. The R and D budget has been cut a bit, and some of us are wondering who is next to go. In many ways I think Jack was a fall-guy for Burns and Smith. They are not innovators and this is a risk business. They got a good product out of him and solid ideas for future products. Sales are slow now, but they'll pick up and Burns and Smith will look good. The new boss has some good ideas. But that will mean he has to make changes to leave his mark. That might set us back a year or so. I'm just not sure what games are being played here.

Jack had this comment after reflecting on his dismissal and his three months of trying unsuccessfully to secure a similar position:

I'm still bitter and baffled about this whole thing. I'm baffled because I put up the product that will eventually save this company. I'm bitter because I got the shaft. Mark and Bill Smith know that, and there's nothing I can do about it. Oh, I sent a zinger letter to the company's top dog, but I didn't even get a reply. I lie awake at night thinking about how those two toads above me will benefit from my work. Smith even had the gall to warn me not to take Pacemaker's trade secrets with me. *Their* secrets? Hah! In this business the next new product is in somebody's head—mine! I'll take that with me to a competitor and bury these clowns. So far though, I'll admit I haven't had any takers.

For Discussion

Discuss and evaluate the context of Jack's dismissal and the way it was handled. What steps could be taken to improve termination procedures at Pacemakers Inc.?

Milton Snoeyenbos
John Wesley Roberts

Ethics and the Termination of Employees

In signing a work contract an employee agrees to provide his abilities, time, and effort in return for a wage. Some work contracts extend additional benefits to employees; for example, most union collective bargaining agreements require the employer to provide "just cause" for dismissal of an employee, i.e., dismissal must be based on factors related to job performance or business necessities. However, less than one-fourth of American workers are presently covered by collective bargaining agreements. Although a few employees have just cause provisions specified in their individually negotiated work contracts, the vast majority of employees, perhaps seventy percent, are not so covered. These employees not only have no contractual dismissal rights, they also have very little in the way of legal rights.

The traditional legal context regarding the at-will employee, i.e., one not having explicit work contract provisions regarding dismissal, is spelled out in the following legal cases:

> . . . employers "may dismiss their employees at will . . . for good cause, for no cause, or even for cause morally wrong, without being thereby guilty of legal wrong." *Payne v. Western & A. R.R.,* 81 Tenn. 507, 519–520 (1884).

> . . . the "arbitrary right of the employer to employ or discharge labor, with or without regard to actuating motives," is a proposition "settled beyond peradventure." *Union Labor Hospital Assn. vs. Vance Redwood Lumber Co.,* 158 Cal. 551, 555, 112 p. 886, 888 (1910).

Over the years, the law has diminished the scope of at-will terminations in eight ways: (1) the National Labor Relations Act prohibits the termination of employees solely on the basis of labor organizing activities; (2) the Civil Rights Act protects individuals from dismissal solely on the basis of race, color, religion, sex, and national origin; (3) the Age Discrimination in Employment Act prohibits firings solely on the basis of age; (4) the Vocational Rehabilitation Act bans dismissals based solely on handicap; (5) the Occupational Safety and Health Act prohibits firing on the basis of an employee's refusal to perform a task the employee reasonably believes to be life-threatening; (6) the aforementioned union-management collective bargaining agreements may protect workers from arbitrary dismissal; (7) terminations based on a reason that violates a significant public policy (e.g., refusal to commit perjury) may provide grounds for a court suit; and (8) refusal to engage in an ethically or legally prohibited act may provide the basis for court protection from unjust dismissal.[1]

Although these laws have undoubtedly prevented many firings, Congress and the courts have actually been fairly conservative in restricting employers' discharge rights. The cornerstone of this conservatism is the doctrine of contractual mutuality:

> An employee is never presumed to engage his services permanently, thereby cutting himself off from all chances of improving his condition; indeed, in this land of opportunity it would be against public policy and the spirit of our institutions that any man should thus handicap himself; and the law will presume . . . that he did not so intend. And if the contract of employment be not binding on the employee for the whole term of such employment, then it cannot be binding upon the employer; there would be lack of "mutuality." *Pitcher v. United Oil and Gas Syndicate Inc.* 174 La. 66, 69, 139 So. 760, 761 (1932).

Just as the employee is free to resign, the employer is free to discharge the at-will employee at any time; there is a symmetry to the relationship. There is no doubt that this is an improvement over the complete asymmetry found in the master-slave relationship. In actuality, however, there is frequently an asymmetry in the employer-employee relationship that is slanted in favor of the employer. In times of high unemployment, or in fields of specialization or industries where there is a labor surplus, it will probably be more difficult for the discharged employee to find a new position than for the firm to hire a new employee. Consequently, the harm to the employee, in terms of economic hardship and psychological disruption, is often greater than the harm to the firm. In spite of this asymmetry, however, it is unlikely that sweeping statutory limitations on the employer's right to discharge will be enacted in the near future, for, as Lawrence Blades has pointed out, "One need not be an extreme cynic to say that employers would not favor such legislation. Nor could organized labor be expected to favor laws which would give individual employees a means of protecting themselves without a union."[2] Thirteen years later, in 1980, Richard Vernon and Peter Gray note that "The termination-at-will rule remains very much alive in its most absolute form in a majority of states . . . . Judicial reluctance to alter the employer's fundamental right to hire and fire remains strong and is likely to continue in the absence of a large-scale public determination that that right is being abused."[3] However, in spite of the current legal status of discharge practices, we can still inquire into the ethics of the matter and consider the question of whether there is a moral basis for restrictions or limitations on the present, broad discharge rights of employers. Let us discuss the ethics of dismissal under the rubrics of just cause, due process, and mitigation of harmful effects.[4]

JUST CAUSE

Although "just cause" is an admittedly vague phrase, let us see if we can sharpen it a bit by picking out some relatively clear-cut cases where discharge is justifiable and then some cases where it clearly is unjustifiable. Doing so will enable us to better discuss borderline cases.

What we might call "business necessity" may provide a sufficient basis for discharge. Automation necessary for competitiveness or survival of the firm, severe market shrinkage, product obsolescence, lack of capital—any number of such factors may require work force reduction. If managers calculate that benefits to the firm, remaining employees, and society at large outweigh the negative consequences to the discharged employees, and if the dismissal procedure is conducted fairly and the harmful effects of dismissal are mitigated, then there are both consequentialist and nonconsequentialist reasons for such dismissals. The key here is that the business necessity must be real; the firm must make a genuine attempt to calculate long-term consequences, the dismissal procedure must be fair, and the firm should make a real attempt to minimize harm to those dismissed. In many such cases there are alternatives to discharge that should be explored. For example, overall utility and fairness may be achieved by reducing everyone's work week by 20% for a period of time rather than discharging 20% of the work force.

In addition, many factors specifically related to job performance provide a just basis for discharge. If an employee is nonproductive, negligent, frequently absent without cause, and engages in disruptive conduct in violation of explicit guidelines, then the employer surely has just cause for dismissal. If internal due process procedures are available to employees, and the employer attempts to mitigate the harmful effects of discharge, then the employer is ethically justified in firing such an employee. From a utilitarian or consequentialist standpoint, the results of such a dismissal and the subsequent replacement with a more responsible employee would benefit fellow workers, the firm, and society at large. The dismissed worker demoralizes his fellows, reduces corporate efficiency, and the cost is passed to the consumer. In addition, the consequences of dismissal may be beneficial to such a discharged employee. Tacit consent to ineffectiveness, negligence, excessive absenteeism, laziness, etc., may only encourage such habits. If such an employee ignores company programs designed to help him, and explicit warnings prove ineffective, dismissal may help the person fully realize that his bad habits require reform.

Putting aside factors related to business necessity, if discharge should be related to job performance, then factors unrelated to job performance should not provide a basis for just discharge. Humans are adept at assuming a variety of roles, and *normally* there are many facets of a person's life, or roles he fulfills, that have little or no relevance to his role as employee. Where such roles do impinge on job performance, it is the criteria of the latter that form the basis for just dismissal.

Although the general principle is clear, namely, that factors unrelated to job performance do not provide a basis for just discharge, it is difficult to catalog all factors not related to job performance. At best we can set out some relatively clear-cut areas of immunity. Discharge is normally not just if it is based on the exercise of a constitutionally protected right. Thus, the employee has the right of free choice in the political arena and the right to free speech on most matters. Of course, if the employee spends so much time exercising his right to promote a political candidate or party that he impairs job performance, then discharge may be justified. Also, the employee should not be discharged for engaging in civic and cultural activities of his choice. On the other hand, where the employer can demonstrate *clearly* that job performance is closely tied to participation in certain sorts of civic and cultural activities, then a request to join may be reasonable. Typically, however, the connection is difficult to establish, and in fairness the employee should be given a wide range of options. Then, too, it should be noted that this principle can be carried to absurdity. The employee cannot be expected to join every organization that is related to job performance; good performance demands time *away* from the job, where a mix of roles can be fulfilled.

Finally, although employees are generally expected to abide by company regulations and procedures, and lawful management directives, no employee should be discharged for refusing to engage in behavior that is illegal or commonly acknowledged to be ethically unacceptable.[5] The manager who refuses to fix prices or lie should not be dismissed on such a basis. There are other areas where employees should have immunity from discharge, but, depending on the type of firm, these should be spelled out generally in an employee rights document and articulated via the firm's due process procedure.

It is important that the firm attempt to spell out as clearly as possible the various job related grounds for dismissal. It should also make these grounds known to its employees, for just cause should include only that conduct the employee knows is subject to discipline. Of course, some just cause grounds are obvious and need not be stated; an employee need not be told that physical assault on his supervisor will not be tolerated. But the employee should be informed of prohibited conduct that he would not reasonably understand to be prohibited. It is also important for employees to understand the enforcement status of a rule. If a firm has a no smoking rule, but the rule is not enforced and numerous employees do smoke on the job, then dismissal based solely on that rule is hardly just.

If we have marked off some clear cases where dismissal is justified and other cases where it is unjustified, it must, nevertheless, be admitted that there are numerous borderline cases, especially in the discharge of managers, where considerable judgment is required. The problem of managerial discharge is serious. James Gallagher claims that an "estimated 6% of the 250,000 executives and managers in major U.S. corporations—about 15,000 people are fired annually."[6] Donald Sweet argues that a total of 100,000 U.S. managers are fired each year.[7] Thomas Jaffe states that when high-level executives leave a firm the "reasons range from ill health and early retirement to irreconcilable policy differences. Sometimes the leaving is voluntary. Mostly the phrases in the press releases are euphemisms for firing."[8] Sweet points out a survey of personnel managers indicating that they are fired for a variety of reasons: "'too emotional,' 'immature,' 'couldn't delegate,' 'not tough enough,' etc. Not one could say that these people were fired for lack of technical competence or deficiency of education, both of which are key considerations when a person is hired."[9] Gallagher, chairman of Career Management Associates, an outplacement firm, claims that "Contrary to conventional belief, job terminations are more often prompted by incompatibility than by incompetence. In seven out of ten outplacement cases we have managed, the fired executive has had a new boss within the previous eighteen months. Different styles, new goals, and conflicting personalities account for more terminations than plant closings, layoffs, and corporate mergers combined."[10]

Apparently, then, "incompatibility" is a major source of managerial dismissals. Now, in certain cases there may be organizational flaws that generate conflicts and incompatibility. Richard Huseman lists three causes of such conflict: (1) organizational incongruence, i.e., built-in opposition between task responsibilities; (2) inadequate performance measures, e.g., a purchasing department evaluated on the basis of the negative measure of excess inventory may fail to purchase adequately and this in turn may lead to conflict with the sales department; and (3) ambiguity, i.e., organizational complexity results in ambiguous communication, allowing employees to read what they want into communications.[11] In such cases, utility for the firm and fairness to its employees dictates that the flaws be remedied, and dismissals based on conflicts originating in such flaws do not have a just cause foundation.

We should note, however, that the comments of Donald Sweet and James Gallagher suggest that frequently it is simply *personality* conflicts or incompatibilities that are responsible for dismissals. Here we should keep in mind a hypothesis of recent management theory: "Organizations ought to thrive on most personal and professional differences, because in the long run they account for the dynamics of organizational growth."[12] If this is true, and if the person being considered for dismissal has a good job performance record, then utility for the firm and fairness to the employee indicate that such personality conflicts are not in themselves a just cause for discharge. At worst, the employee should be transferred to a position where such a conflict or difference either will not occur or can be used to advantage. Of course, some deep-seated, intractable personality differences may not lead to corporate growth. This is especially true at the top management level, where fundamental personality differences related to conflicting organizational objectives and strategies may harm the firm and its employees. Furthermore, in some top management slots transfer without demotion may be impossible, and the demotion may be unacceptable to the employee. In such circumstances one suspects that job performance frequently suffers and forms the basis for a just dismissal. But even if not, an overall assessment of utility may permit just discharge.

To summarize, we have suggested that business necessity and factors directly related to job performance provide a justifiable basis for dismissal. We also marked off several aspects of an employee's life that have little or no relevance to the employment relationship, and, hence, dismissals based on such factors do not have a just cause basis. Incompatibilities based on organizational flaws call for elimination of the flaw and do not provide just foundation for dismissal. Moreover, personality conflicts are not themselves a just cause for dismissal; in some cases transfer, not termination, is the answer. But in other cases personality conflicts may lead to disutility and thus provide a basis for just dismissal.

Finally, an employer should not only have just cause for terminating an employee, he should state in writing the reasons for discharge. No person should have to experience the following:

> Do you have any idea why you were fired? — I think ultimately because they didn't like me. I think it's probably that simple. There are still people in the company who are quasi alcoholics or who don't do any work. They're still there. And people who don't make waves. I had a lot of people working for me, and I was under a lot of pressure. I'm probably the kind of person who under those circumstances is not invisible. Probably what it came down to was simply that I was not liked. But I don't really know.[13]

There is no moral basis for the anxiety, self-doubt, and resentment often caused by such terminations. Dismissal may be justified in some cases, but the discharged employee cannot learn from the action if he does not understand its rationale. In addition, a written explanation of reasons for dismissal would encourage the manager to give the same reasons to his superiors, the discharged employee, and those responsible for the firm's due process procedure, the second element in an ethical discharge system.

DUE PROCESS

The right to due process in discharge cases is based squarely on fairness to the employee affected and on utility for the company. As we have noted, fairness and utility require a just cause discharge; adequate due process helps assure both. In fairness to the employee, due process may unmask an unjust discharge; furthermore, the unjust firing of a person with a good job performance record will probably have disutility for the firm. And, insofar as it assures other workers that dismissal decisions are not arbitrary, due process increases employee morale, which has overall utility. Finally, the checks and balances of a good due process procedure encourage a more objective decision.

Objectivity is clearly needed in discharge cases. As we have noted, personality differences often play a central role in such cases, and emotion may cloud balanced judgment. Then, too, management texts and management training mention very little about the practice of discharge and almost nothing about the ethics of discharge. As a result, most managers are not prepared to adopt the synoptic viewpoint necessary for an objective decision. This is especially true of lower level managers, who may have a limited perspective of the whole organization and the breadth of its responsibilities.

David Ewing has provided a succinct list of the characteristics of an ethical due process system:

1. It must be a procedure; it must follow rules. It must not be arbitrary.
2. It must be visible, well-known enough so that potential violators of rights and victims of abuse know it.
3. It must be predictably effective. Employees must have confidence that previous decisions in favor of rights will be repeated.
4. It must be "institutionalized." That is, it must be a relatively permanent fixture in the organization, not a device that is here today, gone tomorrow.
5. It must be perceived as equitable. The standards used in judging a case must be respected and accepted by a majority of employees, bosses as well as subordinates.
6. It must be easy to use. Employees must be able to understand it without fear that procedural complexities will get the best of them.
7. It must apply to all employees.[14]

Although there are a variety of ways that an ethical due process system can be institutionalized, and the best method will be somewhat dependent on the size and type of the firm, the following is offered as a procedure that promises objectivity and fairness for a relatively large firm. The firm's Ethics and Social Responsibility Committee of the Board of Directors (constituted by an equal number of inside and outside directors) selects a termination hearing panel of two company members and one member from the firm's legal counsel. Employees who have received a termination notice receive a written explanation for the termination five days before its effective date. Within this period the employee may elect to contest the dismissal by submitting a request for a termination hearing to the panel. The panel sets a hearing date ten to fourteen days after the effective termination date. The employee has the right to select a member of the firm's legal staff, a member of management, or an outside counsel to represent his case, and can make his selection any time after he has informed the panel that he requests a hearing. The manager who fired the employee is also entitled to representation. The member from the firm's outside legal counsel presides over the hearing. Both sides are entitled to call witnesses or additional resource people, and these may be cross-examined. A stenographer is present to record the hearing. The hearing panel renders its decision within ten days. If the decision favors the employee, it is binding on management; if it favors management, it does not abrogate the employee's right to seek relief or legal remedy from state or federal courts. If the decision favors the employee, no record of the termination or proceedings are retained in the employee's personnel file.

MITIGATION OF HARMFUL EFFECTS

Even though a dismissal is based on just cause and the employee has received due process, the employer still has an obligation to mitigate the harmful effects of dismissal. The obligation is in part based on the asymmetry in the employment relationship that we previously mentioned. It is generally more difficult for the dismissed employee to find a new position than for the firm to hire a new employee. And this asymmetry may still obtain even though the employer does mitigate the situation through his contribution to unemployment compensation, for, in addition to his economic loss, the psychological effect of discharge on an employee is often devastating. Sweet says, "there are three very traumatic separations in our life: divorce, the death of a loved one, and the separation that experts estimate faces 100,000 executives every year—separation from their jobs."[15] Fairness often dictates that the firm should help alleviate this harm. Utility also points in the direction of mitigating the harmful effects of discharge; Angelo Troisi nicely captures the shock of termination and the overall utility to be gained from mitigation:

> Although the emotional impact of being fired varies with the individual, studies show that the trauma associated with termination is so great that it can be compared in intensity to divorce or the death of a loved one. Shock, depression, anger, self-pity, confusion, and loss of identity are some common feelings and reactions. The person is filled with anxiety and self-doubt about the prospects of finding a new job, the reactions of family and peers, and finances. The individual may be extremely bitter and negative about the future to the point of seeking revenge. He or she may go to work for a customer or competitor, file a lawsuit against the company, or spread malicious rumors. Since such negative actions can substantially damage a company's reputation and can have serious

effect on its recruiting efforts, community image, and employee morale and loyalty, it is in a company's best interests to handle terminations as positively as possible.[16]

The precise type of help the firm should provide a dismissed employee will depend on the circumstances: financial aid, employment references, logistical support in finding a new job, and job search training all may play a constructive role.

In concluding, we would point out that, although we have stressed termination costs to the employee, there are also costs to the employer. In the case of unjust dismissals, where an employee has a good job performance record, discharge may reduce efficiency. And many dismissals are harmful to morale and company image. Even just dismissals entail a waste of training and often a disruption of continuity. So, management should take a close look at what is causing terminations and resignations. It should start with a close look at its selection and performance appraisal systems: "a major factor in separations may be underhiring and overhiring . . . a great deal of the agony of separation could be eliminated by working harder at the front end — the selection process. Making sure not only that candidates *can* do the job, which is the easy part of the procedure, but that they *will* do the job."[17] Troisi asks three questions related to performance that if sufficiently answered, would prevent many terminations and resignations:

1. Was the employee's job description regularly reviewed to determine if the employee was performing the duties prescribed?
2. Was the correlation between the employee's salary and his job description reviewed?
3. Were the employee's performance reviews carefully studied?[18]

In addition, it seems reasonable to say that improvements in the quality of work-life would often reduce dismissals and resignations. Our main point here, then, is that even if the firm has an ethical discharge system, with just cause, due process, and mitigation mechanisms, the best solution to the problem is to structure the firm so that the dismissal issue seldom arises.

NOTES

1. Richard G. Vernon and Peter S. Gray, "Termination at Will — The Employer's Right to Fire," *Employee Relations Law Journal,* vol. 6, no. 1 (Summer, 1980), pp. 25–40.

2. Lawrence E. Blades, "Employment at Will vs. Individual Freedom: On Limiting the Abusive Exercise of Employer Power," *Columbia Law Review,* vol. 67, no. 8 (December, 1967), p. 1434.

3. Vernon and Gray, "Termination at Will — The Employer's Right to Fire," p. 39.

4. Thomas Garrett, *Business Ethics* (New York: Appleton-Century-Crofts, 1966), pp. 46–50.

5. In 1981 a law titled the Whistle-Blowers Protection Act was implemented in Michigan. The law makes it illegal for an employer to discharge or threaten a worker or to discriminate in salary, benefits, privileges, or location of employment because an employee has reported a violation of law to any public body. Courts are empowered to order reinstatement, along with seniority, back pay, and damages.

6. James J. Gallagher, "What Do You Owe the Executive You Fire?" *Dun's Review,* vol. 113, no. 6 (June, 1969), p. 109.

7. Donald H. Sweet, "What's Wrong with Being Fired?" *Personnel Journal,* vol. 58, no. 10 (October, 1979), p. 672.

8. Thomas Jaffe, "Is There Life After Downfall?" *Forbes,* vol. 124, no. 10 (November 12, 1979), p. 241.

9. Sweet, "What's Wrong with Being Fired?" p. 672.

10. Gallagher, "What Do You Owe the Executive You Fire?" p. 109.

11. Richard C. Huseman, "Interpersonal Conflict in the Modern Organization," in *Readings in Interpersonal and Organizational Communication,* edited by Richard C. Huseman, Cal M. Logue, and Dwight L. Freshley (Boston: Holbrook Press, 1973), 2nd edition, pp. 192–193.

12. Stephen S. Kaagen, "Terminating People From Key Positions," *Personnel Journal,* vol. 57, no. 2 (February, 1978), p. 96.

13. Harry Maurer, *Not Working* (New York: Holt, Rinehart and Winston, 1979), p. 20.

14. David W. Ewing, *Freedom Inside the Organization* (New York: E. P. Dutton, 1977), p. 156.

15. Sweet, "What's Wrong with Being Fired," p. 672.

16. Angelo M. Troisi, "Softening the Blow of 'You're Fired,'" *Supervisory Management,* vol. 25, no. 6 (June, 1980), p. 16.

17. Sweet, "What's Wrong with Being Fired," p. 672.

18. Troisi, "Softening the Blow of 'You're Fired,'" p. 14.

Selected Bibliography

Arvey, R. *Fairness in Selecting Employees.* Reading, Mass.: Addison-Wesley, 1979.

Barry, V. *Moral Issues in Business.* 2nd ed. Belmont, Cal.: Wadsworth, 1982, ch. 4.

Bittker, B. *The Case for Black Reparations.* New York: Vintage Books, 1973.

Cohen, M., Nagel T., and Scanlon, T., eds. *Equality and Preferential Treatment.* Princeton: Princeton University Press, 1977.

Davidson, K., Ginsburg, R., and Kay, H., eds. *Sex-Based Discrimination: Text, Cases, and Materials.* St. Paul, Mn.: West Publishing Co., 1974.

Dessler, G. *Personnel Management.* 2nd ed. Reston, Va.: Reston Publishing, 1981.

Garrett, T. *Business Ethics.* Englewood Cliffs, N.J.: Prentice-Hall, 1966, ch. II.

Goldman, A. *Justice and Reverse Discrimination.* Princeton: Princeton University Press, 1979.

Gross, B., ed. *Reverse Discrimination.* Buffalo: Prometheus Books, 1977.

Meyer, J., and Donaho, M. *Get the Right Person for the Job.* Englewood Cliffs, N.J.: Prentice-Hall, 1979.

Pigors, P., and Myers, C. *Personnel Administration.* 5th ed. New York: McGraw-Hill, 1965.

"Protecting At-Will Employees Against Wrongful Discharge: The Duty to Terminate Only in Good Faith." *Harvard Law Review,* 93 (June, 1980), 1816–44.

Robbins, S. *Personnel: The Management of Human Resources.* Englewood Cliffs, N.J.: Prentice-Hall, 1978.

Stanton, E. *Successful Personnel Recruiting and Selection.* New York: Amacom, 1977.

Summers, C. "Individual Protection Against Unjust Dismissal: Time for a Statute." *Virginia Law Review,* 62 (April, 1976), 481–532.

5

EMPLOYEE RIGHTS

INTRODUCTION

Corporations are goal oriented and hierarchically organized, which places a premium on efficiency and the attendant employee obligations of loyalty, obedience, and confidentiality. In recent years it has been argued that employees have certain rights that cannot morally be overridden on grounds of efficiency. This chapter explores some of the moral rights that have been proposed.

In "Privacy in the Corporation," Humber first differentiates moral from legal rights and then focuses on the moral right to privacy within the corporate context. His essay points out the difficulties corporations have in formulating and applying specific guidelines once a decision is made to acknowledge privacy rights. He concludes by recommending a general course of action, which firms can adopt, to resolve the central problems that arise in balancing the moral right to privacy with other corporate interests and rights. The case studies in this section explore two areas of concern with respect to privacy: a general moral issue concerning the kinds of employee data firms should be allowed to gather and retain, and the issue of defining the morally permissible means used to gather such data.

If a corporation is engaged in immoral or illegal activity, does an individual in that firm have a right or obligation to blow the whistle? Gene James clarifies the nature of whistle blowing, discussing a variety of legal and practical constraints on the activity, and defends the practice against criticisms. The case study discusses an actual whistle blowing situation and invites discussion of the corporation's response.

Today's workers enjoy relatively high pay and job security, yet many not only want but believe they have a right to jobs that are stimulating and enable them to maximize their potential. As the Lordstown case points up, however, there is often considerable disparity between what employers and employees take to be employee rights or management responsibilities in the area of job quality. Robert Schappe's article explores some of the arguments management and union representatives employ against implementation of job enrichment programs that encourage more employee autonomy and responsibility.

In "A Proposed Bill of Rights," David Ewing sets out nine specific rights he believes corporations should implement. Mark Woodhouse amends and articulates Ewing's proposals. Donald Martin, on the other hand, contends that the argument for corporate employee rights rests on a faulty analogy between corporations and governments; such corporate employee rights, he concludes, are neither justified nor needed.

One of Ewing's proposed employee rights is the right to due process regarding grievances. Maurice Trotta and Harry Gudenberg provide information on grievance procedures in nonunion contexts.

Privacy

Employee Records at Fantenetti Valve Corporation

Fantenetti Valve Corporation, headquartered in Patterson, New Jersey, is a specialty valve manufacturer with 1981 sales of $426 million. Unlike many of its competitors, Fantenetti does not mass produce standard valves, but instead focuses primarily on research and design work; it employs a relatively high percentage of scientific and technical personnel and spends about 6% of its annual sales on research. Most of its manufacturing is subcontracted with other firms. Fantenetti is not unionized. We interviewed Ross Mills, personnel manager at Fantenetti Valve Corporation, concerning that company's policy on employee records.

QUESTION: We hear a lot about files on employees these days Ross; what's the need for them in a firm such as Fantenetti?

MILLS: We are a large, technologically based firm, with about 6,000 employees in five states. Our technical data are our lifeblood, and we simply have to minimize risk with respect to trade secrets, formulas, marketing plans, and our growth strategies. Since most of the risk relates to the background and experiences of our employees, we must have data about them. We're in a tough position. We try to be sensitive to people's rights, but managers cannot make rational decisions without data, and this includes data on people — we certainly would be open to criticism if we acted without benefit of information on the people we hire and employ.

QUESTION: How do you get the data you want, and what's included?

MILLS: Well, each person's an individual. What's relevant in one case may not be relevant in another. So, at the time of application we ask the applicant to sign the following authorization:

I understand that my employment at Fantenetti Valve Corporation is subject to verification of previous employment, data provided in my application, and any related documents, and will be contingent on my submitting to and passing both a physical examination administered by a company appointed physician and whatever psychological tests are authorized by Fantenetti Valve Corporation. I authorize educational institutions, law enforcement authorities, employers, and all organizations and individuals having information relevant to my employment at Fantenetti Valve Corporation, to provide such information. I release all organizations and individuals, including Fantenetti Valve Corporation, from any liability in connection with the release of information about me. I understand that an investigative report may be made by, or authorized by and submitted to, Fantenetti Valve Corporation, and that this report might include information concerning my character, reputation, and mode of living.

This gives us some flexibility on the data we collect about each applicant; what's important in the case of one person may not be with another.

QUESTION: But isn't this just too broad? Doesn't it authorize you to gather any data in whatever way without incurring any liability at all?

MILLS: Our experience is that you never know where an investigation will lead. So you need a blanket authorization. Of course we don't do anything outside the law. And once we hire someone, he's free to inspect his dossier anytime and to insert comments. I suppose we are unfair to some applicants. We do hire professionals to run our tests and background checks. And where we have only a few applicants we may invite in an otherwise promising candidate who has a few bad spots on his record. We sit down, talk about, and maybe clarify the problem. But, you know, in most cases we are swamped with candidates, so we can quickly narrow the list to the cream of the crop, most of whom have no problems with previous employers, school records, credit bureaus, health, and so on. But let me add that we also base our decisions on objective tests that we administer regarding aptitude, intelligence, and personality.

QUESTION: Aren't some of these sorts of tests of doubtful validity, especially personality tests?

MILLS: Let me say that we are an equal opportunity employer. We do some federal work, and we've always met Equal Employment Opportunity Commission (EEOC) and Office of Federal Contract Compliance (OFCC) guidelines. Beyond that, we are a scientific company. We believe in science. We believe that personality traits are measurable. You may have a person with the aptitude and brains for a job, but he has a personality flaw. In our sensitive business it's important that we measure a person's maturity, stability, and compatibility. Personality tests aren't infallible, but they're better than just a hunch about a person. They give us some idea about areas of a person's adequacy and inadequacy. They also help place people, to fit them into the right corporate slot.

QUESTION: Don't some of these tests touch on variables like masculinity/ femininity? Are you interested in this sort of adequacy?

MILLS: It might be relevant.

QUESTION: Is homosexuality a thing of interest here?

MILLS: It may be; you can't generalize. You have to look at each case as it comes up.

QUESTION: But in these cases aren't you faced with an invasion of privacy?

MILLS: There's no law requiring a quota of homosexuals. Beyond that we do take each case on its own merits. And that right has to be set against our right to gather relevant information.

QUESTION: Does all this data become part of one's permanent file?

MILLS: Yes, but he always has access to it, and can insert comments. We don't try to stereotype people with tests. Files are constantly updated. Everyone is evaluated annually, and the employee sees and signs his evaluation. He may add comments. Other data is constantly added: letters of commendation or warning, relevant memoranda, newspaper clippings, employee suggestions, health insurance information, and so on.

QUESTION: Do you separate job performance data from personal information?

MILLS: No. It's all related to job performance.

QUESTION: Can the employee see anything in his file at any time?

MILLS: There are only two things he cannot see. We have a form that compares workers for merit raises, promotions, and layoffs. Since this data is comparative, and includes personal information on several employees, it is not available. We also have a corporate development plan that contains management's general opinion of an individual's potential, any long-range plans the company might have regarding the employee, and a list of possible replacements. This isn't available either. But let me add that we're practically required to keep such files. We have to promote minorities, and so we have to get the data. To compare people and groups we have to have data on everyone.

QUESTION: Who has access to these files?

MILLS: A superior has access to the file of any subordinate responsible to him on the organizational chart. Those people designated "senior manager" have access to the file of anyone below that level. You must have this sort of access to facilitate the information flow. We're a "people" company, and we have to get the right people in the right jobs.

QUESTION: Do you allow outsiders access to your employee files?

MILLS: You have to. The Occupational Safety and Health Administration (OSHA) requires health information. The IRS wants payroll data. The Defense Department examines our security checks. I could go on. The police and the courts can get certain data. We also generally agree to provide data on job title, salary, and length of service to the credit bureaus and investigating agencies that screen our applicants. We don't release any other information unless the employee agrees to it.

For Discussion

Has Ross Mills presented an acceptable defense of Fantenetti's policies regarding employees' records? In what areas is his defense strong? In what areas is it weak? If it was your responsibility to redesign Fantenetti's employee record procedures, what changes would you make? Why?

Surveillance at Unitex Distributors of America Inc.

Unitex Distributors operates 157 convenience food stores in the south and operates concessions at 26 large airports in the U.S. We interviewed Marvin Bell, Unitex's vice-president responsible for security.

QUESTION: Mr. Bell, Unitex is known as a security conscious firm; explain some of your precautions and the reasons for them.

BELL: We're in two low profit margin businesses, and we found that 1–2% of sales were lost to shoplifting and employee pilferage. Since we began closed circuit surveillance, tightened our investigations of job seekers, and introduced periodic polygraph tests, our loss ratio is down to a fraction of a percent in areas where we can use these methods.

QUESTION: How do you screen applicants? What are you looking for?

BELL: We hire an investigative agency to run a check on each applicant who passes our initial screen tests. We want to know whether the person is stable and honest: What's his work record like? Is he extravagant? Does he pay his debts? Is his home life stable? Has he committed crimes? Is he healthy? — things like that. We also screen the applicant with a polygraph test administered by a professional. Here we try to catch any undetected crimes, dishonest tendencies, intentions with regard to job permanency, problems with drugs, family stability, and so on.

QUESTION: Doesn't this amount to an invasion of privacy?

BELL: Not really. We don't force anyone to apply with or work for us. It's all on the up and up. To be processed each applicant must accept and sign the following:

As part of my application I agree to voluntarily submit to a polygraph test, and, if accepted, I agree to voluntarily submit from time to time to polygraph tests, in all cases releasing and indemnifying my employer, Unitex Distributors of America Inc., and any persons in any way connected therewith, of any and all liability with respect thereto.

So it's all voluntary. We aren't coercing these people.

QUESTION: But is this truly voluntary? You either take the polygraph or you are not hired. Or if you are employed, you take it or you are fired. Doesn't this go against the Fifth Amendment right to remain silent and to not incriminate oneself? Doesn't it amount to an unreasonable search that the Fourth Amendment bans? And isn't it a form of coerced expression that violates the First Amendment?

BELL: Those amendments relate to the government's actions, to court cases and the like. If the polygraph turns up a thief, we know it isn't admissible in court. In most cases we don't prosecute, we just fire the person. There's no federal law prohibiting the polygraph, so we are within our rights and the law. Now some states do have laws banning polygraph tests, but there our loss ratio is much greater than in states where we can test prospective employees. We think those laws should be repealed. And, before you say it, the reason is not just profit. That's part of it, of course; Unitex has a responsibility to its shareholders. But each outlet is a profit center that sets its own prices and pays its own wages. A thief raises the cost to customers of that outlet and reduces wages to its employees. Is that fair? Does a thief have that right? If it's legal, if it exposes and prevents theft, if it benefits customers and honest employees as well as Unitex, then don't we have an obligation to use the polygraph?

QUESTION: One doesn't have a right to steal, but the issue is whether your investigative methods invade peoples' privacy.

BELL: Well, these rights aren't inalienable; they have to be balanced. A couple of years ago a truckload of goods was stolen. It had to be an inside job, and two people had keys. We couldn't polygraph in that state, and we wound up firing both employees. In all probability only one was guilty. You can't take losses of that magnitude in this business; but why should the innocent suffer? Only the guilty, not the innocent, need to worry about a polygraph.

QUESTION: But is that true? I've heard that the polygraph is only about 90% accurate. So some thieves will not get caught; but, if there are only a few thieves, a much larger number of innocent people will fail the test.

BELL: That's a problem. We always use licensed experts employed by a professional investigative agency. In the hands of an expert, we believe the polygraph is about 98% accurate. And usually corroborating evidence is available. If the test shows someone is guilty, you test his fellow employees. Usually they know. So you usually have independent evidence—maybe a TV monitor reveals suspicious behavior. But I think you are really missing the point. We don't want to catch people, any more than you want to catch your kids doing something wrong. You need some rules or guidelines so people won't misbehave. You try to encourage them not to misbehave. Our methods do that.

QUESTION: But do they? Haven't studies shown that people today want more respect and responsibility, that they want to be trusted, and that they produce better if they are trusted?

BELL: Frankly, I don't put much stock in any of these studies. Common-sense tells us that there's a little larceny in all of us. That little larceny can ruin a low-margined business. Surveillance, the polygraph—these really help people. They deter some people from crime. But if a person steals, he gets caught. When faced with the evidence he usually confesses. We don't automatically fire him. Confession is good for the soul; if the transgression isn't too serious, we often retain and retrain the person. But the main point is deterrence. We've even hired some people with prison records, people with dispositions to crime, and some of them are grateful for our surveillance because it keeps them on the straight and narrow. Some of them are very loyal. Of course, we want loyal employees, but we only want the loyalty of honest people. We do trust the people we keep, and we have a solid basis for trusting them. They know their fellow employees can be trusted. The fact that our losses have been cut means we are seeing more responsible behavior from our employees. That not only flows to the bottom line, it also results in increased wages—you don't want to overlook the motivation of money.

QUESTION: You speak of trust, Mr. Bell; you trust your employees because they're polygraphed. But do they trust you? The top management of Unitex isn't polygraphed is it?

BELL: Well, they could be; we haven't had problems at that level yet, but we wouldn't rule out use of the polygraph at any level. But most of our upper-level managers come up the Unitex ladder; we promote from within. These people have a real stake in the firm, and a lot to lose. We don't have any evidence that they stray.

For Discussion

Does Mr. Bell make a good case for the surveillance and polygraph policies of Unitex? What are the strengths of his position? What are the weaknesses? If you were managing Unitex what practices would you retain? Why? What policies would you change? Why?

James M. Humber

Privacy in the Corporation

In our society we speak very loosely of "rights." Much of the discussion of the right to privacy in the literature reflects this looseness. Few commentaries on the right to privacy in corporations clearly distinguish between legal and moral rights, or attempt to explore the complex relationships between these different rights. Indeed, more often than not the two kinds of rights are confused.[1] Furthermore, the concept of a "moral right" is problematic. Are humans "endowed" with "inalienable" moral rights, or are moral rights ascribed to us by society? Philosophers have argued this issue for years; but those who discuss the right to privacy avoid the fray and rarely, if ever, tell us which theory of rights they accept.

In an essay of this length I cannot begin to resolve, or even take note of, all the problems involved in discussions of moral and legal rights. However, what I can and will attempt to do is the following: First, I will distinguish between moral and legal rights in general, and, in particular, the moral and legal right to privacy. Next, I will narrow my discussion to the *moral* right to privacy, and consider some of the problems involved in understanding and implementing such a right within the corporate structure. Finally, I will recommend a course of action aimed at resolving the more important problems corporations must face as they attempt to balance the moral right to privacy against opposing corporate interests.

I. RIGHTS: MORAL AND LEGAL

Ordinarily, statements about rights and statements about duties are taken to be reciprocal. For example, if I have a legal right to vote, one might say that society has a legal duty not to interfere with my voting. Similarly, if I have a moral right not to be killed, then it could be claimed that other persons have a moral duty not to kill me. In addition, rights and duties can be viewed as absolute or as *prima facie*. If my right not to be killed is absolute, then there are absolutely no circumstances under which one's duty not to kill me would not hold. (In essence, to kill me *must* be to do something wrong.) On the other hand, if my right not to be killed is merely *prima facie*, then if I am killed by another, there is nothing more than a presumption that my killer has done something wrong. That is to say, it is understood that there may be circumstances under which a person's duty not to kill me could be "overridden" or "negated," so that he or she could kill me and do nothing wrong (e.g., my killer might have to kill me in order to avoid his or her own death).

In our society few rights (legal or moral) are granted absolute status. However, a *prima facie* right is a right nonetheless. On the other hand, there are cases where we possess moral rights without corresponding legal rights, and *vice versa*. It is in these cases that the distinction between moral and legal rights is most clearly evidenced. For example, most people would agree that we have a moral duty to tell the truth, and that we have a (moral) right not to be lied to. However, we have no general legal obligation to tell the truth. For example, assume that you must catch a train in order to be present for a job interview, and that you ask me what time the train leaves. I dislike you and straightforwardly lie about the train schedule. Because of my lie you miss the train and do not make your interview. In this case you cannot take me to court and claim that I have violated one of your legal rights. Still and all, I have done something morally wrong; there is no justification for violating my moral duty to tell you the truth. Or to put it another way, you have a moral right to be told the truth (even though you have no legal right), and in the case at hand the circumstances are not such that I can morally justify violating that right.

If there are cases where we possess moral rights without corresponding legal rights, there also are cases where we have legal rights and no corresponding moral rights. Let us say, for instance, that I buy a used car only after the salesman gives me his "personal assurance" that he will make all necessary repairs within the first six months of my ownership. I secure a loan from the car dealership, and, after paying $500 down and making three monthly payments, my car's transmission falls out. When I return the car to the salesman and demand that he fix the transmission he refuses. I withhold my fourth month's car payment and use that money to repair the car. The salesman responds by repossessing my car. In this case the salesman does not act illegally; indeed, he has a legal right either to be paid or to be given title to my car. From the moral point of view, however, his right to repossess my car is questionable, for he has not kept his promise to repair my car when necessary.

II. Privacy Rights: Legal and Moral

Companies doing business in the United States have no choice but to recognize a legal right to privacy, for that right has been held to be constitutionally guaranteed.[2] In addition, some states have passed legislation attempting to protect the employee's right to privacy.[3] Thus, unless a corporation is willing to break the law, it must do its utmost to ensure that its policies and practices accord with requirements set by law. Of course, this is not a simple procedure; there are times when the best lawyer can do no more than make an educated guess as to what is and is not required or prohibited by law. For example, a California law gives employees the right to inspect personnel files that are "used or have been used to determine that employee's qualifications for employment, promotion, and additional compensation, or termination. . . ."[4] Does this mean that *no* information in an employee's file can be kept "company confidential"? Or does it mean that no *personal* information can be kept from an employee? If the latter, what is meant by "personal information"? Are a company's salary forecasts for an employee personal information (after all, they may be used to determine the employee's additional compensation), or are they rather business planning information? Until the matter is tested in court, no one can be *absolutely* sure whether such forecasts are legally classifiable as personal information, or as business planning information. Furthermore, no lawyer can be expected to anticipate all the new directions the law will take. For instance, some legal scholars were quite surprised to discover that the right to privacy was used as a justification for allowing women the right to abort in the first and second trimesters of pregnancy.[5] Thus, a corporate law firm may have very good reasons to believe that certain corporate practices do not violate the legal right to privacy, and yet discover (to its dismay) that the court does not share its opinion.[6]

A corporation must grapple with difficult problems as it attempts to set its policies and practices foursquare with the law. As difficult as these problems are, however, they pale in comparison to the problems that arise once a corporation evidences a concern for the moral right to privacy; in many ways legal rights are less problematic than moral rights. The former are determined by statute and by case law; as such, they are fairly determinate, easily accessible, and uniformly applicable. In addition, they are subject to final arbitration; ultimately, the law is what the court says it is. Moral rights enjoy none of these advantages: moral views differ; the "moral law" is informal and indeterminate; and most troublesome of all, there is no group of moral "experts" empowered to serve as an ultimate court of appeal in resolving moral disputes. Because all moral rights share these characteristics, corporate attempts to formally recognize a moral right to privacy face numerous problems. It is to the most important of these problems that we must now direct our attention.

III. Problems Involved in Understanding and Implementing the Moral Right to Privacy in the Corporation

Although any attempt to recognize a moral right to privacy within the corporate setting will generate problems, there seems to be a general feeling among corporate executives that such action is advisable. There are at least three reasons for this. First, as many managers realize, failure to acknowledge a moral right to privacy may well foster employee discontent.[7] Second, those companies exhibiting little or no concern for employee privacy beyond what is mandated by law risk projecting a bad public image. Finally, and most importantly, privacy concerns have prompted, and will continue to prompt, a swirl of legislative activities;[8] thus, if corporations do not act to provide some corporate mechanisms for avoiding and resolving privacy disputes, they may well find themselves hamstrung by severely restrictive privacy legislation.[9]

Once a company acknowledges that its own interests are served by concerning itself with the moral right to privacy, a host of problems must still be faced. Virtually all of these problems arise because, as we have seen, moral rights are quite different from legal rights. Moral rights are informal and indeterminate. They cannot be found "written down" in a moral constitution somewhere; and as a consequence, each corporation is left to its own devices as it attempts to understand the moral right to privacy. What exactly is that right, and how far does it extend? There appears to be general agreement that the right refers to the control an individual has over personal information; but once one proceeds beyond this point agreement breaks down. The major reason for disagreement is that different people accept different moral theories, and moral commitments affect one's views concerning moral rights. To illustrate this point, let us consider the importance that the right to privacy would have for advocates of two very different moral theories.[10]

Many persons argue for a moral right to privacy by appealing to consequences. According to Stanley I. Benn:

> The usual arguments against wiretapping, bugging, a National Data Center, and private investigators rest heavily on the contingent possibility that a tyrannical government or unscrupulous individuals might misuse them for blackmail or victimization. The more one knows about a person, the greater one's power to damage him.[11]

The argument here is that failure to recognize a right to privacy will, in all likelihood, produce more harm than good, and that as a consequence we ought to recognize such a right. As Benn realizes, however, this argument rests upon the "contingent possibility" that someone might misuse information secretly obtained. As such, we can imagine circumstances in which the argument would have little or no force. For example, let us say that I own a small business, that I interview all candidates for jobs in my company, and that only I have access to personnel files. I know that I would never misuse the employee information I have accumulated, and that the possibility of this information being misused by anyone else is virtually *nil*. Furthermore, my past experience has been that secretly obtaining personal information regarding sexual preferences, drinking habits, religious affiliations, etc., has been extremely helpful to me in hiring trustworthy employees. In these circumstances, I might well conclude that recognition of a right to privacy would do more harm than good, and so hold that there is no such right to be accorded those who seek employment in my business.

If we attempt to ground the moral right to privacy on considerations of consequences, there may be circumstances in which we would not want to recognize that right. But we are not forced to appeal to consequences in order to justify recognition of a moral right to privacy. For example, Benn argues that the moral right to privacy is founded on the principle of respect for persons. On this view:

> It is not just a matter of a fear to be allayed by reassurances (concerning the possible misuse of secretly obtained information), but a resentment that anyone—even a thoroughly trustworthy official—should be able to satisfy any curiosity, without the knowledge let alone the consent of the subject. For since what others know about him can radically affect a man's view of himself, to treat the collation of personal information about him as if it raised purely technical problems of safeguards against abuse is to disregard his claim to consideration and respect as a person.[12]

To ground the right to privacy on the principle of respect for persons is not to found that right on "contingent possibilities." Thus, if one accepts such an interpretation he or she must acknowledge that at least a *prima facie* right to privacy is *always* possessed by *all* persons. And even if one is convinced (as was the owner of the small business in our earlier example) that no harmful consequences would flow from secretly collecting information about another person's sex life or religious preferences, he or she must allow that action of this sort is morally questionable because it violates the right to privacy that all persons possess.[13]

Because the moral right to privacy is subject to various interpretations, any corporation wanting to recognize such a right must first decide how it wants, generally, to understand that right. That is to say, the corporation must determine whether it considers the right to privacy to be grounded on considerations of consequences, respect for persons, or some other foundation. Once a corporation has cleared this hurdle, however, it faces further difficulties. These problems arise because the moral right to privacy is commonly understood to be *prima facie* and not absolute. To say that privacy is a *prima facie* right is to acknowledge that there are circumstances in which it may be "overridden." Or to put it another way, it is to admit that there may be cases where it would be morally permissible to invade someone's privacy. The difficulty with all this, however, is that two or more people can: a) agree in their general understanding of the moral right to privacy, b) agree that the right is *prima facie,* and yet c) disagree completely as to what sorts of conditions justify overriding that right. To see how this can happen, it may be useful to examine an actual set of corporate privacy guidelines.

Probably no corporation has spent more time, money, and effort developing corporate guidelines regarding privacy than International Business Machines. IBM hired a consultant, Professor Paul Westin of Columbia University, an acknowledged expert on privacy, and did all that it could to achieve a comprehensive understanding of the moral right to privacy.[14] The end product of IBM's study—the corporation's guidelines to privacy—may well serve as a model for other businesses and industries. The following summarizes, in a very rough fashion, a number of IBM's most important views on employee privacy.

A. Only job-related facts about employees may be collected and kept in personnel files.

B. Employees have a right to see most of the information in their personnel files, and they are entitled to know how that information is being used.

C. Information over three years old is purged from personnel files.

D. No employee's conversation may be recorded or monitored without that employee's consent and knowledge.

E. Employers are restricted in the means they can use to "check up" on employees, e.g., they cannot hire an investigator to follow an employee on a trip.

F. Personality and general intelligence tests may not be used by the personnel department.

G. Lie detectors can only be used if an employee gives his/her permission for their use. If the employee does not give his/her permission, this decision cannot be used against the employee.

H. Use of personal files within the corporation must be classified.

I. No information on an employee is given to an outsider unless the employee consents, or the requestor can furnish proper identification, prove his or her legal authority, and demonstrate that they need the information sought.

J. Information that is less than three years old and included in an employee's personnel file cannot be destroyed without the employee's consent.

IBM's attempt to formulate a comprehensive set of guidelines to privacy is laudable. Nevertheless, it is clear that different people can accept these guidelines and disagree as to what sorts of investigations they permit. For example, consider a problem that could arise under guideline A. The problem is one noted by Frank Cary, chairman and chief executive officer of IBM.

> Suppose one of our managers got an anonymous letter giving strong indication that an employee was a child beater. The manager might judge this to be a private matter and not investigate. Of course he would be wrong. Humanitarian considerations aside, an accusation such as this, if true, might affect both the employee's performance and — if there were contact with customers — ability to represent IBM.[15]

For Cary it is clear that an anonymous charge of child beating warrants investigation, because if the charge were true it could affect the employee's job performance. However, for a number of reasons one might want to disagree with Cary's judgment. First, the charge is anonymous; one could argue that charges from anonymous parties do not justify intrusions into areas of one's life that do not obviously and directly relate to one's job description. Second, one could claim that IBM's only interest is in its employees' *job performances,* not in the *causes* for its employees' successes and failures. Or to put it another way, investigation into the child beating charge is not called for, because means are readily available to determine whether or not the employee is accomplishing the tasks he or she has been assigned. Indeed, if Cary feels that he has a right to investigate anything that *might* affect job performance, this gives him license to intrude into virtually *any* area of his employees' lives. After all, if an employee is upset about his daughter being unwed and pregnant, or his wife overcharging a credit account, he might well perform poorly on the job. Should Cary be permitted to investigate these areas of his employees' lives too?

The point is not that Cary is wrong in judging that an anonymous child beating charge justifies collecting information about otherwise private areas of his employees' lives. The point is that it is a personal judgment whether such a charge justifies "overriding" an employee's right to privacy, and that as a consequence those empowered to apply IBM's guidelines may evidence honest and deepseated disagreement as to how this ought to be done. But if this is so, those corporations which formulate and employ a formal set of corporate privacy guidelines also must set some general policy for the application of those guidelines. Otherwise the corporation will not have one set of guidelines, but as many sets as there are people interpreting and applying them.

Finally, once a corporation has formulated its corporation privacy guidelines and has set some policy for applying these standards, there is a third set of problems it must face. These problems arise because the moral right to privacy is affected by contingencies of time, place, and culture. One hundred years ago we did not worry about computers, tape recordings, and lie detectors, for these machines did not exist. In addition, we did not have the attitude (which seems to be evolving today), that elected officials' tax records are public property. In short, societal attitudes and circumstances change; what is not considered a violation of one's moral right to privacy at one time and place may be so considered in another, and *vice versa*. As a result, corporations must develop a procedure for modifying or extending their guidelines so as to cover new cases that arise because of changing circumstances and attitudes. Without such a procedure, the net effect would be that new cases would be decided in a totally *ad hoc* manner, without reference to any guidelines at all. And it is precisely this condition that a corporation seeks to avoid when it develops a formal set of guidelines reflecting the organization's understanding of the moral right to privacy.

IV. RECOMMENDATION FOR UNDERSTANDING AND IMPLEMENTING THE MORAL RIGHT TO PRIVACY IN THE CORPORATION

We have seen that there are at least three reasons motivating a corporation to go beyond what is required by law and to recognize that its employees have a moral right to privacy: 1) such action creates a good public image; 2) it significantly reduces the possibility of disputes with employees over privacy related issues; and 3) it provides a means for resolving privacy disputes within the corporation, thus obviating the need for restrictive privacy legislation. In addition, we have seen the problems that recognition of a moral right to privacy raises for a corporation: a) the organization must develop a general understanding of the moral right to privacy; b) it must develop a general policy for the application of its guidelines; and c) it must formulate procedures for extending its guidelines to new cases. A truly successful program for recognizing the moral right to privacy within the corporation will accomplish goals 1) through 3) while at the same time resolving problems a) through c). It may be that no program can totally realize all of these ends.[16] I believe, however, that the following program holds out some hope of success.

First, I recommend that each organization look upon itself as a microsociety existing within, and at the pleasure of, the macro-society. Realization of this fact makes it clear that businesses and industries must obey existing statutory law. Thus, the first step any corporation must take is to get clear as to current privacy legislation, and do its utmost to ensure that its procedures concerning privacy are in accord with all legal requirements.

Second, corporations need to arrive at some general understanding of what they take the moral right to privacy to be. Because moral rights are informal and indeterminate, each corporation can — indeed must — determine this on its own. There is no indisputably "correct" interpretation of the moral right to privacy; corporations may adopt their own methods for arriving at their various interpretations of the privacy right. In the end, however, it is absolutely essential that a formal set of privacy guidelines be written, and that this be distributed to all employees and made available to all job applicants. Furthermore, it should be clearly stated that the corporation's guidelines apply equally to *all* persons on the company payroll. For example, if the guidelines state that union workers who call in sick may be called at home or "checked up on" in other ways, such actions would also be permitted when the company president failed to show up for work.

A number of advantages would be secured if corporations were to proceed along the lines just noted. First, the requirement that the corporate guidelines be distributed to all employees and be made available to all job applicants helps ensure employee consent for these guidelines. It is generally recognized that there is no invasion of a person's privacy if that person freely consents to share information about himself. If we look upon a corporation as a micro-society, we can say that employees who are aware of their corporation's privacy guidelines and do not resign tacitly agree to accept them (much like the citizens of a state tacitly "sign" the social contract). Thus, if the guidelines were strictly adhered to, no employee could complain that his/her privacy was being invaded. After all, he/she has tacitly agreed that the corporation's guidelines determine his/her right to privacy in the corporation; and if those guidelines are not violated, his/her privacy has been respected.

Second, it seems clear that within any corporation, privacy guidelines would have to be approved and set in place by top-level management. Making the guidelines applicable to these managers assures that they will be honest and truthful in their understanding of the moral right to privacy. That is to say, it forestalls the possibility that top-level management will interpret the moral right to privacy in a very weak fashion for middle-level management and below, and then interpret that right in a much more strict fashion when they apply it to themselves.

Finally, if a corporation's privacy guidelines applied equally to everyone in the corporation, employees would not feel that they were being treated unfairly or that there were two rights to privacy: one for themselves and one for top-level management. This would do much to avoid employee discontent.

Obviously, if a corporation's privacy guidelines are to apply equally to all employees, there must be some mechanism within the corporation to assure such equality of application. What seems to be called for is a privacy court, similar to the macro-society's judicial system. This court would have at least one representative from all major groups within the organization, e.g., union workers, management, research and development. In addition to ensuring that the guidelines are applied to everyone in the corporation, this court also would be responsible for interpreting and applying the corporation's guidelines, and extending them to new cases. As decisions of these sorts are made, they could be kept on file and used as precedents for later decisions.[17] This would solve the problems of developing a general policy for applying the guidelines, and formulating procedures for extending these guidelines to new cases (b and c).

Development of a privacy court within a corporation would not be an easy matter; there is no obviously "correct" method of operation for such a court. That is to say, one corporation might want all court decisions to be made in accordance with a majority rule doctrine, while another company might insist that a representative of top management serve as judge and final decision maker, with all other court members merely offering opinions and advice. Each corporation would have to work out its own method of operation. Each granting this, however, there do not seem to be any insuperable problems involved in setting up privacy courts within business organizations. Furthermore, if a privacy court were made operational in a corporation, and if knowledge of the judicial procedure for the application and extension of the guidelines were made available to all employees and job applicants, along with copies of the corporate privacy guidelines, employees who did not resign could be said to have tacitly consented to the corporation's judicial procedure as well as to its guidelines. In short, all problems involved in understanding and implementing the moral right to privacy in the corporation would be solved. And as these problems are solved, the goals the corporation had in mind when it decided to recognize the moral right to privacy would also be realized. Specifically: 1) the corporation would acquire a good public image; 2) it would minimize disputes over privacy concerns; and 3) it would provide a mechanism within the corporation for resolving disputes that do arise, thus making it less likely that society would pass laws imposing its views of privacy upon the corporation.

NOTES

1. To take just one example, International Business Machines has guidelines to employee privacy which clearly are intended to go beyond the law and specify *moral* standards for corporate behavior (see "IBM's Guidelines to Employee Privacy," *Harvard Business Review,* Vol. 54, no. 5 (1976), pp. 82–90). When David Ewing discusses these guidelines, however, he contends their acceptance would not "hobble management in its security efforts" because (among other things) "where the checking of purses, briefcases, and bundles is legal today, it would still be legal" (David Ewing, *Freedom Inside the Organization* (E. P. Dutton: 1977), p. 137). But IBM is not making law when it formulates corporate guidelines to privacy; it is merely setting internal corporate policy relevant to its employees' *moral* right to privacy. Thus the question Ewing should ask is: "Do IBM's guidelines reflect what is morally right (so that security is morally justified in inspecting bundles, etc.), or does the moral right to privacy, when properly interpreted, prohibit such searches (in which case IBM's guidelines ought to proscribe such inspections)?"

2. *Griswold v. State of Connecticut* 381 U.S. 479, 85 S. Ct. 1678 (1965).

3. For example, seven states have laws giving private employees the right to see their personnel files. "Privacy at Work," *Wall Street Journal,* May 12, 1980, p. 26.

4. Virginia Schein, "Privacy and Personnel: A Time for Action," *Personnel Journal,* Vol. 55, no. 12 (1976), p. 606.

5. John Ely, "The Wages of Crying Wolf," *The Yale Law Journal,* Vol. 82 (1973), pp. 923–937.

6. For further problems encountered by businesses and industries as they attempt to implement the legal right to privacy see Schein, *op. cit.*

7. For an example of such discontent see Vincent Barry's account of the strike at Adolph Coors brewery in 1977. V. Barry, *Moral Issues in Business* (Wadsworth: 1979), p. 149.

8. See Schein, *op. cit.*, p. 604.

9. This seems to be the principal motivation behind IBM's concern with privacy. In explaining his company's interest in privacy, Frank Cary, chairman and chief executive of IBM says: "When I became chairman, it seemed to me that this subject (privacy) was going to become an issue for us, as auto safety has become a major issue for Ford and General Motors" ("IBM's Guidelines to Employee Privacy," *op. cit.*, p. 82). The major auto makers did not set strict enough auto safety standards for themselves, and this prompted legislation governing their actions. Apparently, Cary wants to avoid a repeat of this scenario.

10. Our purpose is served by considering only two moral theories. It should be noted, however, that there are numerous moral theories and hence numerous interpretations of the moral right to privacy. For a brief discussion of the right to privacy as it relates to a wide variety of moral theories see Barry, *op. cit.*, pp. 160–163.

11. Stanley I. Benn, "Privacy, Freedom, and Respect for Persons," in R. Wasserstrom (ed.), *Today's Moral Problems* (Macmillan: 1975), p. 5.

12. *Ibid.*, p. 9.

13. For a good example of how prior moral commitments can affect one's view of the strength and scope of the moral right to privacy see E. Pattullo, "The Limits of the 'Right' of Privacy," and R. Veatch, "Limits to the Right of Privacy: Reason, Not Rhetoric," *IRB*, Vol. 4, no. 4 (1982), pp. 3–7.

14. Although the evidence is not conclusive, it appears that IBM has decided that the moral right to privacy is grounded on respect for persons. For example, in discussing his corporation's privacy guidelines, Frank Cary, chairman of IBM, says: "There's absolutely no taping of a person's conversations on the telephone without express permission. . . . I consider this a simple matter of respect for the individual." ("IBM's Guidelines to Employee Privacy," *op. cit.*, p. 89.)

15. *Ibid.*, p. 84.

16. IBM probably has devoted more time and energy to privacy related issues than any other corporation; and its program does not achieve all of the goals specified. IBM has resolved problem a; but as far as I can tell it has not solved problems b or c. Because IBM has solved problem a it has accomplished goal 1. However, so long as problems b and c remain unresolved, goals 2 and 3 remain unrealized.

17. For example, in the case cited earlier by Frank Cary, the privacy court would decide whether or not an anonymous charge of child beating would warrant investigation. And its holding in this case would have an influence on a later case in which an employee was charged with, say, wife beating or use of prostitutes.

Corporate Policy Statements

Employe Records. General Motors believes that its employes' private personal activities are not properly the concern of GM so long as they do not adversely affect attendance, job performance, working relationships with fellow employes, or the public image of the Corporation.

General Motors does not consider such procedures as polygraph tests proper in the evaluation of job candidates, nor does the Corporation include in personnel records non-business-related information, unless submitted or authorized in writing by the employe. Nonetheless, compliance with government regulations and administration of labor agreements and employe-benefit programs have greatly increased the amount of personal data GM is required to record.

GM policy dictates that such records be treated with the same strict confidentiality accorded to all GM's proprietary information. Any employe may examine his or her own personnel record.

Employes are advised, upon inquiry, of the kinds of files and data which the Corporation must maintain concerning them. These may contain personally identifiable information only if it is relevant and necessary to the proper administration of the business or to compliance with the law or government regulation.

All written information about employes is to be recorded and maintained accurately, factually, and objectively. Employes have the opportunity to correct or amend any information concerning themselves, to ensure accuracy and fairness. Furthermore, GM personnel whose job responsibilities legitimately permit them access to such information are directed to protect employe records from unauthorized release, transfer, access, or use.

Personally identifiable information must not be disclosed outside the Corporation unless the employe consents, with the following exceptions: the *fact* of employment may be verified for employe credit approval; *dates* of employment may be verified for employment reference checks; an employe's elected bargaining representative may be entitled by labor contract

279

to certain information; and a law or a court order may require disclosure of certain information.

General Motors

IBM has four basic practices concerning the use of personal information about employees: To collect, use and retain only personal information that is required for business or legal reasons; To provide employees with a means of ensuring that their personal information in IBM personnel records is correct; To limit the internal availability of personal information about an individual only to those with a clear business need to know; and to release personal information outside IBM only with approval of the employee affected, except to verify employment or to satisfy legitimate investigatory or legal requirements. But even with these practices, not every case can be covered. What constitutes a legitimate business need for a particular piece of information? Should information about an employee ever be released without his or her knowledge, even if it might be to his or her benefit? Ultimately, you must balance the right of the organization to use information for valid business purposes with the individual's right to privacy. Your own conscience and judgment and the advice of your management and of IBM Personnel all should be considered in this delicate area.

IBM

The nature of the services offered by American Express Company necessitates collection and retention of a substantial amount of personal information about the individuals to whom services are provided. We must avoid any unjustifiable intrusion on an individual's right to privacy. We must strive for a reasonable balance between the operational needs of our businesses and the personal needs of individuals. In an effort to attain such a balance we will be guided by the following principles with regard to the collection, custody and distribution of personal information concerning the individuals to whom we provide services. (1) Obtain only that personal information which is necessary and relevant to the conduct of our business; (2) Use only lawful means to collect information; obtain it directly from the individual to the extent practicable; and make reasonable efforts to assure the reliability of information acquired from others; (3) Explain the general uses of personal information to all individuals who question the reasons that they provide such information, and refrain from using the information for other purposes without informing the individual; (4) Establish appropriate administrative, technical, and physical safeguards to assure that access to records is limited to those who are authorized and that information is disseminated only by and to those with a legitimate business purpose or regulatory function, or where disclosure is required by subpoena or other legal process; (5) Provide personal data records with secure storage and ensure that personnel who are involved with custody or maintenance of such records are aware of their responsibility to preserve their confidentiality; (6) Promptly notify the individual in the case where records are subpoenaed, unless specifically prohibited from doing so by court order. Respond according to the law, but wait the full length of time allowed by the subpoena before providing the information in order to allow the individual the opportunity to exercise his or her rights; (7) Advise the individual of the Company's policy with respect to mailing lists and provide the individual with the opportunity to have his or her name removed from such lists; (8) Respond to all individuals who question the reasons that adverse determinations have been made about them, and advise them of the nature of information acted upon, except for information which relates to the investigation of an insurance claim or of a possible criminal offense. This will, of course, be subject to ethical considerations and applicable laws; (9) Upon request, except with regard to insurance claims investigations, and within a reasonable period of time, advise an individual of factual data (maintained about that person) such as residence, address, place of employment, etc., and give the individual the opportunity to verify this factual data and to provide corrected or amended information where appropriate; (10) Review periodically corporate policy regarding the collection, retention, use and protection of individually identifiable data to ensure that this policy is in keeping with the shifting needs of both the business and the individual.

American Express Co.

Whistle Blowing

Dan Gellert: Whistle Blower

By 1972, Dan Gellert had been a pilot for twenty-five years, the last ten with Eastern Air Lines. Eastern had sent Gellert to the Air Force Safety School, the Army Crash Survival Investigators Course, and the Aerospace Systems Safety Course; in addition to flying scheduled flights, he also was involved in flight training and engineering safety for Eastern. In the summer of 1972, when Gellert was undergoing flight training for the Lockheed L–1011 (Tri-Star), his roommate was in a flight simulator when the autopilot and flight instrumentation disengaged, crashing the flight on a simulated landing. Gellert's roommate reported the incident to Eastern's flight-operations managers.

In September 1972, Gellert was flying an L–1011 with 230 passengers aboard; cruising on autopilot at 10,000 feet when:

> . . . I accidentally dropped my flight plan. As I bent down to pick it up, my elbow bumped the control stick in front of me. Suddenly the plane went into a steep dive—something that shouldn't have occurred (on autopilot). Fortunately, I was able to grab the control stick and ease the plane back onto course.
>
> What had happened, I realized, was that in bumping the stick, I had tripped off the autopilot. Instead of holding the plane at 10,000 feet, it had switched from its "command mode" to "control wheel steering." As a result, when the stick moved forward, causing the plane to dive, the autopilot, rather than holding the aircraft on course, held it in the dive.
>
> There was no alarm system to warn me that the plane was off course. If I hadn't retrieved my flight plan quickly, observing the dive visually when I sat up in my seat, the plane could easily have crashed. Even more alarming, as I eased the plane back onto course, I noticed that the autopilot's altimeter indicated that the plane was flying at 10,000 feet—the instrumentation was giving me a dangerously false reading.

Gellert made a verbal report to Eastern's management, which promised him it would look into the matter.

On December 29, 1972, an Eastern L-1011, operating as flight 401 from New York to Miami, crashed into the Everglades, 18 miles from Miami's International Airport. Of the 163 passengers and 13 crew aboard, 93 passengers and 5 crew members were fatally injured.

When Gellert learned of the accident, he suspected the autopilot problem he had experienced might have contributed to the accident, and he outlined the problems with the L-1011 autopilot in a two-page memorandum sent to the top three people at Eastern: Floyd Hall, board chairman; Samuel Higgenbottom, president of operations; and Frank Borman, vice-president of operations. In February 1973, he received a reply from Borman stating it was doubtful that any one procedure caused the accident.

Shortly thereafter, Gellert sent copies of his memorandum to his union, the Airline Pilots Association (ALPA), and to the National Transportation Safety Board (NTSB), which was about to hold hearings on the crash. The NTSB called on Gellert to testify, and he stressed the autopilot problem.

Gradually the crash scenario was pieced together. Flight 401 was making its landing approach when a lightbulb that is supposed to light when the landing gear is down and locked into place failed to light up. The crew switched the plane to autopilot at 2,000 feet, and the Second Officer went to check whether the landing gear was down and locked. A warning chime would sound if the plane diverged from the 2,000 feet level, and the autopilot had its own annunciator signal to indicate the altitude it had been set for. The chime, however, was so faint that it could barely be heard on the recovered cockpit voice recorder tape. Furthermore, it sounded only near the Second Officer's seat—and he was below, checking on the landing gear when it sounded.

A critical part of the testimony related to the autopilot's operation. An ALPA representative questioned an L-1011 technical expert on the issue Gellert had raised:

> QUESTION: Were the crew members taught that with the autopilot engaged in command mode, altitude hold engaged, that a slight bump or pressure on either steering yoke would disengage the altitude hold portion, would or could disengage the altitude hold portion of the autopilot?

> ANSWER: They were not taught that. As a matter of fact, I don't think that very many people were aware of this until after the accident.

> QUESTION: I agree. If there is a disconnect of this sort, an inadvertent disconnect, or however you want to call it, what indication is there?

> ANSWER: Your indication would be the annunciator in front of your particular seat. The prism would flip over; you wouldn't have the altitude showing.

> QUESTION: Does the light in the altitude hold selector switch go out, or does it stay on?

ANSWER: It should go out.

QUESTION: And I believe you have just said what the indication was in the annunciator panel.

ANSWER: Right.

QUESTION: Is there any indication in the AFCS (Avionics Flight Control System) warning annunciator panel?

ANSWER: I don't think so.

QUESTION: Does the autopilot aural disengage warning light sound, the wailer?

ANSWER: No, sir.

QUESTION: Does the autopilot engage lever drop in this case?

ANSWER: Negative.

QUESTION: What is the primary indication that the altitude hold has engaged when the altitude switch is pushed?

ANSWER: The way we teach it and use it, if you push the switch in to switch light and watch the annunciator for the prism to flip over, showing the altitude, this informs you that you are in effect in altitude hold.

QUESTION: Are you aware that there have been cases where the AFCS mode annunciator on the corresponding side to the engaged autopilot indicated altitude hold disengagement while the opposite side mode annunciator panel still indicated that the altitude hold was engaged?

ANSWER: I have heard this, but I have not personally seen it, so it would be hearsay.

QUESTION: Are you aware that the First Officer cannot see the captain's annunciator panel if they are both in the correct position in their seats?

ANSWER: Affirmative.

QUESTION: Assuming that these cases are correct, could you agree that this is a highly undesirable fault in the annunciator system?

ANSWER: I have to think about that for a minute.

QUESTION: The one says it is on and one says it is off, and one pilot cannot see the other's?

ANSWER: We have other redundant characteristics. It would still be undesirable, though.

The issue finally boiled down to the possible autopilot problem and/or flight-crew distractions with the landing gear. In the end, the NTSB ruled the crash was not the result of a single error, but was "the cumulative result of several minor deviations from normal operating procedures which triggered a sequence of events with disastrous results." The decision was that the crew failed to monitor the flight instruments during the last four minutes of flight. The landing gear problem had drawn the attention of the crew, and as the pilots peered into the bay one of them apparently pressed against the control yoke, dislodging the autopilot. Still distracted, they never realized Flight 401 was in a slow descent.

In July 1973, after the NTSB released its findings, Eastern decided to modify the autopilot design. The amount of pressure necessary to disengage the autopilot was to be increased and the warning light was to be altered. The alterations took some time to implement.

In December 1973, Dan Gellert was flying an L-1011 when the autopilot twice disengaged when it should not have; one involved a close call coming into Atlanta. Gellert wrote a 12-page petition to the NTSB explaining the continuing problem. The NTSB queried Eastern, which replied that it was making the necessary changes in the L-1011.

In early 1974, Gellert was demoted to co-pilot. Twice a year pilots bid on routes, and Eastern claimed Gellert returned a blank bid sheet, which entailed a demotion to co-pilot. Gellert claimed he had not returned a blank bid sheet. Gellert protested to Borman, who responded by grounding Gellert for medical reasons. Gellert filed a grievance against Eastern. The ALPA-Eastern contract provides that a pilot grievance must be brought before the Eastern Airlines Pilots System Board of Adjustment (ESBA), which has the power to settle any dispute. ESBA is comprised of two members from ALPA and two from Eastern's management. Deadlocks are resolved by an independent arbiter. After seven months ESBA ruled in favor of Gellert and he was reinstated as a pilot in 1975.

Shortly thereafter Eastern sent Gellert a letter informing him that he should have gone through internal grievance procedures and reminded him that he could be terminated for not following procedures. Gellert felt this was contrary to the ALPA contract and federal air regulations, and filed a civil suit against Eastern for $1.5 million charging "intentional infliction of mental stress."

In June 1976, Gellert's attorney took depositions from Borman and other senior management at Eastern. In July 1976, Gellert was suspended for being unavailable for a flight. He filed a grievance. The ESBA held a hearing, and Gellert cancelled an Eastern flight to attend. The ESBA ruled in Gellert's favor, but Eastern suspended him for the flight he missed to attend the ESBA hearing. Gellert filed another grievance, and again ESBA ruled in his favor. In January 1977, he completed a flight and was told he was slated to pilot another flight in four hours. When he protested that this was unsafe, he was removed from the flight, and two days later he was suspended for a month. Again, Gellert filed and won a grievance from ESBA. The Board cited a previous ruling requiring eight hours rest between flights, and stating that federal air regulations require a pilot to remove himself from any flight, for any reason, should he feel unable to fly the aircraft.

In May 1977, Gellert was grounded indefinitely and told to report for a medical examination in Miami. He received the letter after the examination and received a disciplinary suspension.

In September 1977, Gellert won his civil suit against Eastern for $1.5 million. Eastern appealed, and a Florida circuit court set aside the verdict. The case is still in appellate courts.

In the meantime, Gellert filed another grievance with ESBA over his grounding for medical reasons. ESBA asked him to submit to a medical examination by Eastern's doctors; Gellert passed three examinations over a period of four months, and ESBA ruled in his favor. Gellert also filed a grievance over his suspension, and ESBA ruled in his favor because post office records showed that Eastern's letter informing Gellert of the medical examination was delivered after the examination was to have taken place.

In June 1978, Gellert filed a $12 million lawsuit against Eastern charging "civil conspiracy to force me out of employment," and in January 1979, he filed a $1 million libel suit against Eastern for comments allegedly made about him by Eastern's publicity director. These cases are pending.

For Discussion

Was Dan Gellert justified in blowing the whistle on Eastern Airlines? Why or why not? Discuss Eastern's response to Gellert's disclosures. Was the response justified? Why or why not? If you were placed in charge of handling Eastern's response to safety related issues, what sort of corporate structure would you implement to deal with them?

SOURCES

John G. Fuller, *The Ghost of Flight 401* (Berkeley: Berkeley Publishing, 1976); "Whistle Blower: Dan Gellert, Airline Pilot," *The Civil Liberties Review,* vol. 5, no. 3 (September–October, 1978), pp. 15–19; Robert J. Serling, *From the Captain to the Colonel* (N.Y.: Dial Press, 1980); Dan Gellert, "Insisting on Safety in the Skies," in *Whistle Blowing,* edited by Alan F. Westin (N.Y.: McGraw-Hill Book Co., 1981), pp. 17–30.

Gene G. James

Whistle Blowing: Its Nature and Justification

Whistle blowing has increased significantly in America during the last two decades. Like blowing a whistle to call attention to a thief, whistle blowing is an attempt by a member or former member of an organization to bring illegal or socially harmful activities of the organization to the attention of the public. This may be done openly or anonymously and may involve any kind of organization, although business corporations and government agencies are most frequently involved. It may also require the whistle blower to violate laws or rules such as national security regulations which prohibit the release of certain information. However, because whistle blowing involving national security raises a number of issues not raised by other types, the present discussion is restricted to situations involving business corporations and government agencies concerned with domestic matters.

I

It is no accident that whistle blowing gained prominence during the last two decades which have been a period of great government and corporate wrongdoing. The Viet Nam war, Watergate, illicit activities by intelligence agencies both at home and abroad, the manufacture and sale of defective and unsafe products, misleading and fraudulent advertising, pollution of the environment, depletion of scarce natural resources, illegal bribes and campaign contributions, and attempts by corporations to influence political

From *Philosophy in Context* 10 (1980):99–117. Reprinted by permission of the publisher.

activities in third world nations are only some of the events occurring during this period. Viewed in this perspective it is surprising that more whistle blowing has not occurred. Yet few employees of organizations involved in wrongdoing have spoken out in protest. Why are such people the first to know but usually the last to speak out?

The reason most often given for the relative infrequency of whistle blowing is loyalty to the organization. I do not doubt that this is sometimes a deterrent to whistle blowing. Daniel Ellsberg, e.g., mentions it as the main obstacle he had to overcome in deciding to make the Pentagon Papers public.[1] But by far the greatest deterrent, in my opinion, is self-interest. People are afraid that they will lose their job, be demoted, suspended, transferred, given less interesting or more demanding work, fail to obtain a bonus, salary increase, promotion, etc. This deterrent alone is sufficient to keep most people from speaking out even when they see great wrongdoing going on around them.

Fear of personal retaliation is another deterrent. Since whistle blowers seem to renounce loyalty to the organization, and threaten the self-interest of fellow employees, they are almost certain to be attacked in a variety of ways. In addition to such charges as they are unqualified to judge, are misinformed, and do not have all the facts, they are likely to be said to be traitors, squealers, rat finks, etc. They may be said to be disgruntled, known troublemakers, people who make an issue out of nothing, self-seeking and doing it for the publicity. Their veracity, life style, sex life and mental stability may also be questioned. Most of these accusations, of course, have nothing to do with the issues raised by whistle blowers. As Dr. John Goffman, who blew the whistle on the AEC for inadequate radiation standards, said of his critics, they "attack my style, my emotion, my sanity, my loyalty, my public forums, my motives. Everything except the issue."[2] Abuse of their families, physical assaults, and even murder, are not unknown as retaliation to whistle blowers.

The charge that they are self-seeking or acting for the publicity is one that bothers many whistle blowers. Although whistle blowing may be anonymous, if it is to be effective it frequently requires not only that the whistle blower reveal his or her identity, but also that he or she seek ways of publicizing the wrong-doing. Because this may make the whistle blower appear a self-appointed messiah, it prevents some people from speaking out. Whistle blowing may also appear, or be claimed to be, politically motivated when it is not.

Since whistle blowing may require one to do something illegal such as copy confidential records, threat of prosecution and prison may be additional deterrents.

II

Not only laws which forbid the release of information but agency law which governs the obligations of employees to employers seems to prohibit whistle blowing.[3] Agency law imposes three primary duties on employees: obedience, loyalty and confidentiality. These may be summed up by saying that in general employees are expected to obey all reasonable directives of their employers, to not engage in any economic activities detrimental to their employers, and to not communicate any information learned through their employment which either might harm their employer or which he might not want revealed. This last duty holds even after the employee no longer works for the employer. However, all three duties are qualified in certain respects. For example, although the employee is under an obligation to not start a competing business, he or she does have the right to advocate passage of laws and regulations which adversely affect the employer's business. And while the employee has a general obligation of confidentiality, this obligation does not hold if he has knowledge that his employer has committed, or is about to commit, a crime. Finally, in carrying out the duty of obeying all reasonable directives, the employee is given the discretion to consult codes of business and professional ethics in deciding what is and is not reasonable.

One problem with the law of agency is that there are no provisions in it to penalize an employer who harasses or fires employees for doing any of the things the law permits them to do. Thus, employees who advocate passage of laws which adversely affect their employers, who report or testify regarding a crime, or who refuse to obey a directive they consider illegal or immoral, are likely to be fired. Employees have even been fired on the last day before their pension would become effective after thirty years of work and for testifying under subpoena against their employers without the courts doing anything to aid them. Agency law in effect presupposes an absolute right of employers to dismiss employees at will. That is, unless there are statutes or contractual agreements to the contrary, an employer may dismiss an employee at any time for any reason, or even for no reason, without being accountable at law. This doctrine which is an integral part of contract law goes all the way back to the code of Hammurabi in 632 B.C., which stated that an organizer could staff his workforce with whomever he wished. It was also influenced by Roman law which referred to employers and employees as "masters" and "servants," and by Adam Smith's notion of freedom of contract according to which employers and employees freely enter into the employment contract so either has the right to terminate it at will. Philip Blumberg, Dean of the School of Law at the University of Connecticut sums up the current status of the right of employers to discharge as follows: "Over the years, this right of discharge has been increasingly restricted by statute and by collective bargaining agreements, but the basic principle of the employer's legal right to discharge, although challenged on the theoretical level, is still unimpaired."[4] The full significance of this remark is not apparent until one examines the extent to which existing statutes and collective bargaining agreements protect whistle blowers. As we shall see below, they provide very little protection. Furthermore, since in the absence of statutes or agreements to the contrary, employers can dismiss employees at will, it is obvious that they can also demote, transfer, suspend or otherwise retaliate against employees who speak out against, or refuse to participate in, illegal or socially harmful activities.

A second problem with the law of agency is that it seems to put one under an absolute obligation to not disclose any information about one's employer unless one can document that a crime has been, or is about to be, committed. This means that disclosing activities which are harmful to the public, but not presently prohibited by law, can result in one's being prosecuted or sued for damages. As Arthur S. Miller puts it: "The law at present provides very little protection to the person who would blow the whistle; in fact, it is more likely to assess him with criminal or civil penalties."[5] All that the whistle blower has to protect himself is the hope that the judge will be lenient, or that there will be a public outcry against his employer so great that he will not proceed against him.

III

There are some laws which encourage or protect whistle blowing. The Refuse Act of 1899 gives anyone who reports pollution one half of any fine that is assessed. Federal tax laws provide for the Secretary of the Treasury to pay a reward for information about violations of the Internal Revenue Code. The Commissioner of Narcotics is similarly authorized to pay a reward for information about contraband narcotics. The Federal Fair Labor Standards Act prohibits discharge of employees who complain or testify about violations of federal wage and hours laws. The Coal Mine Safety Act and the Water Pollution Control Act have similar clauses. And the Occupational Safety and Health Act prohibits discrimination against, or discharge of, employees who report violations of the act.

The main problem with all these laws, however, is that they must be enforced to be effective. The Refuse Act of 1899, for example, was not enforced prior to 1969 and fines imposed since then have been minimal. A study of the enforcement of the Occupational Safety and Health Act in 1976 by Morton Corn,[6] then an Assistant Secretary of Labor, showed that there were 700 complaints in FY 1975 and 1600 in FY 1976 by employees who claimed they were discharged or discriminated against because they had reported a violation of the act. Only about 20% of these complaints were judged valid by OSHA investigators. More than half of these, that is to say, less than three hundred, were settled out of court. The remaining complaints were either dropped or taken to court. Of the 60 cases taken to court at the time of Corn's report in November 1976, one had been won, eight lost and the others were still pending. Hardly a record to encourage further complaints.

What help can whistle blowers who belong to a union expect from it? In some cases unions have intervened to keep whistle blowers from being fired or to help them gain reinstatement. But for the most part they have restricted themselves to economic issues, not speaking out on behalf of free speech for their members. Also, some unions are as bad offenders as any corporation. David Ewing has well stated this problem. "While many unions are run by energetic, capable, and high-minded officials, other unions seem to be as despotic and corrupt as the worst corporate management teams. Run by mossbacks who couldn't care less about ideals like due process, these unions are not likely to feed a hawk that may come to prey in their own backyard."[7]

The record of professional societies is not much better. Despite the fact that the code of ethics of nearly every profession requires the professional to place his duty to the public above his duty to his employer, very few professional societies have come to the aid of members who have blown the whistle. However, there are some indications that this is changing. The American Association for the Advancement of Science recently created a standing committee on Scientific Freedom and Responsibility which sponsored a symposium on whistle blowing at the 1978 meeting and is encouraging scientific societies and journals to take a more active role in whistle blowing situations. A sub-committee to review individual cases has also been formed.[8]

Many employees of the federal government are in theory protected from arbitrary treatment by civil service regulations. However, these have provided little protection for whistle blowers in the past. Indeed, the failure of civil service regulations to protect whistle blowers was one of the factors which helped bring about the Civil Service Reform Act of 1978. This act explicitly prohibits reprisal against employees who release information they believe is evidence of: (a) violation of law, rules, or regulations, (b) abuse of authority, mismanagement, or gross waste of funds, (c) specific and substantial danger to public health or safety. The act also sets up mechanisms to enforce its provisions. Unfortunately, it excludes all employees of intelligence agencies, even when the issue involved is not one of national security, except employees of the FBI who are empowered to go to the Attorney General with information about wrongdoing. Although it is too early to determine how vigorously the act will be enforced, it seems on paper to offer a great deal of protection for whistle blowers.

Although state and local laws usually do not offer much protection, thanks to a series of federal court decisions, people who work for state and municipal governments are also better off than people who work for private corporations. In the first of these in 1968 the Supreme Court ordered the reinstatement of a high school teacher named Pickering who had publicly criticized his school board. This was followed by a 1970 district court decision reinstating a Chicago policeman who had accused his superiors of covering up thefts by policemen. In 1971 another teacher who criticized unsafe playground conditions was reinstated. And in 1973 a fireman and a psychiatric nurse who criticized their agencies were reinstated. In all of these decisions, however, a key factor seems to have been that the action of the employee did not disrupt the morale of fellow employees. Also no documents of the organizations were made public. Had either of these factors been different the decisions would have probably gone the other way.[9]

Given the lack of support whistle blowers have received in the past from the law, unions, professional societies, and government agencies, the fear that one will be harassed or lose one's job for blowing the whistle is well founded, especially if one works for private industry. Moreover, since whistle blowers are unlikely to be given favorable letters of recommendation, finding another job is not easy. Thus despite some changes for the better, unless there are major changes in agency law, the operation and goals of unions and professional societies, and more effective enforcement of laws protecting government employees, we should not expect whistle blowing to increase significantly in the near future. This means that much organization wrongdoing will go unchecked.

IV

Whistle blowing is not lacking in critics. When Ralph Nader issued a call for more whistle blowing in an article in the *New York Times* in 1971, James M. Roche, Chairman of the Board of General Motors Corporation responded:

> Some of the enemies of business now encourage an employee to be disloyal to the enterprise. They want to create suspicion and disharmony and pry into the proprietary interests of the business. However this is labelled — industrial espionage, whistle blowing or professional responsibility — it is another tactic for spreading disunity and creating conflict.[10]

The premise upon which Roche's remarks seem to be based is that an employee's only obligation is to the company for which he works. Thus he sees no difference between industrial espionage — stealing information from one company to benefit another economically — and the disclosure of activities harmful to the public. Both injure the company involved, so both are equally wrong. This position is similar to another held by many businessmen, viz., that the sole obligation of corporate executives is to make a profit for stockholders for whom they serve as agents. It is tantamount to saying that employees of corporations have no obligations to the public. However, this is not true because corporations are chartered by governments with the expectation that they will function in ways that are compatible with the public interest. Whenever they cease to do this, they violate the understanding under which they were chartered and allowed to exist, and may be legitimately penalized or even have their charters revoked. Furthermore, part of the expectation with which corporations are chartered in democratic societies is that not only will they obey the law, but in addition they will not do anything which undermines basic democratic processes. Corporations, that is, are expected to be not only legal persons but good citizens as well. This does not mean that corporations must donate money to charity or undertake other philanthropic endeavors, although it is admirable if they do. It means rather than the minimum conduct expected of them is that they will make money only in ways that are consistent with the public good. As officers of corporations it is the obligation of corporate executives to see that this is done. It is only within this framework of expectations that the executive can be said to have an obligation to stockholders to return maximum profit on their investments. It is only within this framework, also, that employees of a corporation have an obligation to obey its directives. This is the reason the law of agency exempts employees from obeying illegal or unethical commands. It is also the reason that there is a significant moral difference between industrial espionage and whistle blowing. The failure of Roche and other corporate officials to realize this, believing instead that their sole obligation is to operate their companies profitably, and that the sole obligation of employees is to obey their directives without question, is one of the central reasons corporate wrongdoing exists and whistle blowing is needed.

Another objection to whistle blowing advanced by some businessmen is that it increases costs, thereby reducing profits and raising prices for consumers. There is no doubt that it has cost companies considerable money to correct situations disclosed by whistle blowers. However, this must be balanced against costs incurred when the public eventually comes to learn, without the aid of whistle blowers, that corporate wrongdoing has taken place. Would Ford Motor Company or Firestone Rubber Company have made less money in the long run had they listened to their engineers who warned that the gas tank of the Pinto and Firestone radial tires were unsafe? I think a good case could be made that they would not. Indeed, if corporate executives were to listen to employees troubled by their companies' practices and products, in many cases they would improve their earnings. So strong, however, is the feeling that employees should obey orders without questioning, that when an oil pipeline salesman for U.S. Steel went over the head of unresponsive supervisors to report defective pipelines to top company officials, he was fired even though the disclosure saved the company thousands of dollars.

I am not arguing that corporate crime never pays, for often it pays quite handsomely. But the fact that there are situations in which corporate crime is more profitable than responsible action, is hardly an argument against whistle blowing. It would be an argument against it only if one were to accept the premise that the sole obligation of corporations is to make as much money as possible by any means whatever. But, as we saw above, this premise cannot be defended and its acceptance by corporate executives in fact provides a justification for whistle blowing.

The argument that employees owe total allegiance to the organizations for which they work has also been put forth by people in government. For example, Frederick Malek, former Deputy Secretary of HEW states:

> The employee, whether he is civil service or a political appointee, has not only the right but the obligation to make his views known in the most strenuous way possible to his superiors, and through them, to their superiors. He should try like hell to get his views across and adopted within the organization—but not publicly, and only until a decision is reached by those superiors. Once the decision is made, he must do the best he can to live with it and put it into practice. If he finds that he cannot do it, then he ought not to stay with the organization.[11]

And William Rehnquist, Justice of the Supreme Court, says "I think one may fairly generalize that a government employee . . . is seriously restricted in his freedom of speech with respect to any matter for which he has been assigned responsibility."[12]

Malek's argument presupposes that disclosure of wrongdoing to one's superior will be relayed to higher officials. But often it is one's immediate superiors who are responsible for wrongdoing. Furthermore, even if they are not, there is no guarantee that they will relay one's protest. Malek also assumes that there are always means of protest within organizations and that these function effectively. This, too, is frequently not the case. For example, Peter Gall who resigned his position as an attorney for the Office of Civil Rights Division of HEW because the Nixon administration was failing to enforce desegregation laws, and who along with a number of colleagues sent a public letter of protest to President Nixon, says in response to Malek that

> as far as I am concerned, his recommended line of action would have been a waste of everyone's time. To begin with, the OCR staff members probably would have made their protest to Secretary Finch if they had felt that Finch's views were being listened to, or acted upon, at the White House. . . .[13]

And in defense of sending the public letter to Nixon he states that:

> A chief reason we decided to flout protocol and make the text of the letter public was that we felt that the only way the President would even become aware of . . . the letter was through publicity. We had answered too many letters—including those bitterly attacking the retreat on segregation—referred unread by the White House . . . to have any illusion about what the fate of our letter would be. In fact, our standing joke . . . was that we would probably be asked to answer it ourselves.[14]

Even when there are effective channels of protest within an organization, there may be situations in which it is justifiable to bypass them. For example, if there is imminent danger to public health or safety, if one is criticizing the overall operation of an agency, or if used standard channels of protest would jeopardize the interests one is trying to protect.

If Justice Rehnquist's remark is meant as a recommendation that people whose responsibility is to protect the health, safety and rights of the American people should not speak out when they see continued wrongdoing, then it must be said to be grossly immoral. The viewpoint it represents is one that Americans repudiated at Nuremberg. Daniel Ellsberg's comments on why he finally decided to release the Pentagon Papers put this point well.

> I think the principle of "company loyalty," as emphasized in the indoctrination within any bureaucratic structure, governmental or private, has come to sum up the notion of loyalty for many people. That is not a healthy situation, because the loyalty that a democracy requires to function is a . . . varied set of loyalties which includes loyalty to one's fellow citizens, and certainly loyalty to the Constitution and to the broader institutions of the country. Obviously, these loyalties can come into conflict, and merely mentioning the word "loyalty" doesn't dissolve those dilemmas. . . . The Code of Ethics of Government Service, passed by both the House and Senate, starts with the principle that every employee of the government should put loyalty to the highest moral principles and to country above loyalty to persons, parties, or government department. . . . To believe that the government cannot run unless one puts loyalty to the President above everything else is a formula for a dictatorship, and not for a republic.[15]

V

Even some people who are favorable to whistle blowing are afraid that it might become too widespread. For example, Arthur S. Miller writes: "One should be very careful about extending the principle of whistle blowing unduly. Surely it can be carried too far. Surely, too, an employee owes his employer enough loyalty to try to work, first of all, within the organization to attempt to effect change."[16] And Philip Blumberg expresses the fear that "once the duty of loyalty yields to the primacy of what the individual . . . regards as the 'public interest,' the door is open to widespread abuse."[17]

It would be unfortunate if employees were to make public pronouncements every time they thought they saw something wrong within an organization without making sure they have the facts. And employees ought to exhaust all channels of protest within an organization before blowing the whistle, provided it is feasible to do so. Indeed, as Ralph Nader and his associates point out, in many cases "going to management first minimizes the risk of retaliatory dismissal, as you may not have to go public with your demands if the corporation or government agency takes action to correct the situation. It may also strengthen your case if you ultimately go outside . . . , since the managers are likely to point out any weaknesses in your arguments and any factual deficiencies in your evidence in order to persuade you that there is really no problem."[18] But this is subject to the qualifications mentioned in connection with Malek's argument.

If it is true, as I argued above, that self-interest and narrow loyalties will always keep the majority of people from speaking out even when they see great wrongdoing going on around them, then the fear that whistle blowing could become so prevalent as to threaten the everyday working of organizations seems groundless. However, Miller's and Blumberg's remarks do call to our attention the fact that whistle blowers have certain obligations. All whistle blowers should ask themselves the following kinds of questions before acting: What exactly is the objectionable practice? What laws are being broken or specific harm done? Do I have adequate and accurate information about the wrongdoing? How could I get additional information? Is it feasible to report the wrongdoing to someone within the organization? Is there a procedure for doing this? What are the results likely to be? Will doing this make it easier or more difficult if I decide to go outside? Will I be violating the law or shirking my duty if I do not report the matter to people outside the organization? If I go outside to whom should I go? Should I do this openly or anonymously? Should I resign and look for another job before doing it? What will be the likely response of those whom I inform? What can I hope to achieve in going outside? What will be the consequences for me, my family and friends? What will the consequences of not speaking out be for me, my family and friends? What will the consequences be for the public? Could I live with my conscience if I do not speak out?

There is one respect in which whistle blowing might be taken too far. However, this requires explanation. Proponents of whistle blowing often write as though it were by definition a morally praiseworthy activity. For example, whistle blowing is defined in the Preface of Nader's book as

> the act of a man or woman who, believing that the public interest overrides the interest of the organization he serves, publicly "blows the whistle" if the organization is involved in corrupt, illegal, fraudulent, or harmful activity. . . .[19]

And Charles Taylor and Peter Branch, defending whistle blowers against the charge that they are traitors say:

> The traitor was always hated, because he was the enemy, but there was a special edge on the scorn that historically made traitors hated everywhere. . . . For the traitor was excoriated as a person without honor of any kind, who, among people willing to die for cause or principle . . . could shuffle back and forth between opposing camps, sniffing for the highest bidder, unmoved by higher loyalty or human bond. . . . Benedict Arnold was hated for defecting . . . , but he was despised as a real traitor because people found out that he had bargained at length over the pension he would receive—and even the number of calico dresses his wife would obtain—for switching sides.

> The whistle-blowers have actually reversed the operation of the classical traitor, as they have usually been the only people in their organizations taking a stand on some kind of ideal.[20]

They go on to argue that whistle blowers have been so successful in winning public admiration that "looking at the problem through the eyes of future whistle-blowers, the dilemmas are likely to center not on the morality of proposed actions but on their utility."[21]

The problem with both this definition and defense of whistle blowing is that they fuse motives with goals. That is, they seem to take for granted that because the whistle blower discloses wrongdoing, his or her motives must be praiseworthy. In fact, people may blow the whistle for a variety of reasons: to seek revenge, gain prosecutorial immunity, attract publicity, etc. Furthermore, from the standpoint of immediate public good, the motives of whistle blowers are unimportant. All that matters is whether the situation is as the whistle blower describes it. That is, does a situation exist which is harmful to the public?

However, consideration of the motives of whistle blowers does raise an interesting problem. To what extent should there be laws which encourage whistle blowing for self-interested reasons? Should there, e.g., be more laws like the federal tax law which furthers disclosure of tax violations by paying informers part of any money that is collected? Do not laws such as these bring about a situation which encourages suspicion, revenge, and profit seeking among citizens? And would not a society which relied heavily on this type of law be "taking whistle blowing too far?" I think that the answer to the last two questions must be affirmative. This does not mean, however, that society should never adopt laws which encourage whistle blowing for base motives. The extent to which a given law furthers spiteful behavior among citizens must be balanced against the amount of good it produces. In some cases, although I do not think in very many, the good clearly outweighs the harm of furthering vengeful behavior.

It would seem that anyone who was in favor of whistle blowing would also be in favor of laws protecting whistle blowers from arbitrary discharge from their jobs. However, Peters and Branch argue that with one exception

> freedom to hire and fire without red tape is essential to good government and . . . potential whistle-blowers should not be promised a world free of risks. Of course, our society should offer everyone a cushion against catastrophic job loss in the form of a decent guaranteed annual income and free health care. Beyond that we resist depriving life of adventure.[22]

The one exception they allow is that of people in situations like that of Dr. Jacqueline Verrett, the FDA employee who informed the press that her superiors were distorting the results of experiments she had performed which showed that cyclamates cause growth deformities in chicken embryos. All other whistle blowers, they say, even those such as Daniel Ellsberg whom they admire greatly, should be subject to being fired. But, exactly why people in situations such as Dr. Verrett's should be treated as exceptions is not made clear. Perhaps they consider threats to people's health more important than other threats to their well-being. Nor do they give any argument to justify why not depriving life of adventure is more important than preventing the discharge of people they claim are usually the most conscientious employees of organizations. Their position also seems to be inconsistent since they saw elsewhere that whistle blowing "should be encouraged, even by . . . employers themselves."[23]

The reason they arrive at such a contradictory position, in my opinion, is that they too fear that whistle blowing might get out of hand. Shortly after making the foregoing remark they say:

> There should be more protection for the whistle-blowers who prove right . . . without making whistle-blowing an automatic free ride. The risk must be preserved, for otherwise whistle-blowing would become banal, the country would be inundated with exposures, and the good cases would become uselessly lost in a sea of bad ones.[24]

This is to abandon the view that all whistle blowers should be fired, in favor of the one that people whose claims turn out to be false should be fired. But should all whistle blowers be fired whose claims turn out to be false? If so, what about those whose claims are partially true and partially false? Their position is a variation of the view that speech should be protected only when what is said is true. I doubt that they would accept this view if applied to the press. As working journalists they are more likely to believe that the press should be penalized only when it can be shown that false statements were made with malicious intent. Why should it be different in the case of whistle blowers? To believe that it should is not only to deprive life of adventure, it is to actively discourage whistle blowing and to allow corporate and governmental wrongdoing to flourish.

Rosemary Chalk, Staff Officer for the American Association for the Advancement of Science, arguing for greater involvement of scientific societies in whistle blowing, is correct, in my opinion, when she says that: "It should not be necessary for the whistle-blower to be 100% correct in order to gain support from his or her professional colleagues. The basis for scientific society involvement should not rest exclusively on whether the whistle-blower is right or wrong, but rather on whether the issue . . . is important in terms of its effect on the public interest."[25] Philip Blumberg is also correct when he says: "The public interest in the free discussion of ideas does not rest on the validity of the point of view expressed. Where dissent involves no unauthorized disclosure, the cost of sanctioning such conduct is low and of prohibiting it, high."[26] But unlike Blumberg, I believe that the area of authorized disclosure should be as wide as possible. This means that the law of agency should be superseded by federal legislation which would prevent employers from discharging or otherwise penalizing whistle blowers unless it can be proven both that their claims are false and were made with malicious intent. However, the situation must be one in which the public interest is at stake. Disclosure of trade secrets, customer lists, plans for marketing, personnel records, etc., should not be protected unless releasing them was necessary for the whistle blowing and the damage resulting is clearly outweighed by benefits to the public.

Many people are opposed to legislation protecting whistle blowers because they believe it unwarranted interference with freedom of contract. However, the traditional doctrine of freedom of contract rested on an assumption of equality between employers and employees which no longer exists. It is far easier today for employers to find another employee than for employees to find a new job. Furthermore, as Lawrence E. Blades has pointed out, the freedom of the individual to terminate his employment is more important than the freedom of employers to hire and fire at will.[27] The rights of the individual to dispose of his labor as he wishes and to be protected from retaliation in exercising his civil rights are fundamental to the existence of democratic societies. The courts have recognized this to some extent by limiting the right of employers to dismiss employees for union activities. The current practice of allowing employers to dismiss employees who are performing their jobs competently and whose sole "offense" is disclosure of situations harmful to the public is, therefore, one that ought to be abolished.

If legislation to protect whistle blowers is effective, it should provide for punitive damages against employers when it can be proven that they dismissed or penalized employees for justified whistle blowing. But how is the employee to show this? Both Blades and Ewing believe that the burden of proof should be on the employee. Blades writes:

> Ordinarily, when both sides present equally credible versions of the facts, the plaintiff will have failed to carry his burden. However, there is the danger that the average jury will identify with . . . the employee. This . . . could give rise to vexatious lawsuits. . . .
>
> Certainly, the employee should not be allowed to shift to the employer the burden of showing that the discharge was motivated by good cause by proving only that he capably performed the duties required by his job and was discharged for no apparent reason. . . . The employee should be required . . . to prove by affirmative and substantial evidence that his discharge was actuated by reasons violative of his personal freedom or integrity.[28]

Both Blades and Ewing qualify their position by suggesting that longevity of service be taken as evidence that an employee was doing his job effectively. Blades says "in cases like *Mims,* where the discharged employee had served the employer for 17 years as a branch manager and 32 years in all, a jury would probably be quite justified in finding little merit in an explanation that the plaintiff was fired for 'chronic' inefficiency and incompetence."[29] And Ewing states: "The longer the employee was on the job, the better his or her case. . . . If management was doing its job, such employees (who have served eight or more years) must have been working competently or they would not have stayed on the payroll all that time."[30]

The problem with these remarks is that if the burden of proof is on the employee to show by "affirmative and substantial" evidence that his discharge was for reasons which violate his personal freedom or integrity, and at the same time, the employer is under no obligation to show that the discharge was for good cause, establishing that an employee has competently performed his job for a number of years would be irrelevant to the issue at dispute. Showing this would be relevant only if the employer were under an obligation to show that he or she had not performed competently. And in cases involving discrimination against, or the firing of, whistle blowers, this is exactly what employers should be required to do. To require that employees show by affirmative and substantial evidence that they were not fired for good reason, when employers are under no obligation to demonstrate why they were fired, is to require a degree of evidence impossible to fulfill. Such a law would offer no protection to whistle blowers and is in fact a reversion to the doctrine of the absolute right of employers to discharge at will which laws protecting whistle blowers should be designed to overcome.

The fear that unless the burden of proof is placed on the whistle blower, vexatious lawsuits will result is unrealistic for two reasons. First, as I argued above, self-interest will always keep the majority of people from engaging in whistle blowing. Second, only employees who could show that an act of whistle blowing preceded their being dismissed or penalized would be able to seek redress under the law.

VI

Laws preventing whistle blowers from being dismissed or penalized are, of course, only one way of dealing with corporate and government wrongdoing. Laws and other measures aimed at changing the nature of organizations to prevent wrongdoing and encourage whistle blowing are equally important. Changing the role of corporate directors, appointing ombudspersons and high-level executives to review charges of wrongdoing, requiring that certain types of information be compiled and retained, and reforming regulatory agencies are some of the proposals which have been advanced for doing this. Unions and professional societies also need to act to further the rights of their members and protect the public good. Professional societies, e.g., should reformulate their codes of ethics to make obligations to the public more central, investigate violations of member's rights, provide advice and legal aid if needed, censure organizations found guilty, attempt to secure legislation protecting member's rights, and in some cases set up central pension funds to free members from undue dependence on the organization for which they work.

Since my primary purposes were to clarify the nature of whistle blowing, defend it against criticisms and show its importance for democratic societies, detailed discussion of the topics mentioned in this section is beyond the scope of this paper. Whistle blowing is not a means of eliminating all organizational wrongdoing. But in conjunction with other measures to insure that organizations act responsibly, it can be an important factor in maintaining democratic freedom.

NOTES

1. See Charles Peters and Taylor Branch, *Blowing the Whistle: Dissent in the Public Interest,* New York, 1972, Praeger Publishers, Chapter Sixteen.

2. Quoted in Ralph Nader, Peter J. Petkas and Kate Blackwell, *Whistle Blowing,* New York, 1972, Grossman Publishers, p. 72.

3. For a discussion of agency law and its relation to whistle blowers see Lawrence E. Blades "Employment at Will vs. Individual Freedom: On Limiting the Abusive Exercise of Employer Power," *Columbia Law Review* 67 (1967), and Philip Blumberg, "Corporate Responsibility and the Employee's Duty of Loyalty and Obedience: A Preliminary Inquiry," *Oklahoma Law Review* 24 (1971), reprinted in part in Tom L. Beauchamp and Norman E. Bowie, *Ethical Theory and Business,* New York, 1979, Prentice-Hall; and Clyde W. Summers, "Individual Protection Against Unjust Dismissal: Time for a Statute," *Virginia Law Review* 62 (1976). See also Nader, *Op. Cit.,* and David W. Ewing, *Freedom Inside the Organization,* New York, 1977, E. P. Dutton.

4. Blumberg, *Op. Cit.,* in Beauchamp and Bowie, p. 311.

5. Arthur S. Miller, "Whistle Blowing and the Law" in Nader, *Op. Cit.,* p. 25.

6. Corn's report is discussed by Frank von Hipple in "Professional Freedom and Responsibility: The Role of the Professional Society," in the *Newsletter on Science, Technology and Human Values,* Number 22, January 1978, pp. 37–42.

7. Ewing, *Op. Cit.,* pp. 165–166.

8. Discussion of the role professional societies have played in whistle blowing can be found in Nader, *Op. Cit.,* von Hipple, *Op. Cit.,* and in Rosemary Chalk, "Scientific Involvement in Whistle Blowing" in the *Newsletter on Science, Technology and Human Values, Op. Cit.,* pp. 47–51.

9. These decisions are discussed by Ewing, *Op. Cit.,* Chapter Six.

10. Quoted in Blumberg, *Op. Cit.,* p. 305.

11. Quoted in Peters and Branch, *Op. Cit.,* pp. 178–179.

12. *Ibid.,* pp. x–xi.

13. *Ibid.,* p. 179.

14. *Ibid.,* p. 178.

15. *Ibid.,* p. 269.

16. Miller, *Op. Cit.,* p. 30.

17. Blumberg, *Op. Cit.,* p. 313.

18. Nader, *Op. Cit.,* pp. 230–231.

19. *Ibid.,* p. vii.

20. Peters and Branch, *Op. Cit.,* p. 288.

21. *Ibid.,* p. 290.

22. Peters and Branch, *Op. Cit.,* p. xi.

23. *Ibid.,* p. 298.

24. *Ibid.*

25. Chalk, *Op. Cit.*, p. 50.

26. Philip Blumberg "Commentary on 'Professional Freedom and Responsibility: The Role of the Professional Society" in the *Newsletter on Science, Technology and Human Values, Op. Cit.*, p. 45.

27. Blades, *Op. Cit.*

28. *Ibid.*, pp. 1425–1426.

29. *Ibid.*, pp. 1428–1429.

30. Ewing, *Op. Cit.*, p. 202.

Job Quality

Problems at Lordstown

As the small car market became more viable and foreign imports increased in the 1960s General Motors (GM) began to map out a strategy to compete for this market segment. Part of its strategy involved design of the Vega, to be assembled at a plant in Lordstown, Ohio. Given the relatively high wages of American auto workers, GM recognized that its ability to compete rested on cost reductions in manufacturing, enhanced product quality, and motivated employees. At Lordstown, GM attempted to (1) install a highly integrated and automated fabrication and assembly facility, (2) introduce numerous cost-cutting design techniques, and (3) employ carefully selected workers in an attractive industrial setting.

The Lordstown plant is integrated and automated. A metal fabricating plant, where stamping and subassembly is done, is linked by conveyor to the assembly line, so the plant is self-contained. Since major subassemblies are constructed before they reach the final assembly line, more automation on the final line is achievable. Unimation Corporation's robots are used extensively on the assembly line; for example, they make ninety-five percent of the 520 spot welds on an auto. One robot on the line can make 130 welds in less than five seconds. The result is a very efficiently designed assembly line. Although the average line produces 55 cars per hour, the Vega line is designed to produce 100 cars per hour.

GM also instituted a variety of other strategies to reduce costs: the Vega's small size enabled engineers to reduce the number of parts per car body from 996 in the average car to 578; many interchangeable parts were used in the four Vega models; and assembly was simplified by the use of certain materials, e.g., a one-piece interior plastic roof eliminated cutting and sewing fabric, and simplified installation.

303

In addition, the plant was designed to attract and employ what GM took to be motivated, quality workers. It is situated in the rolling hills of northeastern Ohio, far from big-city problems. GM carefully screened applicants, seeking and obtaining mainly young, white workers with better than average education. The average age of the Lordstown employees in 1971 was twenty-five. Of its 7,700 workers, less than 500 were women and about 100 were black. Including fringe benefits, wages in 1970 averaged $56 per day; even the lowest paid employee was in the top third strata of income for U.S. workers. GM's plant was also designed to enhance work quality. Automation itself eliminated many physically difficult line jobs. The line's conveyor was height adjusted along its mile length to provide a comfortable working height. The line was computer controlled to give each worker time to do his job properly.

GM began operating the Lordstown plant in mid-1970. Things went relatively well through the shake-down phase; but during 1971, GM did not achieve its planned rate of 100 cars per hour on the Lordstown line. In October 1971, GM placed the General Motors Assembly Division (GMAD) in charge of the Lordstown plant — replacing Fisher Body and the Chevrolet Division. The assignment was in line with overall GM policy, since GMAD had assumed control of nearly all GM assembly plants since 1968.

GMAD had a hard-nose reputation. Leonard Woodcock, then United Auto Workers (UAW) president, labeled GMAD as "probably the roughest, toughest division at GM." GMAD has a computerized ranking system for the assembly plants it manages. The performance of each plant is assessed on a daily basis, and the twenty GMAD plants are ranked monthly for efficiency and quality. Those plants ranked in the lowest third are given special attention by GMAD's top management. Since there are no final goals, and one plant's movement out of the lower third in rank results in another plant being placed in the lower third, there is continual pressure to improve productivity.

Upon taking over the Lordstown plant GMAD assigned work standard engineers to recalculate the time required to perform particular jobs. Certain performance standards were raised and a speed-up of the line was instituted. In addition some workers were laid off. GMAD claimed 400 employees in a workforce of 7,700 were laid off, but the union claimed the total was close to 700. GMAD also cancelled certain local agreements that the previous management had made with UAW Local 1112, claiming that new management had the right to reorganize jobs to improve efficiency. To head off anticipated problems, GMAD held informal meetings with workers to explain the new procedures. To increase motivation and productivity, GMAD's foremen were trained in leadership effectiveness and told to make every effort to know their workers as individuals and try to get them to do their jobs.

By early 1971, however, it was apparent that serious problems existed. Absenteeism and the number of grievances filed both increased. Gary Bryner, president of Local 1112, claimed that whereas 300 grievances were filed against the previous management, 5,000 grievances were filed against

GMAD. Quality was also reduced. Autos rolled off the line with unfinished upholstery, uneven or scratched paint jobs, dented bodies, loose wires, and missing bolts. Cases of sabotage surfaced: slit upholstery, trunk keys broken off in the trunk lock, cut wires, screws left in brake drums, and metal parts placed to rattle in fender compartments.

In early 1972, GM made public charges of sabotage. A week later Local 1112 leaked a story to the press that GM was shipping defective Vegas to dealers. GM hotly denied the charge, and GM dealers claimed that they noticed no decline in Vega quality, but GM was forced to increase quality control expenditures at Lordstown and it employed stricter disciplinary measures. Reprimands, disciplinary suspensions, and dismissals increased. When the repair shop lot was filled, entire shifts were sent home with loss of pay. In February 1972 the union called a strike vote. It claimed that ninety-seven percent of the 6,550 members voting (out of a total of 7,900 eligible to vote) supported the strike.

During March 1972 negotiations were conducted. The union complained about: (1) the speed-up; (2) layoffs; (3) extra tasks assigned to the remaining workers in alleged violation of the 1970 GM-UAW contract, which specified job descriptions in detail; (4) disciplinary tactics, especially the sending home of entire shifts; (5) mandatory overtime required by GMAD on certain days to make up for lost production; and (6) dehumanizing work conditions, monotony, boredom, and lack of job quality. GM countered that: (1) the speedup was necessary to meet competition, especially foreign competition, and still make a profit; (2) layoffs only eliminated duplicated jobs; (3) no contract violation occurred; (4) disciplinary measures were justified to curb incomplete assembly and sabotage; (5) overtime was the only means available to realize production goals; and (6) automation had eliminated most excessively monotonous line jobs at Lordstown. Much of the controversy centered on issue (6), the union's allegation of "dehumanizing" work conditions. Here are some comments from participants in the dispute and knowledgeable sources:

GEORGE WALLIS, RANK AND FILE: We want a normal work rate out there; we don't want a guy killing himself by speeding around out there on a shift. Okay? A normal pace—not hustling, normal. At 100 cars an hour you've got thirty-six seconds for your task. Now if you give a guy two tasks, he's got eighteen seconds. The job was boring before, now it's boring and hectic.

JOE ALFONA, ABSENTEE REPLACEMENT OPERATOR: Well, like all men when when they used to work, they had a specific job to do. They told them to shove 100 tons of coal within x amount of time, and that's what they did. And they left them alone. But like now they tell you to "Put in ten screws," and you do it. Then, a couple of weeks later, they say "Put in fifteen; and next they say, "Well, we don't need you no more, give it to the next man." From day to day, you don't know what your job's going to be. They always either add to your job or take a man off. I mean management's word is no good. They guarantee you — they write to the union — that this is the settlement on the job, this is the way it is going to run — 103 cars an hour, and we're the only ones in the world who could do that pace. Know what I mean? They agree that so many men are going to do so many things, period! Fine, the union will buy that because they negotiated it. Two weeks later management comes down and says, "Hey, listen, let's add something else to that guy." They don't even tell the union. And management says, if you don't do it, they'll throw you out, which they do. No problem. Zap! away you go . . .

Duane Messner, assembler: It's like the Army. They even use the same words, like "direct order." Supposedly you have a contract, so there's some things that they can't make you do — except if the foreman gives you a direct order. You do it or you're out; they fire you or give you a DLO (disciplinary layoff). Like this foreman comes over and says, "Pick up that paper." So I says, "That's not my job." He says, "I'm giving you a direct order to pick up that paper." Finally he takes me up to the office and my committeeman comes over and tells me I could lose my job because you can't refuse a direct order. Just like the Army. No, it's worse because you're welded to the line.

Ron Alcoff, buffer: They could let you do your job your way. You work at it day in and day out. But they don't. You do it their way, even if you could do it better. And you're tied down; you do that one thing day in, day out, hour after hour. You're like in a jail cell — except they have more time off in prison.

Frank Perinski, assembler: Every young unskilled worker in the plant wants out. This whole generation has been taught by their parents to avoid the line, to go to college to escape it, but now some of them are trapped here. They can't face it; they hate to go in there.

Jim Clauson, assembler: If you were about twenty-two and had this job where you were dealt with like a machine and you had thirty years of it ahead of you, how would you feel? Then they want to turn you into more of a robot, give you three tasks instead of two with the same time.

Reese Orlosky, buffer: I object to job regimentation, and the lack of job involvement and initiative needed for the work, and GMAD's controls. Miss a day and they'll question you. They're not paying you but they'll question you. And the company never could understand why we don't want a day's work plus overtime. We want forty hours and that's it.

Tom Orlosky (Reese's father): These kids who come up today want to sit on their fantails eight hours a day. They think the plant owes them a living. When I was young you put in a day's work, no question about it.

JAMES ROCHE, GM CHAIRMAN: To be viable we cannot tolerate employees who reject responsibility and fail to respect essential disciplines and authority. Management and the public have lately been shortchanged; we have a right to more than we have been receiving. GM increased its investment per hourly worker from $5,000 in 1950 to $24,000 in 1969, to improve both productivity and working conditions, but tools and technology mean nothing if the worker is absent from his job. Absenteeism and poor work habits affect efficiency and quality. We must receive the fair day's work for which we pay the fair day's wage.

ED BRAMBLETT, GM VICE PRESIDENT FOR PERSONNEL: Absenteeism and complaints occur not because jobs are dull, but because of the nation's economic abundance, and the high degree of security and the many social benefits the industry provides. Labor has made impressive gains. The young should show more appreciation for what they have instead of insisting on even more benefits and improvements.

DELMAR LANDEN, GM DIRECTOR OF EMPLOYEE RESEARCH: Absenteeism and allied production problems are only symptoms of the trouble. For too long the automobile industry assumed economic man was served if the pay was okay. It didn't matter if the job was fulfilling. Once the pay is good, though, higher values come into play. Other satisfactions are required.

GARY BRYNER, PRESIDENT OF UAW LOCAL 1112 AT LORDSTOWN: The attitude of young people is going to compel management to make jobs more desirable in the workplace and to fulfill the needs of the man. The management concern is for productivity and profits. Ours is for the employee. There's got to be a blending. Management has to face the fact that the attitude that a guy goes to work and slaves to get his wage is passe. The guys want to feel like they're making real contributions. They don't want to feel like a part of the machines.

KEN BANNON, A UAW VICE-PRESIDENT: The pace at which people are compelled to work and the monotony of many jobs have their effect both on the worker and on the product. New and younger workers will be less attracted to repetitive and uninteresting or physically arduous routine tasks. The traditional concept that hard work is a virtue and a duty, which older workers have adhered to, is not applicable to younger workers, and the concepts of the younger labor force must be taken into account.

WALTER REUTHER, FORMER PRESIDENT OF THE UAW: Young workers get three or four days' pay and figure, well, I can live on that. I'm not really interested in these material things anyhow. I'm interested in the sense of fulfillment as a human being. The prospect of tightening up bolts every two minutes for eight hours for thirty years doesn't lift the human spirit. The young worker feels he's not master of his own destiny. He's going to run away from it every time he gets a chance.

DOUGLAS FRASER, A UAW VICE-PRESIDENT: Adding additional tasks on the line may make the job more difficult, not more satisfying. Some say you should change a guy's job every day. Well, an auto worker would kill you for saying that. Ask a guy in the labor pool who takes a different job every day. He will tell you its harder to keep up. In some cases the absenteeism and problems have been caused almost exclusively by high overtime. The young workers won't accept the same old kind of discipline their fathers did.

ED REINGOLD, *Time* MAGAZINE'S DETROIT BUREAU CHIEF: There has been much talk of "job enrichment," assigning a worker more tasks in order to give him a sense of fulfillment. But some union leaders charge that "enriching" a worker's job by making him do two jobs, each thirty times an hour instead of one job sixty times an hour is a "con." At Lordstown the workers want more time to do their single, simple job— and that is certainly the opposite of what many outsiders think they want. Many workers complain that they do not want to work as hard as they are being asked to. It may well be that what were considered ordinary norms in the past are no longer acceptable.

BARBARA GARSON, AUTHOR OF *All the Livelong Day*: The underlying assumption in an auto plant is that no worker wants to work. The plant is arranged so that employees can be controlled, checked, and supervised at every point. The efficiency of an assembly line is not only in its speed but in the fact that the workers are easily replaced. This allows the employer to cope with high turnover. But it's a vicious cycle. The job is so unpleasantly subdivided that men are constantly quitting and absenteeism is common. Even an accident is a welcome diversion. Because of the high turnover, management further simplifies the job, and more men quit. But the company has learned to cope with high turnover. So they don't have to worry if men quit or go crazy before they're forty.

CARL MARTIN, AUTO INDUSTRY CONSULTANT: Constant, repetitive work is being resisted by workers, and when you put in tough management to make a car every forty seconds, instead of fifty-five, the whole thing falls apart. You can't take a young man, average age of twenty-two, and subject him to the dreadful, dismal future of a production line.

MILTON NIEBARS, AUTO INDUSTRY CONSULTANT: Everyone concedes these new workers at Lordstown are probably the best-educated, brightest workforce that ever came into an auto plant. But no matter how you cut up the work, line jobs are dull. You can either automate completely and get rid of the problem by getting rid of the dull jobs, or you can keep the lines and hire dull people to do the dull jobs. But I question whether you can find a middle course today.

The Lordstown strike was over in twenty days. Financially, neither side wanted a strike. GM lost production of 1,500 Vegas a day and it lost $50 million in total production, while the union strike fund was low. The settlement contract was approved by seventy percent of the voting union members, although only 2,940 of 7,700 eligible members voted. Gary Bryner allowed that only 400 layoffs had occurred but claimed 240 jobs had been restored by the settlement. GMAD said 150 workers had been rehired.

Workers who had been sent home for failure to meet performance standards received back pay in instances where standards had been changed. GMAD reserved the right to improve efficiency by altering performance standards.

For Discussion

From a moral point of view discuss GM's management style in handling the Lordstown dispute, and its workers' response. What steps could be implemented to improve the situation at Lordstown? Discuss the pros and cons of implementing a job enrichment program at Lordstown. Are there steps beyond, or in addition to, job enrichment that should be implemented at Lordstown? Why or why not?

SOURCES

Judson Gooding, "Blue-Collar Blues on the Assembly Line," *Fortune,* vol. LXXXII, no. 1, July, 1970, pp. 69ff; "GM's Mini: The Very Model of Automation," *Business Week,* August 8, 1970, p. 26; Agis Salpukas, "Extra Work Prompts Vote to Strike at GM Plant," *New York Times,* Feb. 3, 1972, p. 38; "Sabotage at Lordstown?" *Time,* Feb. 7, 1972, p. 76; Russell W. Gibbons, "Showdown at Lordstown," *Commonweal,* vol. XCV, no. 22 (March 3, 1972), pp. 523-4; "The Spreading Lordstown Syndrome," *Business Week,* March 4, 1972, pp. 69-70; B. J. Widick, "The Men Won't Toe the Vega Line," *Nation,* March 27, 1972, pp. 403-4; "Vega Strike Ends, but the Issue Still Boils," *Business Week,* April 1, 1972, p. 23; Agis Salpukas, "GM's Toughest Division," *New York Times,* April 16, 1972, p. 1; "Why One Worker Sticks With a Job He Finds Dull," *Life,* Sept. 1, 1972, pp. 34-6; "The Will to Work and Some Ways to Increase It," *Life,* Sept. 1, 1972, pp. 38-9; "Job Monotony Becomes Critical," *Business Week,* Sept. 9, 1972, p. 108; Barbara Garson, *All The Livelong Day* (N.Y.: Doubleday, 1972); Bennett Kremen, "Lordstown—Searching for a Better Way of Work," *New York Times,* Sept. 9, 1973, sec. 3, pp. 1 and 4; "The Lordstown Experiment," in Robert J. Litschert and Edward A. Nicholson, *The Corporate Role and Ethical Behavior* (N.Y.: Mason/Charter, 1977), pp. 199-213.

Robert H. Schappe

Twenty-Two Arguments Against Job Enrichment

The arguments against job enrichment which are presented here have arisen primarily in industrial organizations with assembly line processes and a long history of organized labor. The information has been collected from such diverse sources as management seminars, industrial consulting situations, academic classrooms, the mass media and informal discussions and is divided into management and labor positions, because the arguments reflect much of the prevalent political philosophy of each side of the organization. These arguments vary along organizational dimensions such as department, function, level and job, as well as along socioeconomic, cultural and personality dimensions. It cannot be said that they represent or typify any particular management or labor position. Sometimes labor and management agree and sometimes they disagree, or at times there is disagreement within labor or within management on the concept of job enrichment. Some of the twenty-two arguments arise as unadulterated resistance while others arise more as inquiries about job enrichment and its implications. It is not likely that all of these reasons would be heard in the same organization, but over many organizations these twenty-two are the ones which recur and persist.

The job enrichment under discussion is essentially that proposed and discussed by Herzberg (1968), Ford (1973), and Myers (1964). It involves modifying job content so that the individual has increased responsibility and autonomy, a wider variety of tasks and more opportunities for achievement and recognition in his work. In effect the work itself becomes a source of motivation for the individual.

From *Personnel Journal* 53 (February, 1974):116–123. Copyright © 1974 by *Personnel Journal*, Costa Mesa, California. All rights reserved. Reprinted by permission of the publisher.

Myers (1971) examined union opposition to job enrichment as a *general* phenomenon in labor-management relations, but was not directly concerned with the *specific* union arguments against enrichment. He suggested four "models" or processes whereby both sides of the organization could more easily attain goals in the common interest of the organization. But in the main, he was concerned with solutions to a *general* problem of union resistance.

An underlying assumption in this article is that if a job enrichment effort is to be implemented, it will be done only after a thorough analysis of the organization has been made and this analysis indicates that enrichment would be a workable solution to existing problems. The next step would be one of explaining job enrichment, clarifying questions about it, and convincing certain individuals of its potential. This is in contrast to situations where job enrichment is being "sold" to an organization as a program, regardless of existing needs.

MANAGEMENT ARGUMENTS AGAINST JOB ENRICHMENT

In the course of discussing job enrichment with management and trying to show how it can solve certain kinds of problems, some very predictable arguments and forms of resistance are offered and when committing these to paper, they can be sequenced or organized in a variety of ways. Those arguments appearing early in this section tend to be general in nature and could apply to other change efforts as well as job enrichment, while those appearing later in the list tend to be arguments peculiar to job enrichment. Usually, when the subject of job enrichment is discussed, members of management assume that it is hourly-rated jobs that are under consideration. Many of the management arguments are presented here from this perspective.

1. GENERAL ARGUMENT AGAINST CHANGE THROUGH JOB ENRICHMENT

This is mentioned mainly because of its pervasiveness and ubiquity in organizations. It may be regarded as some global resistance to change or viewed as a sum of several specific arguments. Underlying this resistance seems to be the feeling that if change is suggested for the way things are to be done in the future, something must have been wrong with the way things were done in the past.

Admittedly, the possibility for needed change may be psychologically painful insofar as it means admitting error. Overcoming this kind of resistance is especially difficult because of the diffusion of the resistance. Treating this general resistance as a summation of several specific arguments makes it more vulnerable as each argument can then be examined and dealt with as a concrete, specific item.

2. No Felt Need For Job Enrichment

If an analysis of the organization reveals that job enrichment could be a meaningful answer to existing problems, the next step is to get certain members of management to admit they have problems which can be dealt with by job enrichment. When there is no felt need or a lack of willingness to admit the need for help, it is common to hear "horror stories" and requests for motivational "Band-Aids." The former are anecdotes about expensive, time-consuming, motivational efforts which the organization tried sometime in the past and which weren't successful. The latter are requests for motivating certain individuals; the 63-year-old sweeper or the chronically absent female assembler. Both of these tactics are commonly used for saving face and keeping problems out of sight. One approach that has been successful in dealing with this type of resistance is to initiate an organizational change strategy (before that of job enrichment) which will promote and foster an atmosphere of trust and mutual acceptance. This is not easy, but it is only when individuals feel free to discuss problems, rather than try to hide them, that solutions can be brought to bear on them.

3. Job Enrichment Is Incompatible with Profits

This is perhaps the oldest and most common reason to be found in any organization. The traditional conception of man at work embodies the notion of a trade-off between satisfaction and earnings. The worker can have it one way or the other, but cannot expect to have both. This has been perpetuated by programs or efforts to increase satisfaction which have not been reflected in organizational earnings. This may be the cardinal item for the success not only of job enrichment, but for any motivational effort designed to change the organization. When the improvement of work content is viewed as an integral aspect of profits rather than something in competition with them, job enrichment can be successful. Satisfaction gained from meaningful work is a means by which the organization can achieve the goal of profits. In short, the amount of change produced by job enrichment ultimately must get translated into the scale of measurement by which the organization is appraised—dollars and cents.

4. Job Enrichment Costs Too Much, Takes Too Much Time

With little research on the cost of job enrichment and its expected financial return, it becomes necessary to turn from empiricism to persuasion to respond to this argument. Job enrichment is an investment which will require an initial expenditure of time (money) by the organization. As an investment it will be some time, probably months, before there is any visible return.

This return may be reflected in different ways: greater productivity, better quality, less scrap, less absenteeism, or other measures of performance. In the long run, it just might cost *less* to motivate people through meaningful work than through extrinsic work context factors which cost real money, but which don't seem to motivate. The entire issue of cost, investment, and profits as they relate to a motivational effort like job enrichment is very complex and cannot be satisfactorily examined here, but treating job enrichment as an investment has met with success in the past when the argument of cost has arisen.

5. JOB ENRICHMENT IS JUST ANOTHER PROGRAM

This is related to Argument 3, but is mentioned because of the word, "Program." This word has a connotation of something starting one day and stopping a few days later. In industry these programs typically involve technical training or behavior modification, with the former concerned with very specific, practical goals and the latter concerned with broader and frequently more elusive goals. People in the plant tend to regard these programs as something extra and not as an integral aspect of their work. If job enrichment is regarded as "just another program," it will be placed well down on the priority list. When this happens, the effort is usually regarded as a personnel department activity and operating managers feel neither identification with it nor commitment to it. Unless there is involvement of operating managers and commitment by them, job enrichment *will* be "just another program."

6. JOB ENRICHMENT HASN'T PROVEN ITSELF YET

The cold pragmatism and practicality that pervades many manufacturing organizations today produces a fear of failure and discourages risk-taking. Members of management are rewarded for producing. This system reduces risk-taking, losses, innovating and maybe profits, and breeds an understandable reluctance to attempt any change strategy like job enrichment. The evidence for the positive effects of enrichment usually is questioned on the grounds of nonrepresentative worker composition and work processes. There is a reasonable quantity of research available to argue for job enrichment, but more is needed in heavy industry, especially where there are assembly-line operations.

7. LACK OF POWER TO ENRICH JOBS

Members of lower and middle management frequently state that they feel impotent to alter job content because they are too far down in the organization, while members of upper management maintain that they feel impotent because they are too far removed from the work itself. The greater the adamance with which these positions are held, the greater the probability that something must be done to prepare the climate before job enrichment is attempted. Management must be ready for job enrichment or it cannot be successfully implemented. When these two groups are able to meet and talk with feelings of mutual trust and confidence, and can begin to share ideas about job design and work content, the authority and knowledge needed to modify certain jobs materializes. This stated feeling of impotence can itself be treated as a symptom of job design problems within lower and middle management and job enrichment can be used effectively for entry into these levels of the organization.

8. JOB INTERDEPENDENCY

This is a very real and complex problem and deserves considerably more space than is available here, but it is touched on briefly for the sake of closure. If the job to be enriched is independent of other jobs, its redesign and enrichment are not so difficult. However, many jobs, especially in assembly, are highly interdependent, and altering one job can change the entire work flow. In this case, several interdependent jobs might be considered simultaneously for enrichment. This does not mean there has to be confusion and chaos when it is introduced. Job redesign can be dealt with by modifying just certain aspects of each job initially, but gradually adding to them over time, with the enrichment process occurring in phases over a period of several months. Another way of handling the redesign of several interdependent jobs is that of setting up a long-term plan so that when one of the enriched jobs is operating smoothly, another of the jobs is phased in for enrichment. It frequently happens that as the enrichment process of interrelated jobs evolves, rethinking and redesigning the whole work flow and work process for that area occurs. If the whole process of job enrichment of interdependent jobs is carefully planned, its execution will be more orderly and the outcome more stable. Research concerned with basic parameters of change is needed in this area.

9. JOB ENRICHMENT INFRINGES ON MANAGEMENT PREROGATIVES

When an employee's job is enriched, he is given increased autonomy and responsibility. This means that certain aspects of his superior's job are now going to be a part of his job. To the extent that the employee is viewed as having a voice in the decision-making, the superior may regard this as an infringement on his job. In a more subtle way the superior will see his job role of "purveyor of rewards" undermined because now, if the work itself provides more rewards, he as the superior will suffer a perceived reduction in power. With enrichment of the subordinates' jobs, the supervisor's job content and role will undergo change and there will be a need for educating individuals to this new role. The supervisor will spend less time checking work and "bossing" people and will be able to spend more time on the real supervisory aspects of his job such as coordinating, communicating, developing and planning.

10. WORKERS DON'T WANT INCREASED JOB ENRICHMENT

This is a very tantalizing assertion because it contains just enough "truth" to make it seem like a good argument. While it is mentioned by both labor and management, the latter tends to use it much more frequently. Furthermore, when it is used by production management, it is as though job enrichment is always for the other guy, the worker. The seductiveness of this argument is that there is, in fact, a significant percentage (which varies with numerous factors including functional area, department, shift, company, and personal matters) of the work force which states that it does not desire the increased responsibility of job enrichment. However, the fallacy here is that many of the people comprising this percentage are not aware of the full meaning of increased responsibility. From the worker's perspective, the typical example of increased responsibility is the harried, over-burdened, first-line production supervisor. Usually the worker does not see increased responsibility as an opportunity for advancement, achievement, recognition or fulfillment on manual or blue collar work. Thus, when a worker is asked if he wants an enriched job and increased responsibility, it is essential that an adequate explanation of its meaning, as well as the alternatives to it, are made available. When this is done, greater confidence can be placed in the interpretation of data on worker attitudes about more responsibility and enriched work.

11. SUBTLE PUNITIVENESS

This argument against job enrichment takes the form of a disdainful attitude toward or contempt for low-skill employees. Certain members of management maintain that since these people have virtually no personal investment of education, training, or experience and are earning high wages, they should be willing to put up with the work they have been assigned. In short, they don't deserve enriched jobs. If you do have some personal investment and have been through the organization's initiation, then the job you're on might be considered for enrichment. When it is shown that a department has its absenteeism rate reduced by 40 percent due to the enrichment of jobs, this subtle punitiveness is less evident.

12. Constrained by the Union Contract

This argument seems to come up toward the end of a discussion and always sounds like a final management plea for the status quo. It can be a good argument because as a form of resistance, it brings about a coalition of labor and management against the threat of change. Some members of management are aware of this, others are not, but if labor is not invited to contribute to rethinking the jobs of its members, they will undoubtedly oppose job enrichment. Why labor would choose to do this is not the issue. However, it must be recognized that labor does have a say about the content of its members' jobs and should be represented in any enrichment effort of these jobs. When this is done, many of the arguments about contract restraints dealing with job content disappear.

13. Constrained by Company Policy

This is another "last-ditch" argument, but it has more the appearance than the substance of an obstacle to job enrichment. If top management is sincere about facing its problems and is genuinely interested in having real changes made, company policy is more likely to accommodate than to impede the enrichment of jobs. Sincerity of commitment can be demonstrated by active involvement and participation of staff members. Without this support, any broad or long-range effect of job enrichment is doubtful.

Labor Arguments Against Job Enrichment

Labor's response to the enrichment of hourly-rated jobs is a product of the labor-management conflict model and reflects labor's traditional mistrust and skepticism for management "motivation programs." Today, the response of some union officers is to dismiss extrinsic factors such as a shorter work week, more time off, and early retirement. In effect, these individuals maintain that workers will tolerate existing working conditions, but only for shorter periods of time. When the management position on job enrichment was outlined, several of the reasons were really inextricably related but for analytical purposes they were parceled out. This also applies to labor arguments against job enrichment.

14. Job Enrichment Is Confusing

There is a continuing lack of resolution in the collective mind of organized labor about the definition, objectives, and rationale behind job enrichment. This is not surprising in light of the many things which have been labeled job enrichment. Keeping people busy has been called job enrichment. Rotating workers through a series of boring jobs has been labeled job enrichment. Giving people more work has been called job enrichment. Adding more of the same kind of boring tasks to a job has been called job enrichment. This confusion about job enrichment is shared by many members of management, but it is mentioned in this section because labor more than management has expressed puzzlement about it. In the sense that it is used by Herzberg (1968), Myers (1964), Ford (1973) and in this article, the preceding definitions are *not* job enrichment. Job enrichment is the redesign of a job for the purpose of introducing a wider variety of tasks, increasing individual autonomy and responsibility, and creating the opportunity to achieve on the job so that work will become intrinsically rewarding and more meaningful to the individual.

15. Job Enrichment Is Not Bread and Butter

This could be argued, but it's probably true. It's not tangible like a dollar bill, not apparent like a day off; it doesn't say anything about job security and doesn't mention fringe benefits. It is not an easily understood concept and its implications seem abstract when conventional concrete measuring devices are employed. The challenge is to translate job enrichment into bread and butter terms.

16. Job Enrichment Is Just Another Manipulative Device

Various efforts at organizational change have been manipulative. Some have been conceived to attain that end while others began honestly, but were later subverted. This is closely related to the line of thinking in Argument 14. Different devices have been called "Job Enrichment," but beneath the verbal veneer could be found the core of manipulation. Job enrichment is seen by many as just another attempt to get more work for no more reward. As the mutual trust of labor and management increases, manipulation and suspicion about manipulation are less likely to occur.

17. Job Enrichment Is Just a Substitute for Tangible Rewards

Used as a substitute for money or other tangible reward, job enrichment would be just another manipulative device, but it is not the intent of job enrichment to be used as a replacement for money. While it is true that job enrichment is based on the hypothesis that the motivation of work comes from the work itself and that money is not an effective motivator, money is a prerequisite for avoiding dissatisfaction on the job.

18. Job Enrichment Means Something Else Will Be Taken Away

Management and labor have historically adhered to a conflict model. This has worked well at some times and ill at others, but unfortunately, prolonged conflict breeds mistrust and suspicion. Every gesture becomes an attack or a feint. Nothing is done without an ulterior motive. Every action of the other must be scrutinized and questioned. If labor softens a demand today, it is merely a set-up for tomorrow. If management gives up something this week, they will take away something next week. Does the enrichment of jobs mean something will be taken away from labor? Job enrichment, per se, does not mean that members of labor must give something up. Activities referred to as job enrichment have been used for abusive purposes and underhanded tactics, but this is not a problem with job enrichment per se. This is a problem of management style and labor-management relations. Having one's job enriched does not mean that something else must be taken away.

19. Job Enrichment Is a Threat to Job Security

The threat that job enrichment poses for labor insofar as it threatens job security is more imaginary than real. Again, labor's rationale would appear to emerge out of the traditional mistrust for any change which management might seek to introduce. To remain competitive, companies have increased efficiency and productive capacity through the introduction of technological devices or processes which have made certain jobs or classes of jobs obsolete. Job enrichment, as an organizational change technique, has not proven its worth to a company as a competitive strategy by eliminating jobs. Rather, it pays off by making work more satisfying and this increased job satisfaction is reflected by monetary savings produced by increased quality, less scrap, or decreased absenteeism, etc. Job enrichment does not have job elimination as a goal.

20. Job Enrichment Conflicts with Contract Job Descriptions

This position asserts that particular jobs have specific boundaries which are inviolable and immutable. This is basically the same argument offered by management in Argument 12, but is used by labor for a different reason. While management tends to use this for arguing against change and for maintaining existing organizational processes, labor uses it for job protection and security. Unfortunately, while a worker's job is indeed protected, the worker himself may be locked into a boring, repetitive, demeaning job. If it can be recognized that management and labor are working toward common goals, both sides should be willing to discuss and share in the enrichment of jobs.

21. MANAGEMENT IS TRYING TO UNDERCUT UNION INFLUENCE

This springs from the very depths of the union as a political power bloc and is most likely to be heard in those places where job enrichment has been introduced, or is being considered, and the union has not been invited to participate in the effort. It is viewed as a threat to the worker's allegiance to labor because management is seen as vying in an underhanded way with the union for the workers' attention. If it appears that a job enrichment effort is having some payoff and is getting good press, the union is going to insist strongly on union involvement in the effort. It is beneficial and productive for labor and management to sit down at the earliest stages and start cooperating in the enrichment effort.

22. JOB ENRICHMENT THREATENS THE UNION INSTITUTION

If job enrichment were to achieve everything that it was supposed to, people would find their work rewarding and meaningful, management philosophy would change, and unions as known today would have no reason to exist. The need for a union as originally conceived and historically maintained would simply not be there. This kind of thinking is more likely to be heard at the highest levels of the union structure and not phrased in those words. Furthermore, it is only in the long run that organized labor would feel a real threat from job enrichment, and the long run impact of job enrichment is yet to be felt and assessed.

TOWARD EFFECTIVE JOB ENRICHMENT

For job enrichment to be effective it must meet the needs of the organization, not the needs of someone who has taken a fancy to it. Only after a thorough analysis of the organization reveals a need for it, should it be attempted. It has met with failure at times and places in the past because it was imposed on a system rather than emerging out of the needs of that system.

Job enrichment won't work if people don't want enriched jobs. This presupposes that the worker rejecting the increased responsibility of an enriched job knows what enrichment is and is aware of some of the alternatives.

When it is introduced to an organization, job enrichment is most usefully regarded as an aid to achieving organizational goals rather than as a "now" or "right" approach which suggests the old approach was in error. It should be regarded as a natural and needed component of the change process in the organization.

Job enrichment will need the support of both top management and labor if it is to be a viable force for change. Lacking either of these will reduce the effort to an exercise to be terminated at the end of the budget year.

The *sine qua non* of a job enrichment effort is its eventual translation into the ultimate measuring scale of the organization—money. This may seem crass and mercenary, but it is reality. To have satisfied people who are proud of their workplace because the work is meaningful is not enough. Eventually, this must be reflected somewhere with a dollar sign, whether it be by reduced absenteeism, improved quality, greater productivity, reduced scrap or whatever. If it does not get translated, then it will not become a part of the existing system.

Job enrichment might profitably be regarded as an investment. As such no immediate payoff should be expected. It will take some time for a return. If we look at industrial history and the length of time it has taken to create some of the existing problems, we can't realistically expect to reverse this course of events within a six-week time period. There is a need for well-conceived and well-designed studies in heavy industry and in large organizations. These must include sensitive measures which reflect both short- and long-term trends, as well as measures which detect time lags between cause and impact on the organizational system. Adequate controls must be provided and awareness must be created of such problems as the old Hawthorne effect and the new Experimenter effect.

After reading through this list of twenty-two arguments against job enrichment, an expected comment might be, "If there's so much resistance to job enrichment, maybe there's good reason not to get involved in it." For several years we have heard about the reasons for introducing job enrichment and the ways of overcoming resistance to it, but the specific arguments for resisting it have not been spelled out. Perhaps by using the negative approach to positive thinking, by enumerating these reasons and becoming aware of them, it will be less difficult to persuade labor and management that job enrichment can provide a possible solution to the continuing problem of motivating people to work.

REFERENCES

Ford, R. N. Job enrichment lessons from AT&T. *Harvard Business Review,* 1973, *51* (1), 96–106.

Herzberg, F. One more time: How do you motivate employes? *Harvard Business Review,* 1968, 46 (1), 53–62.

Myers, M. S. Who are your motivated workers? *Harvard Business Review,* 1964, 42 (1), 73–88.

Myers, M. S. Overcoming union opposition to job enrichment. *Harvard Business Review,* 1971, 49 (3), 37–49.

Corporate Policy Statement

Quality of work life is not merely an employe *program* at General Motors; it is both a goal and a continuing process. As a *goal,* QWL is GM's commitment to the creation of jobs and work environments which are satisfying for GM people at all levels. This philosophy is reflected in the Corporation's employment policies and in its commitment to improve not only physical working conditions and the rewards of work, but work itself, by encouraging employe involvement on the factory floor and in the office; better working relationships, particularly between employes and their supervisors; more cooperation between unions and management; and smoother integration of technology with people.

As a continuing *process,* QWL seeks to involve General Motors' vast human resources actively in achieving its goals. Through personal involvement, employes can contribute more to GM's success and, at the same time, increase their own satisfaction, pride in accomplishment, and personal growth. The QWL process encourages people to respect one another, treat each other fairly, and to solve problems cooperatively — helping one another and GM to grow and develop.

To assure that Quality of Work Life has fundamental, day-to-day meaning, each GM unit has established:

- a group to oversee the QWL process
- a statement of long-term QWL objectives
- regular QWL assessment
- seminars and other activities to disseminate QWL techniques
- internal resources and skills adequate to make the process work.

In ten years of experience, GM has identified several elements required for QWL success. The firm commitment of top management — without which little of lasting value can be expected or accomplished — is essential. Another key is the participation of the unions which represent hourly employes. (QWL became a joint effort of General Motors and the UAW in 1973, with the establishment of a joint national QWL Committee.) Effective two-way communication — particularly face-to-face communication at all levels — is critical to a successful program. And so are innovation in organizational structures, training, and performance appraisal effective ways to address employes' concerns.

But, as GM has discovered, there is no single "best" organizational system or design; what is right for one group of employes may not suit another. In some GM plants, QWL programs have encouraged employe responsibility and involvement through 'team' involvement, in which employes themselves may take on responsibility for such matters as:

- training team members
- assessing individual team members' performance
- contributing to the selection of new employes
- selecting team leaders
- maintaining tools and equipment within process standards
- forecasting efficiency, scrap, and manpower requirements within an operating area.

QWL principles may be applied differently in other plants, but General Motors is committed to implementing them in every GM unit.

Serious challenges in the 1980s will test the adaptability of people and organizations as they attempt to improve the quality of work life. Most serious is the nation's struggle to compete in the worldwide marketplace — with the attendant need to increase national productivity.

A concurrent challenge is to provide American workers, whose material work rewards have steadily improved, with more personal fulfillment from the work experience itself.

General Motors

Employee Bill of Rights

David W. Ewing

A Proposed Bill of Rights

What should a bill of rights for employees look like?

First, it should be presented in the form of clear and practical injunctions, not in the language of desired behavior or ideals.

In 1789, when James Madison and other members of the first U.S. Congress settled down to write the Bill of Rights (the first ten amendments to the Constitution), Madison insisted on using the imperative "shall" instead of the flaccid "ought," which had been used in the declaration of rights by the states, from which the ideas for the federal Bill of Rights were taken. For instance, where Virginia's historic Declaration of Rights of 1776 stated that "excessive bail ought not to be required," and where the amendments proposed in 1788 by Virginia legislators were identically worded, the amendment proposed by Madison (and later accepted) read: "Excessive bail shall not be required. . . ."

The imperative has precisely the same advantage in a bill of rights for members of a corporation, government bureau, university administration, or other organization. An analogy is a traffic light. It does not contain various shades of red but just one shade which means clearly and unequivocally, "Stop." Nor does a stop sign say "Stop If Possible" or "Stop If You Can." It says simply "Stop."

Second, as a general rule, it is wise to phrase a bill of rights in terms of negative injunctions rather than positive ones. A bill of rights does not aim to tell officials what they can do so much as it aims to tell them what they cannot do. It is not like the delegation of powers found in constitutions.

Here again it is instructive to recall the writing of the federal Bill of Rights in 1789. Madison insisted that the positive grants of government powers had been well provided for in the main body of the Constitution and did not need to be reiterated in the first ten amendments.

In addition, a "Thou shalt not" type of commandment generally can be more precise than a "Thou shalt" type of commandment; the latter must be worded and interpreted to cover many possibilities of affirmative action. Since it is more precise, a "Thou shalt not" injunction is more predictable— not quite as predictable as a traffic light, but more so than most positive injunctions can be.

Also, since it is more limited, a negative injunction is less of a threat to the future use of executive (and legislative) powers. For instance, the injunction "Congress shall make no law respecting an establishment of religion" (first item in the U.S. Bill of Rights) inhibits Congress less, simply because it is so precise, than a positive command such as "Congress shall respect various establishments of religion" (rejected by the Founding Fathers when proposed in the 1789 discussions), which is more protean and expansible.

Third, an organization's bill of rights should be succinct. It should read more like a recipe in a cookbook than the regulations of the Internal Revenue Service. It is better to start with a limited number of rights that apply to familiar situations and that may have to be extended and amended in a few years than try to write a definitive listing for all time. Rights take time to ingest.

Fourth, a bill of rights should be written for understanding by employees and lay people rather than by lawyers and personnel specialists. It should not read like a letter from a credit company or a Massachusetts auto insurance policy. If an organization desires to make everything clear for experts, it could add a supplement or longer explanation that elaborates in technical terms on the provisions and clarifies questions and angles that might occur to lawyers.

Fifth, a bill of rights should be enforceable. Existence as a creed or statement of ideals is not enough. While creeds indeed may influence behavior in the long run, in the short run they leave too much dependent on good will and hope.

The bill of rights that follows is one person's proposal, a "working paper" for discussion, not a platform worked out in committee. As the short commentaries indicate, these proposed rights encapsulate parts of the discussion and reasoning in preceding chapters. The slight variations in style are purposeful—partly to reduce monotony and partly to suggest different ways of defining employee rights and management prerogatives.

1. *No organization or manager shall discharge, demote, or in other ways discriminate against any employee who criticizes, in speech or press, the ethics, legality, or social responsibility of management actions.*

Comment: This right is intended to extend the U.S. Supreme Court's approach in the *Pickering* case to all employees in business, government, education, and public service organizations.

What this right does not say is as important as what it does say. Protection does not extend to employees who make nuisances of themselves or who balk, argue, or contest managerial decisions on normal operating and planning matters, such as the choice of inventory accounting method, whether to diversify the product line or concentrate it, whether to rotate workers on a certain job or specialize them, and so forth. "Committing the truth," as Ernest Fitzgerald called it, is protected only for speaking out on issues where we consider an average citizen's judgment to be as valid as an expert's—truth in advertising, public safety standards, questions of fair disclosure, ethical practices, and so forth.

Nor does the protection extend to employees who malign the organization. We don't protect individuals who go around ruining other people's reputations, and neither should we protect those who vindictively impugn their employers.

Note, too, that this proposed right does not authorize an employee to disclose to outsiders information that is confidential.

This right puts publications of nonunionized employees on the same basis as union newspapers and journals, which are free to criticize an organization. Can a free press be justified for one group but not for the other? More to the point still, in a country that practices democratic rites, can the necessity of an "underground press" be justified in any socially important organization?

2. *No employee shall be penalized for engaging in outside activities of his or her choice after working hours, whether political, economic, civic, or cultural, nor for buying products and services of his or her choice for personal use, nor for expressing or encouraging views contrary to top management's on political, economic, and social issues.*

Comment: Many companies encourage employees to participate in outside activities, and some states have committed this right to legislation. Freedom of choice of products and services for personal use is also authorized in various state statutes as well as in arbitrators' decisions. The third part of the statement extends the protection of the First Amendment to the employee whose ideas about government, economic policy, religion, and society do not conform with the boss's. It would also protect the schoolteacher who allows the student newspaper to espouse a view on sex education that is rejected by the principal, the staff psychologist who endorses a book on a subject considered taboo in the board room, and other independent spirits.

Note that this provision does not authorize an employee to come to work "beat" in the morning because he or she has been moonlighting. Participation in outside activities should enrich employees' lives, not debilitate them; if on-the-job performance suffers, the usual penalties may have to be paid.

3. *No organization or manager shall penalize an employee for refusing to carry out a directive that violates common norms of morality.*

Comment: The purpose of this right is to take the rule of the *Zinman* case a step further and afford job security (not just unemployment compensation) to subordinates who cannot perform an action because they consider it unethical or illegal. It is important that the conscientious objector in such a case hold to a view that has some public acceptance. Fad moralities — messages from flying saucers, mores of occult religious sects, and so on — do not justify refusal to carry out an order. Nor in any case is the employee entitled to interfere with the boss's finding another person to do the job requested.

4. *No organization shall allow audio or visual recordings of an employee's conversations or actions to be made without his or her prior knowledge and consent. Nor may an organization require an employee or applicant to take personality tests, polygraph examinations, or other tests that constitute, in his opinion, an invasion of privacy.*

Comment: This right is based on policies that some leading organizations have already put into practice. If an employee doesn't want his working life monitored, that is his privilege so long as he demonstrates (or, if an applicant, is willing to demonstrate) competence to do a job well.

5. *No employee's desk, files, or locker may be examined in his or her absence by anyone but a senior manager who has sound reason to believe that the files contain information needed for a management decision that must be made in the employee's absence.*

Comment: The intent of this right is to grant people a privacy right as employees similar to that which they enjoy as political and social citizens under the "searches and seizures" guarantee of the Bill of Rights (Fourth Amendment to the Constitution). Many leading organizations in business and government have respected the principle of this rule for some time.

6. *No employer organization may collect and keep on file information about an employee that is not relevant and necessary for efficient management. Every employee shall have the right to inspect his or her personnel file and challenge the accuracy, relevance, of necessity of data in it, except for personal evaluations and comments by other employees which could not reasonably be obtained if confidentiality were not promised. Access to an employee's file by outside individuals and organizations shall be limited to inquiries about the essential facts of employment.*

Comment: This right is important if employees are to be masters of their employment track records instead of possible victims of them. It will help to eliminate surprises, secrets, and skeletons in the clerical closet.

7. *No manager may communicate to prospective employers of an employee who is about to be or has been discharged gratuitous opinions that might hamper the individual in obtaining a new position.*

Comment: The intent of this right is to stop blacklisting. The courts have already given some support for it.

8. *An employee who is discharged, demoted, or transferred to a less desirable job is entitled to a written statement from management of its reasons for the penalty.*

Comment: The aim of this provision is to encourage a manager to give the same reasons in a hearing, arbitration, or court trial that he or she gives the employee when the cutdown happens. The written statement need not be given unless requested; often it is so clear to all parties why an action is being taken that no document is necessary.

9. *Every employee who feels that he or she has been penalized for asserting any right described in this bill shall be entitled to a fair hearing before an impartial official, board, or arbitrator. The findings and conclusions of the hearing shall be delivered in writing to the employee and management.*

Comment: This very important right is the organizational equivalent of due process of law as we know it in political and community life. Without due process in a company or agency, the rights in this bill would all have to be enforced by outside courts and tribunals, which is expensive for society as well as time-consuming for the employees who are required to appear as complainants and witnesses. The nature of a "fair hearing" is purposely left undefined here so that different approaches can be tried, expanded, and adapted to changing needs and conditions.

Note that the findings of the investigating official or group are not binding on top management. This would put an unfair burden on an ombudsperson or "expedited arbitrator," if one of them is the investigator. Yet the employee is protected. If management rejects a finding of unfair treatment and then the employee goes to court, the investigator's statement will weigh against management in the trial. As a practical matter, therefore, employers will not want to buck the investigator-referee unless they fervently disagree with the findings.

In Sweden, perhaps the world's leading practitioner of due process in organizations, a law went into effect in January 1977 that goes a little farther than the right proposed here. The new Swedish law states that except in unusual circumstances a worker who disputes a dismissal notice can keep his or her job until the dispute has been decided by a court.

Every sizable organization, whether in business, government, health, or another field, should have a bill of rights for employees. Only small organizations need not have such a statement — personal contact and oral communications meet the need for them. However, companies and agencies need not have identical bills of rights. Industry custom, culture, past history with employee unions and associations, and other considerations can be taken into account in the wording and emphasis given to different provisions.

For instance, Booz, Allen and Hamilton, the well-known consulting company, revised a bill of rights for its employees in 1976 (the list included several of the rights suggested here). One statement obligated the company to "Respect the right of employees to conduct their private lives as they choose, while expecting its employees' public conduct to reflect favorably upon the reputation of the Firm." The latter part of this provision reflects the justifiable concern of a leading consulting firm with outward appearances. However, other organizations — a mining company, let us say, or a testing laboratory — might feel no need to qualify the right of privacy because few of their employees see customers.

Mark B. Woodhouse

Implementing Employee Rights: A Critique

Historically, the topic of employee rights tends not to be addressed by management except in times of a local crisis or contract negotiation; seldom does management take the initiative. Thus Mr. Ewing's delineation of an Employees' "Bill of Rights" from the perspective of management is a welcome proposal and worthy of serious attention.[1] It is difficult to take exception to any of the individual principles Ewing presents; none should be deleted. The overriding problem with his proposal is not what he does say, but what he fails to say in spelling out the necessary amendments and qualifications to make their implementation both fair and realistic.

1. Ewing begins by proposing that management shall not discriminate against any employee "who criticizes, in speech or press, the ethics, legality, or social responsibility of management actions." This presumably would protect the employee who, for example, publicly questions his firm's decision not to hire more minorities, but it would not protect the employee who criticizes a manager's legitimate business decisions. Ewing leaves the term 'criticize' rather open-ended, when its connection with truth and sound reasoning should be stressed. The individual should be willing to provide *evidence* for his criticism of management, and, as a corollary, no employee should abuse the right of free speech by knowingly communicating falsehoods about the company or its employees, irrespective of the subject matter in question.

Secondly, if a company is large enough to be affected by public criticism from its employees, then it needs to establish some *internal* channels or hearing procedures that address the issue. For we might want to say that rights of the employee who makes a sincere and well-reasoned case to management before going public (should that prove necessary) are more secure

328

than those of the employee who does not avail himself of such internal procedures. The employee does have a legal obligation to be loyal to his employer, and he also has a *prima facie* moral obligation to be loyal. Correlatively, the firm has an obligation to see that reasonable dissent can be voiced through internal channels. If the firm has an internal grievance or hearing mechanism, the employee's duty to be loyal obliges him to use that mechanism before voicing public criticism.

Another important factor relates to the seriousness of the alleged management act. If a manager steals his firm's pencil, this act hardly deserves a letter to the local newspaper's editor. The seriousness of the offense must be taken into consideration. The employee's motive is also a relevant factor; the firm should not sanction the free speech of an employee who deliberately sets out to embarrass the company and does not act from a reasonable sense of good will.

Criticisms of the firm, then, should be voiced only if they are: (1) of a serious nature, e.g., the management act harmed or will harm individuals or society; (2) based on an appropriate motive; (3) grounded on evidence; and (4) voiced through appropriate internal channels prior to external criticism.

2. In his second proposal, Ewing suggests that "no employee shall be penalized for engaging in outside activities of his or her choice after working hours. . . ." This includes buying the competitor's products, working for certain civic clubs, or even espousing particular political, social, or religious views (which may be contrary to those of top management). The intent of this proposal is well-taken. Implementing it in particular cases, however, requires that each firm spell out in advance the ground-rules regarding such activities, and in a way that takes into account its unique circumstances.

Ewing's rule works best in cases where there is no connection between the company's business interest and the outside activities of the employee. Establishing a connection (or nonconnection), however, can be difficult. For example, some firms may have such a vested interest in their public image that certain kinds of activities may be ruled out, e.g., those with even the slightest racist overtones, or a political action group advocating the legalization of marijuana. To take a specific case, if the vice-president of a black owned and managed firm were caught contributing time or money to the KKK, his firm might very well face a boycott of its products, especially in the black community. Hence, some restrictions on his outside interests are justified. In all such cases, the restrictions should be commensurate with the employee's level of responsibility.

As a corollary to his proposal, we might want to insist that every employee has a right to a statement regarding acceptable levels of job performance, perhaps with some grading, e.g., levels necessary to keep one's position versus levels necessary to advance. In this way we have some framework to judge how much outside activity is "too much," namely, when it begins to detract from the employee's ability to meet these levels. We might also add the proviso that no company shall place its employees in a double bind by requiring (either formally or by tacit prescription) that the employee participate in certain activities that would in turn have the effect of limiting or reducing job performance.

3. Ewing proposes that no employee shall be penalized "for refusing to carry out a directive that violates common norms of morality." Depending upon how broadly or narrowly we interpret "common norm" (How much public acceptance is necessary?) this principle turns out to be obvious or only arbitrarily enforceable. Hence, some bill of particulars needs to be spelled out in advance to address the kinds of moral dilemmas that an employee is likely to encounter in the course of doing his job, e.g., the paying of bribes to foreign clients.

An enlightened organization might consider carrying Ewing's proposal one step further by insisting that no manager shall place a subordinate in the position of having to refuse an unethical or illegal directive in the first place. For the natural desire to please may compromise employees up and down the line. The problem with meeting this objective, of course, is aggravated in some cases by the sharp though shifting distinction drawn between corporate and public morality. Our common understanding of what is unethical in the public sphere all too often may be suspended in company thinking to the extent that, say, a directive to lie or to withhold relevant information in some circumstances is simply not viewed as "unethical." And of course if it is not viewed as unethical by the company, then the employee's right of refusal is on shakier grounds.

4. In his next proposal, Ewing seeks to preserve the employee's right to privacy, including freedom from recordings made without his consent, and polygraph or personality tests. This proposal is so broad as to constitute at best only a point of departure. To begin, some provision must be made for jobs that deal with security matters or with information that is highly classified, whether by the government or by the company. The company's right to preserve its own legitimate interests, e.g., those involving trade secrets, surely will take precedence in some *limited* areas. And here it is the responsibility of upper management to spell out the conditions in advance.

Secondly, even in cases not involving classified material surveillance may be justified, for example, in situations of petty thievery. To be sure, it takes time to spell out *conditions* in detail, but some mechanism must be in place to stipulate those under which an invasion of privacy may be warranted. This mechanism will tell us, in reasonably specific ways, how to distinguish between arbitrary or capricious "fishing trips" on the one hand, and job-related problems on the other. This mechanism will also tell us about the *means* of surveillance to be undertaken in situations where it is justified. These, too, should be ethical. For example, tapping a home phone would generally be excluded as a means, even though it might accidentally provide some information.

The matter of requiring personality or intelligence tests certainly can be a sensitive issue, but surely we do not wish to rule them out on the basis of an unqualified employee right to privacy. The criteria for requiring these tests should stipulate a clear connection between what the test can show on the one hand and what a particular job requires on the other. Being a commodities broker, for example, does require certain personality traits. Still, the right to privacy is not to be taken lightly. Hence, we need a corollary stating that any employee (or prospective employee) who refuses on grounds of privacy to take reasonable tests related to the job will not be discriminated against.

5. Ewing's fifth proposal would grant employees freedom from unnecessary searches and seizures. Their desks, files, etc., may not be arbitrarily inspected. Our concerns here parallel those expressed earlier. Ewing views such inspections as necessary and justified in those cases where a management decision must be made "in the employee's absence." (Does this mean while the employee happens to be away, or that the absence is necessary for the decision?) What kinds of management decisions are at stake here? Those pertaining to everyday business matters, to the employee's own record, or both? Whose permission is required? Ought there to be a second party present? Should the search occur only when the decision could not wait? Who is to take responsibility for what is done with the information? Of course, Ewing cannot give answers to these questions in advance. But any company that adopts his Bill of Rights will need to address them.

6. Ewing proposes that no organization "may collect and keep on file information about an employee that is not relevant and necessary for efficient management." Employees may challenge the relevance or accuracy of the information, and outsiders shall not be given access to its contents. The primary problem here consists in spelling out, in advance, what kind of information is both "relevant and necessary" for "efficient" management. Left unqualified, such stipulations open the way for monumental abuses by managers whose perception of efficiency is not sufficiently tied to actual job performance.

More importantly, however, there is a potentially self-destructive mechanism in Ewing's proposal when we note that the employee may not examine those personal evaluations which are not otherwise obtainable without the promise of confidentiality. But such evaluations are in many cases the *heart* of an employee's file. How are we to screen for irrelevance, inaccuracy, or other abuses here? If the employee's job security and advancement depend primarily upon what others are secretly saying about him in confidential reports, then Ewing's proposal may amount to a very low grade (some might say meaningless) "right." What we give with one hand, we take away with the other.

One daring way to deal with this problem would be to require that managers making personal evaluations be trained to make clear, tightly reasoned, and balanced evaluations using good interpersonal skills on a "face to face" basis. They would do this in conjunction with placing written evaluations in the employee's file. In all but special circumstances, this requirement makes sense for two reasons. First, it can make for better managers because they are, figuratively speaking, forced to "live with what they say." Secondly, if (per proposal #8) the employee must be given a written statement of the reasons for his discharge or demotion, then there seems to be less point in taking refuge in confidentiality early on. At the very least, we might permit the employee access to evaluations with names withheld, rather than denying access altogether.

7. Ewing next proposes that prospective employers shall not be given "gratuitous opinions" from ex-managers that would have the effect of blacklisting the employee. Presumably "gratuitous" means "unwarranted." Again, the problem for the corporation adopting this proposal will be to spell out in advance exactly what kind of information will be given to prospective employers along with some explanation of why the disclosure is warranted. The facts of employment, for example, are relatively noncontroversial; so-called "work habits" are a more sensitive area. Generally, it seems best to limit inquiries to factual information, and allow the employee to waive his right to confidentiality on interpretive matters, if he so desires. After all, a broader perspective on his job-performance might enhance his future employment possibilities. Furthermore, the company may wish to address the issue of whether, as a matter of policy, employees may request a copy of the information that has been forwarded. Providing this option would be the strongest way to help keep gratuitous material from following the employee.

8. Ewing proposes that the employee has the right to a written statement of the reasons for being fired or demoted. As a corollary to this, we might add that the employee also has a right to a written statement of his *current status* with the company, including occasional unscheduled evaluations in special circumstances, e.g., where he is being approached by other firms. The principal difficulty here is to make the reasons specific enough to be significant. It is far too easy to deal in generalities in such matters. That Jones did not live up to management's expectations, for example, means nothing unless we know what management's expectations initially were, and we are then given specific instances of the actions that did not fit prospective goals.

9. In what is perhaps the most important proposal in his entire Bill of Rights, Ewing stipulates that every employee with a specific grievance involving any of the other rights is entitled to "a fair hearing before an impartial official, board, or arbitrator." But senior managers are not automatically impartial magistrates; we are only one step removed from the analogous legal situation of a judge presiding at his own trial. For whatever the reasons, in most *any* type of organization those with higher rank, seniority, responsibility, etc., have a way of coming out ahead when their decisions regarding fair treatment of subordinates are called into question by those subordinates. Perhaps this is inevitable. If so, however, then some very clear procedural mechanism must be put in place to guarantee that those hearing the case have no direct or indirect stake in the outcome. To

help ensure impartiality, members of this board should include peers, outsiders, and senior managers who, where possible, are at least several levels removed from the area of controversy and from a different area of operations. Most importantly, it must be made very clear that from the highest levels on down the company has a demonstrable long-term interest in implementing, refining, and enforcing any employee Bill of Rights. Without that clarity and commitment, all talk about employee rights will be just that—talk.

NOTE

1. David Ewing, "A Proposed Bill of Rights," *Freedom Inside the Organization: Bringing Civil Liberties to the Workplace* (New York: E. P. Dutton, 1977), Chapter 9. For further criticism, see Staughton Lynd's "Company Constitutionalism?," *The Yale Law Journal,* Vol. 87, No. 4 (March, 1978).

Donald L. Martin

Is an Employee Bill of Rights Needed?

The perception of the corporation as an industrial form of government in which management plays the role of the governor and labor the role of the governed has been particularly popular since the end of World War II. "Industrial democracy" has been the slogan of the labor movement in the industrial relations community. This analogy has recently given rise to demands for an "Employee Bill of Rights." Such a bill would guarantee the worker the same *due process* that the Constitution guarantees the citizen. It would protect the worker from the arbitrary and inequitable exercise of managerial discretion.

WHERE THE INDUSTRIAL DEMOCRACY ANALOGY FALTERS

But, the industrial democracy analogy surely must be false. Two important considerations obviate it. First, a crucial distinction between government at any level and private economic organization, corporate or otherwise, is the right entrusted to government to exercise legitimate and reasonable force in its relations with its citizens. Second, the cost to a citizen of switching affiliation between governments is far greater than the cost to an employee of switching affiliations between firms. Since governments will surely violate public trust through their police powers, and since the costs to citizens of changing leaders or residences are relatively high, citizens will seek institutions to insulate themselves from the arbitrary and exploitative use of such powers by their elected and appointed representatives. These institutions include the first ten amendments to the United States Constitution (the Bill of Rights) and the Fourteenth Amendment (guaranteeing due process).

THE PROBLEM OF THE MONOPSONISTIC LABOR MARKET

Something close to an analogous use of exploitative power in the private sector occurs in the world of monopsonistic labor markets. In those labor markets, would-be employees have few, if any, alternative job opportunities, either because of an absence of immediate competitive employers or because of the presence of relatively high costs of moving to available job alternatives in other markets. With few or no job alternatives, workers are more likely to be the unwilling subjects of employer prejudice, oppression, and personal discretion than if labor market competition prevails.

No one would claim that the American economy is completely free of monopsony power. There is not a shred of evidence, on the other hand, that such power exists in the large American corporation of today. Indeed, there is impressive evidence to suggest that monopsony is not likely to be found in large, private corporations. Robert Bunting's examination of labor market concentration throughout the United States among large firms, for example, finds that employment concentration (measured by the fraction of total employees in a geographic area who are employed by the largest reporting firm in that area) is related inversely to labor market size, while firm size is correlated positively with labor market size. . . .

THE NATURE OF EMPLOYER-EMPLOYEE AGREEMENTS

The Constitution of the United States does not extend the Bill of Rights and the due process clause of the Fourteenth Amendment to the private sector unless agents of the latter are performing public functions [*Marsh v. State of Alabama,* 66 S. Ct. 276 (1946)]. Instead of interpreting this limitation as an oversight of the founding fathers, the preceding discussion suggests that the distinctive treatment accorded governments reflects the conscious belief that market processes, more than political processes, yield a degree of protection to their participants that is closer to levels that those participants actually desire. It also suggests that this inherent difference justifies the institutionalization of civil liberties in one form of activity (political) and not in the other form (market).

This interpretation is consistent with the repeated refusal of the United States Supreme Court to interfere with the rights of employers and employees (corporate or otherwise) to make mutually agreeable arrangements concerning the exercise of civil liberties (otherwise protected under the Constitution) on the job or in connection with job-related activities. (The obvious legislative exceptions to this generalization are the Wagner Act of 1935 and the Taft-Hartley Act of 1947. These acts proscribe the free speech rights of employers with regard to their possible influence over union elections on their own property, while allowing labor to use that same property for similar purposes.)

In the absence of monopsonistic power, the substantive content of an employer-employee relationship is the result of explicit and implicit bargaining that leaves both parties better off than they would be if they had not entered into the relationship. That both are better off follows because each is free to end the employment relationship at will—unless, of course, contractual relationships specify otherwise. Americans have demonstrated at an impressive rate a willingness to leave current employment for better pecuniary and nonpecuniary alternatives. During nonrecessionary periods, employee resignations contribute significantly to turnover statistics. In an uncertain world, the workers who resign generate valuable information about all terms and conditions under which firms and would-be employees can reach agreement.

THE COSTS OF WORKPLACE CIVIL LIBERTIES

If information about each party to employment and information about potential and actual performance are costly, both firms *and* employees seek ways to economize. Indeed, the functions of a firm, from the viewpoint of employees, are to screen job applicants and to monitor on-the-job activities. A firm's final output is often a result of the joint efforts of workers rather than a result of the sum of the workers' separate efforts. This jointness of production makes individual effort difficult to measure, and on-the-job shirking becomes relatively inexpensive for any given employee. The reason is precisely that all employees must share the cost of one employee's "goldbricking." As a consequence, shirking, if done excessively, threatens the earning opportunities of other workers. Other white collar crimes, such as pilfering finished products or raw materials, have similar consequences.

To protect themselves from these threats, workers use the firm as a monitoring agent, implicitly authorizing it to direct work, manage tools, observe work practices and other on-the-job employee activities, and discipline transgressors. If employers function efficiently, the earnings of workers will be higher than if the monitoring function were not provided.

Efficient *employer* activities, however, may appear to others, including some employees, to be flagrant violations of personal privacy from the perspective of the First, Fourth, Fifth, and Ninth Amendments to the Constitution. These employer activities, on the contrary, are the result of implied agreements between employers and employees, consummated by demand and supply forces in the labor market. The reduction in personal liberty that workers sustain in a firm has a smaller value for them, at the margin, than the increase in earning power that results. Thus, limitations on personal liberty in a firm, unlike such limitations in governments, are not manifestations of tyranny; they are, instead, the product of a mutually preferred arrangement.

It should not be surprising that higher-paying firms and firms entrusting more valuable decision-making responsibility to some employees would invest relatively more resources than would other firms in gathering potentially revealing information about the qualifications of prospective employees and about the actions of existing employees. Since the larger a firm is, by asset size or by employee number, the more likely it is to be a corporation, it should also not be surprising that corporations are among the firms that devote relatively large amounts of resources to gathering information of a personal nature about employees.

Prohibiting the gathering of such information by superimposing an "Employee Bill of Rights" on the employment relationship has the effect of penalizing a specific group of employees. This group is composed of those persons who cannot otherwise compete successfully for positions of responsibility, trust, or loyalty because the high cost of information makes it unprofitable for them to distinguish themselves from other workers without desirable job characteristics. Thus, federal protection of the civil liberties of employees in the marketplace may actually harm those who wish to waive such rights as a less expensive way of competing.

Under an "Employee Bill of Rights," the process of searching for new employees and the process of managing existing employees are relatively more costly for an employer. This greater cost will be reflected not only in personnel policy but also in the cost of producing final outputs and in the price consumers pay for them. An effect of an "Employee Bill of Rights" would be limited dimensions on which employees may compete with each other. Although there are precedents for such limitations (for example, federal minimum wage laws), it is important to recognize that this kind of protection may have unintended effects on the welfare of large numbers of employees. The anticompetitive effects of institutionalizing due process and civil liberties have long been recognized by trade unions. These effects constitute an important reason for the interest unions have in formalizing the procedures employers use in hiring, firing, promoting, demoting, rewarding, and penalizing union employees. It is false to argue, nevertheless, that an absence of formal procedures and rules in nonunionized firms is evidence that workers are at the mercy of unfettered employers, or that workers are more likely to be exploited if they are located in corporations rather than in noncorporate forms of organization.

Even the most powerful corporations must go to an effectively competitive labor market for their personnel. Prospective employees see arbitrary and oppressive personnel policies as relatively unattractive working conditions requiring compensation of pecuniary and nonpecuniary differentials over and above what they would receive from alternative employments.

Those workers who want more certainty in the exercise of civil liberties pay for that certainty by forgoing these compensating differentials. This reasoning suggests that the degree of desired democracy in the labor market is amenable to the same forces that determine wages and working conditions. There is neither evidence nor persuasive arguments that suggest that workers in large corporations somehow have been excluded from the process that determines the degree of democracy they want.

Maurice S. Trotta
Harry R. Gudenberg

Resolving Personnel Problems in Nonunion Plants

The manager of an electronics division at a United States Air Force base attended a conference on how to resolve employee grievances. The conference leader outlined a typical problem and asked the manager how he would handle it. The Air Force man gave his decision, and when asked to state his reasons for it, he replied: "It was a gut reaction." Pressed to explain "gut reaction," he was unable to do so. During the subsequent discussion many of his colleagues disagreed with his solution, and he later admitted that (1) this was the first time his personnel decisions had ever been questioned and analyzed, and (2) he now realized that making a sound personnel decision was a complex process.

Highly competent and intelligent, this electronics engineer had honestly felt that his personnel decisions were fair and sound. He was able to make sound technical decisions, but his ability to make sound personnel decisions was questionable.

CONFLICT ANALYSIS: THE DECISIONAL PROCESS

If managers were trained how to handle personnel problems and were taught something about the decisional process, many personnel grievances that now come up for adjudication would never materialize in the first place. This is a view held by experienced arbitrators, and a reading of arbitration awards published by the Bureau of National Affairs and Commerce Clearing House will confirm it.

It should also be emphasized, however, that the same lack of training among shop stewards and other union officers also provokes many grievances that are eventually submitted to arbitration.

Conflict results when two parties view the same situations, but come to different decisions. Thus, the first step toward conflict resolution is to analyze why the parties reached different conclusions. Such an effort is one of the functions of the arbitral process.

In most situations both sides believe their conclusions are sound and fair. But the arbitrator, in reviewing the reasons why two persons or sides have reached different conclusions, will often discover that there is a dispute as to facts or that lack of communication has created misunderstandings. He may also find that basic assumptions rested on shaky facts, that opinions were formed upon scanty evidence or stated by persons not competent to form a reliable opinion, and that the parties' concepts of what is a proper employee-employer relationship are diametrically opposed. Personality conflicts also cause problems.

*   *   *

TRENDS IN RESOLVING PERSONNEL PROBLEMS

Whenever people are supervised, personnel problems will inevitably arise. Top management invariably expresses desire for equitable personnel decisions and assumes that personnel decisions made by middle management are sound and fair and do not need to be reviewed. On the basis of arbitration awards, however, it appears that the assumption underlying this traditional approach is not always warranted.

A large percentage of cases processed through grievance-arbitration procedures is decided in favor of the grievant. For example, a recent survey found that in cases involving faculty members of institutions of higher education, 40 percent of the grievants were successful, 30 percent of all issues arbitrated involved discharge, discipline, and tenure problems of faculty, and 24 percent involved merit rates, promotion, and demotion. (Approximately the same percentages are applicable to cases submitted to arbitration by business and industry.) . . .

Experience has also shown that a company or institution will have high turnover—with resultant higher labor costs and lower efficiency—if employees believe their personnel problems are consistently handled arbitrarily, with no right to an impartial review of decisions believed to be unfair. To avoid this problem, nonunion plants and nonprofit institutions are tending to establish impartial appeal procedures. . . .

TYPICAL GRIEVANCE PROCEDURES

Grievance policies adopted by nonunion companies and organizations prescribe a wide range of appeal and decision procedures. Some enunciate relatively informal "open door" policies that are briefly stated in one or two paragraphs in employee handbooks. Others provide a lengthy, formalized series of checks and balances designed to assure fair treatment of workers who believe they have been wronged in one way or another.

An informal survey conducted by the authors among some 100 companies and institutions showed that most firms contacted had installed basically formalized procedures terminating in a final decision by the general manager. But a few had adopted procedures utilizing impartial arbitration along the lines specified in union contracts.

An informal "open door" policy utilized by some firms is illustrated by the following compact statement from an employee handbook:

> All problems should be taken up initially with the employee's immediate supervisor. Most of the problems will be settled at this point to the satisfaction of the employee. There may be times, however, when the nature of the problem is such that the supervisor may not be able to give an immediate answer. In those instances where the immediate supervisor is unable to solve the problem within two working days following the date of presentation by the employee, the employee may review the problem with his departmental manager or superintendent. In situations where, after having discussed his problem with this immediate supervisor and departmental manager or superintendent, an employee still has questions, he may take the problem to the personnel manager for disposition.

Other, less informal grievance procedures extend the route for appeal past the personnel or employee relations manager to the general manager. For example, one company prescribed a three-step procedure similar to the one quoted above, but added a fourth step as follows:

> If the Employee Relations Manager is unable to give you an answer that resolves your problem, he will be happy to get you an appointment with the General Manager, who will give a fair and just answer to your problem after reviewing the facts.

This company then assured employees that use of the grievance procedures would not jeopardize them in their jobs.

> If you follow these steps, no one may criticize you, penalize you, or discriminate against you in any way. If you have a very personal problem that you wish to discuss with the Employee Relations Manager or any member of management, just tell your immediate supervisor of this fact, and he will get you an appointment.

One of the more formal, detailed grievance procedures reported in the survey is illustrated below. Note how it carefully specifies action time requirements for both the employee and supervisors and states that all decisions are to be handed down in writing.

ONE COMPANY'S "ACTION REVIEW" OF SALARIED EMPLOYEES' GRIEVANCES

POLICY. It is our policy to provide a pleasant working environment for all employees. This is achieved by developing and maintaining cooperative working relationships among employees based on mutual respect and understanding. We recognize the need for a procedure that will allow employees to call attention to work-related matters that they feel need correction. The following procedure may be used for resolving such work-related problems.

PROCEDURE. A grievance is defined as an alleged violation by the company of its established policies and/or practices with respect to wages, hours, or conditions of work, or where an employee claims that the company has shown discrimination among employees in the application of its policies and/or practices.

It is the employee's right to make his grievances known. Any employee who feels that he has a just grievance is encouraged to make use of the following procedure with the guarantee that in so doing he will in no way place his standing or job in jeopardy. If the basis of his complaint is found valid, immediate steps will be taken to correct the matter.

The Employee Relations Specialist is available upon request by the employee to assist in preparation and presentation of grievances at any step. The employee should be advised of this service.

STEP 1. IMMEDIATE SUPERVISOR

A. The employee normally is expected to present his grievance to his immediate supervisor either verbally or in writing, but must do so within three working days of the alleged violation.

B. In unusual cases where the grievance is of a personal nature, the employee may discuss it with the Employee Relations Specialist. The Employee Relations Specialist will then arrange a meeting between the employee and his supervisor, and the Employee Relations Specialist will attend if the employee so requests.

C. The immediate supervisor will, within three working days, give the employee an answer (in writing if the employee so requests).

To retain flexibility and to reduce the number of formal steps in this procedure, the immediate supervisor should confer with all appropriate line management below the level of Department Head where it is deemed necessary. The answer given to the employee will then represent the combined opinion of the section head, foreman, assistant foreman, etc.

STEP 2. DEPARTMENT HEAD

A. If the grievance is not resolved in Step 1 above, the employee may, within three working days, state his grievance in writing. Grievance forms may be obtained from the immediate supervisor or the office of the Employee Relations Specialist.

B. The immediate supervisor will add his answer to the written grievance and immediately submit it to the Department Head.

C. The Department Head will, within three working days, meet with the employee.

All levels of supervision involved in the Step 1 answer shall initial the written grievance before it is sent to the Department Head.

The Employee Relations Specialist shall be notified by the immediate supervisor of any grievance reduced to writing for Step 2 consideration.

The Department Head will discuss the grievance with the immediate supervisor and other appropriate supervisors before meeting with the employee and may call the immediate supervisor into the meeting to clear up any conflicting information given by the employee during the meeting.

STEP 3. GENERAL MANAGEMENT REVIEW

A. If the grievance is not resolved in Step 2 above, it may be referred to the Director of Personnel who will, within five working days, establish a date for a meeting with the General Manager and the employee.

The Department Head shall refer the grievance to the Director of Personnel in all cases requiring Step 3 consideration. The Director of Personnel shall contact the employee to orient him to his Step 3 session with the General Manager.

The General Manager will discuss the grievance with the immediate supervisor and other appropriate supervisors before meeting with the employee and may call the immediate supervisor into the meeting to clear up any conflicting information given by the employee during the meeting.

B. After hearing the facts presented by the parties, the General Manager will, within five working days, render his decision in writing to the employee through the employee's immediate supervisor.

*   *   *

KEY ELEMENTS OF GRIEVANCE PROCEDURES

To be effective, employee grievance procedures should contain the following features:

- Three to five steps of appeal, depending upon the size of the organization. Three steps usually will suffice.
- A written account of the grievance when it goes past the first level. This facilitates communication and defines the issues.
- Alternate routes of appeal so that the employee can bypass his supervisor if he desires. The personnel department may be the most logical alternate route.
- A time limit for each step of the appeal so that the employee has some idea of when to expect an answer.
- Permission for the employee to have one or two co-workers accompany

him at each interview or hearing. This safety-in-numbers approach helps overcome fear of reprisal.

Employees are entitled to know the reasons for decisions affecting them. Thus some procedure is necessary to examine the basis for decisions that employees believe to be unfair.

Personnel decisions are frequently unfair because the manager is not trained in the decisional process and is unaware of his biases. Therefore, when a grievance procedure gives the final say to a management representative, that executive or supervisor should be required to take an intensive course in the decisional process in order to improve the chances for a sound personnel decision.

SELECTED BIBLIOGRAPHY

Barry, V. *Moral Issues in Business.* Belmont, Cal.: Wadsworth, 1979, chs. 4 and 5.

Bendix, R. *Work and Authority in Industry.* Berkeley: University of California Press, 1974.

Bok, S. "Whistleblowing and Professional Responsibility." *New York Education Quarterly,* 4 (1980), 2-7.

Bowie, N. "The Moral Contract Between Employer and Employee," in *Ethical Theory and Business.* 2nd ed. Beauchamp, T., and Bowie, N., eds. Englewood Cliffs, N.J.: Prentice-Hall, 1983, pp. 150-154.

Davis, L., and Taylor, J. *Design of Jobs.* London: Penguin Books, 1972.

Ewing, D. *Freedom Inside the Organization.* New York: McGraw-Hill, 1977.

Miller, A. *The Assault on Privacy: Computers, Data Banks and Dossiers.* Ann Arbor: University of Michigan Press, 1971.

Nader, R., Petkas, P., and Blackwell, K. *Whistle Blowing.* New York: Grossman, 1972.

O'Neil, R. *The Rights of Government Employees.* New York: Avon Books, 1978.

Taylor, J. *The Quality of Working Life: An Annotated Bibliography.* Los Angeles: UCLA Press, 1973.

Walters, K. "Your Employees' Right to Blow the Whistle." *Harvard Business Review,* 53 (July–August, 1975), 26 ff.

Walton, R. "How to Counter Alienation in the Plant." *Harvard Business Review,* 50 (November–December, 1972), 70-81.

Westin, A., ed. *Whistle Blowing: Loyalty and Dissent in the Corporation.* New York: McGraw-Hill, 1981.

Westin, A., and Salisbury, S., eds. *Individual Rights in the Corporation.* New York: Pantheon Books, 1980.

6

ETHICS AND THE ACCOUNTING PROFESSION

INTRODUCTION

Professionals, such as lawyers or doctors, are generally hired for their expertise; it is assumed that they have command of a complex body of knowledge that the client seeks to utilize. Since the client is rarely in a position to appraise the quality of the service received, he must trust the professional's competence. While engaged in a professional relationship, the expert is expected to serve his client's interests and not his own. To ensure public confidence and trust, the professions have formed associations that develop and enforce standards of competence and codes of professional ethics.

Public confidence is especially important to those in the accounting profession because businesses whose financial statements are audited pay for the accountant's services rather than those who use such statements. Clearly, then, those who use the information received from the statements need an independent review of the materials provided; and it is important for the profession to assure the independence of its members as well as their competence in order to maintain public confidence.

Abraham Briloff charges the accounting profession with serving the vested interests of accountants and their clients rather than the public interest. If, as is the case at present, the profession establishes accounting standards and the client hires the accountant, Briloff believes the system will be skewed against users of the audited firm's financial statements. In particular, he argues that self-enforcement of the profession's code of ethics has been lax. To remedy the situation, he proposes a thorough restructuring of the accounting profession.

Snoeyenbos and Dillon discuss in some detail the accounting profession as it is presently structured, while paying particular attention to those sections of the American Institute of Certified Public Accountants' Code of Professional Ethics that address the issues of independence, objectivity, and integrity. Taking up Briloff's criticisms, they argue that the code together with the technical accounting and auditing standards of the profession provide a viable structure for assuring competence and independence.

In contrast with independent accountants, who are not employees of the firms whose financial statements they audit, management (or internal) accountants are employed by the firms for which they do audit work. As agents, management accountants lack independence; in effect they lack full professional status. John F. Nash and Roger H. Hermanson point out certain ethical problems management accountants must face because of their divided loyalties to employers, to the profession, and to society at large. They suggest that these problems could be at least partially alleviated by granting management accountants full professional status. The authors point out, however, that there are other ethical problems that arise for any individual who has full professional status but is employed by a business.

Abraham Briloff

How Accountants Can Recover Their Balance

Early 1977 witnessed the promulgation of a 1,760-page document, the staff study by Senator Metcalf's Subcommittee of Reports, Accounting, and Management. Entitled *The Accounting Establishment,* the study followed by a matter of months another congressional criticism of the accounting scene, this one from Congressman John E. Moss's Subcommittee on Oversight and Investigation. These reports, as well as other factors like the profession's obvious failure to regulate itself, will undoubtedly lead to critical changes in the organization, structure, and functioning of accounting.

In particular, the Metcalf Committee report observes:

> The Federal Government has an important responsibility to ensure that publicly-owned corporations are properly accountable to the public. Existing accounting practices promulgated or approved by the Federal Government have failed to fulfill that responsibility adequately.

This awareness of the existence of the accounting profession is itself a remarkable shift in attitude. Less than a decade ago, a sociologist's study of attitudes toward accounting and accountants would have indicated that the former is a dismal and arcane art, while the latter would have been depicted in the Dickensian stereotype of a one-dimensional man with celluloid collars and cuffs. The respondents to the sociologists's inquiry might not have been certain that the accountant breathed—and whether he did or did not hardly mattered.

From the *Business and Society Review,* 24 (Winter 1977–78):64–68. Copyright © 1978 by Warren, Gorham, and Lamont Inc., 210 South Street, Boston, Mass. All rights reserved. Reprinted by permission of the publisher.

The mere recognition of our profession's crucial role in the effective functioning of government and business should call forth cheers. Regrettably, my colleagues have not generally seen this awareness in the same light. All too frequently they have looked upon the Moss and Metcalf reports with suspicion and resentment. Instead of seeing these developments as challenges calling for improvement, accountants generally have seen them merely as threats—which they are for those irrevocably committed to the status quo.

This greater awareness was undoubtably born out of crises—the Penn Central collapse, the Equity Funding scandal, disclosures of enormous corporate bribes at home and abroad—all treated with benign neglect by the auditors. Further, the "energy crisis" brought forth still-unanswered questions about the economics of the energy industry—questions that should properly have been answered by the keepers of the books.

So it is that, to a greater degree than at any time since double entry was discovered around 1492, the accounting profession is in a state of flux. Will the profession rise to the challenge, or will it sink to the bottom and become virtually useless?

At the very root of the accounting profession's dilemmas is the failure of its organizations, especially the American Institute of Certified Public Accountants, to fulfill the self-regulatory standard presumed for a profession. While the AICPA has been devoting much of its resources to the pursuit of accounting principles, it has, to all intents and purposes, ignored the principles of the accountant. Except for occasional platitudinous nods, the Institute has chosen to ignore the most serious transgressions on the part of its members, especially when these have been perpetrated by Establishment firms who provide financial and logistical support for the AICPA.

I am, of course, ever mindful of the Institute's highly structured ethics apparatus. This includes a Professional Ethics Executive Committee and its subcommittees, and the Professional Ethics Division, with trial boards and subboards. What has this remarkable superstructure of committees, divisions, and the like have been doing over these recent turbulent and critical years? Over the seven-and-a-half year period from 1970 through 1977 there have been 121 suspensions or expulsions of members for violating the AICPA's code of Professional Ethics. All of these suspensions or expulsions have occurred because of serious transgressions. But search the record as carefully as you might, and, except for those convicted in criminal proceedings in the Equity Funding and National Student Marketing frauds, you will not find the profession's sanctions being meted out to those who have perpetrated the profession's *causes celebres,* such as Penn Central, Investors Overseas, and corporate bribery.

Even those convicted of felonies in Continental Vending got off lightly. True, the three CPA's were expelled by the AICPA after their conviction was upheld by the Supreme Court. But the AICPA, which had no alternative under the rules, took the action begrudgingly and anonymously.

And when Nixon granted these accountants Christmas 1972 pardons, the AICPA restored them to good standing.

In light of this failure of self-regulation, both the Moss and Metcalf reports repeatedly raise the question: Who should determine the underlying precepts of accountancy, its Generally Accepted Accounting Principles? Should the profession make this determination or should Congress and government agencies? Presently, this responsibility is presumed to be lodged within the accounting profession's Financial Accounting Standards Board (FASB), with some important oversight by the Securities and Exchange Commission.

WHO SHALL SET THE PRINCIPLES?

I believe that the determination of accounting principles cannot be confined to either the private or the public sector. Accounting principles are polyglot. They represent the conglomeration of sociology, history, economics, communications, philosophy, law, mathematics, taxation, and accounting converging on itself. It therefore seems reasonable that no single narrow group should set Generally Accepted Accounting Principles (GAAP).

For the same reason, the accounting profession should abandon its quest for a single rule for each type of accounting transaction. There is just too much diversity to contend with. Instead I would unshackle accountants from the bonds of uniformity and leave it to the marketplace of ideas to judge the quality of the principles in practice.

The danger of such a system is that it might produce a race for the bottom, in which accountants applied the weakest possible principles in order to please their corporate clients. To avoid this trap, I would shift the responsibility for financial statements from where it is now (i.e., in management) to the independent auditor. I would want him, on the basis of his credentials and his professional responsibility and integrity, to assert that, from the alternatives in the Good Book of GAAP, he has applied the principles that he deemed to be most appropriate and fairest under the circumstances.

At present, the words used by the auditor when he "certifies" the financial statements make it appear that this is precisely what he is doing. But, in fact, the auditor's certification that the financial statements describe the financial condition and operations fairly is specious. While the profession usually prefers to gloss over the auditor's abdication of primary responsibility for the financial statements, when it suits the profession's purposes this fact is permitted to surface. That usually occurs in litigation when an accountant is found with his procedures down. It was emphasized by AICPA Chairman Michael Chetkovich when he defended the profession in a letter to Senator Sam Nunn, a member of the Metcalf Committee. Chetkovich rationalized the current attacks against the "Accounting Establishment" in this way:

It is not surprising that public accountants have been targets of such attention since they are important to the process of financial disclosure. Much of the criticism has its origins in the misconception that financial statements are prepared by auditors. The preparation of financial statements is the responsibility of management. The auditor's responsibility is to examine them for conformity with generally accepted accounting principles.

The profession would be on the road to recovering its credibility if this confession were appended to every certificate with which the auditor presently graces his clients' financial statements. It could serve as the "skull and bones" to warn the user that the product could be fatal if swallowed.

The selection of alternatives from the book of GAAP should not be made in an environment of intimacy between the auditor and the client's management. Instead I would have these determinations made consistent with the "Sunshine Standards" presumed to apply to governmental deliberations; they should be open covenants openly arrived at and would then become a matter of public record. Management should not be permitted to squeeze a contrived transaction into a particular accounting alternative in order to achieve a preconceived accounting consequence. This "new wine into old bottles" phenomenon should be recognized by the auditor whenever it occurs, and he should then apply a fairer alternative.

I want the auditor to become the historian for the corporate enterprise. His dedication and commitment in the writing of the corporation's history should parallel that expected from the traditional historian when he writes about politics. Moreover, I would assign a new and higher responsibility to the profession's Financial Accounting Standards Board. If the board is no longer to set standards for *accounting,* I would look to it to oversee the standards of the *accountant.* The board would diligently review the accounting alternatives which are being applied in practice. The FASB would ask, "Did the auditor apply the best alternatives available in the book of Generally Accepted Accounting Principles? If not, why not?" This oversight responsibility should serve to avoid the race for the bottom, which might result from auditors competing to accommodate any improper proclivities on the part of their clients' managements.

Who Shall Set the Standards?

Just as there are problems with current accounting principles, so are there difficulties with standards for accountants themselves. As mentioned before, the auditor should have the responsibility for choosing among accounting alternatives. Moreover, he has responsibility for ferreting out questionable and fraudulent transactions.

But the sine qua non of accounting standards is the need for true independence of the auditor from his client's management. As SEC Chairman Harold M. Williams testified before the Metcalf Committee:

The issue of independence arises in various ways. For example, an accounting firm's challenge to Commission (SEC) requests for information may impact upon independence. There should be no question, under existing law, of the Commission's right to obtain information from accountants in its oversight role and law enforcement investigations. . . . When an accountant resists the Commission's efforts to secure information primarily because the client so desires, this action reflects adversely on his independence.

There are many cases, such as Yale Express and Penn Central, where I believe the independent audit function was seriously compromised by peripheral services (i.e., consulting or tax advising or tax advocacy), performed by the audit firm. Although the Accounting Establishment has in the past resisted such ideas, there are now some indications that the profession is ready to accept them. The SEC is considering a requirement that the auditor at least disclose any multiplicity of services, a rule that I believe would have a salutary effect.

I would go further. I would absolutely proscribe the performance of any peripheral services by any firm which derives, say, more than 50 percent of its fees from the audit of large corporations. I would prohibit these firms from performing any peripheral services for any client at all. Yet I would expect these firms to maintain their sophisticated expertise in all areas of management effectiveness—possibly to an even greater degree than at present—in order to cope with the expanding universe of constituents to whom the accountants will be presumed to relate. All of this expanded expertise should be subsumed in the independent audit function.

By way of a quid pro quo, I would then restrict the right to audit large public-owned corporations to these "restricted auditing firms." For the realities of the situation are that the manpower, expertise, and the special qualities essential to conducting a major audit exist in relatively few firms. There is already an oligopoly of auditors. As the Metcalf Study noted, "85% of the 2,641 corporations listed on the New York Stock Exchange and the American Exchange are clients of the 'Big-Eight' firms."

It is likely that these eight firms, along with perhaps six others, will monopolize the auditing of large corporations. It may well be that this monopoly is inexorable. My proposals, recognizing this underlying reality, are aimed at constraining and regulating the natural monopoly. I also see much merit in the proposals put before the Metcalf Committee by John C. Biegler, the managing partner of the Establishment firm of Price Waterhouse and Co. He and his firm, he said, would join in sponsoring legislation to provide for:

—a new registration program requiring periodic reviews of the performance for each independent accounting firm auditing financial statements of publicly-owned companies;

—public disclosure of the financial statements and other operating data of such accounting firms;

—open public meetings of those bodies promulgating accounting and auditing standards; and

—support for the SEC's review of the extent of management advisory services properly offered by independent accounting firms.

These Price Waterhouse proposals, if implemented with oversight by the SEC, would make clear that auditors of publicly owned corporations straddle both the public and private sectors of our society.

A STEP IN THE RIGHT DIRECTION

In another move to strengthen the auditor's independence of the New York Stock Exchange, the SEC, the American Institute of CPA's, and the major accounting firms have all recommended that all publicly owned corporations have an audit committee composed of independent directors. I heartily agree, but I see at least two major obstacles in the effectiveness of this plan.

First, how do we define an "independent director"? At present, all directors who are not part of management are categorized as independent. But that means, for example, that a partner in the corporation's law firm who is intimately involved, sometimes on a day-to-day basis, with corporate management in its decision-making could be an "independent director." And this, mind you, despite the fact that his status in his law firm might be predicated on the firm's keeping that corporate client. Or we might also find an executive of the corporation's lead bank characterized as an "independent director"—even where that bank not only lends money to the corporation but also helps finance some highly sophisticated transactions involving the corporation. Would people with these kinds of conflicts of interest be serving on "independent audit committees"? Would they be among the first to "blow the whistle" on financial statements that reflect distortions arising from contrived transactions, when these might have been facilitated (or even conceived) by counsel and financed by the lead bank?

My confidence in the independent audit committee, as presently conceived and structured, is not enhanced when I read in the findings of Lockheed's Special Review Committee that partners of the independent audit firm conferred with the audit committee of the corporation in early 1973. The auditors were anxious about the payments for mounting foreign commission. After being rebuffed by corporate management, the auditors consoled themselves with a very ambiguous footnote to Lockheed's 1972 financial statements. By all means, let there be truly independent audit committees, comprising knowledgeable directors who are willing to commit much time and energy to fulfilling their responsibilities. When major corporations are involved, regulatory agencies should watch these committees carefully. The committees should be supported by independent experts to help comprehend what is laid before them, to ask the right probing questions, and to make certain that the responses from the auditor and management are full and fair. Such a procedure might be costly, but the cost/benefit ratio for shareholders and creditors and society at large would be favorable.

A Profession Goes to School

In accordance with accounting's new role, those who aspire to enter the profession must have a new education. This training will, of course, have to deal with the changing technical and technological aspects of the profession. In addition, I would expect a far greater emphasis on the philosophic aspects of accounting. This training should try to instill a commitment to a full and sensitive philosophy of auditing and the auditor, corresponding to the philosophy of history and that of the historian. Those who are teaching accounting (or any other) subject must recognize the values implicit in the disciplines, and they must develop the techniques and competence to impart these values continuously and pervasively.

These measures alone will not be enough. We must, finally, correct the profession's self-regulatory process. To break the Big Eight's oligopolistic hold on the profession's disciplinary and self-regulatory proceedings, we must establish an independent disciplinary apparatus, adequately funded and fully staffed. The independent board would be expected to take notice of deviations from the established standards of conduct. Such a board should proceed with its inquiry and judgment independent of any other proceedings before the courts or regulatory agencies.

All of my recommendations are predicated on the notion that the independent auditor has been designated as society's surrogate. He must probe deep inside the corporate organization in order to write the corporate history. But instead of this the profession has, in many ways, taken on the attributes of the major corporations it is supposed to audit. In pursuing their own interests and failing to limit their own misconduct, accounting firms have failed to insure that corporate management's actions are undertaken with Visibility and Accountability.

Milton Snoeyenbos
Ray D. Dillon

Independence and the AICPA Code of Professional Ethics

Professions are generally characterized by:

1. possession of a technical body of knowledge;
2. a professional association establishing
   a. competence requirements for entry into the profession;
   b. technical standards for use of the body of knowledge;
   c. an ethical code;
   d. a mechanism for enforcement of the code;
3. a commitment to socially responsible behavior.

After some general comments on the accounting profession and its technical standards, this paper focuses on (2c) with a particular emphasis on those sections of the American Institute of Certified Public Accountants' (AICPA) Code of Professional Ethics which discuss the concepts of independence, integrity, and objectivity. The focus throughout is on independent auditors (or certified public accountants, CPA's), and not on internal auditors who act as agents for organizations.

Businesses and other organizations make claims concerning their activities by issuing financial statements; investors, government agencies, creditors, and other interested parties base a variety of decisions on these statements. Because financial data are complex and voluminous, and because those who use it seldom have direct access to the data, which may be biased in favor of the provider, there is a need for an independent review of the provider's claims.

Although there are a variety of possible review mechanisms, including governmental review, our society has selected public accounting firms hired by providers of financial statements to perform the audit function. Even though the Security and Exchange Commission (SEC) has legislative authority to promulgate generally accepted accounting principles (GAAP), it has consistently relied on the accounting profession to develop these principles. The Financial Accounting Standards Board (FASB), a body consisting of a majority of CPAs, formulates the GAAP that must be followed by accountants when preparing financial statements. In a sense, then, society has granted a monopoly to independent auditors in return for the assurance that they will perform their tasks with competence, independence, and a sense of public responsibility.

The AICPA attempts to assure the *competence* of independent auditors by specifying entry-level requirements for admittance to the profession and by establishing generally accepted auditing standards (GAAS) for use by CPAs. Thus, passage of the CPA examination (which covers, in part, both GAAS and GAAP) was established as a minimum requirement for admittance to the profession, and the AICPA has recently recommended that candidates have five years of college training. GAAS were developed to assist the CPA in attesting to whether financial statements were prepared in accordance with GAAP and fairly reflect the activities of the organization.

The GAAS provide a major basis for the profession's social responsibilities — the client's and the user's need for reliable information — and there are three types of such standards.[1] The *general standards* require that auditors have adequate proficiency, maintain independence, and exercise professional care in job performance. *Field work standards* require that the auditor: (1) adequately plan and supervise work, (2) properly evaluate the audited firm's internal control mechanism, and (3) gather sufficient evidence to afford a reasonable basis for an opinion. *Reporting standards* specify guidelines for the auditor's report. Although the GAAS are general, the AICPA issues specific interpretations of the standards from time to time.[2] The AICPA also issues industry audit guidelines for specific industries or areas, e.g., Medicare audits. CPAs must attest that financial statements are prepared according to GAAP promulgated by the FASB. The FASB is a body independent from the AICPA and is comprised of four CPAs and three individuals highly qualified in accounting but not necessarily CPAs. The profession's entry requirements and technical standards as set forth in GAAS and GAAP establish a basis for professional competence and accountability to society, and also provide guidelines for job performance.

If users of financial statements and the public in general expect, and have a right to expect, that accountants be competent, then there is a concomitant right to expect these professionals to be *independent*. We will examine the concept of independence in some detail as it is discussed in the AICPA's Code of Professional Ethics (COPE).[3] Our aim is to show how the profession's technical standards and COPE combine to provide a basis for independence in the accounting profession as it is presently structured.

The COPE for the American Institute of Certified Public Accountants has three parts: concepts of professional ethics, rules of conduct, and interpretations of the rules. The part dealing with concepts is a general essay on the responsibilities of the profession. Since it suggests behavior that goes beyond the formal rules, this section does not establish enforceable standards. The section on rules does establish enforceable standards, and the AICPA's trial board ". . . may, after a hearing, admonish, suspend, or expel a member who is found guilty of infringing any of the by-laws or any provisions of the Rules of Conduct."[4] The third part of the COPE lists specific interpretations of the rules issued by the AICPA's division of professional ethics. The interpretations delineate guidelines for the scope and applicability of the rules of conduct.

In the first part of the COPE it is stated that "a certified public accountant should maintain his integrity and objectivity, and, when engaged in the practice of public accounting, be independent of those he serves."[5] Independence is said to be defined in terms of integrity and objectivity, and the COPE goes on to say that:

> Integrity is an element of character which is fundamental to reliance on the CPA. This quality may be difficult to judge, however, since a particular fault of omission or commission may be the result either of honest error or a lack of integrity.[6]

> Objectivity refers to a CPA's ability to maintain an impartial attitude on all matters which come under his review. Since this attitude involves an individual's mental processes, the evaluation of objectivity must be based largely on actions and relationships viewed in the context of ascertainable circumstances.[7]

Although the COPE regards integrity and objectivity as "not precisely measurable," they are elucidated more clearly in Rule 102:

> *Integrity and objectivity.* A member shall not knowingly misrepresent facts, and when engaged in the practice of public accounting . . . shall not subordinate his judgment to others.[8]

Of the two aspects of independence, integrity rests fundamentally on honesty and objectivity on the charge to the CPA to not subordinate his judgment.

Now *Webster's Seventh New Collegiate Dictionary* helps clarify the concept of independence for us; to be independent is to be "not dependent: as, not subject to control by others, not looking to others for one's opinions or for the guidance of one's conduct." In this sense the auditor should not be subordinate to the provider whose financial statements he audits. Legally he is not an agent of that firm, and hence does not have the agent's duties of loyalty and obedience to the firm. From an ethical and social point of view the auditor is to review the provider's claims to assure users that these claims are both fair and meet professional standards. If the auditor subordinates his judgment to that of the provider, such assurance would be undercut.

Insistence on independence from the provider is especially important given the fact that the provider selects the auditor and pays his fees. The auditor, then, should assume responsibility for his own opinion based upon standards of the profession.

It follows that the auditor must also be independent of vested interests, personal interest, and third party interests or relationships that might impair his professional judgment. The auditor has the same obligation to the provider that he has to users: to establish that the provider's financial statements are fair and meet professional standards. If he subordinates his judgment to his own interests or the interests of third parties or users, he fails in his professional obligation to both the provider and the potential user. It is in this sense that the auditor is to remain objective; he is to focus on the evidence in light of his profession's standards and not subordinate his judgment to anyone.

Objectivity, or impartiality, however, is not sufficient to establish independence in the AICPA's use of the concept; the auditor must also act with integrity. Again, *Webster's Seventh* helps us: "integrity" means "an unimpaired condition, adherence to a code of . . . values, the quality or state of being complete or undivided." The last phrase is important. The auditor must base his opinions on the facts, not just a select set of facts, but the complete set of relevant facts in accordance with professional standards.

The casual reader of the Code of Professional Ethics might note that although it discusses objectivity at length, it has little to say about integrity. It is the case, however, that Rules 202 and 203 commit the auditor to compliance with GAAS and GAAP. The fieldwork standards of GAAS read as follows:

1. The work is to be adequately planned and assistants, if any, are to be properly supervised.
2. There is to be a proper study and evaluation of the existing internal control as a basis for reliance thereon and for the determination of the resultant extent of the tests to which auditing procedures are to be restricted.
3. Sufficient competent evidential matter is to be obtained through inspection, observation, inquiries, and confirmations to afford a reasonable basis for an opinion regarding the financial statements under examination.[9]

If the auditor intentionally or unintentionally fails to gather enough evidence to make an objective opinion, (3) is violated. Failure to disclose a material fact known to him but not indicated in the financial statements, the disclosure of which would be necessary to make the statements not misleading, also results in a violation of (3). If the auditor fails to report a material misstatement that he knows to be present in the financial statements, (3) is violated. Because of (2) the auditor cannot claim that a failure to satisfy (3) rests on an inadequate internal control system in the firm he audits. Standard (1) precludes dishonesty that might be masked by a claim of inadequate planning or supervision. In addition, the reporting standards of GAAS require audit reports to be in accordance with GAAP, which precludes a failure to direct attention to any material departure from GAAP. Thus, the requirement of integrity is built into the profession's technical and ethical standards. Of course, this is not to say that all accountants maintain integrity, but it does mean that the profession has standards to deal with those who do not.

The Code of Professional Ethics explicitly delineates and precludes a number of contexts in which objectivity might be impaired. Most of these involve conflict of interest situations in which the auditor might be tempted to subordinate professional judgment to personal interests. Thus, Rule 101A states that independence is impaired if the auditor has: (1) a material financial interest in the client, (2) a material financial business investment with the client, or (3) a loan from the client.[10] Rule 101B bans relationships in which the auditor has been or is in effect a management member of the audited firm during the time period covered by the audit.[11] Interpretations of Rule 101 provide specifics regarding its scope.[12] For example, a direct financial interest in a client refers to ownership by an auditor or member of his immediate family. But the COPE requires independence in *appearance* as well as independence in fact. Consequently, it states that appearance of independence is impaired if the following close kin have a material financial interest in or business relationship with a client: nondependent children, brothers and sisters, grandparents and parents, parents-in-law, and the respective spouses of any of the foregoing.

Rule 101 prohibits an auditor from serving the client as a director, officer, or employee, but it does not ban the auditor from serving the client in certain capacities other than the audit function. Two such areas have been addressed by the AICPA in recent years: tax services and management advisory services.

If an auditor prepares a client's taxes, therein acting as the client's advocate, and also makes an audit of the client's financial statements, the possibility of a conflict of interest emerges that threatens independence. It should be noted, however, that although the CPA has a primary responsibility to the client in the tax area, part of his responsibility is to advise the client to avoid underpayment or concealment, which can lead to penalties or fraud charges. Thus, the CPA's duties to the client need not negate his duties to the government and general public. In fact, the U.S. Treasury requires tax preparers to sign the following affidavit:

> Under penalties of perjury, I declare that I have examined this return, including accompanying schedules and statements, and to the best of my knowledge and belief it is true, correct, and complete. Declaration of preparer (other than taxpayer) is based on all information of which he has any knowledge.[13]

To reinforce the CPA's commitment to this statement and his professional obligations, the AICPA has issued specific guidelines on tax practice.[14]

For example, the CPA should sign a return if he prepares it, and he should prepare it based on evidence and professional competence. If an error is detected, the CPA should advise the client and recommend corrective action. If a CPA represents a client in an administrative action with respect to a tax return known to contain an error, the CPA should request his client's permission to reveal the error to the IRS. Failing to secure permission, the CPA may be obligated to withdraw from the engagement.

CPAs often provide management services for clients in areas other than audits or tax work. Some of this work is related to accounting, e.g., studies of internal control of financial activities or accounting systems, whereas some services may not be so related, e.g., marketing surveys or production control. In any such area the CPA has an obligation to provide competent service. He also has an obligation to retain his independence. Via Rule 101B the CPA is prevented from being an employee of an audited client; therefore, the CPA must act as an *advisor* to management, not as an agent. If he acts as an advisor, making recommendations and pointing out alternatives and their consequences, but leaving the final decision and implementation to management, then his objectivity as an auditor of that firm need not be impaired.

To strengthen independence in advisory contexts, the AICPA has issued standards that go beyond Rule 101B.[15] Before he provides a service, the CPA must inform his client of any reservations he has regarding anticipated benefits. The CPA must be competent in the service provided, he must exercise due care in planning and performing the service, and he must base recommendations on sufficient evidence. Furthermore, he must communicate all significant results to the client.

Interesting cases arise when a client either does not have internal personnel qualified to review and assess a CPA's recommendation or the client participates in only a limited way in the consulting process. In the former case, the CPA's recommendation might be tantamount to a management decision; after all, he is the only expert involved. Rule 101B, however, does not allow such an engagement, since it prevents the CPA from service in which he acts in a "capacity equivalent to that of a member of management."[16] Where the client participates in a limited way in the advisement process, the AICPA recommends that "sufficient expertise be available in the client organization to fully comprehend the significance of the changes made during implementation."[17]

In our opinion the AICPA, through its COPE and additional supplementary *Statements,* has provided an adequate specification of the concepts of professional competence and independence. The standards specified in the COPE and the AICPA's supplementary *Statements* provide guidelines for appropriate behavior, and criteria for enforcement action when behavior is inappropriate.

The accounting profession is not, however, without its critics. The controversies surrounding Lockheed, Equity Funding, Ampex, National Student

Marketing, Penn Central, the Watergate revelations, and so forth, have focused criticism on four areas of the profession: (1) the problem of independence from the client when the client contracts with the auditor and can dismiss him at will, (2) whether the COPE is adequately enforced at present and whether the profession can be expected to fully enforce its standards, (3) the issue of who should determine the precepts of accounting, and (4) whether the profession should allow CPAs to perform peripheral services such as tax work and advisory work.[18]

Critics charge that clients exert a dominant influence over auditors because they contract with them and can dismiss them at will. The upshot is said to be an asymmetry of power that too often undermines the auditor's independence. The critics' remedy frequently is to suggest that the client/auditor contract be severed, and the auditor made truly independent by affording him public employee status. The idea is that the auditor's neutrality would be ensured in his relationship with providers and users of financial statements.

This argument, however, overlooks the fact that the government itself is a major user of financial statements. Hence, the problem of independence would emerge in a new context. There are problems with the present system, but it seems likely that the potential for abuse is greater if auditors are placed under governmental controls. There is a recent case that points up the possible Orwellian implications of the critics' suggestion. At the height of the improper payments scandal that resulted from the Watergate investigations, the IRS required of 1,200 large corporations that they submit with their tax returns answers to questions about possible improper payments. The IRS also requested such responses from the companies' auditors, under threat of criminal charges for false responses. Furthermore, it threatened to refuse to finalize its examination of the firms' returns unless the auditors' statements were received. Clearly, the threat to the private sector, which is serious enough in the above case, would be magnified if auditors were government employees. At present, the CPA is not an employee of the provider, the government, or other users. It is doubtful that making him an employee of a major user of financial statements would strengthen his independence.

If the critics' remedy is too extreme, this does not mean that their criticism of the profession entirely lacks force; there are troublesome cases where independence has been affected because of the asymmetry of power in the client/auditor relationship. The answer is to strengthen the auditor's independence. This can best be accomplished by the development of more detailed interpretations of the COPE and the articulation of additional *Statements* covering new areas where independence is threatened. In addition, the COPE should be vigorously enforced. The necessity for strict enforcement is twofold: it strengthens the auditor's independence by making it less likely that he will succumb to pressure, and it reduces the client's power through an awareness that high professional standards are maintained and that a more compliant auditor will not likely be found by "shopping around."

Are the COPE's standards adequately enforced at present? Some critics say no. Abraham Briloff surveyed the disciplinary actions of the AICPA trial board from 1970 to 1977 and argues that the 121 actions were insufficient for the amount of sin that occurred during that period.[19] The question, however, is whether the sin is *accounting* sin. Briloff seems to believe that audits should be performed to uncover the sin of fraud. At present the purpose of the audit is to provide an independent opinion on the conformity of financial statements to GAAP in accordance with GAAS. If so, Briloff's concern about the number of trial board actions may be unfounded. Given the present structure of the profession, auditors may simply be doing their job well; furthermore, our utility considerations suggest the auditor's role should not be expanded to the detection of all fraud. On the other hand, if Briloff is correct, then by all means enforcement should be more vigorous, for it is primarily via enforcement of the COPE that independence can be strengthened. The AICPA has a clear statement on fraud detection: under GAAS "the independent auditor has the responsibility, within the inherent limitations of the audit process, to plan his or her examination to search for errors or irregularities that would have a material effect on the financial statements."[20] The CPA who fails to detect fraud that would have been uncovered if GAAS had been followed is held responsible for damages the client incurs. But clearly the auditor cannot be held responsible for detecting immaterial fraud; the cost would be enormous if the auditor had to establish evidence sufficient to *guarantee* that no fraud existed at, say, IBM. Similarly, although the auditor has the obligation to make a "proper study and evaluation of the (firm's) existing internal control,"[21] management can override internal controls, and engage in collusion or other improper actions. If total responsibility for detection of such activities were placed on the auditor, his detective work would be very expensive. Although utility calculations are difficult in this area, the above reasoning suggests that the present fraud detection responsibilities of auditors are appropriate.

Critics of accounting claim that GAAP and GAAS are "the writings of persons who have impacted into them their own particular vested interests, and those of their clients,"[22] and the profession itself should not determine these basic precepts of accounting and auditing. Now part of this criticism rests on an alleged threat to independence because of self-interest. But, as we have argued, if the proposed remedy is governmental specification of standards, one threat to independence is replaced by another. The other basis of this criticism is that the standards exhibit a degree of flexibility that leads to auditor abuse in terms of self-interest. Two remedies have been proposed. One is that whoever sets the standards should set very specific standards that severely limit accounting and auditing alternatives. The problem here is that the factors that auditors attempt to record are dynamic; to strap the auditor with inflexible standards over time raises the possibility that he will record an illusion. The Interstate Commerce Commission required strict, uniform accounting standards for railroads in 1914, at which time the system was widely regarded as a model accounting system. Half a century later the system was essentially still in use but very dated. In following the dated standards, many railroads' financial statements were no longer in accordance with current GAAP. Adherence to overly rigid standards in this case has not led to high levels of utility for the railroads or for users of their statements. The other remedy, suggested by Briloff, is to: (1) abandon the quest for tight rules and "leave it to the marketplace of ideas to judge the quality of the principles in practice," (2) shift responsibility for the financial statements from management to the auditor, and (3) assign the FASB responsibility to review accounting alternatives in practice.[23] The danger with (1), however, is that if standards are loose, statements within an industry might not be comparable. With respect to (3), if there are a variety of principles and the FASB, with Briloff, is to ask "Did the auditor apply the best principles? . . . If not, why not?" the FASB is assigned an open-ended task.[24]

Indeed, there is this dilemma for auditors: if standards are too flexible, comparability is impaired; but if they are too rigid, they probably will not capture the dynamics of business. Hence, standards with some flexibility are required, whoever sets them. Our view is that the AICPA does attempt to walk the proper line between rigidity and anarchy. Furthermore, since the FASB is independent from the AICPA and does have outside representation, it is not solely the profession that determines GAAP. Finally, the COPE's strongest strictures are in the area of conflicts of interest. With an adequately enforced ethical code the present system is probably our best alternative.

The final major criticism is that peripheral services represent a serious enough threat to independence that they ought to be precluded.[25] If holding a financial interest in an audited firm is banned by the COPE, so, it is claimed, should peripheral services. Now a counter to this argument is that there is increasing demand for expertise, and accountants have skills that can directly benefit society. We want the best advisor available to provide management with advice regarding a cost accounting system, and that person will in all probability be a CPA. Thus, utility for society as well as for the firm favors allowing CPAs to provide tax and management advisory services. But there is no utility for society in having any particular individual own a firm's stock. Thus, utility considerations suggest that the situations are not exactly analogous.

The Code of Professional Ethics does specify that "When a CPA expresses an opinion on financial statements, not only the fact but also the appearance of integrity and objectivity is of particular importance."[26] Critics contend that at least the appearance of independence is threatened when the auditor of a firm also provides peripheral services. Given the utility to society in having experts advise management, however, this is more an argument that favors strengthening the independence criteria for auditors rather than preventing use of their services. The AICPA's recent *Statements* concerning tax practice and management advisory services are a step in this direction; if they are linked to a vigorous enforcement mechanism, independence should be preserved.

GAAP, GAAS, and the COPE will most certainly require future modifications; but this is simply a corollary of the dynamism of the profession, the organizations it audits, and users' needs. In our opinion, the AICPA is the most viable vehicle available for maintaining high standards in a changing context.

REFERENCES

1. *AICPA Professional Standards*, vol. 1 (Chicago: Commerce Clearing House, 1979), AU Sections 200, 300, 400, and 500. Material from COPE, GAAP, and GAAS is paraphrased unless it is directly quoted. Both paraphrased and quoted sources are cited.

2. Ibid., AU Section 9000 ff.

3. *AICPA Professional Standards*, vol. 2 (Chicago: Commerce Clearing House, 1977).

4. Ibid., ET Section 92, p. 4381.

5. Ibid., ET Section 52, p. 4291.

6. Ibid., ET Section 52, p. 4291.

7. Ibid., ET Section 52, p. 4291.

8. Ibid., ET Section 102, p. 4421.

9. *AICPA Professional Standards*, vol. 1, AU Section 300 ff.

10. *AICPA Professional Standards*, vol. 2, ET Section 101, p. 4411.

11. Ibid., pp. 4411–4412.

12. Ibid., pp. 4411-3, ff.

13. *AICPA Professional Standards*, vol. 1, TX Section 111, p. 2811.

14. Ibid., TX Section, p. 2701, ff.

15. Ibid., MS Section, p. 2201, ff.

16. *AICPA Professional Standards*, vol. 2, ET Section 101, pp. 4411-3.

17. *AICPA Professional Standards*, vol. 1, MS Section 430, p. 2556.

18. These criticisms are clearly and forcefully stated in: Abraham Briloff, "How Accountants Can Recover Their Balance," *Business and Society Review*, No. 24 (Winter, 1977-78), pp. 64-68; Abraham Briloff, "Codes of Conduct: Their Sound and Fury" in *Ethics, Free Enterprise*, and *Public Policy* (N.Y.: Oxford University Press, 1978), edited by Richard T. DeGeorge and Joseph A. Pichler, pp. 264-287.

19. Briloff, "Codes of Conduct: Their Sound and Fury," pp. 272-76.

20. *AICPA Professional Standards*, vol. 1, AU Section 327, pp. 323-2.

21. Ibid., AU Section 320, p. 241.

22. Briloff, "Codes of Conduct: Their Sound and Fury," p. 267.

23. Briloff, "How Accountants Can Recover Their Balance," pp. 65-66.

24. Ibid., p. 66.

25. Ibid., p. 67.

26. *AICPA Professional Standards*, vol. 2, ET Section 52, p. 4292.

John F. Nash
Roger H. Hermanson

Ethics and Management Accountants

STATUS OF THE INTERNAL ACCOUNTANT

Much has been said and written about ethics in public accounting. A major role of the American Institute of Certified Public Accountants (AICPA) has been to promulgate a comprehensive code of ethics that governs the conduct of its members. The AICPA Code of Professional Ethics limits the freedom of CPAs but, at the same time, provides protection for these professionals when they are under pressure to behave in some questionable manner by clients, or when they are criticized for their actions. In contrast, other branches of the accounting profession — notably internal or management accountants — have no recognized code of ethics. While this situation provides them with greater flexibility, it also leaves them without adequate defenses against external pressures. Sometimes they are unsure of what their response should be when faced with particular ethical choices. Part of the problem stems from the fact that the management accountant has divided loyalties: to the employer on the one hand, and to the profession and society on the other.

The managerial accountant is an employee of the company and owes a direct loyalty to the employer. In contrast to the independent auditor, who is expected to remain detached — even aloof, the managerial accountant cannot be an impartial observer of the company's fortunes; he must be committed to the attainment of organizational goals. The management accountant must be directly involved in the company's survival and development. The success of the organization is as much the responsibility of the controller as it is that of the sales manager or the purchasing agent. The managerial accountant is responsible for satisfying management's information

366

needs in the same way that the sales manager satisfies its revenue needs and the purchasing agent satisfies its needs for materials.

Ethical Problems in Internal Accounting

There would seem to be three main areas in which the managerial accountant might be faced with difficult ethical decisions:

1. the validity of reported accounting data,
2. confidentiality and insider information,
3. complicity in irregular practices.

In the first of these areas it is generally expected that data presented in accounting reports, whether directed to users outside the company, to employees, or to management, should be fair, where "fairness" includes the qualities of objectivity and neutrality or freedom from bias. Here, the consensus seems to be that the accountant should adhere to the same standards when preparing management reports or payroll data as when preparing external financial statements. Neutrality is perhaps less important in the case of management reports, because the requirements of one user can presumably be met without impairing the usefulness of data supplied to other users. The multiplicity of internal reports clearly provides more flexibility in this regard than a single set of external statements. Similar arguments no doubt could be made concerning data supplied to employees. Understandability or clarity is another area where there is more flexibility in the case of management reporting. Footnotes to published financial statements often seem to be phrased to withstand legal assault rather than to communicate information clearly. In contrast, explanatory material in management reports can be written in a simpler, more direct style, because possible looseness in the wording would have less serious consequences.

Conceivably, an accountant might be tempted to falsify data because of personal motivation, such as a vendetta against a particular manager or group. Fortunately, there is little evidence that this type of problem occurs at all frequently.

The second area, confidentiality, appears to present a more common ethical problem than falsification of data. Accountants apparently are more disposed (or perhaps are more often tempted) to disclose information of a confidential or proprietary nature than they are to make changes in the data. A related problem is the use of insider information for personal advantage. The courts have heard cases in which accountants have derived material gain (usually by trading company stock) from information not available outside the company; in at least one case, attempts were made to deny correct reports that would have reduced the likely gains. Court decisions have confirmed that accountants are subject to the same restrictions as other executives with regard to seeking profit from confidential, inside information.

The third, and probably most important, area in which the managerial accountant is faced with ethical decisions is complicity in the irregular practices of others in the organization. Irregular practices involving business people in general are widely believed to be rampant in our society. Irregularities range from minor exaggeration in the filing of individual expense claims and tax returns to major fraud in corporate reporting. They include price-fixing and other actions designed to frustrate the effects of free competition, concealment of political campaign contributions, misrepresentation of the extent of a company's oil reserves, embezzlement of assets, and bribery of political and foreign officials.

Few of these practices could be carried on without the involvement, whether knowing or otherwise, of the company's internal accountants. In some cases, accountants have faced charges of suspected complicity when major incidents have come to light.[1] In other cases, e.g., those involving falsified personal-expense claims, the accountant may believe that an irregular practice is widespread but not have enough evidence to challenge any particular claim. With regard to this last example, the ethical position of the accountant is made more difficult because of the attitudes of society regarding such practices. The prevailing attitude seems to be, "Everyone else does it, so why shouldn't I?" The accountant may feel a strong tension between personal values of honesty and integrity on the one hand, and socially condoned irregularities on the other—especially since law enforcement offers scant help in stamping out such irregularities.

PROPOSALS FOR A CODE OF ETHICS FOR INTERNAL ACCOUNTANTS

From time to time, proposals have been made for a code of ethics for the managerial accountant.[2] This idea is not totally divorced from the question of licensing. Indeed, in the absence of a recognized licensing body, it becomes difficult to enforce an ethical code and to adjudge suspected violators. However, it is not out of place to explore the general area of managerial-accounting ethics in its own right. The more thoroughly it is discussed, the easier it will be to codify the principal rules, if that becomes necessary, and to seek acceptance of them by a regulatory authority or professional association.

THE NEED FOR RECOGNITION OF PROFESSIONAL STATUS

At least part of the present dilemma would be avoided if internal accountants were given full recognition as professional persons. Although internal accountants see themselves as professionals, many other groups, including management, may not. Rather, these groups tend to regard the management accountants simply as employees having primary obligations of loyalty, obedience, and confidentiality to the firm.

The full professional has obligations to standards set *outside* the firm. There may well be conflicts between the standards of the profession and the organizational goals of the firm in which the internal accountant is an agent. For instance, the firm may desire financial statements that bias the reported profit performance, while the profession promotes reporting practices that are fair to all parties.

In a firm, the professional must sacrifice some professional autonomy and conform to the administrative or bureaucratic rules of the organization. However, because of extensive training, the professional expects to be given some latitude with respect to the *means* to achieve certain organizational goals. This latitude may conflict with organizational procedures, which specify exactly what is to be done and how it is to be carried out.

If organizational procedures require a violation of professional standards, the professional may have a serious problem or conflict. For example, organizational procedures may specify that financial statements are to be available during the first week of January, but this may not allow the accountant enough time to verify the accuracy of some of the amounts to be reported. Thus, the internal accountant, in following standards of the profession, may be in conflict with the organization with respect to both the organizational goals of the firm and the means to bring about such goals.

An organization is typically hierarchical in authority. The internal accountant may be involved (and almost always will be) in a situation in which the supervisor is not a professional accountant. The professional's authority is based on competence, on the fact that the professional possesses a relatively complete battery of specialized, technical skills. As such, the internal accountant is capable of operating with autonomy and may ask fellow professionals for advice, but he doesn't expect to receive orders from fellow professionals. In the firm, however, the professional is subject to orders — often from people who are *not* professionals in the same discipline. These orders may direct the internal accountant to do things that are in conflict with standards of the profession. For instance, the internal accountant may be ordered to record sales of 1982 as sales of 1981 so as to improve reported earnings in 1981. Alternatively, the internal accountant may be directed to label illegal bribery payments to foreign government officials as advertising expenses or promotional fees.

CONCLUSION

Management accountants face a range of ethical problems that stem partly from their necessarily divided loyalties: to their employers, and to the accounting profession and society at large. Their ambiguous professional status makes matters worse. When confronted by ethical decisions they are often unsure as to what to do, and have no formal code of ethics or strong professional body to defend them.

The problem is by no means an easy one to deal with, but the solution seems to lie primarily in strengthening the professional status of the management accountant. A uniform code of ethics, which is accepted by the accounting profession as well as by management, and possibly a system of licensing would go a long way toward removing pressure on internal accountants to become involved in unethical practices and to make them more secure when they refuse to do so.

NOTES

1. See, for example, Escott v. BarChris Construction Co., 283 F. Supp. 643 (1968).

2. See, for example, Joyce C. Lambert, "Proposed Code of Professional Conduct," *Management Accounting,* February 1974, pp. 19–22; Stephen E. Loeb, Roger H. Hermanson, and Martin E. Taylor, "Ethical Standards: The Industrial Accountant," *Atlanta Economic Review,* September–October 1977, pp. 11–16; John F. Nash and Roger H. Hermanson, "Wanted: A Code of Ethics for Internal Accountants," *Business,* November–December 1980, pp. 12–17.

SELECTED BIBLIOGRAPHY

American Institute of Certified Public Accountants. *Code of Professional Ethics.* New York: AICPA, Inc., 1972.

Arens, A., and Loebbecke, J. *Auditing.* Englewood Cliffs, N.J.: Prentice-Hall, 1976, chs. 1–2.

Bailey, L. *Contemporary Auditing.* New York: Harper & Row, 1979, chs. 1–3.

Briloff, A. "Codes of Conduct: Their Sound and Their Fury," in *Ethics, Free Enterprise, and Public Policy.* De George, R., and Pichler, J., eds. New York: Oxford University Press, 1978, pp. 264–287.

Carey, J., and Doherty, W. *Ethical Standards of the Accounting Profession.* New York: American Institute of Certified Public Accountants, Inc., 1966.

Carmichael, D., and Swieringa, R. "The Compatibility of Auditing Independence and Management Services – An Identification of Issues." *The Accounting Review* (October, 1968), 697–705.

Causey, D. *Duties and Liabilities of Public Accountants.* Homewood, Ill.: Dow Jones-Irwin, 1982.

De Marco, V. "How Internal Auditors Can Help CPAs Stamp Out Illegal Acts." *The Internal Auditor* (February, 1978), 60–65.

Graese, C. "Accounting, Accountants, and Managers," in *The Ethics of Corporate Conduct.* Walton, C., ed. Englewood Cliffs, N.J.: Prentice-Hall, 1973, pp. 146–159.

Loeb, S., ed. *Ethics in the Accounting Profession.* Santa Barbara: Wiley, 1978.

Taylor, D., and Glezen, G. *Auditing.* New York: Wiley, 1979, chs. 1–3.

Windal, F., and Corley, R. *The Accounting Professional: Ethics, Responsibility and Liability.* Englewood Cliffs, N.J.: Prentice-Hall, 1980.

7

BUSINESS AND
THE CONSUMER

INTRODUCTION

In producing and marketing goods and services, the firm incurs moral and legal obligations to the consumer. The consumer also has responsibilities with regard to the use of a product. This chapter discusses two key issues in the relationship between business and the consumer: product safety and advertising.

Until 1916 a manufacturer was not legally liable for an injury to a consumer unless there was privity (private knowledge) of contract between manufacturer and consumer, i.e., purchasers could sue only those who sold an item directly to them. Since few manufacturers sold goods directly to the public, they were immune from suit. Conrad Berenson discusses the shift from *caveat emptor* (let the buyer beware) to *caveat venditor* (let the seller beware) since 1916 in his discussion of the current liability theories of negligence, breach of warranty, and strict liability. Negligence places the burden of proof on the consumer, since he must prove that the manufacturer was negligent and that this carelessness caused the injury. Strict liability, the dominant current theory, only requires that the consumer prove the product was defective and caused the injury. Strict liability is grounded primarily in utilitarian considerations; it encourages manufacturers to make safe products, which reduces accidents. Taking this argument one step farther, Beverly Moore advocates the theory of absolute liability, i.e., the producer is liable for any injury, regardless of fault.

The recent expansion of manufacturers' liability has not been without costs, as Berenson points out, and the courts have wrestled with this problem. If consumers win excessively large judgments, prices will escalate; but if consumers go uncompensated, manufacturers will have little incentive to make safer products. The cases discussed in this section illustrate how two courts recently addressed this issue.

Advertising has been subject to perhaps more criticism than any other business practice; the section on advertising discusses the central criticisms. Jules Henry charges that advertisers operate on the principle that any form of persuasion resulting in the sale of products is acceptable whether or not it provides information to the consumer. Furthermore, he claims that advertising rests on psychological assumptions about humans that in the long run debase important human values.

In response, Phillip Nelson argues that all advertising does provide information to the consumer, and hence it benefits society. Although he allows that some deceptive advertising does occur in a free market, he argues that active government intervention in policing advertisements is not likely to have social utility and may actually lead to increased deception. Theodore Levitt contends that humans do not seek unvarnished truth and literal functionality in selecting products; consumers choose the functional expectations that they associate with a product. Advertising, like art, conveys a picture of what life might be like, not a picture of reality; hence neither art nor advertising can be judged by the correspondence criterion of truth. While outright falsehoods and deceptions should be precluded from advertising, Levitt argues that the embellishment criticized by Henry is part of what prevents our lives from being drab and dull. The legal case in this section discusses a specific instance of alleged deception or misrepresentation.

John Kenneth Galbraith argues that the standard free market account of advertising is mistaken. On that account people have wants, and advertising provides information so that consumers can make rational choices to satisfy their antecedent wants. Galbraith argues that the market does not respond to consumer wants, rather, it creates the wants via advertising. Thus, there is an asymmetry between producer and consumer that undercuts the free market conception of consumer sovereignty; the producer creates both the desire for a product and the product to satisfy the desire.

Robert L. Arrington takes up the question of whether advertisers manipulate and control the behavior of consumers, and hence violate their autonomy. He analyzes four concepts central to the debate—autonomous desire, rational desire, free choice, and control—and argues that advertising itself does not intrinsically or frequently violate the consumer's autonomy in any of the relevant senses of this concept.

Product Safety

Case Study

Biss v. Tenneco Inc.

Robert Biss was injured when a loader he was operating went off the road, collided with a telephone pole, and pinned him between the loader and the pole. Shortly before he died, Biss told witnesses that he lost control of the loader. Mrs. Biss brought suit against Tenneco, the loader's manufacturer, based on an alleged design defect in the loader since it was not equipped with a rollover protection structure, known as a ROPS.

The action involved a so-called "second collision" issue; that is, the claim was not that the loader itself had a design defect, thus causing the accident, but that there was a design defect that caused or enhanced the injuries arising from the accident. Tenneco, it was claimed, should have provided a ROPS as standard, rather than optional, equipment, and its failure to do so constituted a design defect that caused or enhanced Biss's injuries arising from the accident.

The New York Supreme Court considered the following to be the applicable rule of law:

> A manufacturer is obligated to exercise that degree of care in his plan or design so as to avoid any unreasonable risk of harm to anyone who is likely to be exposed to the danger when the product is used in the manner for which the product was intended, as well as unintended yet reasonably foreseeable use.

The court reasoned that manufacturers are not obligated to provide accident proof merchandise but they are required to exercise reasonable care. There was no defect in the loader itself, and a ROPS was available to

409 N.Y.S. 2d 874 (A.D. 1978)

the purchaser, Vincent Centers, for whom Biss worked. Accordingly, the court ruled:

> That being so, defendants had fulfilled their duty to exercise reasonable skill and care in designing the product as a matter of law when they advised the purchaser that an appropriate safety structure for the loader was available.

The court pointed out that injury from a rollover accident is posed by the use of construction equipment, but noted that the danger varies according to the job and site for which the equipment is used:

> It is not a danger inherent in a properly constructed loader. Neither is it a danger which the manufacturer alone may discover or one which he is more favorably positioned to discover. If knowledge of the available safety options is brought home to the purchaser (Vincent Centers) the duty to exercise reasonable care in selecting those appropriate to the intended use rests upon him. He is the party in the best position to exercise an intelligent judgment to make the trade-off between cost and function, and it is he who should bear the responsibility if the decision on optional safety equipment presents an unreasonable risk to users. To hold otherwise casts the manufacturer and supplier in the role of insurers answerable to injured parties in any event, because the purchaser of the equipment for his own reasons, economic or otherwise, elects not to purchase available options to ensure safety.

Mrs. Biss's suit against Tenneco was dismissed, 3–0.

For Discussion

What theory of product liability has the court applied in this case? Do you agree with this theory? Why or why not? Do you agree with the court's decision in this particular case? Why or why not? If Mrs. Biss sued Vincent Centers, rather than Tenneco, do you believe she should (legally and morally) win? Why or why not?

Austin v. Ford Motor Co.

A variation of the second collision issue was presented in the case of Barbara Austin, who died in a one-car accident. A motorist testified that Ms. Austin passed him when he was travelling at a speed of 65 to 70 mph. The Austin auto, a Ford, was estimated to have been going 20 to 25 mph faster than the vehicle she passed — a speed of approximately 90 mph — when her car left the road, rolled over twice, and landed on its top. Ms. Austin was thrown from her car and killed. A state police officer found a portion of Austin's seatbelt on the ground and a portion still attached to the front seat.

The plaintiffs, Ms. Austin's children, produced two witnesses who provided evidence that she was wearing a seatbelt, and that a defective belt was a cause of death. According to the testimony of a state police technician, a microscopic examination of the belt showed that the webbing had been irregularly cut through. He said that a sharp instrument was needed to cut the belt, that the cut portion was not normally visible, and that nothing in the auto could have caused the cut. An engineer testified to the probable causal connection between the seatbelt's breaking and Austin's death. Ford countered that it was probable that the impact of the accident was of sufficient force to cause Austin's death.

The court's opinion focused on the issue of causation:

> The accident was a grievous one and the facts support a finding of negligent driving by the decedent. But the heart of the case is causation, not of the accident but of the death. In an action such as this, is it a permissible inference or

---

273 N.W. 2d 233 (1979)

conclusion that decedent's negligent driving was a cause of her death? . . . The court is persuaded to the conclusion that it is not.

The court distinguished the cause of the accident from the cause of Austin's death. Ms. Austin's negligence caused the accident, but, since seat belts are designed to protect the wearer in the event of a collision, including a collision that is caused by the driver's own negligence, the court regarded Austin's negligent driving as an irrelevant factor in assessing the cause of her death. The court reasoned that Austin would have survived the accident had the seatbelt not been dangerously defective, and hence the defective seatbelt was a cause of death.

> . . . Ford's negligence in furnishing an unsafe and defective seatbelt was found to be a cause of the death of Barbara Austin and there is no evidence to show that Barbara Austin's own negligence contributed to her death. . . .

Judge Coffey dissented from the majority's opinion:

> The jury found that her (Austin's) excessive speed was the cause of her injuries. How can it be said that her negligence in driving 90 mph, which caused the accident, was not a cause of her death? The answer of the majority is that seat belts are designed to protect the wearer from injuries suffered in an accident which may be the wearer's fault. . . . As a policy matter, the majority has decided in this case that negligence as the cause of the accident (and therefore the injuries) of the deceased will not be compared with the product liability imposed on the manufacturer for the failure of the seat belt. I have reservations about the wisdom of this policy. When applied to the theory that an injury would have been prevented if the injured party had worn a seat belt, its corollary will result in re-introducing a form of assumption of risk into Wisconsin law.

For Discussion

What theory of product liability has the court applied in this case? Do you agree with this theory? Why or why not? Do you agree with the majority or the dissenting opinion in this case? Why do you agree with one opinion and disagree with the other?

Conrad Berenson

The Product Liability Revolution

One of the more significant marketing developments of the last decade—both from the consumer's and producer's view—is the new concept of *product liability.*[1]

The age-old phrase, "let the buyer beware," has been changed to "let the manufacturer and the seller be sued." This is dramatically shown by the well over 100,000 product liability cases introduced in the United States courts in 1969. Estimates for 1971 range up to 250,000 cases. The figures themselves are only significant because they reflect an enormous increase from the few thousand cases of a decade ago; many of these cases amount to big money, with some individual awards exceeding $100,000.

The rise in legal activity against manufacturers and sellers of a broad variety of products and concomitant changes in the law are of grave importance to marketers. Marketing managers, advertising managers, sales managers, product managers, customer service supervisors, and others in the marketing organization are all affected by the changes in our society, by the proliferation of lawsuits, and by the changes in our laws which have resulted in these suits. This article will examine some of the product liability considerations which are important to marketers and consumers, and show how new attitudes toward product liability will affect marketing performance.

CAUSES OF LIABILITY REVOLUTION

What are the reasons for this tremendous increase in legal activity and for the changes in the law?

From *Business Horizons* 15 (October 1972). Copyright © 1972, by the Foundation for the School of Business at Indiana University. Reprinted by permission.

1. Many products today, certainly far more than in prior decades, are packaged so that the consumer cannot examine them. Because the consumer is prevented from examining the merchandise, the courts have placed the responsibility on the vendor and the maker.

2. Many products today are so technically sophisticated that the average consumer simply cannot be expected to have the knowledge to properly appraise them and to reach reasonable conclusions as to safety, quality, price, suitability, and so on. Consider for a moment the complexity of a modern day television set, a hi-fi, or even an electric can opener.

3. Advertising has grown. In the United States it is now a more than $23 billion a year industry — much of this in the form of a wide variety of claims urging that the consumer take action and purchase Product A, B, or C, instead of E, F, and G, because of real or imagined attributes. Subjected to this enormous barrage in the media, the average person often does not know how to make a rational purchasing choice.

4. The transaction between the ultimate consumer and the one who immediately sells to him is usually a transaction between parties who often do not know each other, and, in fact, have never even seen each other. The day when you went to the local grocer, whom you had known well all your life and upon whose recommendation you could rely completely, is long past. Clerks in supermarkets may scarcely know where the merchandise is located, nor can they tell you anything about the nature of the contents of those glamorously designed packages, or the reliability of their manufacture.

5. The emergence of national distribution networks has perhaps caused some manufacturers to be less careful in the design and quality of their product. Their business ethics may have changed too. Their feeling, for example, may have been conditioned by the fact that most of their customers do not know them and neither do their customers' friends, so there will be no personal problems due to a faulty product. This was not so 100 years ago, when many manufacturers sold within a very small geographic area and were known personally to many of their customers.

6. The plethora of product innovations makes even the most sophisticated buyer a loser in the race to keep informed about the attributes of new products. For example, the average supermarket contains between 7,000 and 9,000 different products — this includes different sizes of the same product. Therefore, even the most energetic supermarket manager who attempts to keep up with product information just in his own store must contend with these thousands of products, as well as the new ones each year, about 20 percent of his stock.

7. With such rapid product innovation, the innovators often make honest errors in design and quality. Since they have not had sufficient experience in producing what they are selling, this inexperience may from time to time injure consumers. Today's sophisticated consumer simply will not sit idly by and accept such injury, whether it be physical or economic.

8. The success of some attorneys who specialize in product liability

claims has encouraged other attorneys to get into the field and injured parties to seek redress.

9. As a result of higher levels of consumer education, as well as political expediency of the moment, a new consumer attitude has developed, which encourages stiff resistance on the part of consumers. Also, consumer groups have organized which actively lobby and sue for legislation and redress.

10. Finally, there is a growing tendency by injured people to seek recovery for damages as assiduously as possible. Forty years ago someone who was bumped lightly by an automobile would dart quickly away in embarrassment, thinking he had been too clumsy. Today, such a bump would immediately be followed by cries for witnesses, ambulances, doctors, and attorneys.

TRADITIONAL PRODUCT LIABILITY APPROACHES

Privity. From the time this nation was established until 1916 the *manufacturer* of most products had absolutely no liability (legal responsibility) for them, except to those customers to whom direct sales were made. The exceptions to this doctrine were those products which could seriously affect human life—food, chemicals, drugs, and firearms. If you had purchased an automobile from a dealer in 1915, and not from a manufacturer, you could have filed a lawsuit for negligence only against the dealer.

In 1916, however, a man named Donald MacPherson was driving a new Buick at 15 miles per hour when one of its wheels fell off. MacPherson was injured and sued Buick for negligence, claiming that the wheel had been defective. MacPherson won, and the case of MacPherson v. Buick Motor Company[2] represents a landmark in the philosophy of *privity of contract.*[3] The approach has since become more permissive in the range and scope of allowable lawsuits. Today, for example, if a wheel falls off your car, you have the opportunity of suing the auto manufacturer or the auto dealer, or both. For products in which the chain of distribution may be longer—for example, a chocolate bar that goes from the manufacturer to a wholesaler to a retailer to the ultimate user—any or all of these parties may be sued through the purchaser, and the possibility for a plaintiff's recovery of any damages awarded is consequently far higher.

The change in legal philosophy has developed because of the changes in marketing methods that have occurred in the past 40 years. The New York Court of Appeals made a statement about this several years ago: "The world of merchandising is, in brief, no longer a world of direct contact; it is, rather, a world of advertising and, when representations expressed and disseminated in the mass communications media and on labels (attached to the goods themselves) prove false, and the user or consumer is damaged by his reliance on these representations, it is difficult to justify the manufacturer's denial of liability on the sole ground of the absence of technical privity." Furthermore, continued the court, these manufacturers make a determined advertising effort to attest "in glowing terms to the qualities and virtues of their products, and this advertising is directed at the ultimate consumer, or at some manufacturer or supplier who is not in privity with them. Equally sanguine representations on packages and labels frequently accompany the article throughout its journey to the ultimate consumer and, as intended, are relied upon by remote purchasers."[4] Accordingly, "It is highly unrealistic to limit a purchaser's protection to warranties made directly to him by his immediate seller. The protection he really needs is against the manufacturer whose published representations caused him to make the purchase."[5]

The court also said: "The policy of protecting the public from injury, physical or pecuniary, resulting from misrepresentations outweighs allegiance to an old and outmoded technical rule of law which, if observed, might be productive of great injustice. The manufacturer places his product upon the market. By advertising and labeling it, he represents its quality to the public in such a way as to induce reliance upon his representations. He unquestionably intends and expects that the product will be purchased and used in reliance upon his express assurance of its quality and, in fact, it is so purchased and used. Having invited and solicited this use, the manufacturer should not be permitted to avoid responsibility, when the expected use leads to injury and loss, by claiming he made no contract with the user."[6]

The New York Court of Appeals is not alone in its attitude on privity—many more courts across the country are also taking views that permit the consumer to have legal access to the manufacturer. As one Connecticut court put it—after first emphasizing the fact that neither the retailer nor the consumer can examine a packaged product, and that both rely upon the product's glittering packaging, in riotous color, and the alluring enticement of the qualities as depicted on labels: "There appears to be no sound reason for depriving a purchaser of the right to maintain an action against the manufacturer. Where the purchaser alleges he was induced to purchase the product—by the misrepresentations in the manufacturer's advertising—and he sustained harm when the product failed to measure up to the express or implied representations, he has that right."[7]

Still another decision contained a lengthy statement about the necessity of protecting the consumer so that "the burden of losses consequent upon use of defective articles is borne by those who are in a position to either control the danger or make an equitable distribution of the losses when they do occur. . . ."[8]

This comment by the court is typical of a growing tendency—even when there is no blame on either side—to hold responsible the party better able to bear a loss. In effect, this new philosophy creates a liability on the part of the producer or seller, even when there has been no fault and no departure from reasonable standards of production control.

In addition to the privity of contract concept, other legal parameters are involved in any consideration of product liability. Some of these are discussed briefly in this article.

Negligence. The concept of negligence, that is, that the product's producer made a mistake, or was careless in its manufacture, has been one of the traditional avenues through which the consumer could sue for injury sustained as a result of using that product. Negligence, however, is not easy to prove. For example, an unsafe product—if designed and produced with reasonable care, skill, and quality control—cannot be said to have been negligently manufactured.

Express Warranty. When selling a product, the manufacturer or retailer almost always represents it as having certain characteristics, and he makes various claims for it. Some of these claims are *express,* that is, explicitly stated to the buyer. It does not matter whether the express claims are written or oral. What is significant is that they are presented to the buyer in an unequivocal manner. The seller's or manufacturer's express warranty is not limited to the warranty card which may accompany the item. Statements on labels, wrappers and cartons, and in advertising, are also express warranties. Manufacturers of goods are liable to the buyer for express warranties even though the consumer does not buy the product directly from them.

Implied Warranty. Simply by selling a certain product to a customer the seller implies that the goods are fit for the ordinary purpose for which such goods are most likely to be used. In addition, those sellers who furnish the customer with a product suitable for his need find that this transaction also falls within the purview of implied warranty. Thus, if you went to a camera store, claimed ignorance, and put yourself under the guidance of a salesman, his statements are implied warranties of the fitness of the camera he recommends for the purpose for which you are buying it.

A landmark automobile case concerns a New Jersey housewife who, while driving the family car purchased less than two weeks previously, was injured when the car went out of control and hit a wall. Although there was *no* proof that the car's manufacturer had been negligent, the court directed the jury to reach a verdict in favor of the driver. The case was appealed, and again the auto manufacturer lost. The New Jersey Supreme Court said: "We hold that under modern marketing conditions, when a manufacturer puts a new automobile in the stream of trade and promotes its purchase by the public, an implied warranty that it is reasonably suitable for use as such accompanies it into the hands of the ultimate purchaser."[9]

STRICT LIABILITY IN TORT—A NEW APPROACH[10]

In the last several years a new theory has evolved that allows lawsuits under the concept of *strict liability in tort.* According to this theory, the manufacturer is liable for unfit products that unduly threaten the consumer's personal safety. The traditional conditions of either negligence or warranty (express of implied) are not required. Now, the manufacturer simply by having produced an unreasonably dangerous defective product, regardless of any other consideration, can be held liable for harm caused to the ultimate user of that product. As with warranties, it does not even matter if the manufacturer took every possible precaution to prevent defects. The liability of the manufacturer does not stem from either contractual or promissory understanding; instead, *liability in tort arises from the fact that the courts are imposing a social responsibility on manufacturers and sellers.* Even if they have exercised all possible care in the preparation and sale of the product they are now held accountable for a consumer's injury; these injuries can be either physical, or, as a result of the physical damage, financial.

Strict liability applies to a seller, contractor, supplier, assembler and manufacturer of all or any components of the distributed product. Unfortunately for the links in the supply chain, contributory negligence is not an acceptable defense in a lawsuit based upon strict liability. The purchaser or user of the defective product usually has to show only that it was defective when it left the control of the seller, although there are even exceptions to this rule.[11]

The situation that established the concept of strict liability was a 1962 California case, Greenman v. Yuba Power Products, Inc.[12] The plaintiff, Mr. Greenman, was seriously injured when a combination power tool (one which could be used as a saw, lathe, and so on) let fly a block of wood that hit him in the forehead. The California Supreme Court said: "A manufacturer is strictly liable in tort when an article he places on the market, knowing that it will be used without inspection, proves to have a defect that causes injury to a human being."[13] The effect of this decision was immediate. All over the country other courts began to rule similarly, particularly in the most populous and industrialized parts of the nation. The case can be considered to have two major areas of influence, legal and social. Legally, its significance is that it obviates the necessity to prove fault on the producer's or seller's part—it is only necessary that the product was defective when sold and that it did cause an injury to person or property. Socially, its significance is found in a quote from the Greenman decision: "The purpose of [strict liability in tort] is to insure that the cost of injuries resulting from defective products are borne by the manufacturers that put such products on the market rather than by the injured persons who are powerless to protect themselves."

When is a Product Defective?

For purposes of the strict liability rule how is a product defined? When is it unreasonably dangerous or defective? The Restatement of Tort says: "The article sold must be dangerous to an extent beyond that which would be contemplated by the ordinary consumer who purchases it with the ordinary knowledge common to the community as to its characteristics."[14] Thus, the emphasis is upon the unusual and unexpected dangers attendant to the use of the product. Whiskey, for example, would not be considered dangerous because it makes people drunk and deteriorates their livers. Nor would butter, even though it can cause excessive cholesterol levels; but a nail imbedded in the butter is unusual and if you ingest it and scratch your intestine, you have exceeded the ordinary danger contemplated by the Restatement of Torts. To prosecute successfully a claim for injury under this strict liability rule, a consumer has only to show that the product was defective when it left the producer's control and that it did, indeed, cause him danger.

Strict Liability Is Not Absolute Liability

The section on defective products should not be interpreted to mean that the producer is liable under all conditions. He does not have *absolute liability*. The product's defect must be proven by the consumer. If there is no defect in the product, but it has caused harm, there is no liability on the part of the maker of the product. Several key cases have zeroed in on the definition of "defect." The Supreme Court of Arizona, for example, ruled that "a defective article is one that is not reasonably fit for the ordinary purposes for which such articles are sold and used."[15] And the Illinois Supreme Court noted that a product is defective when it does not perform as one might reasonably expect it to in view of its characteristics and intended function.[16]

The concept of strict liability in tort does not state that anyone harmed by the use of a product can recover damages from the product's maker or seller. These links in the channel of distribution are not *insurers* of the ultimate consumer. The latter must first demonstrate that there was *fault* in the production or design of the product and that the defect was present when it left the control of the maker or seller.

What Products Are Included under Strict Liability?

It is obvious from the many court decisions in the last few years that all types of products are included under the purview of the strict liability doctrine. There is no limit to the products which can, if defective, become dangerous to the user or to his property. What can one do, however, with products necessarily unavoidably dangerous to the user? In this category would fall such items as a knife, hammer, whiskey, cigarettes, and automobiles. Can we hold the manufacturer of an automobile liable for the way people drive it? Do we hold the producer of a hammer responsible if somebody smashes his thumb with it? The vaccine for rabies, for example, often causes intense suffering when it is administered, and sometimes even results in paralysis and death. It is used, of course, because the alternative is an extremely painful death, but what about the producer of this rabies vaccine? Is he responsible for the pain and suffering to those who use it?[17]

It is important to remember that selling a product of merchantable quality does not mean that one is selling a *perfect* product. What it means is that the product is free from serious and unusual defects. Accordingly, one could expect to find a fish bone in fish served in a restaurant, or chicken bones in chickens. In these examples one would not have a viable case against the producer or seller of the food. In reviewing a broad range of liability cases involving many many products, William L. Prosser of the University of California, concluded: "There is no strict liability when the product is fit to be sold and reasonably safe for use; but it has inherent dangers that no human skill or knowledge has yet been able to eliminate."[18]

THE FORESEEABILITY DOCTRINE

As the law of product liability is currently being developed, it appears quite likely that not only will manufacturers and sellers be held responsible for known risks of harm to consumers, but also for those risks which may be reasonably foreseen. The logic behind this is demonstrated in a statement by Arnold B. Elkind, a noted negligence lawyer, when he was head of the National Commission on Product Safety. Mr. Elkind said: "A manufacturer is best able to evaluate the risks inherent in his product and figure out ways to avoid them."[19]

A recent decision of the Kentucky Court of Appeals provides further insight into the development of the foreseeability doctrine.[20] It held that a manufacturer of vacuum cleaners designed to be used in 115 volt outlets was liable when a user of its product plugged the vacuum cleaner into a 220 volt circuit. The vacuum cleaner blew up. Despite the fact that the label clearly stated that the vacuum was to be plugged into 115 volt outlets only, the court still held the producer responsible because of the latter's failure to warn that plugging it into greater voltage was to invite disaster. In short, it is not sufficient to say "Don't do it" but you have to say why you should not do it, and what will happen if you do. The analogy used by the court was "It may be doubted that a sign warning "Keep off the grass" could be deemed sufficient to apprise a reasonable person that "the grass was infested with deadly snakes."

HOW GOOD MUST A PRODUCT BE?

It is reasonable to ask ourselves how good a product actually must be in order for the manufacturer to avoid many of the risks of product liability. Some insight into this can be obtained by examining the criteria proposed by Dickerson. Dickerson concluded that the product is legally defective if it meets the following conditions:[21]

1. The product carries a significant physical risk to a definable class of consumer, and the risk is ascertainable at least by the time of trial.

2. The risk is one that the typical member of a class does not anticipate and guard against.

3. The risk threatens established consumer expectations with respect to a contemplated use and manner of use of a product in a contemplated minimum level of performance.

4. The seller has reason to know of the contemplated use and possibly, where injurious side effects are involved, has reasonable access to knowledge of a particular risk involved.

5. The seller knowingly participates in creating the contemplated use or in otherwise generating the relevant consumer expectations in the way attributed to him by the consumer.

WHO IS RESPONSIBLE FOR FAULTY PRODUCTS?

It has been written that, "The housewife who sells a jar of jam to a neighbor, or the man who trades in a used car on the purchase of a new one will obviously stand on a very different footing so far as the justifiable reliance of third persons is concerned. It is also very probable that the rule will not apply to sales outside of the usual course of business such as execution sales, or the bulk sale of an entire stock of goods for what they will bring after bankruptcy or a fire."[22]

Who then is liable? Well, to begin with, the manufacturer of the item. He, of course, is the most obvious. On the other hand, one who merely assembles the parts as opposed to actually having the machinery which makes them is also responsible for the safe and suitable performance of the product.[23] Also, each one who makes a component part of a final product, assuming that that component does not undergo change (and this is an extremely frequent occurrence) is responsible. While in most jurisdictions the retailer has also been held accountable under the theory of strict liability, there are a few exceptions in which certain courts have ruled that if products are sold in sealed containers the retailer is not necessarily responsible.[24] Here too there has been occasional disagreement as to this general interpretation.

If a seller of a product advertises that he has "manufactured" that product, or he has, simply by not saying otherwise, represented himself to be the manufacturer, he finds that he has the same responsibilities as the manufacturer.[25] Sub-assemblers and component part manufacturers are responsible for the products in the same sense as a fully integrated manufacturer and seller of a product. The co-equal responsibility of the suppliers of raw materials, sub-assemblies, assemblies, and entire operating systems is such that a few years ago a product's marketers were able to select their vendors, materials and components on the basis of price, speed of delivery, quality, and service—today they can no longer do this. Times have changed. They now have to add to their original purchasing criteria the determination of whether or not the prospective vendors' insurance is sufficient to cover any claims for damage, which might reasonably result from the use of his products. After all, if there may be a lawsuit, and if the injured consumer has the choice of suing the marketer or his supplier, he is obviously going to pick the one who is financially able to pay his claim for damages. If the vendor of the components, raw materials, sub-assemblies, and so on skirts the thin edge of financial responsibility in this respect, then the seller is likely to be "it." The watchwords for him are: "Be careful."

At the same time that this new criterion has to be added to the traditional list of the intelligent purchaser, the time tested criterion of quality control must be put under renewed surveillance. Some buyers, in fact, have recently gone to the extent of placing inspectors in their suppliers' plants to see to it that those items which they buy are of consistently high quality. It is very difficult to produce an item which is trouble free if the raw materials or components are not up to the desired standards.

THE EFFECT UPON THE PRODUCER

All that has been said in this article affects the producer of consumer goods and services. There are certain effects, however, which have not yet been described. One is the additional risk to the *innovative* producer and seller. Obviously, the first producer of a consumer good which can be potentially dangerous, for example, television sets and electric irons, is in a different position regarding product liability than those who follow him. The first one must expend a good deal more time, effort, and money to establish production controls. He has to design for safety (both in the product and in its labeling and packaging), advertise the product properly so as not to mislead the buyer, and so on. Those firms which copy innovations later on can also copy the safeguards and designs in packaging and labeling, advertising, and quality control. Hence, their risks and their costs of operation will be lower. The result may well be a considerable diminution of innovator enthusiasm. Indeed, this has certainly happened in the last several years in the domestic drug industry, where today to get a drug approved by the Food and Drug Administration a rather lengthy, costly, and risky procedure must be followed. This may all be to the good of society in the long run, since many drugs which came out in years prior were less useful than their producers claimed. On the other hand, it is likely that some useful consumer products may either never emerge on the marketplace, or if they do it will be at a later time than was technically possible.

For all producers and sellers, not just innovators, there has been, since the expansion of the concept of strict liability, an increase in cost. The next time the reader wonders why some consumer items have gone up in cost he should remember that someone has to pay for the product liability insurance that so many items now require. Due to production and quality control measures designed to minimize faulty product design and performance there are additional costs to all producers and sellers. Too, legal fees, which can be quite expensive, must be paid for by everyone in the channel of distribution, from the producer to the consumer. For example, prior to its distribution, many advertisers now have each advertisement checked by a lawyer.

PRODUCTS LIABILITY INSURANCE

The risk that a producer or seller of any product can be hit with a claim for a catastrophic sum — one which could wipe out the entire net worth of the firm — is a real one. Obviously, manufacturers and marketers have begun to turn to products liability insurance as a means of dealing with the probability that the company will be involved in a damaging lawsuit.

The concept of products liability insurance is about 50 years old. In its early days it was generally confined to products designed for human consumption. Its primary feature was to protect the producers of such products against the fact that an occasional insect, piece of metal, chunk of glass, and so on would be in the food or drink. With the recent increased scope and activity of product liability, the coverage of products liability insurance has been extended to virtually every product category. Indeed, the total annual amount of insurance premiums for such coverage is probably about $100 million just in the United States. This is a big business which has developed in response to a major problem. Both the business and the problem will enlarge considerably before a stable level of activity is reached.

THE FUTURE

In the past several decades the law of product liability has changed enormously. It is reasonable to assume that some time in the near future liability will be imposed on the producer's or marketer's product without regard as to whether or not there was a defect in that product. After all, a certain amount of precedence has already been set by the fact that "no fault" insurance is now in effect in some parts of the country and is likely to sweep the nation within the next few years.

In addition, a number of recent product liability suits have evoked comments from the courts to the effect that the burden for payment and the burden of pain should be shifted to those who can bear it best. This almost always is the manufacturer and the seller, not the consumer. The implications for marketers are clear. The number of inputs which together comprise the ingredients of the marketing mix must now be expanded by one. Consideration of product liability must be included. The failure to do so can have a catastrophic effect upon the financial security of the firm. While product liability considerations may reduce innovation for some, it is better for them to have a reduced rate of innovation than to be wiped out entirely.

NOTES

1. *Product liability* simply means the legal responsibility of a manufacturer or marketer of a product to compensate a consumer who has been "harmed" by the product.

2. MacPherson v. Buick Motor Company, 217 N.Y. 382, 111 N.E. 1050 (1916).

3. Privity is a legal concept. Its effect was to allow lawsuits only between those who purchased an item and those who sold it *directly* to them. Users other than the purchasers, or sellers more distant in the channel of distribution, could not be parties to a suit for injury arising from the use of that product.

4. Randy Knitwear v. American Cyanamid Company, 181 N.E. 2d 402 N.Y. (1962).

5. Ibid.

6. Ibid.

7. Connolly v. Hagi, 188 Atl. 2d 884 (Conn., 1963).

8. Henningsen v. Bloomfield Motors, Inc., 161 A. 2d 81–84 (1960).

9. Henningsen v. Bloomfield Motors, Inc., ibid. 84.

10. Tort is the legal term used to denote one form of a personal injury.

11. Vandermark v. Ford Motor Company, 61 Cal. 2d 256 (1964).

12. Greenman v. Yuba Power Products, Inc., 59 Cal. 2d 57, 377 P. 2d 897, 27 Cal. Rptr. 697 (1963).

13. Ibid.

14. "Injuries Caused by Products: Effects of Strict Liability," *National Underwriter* (December 1, 1967), p. 11.

15. Baily v. Montgomery Ward, 431 P. 2d 108 (1967).

16. Dunham v. Vughan and Bushnell Manufacturing Company, 86 Ill. App. 2d 315 (1967); 42 Ill. 2d 339 (1969).

17. Carmen v. Eli Lilly & Company, 109 Ind. App. 76, 32 N.E. 2d 729 (1941).

18. William L. Prosser, "The Fall of the Citadel" (Strict Liability to the Consumer) *Minnesota Law Review,* Vol. 50, No. 5 (April 1966), p. 812.

19. "The Long Reach of Liability," *Business Week,* No. 2088 (September 6, 1969), p. 95.

20. Ibid.

21. Reed Dickerson, "Products Liability: How Good Does a Product Have to Be?" *Indiana Law Journal,* Vol. 42 (1967), p. 331.

22. Prosser, "The Fall of the Citadel" (Strict Liability to the Consumer) *Minnesota Law Review,* Vol. 50, No. 5 (April 1966), p. 812.

23. Putman v. Erie City Manufacturing Company, 338 Fed. 2d 911 (5th Cir. 1964).

24. Esborg v. Bailey Drug Company, 61 Wash. 2d P. 2d 298 (1963).

25. Ibbetson v. Montgomery Ward & Company, 171 Ill. App. 355 (1912).

Beverly C. Moore, Jr.

Product Safety: Who Should Absorb the Cost?

Product safety will be an important concern of the consumer movement until effective steps are taken to reduce the cost of accidents. Cost estimates for 1970 for three major categories of accidents are $5.5 billion for household product accidents (National Commission on Product Safety), $8 billion for work-related accidents (National Safety Council), and $16.2 billion for automobile accidents (Insurance Information Institute). The $30 billion total, encompassing 105,000 deaths and 390,000 permanent disabilities, is a substantial understatement.

In addition to significant underreporting, particularly of work-related accidents, such intangible damages as pain and suffering and the noneconomic value of lives lost are excluded. The comprehensive total cost of accidents in the United States may be in the vicinity of $50 billion, excluding the cost of administering a compensation system.

Presumably there will continue to be accident costs as long as there are accident prevention costs which are greater. These prevention costs are generally of two kinds:

One, *human carefulness,* in addition to having a relatively finite potential for further perfectibility, appears to be becoming more costly to exercise in a world which is increasingly complex, full of gadgets, warnings, directions, and distractions.

The other, *product design,* has quite the opposite potential. Its perfectibility—ultimately in preventing negligent, even intentionally caused accidents—and the cost of its perfectibility, is dependent solely on the progress

Reprinted by permission from *Trial* magazine (January/February, 1972), The Association of Trial Lawyers of America.

of technology. Judging from the recent past, one can expect that technological progress, given the proper incentives, will be steady and dramatic.

It can be reliably forecast, therefore, that primarily through improvements in product design, accident prevention costs, and thus the net cost of accidents, will be reduced over time.

The pace at which that development unfolds depends upon what external pressures are brought to bear upon the corporations which design products (or employ workers or perform services).

Competition—the external force upon which we generally rely to spur product improvements and cost-saving technologies—is not always or even usually effective in forcing product safety improvements. Competition can work to the extent that the safety improvement is substantial enough to be noticed by a significant number of consumers who will pay the higher cost necessitated by the improvement in order to avoid a cognizable accident risk. Examples could be cited where this has occurred, but generally the consumer lacks the information to evaluate such particularized criteria.

While the problem could be ameliorated somewhat by mandatory disclosure of accident risk information at point of purchase; a further problem remains: Accident-prone products are often produced by oligopolistic firms which compete sluggishly, if at all, in safety improvements.

With a single adjustment, however, competition could be harnessed as the prime lever of cost-effective safety improvements—irrespective of consumer ignorance of accident risks, irrespective of the general absence of competition within oligopolistic industries.

The adjustment is to transfer the entire cost of a product's accidents from its victims to the producer, regardless of fault. By forcing corporations to internalize their social costs—i.e., treating them as ordinary business expenses—the price mechanism will force the adoption of cost-effective safety improvements.

Suppose, for example, that the auto industry was saddled with $20 billion annually for accident costs, not to mention an additional $10 billion liability for air pollution damage and other externalities. The average price of an automobile would increase by $2000. Sales would drop dramatically as consumers would resort to mass transit and other less costly means of transportation. This state of affairs would persist until the industry developed a car safe enough to reduce its damage liability to the point at which prices could be lowered sufficiently to generate a profitable sales volume.

One suspects that safer cars would soon be on the market. The continuing solvency of General Motors would depend upon that. And if, perchance, the industry is unable to reduce net accident costs sufficiently to stay in business, then it will have been demonstrated that automobiles have been economically feasible instrumentalities only by virtue of their costs being subsidized by their accident victims.

From the accident victim's viewpoint, this "enterprise liability" concept differs markedly from present and proposed compensation systems.

• It differs from the fault system in that not 42%, but 100%, of accident victims' economic losses are compensated.

• It differs from workmen's compensation formulas in that there is no schedule of maximum benefits preventing the victim from recovering his full economic and intangible losses.

• It differs from strict products liability doctrine in that no defect need be established.

Enterprise liability goes beyond no-fault in two important aspects:

First, except for very small or new firms, the producers of accident-prone products would be prohibited from resorting to liability insurance to spread their accident-damage risks. In light of the ultimate objective, these corporations cannot be permitted to avoid the safety competition touched off when an individual firm lowers its price after implementing a damage-reducing product-design change.

Second, enterprise liability would not tolerate any exceptions to no-fault principles, such as denial of compensation to drunk drivers.

There is no attempt here to be solicitous of accident victims generally or of drunk drivers in particular, or to impute "blame" to the auto industry. From society's perspective, any benefits to victims are purely incidental to the overriding purpose (which compensation serves) – preventing acidents so that there will ultimately be no victims to compensate.

This is accomplished by imposing the cost of any general category of accidents upon the party (i.e., producer or victim) who is best able to prevent that class of accidents. We have assumed that the producer will usually be that party.

In the case of automobile accidents, one is initially impressed with the argument that the fear of the accident itself is a sufficient deterrent to negligent driving even if the driver is assured of compensation for his own negligence. Likewise, there is no good reason for supposing that placing the loss upon the drunk driver will deter drunk driving to a greater extent then placing it upon the manufacturer according to the general rule. After all, the drunk driver persists, notwithstanding our having held him liable before.

It seems much more promising to encourage the industry to develop devices which will render intoxicated persons unable to operate a parked motor vehicle. Nor is this to say that additional measures, such as traffic fines and license suspensions, should not continue to act as a deterrent to individual carelessness.

Although the concept of internalizing social costs has been advocated by economists as a means of solving our pollution problems, it has not been seriously proposed, even by consumer advocates, as a means of reducing accident costs.

(There has been considerable academic discussion. *See* G. Calabresi, *The Costs of Accidents* (1970); Reviewed in 80 *Yale L.J.* 647 (1971), 84 *Harv. L. Rev.* 1322 (1971); Coase, "The Problem of Social Cost," 3 *J.L. & Econ.* 1 (1960).)

The traditional approach, advocated by the Product Safety Commission and already incorporated into federal auto safety legislation, has instead been to authorize a government agency to promulgate and enforce standards.

These may bring about a reduction in accident costs. But the cost-internalization alternative will generally bring about an even greater accident-cost reduction, and it will accomplish this result with a minimum of prevention costs.

The reasons for the superiority of cost internalization are not difficult to discern. At worst the government agency will become the captive of its regulatees. Congressional appropriations will be minimal, and sanctionless "voluntary compliance" will become the enforcement mode. At best, agency standard setting will be cumbersome and crude.

The basic dilemma is that regulators must operate in a milieu of static technology. Even if the standard that is promulgated—the air bag, for example—is or appears to be the most cost-effective means of reducing accidents at the time of its adoption, a more advanced technology may be developed shortly thereafter. Even if the agency is vigilant to replace the old standard with the new, there will always be some lag.

Also under cost internalization, the pressure to develop new technology is on the industry, where the greatest expertise presumably resides. Under the standards approach, however, this onus is placed upon the agency, which is likely to adopt a standard which either prevents too few accidents or is more costly than necessary with respect to the accidents it does prevent.

Under cost internalization, the industry has an incentive to do neither, but rather to follow the course which will reduce its damage liability at least cost to the consumer.

This is not to say that government standards can play no desirable role. Standards may complement cost internalization in cases where the accident damage cannot be measured with sufficient precision or where there is a small but real possibility of planetwide disaster—if the polar ice caps were to melt on account of increased atmospheric carbon dioxide levels attributable to fuel combustion, for example.

A relatively sure and simple legal apparatus can be fashioned to internalize accident costs without reliance upon government discretion.

A product safety commission would be established with a mandate to gather accident data to be used as evidence in private class-action lawsuits. These actions would seek recovery from the corporate defendants of a lump-sum damage fund (plus attorneys fees and claims administration costs) in behalf of the class as an entity. Individual accident victims would then file claims against the fund, just as they would against a fire insurance company. In the likelihood that not all individual claims will be filed, the remainder of the damage fund will revert in trust "to the benefit of accident victims generally," to be disbursed under court supervision.

The data-collecting agency would be empowered to order corporations, doctors and hospitals to comply with accident reporting procedures. If the agency failed to gather the data necessary to establish class-action damages, any private citizen could file suit to compel the agency to act. If the citizen suit was successful, the agency would be ordered to pay the plaintiff's attorney's fees and expenses, plus a cash bonus to reward his initiative as a private attorney general.

No doubt it will be argued that the higher product costs resulting from cost internalization would be "regressive." This objection is really that *all* prices are regressive—for bread, postage stamps, whatever. To allocate resources most efficiently, prices should reflect costs. The costs of product accidents, pollution and other externalities are no less "costs" than are the costs of labor, land, and capital.

Nor must one resign himself to the inevitability of disproportionately burdening the poor with the cost of accidents. The reason why it is desirable to internalize those costs is that a net economic gain is thereby produced which can be directly transferred to the poor.

To illustrate, suppose that the total annual cost of accidents is $60 billion, including pain and suffering, other intangibles and administration of a compensation system. Suppose further that two-thirds, or $40 billion, of that cost could be eliminated at a prevention cost of $20 billion, leaving a net gain of $20 billion. Through a negative income tax device this sum could then be used to supplement the incomes of low-income persons to an extent which would far outweigh the regressive impact of higher product prices.

Corporate Policy Statement

We are committed to exercising responsible care for our products both in manufacturing and distribution and later in their handling by distributors and use by our customers. This means assessing the environmental impact of the products and then taking appropriate steps to protect employee and public health, and the environment as a whole. In addition to a safe production and distribution, as well as judicious customer use, it means we have a continuous concern for the ultimate disposal of our products in the environment. We expect Research and Development to: Direct Dow development activity to product applications which permit safe handling, use and disposal. Determine that product testing is conducted at each stage of product development so that safety hazards and both short and long range environmental effects can be assessed before critical decision points. Give primary consideration to human safety and potential environmental hazards in selecting products for development and sale. In so doing, Dow employees, customers, plant communities and the public at large must be considered, as well as both short and long range environmental hazards in the distribution, use and eventual disposal of our products. Provide information to production, distribution and marketing personnel so that employees, distributors of our products, and customers may be instructed in the safe handling, use and disposal of our products. We expect Manufacturing to: Adhere to Dow's Global Pollution Control Guidelines and Company safety standards. Carefully review, before adoption, product specifications or process changes which may alter product properties, utility or quality, including product impurities. . . . We expect Marketing to: Furnish customers and distributors of Dow products appropriate information to foster the safe handling, use and disposal of Dow products. . . . Alert Dow personnel immediately to problems of use involving human or environmental safety and assist in modifications of either products or use patterns, as required, to correct these problems. We expect Distribution to: Assess the safety and environmental impact to determine that appropriate steps will be taken while our products are being stored and transported in order to protect persons, property and the total environment. . . . Select carriers, warehouses and terminals to perform distribution functions consistent with Dow policies and guidelines.

Dow Chemical Co.

Advertising

FTC v. Colgate-Palmolive Co.

Colgate-Palmolive engaged the Ted Bates advertising agency to develop an advertising campaign based on the slogan "Rapid Shave outshaves them all." The result was a series of three one-minute commercials in which it was claimed that Rapid Shave could soften even the toughness of sandpaper. The test showed Rapid Shave being applied to what was claimed to be sandpaper. The ad used these words: "To prove Rapid Shave's super-moisturizing power, we put it right from the can onto this tough, dry sandpaper. It was apply, soak, and off in a stroke." Simultaneously, the viewer saw a razor shave the surface, leaving it completely smooth. But the actual surface was not sandpaper, rather, plexiglas to which sand had been applied, because, it was claimed, sandpaper looks like ordinary colored paper when shown on television. Evidence brought to the attention of the Federal Trade Commission (FTC) also showed that, although Rapid Shave could actually shave the sand from real sandpaper, it could do so only after a soaking period of about 80 minutes, rather than the few moments shown on television.

In 1960 the FTC issued a complaint against Colgate and Bates claiming the commercials were false and deceptive. The hearing examiner dismissed the complaint, reasoning that neither misrepresentation—concerning moistening time or the identity of the shaved surface—would mislead the public. In 1961 the FTC reversed the hearing examiner, claiming that since Rapid Shave could not shave actual sandpaper in the time depicted in the ads, the product's moisturizing power had been misrepresented. The Commission also held that undisclosed use of a plexiglas substitute was deceptive.

U.S. Sp. Ct., 1965. 380 U.S. 374, 85 S. Ct. 1035, 13 L. Ed. 2d904.

In 1962 the First Circuit Court of Appeals twice upheld the FTC order against misrepresentation relating to the time factor, and Colgate conceded this issue. But the Appeals Court refused to allow enforcement of the FTC's claim of misrepresentation regarding the plexiglass substitution. The issue facing the Supreme Court then was whether a commercial (portraying tests that supposedly confirm the claims made for a product) may use simulated props and devices that differ from materials the defendants originally claimed to be using in the tests.

A majority of the Supreme Court decided against Colgate. Television commercials that include a test were ruled deceptive if the test uses materials other than those which it purports to use. The majority argued mainly by analogy. Similar cases established that it is deceptive: (1) to state falsely that a product ordinarily sells for an inflated price but that it is being offered at a reduced price, even if the offered price represents the product's actual value, (2) to conceal that a product has been reprocessed even though it is as good as new; and (3) for a seller to misrepresent to the public that he is in a certain line of business, even though the misstatement in no way affects the quality of a product. Speaking for the majority, Chief Justice Warren went on to say:

> Respondents . . . insist that the present case is not like any of the above, but is more like a case in which a celebrity or independent testing agency has in fact submitted a written verification of an experiment actually observed, but, because of the inability of the camera to transmit accurately an impression of the paper on which the testimonial is written, the seller reproduces it on another substance so that it can be seen by the viewing audience. This analogy ignores the finding of the Commission that in the present case the seller misrepresented to the public that it was being given objective proof of a product claim. In respondents' hypothetical the objective proof of the product claim that is offered, the word of the celebrity or agency that the experiment was actually conducted, does exist; while in the case before us the objective proof offered, the viewer's own perception of an actual experiment, does not exist. . . .
>
> The Court of Appeals has criticized the reference in the Commission's order to "test, experiment or demonstration" as not being capable of practical interpretation. It could find no difference between the Rapid Shave commercial and a commercial which extolled the goodness of ice cream while giving viewers a picture of a scoop of mashed potatoes appearing to be ice cream. We do not understand this difficulty. In the ice cream case the mashed potato prop is not being used for additional proof of the product claim, while the purpose of the Rapid Shave commercial is to give the reviewer objective proof of the claims made. If in the ice cream hypothetical the focus of the commercial becomes the undisclosed potato prop and the viewer is invited, explicitly or by implication, to see for himself the truth of the claims about the ice cream's rich texture and full color, and perhaps compare it to a "rival product," then the commercial has become similar to the one now before us. Clearly, however, a commercial which depicts happy actors delightedly eating ice cream that is in fact mashed potatoes . . . is not covered by the present order.

Justice Harlan spoke for the minority, and in favor of Colgate, in the 7-2 decision:

> The only question here is what techniques the advertiser may use to convey essential truth to the television viewer. If the claim is true and valid, then the technique for projecting that claim, within broad boundaries, falls purely within the advertiser's art. The warrant to the Federal Trade Commission is to police the verity of the claim itself. . . .
>
> I do not see how such a commercial can be said to be "deceptive" in any legally acceptable use of that term. The Court attempts to distinguish the case where a "celebrity" has written a testimonial endorsing some product, but the original testimonial cannot be seen over television and a copy is shown over the air by the manufacturer. . . . But in both cases the viewer is told to "see for himself," in the one case that the celebrity has endorsed the product; in the other, that the product can shave sandpaper; in neither case is the viewer actually seeing the proof; and in both cases the objective proof does exist, be it in the original testimonial or the sandpaper test actually conducted by the manufacturer. In neither case, however, is there a material misrepresentation, because what the viewer sees *is* an accurate image of the objective proof. . . .
>
> It is commonly known that television presents certain distortions in transmission for which the broadcasting industry must compensate. Thus, a white towel will look a dingy gray over television, but a blue towel will look a sparkling white. On the Court's analysis, an advertiser must achieve accuracy in the studio even though it results in an inaccurate image being projected on the home screen. . . . Would it be proper for respondent Colgate, in advertising a laundry detergent, to "demonstrate" the effectiveness of a major competitor's detergent in washing white sheets; and then "before the viewer's eyes," to wash a white (not a blue) sheet with the competitor's detergent? The studio test would accurately show the quality of the product, but the image on the screen would look as though the sheet had been washed with an ineffective detergent. All that has happened here is the converse: a demonstration has been altered in the studio to compensate for the distortions of the television medium, but in this instance in order to present an accurate picture to the television viewer.

For Discussion

Analyze carefully the reasoning of Justices Warren and Harlan. In your opinion which Justice presents the best argument? Why? Pay attention to their uses of "misrepresentation" and "deception." Do you yourself believe Colgate's advertisement was deceptive? If so, what aspects were deceptive, and why were they deceptive? If you believe the advertisement was not deceptive, what is the basis for your claim? What additional arguments can you provide for your view beyond the arguments presented by the justices?

The Advertising Code of American Business

We hold that advertising has a responsibility to inform and serve the American public and to further the economic life of this nation. Believing this, the following principles are hereby affirmed.

1. **Truth**
   Advertising shall tell the truth, and shall reveal material facts, the concealment of which might mislead the public.
2. **Responsibility**
   Advertising agencies and advertisers shall be willing to provide substantiation of claims made.
3. **Taste and Decency**
   Advertising shall be free of statements, illustrations, or implications which are offensive to good taste or public decency.
4. **Disparagement**
   Advertising shall offer merchandise or service on its merits, and refrain from attacking competitors or disparaging their products, services or methods of doing business.
5. **Bait Advertising**
   Advertising shall be bona fide and the merchandise or service offered shall be readily available for purchase at the advertised price.
6. **Guarantees and Warranties**
   Advertising of guarantees and warranties shall be explicit. Advertising of any guarantee or warranty shall clearly and conspicuously disclose its nature and extent, the manner in which the guarantor or warrantor will perform and the identity of the guarantor or warrantor.
7. **Price Claims**
   Advertising shall avoid price or savings claims which are unsupported by facts or which do not offer bona fide bargains or savings.
8. **Unprovable Claims**
   Advertising shall avoid the use of exaggerated or unprovable claims.
9. **Testimonials**
   Advertising containing testimonials shall be limited to those of competent witnesses who are reflecting a real and honest choice.

Jules Henry

Cultural Factors in Advertising

Advertising is not a strange fever boiling up from the concrete swamps of Madison Avenue; rather it is a perfectly intelligible cultural form emerging logically from the configuration of contemporary life. . . .

Three Types of Society

From the standpoint of truth, only three types of society are possible: the verdical, the mendacious, and the pseudo-veridical. The veridical society, one in which people tell the truth all the time, is probably found only in monasteries or nunneries. Mendacious societies, *i.e.,* societies in which people never tell the truth, are equally rare. Only one is known to me — Alor, a complex of villages on a small island in the Dutch East Indies. There nobody tells the truth, nobody is expected to tell the truth, and children learn to lie as soon as they are able to walk. More common in the world however, is the pseudo-veridical society, the type in which truth is an ideal honored as often in the breach as in the observance. Contemporary United States — like most of the world called "civilized" — belongs to this largest class of societies. But though we share the qualities of pseudo-veridity with most of the world, it is clear that calculated product redundance and other peculiarities of our economy have played very important parts in giving our own pseudo-veridity a unique and spicy quality. Since products are redundant, it is clear that unique verbal methods must be developed to make them appear to be different from one another. Since we are ruled by consumption autarchy, on the other hand, still other forms of reasoning must evolve in order to sell a home market always in danger of being saturated. And since the high-rising standard of living has become something like a moral imperative, special forms of reasoning have to be used in order to convince a person that his moral qualities would indeed be enhanced were he to acquire a given product. Such phenomena arise readily in a world in which the progress of ethics has been joyously downhill. . . .

Advertising operates on a series of principles, not all of them quite conscious, which I shall call not a system but a *mélange*. Let us enumerate some of them.

Pecuniary Pseudo-Truth

Since the entire advertising idea-mélange is devoted to pecuniary purposes, I prefix all components with the word "pecuniary." A pecuniary pseudo-truth is a false statement made as if it were true but not intended to be believed. No proof is offered for the pecuniary pseudo-truth and no one looks for it. Its proof is that it sells merchandise; if it does not, it is false. Examples of pecuniary pseudo-truth are: (1) Alpine cigarettes "put the men in menthol"; (2) ". . . everybody's talking about the new *Starfire* automobile." (3) A woman wearing a *Distinction* foundation will look so beautiful that other women will want to kill her.

Obviously none of these statements is true, the advertisements are not to be believed, and nobody in his right mind will believe them. They are pecuniary pseudo-truth.

Pecuniary Para-Poetic Hyperbole

A para-poetic hyperbole is something like poetry, with high-flown figures of speech, but is not poetry. Examples are: (1) *Pango peach* cosmetic color comes "from east of the sun . . . west of the moon where each tomorrow dawns . . . is succulent on your lips and sizzling on your finger tips" and will be one's "adventure in paradise." (2) 7 *Crown* whiskey "holds within its depths a world of summertime." (3) The use of *The Look* eyeshadow will make a woman's eyes "jungle green . . . glittery gold . . . flirty eyes, tiger eyes."

An essential feature of a para-poetic hyperbole is that it is deliberately chosen because it is cliché: when you are trying to sell eyeshadow to a working girl or whiskey to an executive, you do not quote Dylan Thomas, but rather seek to jog them on the exposed funny-bone of their goofy elementary and high-school fantasy.

PECUNIARY LOGIC

Pecuniary logic is a proof that is not a proof but is intended to be for commercial purposes. For example, the truth value of the statement in the advertising copy for Old Crow whiskey to the effect that when the Confederate General Basil Duke arrived in New York after the war, "Old Crow quite naturally would be served" rests on the shaky grounds that he "esteemed it 'the most famous whiskey ever made in Kentucky.'" And *Butyl* tries to convince us that it is a valuable ingredient in tires because "major tire marketers . . . are now bringing you tires made of this remarkable material." When one is asked to accept the literal message of a product on the basis of shadowy evidence, I dub it *pecuniary logic*.

There is nothing basically novel in pecuniary logic, for most people use it more or less all the time in their everyday life. What business has done is to adopt one of the commoner elements of folk thought and to use it for selling products to people who think this way all the time. This kind of thinking—that accepts proof that is not proof—is an *essential* intellectual factor in our economy, for if people were careful thinkers, it would be difficult to sell anything. From this it follows that in order for our economy to continue in its present form, people must learn to be fuzzy-minded and impulsive, for if they were clear-headed and deliberate, they would rarely put their hands in their pockets; or if they did, they would leave them there. If we were all gifted logicians, the economy would not survive; and herein lies a terrifying paradox, for *in order to exist economically as we are, we must try by might and main to remain stupid.*

*   *   *

It is now obvious that advertising cannot be expected either to seek or to present truth as we understand it from the point of view of the more orthodox philosophies of our civilization. Rather, advertising, since it pivots on what must sell, must have a truth-system related to the iron requirements of sales. Let us therefore give some attention to the problem of *pecuniary truth*.

Americans are not obsessive truth-seekers; they do not yearn to get to the bottom of things; they are willing to let absurd or merely ambiguous statements pass. And this undemandingness that does not insist that the world stand up and prove that it is real, this air of relaxed woolly-mindedness, is a necessary condition for the development of a revolutionary mode of thought herein called *pecuniary philosophy*. There is as yet only a dim awareness of this as a coherent, self-consistent system among the creative sparks of Madison Avenue. The relaxed attitude toward veracity (or mendacity, depending on the point of view) and its complement, pecuniary philosophy, are important to the American economy for they make possible an enormous amount of selling that could not otherwise take place.

Every culture creates a philosophy out of its own needs, and ours has produced an orthodox philosophy based on a truth verifiable by some primordial objective criterion and another derived from an irrational need to sell. The heart of truth in the orthodox philosophy was God or His equivalent, the heart of truth in pecuniary philosophy is contained in the following three postulates:

Truth is what sells.

Truth is what you want people to believe.

Truth is that which is not legally false.

The first two postulates are clear but the third probably requires a little explaining and a good example. A report in *Science* on the marketing practices of the *Encyclopaedia Britannica* is just what we need at this point.

> One of the tasks of the Federal Trade Commission, according to the Encyclopaedia Britannica, is to order business organizations to stop using deceptive advertising when such organizations are found to be so engaged. A few weeks ago Encyclopaedia Britannica Inc., was ordered by the Federal Trade Commission to stop using advertising that misrepresents its regular prices as reduced prices available for a limited time only. . . .
>
> Some of the company's sales practices are ingenious. The FTC shows, for example, how the prospective customer, once he has gained the impression that he is being offered the Encyclopaedia and accessories at reduced prices, is led to believe that the purported reduced prices are good only for a limited time. This is done by two kinds of statements, *each one being true enough if regarded separately.*
>
> The first kind of statement, which appears in written material, says such things as "This offer is necessarily subject to withdrawal without notice."

Science explains that the second kind of statement is made by the salesman when he applies pressure to the prospective customer by telling him he will not return. The Federal Trade Commission, in enjoining the *Encyclopaedia* from using this kind of sales technique, argued that the first statement plus the second created the impression in the customer's mind that if he does not buy now, he will lose the opportunity to buy at what he has been given to think is a reduced price. Actually, *Science* points out, it is not a reduced price, for the price has not changed since 1949. Since it is literally true that a business has the right to raise prices without advance notice, the *Encyclopaedia* advertisement is not legally false even though it reads like a warning that prices will go up soon. I have coined the term *legally innocent prevarication* to cover all statements which, though not legally untrue, misrepresent by implication.

PECUNIARY FOLK-PSYCHOLOGY

In this section I do not deal with the psychological concepts and instruments that advertising uses to manipulate desire. Rather I examine what might be called its folk-psychology or, perhaps, its assumptions and mental strategy; and I use for this purpose the notions developed by a great classicist of Madison Avenue, Rosser Reeves of Ted Bates, Inc., one of the largest agencies in New York. Reeves' book, *Reality in Advertising,* had a phenomenal sale, and he credits it with having attracted many customers, even from Pakistan. Reeves' psychology is free of academic frills and has a massive simplicity. We can readily understand why he is one of the vice-presidents of Ted Bates.

The fundamental concepts of pecuniary psychology are the "brain box" or, more simply, "the head," and "penetration." The head is a repository for advertising "claims" or "messages," and these enter the head by virtue of their penetrating power. Quotes from Reeves' book will make the matter clear:

> There is a finite limit to what a consumer can remember about 30,000 advertised brands. . . .
>
> It is as though he carries a small box in his head for a given product category. . . .
>
> Do you doubt this?
>
> Then, take one man and subject him to an exhausting depth interview. Measure his total memory of advertising in any one field — be it cereals, razor blades or beer. . . . You will be able to chart the size of the theoretical box in his head. Now, do this with tens of thousands of people. . . .
>
> You will be able to see the tremendous difficulty of owning a bit of space in the box.
>
> Our competitor's penetration is moving down as we seize a larger and larger share of the consumer's brain box.

Thus pecuniary psychology pivots, like any system of thought, on a conception of mind.

Other important concepts are: the advertiser's "claim"; "finiteness" of head content; "measurability" of head content; transitoriness. Transitoriness is really an implicit underlying idea or parameter extracted from Reeves' thinking by me. Fundamentally it implies impermanence, instability, evanescence — disloyalty, so to speak, of consumers, for consumers are viewed — rather ungratefully, I think — as being constantly on the verge of deserting one product for another, just like people among themselves. It seems to me that Reeves is a little confused in his attitude here, for not "product loyalty" but product *dis*loyalty is the foundation of our economy. After all, if everyone stuck with the product he bought but once, how would dozens of other manufacturers enter the field with identical ones? And where would Reeves be? His inability to grasp the importance to our entire way of life of this *socially necessary evanescence* seems a curious weakness in one so brilliant.

The conception of the head or box involves the hidden assumption of mental passivity, for the brain box is conceived of as an inert receptacle which the advertiser enters by penetration, *i.e.,* his "campaign" gets a claim inside the box. Reeves must be right, for if the box were not relatively inert, advertising would be a failure.

Since many products are very similar to one another and hence must compete intensely for the same brain boxes, struggles develop between claims. I have called these struggles "The Wars of Pecuniary Claims."

In the battles of The Wars of Pecuniary Claims, the consumer is passive while the wars are fought by claims competing for the consumer's brain box. It is something like a fort which, though inanimate, is a provocation to the adversaries because of its strategic importance. Triumph means that the victor plants his flag—symbolizing beer, electric razors, soap, toothpaste, et cetera—on the consumer's head encasing the winning claim: he has been penetrated. My simile is not quite perfect because while generals in traditional wars understand that fortresses may be destroyed in the struggle for them, Reeves does not discuss the possibility of the destruction of the consumer.

Up to this point, I have stated the central features of our economy that give to advertising its fateful thrust; I have examined some of its peculiarities as a method of thinking about products, and I have analyzed what might be called its metapsychology. I have said nothing, however, about its handling of values.

Advertising uses for pecuniary purposes, *i.e.* to expand sales, almost anything in the human head: if a person has feelings of inferiority, advertising finds a way to exploit this to sell him something; if he is worried advertising is there with product therapy and thus converts his worries into dollars. If a person is sick and tired of staying home, advertising will tell him how to travel; and if he is bored with running around, advertising will instruct him in how to have a good time as a home-body, while spending money. This process of converting all human weaknesses and strivings into cash, this Midas-touch of advertising, I have called *monetization*. This section deals with the problem of the monetization of values.

Since values like love, truth, the sacredness of high office, God, the Bible, motherhood, generosity, solicitude for others, and so on are the foundation of Western culture, anything that weakens or distorts them shakes traditional life. The traditional values are part of traditional philosophy; but pecuniary philosophy, far from being at odds with them, appears to embrace them with fervor. But this is the embrace of a golden grizzly bear; for as it embraces the traditional values, pecuniary philosophy chokes them to death. The specific choking mechanism is *monetization*.

Let us consider the following advertisement for a popular woman's magazine: Against a black sky covering almost an entire page in *The New York Times* is chalked the following from the New Testament: "Children, love ye one another." Below, the advertising copy tells us that the magazine will carry in its next issue parables from five faiths, and that

> Such spiritual splendor, such profound mystical insight, seem perfectly at home in the pages of the magazine, where the editorial approach is all-inclusive, universal, matching the infinite variety of today's existence.

Guilt by association is familiar enough to the American people through the work of various sedulous agencies of Government. Magazine, however, has discovered its opposite—*glory* by association, or, in the language of this work, pecuniary transfiguration, since "spiritual splendor" and "mystical insight" are traits of holy books, and since examples of these are printed in Magazine. Magazine is by that fact a kind of holy book. This is what I mean by the use of values for pecuniary purposes; this is value distortion through monetization.

In their wars of survival, pecuniary adversaries will use anything for ammunition—space, time, the President, the Holy Bible, and all the traditional values. Monetization waters down values, wears them out by slow attrition, makes them banal, and, in the long run, helps Americans to become indifferent to them and even cynical. Thus the competitive struggle forces the corruption of values. . . .

I have, perhaps, burdened this article with too many new expressions; yet it seemed necessary to do this in order to make clear the fact that pecuniary philosophy is a more or less systematic method of thinking, as well as a way to make money. So I have spoken of pecuniary pseudo-truth, which is a statement nobody is expected to believe but which is set down as if it were to be believed. Pecuniary logic was defined as a statement made to be believed but backed up by shadowy proof, and para-poetic hyperbole was described as being poetry but not quite poetry, its function being to make a product appear rather dreamlike and to transmute it. Pecuniary psychology is the "scientific" base of pecuniary philosophy, and its central concepts are the head or "brain box," penetration, and the claim.

This brings us to pecuniary philosophy's conception of man. Man—or, rather, his brain box—is finite, but at the same time, infinite. The brain box is finite with respect to the number of claims it can contain at the same time, but it is infinite in the things it may desire. Claims and perceptions (of products) surge in and out of the brain box like the tides of an ocean moving up and down a passive beach. Put another way, man is supine while the external culture in the form of products and claims molds him to desire. Thus if the culture (*i.e.,* advertising) requires that man stay at home consuming electric organs and barbecue pits, he can readily be gotten to do so if advertising paints mellow pictures of home and family; and if, on the other hand, it is desired that he drive around and use up gasoline, man, in the pecuniary conception, will readily be brought to that too simply through "promoting" the beauties of automobile travel. If he takes his coffee weak, he will drink it strong if advertising admonishes him to do so. If, smoking mentholated cigarettes, he fears for his masculinity, he will lose his fears if he is told that *Alpine* "put the men in menthol"!

Insatiably desiring, infinitely plastic, totally passive and always a little bit sleepy; unpredictably labile and disloyal (to products); basically wooly-minded and non-obsessive about traditional truth; relaxed and undemanding with respect to the canons of traditional philosophy, indifferent to its values and easily moved to buy whatever at the moment seems to help his underlying personal inadequacies—this is pecuniary philosophy's conception of man and woman in our culture.

Considering the enormous success of many of the advertising campaigns discussed here, I am not prepared to say that the advertisers are wrong.

*   *   *

Phillip Nelson

Advertising and Ethics

THE MARKET SYSTEM AND ADVERTISING

There are two possible routes one can take to ethics. One can exhort
others to take account of social well-being in their behavior — "to love one
another" and act accordingly. Or one can try to design institutions such that
people will, indeed, benefit society, given the motivations that presently
impel their behavior. Most economists, whatever their political position,
adopt the latter view; ethical behavior is behavior that, in fact, benefits
society, not necessarily behavior that is motivated to benefit society.

Those of us who advocate the market as an appropriate institution are
following the lead of Adam Smith: that the market, more or less, acts as if
there were an invisible hand, converting individual actions motivated by the
pursuit of private gain into social benefit. The selfish employer, for example,
callously firing employees when he no longer needs them, helps in the
reallocation of labor to activities where it is more useful.

This is not the stuff of poetry. In novels — and quite possibly in the interpersonal relations upon which novels generally focus — selfish people act in
ways disastrous to those around them. But novels are hardly the basis for
determining social policy, though novelists and their compatriots, literary
critics, are often in the forefront in the espousal of "social causes." They
have been the consciences of society. Because of their focus on motivation,
they have generated a guilt complex when guilt is totally unjustified.

From *Ethics, Free Enterprise, and Public Policy: Original Essays on Moral Issues in Business*
by Richard T. DeGeorge and Joseph A. Pichler. Copyright © 1978 Oxford University Press,
Inc. Reprinted by permission.

It must be admitted that the market is not a perfect instrument, that the invisible hand wavers a bit. Some individual actions will not lead to social well-being. However, popular perceptions tend to exaggerate market imperfections. For example, the available evidence indicates that the monopoly problem is not terribly serious in the United States. More importantly, the popular view fails to evaluate the problems of alternative institutions. The record of government regulation to make the market behave has been distinguished by case after case where the cure has been worse than the disease, where often there has been no disease at all.

I want to look at the ethics of advertising, given this perspective. Advertising is ethical not because of the motivations of its practitioners but because of the consequences of its operation. The invisible hand strikes again! The market power of consumers will force advertisers to act in ways that benefit society. Advertising will by no means be an "ideal" institution. But it will do an effective job of getting information to consumers.

Advertising bothers its critics not only because its practitioners are selfishly motivated. The advertising itself is often distasteful. Celebrities endorse that brand that pays them the highest price. Advertisers lie if it pays. Advertisers often make empty statements. Nobel prizes for literature have not yet been awarded to the classics of the advertising art. But the crucial question is not whether advertising is aesthetically satisfying, or whether its practitioners are noble, or even whether they occasionally lie. The question is whether advertising generates social well-being. Some of the former questions are not irrelevant in determining the answer to the latter question. In particular, as I discuss later, the role that truth plays in generating socially useful advertising is an important question.

ADVERTISING AND INFORMATION

Before resolving the fundamental ethical issue about advertising, it is important to understand how advertising behaves. I support a simple proposition about the behavior of advertising: that all advertising is information. This is not a statement with which the critics of advertising would agree. What bothers them is that advertising is paid for by the manufacturers of the brands whose products are being extolled. How can information be generated by such a process? Clearly, some kind of mechanism is required to make the self-interested statements of manufacturers generate information. But such a mechanism exists—consumer power in the product markets.

The nature of consumer control over advertising varies with the character of consumer information. Consumers can get some information about certain qualities of products prior to purchase. For example, they can try on a dress, find out about the price of the product, or see how new furniture looks. I call these "search qualities." In the case of search qualities, a manufacturer is almost required by the nature of his business to tell the truth.

The consumer can determine before he buys the product whether indeed this is the dress or the piece of furniture that has been advertised; and in consequence, it will pay the advertiser to be truthful. This is a situation where the famous ditty of Gilbert and Sullivan would be appropriate:

> This haughty youth, he tells the truth
> Whenever he finds it pays;
> And in this case, it all took place
> Exactly like he says.

Now, there are other qualities that the consumer cannot determine prior to purchase. It is very difficult for the consumer to determine the taste of a brand of tuna fish before he buys the tuna fish, or to determine how durable a car will be until he's experienced it; but even in these cases, the consumer can get information about a product. The character of his experiences when using the brand will generate information to the consumer. This information will not be useful for initial purchases, but it will govern whether the consumer repeatedly purchases the brand or not. The repeat purchase of consumers provides the basis of consumer control of the market in the case of "experience qualities."

In this case, there will be certain characteristics of the advertising which are truthful. It will pay the advertiser to relate correctly the function of the brand. It pays the manufacturer of Pepto-Bismol to advertise his brand as a stomach remedy rather than as a cure for athlete's foot because, obviously, he is going to be able to get repeat purchases if Pepto-Bismol does something for stomachs and people are taking it for stomachs. If they're taking the stomach remedy for athlete's foot, they're in trouble. So the effort to get repeat purchasers will generate a lot of truthfulness in advertising. Another example: it pays the manufacturer of unsweetened grapefruit juice to advertise the product as unsweetened. This is the effective way to get repeat purchases; hence people can believe it.

There are other qualities about the brand for which the incentive of truthfulness does not exist. It pays the manufacturer of Pepto-Bismol to advertise his brand as the most soothing stomach remedy even if it were the least soothing stomach remedy around. It pays somebody to say that a piece of candy tastes best even if the candy has an unpleasant taste. Even here, however, there is information for the consumer to obtain through advertising. The advertising message is not credible, but the fact that the brand is advertised is a valuable piece of information to the consumer. The consumer rightly believes that there is a positive association between advertising and the better buy. The more advertising he sees of the product, the more confidence he has prior to purchasing the product. Simply put, it pays to advertise winners. It does not pay to advertise losers. In consequence, the brands that are advertised the most heavily are more likely to be the winners.

The mechanism that is operating is the repeat purchasing power of the consumer. Brands that are good after purchase will be brands that consumers buy more. In consequence, there is a negatively sloped demand curve. People buy more as the price per unit of utility of a good goes down, even when it takes experience on the part of consumers to determine this utility. As quantity goes up, the amount of advertising will also go up. This is a well-established relationship.[1] The positive association between quantity and advertising and the negative association between quantity and price per unit of utility generates a negative association between advertising and price per unit of utility. In other words, the "better buys" advertise more; and, in consequence, the *amount* of advertising provides information to consumers.

Considering that we have no direct measure of "better buys," there is a good deal of evidence to support this proposition. First, it pays a firm to expand its sales if it can produce what consumers want more cheaply than other firms. It can increase its sales either by increasing advertising or lowering prices. I maintain that it does both at the same time, just as plants usually increase both their capital and their labor when they expand output on a permanent basis. But the critics say that the larger selling brand advertises more, therefore, it charges more to cover the costs of advertising.

The only way the critics could be right is if diminishing returns in advertising did not exist. By diminishing returns in advertising, I mean that the more a manufacturer spends on advertising, the less he gets in additional sales per dollar of advertising. When there are diminishing returns, the advertising of the larger selling brand is less efficient; it gets fewer sales per dollar. When advertising is less efficient in that sense, the larger advertiser will have a greater incentive to get additional sales by lowering the price. With diminishing returns in advertising, then, the larger selling brand both advertises more and gives greater value per dollar. There is considerable evidence that there are, indeed, diminishing returns in advertising.[2]

There is a second strand of evidence in support of my position. One can successfully predict which products get advertised most intensively by assuming that advertising provides information in the way I have described. It can be shown that it requires more advertising to provide the indirect advertising for experience goods than the direct advertising of search goods. Indeed, the advertising/sales ratios are greater for experience goods than search goods.

There is another important piece of evidence that winners are advertised more. If it is true that the larger-selling brand provides better value per dollar on the average than smaller-selling brands, wouldn't it pay a brand to advertise its rank in its product class more, the higher the rank? Consumers would prefer to buy top sellers rather than bottom sellers. The evidence is overwhelming that more brands say that they are Number One than declare any other rank.

One could argue, I suppose, that consumers are brainwashed into believing that larger-selling brands are better, when the contrary is true. But how could this be? A lot more advertisers have an interest in brainwashing the consumers into believing the contrary. Yet, the "big is beautiful" message wins. The only reasonable explanation is that this is the message which is confirmed by the consumers' own experiences. The brainwashing explanation is particularly hard to accept, given the industries in which brands most frequently advertise their Number One status. It pays consumers to make much more thoughtful decisions about durables than non-durables because the cost to them of making a mistake is so much greater in that case. Yet, the "I am Number One" advertising occurs more frequently for durables than for non-durables.[3] Even more convincing is the evidence that the advertising of Number One rank is not confined to possibly gullible consumers. That same message is used in advertising directed to businessmen. They too must have been brainwashed if the critics are right. But such soft-headed businessmen could hardly survive in the market.

The evidence seems inescapable: larger-selling brands do, on the whole, provide the better value per dollar. The evidence also shows — and all would admit — that larger-selling brands advertise more. In consequence, the more advertised brands are likely to be the better buys.

It is frequently alleged that advertised brands are really no better than non-advertised brands. A case that is often cited in this connection is Bayer Aspirin. But aspirins do, indeed, vary in their physical characteristics. Soft aspirins dissolve in the stomach both more rapidly and more certainly than hard aspirins. In consequence, the soft aspirin are better. They are also more expensive to produce. It is no accident that the most heavily advertised brand of aspirin is a soft aspirin. Of course, there are also non-advertised soft aspirins that sell for less than Bayer Aspirin. But the issue is not whether the best unadvertised aspirin is as good as the most heavily advertised aspirin. The issue is whether purchasing one of the more heavily advertised aspirins at random gives one a better product, on the average, than getting an unadvertised aspirin at random. The existence of unadvertised soft aspirin, when the consumer does not know which aspirin fits into that category, is of little help to the consumer.

Advertising can provide this information without consumers being aware of its doing so. Advertising as information does not require intelligent consumer response to advertising, though it provides a basis for such intelligent response. Consumers who actually believe paid endorsements are the victims of the most benign form of deception. They are deceived into doing what they should do anyhow.

It does not pay consumers to make very thoughtful decisions about advertising. They can respond to advertising for the most ridiculous, explicit reasons and still do what they would have done if they made the most careful judgments about their behavior. "Irrationality" is rational if it is cost-free.

Whatever their explicit reasons, consumers' ultimate reason for responding to advertising is their self-interest in so doing. That is, it is no mere coincidence that thoughtful and unthoughtful judgments lead to the same behavior. If it were not in consumers' self-interest to respond to advertising, they would no longer pay attention to advertising. It is in this context that we can examine the question of whether true or false advertising statements should be protected by the right of free speech.

DECEPTIVE ADVERTISING, REGULATION, AND FREE SPEECH

A lot of people think that there is far too much deceptive advertising and that active government intervention, policing every advertisement, is necessary to improve advertising.

But the amount of deceptiveness in advertising can be easily exaggerated if one simply looks at the incentives of the advertiser to deceive without considering the incentives of consumers not to be deceived. The circumstances under which advertisers have the greatest incentives to deceive if consumers believed them are precisely the circumstances under which consumers would be least inclined to believe advertising. Deception requires not only a misleading or untrue statement but somebody ready to be misled by that statement.

One possible source of deceptive advertising is consumer confusion. Though the decision rules that consumers need follow to avoid being deceived by advertising are relatively simple, some consumers will possibly be confused. They will possibly be gullible when they should not be, and inappropriately skeptical at other times.

But let us suppose that one tries to remove these deceptions by active government intervention to prohibit advertising that deceived anybody. Short of eliminating all advertising, such a government role would be self-defeating. Whatever the standards for fraudulence in advertising, it is unlikely that all consumers will know those standards. If the relatively simple decision rules necessary to avoid deception without government intervention are too confusing to some consumers, how much more confusing is the law on fraud? I know of no simple (or complicated) decision rule that would tell a consumer which advertising claims are legally required to be valid and which are not, or which advertisements are legally misleading and which are not.

The more the law protects against fraud, the more people think the law protects against fraud. Misinterpretation of the law's domain will exist, no matter how extensive that domain. Indeed, I believe, there is probably more deceptive advertising when laws on fraud exist than when they do not. Consumer market power generates information from advertising precisely because that information is in the self-interest of producers to provide. Hence, there is little incentive for deceptive advertising under the aegis of consumer market power. In contrast, state police power, involving the expenditure of resources, will never be enforced vigorously enough to eliminate all incentives for fraudulent advertising even in terms of the legal definition of fraud that prevails at the moment.

I am not saying that these laws against deceptive advertising are pointless. I am only asserting that most people have missed their point. The virtue of these laws is not that they reduce deceptive advertising. Rather, it is that they can make more information available to consumers than they would otherwise receive. Take, for example, the law prohibiting the mislabeling of the fabric content of clothing. If that law is sufficiently enforced, consumers will believe that a clothing label is usually correct. This will provide an incentive for some manufacturer to mislabel — unless the law is enforced so vigorously that nobody gains from breaking it (a non-optimal level of law enforcement). In the absence of the law, no one could trust any clothing label that it was not in the self-interest of the producer to specify correctly. Hence, these clothing labels, though incorrect, would not deceive many people. This law is not reducing deception in advertising, but it is enabling consumers to determine in many instances the fabric content of their clothing from the label. Laws can achieve the objective of more direct information at the price of both enforcement costs and costs to the consumer of being deceived where otherwise he would be appropriately distrustful.

Laws against fraudulent advertising are trying to accomplish something very important. People who feel that advertising is often wasteful have some real basis for that feeling. In the same sense that the engineer rates some kinds of engines as inefficient, the economist can declare that advertising is inefficient, that there is a significant potential for the improvement of advertising's performance. Whether that potential can be realized economically or not is, of course, another question. An inefficient motor may be the best motor we have. The indirect information which dominated the advertising of experience goods is inefficient compared to direct information. (By indirect information, I mean the information contained in the *fact* that the brand advertises. This is in contrast to direct information, which is the specific information contained in the advertising message.) First, direct information tells the consumer more, as evidenced by his preference for direct information. Second, more advertising is required to transmit indirect information than direct information. Any increase in the proportion of direct information in the advertising of experience goods would be an increase in advertising's efficiency. Laws that increase the range of believable statements in advertising can help advertising do a better job — unless, of course, they create even worse problems.

There are, indeed, some serious drawbacks to the way in which the Federal Trade Commission has been enforcing the law against fraudulent advertising. Hyperbole plays a useful role in advertising. Exaggeration makes advertising more memorable. The more memorable the advertising, the more efficient it will be from both a private and social point of view, simply because memorability makes advertising perform its information function better. The Federal Trade Commission seems bent on eliminating these exaggerations. Take, for example, the famous case of the sandpaper shave. The FTC ruled that Rapid Shave must cancel this advertisement on the grounds that the conditions of the experiment were not quite kosher. An exceedingly memorable advertisement was eliminated. I believe virtually no new source of direct information was created by this decision.

Take another case on which the FTC would be on stronger ground: advertisements comparing Shell's performances with and without TCP, a gasoline additive. Obviously, it is an irrelevant comparison because Shell without TCP is not an option facing consumers. What harm is done by eliminating this advertisement? Its very existence suggests that it is a memorable advertisement. What good is done by this act? Nothing, by itself. The FTC would have to police carefully all advertisements using any purported tests or surveys to determine both the relevance and the appropriateness of the study design. Even then, it would take consumers quite a while to begin to believe the data quoted by advertisers, because it has been in their interest to distrust these data for so long. This herculean effort by the FTC would, in the process, have the unfortunate by-product of eliminating lots of memorable advertising.

An Alternative Proposal

Can we do better? Laws designed to prevent deceptive advertising are not necessarily the best laws to help open up new bases of believable statements in advertising. The more strictly laws on fraud are interpreted, the less the opportunity for hyperbole, with its very real information payoff to society.

I think it is possible to design laws that at the same time: (1) create new bases for direct information, (2) allow hyperbole as much sway as the market desires, and (3) reduce enforcement costs as compared with the present legal structure. Remember, that is the heart of the problem. Advertisers provide indirect information for experience goods because, in the absence of laws, they are limited in the kinds of direct information they can authenticate. Let us attack that problem in the most direct way possible.

Let us create a dual set of standards for advertising authenticity. Suppose the advertiser were to utter some magic words such as, "We guarantee the validity and relevance of the information contained in this commercial." Then he would be strictly accountable in the courts for that information. Not only must that information be true, but it must not be misleading. Without such magic words, the advertiser is not accountable. Such a legal structure accomplishes the same objective as government authentication of advertising messages. The only differences are that the authentication process occurs after the advertisement rather than before, and the courts are the functioning government agency rather than the FTC.

This system seems to me to be vastly preferable to the present vigorous policing policies of the FTC against purportedly misleading advertising. It permits the authentication of direct information without destroying the effectiveness of indirect information. Certainly, the criterion that the FTC uses in policing advertising—does it mislead any consumers?—seems a self-defeating criterion to employ. The very act of policing makes other advertisements misleading to some consumers who would not have been previously misled.

It seems to me that, worthy though it may be, the goal of converting the advertising of experience quality from indirect information cannot be completely achieved. Therefore, one has to remember that indirect information still has a role to play. One must be on guard against destroying the effectiveness of this indirect information while pursuing the goal of improving the information content of advertising.

In that sense, I am in favor of virtue rather than vice. But vice is not utterly vicious in its consequences. Consumers are, on the whole, better off as a result of being exposed to the essentially empty messages of experience goods advertising. That advertisements contain all sorts of non-credible statements does not prevent these advertisements from serving a social purpose, though that purpose could be better served if more credible statements were part of advertising.

Many of those who attack advertising are really attacking the market system in general. "Advertisers," they say, "are constantly pushing products which consumers either do not need or are positively harmful to them. For shame!" But these are always products that the consumer wants. Otherwise, the advertising could not succeed. In consequence, this is not an attack on advertising so much as an attack on consumer free choice.

It seems to me that consumer choice is the best way we have to determine what is valuable to consumers. Admittedly, consumers will make many mistakes in their choices. The information shortage that confronts consumers in their choice of brands is matched by the information shortage they face in choosing products. But consumers have a strong incentive to try to make the best decision, since their own well-being is at stake.

On the whole, government agencies will have even more severe information problems about which products are valuable to consumers than will consumers themselves. Consumers will, in general, know more about their own idiosyncracies than will any regulatory agency. The only class of cases in which the government could know more is that in which individual differences among consumers are largely irrelevant—not a very large class of cases.

While it is conceivable that in certain situations regulatory agencies will know more than will consumers, it is inconceivable that regulatory agencies will have as strong incentives to make the right choice as will consumers. Government officials are, on the whole, interested in their own well-being. Their own well-being is not closely related to consumer well-being because the voting market is a seriously defective market. People in general will have less incentive to acquire information as voters than they do as consumers, because the individual returns to them of voter information are less than the returns to them as individuals of consumer information. In consequence, government incentives to make decisions maximizing the well-being of voters are generally less than the incentives of consumers to achieve the same objective. In consequence, government decisions are likely to be worse than those of consumers.

The record of government regulation of consumer decisions is not one to encourage the case for government interference with consumer choice. Peltzman, for example, finds that the regulation of drugs by the Federal Drug Administration has made consumers far worse than they would have been otherwise.[4]

As far as advertising is concerned, the attack on consumer choice is particularly pointless. There is nothing in the process of advertising that makes advertisers systematically advertise the products that are bad for consumers rather than the products that are good for consumers. However, there is a process that seems to generate that result.

Advertising volume will be concentrated in the advertising of products that most consumers want rather than the products that satisfy minority taste. Best-sellers will be advertised more than poetry. Most critics of consumer choice would like consumers to have the tastes developed by a combined Ph.D. in English, art history, and music. Even supposing that Mozart provides more enjoyment than Elvis Presley, if one has developed the taste for Mozart, it is not clear whether such investment pays. It is assuredly clear that providing Mozart for people who prefer Presley will not work, since the Presleyites simply will not listen. The critics mistakenly attack advertising as catering to the products that are popular rather than unpopular. They are mistaken not so much in their facts as in the inference they draw from this feature of advertising.

Furthermore, advertising is in many ways more useful to minor segments of the market than to majority groups. The continuation of activities for minor segments of the market is more dependent on advertising than is the continuation of majority activities. The smaller the group, the more difficult is the information problem of matching audience and activity. Anything which reduces that information problem — as does advertising — will tend, therefore, to be of particular benefit to minority groups.

While a critic (if pressed) might admit all of the above, he could still assert that an ethical advertiser should refuse to advertise a product which is not useful to consumers. This would be a largely pointless protest upon the part of advertisers unless many advertisers operated in this fashion since, otherwise, the consequence would be that somebody else, of roughly the same competence, would do the job at roughly the same price. If enough advertisers behaved this way, the price of "unethical" advertising would go up to some extent; but given actual behavior, the ethical advertiser would be making little social contribution.

It is even questionable whether advertising dominated by this much love of humanity is desirable or not. It is a maxim that, in a full-information world, the more people love one another, the better. (Becker's work on marriage and social interaction bears this out.[5]) But with less than full information, this proposition no longer necessarily holds. One of the great advantages of selfish behavior in a market system is that it requires limited information to do a good job. The advertiser simply has to know how to advertise and at what price his services are demanded. But, now, let us convert the advertiser to a philanthropist, to a man who insists that he will advertise only those products which are best for consumers. To do his job right, he must now determine what are the consequences to consumers of all the alternative products that they face. The investments in necessary information required would be enormous, and a great deal of social waste would result. I would also be afraid of the results. The decisions people make about what others ought to consume differ in systematic ways from the decisions they make about what they themselves want. The fun in life tends to be eliminated in decisions for others. Sermons would be advertised heavily. Candy not at all. There are advantages to the maxim: Advertisers, stick to your copy.

NOTES

1. This is borne out by data from the Internal Revenue Service *Source Book of Income,* 1957. For every industry, firms with larger sales advertise more.

2. See Phillip Nelson, "Advertising as Information Once More" (forthcoming).

3. In the May, 1955 issue of *Life* magazine, there were twelve durable and three non-durable "I am Number One" advertisements.

4. Sam Peltzman, "An Evaluation of Consumer Protection Legislation: the 1962 Drug Amendments," *Journal of Political Economy,* Vol. 81, No. 5 (September, 1973), pp. 1049–1051.

5. Gary Becker, "A Theory of Social Interaction," *Journal of Political Economy,* Vol. 82 (November, 1974), pp. 1063–1093.

Theodore Levitt

Advertising and Its Adversaries

The purposeful transmutation of nature's primeval state occupies all people in all cultures and all societies at all stages of development. Everybody everywhere wants to modify, transform, embellish, enrich, and reconstruct the world around him—to introduce into an otherwise harsh or bland existence some sort of purposeful and distorting alleviation. Civilization is man's attempt to transcend his ancient animality; and this includes both art and advertising.

It will be said that art has a higher value for man because it has a higher purpose. True, the artist is interested in philosophic truth or wisdom, and the ad man in selling his goods and services. Michelangelo, when he designed the Sistine chapel ceiling, had some concern with the inspirational elevation of man's spirit, whereas Edward Levy, who designs cosmetics packages, is interested primarily in creating images to help separate the unwary consumer from his loose change.

But this explanation of the difference between the value of art and the value of advertising is not helpful. Is the presence of a "higher" purpose all that redeeming? Consider: while the ad man and designer seek only to convert the audience to their commercial custom, Michelangelo sought to convert its soul. Which is the greater blasphemy? Who commits the greater affront to life—he who dabbles with man's erotic appetites, or he who meddles with man's soul? Which is the easier to judge and justify?

Where have we arrived? Only at some common characteristics of art and advertising. Both are rhetorical, and both literally false; both expound an

Excerpted by John S. Wright from an address before the 1971 annual meeting of the American Association of Advertising Agencies, May 1971. Reprinted by permission of the author.

emotional reality deeper than the "real"; both pretend to "higher" purposes, although different ones; and the excellence of each is judged by its effect on its audience—its persuasiveness, in short. I do not mean to imply that the two are fundamentally the same, but rather that they both represent a pervasive, and I believe *universal*, characteristic of human nature—the human audience *demands* symbolic interpretation in everything it sees and knows.

The consumer refuses to settle for pure operating functionality. For a woman, dusting powder in a sardine can is not the same product as the identical dusting powder in an exotic Paisley package. For the laboratory director, the test equipment behind an engineer-designed panel just isn't as "good" as the identical equipment in a box designed with finesse. We do not choose to buy a particular product; we choose to buy the functional expectations that we attach to it.

Whatever symbols convey and *sustain* these promises in our minds are therefore truly functional. The promises and images which imaginative ads and sculptured packages induce in us are as much the product as the physical materials themselves. To put this another way, these ads and packagings describe the product's fullness for us: in our minds, the product becomes a complex abstraction which is, as Immanuel Kant might have said, the conception of a perfection which has not yet been experienced.

But all promises and images, almost by their very nature, exceed their capacity to live up to themselves. As every eager lover has ever known, the consummation seldom equals the promises which produced the chase.

Everyone in the world is trying in his special personal fashion to solve a primal problem of life—the problem of rising above his own negligibility, of escaping from nature's confining, hostile, and unpredictable reality, of finding significance, security, and comfort in the things he must do to survive. Many of the so-called distortions of advertising, product design, and packaging may be viewed as a paradigm of the many responses that man makes to the conditions of survival in the environment. Without distortion, embellishment, and elaboration, life would be drab, dull, anguished, and at its existental worst.

Consumption is man's most constant activity. It is well that he understands himself as a consumer.

The object of consumption is to solve a problem. Even consumption that is viewed as the creation of an opportunity—like going to medical school or taking a singles-only Caribbean tour—has as its purpose the solving of a problem. At a minimum, the medical student seeks to solve the problem of how to lead a relevant and comfortable life, and the lady on the tour seeks to solve the problem of spinsterhood.

The "purpose" of the product is not what the engineer explicitly says it is, but what the consumer implicitly demands that it shall be. Thus the consumer consumes not things, but expected benefits—not cosmetics, but the satisfactions of the allurements they promise; not quarter-inch drills, but quarter-inch holes, not stock in companies, but capital gains; not numerically controlled milling machines, but trouble-free and accurately smooth metal parts; not low-cal whipped cream, but self-rewarding indulgence combined with sophisticated convenience.

The significance of these distinctions is anything but trivial. Nobody knows this better, for example, than the creators of automobile ads. It is not the generic virtues that they tout, but more likely the car's capacity to enhance its user's status and his access to female prey.

Whether we are aware of it or not, we in effect expect and demand that advertising create these symbols for us to show us what life *might* be, to bring the possibilities that we cannot see before our eyes and screen out the stark reality in which we must live. We insist, as Gilbert put it, that there be added a "touch of artistic verisimilitude to an otherwise bald and unconvincing narrative."

In a world where so many things are either commonplace or standardized, it makes no sense to refer to the rest as false, fraudulent, frivolous, or immaterial. The world works according to the aspirations and needs of its actors, not according to the arcane or moralizing logic of detached critics who pine for another age—an age which, in any case, seems different from today's largely because its observers are no longer children shielded by protective parents from life's implacable harshness.

To understand this is not to condone much of the vulgarity, purposeful duplicity, and scheming half-truths we see in advertising, promotion, packaging, and product design. But before we condemn, it is well to understand the difference between embellishment and duplicity and how extraordinarily uncommon the latter is in our times. The noisy visibility of promotion in our intensely communicating times need not be thoughtlessly equated with malevolence.

Thus the issue is not the prevention of distortion. It is, in the end, to know what kinds of distortions we actually want so that each of our lives is, without apology, duplicity, or rancor, made bearable. This does not mean we must accept out of hand all the commercial propaganda to which we are each day so constantly exposed, or that we must accept out of hand the equation that effluence is the price of affluence, or the simple notion that business cannot and government should not try to alter and improve the position of the consumer vis-à-vis the producer. It takes a special kind of perversity to continue any longer our shameful failure to mount vigorous, meaningful programs to protect the consumer, to standardize product grades, labels, and packages, to improve the consumer's information-getting process, and to mitigate the vulgarity and oppressiveness that is in so much of our advertising.

But the consumer suffers from an old dilemma. He wants "truth," but he also wants and needs the alleviating imagery and tantalizing promises of the advertiser and designer.

Business is caught in the middle. There is hardly a company that would not go down in ruin if it refused to provide fluff, because nobody will buy pure functionality. Yet, if it uses too much fluff and little else, business invites possibly ruinous legislation. The problem therefore is to find a middle way. And in this search, business can do a great deal more than it has been either accustomed or willing to do:

> It can exert pressure to make sure that no single industry "finds reasons" why it should be exempt from legislation restrictions that are reasonable and popular.

> It can support legislation to provide the consumer with the information he needs to make easy comparison between products, packages and prices.

> It can support and help draft improved legislation on quality stabilization.

> It can support legislation that gives consumers easy access to strong legal remedies where justified.

> It can support programs to make local legal aid easily available, especially to the poor and undereducated who know so little about their rights and how to assert them.

> Finally, it can support efforts to moderate and clean up the advertising noise that dulls our senses and assaults our sensibilities.

It will not be the end of the world or of capitalism for business to sacrifice a few commercial freedoms so that we may more easily enjoy our own humanity. Business can and should for its own good, work energetically to achieve this end. But it is also well to remember the limits of what is possible. Paradise was not a free-goods society. The forbidden fruit was gotten at a price.

John Kenneth Galbraith

The Dependence Effect

The notion that wants do not become less urgent the more amply the individual is supplied is broadly repugnant to common sense. It is something to be believed only by those who wish to believe. Yet the conventional wisdom must be tackled on its own terrain. Intertemporal comparisons of an individual's state of mind do rest on technically vulnerable ground. Who can say for sure that the deprivation which afflicts him with hunger is more painful than the deprivation which afflicts him with envy of his neighbor's new car? In the time that has passed since he was poor, his soul may have become subject to a new and deeper searing. And where a society is concerned, comparisons between marginal satisfactions when it is poor and those when it is affluent will involve not only the same individual at different times but different individuals at different times. The scholar who wishes to believe that with increasing affluence there is no reduction in the urgency of desires and goods is not without points for debate. However plausible the case against him, it cannot be proven. In the defense of the conventional wisdom, this amounts almost to invulnerability.

However, there is a flaw in the case. If the individual's wants are to be urgent, they must be original with himself. They cannot be urgent if they must be contrived for him. And above all, they must not be contrived by the process of production by which they are satisfied. For this means that the whole case for the urgency of production, based on the urgency of wants, falls to the ground. One cannot defend production as satisfying wants if that production creates the wants.

Were it so that a man on arising each morning was assailed by demons which instilled in him a passion sometimes for silk shirts, sometimes for kitchenware, sometimes for chamber pots, and sometimes for orange squash, there would be every reason to applaud the effort to find the goods, however odd, that quenched this flame. But should it be that his passion was the result of his first having cultivated the demons, and should it also be that his effort to allay it stirred the demons to ever greater and greater effort, there would be question as to how rational was his solution. Unless restrained by conventional attitudes, he might wonder if the solution lay with more goods or fewer demons.

So it is that if production creates the wants it seeks to satisfy, or if the wants emerge *pari passu* with the production, then the urgency of the wants can no longer be used to defend the urgency of the production. Production only fills a void that it has itself created.

II

The point is so central that it must be pressed. Consumer wants can have bizarre, frivolous, or even immoral origins, and an admirable case can still be made for a society that seeks to satisfy them. But the case cannot stand if it is the process of satisfying wants that creates the wants. For then the individual who urges the importance of production to satisfy these wants is precisely in the position of the onlooker who applauds the efforts of the squirrel to keep abreast of the wheel that is propelled by his own efforts.

That wants are, in fact, the fruit of production will now be denied by few serious scholars. And a considerable number of economists, though not always in full knowledge of the implications, have conceded the point. In the observation cited at the end of the preceding chapter, Keynes noted that needs of "the second class," i.e. those that are the result of efforts to keep abreast or ahead of one's fellow being "may indeed be insatiable; for the higher the general level, the higher still are they."[1] And emulation has always played a considerable role in the views of other economists of want creation. One man's consumption becomes his neighbor's wish. This already means that the process by which wants are satisfied is also the process by which wants are created. The more wants that are satisfied, the more new ones are born.

However, the argument has been carried farther. A leading modern theorist of consumer behavior, Professor Duesenberry, has stated explicitly that "ours is a society in which one of the principal social goals is a higher standard of living . . . [This] has great significance for the theory of consumption . . . the desire to get superior goods takes on a life of its own. It provides a drive to higher expenditure which may even be stronger than that arising out of the needs which are supposed to be satisfied by that expenditure."[2] The implications of this view are impressive. The notion of independently established need now sinks into the background. Because the society sets great store by ability to produce a high living standard, it evaluates people by the products they possess. The urge to consume is fathered by the value system which emphasizes the ability of the society to produce. The more that is produced, the more that must be owned in order to maintain the appropriate prestige. The latter is an important point, for, without going as far as Duesenberry in reducing goods to the role of symbols of prestige in the affluent society, it is plain that his argument fully implies that the production of goods creates the wants that the goods are presumed to satisfy.

III

The even more direct link between production and wants is provided by the institutions of modern advertising and salesmanship. These cannot be reconciled with the notion of independently determined desires, for their central function is to create desires — to bring into being wants that previously did not exist.[3] This is accomplished by the producer of the goods or at his behest. A broad empirical relationship exists between what is spent on production of consumer goods and what is spent in synthesizing the desires for that production. A new consumer product must be introduced with a suitable advertising campaign to arouse an interest in it. The path for an expansion of output must be paved by a suitable expansion in the advertising budget. Outlays for the manufacturing of a product are not more important in the strategy of modern business enterprise than outlays for the manufacturing of demand for the product. None of this is novel. All would be regarded as elementary by the most retarded student in the nation's most primitive school of business administration. The cost of this want formation is formidable. In 1956, total advertising expenditure — though, as noted, not all of it may be assigned to the synthesis of wants — amounted to about ten billion dollars. For some years, it had been increasing at a rate in excess of a billion dollars a year.[4] Obviously, such outlays must be integrated with the theory of consumer demand. They are too big to be ignored.

But such integration means recognizing that wants are dependent on production. It accords to the producer the function both of making the goods and of making the desires for them. It recognizes that production, not only passively through emulation, but actively through advertising and related activities, creates the want it seeks to satisfy.

The businessman and the lay reader will be puzzled over the emphasis which I give to a seemingly obvious point. The point is indeed obvious. But it is one which, to a singular degree, economists have resisted. They have sensed, as the layman does not, the damage to established ideas which lurks in these relationships. As a result, incredibly, they have closed their eyes (and ears) to the most obtrusive of all economic phenomena, namely, modern want creation.

This is not to say that the evidence affirming the dependence of wants on advertising has been entirely ignored. It is one reason why advertising has so long been regarded with such uneasiness by economists. Here is something which cannot be accommodated easily to existing theory. More pervious scholars have speculated on the urgency of desires which are so obviously the fruit of such expensively contrived campaigns for popular attention. Is a new breakfast cereal or detergent so much wanted if so much must be spent to compel in the consumer the sense of want? But there has been little tendency to go on to examine the implications of this for the theory of consumer demand and even less for the importance of production and productive efficiency. These have remained sacrosanct. More often, the uneasiness has been manifested in a general disapproval of advertising and advertising men, leading to the occasional suggestion that they shouldn't exist. Such suggestions have usually been ill received.

And so the notion of independently determined wants still survives. In the face of all the forces of modern salesmanship, it still rules, almost undefiled, in the textbooks. And it still remains the economist's mission — and on few matters is the pedagogy so firm — to seek unquestioningly the means for filling these wants. This being so, production remains of prime urgency. We have here, perhaps, the ultimate triumph of the conventional wisdom in its resistance to the evidence of the eyes. To equal it, one must imagine a humanitarian who was long ago persuaded of the grievous shortage of hospital facilities in the town. He continues to importune the passersby for money for more beds and refuses to notice that the town doctor is deftly knocking over pedestrians with his car to keep up the occupancy.

And in unraveling the complex, we should always be careful not to overlook the obvious. The fact that wants can be synthesized by advertising, catalyzed by salesmanship, and shaped by the discreet manipulations of the persuaders shows that they are not very urgent. A man who is hungry need never be told of his need for food. If he is inspired by his appetite, he is immune to the influence of Messrs. Batten, Barton, Durstine & Osborn. The latter are effective only with those who are so far removed from physical want that they do not already know what they want. In this state alone, men are open to persuasion.

IV

The general conclusion of these pages is of such importance for this essay that it had perhaps best be put with some formality. As a society becomes increasingly affluent, wants are increasingly created by the process by which they are satisfied. This may operate passively. Increases in consumption, the counterpart of increases in production, act by suggestion or emulation to create wants. Or producers may proceed actively to create wants through advertising and salesmanship. Wants thus come to depend on output. In technical terms, it can no longer be assumed that welfare is greater at an all-round higher level of production than at a lower one. It may be the same. The higher level of production has, merely, a higher level of want creation necessitating a higher level of want satisfaction. There will be frequent occasion to refer to the way wants depend on the process by which they are satisfied. It will be convenient to call it the Dependence Effect.

We may now contemplate briefly the conclusions to which this analysis has brought us.

Plainly, the theory of consumer demand is a peculiarly treacherous friend of the present goals of economics. At first glance, it seems to defend the continuing urgency of production and our preoccupation with it as a goal. The economist does not enter into the dubious moral arguments about the importance or virtue of the wants to be satisfied. He doesn't pretend to compare mental states of the same or different people at different times and to suggest that one is less urgent than another. The desire is there. That for him is sufficient. He sets about in a workmanlike way to satisfy desire, and accordingly, he sets the proper store by the production that does. Like woman's, his work is never done.

But this rationalization, handsomely though it seems to serve, turns destructively on those who advance it once it is conceded that wants are themselves both passively and deliberately the fruits of the process by which they are satisfied. Then the production of goods satisfies the wants that the consumption of these goods creates or that the producers of goods synthesize. Production induces more wants and the need for more production. So far, in a major tour de force, the implications have been ignored. But this obviously is a perilous solution. It cannot long survive discussion.

Among the many models of the good society, no one has urged the squirrel wheel. Moreover, as we shall see presently, the wheel is not one that revolves with perfect smoothness. Aside from its dubious cultural charm, there are serious structural weaknesses which may one day embarrass us. For the moment, however, it is sufficient to reflect on the difficult terrain which we are traversing. In Chapter VIII, we saw how deeply we were committed to production for reasons of economic security. Not the goods but the employment provided by their production was the thing by which we set ultimate store. Now we find our concern for goods further undermined. It does not arise in spontaneous consumer need. Rather, the dependence effect means that it grows out of the process of production itself. If production is to increase, the wants must be effectively contrived. In the absence of the contrivance, the increase would not occur. This is not true of all goods, but that it is true of a substantial part is sufficient. It means that since the demand for this part would not exist, were it not contrived, its utility or urgency, *ex* contrivance, is zero. If we regard this production as marginal, we may say that the marginal utility of present aggregate output, *ex* advertising and salesmanship, is zero. Clearly the attitudes and values which make production the central achievement of our society have some exceptionally twisted roots.

Perhaps the thing most evident of all is how new and varied become the problems we must ponder when we break the nexus with the work of Ricardo and face the economics of affluence of the world in which we live. It is easy to see why the conventional wisdom resists so stoutly such change. It is a far, far better thing to have a firm anchor in nonsense than to put out on the troubled seas of thought.

NOTES

1. J. M. Keynes, *Essays in Persuasion,* "Economic Possibilities for Our Grandchildren" (London: Macmillan, 1931), p. 365.

2. James S. Duesenberry, *Income, Saving and the Theory of Consumer Behavior* (Cambridge, Mass.: Harvard University Press, 1949), p. 28.

3. Advertising is not a simple phenomenon. It is also important in competitive strategy and want creation is, ordinarily, a complementary result of efforts to shift the demand curve of the individual firm at the expense of others or (less importantly, I think) to change its shape by increasing the degree of product differentiation. Some of the failure of economists to identify advertising with want creation may be attributed to the undue attention that its use in purely competitive strategy has attracted. It should be noted, however, that the competitive manipulation of consumer desire is only possible, at least on any appreciable scale, when such need is not strongly felt.

4. In 1966, they were 16.5 billion dollars. The increase in the three years preceding was also by about one billion a year.

Robert L. Arrington

Advertising and Behavior Control

Consider the following advertisements:

(1) "A woman in *Distinction Foundations* is so beautiful that all other women want to kill her."

(2) Pongo Peach color from Revlon comes "from east of the sun . . . west of the moon where each tomorrow dawns." It is "succulent on your lips" and "sizzling on your finger tips (And on your toes, goodness knows)." Let it be your "adventure in paradise."

(3) "Musk by English Leather—The Civilized Way to Roar."

(4) "Increase the value of your holdings. Old Charter Bourbon Whiskey—The Final Step Up."

(5) Last Call Smirnoff Style: "They'd never really miss us, and it's kind of late already, and it's quite a long way, and I could build a fire, and you're looking very beautiful, and we could have another martini, and it's awfully nice just being home . . . you think?"

(6) A Christmas Prayer. "Let us pray that the blessings of peace be ours—the peace to build and grow, to live in harmony and sympathy with others, and to plan for the future with confidence." New York Life Insurance Company.

These are instances of what is called puffery—the practice by a seller of making exaggerated, highly fanciful or suggestive claims about a product or

From *Journal of Business Ethics*, 1 (February 1982): pp. 3–12. Copyright © 1982 by D. Reidel Publishing Co. Reprinted by permission of *The Journal of Business Ethics*.

service. Puffery, within ill-defined limits, is legal. It is considered a legitimate, necessary, and very successful tool of the advertising industry. Puffery is not just bragging; it is bragging carefully designed to achieve a very definite effect. Using the techniques of so-called motivational research, advertising firms first identity our often hidden needs (for security, conformity, oral stimulation) and our desires (for power, sexual dominance and dalliance, adventure) and then they design ads which respond to these needs and desires. By associating a product, for which we may have little or no direct need or desire, with symbols reflecting the fulfillment of these other, often subterranean interests, the advertisement can quickly generate large numbers of consumers eager to purchase the product advertised. What woman in the sexual race of life could resist a foundation which would turn other women envious to the point of homicide? Who can turn down an adventure in paradise, east of the sun where tomorrow dawns? Who doesn't want to be civilized and thoroughly libidinous at the same time? Be at the pinnacle of success—drink Old Charter. Or stay at home and dally a bit—with Smirnoff. And let us pray for a secure and predictable future, provided for by New York Life, God willing. It doesn't take very much motivational research to see the point of these sales pitches. Others are perhaps a little less obvious. The need to feel secure in one's home at night can be used to sell window air conditioners, which drown out small noises and provide a friendly, dependable companion. The fact that baking a cake is symbolic of giving birth to a baby used to prompt advertisements for cake mixes which glamorized the "creative" housewife. And other strategies, for example involving cigar symbolism, are a bit too crude to mention, but are nevertheless very effective.

Don't such uses of puffery amount to manipulation, exploitation, or downright control? In his very popular book *The Hidden Persuaders*, Vance Packard points out that a number of people in the advertising world have frankly admitted as much:

> As early as 1941 Dr. Dichter (an influential advertising consultant) was exhorting ad agencies to recognize themselves for what they actually were—"one of the most advanced laboratories in psychology." He said the successful ad agency "manipulates human motivations and desires and develops a need for goods with which the public has at one time been unfamiliar—perhaps even undesirous of purchasing." The following year *Advertising Agency* carried an ad man's statement that psychology not only holds promise for understanding people but "ultimately for controlling their behavior."[1]

Such statements lead Packard to remark: "With all this interest in manipulating the customer's subconscious, the old slogan 'let the buyer beware' began taking on a new and more profound meaning."[2]

B. F. Skinner, the high priest of behaviorism, has expressed a similar assessment of advertising and related marketing techniques. Why, he asks, do we buy a certain kind of car?

Perhaps our favorite T.V. program is sponsored by the manufacturer of that car. Perhaps we have seen pictures of many beautiful or prestigeful persons driving it—in pleasant or glamorous places. Perhaps the car has been designed with respect to our motivational patterns: the device on the hood is a phallic symbol; or the horsepower has been stepped up to please our competitive spirit in enabling us to pass other cars swiftly (or, as the advertisements say, 'safely'). The concept of freedom that has emerged as part of the cultural practice of our group makes little or no provision for recognizing or dealing with these kinds of control.[3]

In purchasing a car we may think we are free, Skinner is claiming, when in fact our act is completely controlled by factors in our environment and in our history of reinforcement. Advertising is one such factor.

A look at some other advertising techniques may reinforce the suspicion that Madison Avenue controls us like so many puppets. T.V. watchers surely have noticed that some of the more repugnant ads are shown over and over again, *ad nauseum*. My favorite, or most hated, is the one about A-1 Steak Sauce which goes something like this: Now, ladies and gentlemen, what *is* hamburger? It has succeeded in destroying my taste for hamburger, but it has surely drilled the name of A-1 Sauce into my head. And that is the point of it. Its very repetitiousness has generated what ad theorists call *information*. In this case it is indirect information, information derived not from the content of what is said but from the fact that it is said so often and so vividly that it sticks in one's mind—i.e., the information yield has increased. And not only do I always remember A-1 Sauce when I go to the grocers, I tend to assume that any product advertised so often has to be good—and so I usually buy a bottle of the stuff.

Still another technique: On a recent show of the television program 'Hard Choices' it was demonstrated how subliminal suggestion can be used to control customers. In a New Orleans department store, messages to the effect that shoplifting is wrong, illegal, and subject to punishment were blended into the Muzak background music and masked so as not to be consciously audible. The store reported a dramatic drop in shoplifting. The program host conjectured whether a logical extension of this technique would be to broadcast subliminal advertising messages to the effect that the store's $15.99 sweater special is the "bargain of a lifetime." Actually, this application of subliminal suggestion to advertising has already taken place. Years ago in New Jersey a cinema was reported to have flashed subthreshold ice cream ads onto the screen during regular showings of the film—and yes, the concession stand did a landslide business.[4]

Puffery, indirect information transfer, subliminal advertising—are these techniques of manipulation and control whose success shows that many of us have forfeited our autonomy and become a community, or herd, of packaged souls?[5] The business world and the advertising industry certainly reject this interpretation of their efforts. *Business Week,* for example, dismissed the charge that the science of behavior, as utilized by advertising, is engaged in human engineering and manipulation. It editorialized to the effect that "it is hard to find anything very sinister about a science whose principle conclusion is that you get along with people by giving them what they want."[6] The theme is familiar: businesses just give the consumer what he/she wants; if they didn't they wouldn't stay in business very long. Proof that the consumer wants the products advertised is given by the fact that he buys them, and indeed often returns to buy them again and again.

The techniques of advertising we are discussing have had their more intellectual defenders as well. For example, Theodore Levitt, Professor of Business Administration at the Harvard Business School, has defended the practice of puffery and the use of techniques depending on motivational research.[7] What would be the consequences, he asks us, of deleting all exaggerated claims and fanciful associations from advertisements? We would be left with literal descriptions of the empirical characteristics of products and their functions. Cosmetics would be presented as facial and bodily lotions and powders which produce certain odor and color changes; they would no longer offer hope or adventure. In addition to the fact that these products would not then sell as well, they would not, according to Levitt, please us as much either. For it is hope and adventure we want when we buy them. We want automobiles not just for transportation, but for the feelings of power and status they give us. Quoting T. S. Eliot to the effect that "Human kind cannot bear very much reality," Levitt argues that advertising is an effort to "transcend nature in the raw," to "augment what nature has so crudely fashioned." He maintains that "everybody everywhere wants to modify, transform, embellish, enrich and reconstruct the world around him." Commerce takes the same liberty with reality as the artist and the priest—in all three instances the purpose is "to influence the audience by creating illusions, symbols, and implications that promise more than pure functionality." For example, "to amplify the temple in men's eyes, (men of cloth) have, very realistically, systematically sanctioned the embellishment of the houses of the gods with the same kind of luxurious design and expensive decoration that Detroit puts into a Cadillac." A poem, a temple, a Cadillac—they all elevate our spirits, offering imaginative promises and symbolic interpretations of our mundane activities. Seen in this light, Levitt claims, "Embellishment and distortion are among advertising's legitimate and socially desirable purposes." To reject these techniques of advertising would be "to deny man's honest needs and values."

Phillip Nelson, a Professor of Economics at SUNY-Binghamton, has developed an interesting defense of indirect information advertising.[8] He argues that even when the message (the direct information) is not credible, the fact that the brand is advertised, and advertised frequently, is valuable indirect information for the consumer. The reason for this is that the brands advertised most are more likely to be better buys—losers won't be advertised a lot, for it simply wouldn't pay to do so. Thus even if the advertising claims made for a widely advertised product are empty, the consumer reaps the benefit of the indirect information which shows the product to be a good buy. Nelson goes so far as to say that advertising, seen as information and especially as indirect information, does not require an intelligent human response. If the indirect information has been received and has had its impact, the consumer will purchase the better buy even if his explicit reason for doing so is silly, e.g., he naively believes an endorsement of the product by a celebrity. Even though his behavior is overtly irrational, by acting on the indirect information he is nevertheless doing what he ought to do, i.e., getting his money's worth. "'Irrationality' is rational," Nelson writes, "if it is cost-free."

I don't know of any attempt to defend the use of subliminal suggestion in advertising, but I can imagine one form such an attempt might take. Advertising information, even if perceived below the level of conscious awareness, must appeal to some desire on the part of the audience if it is to trigger a purchasing response. Just as the admonition not to shoplift speaks directly to the superego, the sexual virtues of TR-7's, Pongo Peach, and Betty Crocker cake mix present themselves directly to the id, bypassing the pesky reality principle of the ego. With a little help from our advertising friends, we may remove a few of the discontents of civilization and perhaps even enter into the paradise of polymorphous perversity.[9]

The defense of advertising which suggests that advertising simply is information which allows us to purchase what we want, has in turn been challenged. Does business, largely through its advertising efforts, really make available to the consumer what he/she desires and demands? John Kenneth Galbraith has denied that the matter is as straightforward as this.[10] In his opinion the desires to which business is supposed to respond, far from being original to the consumer, are often themselves created by business. The producers make both the product and the desire for it, and the "central function" of advertising is "to create desires." Galbraith coins the term 'The Dependence Effect' to designate the way wants depend on the same process by which they are satisfied.

David Braybrooke has argued in similar and related ways.[11] Even though the consumer is, in a sense, the final authority concerning what he wants, he may come to see, according to Braybrooke, that he was mistaken in wanting what he did. The statement 'I want x,' he tells us, is not incorrigible but is "ripe for revision". If the consumer had more objective information than he is provided by product puffing, if his values had not been mixed up by motivational research strategies (e.g., the confusion of sexual and automotive values), and if he had an expanded set of choices instead of the limited set offered by profit-hungry corporations, then he might want something quite different from what he presently wants. This shows, Braybrooke thinks, the extent to which the consumer's wants are a function of advertising and not necessarily representative of his real or true wants.

The central issue which emerges between the above critics and defenders of advertising is this: do the advertising techniques we have discussed involve a violation of human autonomy and a manipulation and control of consumer behavior, *or* do they simply provide an efficient and cost-effective means of giving the consumer information on the basis of which he or she makes a free choice. Is advertising information, or creation of desire?

To answer this question we need a better conceptual grasp of what is involved in the notion of autonomy. This is a complex, multifaceted concept, and we need to approach it through the more determinate notions of (a) autonomous desire, (b) rational desire and choice, (c) free choice, and (d) control or manipulation. In what follows I shall offer some tentative and very incomplete analyses of these concepts and apply the results to the case of advertising.

(a) *Autonomous Desire.* Imagine that I am watching T.V. and see an ad for Grecian Formula 16. The thought occurs to me that if I purchase some and apply it to my beard, I will soon look younger—in fact I might even be myself again. Suddenly I want to be myself! I want to be young again! So I rush out and buy a bottle. This is our question: was the desire to be younger manufactured by the commercial, or was it 'original to me' and truly mine? Was it autonomous or not?

F. A. von Hayek has argued plausibly that we should not equate nonautonomous desires, desires which are not original to me or truly mine, with those which are culturally induced.[12] If we did equate the two, he points out, then the desires for music, art, and knowledge could not properly be attributed to a person as original to him, for these are surely induced culturally. The only desires a person would really have as his own in this case would be the purely physical ones for food, shelter, sex, etc. But if we reject the equation of the nonautonomous and the culturally induced, as von Hayek would have us do, then the mere fact that my desire to be young again is caused by the T.V. commercial—surely an instrument of popular culture transmission—does not in and of itself show that this is not my own, autonomous desire. Moreover, even if I never before felt the need to look young, it doesn't follow that this new desire is any less mine. I haven't always liked 1969 Aloxe Corton Burgundy or the music of Satie, but when the desires for these things first hit me, they were truly mine.

This shows that there is something wrong in setting up the issue over advertising and behavior control as a question whether our desires are truly ours *or* are created in us by advertisements. Induced and autonomous desires do not separate into two mutually exclusive classes. To obtain a better understanding of autonomous and nonautonomous desires, let us consider some cases of a desire which a person does not *acknowledge* to be his own even though he *feels* it. The kleptomaniac has a desire to steal which in many instances he repudiates, seeking by treatment to rid himself of it. And if I were suddenly overtaken by a desire to attend an REO concert, I would immediately disown this desire, claiming possession or momentary madness. These are examples of desires which one might have but with which one would not identify. They are experienced as foreign to one's character or personality. Often a person will have what Harry Frankfurt calls a second-order desire, that is to say, a desire *not* to have another desire.[13] In such cases, the first-order desire is thought of as being nonautonomous, imposed on one. When on the contrary a person has a second-order desire to maintain and fulfill a first-order desire, then the first-order desire is truly his own, autonomous, original to him. So there is in fact a distinction between desires which are the agent's own and those which are not, but this is not the same as the distinction between desires which are innate to the agent and those which are externally induced.

If we apply the autonomous/nonautonomous distinction derived from Frankfurt to the desires brought about by advertising, does this show that advertising is responsible for creating desires which are not truly the agent's own? Not necessarily, and indeed not often. There may be some desires I feel which I have picked up from advertising and which I disown—for instance, my desire for A-1 Steak Sauce. If I act on these desires it can be said that I have been led by advertising to act in a way foreign to my nature. In these cases my autonomy has been violated. But most of the desires induced by advertising I fully accept, and hence most of these desires are autonomous. The most vivid demonstration of this is that I often return to purchase the same product over and over again, without regret or remorse. And when I don't, it is more likely that the desire has just faded than that I have repudiated it. Hence, while advertising may violate my autonomy by leading me to act on desires which are not truly mine, this seems to be the exceptional case.

Note that this conclusion applies equally well to the case of subliminal advertising. This may generate subconscious desires which lead to purchases, and the act of purchasing these goods may be inconsistent with other conscious desires I have, in which case I might repudiate my behavior and by implication the subconscious cause of it. But my subconscious desires may not be inconsistent in this way with my conscious ones; my id may be cooperative and benign rather than hostile and malign.[14] Here again, then, advertising may or may not produce desires which are "not truly mine."

What are we to say in response to Braybrooke's argument that insofar as we might choose differently if advertisers gave us better information and more options, it follows that the desires we have are to be attributed more to advertising than to our own real inclinations? This claim seems empty. It amounts to saying that if the world we lived in, and we ourselves, were different, then we would want different things. This is surely true, but it is equally true of our desire for shelter as of our desire for Grecian Formula 16. If we lived in a tropical paradise we would not need or desire shelter. If we were immortal, we would not desire youth. What is true of all desires can hardly be used as a basis for criticizing some desires by claiming that they are nonautonomous.

(b) *Rational Desire and Choice.* Braybrooke might be interpreted as claiming that the desires induced by advertising are often irrational ones in the sense that they are not expressed by an agent who is in full possession of the facts about the products advertised or about the alternative products which might be offered him. Following this line of thought, a possible criticism of advertising is that it leads us to act on irrational desires or to make irrational choices. It might be said that our autonomy has been violated by the fact that we are prevented from following our rational wills or that we have been denied the "positive freedom" to develop our true, rational selves. It might be claimed that the desires induced in us by advertising are false desires in that they do not reflect our essential, i.e., rational, essence.

The problem faced by this line of criticism is that of determining what is to count as rational desire or rational choice. If we require that the desire or choice be the product of an awareness of *all* the facts about the product, then surely every one of us is always moved by irrational desires and makes nothing but irrational choices. How could we know all the facts about a product? If it be required only that we possess all of the *available* knowledge about the product advertised, then we still have to face the problem that not all available knowledge is *relevant* to a rational choice. If I am purchasing a car, certain engineering features will be, and others won't be, relevant, *given what I want in a car*. My prior desires determine the relevance of information. Normally a rational desire or choice is thought to be one based upon relevant information, and information is relevant if it shows how other, prior desires may be satisfied. It can plausibly be claimed that it is such prior desires that advertising agencies acknowledge, and that the agencies often provide the type of information that is relevant in light of these desires. To the extent that this is true, advertising does not inhibit our rational wills or our autonomy as rational creatures.

It may be urged that much of the puffery engaged in by advertising does not provide relevant information at all but rather makes claims which are not factually true. If someone buys Pongo Peach in anticipation of an adventure in paradise, or Old Charter in expectation of increasing the value of his holdings, then he/she is expecting purely imaginary benefits. In no literal sense will the one product provide adventure and other increased capital. A purchasing decision based on anticipation of imaginary benefits is not, it might be said, a rational decision, and a desire for imaginary benefits is not a rational desire.

In rejoinder it needs to be pointed out that we often wish to purchase subjective effects which in being subjective are nevertheless real enough. The feeling of adventure or of enhanced social prestige and value are examples of subjective effects promised by advertising. Surely many (most?) advertisements directly promise subjective effects which their patrons actually desire (and obtain when they purchase the product), and thus the ads provide relevant information for relevant choice. Moreover, advertisements often provide accurate indirect information on the basis of which a person who wants a certain subjective effect rationally chooses a product. The mechanism involved here is as follows.

To the extent that a consumer takes an advertised product to offer a subjective effect and the product does not, it is unlikely that it will be purchased again. If this happens in a number of cases, the product will be taken off the market. So here the market regulates itself, providing the mechanism whereby misleading advertisements are withdrawn and misled customers are no longer misled. At the same time, a successful bit of puffery, being one which leads to large and repeated sales, produces satisfied customers and more advertising of the product. The indirect information provided by such large-scale advertising efforts provides a measure of verification to the consumer who is looking for certain kinds of subjective effect. For example, if I want to feel well dressed and in fashion, and I consider buying an Izod Alligator shirt which is advertised in all of the magazines and newspapers, then the fact that other people buy it and that this leads to repeated advertisements shows me that the desired subjective effect is real enough and that I indeed will be well dressed and in fashion if I purchase the shirt. The indirect information may lead to a rational decision to purchase a product because the information testifies to the subjective effect that the product brings about.[15]

Some philosophers will be unhappy with the conclusion of this section, largely because they have a concept of true, rational, or ideal desire which is not the same as the one used here. A Marxist, for instance, may urge that any desire felt by alienated man in a capitalist society is foreign to his true nature. Or an existentialist may claim that the desires of inauthentic men are themselves inauthentic. Such concepts are based upon general theories of human nature which are unsubstantiated and perhaps incapable of substantiation. Moreover, each of these theories is committed to a concept of an ideal desire which is normatively debatable and which is distinct from the ordinary concept of a rational desire as one based upon relevant information. But it is in the terms of the ordinary concept that we express our concern that advertising may limit our autonomy in the sense of leading us to act on irrational desires, and if we operate with this concept we are driven again to the conclusion that advertising may lead, but probably most often does not lead, to an infringement of autonomy.

(c) *Free Choice.* It might be said that some desires are so strong or so covert that a person cannot resist them, and that when he acts on such desires he is not acting freely or voluntarily but is rather the victim of irresistible impulse or an unconscious drive. Perhaps those who condemn advertising feel that it produces this kind of desire in us and consequently reduces our autonomy.

This raises a very difficult issue. How do we distinguish between an impulse we *do* not resist and one we *could* not resist, between freely giving in to a desire and succumbing to one? I have argued elsewhere that the way to get at this issue is in terms of the notion of acting for a reason.[16] A person acts or chooses freely if he does so for a reason, that is, if he can adduce considerations which justify in his mind the act in question. Many of our actions are in fact free because this condition frequently holds. Often, however, a person will act from habit, or whim, or impulse, and on these occasions he does not have a reason in mind. Nevertheless he often acts voluntarily in these instances, i.e., he could have acted otherwise. And this is because if there *had been* a reason for acting otherwise of which he was aware, he would in fact have done so. Thus acting from habit or impulse is not necessarily to act in an involuntary manner. If, however, a person is aware of a good reason to do *x* and still follows his impulse to do *y*, then he can be said to be impelled by irresistible impulse and hence to act involuntarily. Many kleptomaniacs can be said to act involuntarily, for in spite of their knowledge that they likely will be caught and their awareness that the goods they steal have little utilitarian value to them, they nevertheless steal. Here their "out of character" desires have the upper hand, and we have a case of compulsive behavior.

Applying these notions of voluntary and compulsive behavior to the case of behavior prompted by advertising, can we say that consumers influenced by advertising act compulsively? The unexciting answer is: sometimes they do, sometimes not. I may have an overwhelming, T.V. induced urge to owns a Mazda RX-7, all the while realizing that I can't afford one without severely reducing my family's caloric intake to a dangerous level. If, aware of this good reason not to purchase the car, I nevertheless do so, this shows that I have been the victim of T.V. compulsion. But if I have the urge, as I assure you I do, and don't act on it, or if in some other possible world I could afford an RX-7, then I have not been the subject of undue influence by Mazda advertising. Some Mazda RX-7 purchasers act compulsively; others do not. The Mazda advertising effort *in general* cannot be condemned, then, for impairing its customers' autonomy in the sense of limiting free or voluntary choice. Of course the question remains what should be done about the fact that advertising may and does *occasionally* limit free choice. We shall return to this question later.

In the case of subliminal advertising we may find an individual whose subconscious desires are activated by advertising into doing something his calculating, reasoning ego does not approve. This would be a case of compulsion. But most of us have a benevolent subconsciousness which does not overwhelm our ego and its reasons for action. And therefore most of us can respond to subliminal advertising without thereby risking our autonomy. To be sure, if some advertising firm developed a subliminal technique which drove all of us to purchase Lear jets, thereby reducing our caloric intake to the zero point, then we would have a case of advertising which could properly be censured for infringing our right to autonomy. We should acknowledge that this is possible, but at the same time we should recognize that it is not an inherent result of subliminal advertising.

(d) *Control or Manipulation.* Briefly let us consider the matter of control and manipulation. Under what conditions do these activities occur? In a recent paper on 'Forms and Limits of Control' I suggested the following criteria:[17]

A person *C* controls the behavior of another person *P iff*

(1) C intends P to act in a certain way A;

(2) C's intention is causally effective in bringing about A; and

(3) C intends to ensure that all of the necessary conditions of A are satisfied.

These criteria may be elaborated as follows. To control another person it is not enough that one's actions produce certain behavior on the part of that person; additionally one must intend that this happen. Hence control is the intentional production of behavior. Moreover, it is not enough just to have the intention; the intention must give rise to conditions which bring about the intended effect. Finally, the controller must intend to establish by his actions any otherwise unsatisfied necessary conditions for the production of the intended effect. The controller is not just influencing the outcome, not just having input; he is as it were guaranteeing that the sufficient conditions for the intended effect are satisfied.

Let us apply these criteria of control to the case of advertising and see what happens. Conditions (1) and (3) are crucial. Does the Mazda manufacturing company or its advertising agency intend that I buy an RX-7? Do they intend that a certain number of people buy the car? *Prima facie* it seems more appropriate to say that they *hope* a certain number of people will buy it, and hoping and intending are not the same. But the difficult term here is "intend." Some philosophers have argued that to intend A it is necessary only to desire that A happen and to believe that it will. If this is correct, and if marketing analysis gives the Mazda agency a reasonable belief that a certain segment of the population will buy its product, then, assuming on its part the desire that this happen, we have the conditions necessary for saying that the agency intends that a certain segment purchase the car. If I am a member of this segment of the population, would it then follow that the agency intends that I purchase an RX-7? Or is control referentially opaque? Obviously we have some questions here which need further exploration.

Let us turn to the third condition of control, the requirement that the controller intend to activate or bring about any otherwise unsatisfied necessary conditions for the production of the intended effect. It is in terms of this condition that we are able to distinguish brainwashing from liberal education. The brainwasher arranges all of the necessary conditions for belief. On the other hand, teachers (at least those of liberal persuasion), seek only to influence their students—to provide them with information and enlightenment which they may absorb *if they wish*. We do not normally think of teachers as controlling their students, for the students' performances depend as well on their own interests and inclinations.

Now the advertiser—does he control, or merely influence, his audience? Does he intend to ensure that all of the necessary conditions for purchasing behavior are met, or does he offer information and symbols which are intended to have an effect only *if* the potential purchaser has certain desires? Undeniably advertising induces some desires, and it does this intentionally, but more often than not it intends to induce a desire for a particular object, *given* that the purchaser already has other desires. Given a desire for youth, or power, or adventure, or ravishing beauty, we are led to desire Grecian Formula 16, Mazda RX-7's, Pongo Peach, and Distinctive Foundations. In this light, the advertiser is influencing us by appealing to independent desires we already have. He is not creating those basic desires. Hence it seems appropriate to deny that he intends to produce all of the necessary conditions for our purchases, and appropriate to deny that he controls us.[18]

Let me summarize my argument. The critics of advertising see it as having a pernicious effect on the autonomy of consumers, as controlling their lives and manufacturing their very souls. The defense claims that advertising only offers information and in effect allows industry to provide consumers with what they want. After developing some of the philosophical dimensions of this dispute, I have come down tentatively in favor of the advertisers. Advertising may, but certainly does not always or even frequently, control behavior, produce compulsive behavior, or create wants which are not rational or are not truly those of the consumer. Admittedly it may in individual cases do all of these things, but it is innocent of the charge of intrinsically or necessarily doing them or even, I think, of often doing so. This limited potentiality, to be sure, leads to the question whether advertising should be abolished or severely curtailed or regulated because of its potential to harm a few poor souls in the above ways. This is a very difficult question, and I do not pretend to have the answer. I only hope that the above discussion, in showing some of the kinds of harm that can be done by advertising and by indicating the likely limits of this harm, will put us in a better position to grapple with the question.

NOTES

1. Vance Packard, *The Hidden Persuaders* (Pocket Books, New York, 1958), pp. 20–21.

2. *Ibid.,* p. 21.

3. B. F. Skinner, 'Some Issues Concerning the Control of Human Behavior: A Symposium', in Karlins and Andrews (eds.), *Man Controlled* (The Free Press, New York, 1972).

4. For provocative discussions of subliminal advertising, see W. B. Key, *Subliminal Seduction* (The New American Library, New York, 1973), and W. B. Key, *Media Sexploitation* (Prentice-Hall, Inc., Englewood Cliffs, N.J., 1976).

5. I would like to emphasize that in what follows I am discussing these techniques of advertising from the standpoint of the issue of control and not from that of deception. For a good and recent discussion of the many dimensions of possible deception in advertising, see Alex C. Michalos, 'Advertising: Its Logic, Ethics, and Economics' in J. A. Blair and R. H. Johnson (eds.), *Informal Logic: The First International Symposium* (Edgepress, Pt. Reyes, Calif., 1980).

6. Quoted by Packard, *op. cit.,* p. 220.

7. Theodore Levitt, 'The Morality (?) of Advertising', *Harvard Business Review* 48 (1970), 84–92.

8. Phillip Nelson, 'Advertising and Ethics', in Richard T. De George and Joseph A. Pichler (eds.), *Ethics, Free Enterprise, and Public Policy* (Oxford University Press, New York, 1978), pp. 187–198.

9. For a discussion of polymorphous perversity, see Norman O. Brown, *Life Against Death* (Random House, New York, 1969), Chapter III.

10. John Kenneth Galbraith, *The Affluent Society*; reprinted in Tom L. Beauchamp and Norman E. Bowie (eds.), *Ethical Theory and Business* (Prentice-Hall, Englewood Cliffs, 1979), pp. 496–501.

11. David Braybrooke, 'Skepticism of Wants, and Certain Subversive Effects of Corporations on American Values', in Sidney Hook (ed.), *Human Values and Economic Policy* (New York University Press, New York, 1967); reprinted in Beauchamp and Bowie (eds.), *op. cit.*, pp. 502–508.

12. F. A. von Hayek, 'The *Non Sequitur* of the "Dependence Effect",' *Southern Economic Journal* (1961); reprinted in Beauchamp and Bowie (eds.), *op. cit.*, pp. 508–512.

13. Harry Frankfurt, 'Freedom of the Will and the Concept of a Person', *Journal of Philosophy* LXVIII (1971), 5–20.

14. For a discussion of the difference between a malign and a benign subconscious mind, see P. H. Nowell-Smith, 'Psycho-analysis and Moral Language', *The Rationalist Annual* (1954); reprinted in P. Edwards and A. Pap (eds.), *A Modern Introduction to Philosophy*, Revised Edition (The Free Press, New York, 1965), pp. 86–93.

15. Michalos argues that in emphasizing a brand name — such as Bayer Aspirin — advertisers are illogically attempting to distinguish the indistinguishable by casting a trivial feature of a product as a significant one which separates it from other brands of the same product. The brand name is said to be trivial or unimportant "from the point of view of the effectiveness of the product or that for the sake of which the product is purchased" (*op. cit.*, p. 107). This claim ignores the role of indirect information in advertising. For example, consumers want an aspirin *they can trust* (trustworthiness being part of "that for the sake of which the product is purchased"), and the indirect information conveyed by the widespread advertising effort for Bayer aspirin shows that this product is judged trustworthy by many other purchasers. Hence the emphasis on the name is not at all irrelevant but rather is a significant feature of the product from the consumer's standpoint, and attending to the name is not at all an illogical or irrational response on the part of the consumer.

16. Robert L. Arrington, 'Practical Reason, Responsibility and the Psychopath', *Journal for the Theory of Social Behavior* 9 (1979), 71–89.

17. Robert L. Arrington, 'Forms and Limits of Control', delivered at the annual meeting of the Southern Society for Philosophy and Psychology, Birmingham, Alabama, 1980.

18. Michalos distinguishes between appealing to people's tastes and molding those tastes (*op. cit.*, p. 104), and he seems to agree with my claim that it is morally permissible for advertisers to persuade us to consume some article *if* it suits our tastes (p. 105). However, he also implies that advertisers mold tastes as well as appeal to them. It is unclear what evidence is given for this claim, and it is unclear what is meant by *tastes*. If the latter are thought of as basic desires and wants, then I would agree that advertisers are controlling their customers to the extent that they intentionally mold

tastes. But if by molding tastes is meant generating a desire for the particular object they promote, advertisers in doing so may well be appealing to more basic desires, in which case they should not be thought of as controlling the consumer.

SELECTED BIBLIOGRAPHY

Aaker, D., and Myers, J. *Advertising Management.* Englewood Cliffs, N.J.: Prentice-Hall, 1975, ch. 17.

Carrubba, E. *Assuring Product Integrity.* Lexington, Mass.: Lexington Books, 1975.

Fletcher, G. "Fairness and Utility in Tort Theory." *Harvard Law Review,* 85 (January, 1972), 537–73.

Gardner, D. "Deception in Advertising: A Conceptual Approach." *Journal of Marketing,* 39 (January, 1975), 40–46.

Gray, I. *Product Liability: A Management Response.* New York: Amacom, 1975, ch. 6.

Greyser, S. "Advertising: Attacks and Counters." *Harvard Business Review,* 50 (March 10, 1972), 22 ff.

Hayek, F. "The Non-Sequitur of the Dependence Effect." *Southern Economic Journal,* 27 (1961), 346–348.

Leiser, B. "The Ethics of Advertising," in *Ethics, Free Enterprise, and Public Policy.* De George, R., and Pichler, J., eds. New York: Oxford University Press, 1978, pp. 173–186.

Lowrance, W. *Of Acceptable Risk.* Los Altos, Ca.: William Kaufmann, 1976.

Lucas, J., and Gurman, R. *Truth in Advertising.* New York: American Management Association, 1972.

Moskin, J., ed. *The Case for Advertising.* New York: American Association of Advertising Agencies, 1973.

Posner, R. "Strict Liability: A Comment." *The Journal of Legal Studies,* 2 (January, 1973), 205–21.

Preston, I. *The Great American Blow-up: Puffery in Advertising and Selling.* Madison: University of Wisconsin Press, 1975.

Sandage, C., and Fryburger, V. *Advertising Theory and Practice.* 9th ed. Homewood, Ill.: Richard D. Irwin, 1975.

Stuart, F., ed. *Consumer Protection from Deceptive Advertising.* Hempstead, N.Y.: Hofstra University, 1974.

Truth in Advertising: A Symposium of the Toronto School of Theology. Toronto, 1975.

Velasquez, M. *Business Ethics.* Englewood Cliffs, N.J.: Prentice-Hall, 1982, ch. 6.

8

BUSINESS AND THE ENVIRONMENT

INTRODUCTION

The focus of attention in this chapter will be on the problems arising out of the conflict between economic and environmental needs. A case study is presented that shows how such a conflict arises when a mining company is charged with polluting a nearby stream. Those speaking for the environment describe the impact of the company's operations on the health of citizens in the area as well as on the fish population of the stream, while representatives for the company point to the economic hazards that would result from further efforts at controlling the pollution. The case study also indicates the kinds of legal constraints operating today with respect to these issues. The case of Macklin Mining Company sets the stage for the debate that follows.

Christopher Stone argues in his essay that the notion of a right ought to be extended to cover natural objects in the environment. Having rights would give these objects legal recourse when they are harmed by pollution and other effects of business operations. Stone illustrates what it would mean for natural objects to have rights, and he argues that the proposed extension of rights to the environment would be part of a larger effort to bestow dignity on creatures—e.g., women and blacks—who formerly were thought of as mere things and the property of others. The position Stone develops could serve as a philosophical basis for a radical defense of the needs of the environment over those of the business community.

Wilfred Beckerman looks at the conflict between the economy and the environment in a very different way. He is convinced that extreme environmentalists have exaggerated the facts about the results of economic growth and the facts about pollution. Pollution can be and is being controlled, he argues, and there are no compelling reasons to believe that economic growth will exhaust our resources in a catastrophic or tragic way. Beckerman feels that one should estimate the costs and benefits involved in pollution control, and that while this approach would turn out to justify some control, it would not support the demand of the "eco-doomsters" for a total stop to economic growth or for a pursuit of extreme measures to eradicate pollution.

Robert Arrington analyses the various dimensions of the ongoing debate between environmentalists and the business community with an eye toward highlighting the complexity of the issue and the difficulties of resolving it. He distinguishes factual from normative or moral questions involved in the debate, and he considers in detail two widely used decision procedures for answering the moral questions: the cost-benefit approach and the rights of nature approach. Arrington argues that both of these procedures have severe problems, and he concludes by offering an alternative suggestion for resolving the moral dispute.

Macklin Mining Company

In 1972 Congress passed the Federal Water Pollution Act, which has as its goal "by 1985, to have no discharges of pollutants into the Nation's waters." Although the Act leaves the primary prevention and enforcement responsibilities to the states, it establishes broad guidelines to which states must conform. It requires industries that discharge pollutants to use the "best practicable" control technology by 1977, and the "best available" technology by 1983; consideration is to be given to the cost of control, the age of the industrial facility, the control process used, and the overall environmental impact of the controls. The law also authorizes loans to help small businesses meet water-pollution control requirements. In addition, it sets water quality standards and requires states to set daily load limits for pollutants that will not impair propagation of fish and wildlife. With respect to enforcement, the law requires polluters to keep proper records, to install and use monitoring equipment, and to sample their discharges. States, upon approval of the Federal Environmental Protection Agency (FEPA), are authorized to enter and inspect any polluting facility. Penalties for violating the law range from $2,500 to $25,000 per day and up to one year in prison for the first offense, and up to $50,000 a day and two years in prison for subsequent violations.

Macklin Mining Company is primarily a coal mining company that operates three mines in Tennessee. Macklin's is a marginal operation, with revenue/net income over the last three years of: 1979, $3.2 million/$22 thousand; 1978, $2.7 million/$6 thousand; 1977, $1.6 million/$26 thousand. The company operates the Macklin mine in Bone County, Tennessee, where it employs 42 people. The mine is situated in a low area near Talk Creek, which flows into the Bone River, four miles downstream.

Because of its setting, Macklin has always had a drainage problem with its Talk Creek mine. Prior to 1973, it dumped mine drainage directly into Talk Creek. In 1973 the Tennessee Pollution Control Administration (TPCA) ordered Macklin to cease dumping into Talk Creek. After two years of negotiation, the company proposed to build a settling pond for drainage adjacent to the mouth of the mine and Talk Creek. The pond was finished in 1976 at a cost of $17,000. By 1977 the river was relatively free of contaminants, and residents reported the return of fish to Talk Creek.

In late 1979, however, the TPCA received reports that Talk Creek was again being polluted, and on February 29, 1980 the TPCA filed a complaint against Macklin, claiming that discharge from the firm's settling pond was responsible for extensive pollution of Talk Creek. Macklin responded, claiming that it was not in violation of the Tennessee statute that prohibits discharge of contaminants into state waters.

The TPCA's complaint was filed with the Tennessee Environmental Council (TEC), which hears such cases and, if the charged party is in violation of law, fixes a penalty. The TEC has broad responsibilities and can assess any combination of the following penalties: (1) a maximum penalty of $25,000 for a violation of the State Pollution Control Act, (2) a maximum penalty of $1,500 for each day the violation continues, (3) institution of a program to bring the violator into compliance with the law, and/or (4) an injunction shutting down the firm until compliance is effected.

A hearing before the TEC was held on August 3, 1980. John Benn, regional manager for the TPCA, presented the state's case. He said that the TPCA initially investigated the complaint of nearby residents, who thought Talk Creek was again being polluted. The initial investigation was delayed by a heavy case load, but on November 29, 1979, Benn said, a TPCA inspector found that, although Talk Creek was of relatively clear appearance above the Macklin mine, it was a dark, reddish color below the firm's settling pond. Photographs showing this were submitted. Subsequent water analysis showed the water above the pond to have a slightly alkaline pH of 7.1, whereas below the pond the pH was a somewhat acidic 6.8. Analysis indicated that the dissolved mineral content (mainly iron) below the pond was 132% greater than above it. The suspended solids count was 267% higher below the pond than above it. Analysis also revealed that the water below the pond had a very low dissolved oxygen content, much lower than above the pond. There were also increased sulphate, chloride, bromide, and phosphate concentrations below the pond. Benn stated that the TPCA repeated these experiments on December 14, 1979, again on January 2, 1980, and a third time on January 8, 1980, with very similar results. Benn testified that on January 14, 1980 a Tennessee State biologist sampled Talk Creek and found that, although there was an abundance of organic life and numerous fish above the Macklin mine, there were no fish discovered in shocking experiments just below the settling pond or at four 1,000 yard intervals below the pond. His investigators and scientists concluded that the absence of dissolved oxygen caused the fish to die.

Benn stated that although inspectors could not directly observe a concentrated flow at any one point, an aerial photograph indicated general seepage along the 170 yards that the settling pond fronts Talk Creek. He concluded by saying that in his opinion the environmental damage was extensive, that it had effectively eradicated life in lower Talk Creek.

Speaking for twelve families who live along lower Talk Creek, Jim Clance said they all worried about their drinking water. He added that the Macklin's "only know money" and that the TEC should "shut 'em down or fine 'em to the gills."

Jim Kelly spoke on behalf of the local sportsmen's association. He said that although he was no expert on environmental matters, his association was very concerned with Macklin's pollution of a very fine fishing stream and he wanted to point out certain aspects of the 1972 Federal Water Pollution Act Amendments (FWPAA). According to these amendments "States must establish the total maximum daily load of pollutants . . . that will not impair propagation of fish and wildlife." Since all fish were killed in Talk Creek, Kelly pointed out that Macklin clearly violated the FWPAA, whatever standards the state set. He also pointed out the FWPAA's provision that "Any citizen or group of citizens whose interests may be adversely affected has the right to take court action against anyone violating an effluent standard or limitation, or an order issued by EPA or a State, under the law." Kelly said his association had retained a lawyer and would take legal action against Macklin if the state failed to act. Finally, he noted the FWPAA provision that "A State's permit program is subject to revocation by EPA, after a public hearing, if the State fails to implement the law adequately." He indicated that his association would also pursue this course of action if the state failed to act.

Jim Robbis, manager of the Talk Creek mine, testified for Macklin. He said there was no health hazard: "The state itself indicated it is an iron problem; nobody ever died from rust in their water. And people don't obtain their oxygen by taking in water."

Robbis said that Macklin installed the settling pond in 1976, that it was built to comply with stringent TPCA specifications, that the TPCA approved it upon completion, and that the company had maintained the pond to state standards. He said that Macklin employed Environmental Monitors, an independent firm, to test the site, and that on September 16, 1979 that firm reported to Macklin and the TPCA that Macklin was in full compliance with the law. He noted that Environmental Monitors had tested the site triannually, as required by law, since 1976, and that it had always been in compliance, except for one period during 1977 when heavy rains caused a small spillover of the settling pond. Robbis added that although Environmental Monitors was scheduled at the site during the third week of January 1980, an equipment breakdown caused the testing firm to delay its check until mid-February. By that time the TPCA had filed its complaint.

Robbis said that he noticed some water discoloration in the creek in mid-October 1979, but he recalled that it extended above the mine and thought it was caused by heavy rains. He added that pockets of iron leech out above the mine periodically, and he didn't think anything of the light red tinge.

John Macklin, president of the firm, then spoke. He said he lived in Bone County all his life, and that he knows all the men at the mine—Bone County's third largest employer. He noted the unemployment rate of over 15% there, pointed out the firm's annual wages totaled over $120,000 in 1979, and said he was especially concerned about six employees who were close to pension eligibility.

He said that the TPCA had not conclusively proven its case. But he added that if his company had violated the letter of the law it was completely unintentional.

Mr. Macklin said that although coal has a bright future, the past three years had been difficult: profits were higher ten years ago than in 1979. Compliance with Occupational Safety and Health Administration and environmental legislation had made the Talk Creek operation marginal. A full fine of $25,000, he noted, would wipe out last year's profit. Fines of $1,500 per day could mean bankruptcy for the entire firm. He pointed out that the pricing situation in the coal industry was rapidly improving, and he believed profits would increase substantially in the next year. An injunction shutting down the mine until compliance could be effected would not only penalize employees, it would wipe out Macklin's chance for the profit necessary to keep the mine open. He could agree to a more extensive test procedure to see if the pond was really responsible for the discharge. If so, there was only one reasonable alternative. A new pond would be constructed south of the present one. The present mine and pond would continue as is until the drainage could be shifted to the new pond in a year or so. This was the only way that Macklin could cover the cost of the new pond. This would mean the discharge into Talk Creek would continue, but the creek had snapped back before and would do so again.

For Discussion

If you were the TEC judge, what judgment would you reach in this case? Why? If you believe Macklin is guilty, what penalty would you assess? Why? What factors must be weighed in making your decision?

Wilfred Beckerman

The Case for Economic Growth

For some years now it has been very unfashionable to be in favor of continued long-run economic growth. Unless one joins in the chorus of scorn for the pursuit of continued economic growth, one is in danger of being treated either as a coarse Philistine, who is prepared to sacrifice all the things that make life really worth living for vulgar materialist goods, or as a shortsighted, complacent, Micawber who is unable to appreciate that the world is living on the edge of a precipice. For it is widely believed that if growth is not now brought to a halt in a deliberate orderly manner, either there will be a catastrophic collapse of output when we suddenly run out of key raw materials, or we shall all be asphyxiated by increased pollution. In other words, growth is either undesirable or impossible, or both. Of course, I suppose this is better than being undesirable and inevitable, but the antigrowth cohorts do not seem to derive much comfort from the fact that, although growth would be unpleasant, we cannot—according to them—go on having it anyway.

Anyway, why bother about logical niceties when the emotional appeals of the antigrowth lobby go down so well with large sections of society. There is something in it for everybody. First, the ordinary man—particularly among the middle classes—is attracted by the antigrowth school, which enables him to demonstrate his moral fiber and aesthetic sensibility at no cost. No specialized knowledge is needed in order to hold one's own in cocktail party conversation about the evils of economic growth. Familiarity with one or two of the latest scientific scare stories (but not with their usual

From "The Case for Economic Growth," *Public Utilities Fortnightly,* 94 (September 26, 1974):37–41. Reprinted by permission of Public Utilities Reports, Inc.

subsequent rebuttals), and references to the Minamata disaster in Japan, or the threat to wildlife that one discovered on one's last safari to Kenya, are quite enough. Secondly, radical youth is attracted to the antigrowth movement by the scope for using the environmental destruction argument as a convenient stick with which to beat the soul-destroying corrupting effect of capitalism. The youths who scribble up "carbon monoxide refreshes" on the walls with cigarettes hanging out of the corners of their mouths obviously do not know that the carbon monoxide concentration in the lungs of a cigarette smoker is about ten times as much as in the lungs of a policeman on traffic duty in the center of most cities. Nor do they know that there have been far worse cases of environmental destruction and pollution in the Soviet bloc countries than in the profit-motivated wicked capitalist world. Thirdly, for the mass media, disaster is always good for news, so that impending mass disaster for the whole human race is too good an issue to miss.

Finally, those members of the scientific community who have a guilt complex about some of the effects of scientific discoveries over the past few decades have ample opportunity to impress a captive audience of amateurs with a demonstration of the new sense of social responsibility among scientists.

Hence it is not entirely surprising that the anti-growth movement has gathered so much support over the past few years even though it is 99 per cent nonsense. Not 100 per cent nonsense. There does happen to be a one per cent grain of truth in it.

This is that, in the absence of special government policies (policies that governments are unlikely to adopt if not pushed hard by communal action from citizens), pollution will be excessive. This is because—as economists have known for many decades—pollution constitutes what is known in the jargon as an "externality." That is to say, the costs of pollution are not always borne fully—if at all—by the polluter. The owner of a steel mill that belches smoke over the neighborhood, for example, does not usually have to bear the costs of the extra laundry, or of the ill-health, that may result. Hence, although he is, in a sense, "using up" some of the environment (the clean air) to produce his steel he is getting this particular factor of production free of charge. Naturally, he has no incentive to economize in its use in the same way as he has for other factors of production that carry a cost, such as labor or capital. In all such cases of "externalities," or "spillover effects" as they are sometimes called, the normal price mechanism does not operate to achieve the socially desirable pattern of output or of exploitation of the environment. This defect of the price mechanism needs to be corrected by governmental action in order to eliminate excessive pollution.

But, it should be noted that the "externality" argument, summarized above, only implies that society should cut out "excessive" pollution; not *all* pollution. Pollution should only be cut to the point where the benefits from reducing it further no longer offset the costs to society (labor or capital costs) of doing so.

Mankind has always polluted his environment, in the same way that he has always used up some of the raw materials that he has found in it. When primitive man cooked his meals over open fires, or hunted animals, or fashioned weapons out of rocks and stones, he was exploiting the environment. But to listen to some of the extreme environmentalists, one would imagine that there was something immoral about this (even though God's first injunction to Adam was to subdue the earth and every living thing that exists in it). If all pollution has to be eliminated we would have to spend the whole of our national product in converting every river in the country into beautiful clear-blue swimming pools for fish. Since I live in a town with a 100,000 population but without even a decent swimming pool for the humans, I am not prepared to subscribe to this doctrine.

Anyway, most of the pollution that the environmentalists make such a fuss about, is not the pollution that affects the vast mass of the population. Most people in industrialized countries spend their lives in working conditions where the noise and stench cause them far more loss of welfare than the glamorous fashionable pollutants, such as PCB's or mercury, that the antigrowth lobby make such a fuss about. Furthermore, such progress as has been made over the decades to improve the working conditions of the mass of the population in industrialized countries has been won largely by the action of working-class trade unions, without any help from the middle classes that now parade so ostentatiously their exquisite sensibilities and concern with the "quality of life."

The extreme environmentalists have also got their facts about pollution wrong. In the Western world, the most important forms of pollution are being reduced, or are being increasingly subjected to legislative action that will shortly reduce them. In my recently published book (*"In Defense of Economic Growth"*)[1] I give the facts about the dramatic decline of air pollution in British cities over the past decade or more, as well as the improvement in the quality of the rivers. I also survey the widespread introduction of antipollution policies in most of the advanced countries of the world during the past few years, which will enable substantial cuts to be made in pollution. By comparison with the reductions already achieved in some cases, or envisaged in the near future, the maximum pollution reductions built into the computerized calculations of the Club of Rome[2] can be seen to be absurdly pessimistic.

The same applies to the Club of Rome's assumption that adequate pollution abatement would be so expensive that economic growth would have to come to a halt. For example, the dramatic cleaning up of the air in London cost a negligible amount per head of the population of that city. And, taking a much broader look at the estimates, I show in my book that reductions in pollution many times greater than those which the Club of Rome purports to be the upper limits over the next century can, and no doubt will, be achieved over the next decade in the advanced countries of the world at a cost of only about one per cent to 2 per cent of annual national product.

When confronted with the facts about the main pollutants, the anti-growth lobby tends to fall back on the "risk and uncertainty" argument. This takes the form, "Ah yes, but what about all these new pollutants, or what about undiscovered pollutants? Who knows, maybe we shall only learn in a 100 years' time, when it will be too late, that they are deadly." But life is full of risk and uncertainty. Every day I run the risk of being run over by an automobile or hit on the head by a golf ball. But rational conduct requires that I balance the probabilities of this happening against the costs of insuring against it. It would only be logical to avoid even the minutest chance of some catastrophe in the future if it were costless to do so. But the cost of stopping economic growth would be astronomic. This cost does not merely comprise the loss of any hope of improved standards of living for the vast mass of the world's population, it includes also the political and social costs that would need to be incurred. For only a totalitarian regime could persist on the basis of an antigrowth policy that denied people their normal and legitimate aspirations for a better standard of living.

But leaving aside this political issue, another technical issue which has been much in the public eye lately has been the argument that growth will be brought to a sudden, and hence catastrophic, halt soon on account of the impending exhaustion of raw material supplies. This is the "finite resources" argument; i.e., that since the resources of the world are finite, we could not go on using them up indefinitely.

Now resources are either finite or they are not. If they are, then even zero growth will not save us in the longer run. Perhaps keeping Gross National Product at the present level instead of allowing it to rise by, say, 4 per cent per annum, would enable the world's resources to be spread out for 500 years instead of only 200 years. But the day would still come when we would run out of resources. (The Club of Rome's own computer almost gave the game away and it was obliged to cut off the printout at the point where it becomes clear that, even with zero growth, the world eventually begins to run out of resources!) So why aim only at zero growth? Why not cut output? If resources are, indeed, finite, then there must be some optimum rate at which they should be spread out over time which will be related to the relative importance society attaches to the consumption levels of different generations. The "eco-doomsters" fail to explain the criteria that determine the optimum rate and why they happen to churn out the answer that the optimum growth rate is zero.

And if resources are not, after all, finite, then the whole of the "finite resources" argument collapses anyway. And, in reality, resources are not finite in any meaningful sense. In the first place, what is now regarded as a resource may not have been so in past decades or centuries before the appropriate techniques for its exploitation or utilization had been developed. This applies, for example, to numerous materials now in use but never heard of a century ago, or to the minerals on the sea bed (e.g., "manganese nodules"), or even the sea water itself from which unlimited quantities of certain basic minerals can eventually be extracted.

In the second place, existing known reserves of many raw materials will never appear enough to last more than, say, twenty or fifty years at current rates of consumption, for the simple reason that it is rarely economically worthwhile to prospect for more supplies than seem to be salable, at prospective prices, given the costs of exploitation and so on. This has always been the case in the past, yet despite dramatic increases in consumption, supplies have more or less kept pace with demand. The "finite resource" argument fails to allow for the numerous ways that the economy and society react to changes in relative prices of a product, resulting from changes in the balance between supply and demand.

For example, a major United States study in 1929 concluded that known tin resources were only adequate to last the world ten years. Forty years later, the Club of Rome is worried because there is only enough to last us another fifteen years. At this rate, we shall have to wait another century before we have enough to last us another thirty years. Meanwhile, I suppose we shall just have to go on using up that ten years' supply that we had back in 1929.

And it is no good replying that demand is growing faster now than ever before, or that the whole scale of consumption of raw materials is incomparably greater than before. First, this proposition has also been true at almost any time over the past few thousand years, and yet economic growth continued. Hence, the truth of such propositions tells us nothing about whether the balance between supply and demand is likely to change one way or the other. And it is this that matters. In other words, it may well be that demand is growing much faster than ever before, or that the whole scale of consumption is incomparably higher, but the same applies to supply. For example, copper consumption rose about forty-fold during the nineteenth century and demand for copper was accelerating, around the turn of the century, from an annual average growth rate of about 3.3 per cent per annum (over the whole century) to about 6.4 per cent per annum during the period 1890 to 1910. Annual copper consumption had been only about 16,000 tons at the beginning of the century, and was about 700,000 tons at the end of it; i.e., incomparably greater. But known reserves at the end of the century were greater than at the beginning.

And the same applies to the postwar period. In 1946 world copper reserves amounted to only about 100 million tons. Since then the annual rate of copper consumption has trebled and we have used up 93 million tons. So there should be hardly any left. In fact, we now have about 300 million tons!

Of course, it may well be that we shall run out of some individual materials; and petroleum looks like one of the most likely candidates for exhaustion of supplies around the end of this century — if the price did not rise (or stay up at its recent level). But there are two points to be noted about this. First, insofar as the price does stay up at its recent level (i.e., in the $10 per barrel region) substantial economies in oil use will be made over the next few years, and there will also be a considerable development of substitutes for conventional sources, such as shale oil, oil from tar sands, and new ways of using coal reserves which are, of course, very many times greater than oil reserves (in terms of common energy units).

Secondly, even if the world did gradually run out of some resources it would not be a catastrophe. The point of my apparently well-known story about "Beckermonium" (the product named after my grandfather who failed to discover it in the nineteenth century) is that we manage perfectly well without it. In fact, if one thinks about it, we manage without infinitely more products than we manage with! In other words, it is absurd to imagine that if, say, nickel or petroleum had never been discovered, modern civilization would never have existed, and that the eventual disappearance of these or other products must, therefore, plunge us back into the Dark Ages.

The so-called "oil crisis," incidentally, also demonstrates the moral hypocrisy of the antigrowth lobby. For leaving aside their mistaken interpretation of the technical reasons for the recent sharp rise in the oil price (i.e., it was not because the world suddenly ran out of oil), it is striking that the antigrowth lobby has seized upon the rise in the price of oil as a fresh argument for abandoning economic growth and for rethinking our basic values and so on. After all, over the past two or three years the economies of many of the poorer countries of the world, such as India, have been hit badly by the sharp rise in the price of wheat. Of course, this only means a greater threat of starvation for a few more million people in backward countries a long way away. That does not, apparently, provoke the men of spiritual and moral sensibility to righteous indignation about the values of the growth-oriented society as much as does a rise in the price of gasoline for our automobiles!

The same muddled thinking is behind the view that mankind has some moral duty to preserve the world's environment or supplies of materials. For this view contrasts strangely with the antigrowth lobby's attack on materialism. After all, copper and oil, and so on are just material objects, and it is difficult to see what moral duty we have to preserve indefinitely the copper species from extinction.

Nor do I believe that we have any overriding moral duty to preserve any particular animal species from extinction. After all, thousands of animal species have become extinct over the ages, without any intervention by mankind. Nobody really loses any sleep over the fact that one cannot now see a live dinosaur. How many of the people who make a fuss about the danger that the tiger species may disappear even bother to go to a zoo to look at one? And what about the web-footed Beckermanipus, which has been extinct for about a million years and which, I believe, was far more attractive and far less likely to eat you than is a tiger.

In fact, I am not even sure that the extinction of the human race would matter. The bulk of humanity lead lives full of suffering, sorrow, cruelty, poverty, frustration, and loneliness. One should not assume that because nearly everybody has a natural animal instinct to cling to life they can be said, in any meaningful sense, to be better off alive than if they had never been born. Religious motivations apart, it is arguable that since, by and large (and present company excepted, of course), the human race stinks, the sooner it is extinct the better.

Of course, one cannot criticize the Club of Rome's computer for not examining such moral issues. Nor can one blame the computer for churning out prophecies of doom when doom-laden assumptions – in flagrant conflict with the factual evidence – are fed into it.

The role of the computer in the whole Club of Rome exercise, in fact, was simply to blind the layman with apparent scientifically based discoveries. This is part of a long-run evolution in the evangelical crusade business. The evangelical crusade business, with its forecasts of doom round the corner if we do not mend our ways, is an old tradition in the United States. And over the years all business in the U.S.A. has become increasingly computerized, so that it is not surprising that even the evangelical crusade business has, in the end, become computerized in the form of the Club of Rome's predictions. Given its association with the Vatican, the choice of name for a club operating in the evangelical crusade business is also very fitting. But it is now time to recognize that the various antigrowth arguments are devoid of true moral sense, of logic, and of any real factual basis. It is time now to return to the analysis of the real problems facing society. These include problems of income distribution, food and population control, housing, education, crime, drugs, racial tolerance, international relations, old-age, and many other serious problems.

Whilst economic growth alone may never provide a simple means of solving any of these problems, and it may well be that, by its very nature, human society will always create insoluble problems of one kind or another, the absence of economic growth will only make our present problems a lot worse.

NOTES

1. Jonathan Cape, London. The U.S.A. edition, under the title *"Two Cheers for the Affluent Society,"* is being published by the St. Martins Press in the fall of 1974.

2. The Club of Rome is an informal international organization of educators, scientists, economists, and others which investigates what it conceives to be the overriding problems of mankind. Its study, "The Limits of Growth," has become the bible of no-growth advocates (Potomac Associates, 1707 L Street, N.W., Washington, D.C., $2.75). The study assembled data on known reserves of resources and asked a computer what would happen if demand continued to grow exponentially. Of course, the computer replied everything would break down. The theory of "Beckermonium"

lampoons this. Since the author's grandfather failed to discover "Beckermonium" by the mid-1800's, the world has had no supplies of it at all. Consequently, if the club's equations are followed, the world should have come to a halt many years ago. "Beckermonium's" foundation is that the things man has not yet discovered are far more numerous and of greater importance than what has been discovered. (Editor's Note.)

Christopher D. Stone

Should Trees Have Standing? —
Toward Legal Rights for
Natural Objects

Throughout legal history, each successive extension of rights to some new entity has been, theretofore, a bit unthinkable. We are inclined to suppose the rightlessness of rightless "things" to be a decree of Nature, not a legal convention acting in support of some status quo. It is thus that we defer considering the choices involved in all their moral, social, and economic dimensions. And so the United States Supreme Court could straight-facedly tell us in *Dred Scott* that Blacks had been denied the rights of citizenship "as a subordinate and inferior class of beings, who had been subjugated by the dominant race. . . ."[1] In the nineteenth century, the highest court in California explained that Chinese had not the right to testify against white men in criminal matters because they were "a race of people whom nature has marked as inferior, and who are incapable of progress or intellectual development beyond a certain point . . . between whom and ourselves nature has placed an impassable difference."[2] The popular conception of the Jew in the 13th Century contributed to a law which treated them as "men *ferae naturae*, protected by a quasi-forest law. Like the roe and the deer, they form an order apart."[3] Recall, too, that it was not so long ago that the foetus was "like the roe and the deer." In an early suit attempting to establish a wrongful death action on behalf of a negligently killed foetus (now widely accepted practice), Holmes, then on the Massachusetts Supreme Court, seems to have thought it simply inconceivable "that a man might owe a civil duty and incur a conditional prospective liability in tort to one not yet

From *Southern California Law Review,* 45 (1972):450, 453–460, 463–464, 480–481, 486–487. Reprinted by permission.

in being."[4] The first woman in Wisconsin who thought she might have a right to practice law was told that she did not, in the following terms:

> The law of nature destines and qualifies the female sex for the bearing and nurture of the children of our race and for the custody of the homes of the world. . . . [A]ll life-long callings of women, inconsistent with these radical and sacred duties of their sex, as is the profession of the law, are departures from the order of nature; and when voluntary, treason against it. . . . The peculiar qualities of womanhood, its gentle graces, its quick sensibility, its tender susceptibility, its purity, its delicacy, its emotional impulses, its subordination of hard reason to sympathetic feeling, are surely not qualifications for forensic strife. Nature has tempered woman as little for the juridical conflicts of the court room, as for the physical conflicts of the battle field. . . .[5]

The fact is, that each time there is a movement to confer rights onto some new "entity," the proposal is bound to sound odd or frightening or laughable. This is partly because until the rightless thing receives its rights, we cannot see it as anything but a *thing* for the use of "us"—those who are holding rights at the time. In this vein, what is striking about the Wisconsin case above is that the court, for all its talk about women, so clearly was never able to see women as they are (and might become). All it could see was the popular "idealized" version of *an object it needed.* Such is the way the slave South looked upon the Black. There is something of a seamless web involved: there will be resistance to giving the thing "rights" until it can be seen and valued for itself; yet, it is hard to see it and value it for itself until we can bring ourselves to give it "rights"—which is almost inevitably going to sound inconceivable to a large group of people.

The reason for this little discourse on the unthinkable, the reader must know by now, if only from the title of the paper. I am quite seriously proposing that we give legal rights to forests, oceans, rivers and other so-called "natural objects" in the environment—indeed, to the natural environment as a whole.

As strange as such a notion may sound, it is neither fanciful nor devoid of operational content. In fact, I do not think it would be a misdescription of recent developments in the law to say that we are already on the verge of assigning some such rights, although we have not faced up to what we are doing in those particular terms. We should do so now, and begin to explore the implications such a notion would hold.

TOWARD RIGHTS FOR THE ENVIRONMENT

Now, to say that the natural environment should have rights is not to say anything as silly as that no one should be allowed to cut down a tree. We say human beings have rights, but—at least as of the time of this writing—they can be executed. Corporations have rights, but they cannot plead the fifth amendment; *In re Gault* gave 15-year-olds certain rights in juvenile proceedings, but it did not give them the right to vote. Thus, to say that the environment should have rights is not to say that it should have every right we can imagine, or even the same body of rights as human beings have. Nor is it to say that everything in the environment should have the same rights as every other thing in the environment.

But for a thing to be *a holder of legal rights,* something more is needed than that some authoritative body will review the actions and processes of those who threaten it. As I shall use the term, "holder of legal rights," each of three additional criteria must be satisfied. All three, one will observe, go towards making a thing *count* jurally—to have a legally recognized worth and dignity in its own right, and not merely to serve as a means to benefit "us" (whoever the contemporary group of rights-holders may be). They are, first, that the thing can institute legal actions *at its behest;* second, that in determining the granting of legal relief, the court must take *injury to it* into account; and, third, that relief must run to the *benefit of it.*

The Rightlessness of Natural Objects at Common Law

Consider, for example, the common law's posture toward the pollution of a stream. True, courts have always been able in some circumstances, to issue orders that will stop the pollution. . . . But the stream itself is fundamentally rightless, with implications that deserve careful reconsideration.

The first sense in which the stream is not a rights-holder has to do with standing. The stream itself has none. So far as the common law is concerned, there is in general no way to challenge the polluter's actions save at the behest of a lower riparian—another human being—able to show an invasion of *his* rights. This conception of the riparian as the holder of the right to bring suit has more than theoretical interest. The lower riparians may simply not care about the pollution. They themselves may be polluting, and not wish to stir up legal waters. They may be economically dependent on their polluting neighbor. And, of course, when they discount the value of winning by the costs of bringing suit and the chances of success, the action may not seem worth undertaking. . . .

The second sense in which the common law denies "rights" to natural objects has to do with the way in which the merits are decided in those cases in which someone is competent and willing to establish standing. At its more primitive levels, the system protected the "rights" of the property owning human with minimal weighing of any values: *"Cujus est solum, ejus est usque ad coelum et ad infernos."* Today we have come more and more to make balances—but only such as will adjust the economic best interests of identifiable humans.

. . . None of the natural objects, whether held in common or situated on private land, has any of the three criteria of a rights-holder. They have no standing in their own right; their unique damages do not count in determining outcome; and they are not the beneficiaries of awards. In such fashion, these objects have traditionally been regarded by the common law, and even by all but the most recent legislation, as objects for man to conquer and master and use—in such a way as the law once looked upon "man's" relationships to African Negroes. Even where special measures have been taken to conserve them, as by seasons on game and limits on timber cutting, the dominant motive has been to conserve them *for us*—for the greatest good of the greatest number of human beings. Conservationists, so far as I am aware, are generally reluctant to maintain otherwise. As the name implies, they want to conserve and guarantee *our* consumption and *our* enjoyment of these other living things. In their own right, natural objects have counted for little, in law as in popular movements. . . .

As I mentioned at the outset, however, the rightlessness of the natural environment can and should change; it already shows some signs of doing so.

Toward Having Standing in Its Own Right

It is not inevitable, nor is it wise, that natural objects should have no rights to seek redress in their own behalf. It is no answer to say that streams and forests cannot have standing because streams and forests cannot speak. Corporations cannot speak either; nor can states, estates, infants, incompetents, municipalities or universities. Lawyers speak for them, as they customarily do for the ordinary citizen with legal problems. One ought, I think, to handle the legal problems of natural objects as one does the problems of legal incompetents—human beings who have become vegetable. If a human being shows signs of becoming senile and has affairs that he is *de jure* incompetent to manage, those concerned with his well being make such a showing to the court, and someone is designated by the court with the authority to manage the incompetent's affairs. The guardian (or "conservator" or "committee"—the terminology varies) then represents the incompetent in his legal affairs. Courts make similar appointments when a corporation has become "incompetent"—they appoint a trustee in bankruptcy or reorganization to oversee its affairs and speak for it in court when that becomes necessary.

On a parity of reasoning, we should have a system in which, when a friend of a natural object perceives it to be endangered, he can apply to a court for the creation of a guardianship. . . .

. . . One reason for making the environment itself the beneficiary of a judgment is to prevent it from being "sold out" in a negotiation among private litigants who agree not to enforce rights that have been established among themselves. Protection from this will be advanced by making the natural object a party to an injunctive settlement. Even more importantly, we should make it a beneficiary of money awards. . . .

The idea of assessing damages as best we can and placing them in a trust fund is far more realistic than a hope that a total "freeze" can be put on the environmental status quo. Nature is a continuous theatre in which things and species (eventually man) are destined to enter and exit. In the meantime, co-existence of man and his environment means that *each* is going to have to compromise for the better of both. Some pollution of streams, for example, will probably be inevitable for some time. Instead of setting an unrealizable goal of enjoining absolutely the discharge of all such pollutants, the trust fund concept would (a) help assure that pollution would occur only in those instances where the social need for the pollutant's product (via his present method of production) was so high as to enable the polluter to cover *all* homocentric costs, plus some estimated costs to the environment *per se,* and (b) would be a corpus for preserving monies, if necessary, while the technology developed to a point where repairing the damaged portion of the environment was feasible. Such a fund might even finance the requisite research and development.

I do not doubt that other senses in which the environment might have rights will come to mind, and, as I explain more fully below, would be more apt to come to mind if only we should speak in terms of their having rights, albeit vaguely at first. "Rights" might well lie in unanticipated areas. It would seem, for example, that Chief Justice Warren was only stating the obvious when he observed in *Reynolds v. Sims* that "legislators represent people, not trees or acres." Yet, could not a case be made for a system of apportionment which *did* take into account the wildlife of an area? It strikes me as a poor idea that Alaska should have no more congressmen than Rhode Island primarily *because there are in Alaska all those trees and acres, those waterfalls and forests.* I am not saying anything as silly as that we ought to overrule *Baker v. Carr* and retreat from one man-one vote to a system of one man-or-tree one vote. Nor am I even taking the position that we ought to count each acre, as we once counted each slave, as three-fifths of a man. But I am suggesting that there is nothing unthinkable about, and there might on balance even be a prevailing case to be made for, an electoral apportionment that made some systematic effort to allow for the representative "rights" of non-human life. And if a case can be made for that, which I offer here mainly for purpose of illustration, I suspect that a society that grew concerned enough about the environment to make it a holder of rights would be able to find quite a number of "rights" to have waiting for it when it got to court.

NOTES

1. Dred Scott v. Sandford, 60 U.S. (19 How.) 396, 404–5 (1856).
2. People v. Hall, 4 Cal. 399, 405 (1854).
3. Schechter, "The Rightlessness of Mediaeval English Jewry," 45 *Jewish Q. Rev.,* 121, 135 (1954) quoting from M. Bateson, *Medieval England,* 139 (1904).
4. Dietrich v. Inhabitants of Northampton, 138 Mass. 14, 16 (1884).
5. *In re* Goddell, 39 Wisc. 232, 245 (1875).

Robert L. Arrington

The Economy/Environment Debate: A Wilderness of Questions

A mining company is accused of polluting a stream and thereby killing off its fish population. In defense of its actions the company claims that it was in conformity with all existing laws, that it already had taken extensive measures to control its pollution, and that any further efforts at eliminating the problem would be so costly as to threaten the company's continued existence and, along with it, the numerous jobs it provides for local residents. Such is a typical case in which the demand for environmental protection comes into conflict with economic needs. It is a type of case we have encountered with increasing frequency in recent years, and it poses moral and political problems of great urgency and difficulty. In this paper I shall attempt to define the dimensions of the issue, consider critically some of the proposed solutions, and offer very briefly what I consider to be the proper framework within which the problem may be resolved.

In trying to understand the conflict between environmental and economic needs, it is necessary from the beginning to grasp the complexity of the issue. There are two fundamentally different dimensions to the problem: on the one hand the factual dimension, while on the other the moral or normative dimension. Consider first the factual aspect. We need to know what in fact is the impact of business and the economy on the environment, and equally what the impact of pollution control will be on business and the economy. In asking for this information, we seek to ascertain the actual state of affairs that does or will exist, without passing judgment on whether the state of affairs is good or bad, or better or worse than some alternative. For example, to return to the instance of the mining company case, we need to know whether the operation of the mine is in fact the cause of pollution in the nearby stream. Can we be sure that something else did not cause it or contribute substantially to this effect? Once we have ascertained the cause or causes of the pollution, we need to inquire into its extent. And then another question arises: what will be the effects of this level of pollution? Does the pollution constitute a health hazard for the people in the area? Are the effects on the natural environment limited to the killing off of the fish population, or will this in turn trigger chemical and biological changes affecting the ecological balance in the area, the balance between the various elements of the environment? Could the upsetting of this balance have more far-ranging consequences for adjacent areas?

Here we have a series of factual questions that can in principle be answered by the natural sciences. Chemistry and biology should be able to provide us with the information needed concerning the basic physical changes involved. Unfortunately, however, we are dealing with a problem whose scope goes beyond that of the traditional scientific disciplines. A study of the impact that an environmental change in one area could have on a quite different area of nature goes beyond the expertise of the traditional disciplines and calls for a new mode of scientific inquiry—the science of ecology. Ecology is still in its infancy, and while its practitioners occasionally make dramatic predictions of widespread environmental disasters, they are able to offer little in the way of hard evidence. Moreover, many of the basic concepts of the new science are questionable. Ecologists like to speak of "balance" and "harmony" in nature, but it is difficult to know what these terms mean. How is one to measure balance and harmony? And are they necessarily desirable? Strictly speaking the latter question is improper if we are attempting to ascertain the facts in a neutral, scientific way. But insofar as ecologists often seem committed to the idea that balance is desirable, this calls into question their status as pure scientists. Given these problems, the task of getting at the environmental facts regarding pollution is not one inspiring optimism.

In addition to the facts about the impact of business practices on the environment, we need to inquire as well into the impact of pollution control on business. Will the mining company in our example really go broke if required to engage in further pollution control measures? Will it have to reduce the number of jobs it currently makes available to the community? Perhaps alternative modes of employment for these workers presently exist or could be developed. We need to know if this is the case. And will pollution control have only negative economic consequences for the mining company? Perhaps it will lead to a streamlining of operations or better community relations, both of which could lead to potential economic gains for the company. Moreover, we need to take into account the impact of further pollution control on the economy of the area as a whole. Such efforts may open up new jobs—in the pollution control business! Again there is the question of the impact on the national (and international) economy. The insolvency of this one coal mine might contribute to the eventual displacement of the coal industry as a supplier of energy and to a concomitant development of new, more efficient, inexpensive, and "pure" forms of energy. But looking at things from a different angle, the requirement that the company increase its control measures may well drive up the price of coal, thereby contributing to a local, national, and international inflationary spiral. Consequently, far more jobs might be lost than those provided in the local community by the coal company. Furthermore, in contributing to inflation, pollution control at the mine might well play a part in diminishing the quality of life for the entire culture.

How are we to find out the facts about the economic consequences of pollution control? Once again we have a science that should be able to help us out—the science of economics. But as everyone knows, except perhaps economists themselves, this science is far from perfect. Economists disagree over the proper theoretical analysis of the economy as well as over the course the future will take. Furthermore, the complexity of the economic environment is hardly less than that of the ecological environment. Recent events surrounding the oil policy of the Organization of Petroleum Exporting Countries (OPEC), for instance, have shown us how dependent any one nation is on the actions of other nations. What happens in Saudi Arabia could have an enormous impact on a coal mine in Tennessee, and vice versa. At this point in time, then, while it is true that the science of economics is more mature than that of ecology, its ability to provide us with the facts pertinent to the relationship between business and environmental pollution does not inspire great optimism.

So far we have been dealing with the factual dimensions of our problem. We have recognized the need to find out what the facts are, and we have also seen how difficult it is to accomplish this task. But there is, we must recall, another dimension to the conflict between business practices and environmental protection—what we have called the moral dimension. This is the normative, as opposed to the factual, aspect of our problem. Once we have ascertained what the facts are—should this ever occur—there still remains the job of evaluating these facts. Are the consequences of pollution and pollution control good or bad? Obviously, one might say, the effects of pollution are bad, but just how bad? And how bad are the effects of pollution control on the economy? What are the rights of businesses to pursue their activities so as to generate profits, and what are the limits to those rights? Here we encounter a host of questions asking, not how things are, but how they ought to be, not what people in fact want, but what it is good and proper for them to want. These are what philosophers call normative questions, and it is with respect to the normative issues arising from the conflict between economic and environmental needs that some of our most difficult problems emerge.

In dealing with these normative issues one of the things we first notice is that people differ radically as to how the issues should be resolved. There is disagreement, not just over the answers to specific questions, but also with respect to the basic evaluative categories or methodologies to be employed. In what follows I wish to consider two opposing evaluative approaches to the economy/environment debate. The first of these approaches, the cost-benefit analysis, is favored by most businesspeople and by some environmentalists. The second approach is taken by those environmentalists who argue that elements of the natural environment — mountains, trees, animals — have rights which should not be violated but that the spread of pollution threatens to violate. I shall refer to this as the rights-of-nature approach. I wish to depict the cost-benefit analysis model and the rights-of-nature model in their extreme versions, and to show the kinds of criticisms that may be brought against each.

The cost-benefit analysis model tells us that we should approach any normative question about what we should do or what it would be best to do by computing the costs and the benefits resulting from the different courses of action open to us. By first determining the cost of each possible action, and the benefits it would bring, we would be in a position to ascertain the overall surplus of the former over the latter or vice versa. After such an analysis has been done for each of the alternative actions, we are in a better position to single out that action yielding the greatest overall balance of benefits over costs. This action should be chosen because it is the best available option and therefore the one we have an obligation to pursue.

Such an approach is an application of a "businessperson's perspective" to the resolution of normative problems. Any time we seek the best course of action in a given context, the answer proposed by the cost-benefit model is one that maximizes profits or minimizes costs. The bottom line is what one should look to when attempting to resolve problems. It should come as no surprise, then, that most businesspeople who contemplate the economy/environment conflict attempt to resolve the issues by using a cost-benefit analysis. They want to know what the economic effects of pollution control will be. Their interests are focused only on the economic gain to be won if the controls are implemented. Such people take very seriously the potential costs of environmental protection: loss of jobs, inflation, and the like. They understand the need to clean up the environment in order to reduce health hazards, for these health hazards are themselves costs that become apparent in the loss of manpower hours. Businesspeople can understand the benefits that accrue from environmental protection when the benefits take the form of recreational facilities, a healthier work force, and so on. What they cannot understand is how one may reasonably be asked to engage in pollution control and other forms of environmental protection when the proposed benefits fail to outweigh the costs involved. They might agree that cleaning up the air by requiring emission controls on cars is a wise and prudent action, to a degree. But when the gains to be achieved in this area become increasingly small, while the costs of achieving cleaner air rise astronomically, then our businessperson rebels. At this point he will view the economic benefits resulting from a limited effort at pollution control to be greater than the economic benefits (minus their attendant costs) of pursuing perfection in this matter.

The use of the cost-benefit model, however, is by no means restricted to businesspeople. Many environmentalists also use it. They will point out that environmental protection brings about enormous economic benefits. There are the items already mentioned: the reduction of health hazards and the reduction of manpower losses resulting from health problems induced by pollution and other environmental problems. But the proponents of the environment may go further and point out that environmental protection generates a new pollution control industry, with its numerous additional jobs and profits. They insist that in calculating the costs and benefits involved in pollution control we must include the benefits that the economy derives from this control and also the costs to the economy that could result from not engaging in control. Hence, they urge, the problem of environmental protection should not be viewed simply as a conflict between the interests of business and the interests of others. They want to show that protecting the environment is, from the standpoint of a cost-benefit analysis, in the interest of everyone. They urge that when *all* the costs and benefits are entered into our calculations, we will see that pollution control and other protective devices are profitable for all of us.

There is another perspective, however, from which many environmentalists view the economy/environment conflict, one which is quite different from the cost-benefit model. Many environmentalists believe that we are under an obligation to protect the environment, not because it will bring benefits to us, but because a failure to do so would violate the rights of natural objects and creatures constituting the environment. Endangered species have a right to exist, these environmentalists argue, and this right to exist imposes on us an obligation or duty not to interfere with the exercise of this right. Likewise, some advocates will argue, wilderness areas, rain forests, and the like have a right to exist, and accordingly we have a duty to preserve them. Such environmentalists are deliberately extending the concept of a right to things previously not considered as having rights. They see this extension as analogous to the extension of rights to slaves, to blacks, to women, to fetuses, and so on. All living creatures, and indeed inorganic entities such as mountains, canyons, and waterfalls, are thought of as having rights to life or existence; it is only species chauvinism to suggest that human beings alone have these rights. To be sure, there are disagreements among these environmentalists as to which natural objects possess rights. Some argue that the concept of a right can only extend to animals, whereas others extend it to include plants, and still others seriously entertain the possibility that inorganic objects like mountains can be brought under the concept. Putting such disagreements and the issues they raise aside, all of these environmentalists agree that environmental protection should be seen as a series of measures to protect the rights of nonhuman inhabitants of the natural world.

It is important to see how radically different this conception of our normative problem is from that of the cost-benefit conception. The latter is interested only in what human beings will gain or lose in the conflict between economic and environmental needs. Human interests are the sole measure of value for this point of view. On the contrary, the rights-of-nature perspective views the "interests" of natural objects, animals, and plants as also constituting a measure of value. Even objects that are not conscious—plants and inorganic natural objects—are thought by some environmentalists to have interests in the sense that they can benefit from preservation measures; these objects can be conceived to have an inherent objective value unrelated to human interests, a value that can and should be supported and protected. That nonhuman objects have such interests or value is seen as the ground for ascribing rights to them. They have a right to the preservation of their interests and value, and we have a duty or obligation to protect that right. To have a right is to have a very important moral status: it is to have a moral entitlement or valid moral claim. To say that someone or something has a right is to say in effect that the exercise of this right must not be tampered with except for extremely important reasons. The status of a right establishes a presumption or prima facie case in favor of its exercise; it imposes on others a duty not to interfere with or prevent that exercise, other things being equal. Rights may indeed be overridden—as we all know, having the right to freedom of speech does not give one freedom to shout "fire" in a crowded theatre—but there must be some very good reason present for not permitting the exercise of a right, and the burden of proof is on the person who would prohibit this exercise. Hence attributing rights to the natural environment creates a very strong moral presumption in favor of preserving it, allowing its inhabitants to remain in existence, and not endangering the conditions under which they thrive. Attributing rights to the environment does not entail protecting it for our sake, but rather protecting it for its *own* sake. If animals and trees and mountains have rights, they have a moral status comparable (but not necessarily equal) to that of human beings; if they have rights, then we must respect them as having an inherent value and dignity. Other things being equal, it would be just as wrong to violate the rights of a tree as it would be to violate the rights of a human being. Even if other things are *not* equal—if, for example, the rights to life and security of human beings take precedent over those of trees, and human needs require that a forest be cut down—recognizing the rights of the trees will induce an attitude of respect toward them, which in all likelihood will lead to stricter limits being placed on such devastation than otherwise would be the case.

Advocates of the rights-of-nature approach to the environment are sensitive to the charge that attributing rights to nonhuman things and species is empty of meaning. They disagree with this charge, but they agree that it is a serious one that requires an answer. Admittedly, human and nonhuman beings differ in that human beings are able to claim and insist upon their rights whereas nonhuman beings are not. Trees do not protest when they are cut down, and the snail darter does not argue that it has the right to continue to exist. But this inability *to claim* rights is irrelevant to the question whether nonhuman beings *have* rights, according to the rights-of-nature advocates, who remind us that not all human beings who have rights are able to claim and demand them. Small children do not have this capacity, and many invalids do not. If one agrees that the human fetus has the right to life, then one also must admit that being able to claim a right is not a necessary condition for having it. In the cases of children, invalids, and fetuses, we appoint others to act in their interests, to represent them in insisting that their rights to be honored. Similarly, nonhuman creatures might have rights which they themselves do not claim but which others, acting in their interests, claim for them. Environmentalists of this school see themselves as doing exactly that—serving as the representatives of the inhabitants of the natural environment which are unable to speak for themselves.

Briefly, let us conjecture how cost-benefit advocates and rights-of-nature advocates would respond to the case in which the mining company is charged with polluting the nearby stream. The rights-of-nature theorists, at least those of the extreme variety, would most likely insist that the company completely clean up its pollutants, ridding the stream of all contaminants. They would base their case on the claim that the stream, the fish in it, and the surrounding natural environment all have a right to exist and to be undisturbed by man. Some cost-benefit analysts might agree with this conclusion, but not with the reasons given for it. They would defend further pollution control on the grounds that the human benefits derived from it justify the needed expenditures: the recreational potentialities of the wilderness area and the beauty it affords human observers would be two of these benefits, in addition, of course, to the health benefits supposedly derived from pollution control. Opponents of further control, such as the owners of the mine, probably would totally ignore the so-called rights of the nonhuman creatures involved. They would be concerned only with the interests of the human beings affected, and while they might agree that some few individuals might derive benefits in the way of recreational activities and aesthetic appreciation from further controls, they would argue that the costs of the controls would far exceed the benefits. Inflation, they would claim, affects everyone. To insist on further controls, thereby bankrupting the mining company, would cause severe hardships to those who would be unemployed as a result; these hardships alone more than override the recreational and aesthetic advantages. Add to these costs the additional hardship placed on the owners of the company and the resulting economic plight of the region, and the case is made for limiting further pollution controls—at least so say the cost-benefit advocates who oppose the environmentalists.

As everyone knows, this kind of debate has been going on for some time now, without any sign that it will be resolved decisively in favor of one party or the other. Rather than jump into such a debate and further defend one side or the other, the reasonable thing to do at this stage is to step back and assess the various normative approaches taken by the participants in the debate. As we will see, both the cost-benefit model and the rights-of-nature model have severe difficulties. Recognizing these difficulties may allow us to understand why the argument has gone on so long without resolution, and it may lead us to urge that the entire economy/environment debate be resolved in a different manner.

First let us consider some of the problems with the cost-benefit model. These problems fall into two broad categories: problems of measurement and problems of value comparison. The first set of difficulties has to do with the general problem of measuring what the costs and benefits of alternative policies and actions will be. The second set has to do with actually comparing and contrasting the different costs and benefits once they are identified.

The cost-benefit model recommends that we predict what the costs and benefits will be for the variety of actions open to us. Assuming that we can know all the options available to us (an assumption that surely can be doubted) the question of our ability to predict the consequences of our actions becomes paramount. We have seen the limitations of both ecology and economics with respect to their predictive powers. Are we really in a position to predict what the results would be of engaging in further pollution control at the mine we have discussed? Are we in any better position with respect to predicting what would happen if we stop further pollution control? A large degree of skepticism is called for here. But if ecology and economics are not able to tell us what the consequences of the alternative actions are, then how can we compute the costs and benefits involved? We must never forget that the costs and benefits of concern to us are those we foresee of the options open to us. Given the dismal state of our factual knowledge in this area, no one should have great confidence in a cost-benefit analysis of the problem.

In addition to this general difficulty regarding measurement, there are two more specific problems. First, how many of the consequences are we to take into account? It is easy enough to imagine that the consequences of any action are infinite in number. What Caesar did in ancient Rome affected the course of Christianity, which in turn affected the industrial revolution, which subsequently led to the current wars of our century, which will lead to a certain pattern of life in the next century, which in turn will help to produce whatever happens thereafter, and thereafter, and thereafter. If one set of consequences of an action, namely those in the immediate future, are relevant to its moral assessment, then why should not the consequences in the more distant future also be important? If my action today leads to a new world war ten years from now, shouldn't that fact be taken into account when calculating the costs and benefits to be derived from my acting in this way? But if future consequences are important, how far into the future are we to project? Obviously, the farther we go the more difficult it is to predict exactly what will happen. Hence the infinite expanse of consequences adds a theoretical difficulty to the task of predicting what the costs and benefits will be.

The second specific problem of measurement has to do with the fact that many different elements enter into the production or cause of an event. A student who attends a certain university does so as a result of the interaction of many causes: his natural interests and abilities, his parents' economic position, the influence that high school teachers and peers have had on his development, the accessibility of the university, and so on. Changing any one of these factors might result in his not attending this university. Likewise with respect to the question of pollution, many factors contribute to its cause, and many ways can be found to reduce it. It is obvious that the operations of the mining company described above do not constitute the sole cause of the ecological and economic consequences of the company's actions. The economic and legal structure of the community, for one thing, enters into the picture. One can imagine the owners of the mine suggesting that the community change its tax laws as a means of acquiring the necessary revenue to engage in pollution control without the threat of bankruptcy. Or the owners might urge that the community purchase new recreation areas for its citizens. Changes such as these would remove some aspects of the undesirable situation that presently exists. Just because the operations of the mining company are in some sense the "direct" cause of the pollution, it does not follow from a cost-benefit perspective that the company should be called on to change its ways. The change that should be recommended, from this perspective, is the one that produces the best overall surplus of benefits over costs. And when we are asked to measure the costs and benefits of the various actions open to us, we should remember that by changing any one of the vast number of factors leading to a desirable or undesirable result we would be engaging in different actions. But this means that the number of actions open to us and in need of assessment with respect to the costs and benefits involved is enormously large. Anything less than a complete assessment of all of them would amount to a compromise favoring some parties over others. But the more or less limitless set of possibilities involved in any particular case does not augur well for achieving a cost-benefit analysis that will be complete and accurate.

Earlier it was said that the cost-benefit model has difficulties with respect to value comparison; it is the age-old problem of comparing apples and oranges. Apples and oranges are different kinds of things, and in many respects it may be difficult to compare them. Apples have features that oranges do not, and vice versa, and whether one prefers an orange to an apple may depend on one's preference for certain of these features rather than others. To be sure, apples and oranges also have some features in common, and this may permit the choice of one over the other because the one chosen possesses more of, or a better instance of, the common feature than does the other. For a grocer, both apples and oranges have an economic value, and he may prefer oranges because they cost him less and sell for more. The grocer assigns a monetary value to both fruits, and having done so he can compute which of the two products will yield a greater profit for him. His accountant may agree with him, because the accountant also places a monetary value on the two fruits. But what if someone values oranges for their medicinal or religious value, regardless of the cost? This person might urge that oranges be made available to purchasers at an affordable price even if the grocer loses money on them. In doing so he would be appealing to a scale of values that emphasized matters of health or spirituality, and he would repudiate the monetary scale of values used by the grocer or at least relegate it to a lower level of significance. In such a case, will the grocer and the "oranges-for-health" advocate ever agree on the costs and benefits to be derived from the sale of oranges at a given price level?

A similar problem arises in the case of the economy/environment confrontation. A person who offers a cost-benefit analysis is likely to assign monetary values to the consequences of the various actions open to him. But there are other kinds of values embodied in these consequences—for instance, the value of health. From the businessperson's perspective, health does have a value, but only an economic one. From a different perspective, health may be seen as having a value in and of itself. For a person who adopts this latter perspective, one cannot compute the costs of pollution just by considering the monetary effects of different actions. Such a person may view the value of good health as being of an entirely different, and higher, order from that of monetary profits and losses. In this case we have a confrontation between two sets of values—health values and economic values—and we do not have a means of deciding between them. A cost-benefit analysis will work only when the same measure of value can be assigned to the different options so as to determine their comparative costs and benefits. The costs and benefits, in other words, must be computed on the same scale of value. When there is no common measure or scale of value—as there is not in the conflict between those who value health for its own sake and those who consider only economic profitability—there can be no bottom line figure to show us what we ought to do.

Let us now turn to some of the problems encountered by the rights-of-nature approach to the economy/environment conflict. Again, there are two basic kinds of problem to be faced. First, there are difficulties involved in determining what rights exist. Second, there are difficulties involved in limiting the rights of different parties when these rights come into conflict.

How do we know what rights are possessed by mountains, trees, and endangered species? Indeed, how do we know what rights human beings have? Philosophers have for centuries debated the question of the origin and foundation of human rights, and there still is no universally accepted answer to it. One answer that commands the respect of many is that human beings have rights to those conditions necessary for the development of a fully human existence and the values inherent in it. Hence, in addition to the right to life it is said that human beings have the right to freedom—without freedom, it is argued, one cannot exercise one's will and intelligence in such ways as to be fully human. This answer presupposes that we have a clear conception of what a fully human existence is; unfortunately, different people and cultures have divergent ideas on this score. Consequently, they find it difficult to agree on what rights human beings have.

But if there are problems of this sort with human beings, how much more difficult it is to determine the rights of nonhuman entities! What are the conditions necessary for the development of fully tree-like existence and the values inherent in it? What is it to be truly a mountain? The questions themselves seem senseless, and that means we have no idea how to answer them. How, then, are we to justify the claim that trees and mountains have rights?

It might be objected that there is no difficulty in acknowledging that all natural beings have the right to life or existence. However difficult it may be to know what else they have a right to, it is undeniable that they cannot flourish as things of their kind unless they exist. So, it is said, the right to life or existence can easily be demonstrated for all natural objects.

But even if we grant this, problems remain. If mountains have the right to existence, what does this require us to do with regard to them? Let us get at the problem here by posing an analogous question with regard to human beings. We believe that human beings have a right to life, but what does this entail? Perhaps we can all agree that having this right entails that we should never intentionally take another person's life. But does it also entail that we should provide people with whatever it takes to keep them alive? Do we have an obligation to prevent people from starving? It is debatable. And do we have an obligation to help people extend their lives by protecting them against disease, even at a very advanced age? Many would answer in the affirmative, but the issue is far from clear. Now consider some analogous questions with regard to the environment. If we grant natural objects in the environment a right to existence, this may mean that we should not deliberately destroy something like a lake or mountain, other things being equal. But what do we do about the natural erosion that eventually will destroy a mountain? What about the drought that dries up a lake? Are we to intervene against these natural causes in order to prevent such natural changes? It could be argued that to do so would be *to go against nature,* not to preserve it; to stand in the way of the fully natural development of lakes and mountains, not to promote this development. (In this regard, one can imagine someone arguing that to prevent disease, especially when it occurs late in life, is to stand in the way of nature taking its course in the case of human life.) It follows that even if we attribute the right to life to nonhuman entities, we are far from clear as to the actions to which we are thus committed.

But even the right not to have one's existence intentionally interfered with can be challenged. This can be illustrated by attending to the second problem faced by the rights-of-nature approach: the problem of limiting the exercise of rights that are in conflict with each other.

The classic case of being denied the right to shout "fire" in a crowded theatre shows how the exercise of one right, the right to freedom of speech, may be limited by another right, the right to personal safety and life. Unfortunately many of our rights come into conflict in this way. The right of a businessperson to sell his product to whomever he pleases comes into conflict with the right of any person to purchase goods at a place licensed to sell to the public. This conflict has been resolved in favor of the latter right, at least legally, but many such conflicts are not so easy to resolve. For some time now a debate has been raging over the difficult issue of whether a fetus has a right to life, and, if so, whether this right takes priority over the mother's right to control her own body. Many would admit that both the fetus and the mother have rights, but in numerous instances both of these rights cannot be honored. In an ideal world we would be able to exercise all of our rights, but in the world as we find it this is not the case. Rights establish a presumption in favor of noninterference, but this presumption may be overridden when a higher right is judged to come into conflict with it.

The economy/environment confrontation is an area in which many different rights come into opposition, both between human beings and between human beings and the environment. Even if we acknowledge that natural entities have a right to exist, this right may come into conflict with the rights of human beings, and we may decide that the latter have priority. Given the need for the intake of food, the right of human beings to life involves violating the right to life of those items in the environment which are consumed. Indeed, insofar as much of nature operates on the principle that one species provides food for another, a conflict of basic rights exists at the very heart of nature. And who is to say whether the right of human beings to a certain minimal level of comfort takes priority over the rights of natural entities to exist? Hence even if mountains, lakes, trees, and animals have the right to exist, it is unclear that this moral status justifies a restriction of human economic activities so as to protect these natural elements.

The conclusion we now must draw is that both the benefit-cost approach and the rights-of-nature approach have severe problems as means of resolving the normative problems we have encountered. What, then, is to be done? First, a few admissions. It has not been proved that neither a cost-benefit analysis nor the rights-of-nature approach can solve our difficulties. Nor has it been shown that no other normative approach exists that could be successful in this respect. Still and all, the problems with our two models are severe, and the likelihood of philosophers agreeing on remedies for them is small. Moreover, these are the major approaches used to deal with the normative disputes arising out of the economy/environment confrontation, and no other candidates are likely to appear in the immediate future. Realistically, then, we find ourselves faced with some severe and urgent normative problems and no favorable prospects for attaining a reliable procedure to resolve them. Thus we must face the issue of what is to be done here and now.

I recommend that the problem be treated in the same way we treat other normative conflicts arising in a pluralistic society, namely by opting for a democratic, political solution. Democracy is a way of dealing with the fact that people disagree and that there is no mutually acceptable decision procedure available for a rational, cognitive resolution of disagreements. People in a democracy will agree to disagree and allow the majority to prevail for the purpose of deciding what is to be done concerning matters of policy and social action. Democracy allows for input into the political process from all points of view; it encourages efforts to convince others of the rightness, using argument and persuasion, of one's position. While acknowledging that agreement based on arguments is unlikely, democracy provides a political solution to policy decisions. Although not the only way of dealing with normative conflict in a political manner — totalitarianism is another — democracy is unique in its capacity to combine a respect for rational arguments with an appreciation of their limits.

Parties to both sides of the economy/environment dispute may be reluctant to turn the issues over to the public for a democratic resolution. Those who believe in the rights of nature may feel that these rights ought not to be subjected to political control and compromise, just as many feel that the rights established in the Bill of Rights are properly beyond the reach of political manipulation. And businesspersons may feel that they have reason on their side when they argue that too much pollution control is simply bad business for all of us. They may feel that what is in the public's interest ought to be determined objectively — by use of cost-benefit analysis — and that it is irrational to put such questions to a vote. But we have seen the problems with both of these positions, and in the end the fairest and wisest means of resolving the dispute may well be to vote on it.

Corporate Policy Statements

Exxon's corporate objectives with respect to environmental conservation are: to assure that our operations and products do not create a significant hazard to public health and are compatible with the environmental, social and economic aspirations and needs of the community; to work in cooperation with outside groups toward a consensus on environmental quality standards which are desirable and attainable; to work actively with government groups to foster and encourage timely development of regulations, with regard to operations and product quality, that are needed to achieve desirable and attainable environmental standards; to adhere to all environmental standards and regulations which may be applicable to our business.

Exxon Corp.

As a matter of policy, no new U.S. Steel facility is built without the inclusion of the latest environmental control technology. . . . By far the largest percentage of U.S. Steel's environmental control investment has been made in providing controls for older facilities. Effective control has been either committed or established over practically all of U.S. Steel's operations, although some problems remain. The most difficult operation for control of emissions continues to be that of cokemaking, but even in this extremely complex area progress is being made. Because adequate technology to control coke oven emissions is not yet available, U.S. Steel has been heavily engaged in research studies to develop control systems. Ovei the past 10 years, U.S. Steel has mined about 174 million tons of coal, and only 3 percent of that total was obtained through strip mining methods. U.S. Steel is no longer engaged in coal stripping activities, although a portion of the coal lands which it owns or leases is being strip mined by others under contractual arrangements. When strip mining operations were being conducted, U.S. Steel complied with all applicable laws and, in fact, considerably exceeded legal requirements in many cases. Its land reclamation work, which involved grading the ground, seeding with fast-growing grasses and finally seeding or planting trees, has been the subject of laudatory articles in a number of publications. The contractual arrangements with others for stripping U.S. Steel coal require compliance with all applicable laws and regulations, as well as reclamation activities by the contractors in accordance with detailed specifications.

U.S. Steel Corp.

Selected Bibliography

Anderson, F. *Environmental Improvement Through Economic Incentives.* Baltimore: Johns Hopkins, 1977.

Barbour, I. *Technology, Environment, and Human Values.* New York: Draeger, 1980.

Barkley, P., and Seckler, D. *Economic Growth and Environmental Decay.* I w York: Harcourt Brace Jovanovich, 1972.

Baumal, W., and Oates, W. *Economics, Environmental Policy, and the Quality of Life.* Englewood Cliffs, N.J.: Prentice-Hall, 1979.

Blackstone, W., ed. *Philosophy and Environmental Crisis.* Athens: University of Georgia Press, 1974.

Brunner, D., Miller, W., and Stockholm, N., eds. *Corporations and the Environment: How Should Decisions Be Made?* Stanford, Cal.: Committee on Corporate Responsibility, 1981.

Chamberlain, N. *Enterprise and Environment.* New York: McGraw-Hill, 1968.

Dorfman, R., and Dorfman, N., eds. *Economics of the Environment.* New York: W. W. Norton, 1977.

Mills, E. *The Economics of Environmental Quality.* New York: W. W. Norton, 1978.

Mishan, E. *The Economic Growth Debate: An Assessment.* London: George Allen & Unwin, 1977.

Passmore, J. *Man's Responsibility for Nature.* New York: Charles Scribner's Sons, 1974.

Rogers, W. *Handbook on Environmental Law.* St. Paul, Mn.: West Publishing Co., 1977.

Scherer, D., and Attig, T., eds. *Ethics and the Environment.* Englewood Cliffs, N.J.: Prentice-Hall, 1983.

Velasquez, M. *Business Ethics.* Englewood Cliffs, N.J.: Prentice-Hall, 1982, ch. 5.

9

MULTINATIONAL CORPORATIONS

INTRODUCTION

Multinational corporations, those that produce and/or market goods in more than one country, pose a host of ethical problems. Should a multinational have one conflict of interest policy and one employee rights policy applicable transnationally, or should these be tailored to the business climate in different countries? How much profit should be repatriated to the country where the firm is headquartered, and how much should be reinvested in the host country? Should products sold be uniform across national boundaries, e.g., should drugs be marketed abroad that do not meet Food and Drug Administration (FDA) safety standards in the U.S.? Should American firms be allowed to operate in countries that are ruled by repressive governments?

Discussion of these issues is complicated by the fact that there is no effective organization for policing multinational operations. In any specific country, laws can be passed to curb practices judged to be immoral and detrimental to society, but critics charge that the absence of a transnational legal body and enforcement mechanism invites multinationals to sidestep moral issues and operate in a purely egoistic fashion.

The case study in this chapter addresses a specific issue, investment in South Africa. Although many American businesspersons believe it is not their task to try to change the policy of foreign governments, it is reasonable to believe that most American businesspersons do not approve of apartheid. Many U.S. multinationals operating in South Africa have adopted the Sullivan principles, which commit them to ending apartheid in their firms. These firms argue that their continued presence in South Africa provides a model for other firms to follow; that the slow progress in ending apartheid is in part due to the U.S. firms' presence; and that U.S. withdrawal would have disutility for South Africa's non-whites. Critics, such as Tim Smith, argue that apartheid violates fundamental human rights, and that the continued presence of U.S. firms only serves to support this tragic state of affairs. Smith believes that U.S. firms should withdraw from South Africa. The aim of multinationals in South Africa, Smith says, "is to do business, not to bring about social changes." Critics claim that the Sullivan principles are essentially window dressing, and furthermore, even if they were effective the firms implementing them would still pay taxes to, and hence support, a government that is committed to apartheid.

Multinationals in South Africa

A Dialogue on Investment in South Africa

The following is a discussion between a critic of corporate investment policies in South Africa (X) and a corporate spokesperson (Y).

X: You will agree, won't you, that apartheid—the separation of races in South Africa—is an immoral policy? A policy that gives 17 percent of the people 87 percent of the land—almost all the good farm land and mineral properties—that forces blacks who work in white areas to be migrant workers subject to "pass" laws, that precludes blacks from organizing unions or political parties, that provides only minimal education for blacks, and that strictly controls the press, is simply an evil policy.

Y: I certainly agree. Don't try to cast me as a defender of apartheid.

X: Well, business is part of the power structure in South Africa, and the power structure supports apartheid. Business isn't trying to change the *status quo*. It uses the cheap labor, and pays the taxes that support apartheid.

Y: Business, especially foreign-owned businesses, cannot write a nation's laws. Critics of multinationals often say that they interfere too much in foreign countries; then in other cases they say companies are not doing enough to force change.

X: But apartheid is so blatantly immoral.

Y: Agreed. But no American firm directly supports apartheid. Most U.S. firms have adopted the Sullivan principles, which commit them to end segregation and improve living conditions for non-whites. Signators are committed to fair employment practices, equal pay for equal work, initiation of training programs for non-whites and promotion programs leading to management slots, and improvement of the quality of employees' lives in the areas of housing, transportation, education, recreation, and health facilities.

X: Most of this is just window-dressing. As American multinationals began getting a lot of heat for being in South Africa, they saw they could use Sullivan's code as a buffer against criticism.

Y: That may be true in some cases, but the code has had an impact. There has been considerable progress in the desegregation of work facilities, in training programs, and in employee housing. Less visible, but still significant, progress is being made in recruitment and promotion.

X: The actual results are skimpy. General Motors had four salaried Africans in 1978 out of 1,100 salaried employees. In 1979 it added four more. And you don't really think the whites will allow blacks to supervise whites in South Africa, do you? Also, the wage gap between blacks and whites is actually growing. You can have a commitment to equal pay for equal work, but it doesn't mean much if blacks aren't given much of a chance to get supervisory positions. Nothing less than a full-blown affirmative action program will reverse the situation. But the government won't allow it. It's flatly illegal.

Y: The Sullivan principles were only initiated in 1977; these things don't happen overnight. But let me cite some cases where progress has been made. Firestone now has 50 blacks in white collar positions. CPC has over 10 percent black managers. Coca-Cola is moving toward a target of 95 percent black employees by 1988. Goodyear has moved over 100 blacks into slots formerly held by whites. It is true that most U.S. firms do not have formal affirmative action programs, but these are cases where in deed, if not in word, companies are moving in that direction. The wage gap is a puzzling thing. The wages for blacks were 37 percent of the wages for whites in 1974, and in 1980 they were 60 percent. But the gap between the two increased from 218 rand per month to 270 rand. Nobody expects that gap to be closed soon, but it will probably be closed some over time.

X: I doubt that. The earnings gap has expanded from 218 to 270 rand per month, but the discretionary income gap increased from 108 to 189 rand per month because the government has seen to it that price inflation has occurred largely in essential consumer goods, and these goods take a far higher percent of the income of blacks than that of whites. You see, here's where we disagree. You say American firms should stay in South Africa because of the premise of the Sullivan principles. I say the principles are not working and will not work, even in the long run, because the South African government is deeply committed to apartheid. The government will never let the Sullivan principles be fully implemented. But even if the principles were acted upon by U.S. firms, that doesn't mean they would be adopted by French, Japanese, or South African firms. Given the climate in South Africa, the firm that adopted the principles would probably be at a competitive disadvantage. And even if all U.S. firms actually implemented the principles, their tax dollars would still be used to support apartheid. These minor changes in U.S. managed firms do not alter the reality of racial discrimination.

Y: Of course, we're not happy with the use of tax dollars to support apartheid. We would rather not pay taxes at all—but they are a reality of doing business anywhere in the world. American multinationals could withdraw but, realistically, what would it accomplish? It would probably have a greater negative impact on blacks than on whites. Some whites would lose their jobs, but since U.S. firms employ more blacks than whites, more blacks would lose their jobs. It is estimated that about 60,000 blacks would lose their jobs. If each worker supports a family of five, about 300,000 people would be directly affected. Of course, other foreign multinationals, along with South African firms, would close the gap by picking up business if U.S. firms withdraw; since these firms will probably not be committed to the Sullivan code, the net effect would most likely be detrimental to blacks. Furthermore, when you talk about apartheid, and say that taxes on American multinationals support it, you must also keep in mind that compliance with the Sullivan code does place U.S. firms in violation of several South African laws. The Factories Act and the Shops and Offices Act, for example, require racially designated signs on toilets, but the Sullivan principles require firms to "remove all race designation signs." Most American firms have complied with the Sullivan code. The Apprenticeship Act establishes committees, comprised equally of industry representatives and white union representatives, to approve apprenticeship training. As a result, almost all apprenticeship training of blacks has been restricted to their homelands where resources are very limited. The Sullivan principles commit U.S. firms to "initiate and expand inside training programs and facilities." Some progress is visible. Ford, for example, had no African apprentices in 1975. By 1978 it had increased its training expenses by 140 percent to over $1 million, $700 thousand of which went for black workers. It had 19 black apprentices by 1978, and 40 by 1981. Now all of this is illegal. But it certainly will expand, and it encourages the breakdown of apartheid.

X: You seem to just assume that U.S. firms are more progressive than other foreign multinationals, or South African firms for that matter. But the evidence isn't all that clear. The government will wink at certain practices, as in the Sullivan principles, but only because doing so keeps U.S. firms in South Africa, and keeping them there furthers the government's long-range goals of racial separation and white dominance. Also, you're off target when you claim that U.S. withdrawal wouldn't accomplish much; it could have a major impact. Six foreign oil firms, including Shell, Mobil, Texaco, and Socal, control 85 percent of South Africa's petroleum market. U.S. firms control three of the country's four major refineries. In 1977, U.S. firms controlled 70 percent of the computer market. American firms play major roles in the mining, electrical, and motor industries. Withdrawal would certainly damage the South African economy.

Y: Some, but withdrawal doesn't mean you pack up your oil refinery and ship it back to the U.S. Due to South African laws you can: (1) sell your holding to (a) a non-South African firm, or (b) a South African firm, or (2) scale down your assets, by repairing instead of replacing machinery, until your assets can be written off. Under foreign exchange laws, on option (2) you lose about 30 percent of any allowable repatriated assets. Option (1) just transfers the assets. Furthermore, there really isn't much technology transfer. In only about half of the American subsidiaries in South Africa is the managing director American. The other half are South Africans. Where you have an American director, it's probable that he's the only American in the subsidiary; most of the rest of top management is South African.

X: Okay, but you would cut them off from the benefits of U.S. research, since not much research and development (R&D) work on new products is done by U.S. firms in South Africa.

Y: True, but foreign multinationals—the British, French, German and Japanese companies—will make the fruits of their R&D work available to the South Africans.

X: You still cannot deny the dominance of the U.S. in areas such as computers and telecommunications. I allow there would be some asset and profit loss to American firms who would withdraw. But the South African market is rather small; the loss wouldn't be great for IBM or Mobil. And when that small loss is compared with the major evil of apartheid, and you factor in that profits now earned support apartheid via taxes paid, the moral issue is clear. In fact, I don't think withdrawal is enough; the U.S. government should impose sanctions on South Africa, and argue for international sanctions in the U.N.

Y: Well, the U.S. has imposed some sanctions. In 1976, sales of U.S. computers to South African governmental departments were curtailed. There are restrictions on U.S. Export-Import Bank resources. Since 1978 the U.S. has curbed sales to the South African military and police. But look at the results. In 1973, IBM held 56 percent of the mainframe computer market in South Africa. By 1978 its market share dropped to 30 percent—largely due to U.S. sanctions. Britain's ICL corporation has been the major benefactor. The U.S. sanctions were attempts to comply with U.N. resolutions of 1963 and 1977 regarding arms exports to South Africa. But foreign multinationals just step in and replace American firms. The British, in particular, have a heavy investment; their export-import trade with South Africa is much more significant than ours. Business with South Africa accounts for only .24 percent of our Gross National Product. So you cannot realistically expect sanctions to be accepted internationally. In other cases the South Africans themselves have picked up the business. The Arab oil producers have embargoed oil sales to South Africa since 1973. Worried that other countries would follow suit, the South Africans built plants to convert their immense coal reserves to oil. While it is true that foreign companies own the bulk of the oil refinery and distribution facilities in South Africa, the country now only needs oil to supply 20 percent of its energy requirements. It is also developing nuclear power capabilities.

X: I just can't believe the 5 million white South Africans are supermen who can develop a modern civilization on their own. They simply must have outside support, especially in the area of high technology. And to constantly argue that if we don't provide it someone else will removes us from the moral sphere altogether. This is a moral issue. Just because others are either unable to recognize the immorality of their acts or unwilling to stop acts they recognize to be immoral, it doesn't follow that we should adopt a "me too" attitude.

Y: I agree that it is a moral issue. But I agree with former U.N. Ambassador Andrew Young when he spoke to South African businesspersons in 1977: "When in Atlanta, Georgia, five banks decided it was bad for business to have racial turmoil, racial turmoil ceased." He added that "100 businesses negotiated an end of apartheid (in the U.S.), in spite of the fact that on the books of law it was still illegal to desegregate anything." U.S. businesses can and will make a moral difference in South Africa; but they can't if they're not there.

X: The analogy is not too persuasive. There never was a fear in the U.S. that blacks would dominate either the economic or political spheres.

For Discussion

In your opinion who got the best of this argument from a moral point of view, X or Y? Explain your answer. What additional considerations can be advanced to support X's viewpoint? Can anything more be said to support Y's viewpoint? What moral position would you adopt on this issue? Explain in detail.

SOURCES

Corporations in South Africa (N.Y.: Praeger, 1977); Clyde Ferguson and William Cotter, "South Africa: What Is To Be Done?" *Foreign Affairs,* vol. 56, no. 2 (Jan., 1978), pp. 253-74; "Restrictions on Exports to Namibia and the Republic of South Africa," Export Administration Bulletin No. 175, U.S. Department of Commerce (Feb. 16, 1978); William McWhirter, "America's South African Dilemma," *Time,* vol. 112, no. 12 (Sept. 18, 1978), pp. 64-68; Roger M. Williams, "American Business Should Stay in South Africa," *Saturday Review* (Sept. 30, 1978), pp. 14-21; Richard Leonard, *Computers in South Africa: A Survey of U.S. Companies* (N.Y. The Africa Fund, 1978); Arndt Spandau, *Economic Boycott Against South Africa: Normative and Factual Issues* (Johannesburg: Univ. of Witwatersrand, 1978); Desaix Meyers, *U.S. Business in South Africa* (Bloomington: Indiana Univ. Press, 1980).

The Case for Staying in South Africa

American business recognizes broad social responsibilities both to its employees and the larger community in which it operates, even though its paramount responsibility is to produce goods and services so efficiently that they thereby earn profits for shareholders. This is as true for corporations abroad as in the United States, and many businessmen are deeply concerned about the complex moral issues that exist in relation to the mandatory classification of races in South Africa. But the points that follow are based on the premise that U.S. business, by remaining in South Africa, directly assists its black employees and can help build a climate within which desired social changes can be implemented:

(1) *American business can contribute directly to the economic and educational advancement of Black South Africans.* Many American companies are taking a leading role in upgrading the economic and social status of their employees in South Africa. Economic growth itself has mandated the utilization of increasing numbers of Blacks (used herein collectively to include coloreds and Indians as well as Black Africans) in ever higher skill categories. Equal pay for equal work is becoming an ever more common practice among U.S. firms and job reservation is being eroded (it only applied to around two percent of all jobs in any event). White trade unions in South Africa seem increasingly willing to have Blacks join in the general prosperity in the society and Blacks may, in the near future, join the unions themselves. Real Black wages in South Africa have shown substantial improvement

From *Business and Society Review,* 15 (Fall 1975), 62–64. Copyright © 1975. Reprinted by permission of *Business and Society Review.*

over the past decades, especially in the modern manufacturing sector — where most U.S. companies operate. U.S. firms are also taking the lead in new educational programs for Black employees and their families. High educational levels can enhance the leadership capacity in the Black community and make more meaningful the internal dialogue of white and Black South Africans on the future directions of that society.

There are, in fact, many things within South African law and custom that U.S. companies are doing to upgrade the economic well-being of Black employees. These include equal pay for equal work; wage increases; job training schemes; more rapid promotions; educational programs for children of employees; improved pension, life, health, and disability insurance programs; housing subsidies; medical care; transportation support; and many others.

(2) *If U.S. firms were to withdraw, the greatest losers would be the local employees of U.S. companies.* Those who would be most hurt by U.S. withdrawal are Black employees who run the risk, should the operation actually close, of losing their jobs. That would not only have devastating consequences for family income (since it is not that easy for Black South Africans to find alternative employment) but would raise the risk of such people being "endorsed out" of the urban areas and sent to remote rural areas called "bantustans" or "homelands" which, in many cases, they have never before seen. Even if an operation did not close, it is not certain that its current employees would be retained by new business management or that their wage and other benefits would be maintained at current levels.

(3) *Large numbers of Black South Africans appear to want U.S. firms to stay and upgrade their employment practices.* The expression of Black views in South Africa is severely restricted. Without a regular political voice, it is impossible to know for certain what Black South Africans really want U.S. firms to do. Certainly there are articulate Black voices advocating withdrawal. But there are other strong Black voices favoring continued U.S. business operations in South Africa, and it is the uniform experience of American businessmen who visit South Africa that nearly all Blacks with whom they talk — both employees and others — want U.S. companies to stay. Similarly, influential Americans with knowledge of South Africa and its Black majority favor constructive involvement in South Africa rather than disengagement.

These include the Panel of the United Nations Association on Southern Africa; the Rev. William Creighton, presiding Bishop of the Episcopal Church in Washington; Congressman Charles Diggs, Chairman of the Subcommittee on Africa of the House Committee on Foreign Affairs; and Roy Wilkins, Executive Director of the NAACP.

(4) *Economic advances can lead to other meaningful changes in the society as a whole.* The advocates of U.S. business withdrawal sometimes

argue that if Black living standards fall, internal pressure against the current systems will build past the breaking point. This is debatable. It is based on conjecture concerning the internal dynamics within South Africa among Black South Africans and between Black and white South Africans that are impossible for outsiders to understand fully. Rising prosperity may accelerate the demand for, and eventually lead to, important changes in the society as a whole for Black South Africans. Such demands may be more forcefully made in periods of rising economic power than during periods of decline, as the recent strikes in Durban indicated. As Blacks get more and better jobs, their power in the South African economy increases and this may result in greater political power.

(5) *The return on American investment in South Africa is good but not extraordinary.* Critics of American business in South Africa sometimes argue that U.S. companies make huge profits because of the low wage levels paid Blacks. The return on investment for individual companies varies tremendously but the average in 1970 was 18 percent of book value. This is certainly a healthy profit margin but not all that unusual when compared with other U.S. foreign investment. For example, U.S. investment in Africa *outside* of South Africa during 1970 averaged a 26 percent rate of return—eight percent higher than in South Africa, itself.

Profits of some manufacturing firms in South Africa are, in fact, kept low because of the limited size of the South African market. Consequently, economies of scale are not often possible because of the relatively small market served.

Much of the criticism about wage rates in South Africa focuses on the mining industry. But only about 10 percent of U.S. investment is in mining, while the balance is in manufacturing, petroleum, and other industries where wages are generally a good deal higher. Increasing numbers of U.S. firms now pay wages that are considerably better than their South African and foreign competition.

(6) *Withdrawal by U.S. firms would not seriously damage the South African economy.* The South African economy is extremely strong and growing more so each year. U.S. business investment constitutes only approximately 14 percent of foreign investment in South Africa (and a much smaller percentage of total investment), while Britain accounts for around 60 percent of foreign capital. If U.S. firms were to withdraw, their operations would most likely be taken over and operated—either by South African or by foreign firms from other countries. Because the United States accounts for such a small percentage of foreign investment in South Africa, and since South Africa, itself, now generates enormous sums of domestic capital, even total U.S. withdrawal would be unlikely to have a severe or lasting impact on the South African economy.

In addition, it is highly unlikely that the South African government would simply allow U.S. companies to "withdraw," take the dollar value of their investment, and return to the U.S. More likely the South African Government would seize the operation and prohibit the repatriation of any rands the U.S. company might acquire in the process.

In short, while it might be theoretically possible for a concerted world-wide investment and trade boycott directed at South Africa, if vigorously enforced, to have a substantial impact on the South African economy, unilateral action by only U.S. firms would have no such important consequences. World-wide economic action against South Africa is extremely unlikely. Britain, with the largest investment and trade relations, shows no signs of changing its policy toward South Africa.

(7) *Even if South Africa's economy were damaged, this would not necessarily produce positive change.* It is impossible to know what would happen even if the South African economy were severely retarded as a result of coordinated foreign economic pressure. Initially, at least, Blacks would be the most severely hurt; and whether the South African Government would change its internal policies in order to placate the foreign economic community is open to serious doubt. The opposite would be more likely to occur in order to satisfy local political reactions from the conservative white community. Experience in some other countries that have been subjected to boycotts indicates that more repressive internal policies often result.

(8) *U.S. foreign policy should be made by the U.S. Government and not by U.S. business.* It is improper for U.S. business to try to influence government changes abroad. This is as inappropriate in South Africa as it is in Chile or Nigeria. Occasionally, economic boycotts or other restrictions on business activity have been used by the U.S. Government as an instrument of our foreign policy. The long economic isolation of China and Cuba would be two good examples; but there is a growing consensus which holds that normal diplomatic, cultural and business relationships can be a more effective force for change than any attempt at economic isolation. U.S. firms *are* currently prohibited by our government from selling military equipment to South Africa, Angola, or Mozambique, and new business investment in Namibia (South-West Africa) is now officially discouraged. But U.S. firms must *follow* the U.S. Government lead in such matters. U.S. business itself should not try to make U.S. foreign policy.

Current U.S. policy neither encourages nor discourages U.S. investment in South Africa and consequently, except with respect to military sales, U.S. firms are free to invest in that country so long as South Africa welcomes such investment. A change in that policy should be initiated, if at all, by the State Department, not unilaterally by individual American companies.

(9) *We should not try to impose our system on others.* Very few countries abroad share all of the characteristics of the political and constitutional

system of the United States and it is wrong for American businessmen or citizens to insist that they change to conform to our own images of what an appropriate governmental system is. Although business should not and cannot be insensitive to clear cases of injustice and discrimination within any foreign society where it operates, the power of business to alleviate such injustices is basically limited to its own employees. Only to a very minor degree does foreign business have power to fight injustices in the community at large, and then only by contributing to legal organizations within the foreign country working to correct such problems.

(10) *Gradual change seems possible in South Africa and disengagement would probably most damage the efforts of those working within South Africa for progress.* It is unlikely that isolation of South Africa will accelerate the process of internal progress toward fuller economic and political rights for South Africa's Black majority. Many argue that it is the example of the outside world that most needs to be brought to the attention of those in South Africa resisting meaningful change. It is the policy of the U.S. Government to encourage and extend such contacts and communication, and U.S. business involvement is one way to further that process.

Higher wages, status, and job opportunities should result in an increase in Black dignity and self-confidence, and U.S. firms can contribute importantly in this area. Withdrawal would probably have no practical impact on either helping the South African Blacks or in helping bring about desirable change. It would, for some, be an important symbolic action in the sense that U.S. business would no longer be accused of "supporting" an undesirable system. But it is highly doubtful that withdrawal would have any tangible impact on changing that system for the better—indeed, the opposite result might follow.

Tim Smith

South Africa: The Churches vs. the Corporations

Are corporate investors in white-ruled southern Africa accomplices in apartheid and oppression or are they forces for change? Over the last decade, U.S. investment in southern Africa has been a subject of vigorous debate within Congress, churches, unions, universities, the black community, and, of course, corporations themselves.

In the mid-1960s, national church bodies began to realize that they were substantial shareholders in U.S. corporations with investments in southern Africa. This led them to research the roles these firms played there. Their findings stunned them. The pattern of American corporate involvement was one of unquestioning complicity in apartheid and colonialism. Church investors began a series of campaigns pressing U.S. corporations to face the social and political implications of investing in white-ruled Africa.

The face of southern Africa has changed dramatically since the mid-1960s. After more than a decade of armed insurrection, Mozambique is independent and Angola, another Portuguese colony, is promised independence November 11. White Rhodesia, which is under a United Nations-sponsored economic boycott, faces growing international isolation and strong internal opposition from Africans. There are rumors that Namibia (South-West Africa), which is illegally occupied by South Africa, may be given independence in the near future.

The "winds of change" are blowing over Africa again and black majority rule is marching south. It is conceivable that South Africa will soon be ringed with independent black states, making it extremely vulnerable to infiltration. The South African government, which recently increased its defense budget fifty percent, has a simple objective: to maintain white rule of the country.

South Africa is notorious for its system of apartheid — separation of the races. Whites are a distinct minority, only 17 percent of South Africa's 25 million people. Compared to the 4.2 million whites, there are 17.7 million Africans, 2.3 million "coloreds," (mixed bloods) and 700,000 Asians.

Nonwhites in South Africa are rightless persons in the land of their birth. Coloreds and Asians suffer discrimination in every walk of life; for example, they cannot own land or hold a job supervising whites. But the situation of Africans is even worse.

The government's goal is to assign all Africans to reservations, or bantustans, which comprise 13 percent of the land. Outside bantustans, Africans are treated as foreigners or "migratory labor units." He — or she — has no rights in "white areas." He cannot vote, cannot own land, and may not have his family with him unless he has government permission. Indeed, in order to limit the number of Africans living in the cities, wives and children are frequently not allowed to follow their husbands and fathers to the cities. If an African loses his job, he must return to a bantustan. At all times he must carry an internal passport, called a passbook, properly stamped or face prosecution.

To control the black majority, the government has also enacted stringent laws governing political activity. The government has the authority to arrest and indefinitely detain persons suspected of political crimes. The two major black political parties have been banned and hundreds of persons detained for political offenses.

Africans provide 55 percent of the manufacturing labor force and 88 percent of the work force in the mines, but strikes by Africans are illegal, and meaningful collective bargaining is outlawed. All facilities in plants are racially segregated, and all the best jobs are set aside for whites.

The impact of these restrictions is reflected in the grinding poverty of the black population. Two-thirds of all Africans in industrial areas live beneath the starvation line. For whites, South Africa is a land of sun and prosperity. For blacks, it is a land of poverty and exploitation.

In South Africa, business finds social stability born of repression, cheap labor, and a very comfortable rate of profit, averaging a 17 percent return on investment. These factors help explain why 350 American companies have flocked to that country, investing $1.2 billion in all.

Churches have been examining the role these companies play in South Africa to see whether they are "partners in apartheid" or catalysts for change.

Since the early 1970s, over two dozen U.S. firms have received a variety of stockholder resolutions from churches requesting, for example, reports disclosing details of their South African operations; establishment of a committee to review these operations; an end of sales to the South African government; and complete withdrawal from the country. These resolutions have pressed for information about starvation wages, poor working conditions, inadequate grievance procedures for workers, company contracts with the government and their bolstering of apartheid.

The beauty of a shareholder resolution is that at company expense the issue to be voted on is sent to all shareholders and thus alerts them to a problem. Numerous institutional investors, including universities, foundations, insurance companies, and pension funds, have written letters to management supporting the churches' resolutions and have voted their shares in favor of them.

In all, twenty companies have prepared a special report on their investments in South Africa and either have sent it to shareholders or will mail it on request. These firms are:

(1) General Motors	(11) Weyerhaeuser
(2) Ford	(12) Colgate-Palmolive
(3) Chrysler	(13) 3M
(4) Mobil	(14) Pfizer
(5) Union Carbide	(15) Eastman Kodak
(6) International Harvester	(16) Caterpillar
(7) IBM	(17) ITT
(8) Burroughs	(18) General Electric
(9) First National City Bank	(19) Caltex
(10) AMAX	(20) Xerox

The churches object to the role of American corporations in South Africa on various grounds:

By investing in South Africa, American companies inevitably strengthen the status quo of white supremacy. American firms have invested in key sectors of the South African economy: autos, rubber, oil, banking, electronics. They pay taxes to the white government to use as it sees fit. They sign contracts with the white government which serve its purposes—e.g., General Motors sells trucks to the South African armed forces. From a historical vantage point, foreign capital has played an important part in the economic development of South Africa and in the consolidation of white power.

As U.S. companies explain, they operate in South Africa at the sufferance and under the laws of the white government. Therefore, they must operate without unduly offending that government. Their aim is to do business, not to bring about social change.

The government, of course, directs and manages the economy with its interests in mind. U.S. investors automatically become part of the economic game plan of the government, as they do in any country. For example, the South African government is engaged in an urgent search for oil, aided by U.S. firms, including Mobil and Caltex. The search is motivated by the country's lack of self-sufficiency in oil, a political and economic liability.

U.S. companies thus become allies of the South African government in fulfilling its political and economic goals.

An investor cannot be neutral in South Africa. The leasing of a computer, the establishment of a new plant, the selling of supplies to the military—all have political overtones. One cannot escape politics in South Africa. And among the country's white community, the overriding goal of politics is maintenance of white control. In the words of Prime Minister John Vorster during the 1970 election campaign: "We are building a nation for whites only. Black people are entitled to political rights but only over their own people—not my people."

American investments in South Africa create a U.S. vested interest in the status quo. Washington defends its cordial relationship with South Africa on the grounds of the favorable balance of trade. State Department officials acknowledge that the more than one billion dollars of U.S. investments in South Africa inevitably affects our diplomatic stance and our policy toward that country.

U.S. firms will work to protect their interests in white southern Africa. For instance, when Union Carbide and Foote Mineral Co. found international economic sanctions blocking them from importing chrome from Rhodesia, they lobbied vigorously in Congress to open U.S. doors to Rhodesian chrome. At the very time that the U.N., African nations, and the African National Council of Rhodesia (a grass-roots movement of Rhodesian blacks) were calling for increased sanctions against a weakened Rhodesian regime, these companies, purporting to know what was best for Africans, urged the breaking of sanctions. This was a classic example of conflict between the vested interest of U.S. corporations and the interests of millions of Africans. The same thing could easily happen in South Africa.

American firms, in using public relations to justify their presence in South Africa, portray that country in a positive light, bolstering the white government's international prestige in the process. American corporations portray South Africa as open to change and reform. Through press releases, mailings to shareholders, public statements, and the like, companies depict their involvement in South Africa as assisting change and bettering conditions for blacks. They are supposedly contributing to an economic growth that inevitably will help Africans. The facts, however, do not back up such arguments.

The idea that business plays a progressive role is seductive. As British economist John Sackur has said, the argument for change through economic expansion provides for both "the prospect of change and the satisfaction of moral qualms at absolutely no cost to anybody." Unfortunately, the premises upon which the argument is based conform neither to the historical reality of economic development under apartheid, nor to a realistic assessment of power relationships and the nature of social change.

In 1960, thousands of South African blacks protested peacefully against the hated passbook laws. At Sharpeville, police opened fire, killing or wounding more than 100 demonstrators. Fearing the country was on the brink of rebellion, many foreign companies left South Africa. However, in a year's time investors had regained confidence, and in the fifteen years since the Sharpeville massacre, U.S. investment in South Africa has boomed. Presumably, we should be able to detect during this period of rapid economic growth the trends which are supposedly at work cracking apartheid. In fact, however, political repression of blacks has grown since 1960, and the wage gap between blacks and whites has widened.

This is not to deny that a small fraction of the nonwhite majority (mostly coloreds and Asians) have filtered into some semiskilled jobs to help meet the needs of an increasingly specialized economy. This small group has benefited from the boom in the white economy. But there certainly has been no real improvement for the black population overall.

The United States pays a political price for corporate investments in South Africa. It is losing much prestige and goodwill in the Third World among nations which view it as putting profits above human welfare. Why jeopardize future African markets by continued investment in South Africa?

For that matter, business itself may come to regret investing in South Africa. Already, major investors are paying a heavy cost in public relations. Growing public scrutiny and controversy in the United States are apt to make the high profits earned in South Africa less enticing in the future. Most American firms with investments in South Africa do only a small portion of their business there. It is the U.S. market (including the black market) that counts, and it would be a mistake to risk losing part of it because of operations in South Africa.

To sum up the view of the churches, U.S. corporations are not neutral in South Africa. They help arm the military forces which stand behind apartheid; they influence U.S. foreign policy to favor white South Africa; and they exploit cheap black labor. They profit from apartheid. Africans take the practices of U.S. corporations as indicating American ideals and values; therefore the entire American system symbolically participates in apartheid.

GETTING BIG OIL OUT OF NAMIBIA

The most successful church challenge to date has been the campaign against U.S. oil company investments off the coast of Namibia (South-West Africa). After a three-year effort by several national church organizations working through the Church Project on U.S. Investments in South Africa, five oil giants decided to withdraw from Namibia. Between November 1974 and January 1975, Continental Oil, Phillips Petroleum, and Getty, comprising one consortium, and Texaco and Standard Oil of California, partners in a second venture, announced they would pull out. Today, no U.S. oil company is in Namibia.

The churches first raised the issue of Namibia in 1972, filing stockholder resolutions with Continental Oil and Phillips, and later with Getty and

Standard Oil of California. The resolutions called for withdrawal from Namibia while it was illegally occupied by South Africa. In addition, the churches held lengthy conversations with Continental Oil and Texaco, bringing stacks of documents to back up their case. It seemed that the churches had done more homework on the implications of investing in Namibia than the companies themselves. Generally, the initial decisions by the five oil companies to explore for oil off the coast of Namibia had been taken without even a sketchy study of the country's political situation. Geological data had been the determining factor in deciding to look for oil there. Of course, the contracts permitting exploration were signed by the South African government, the occupying power.

The churches raised several arguments against the investment: The illegality of the occupation was stressed and the oppression of the Namibian people described. The churches pointed out that any investment gives support to South Africa's illegal policy. And if oil were found, South Africa's interest in retaining control would increase.

However, it is unlikely that humanitarian arguments carried much weight in corporate board rooms. But the question of who legally governed Namibia did seem to trouble the oil companies. Both the International Court of Justice and the United Nations had called on South Africa to give Namibia its independence. The U.N. had recognized the Council for Namibia as the legal government of the country. The Security Council had asked all nations to cease any acts which would legitimize South Africa's occupation. The churches argued that investment by the oil companies was just such an act.

Another important factor seemed to be the U.S. Government policy of discouraging investment in Namibia. Church critics were able to argue that such investments flaunted U.S. policy as well as the U.N.'s position. SoCal's representative specifically mentioned the U.S. position on Namibia in explaining the company's withdrawal. He also speculated that the South African government would be unable to do the drilling itself and that other oil companies were unlikely to move in to take SoCal's place. He added that SoCal would not return until the political situation was clarified.

Another factor may have been the decree on natural resources, issued by the Council for Namibia, declaring that investment in Namibia without the Council's approval was illegal and that without it the exploitation of Namibian resources was virtual theft.

Not mentioned by any of the companies was the sizable shareholder vote the church resolutions urging withdrawal had received. Investors such as the Ford and Carnegie foundations, Aetna Life Insurance, and Princeton, Harvard, and Yale all supported the proposal. At Continental Oil, one vote in ten went against management, and at Phillips, in 1974, the vote was close to 6 percent in favor of the resolution. While these may not seem like many votes, in the world of largely uncritical shareholders they verge on a minor investor revolt.

Finally, a number of companies invoked standard business logic, arguing that there were other places of higher priority to spend exploration money. Nonetheless, all the companies admitted the signs of oil were good off Namibia.

While it is virtually impossible to analyze what effect three years of religious campaigning had, clearly the points the churches brought to the companies' attention became factors which they had to weigh in deciding whether to stay in Namibia. If the churches did nothing more than make management look at the realities of southern Africa and examine their part in lending legitimacy to the occupation of Namibia, they would still have a significant accomplishment to their credit.

The last five years have seen a noticeable increase in Christian activism directed against corporate investment in southern Africa. This activism is likely to continue to grow as long as U.S. corporations continue to support white minority rule. The role of U.S. companies in southern Africa will come under increasing scrutiny and more widespread stockholder challenge in the years ahead.

SELECTED BIBLIOGRAPHY

Barnet, R., and Mueller, R. *Global Reach: The Power of Multinational Corporations.* New York: Simon and Schuster, 1974.

Bowie, N. "When in Rome, Should You Do as the Romans Do?" in *Ethical Theory and Business.* 2nd ed. Beauchamp, T., and Bowie, N., eds. Englewood Cliffs, N.J.: Prentice-Hall, 1983, pp. 276-279.

De George, R. *Business Ethics.* New York: Macmillan, 1982, ch. 14.

Eells, R. *Global Corporations.* London: Collier Macmillan, 1972.

Elbinger, L. "Are Sullivan's Principles Folly in South Africa?" *Business and Society Review,* 30 (Summer, 1979), 34-40.

Kindleberger, C. *American Business Abroad.* New Haven: Yale University Press, 1969.

Lemon, A. *Apartheid: A Geography of Separation.* Westmead, England: Saxon House, 1976.

Meyers, D. *U.S. Business in South Africa: The Economic, Political, and Moral Issues.* Bloomington: Indiana University Press, 1980.

Musiker, R. *South Africa.* Santa Barbara, Cal.: Clio, 1979.

Schmidt, E. *Decoding Corporate Camouflage.* Washington, D.C.: Institute for Policy Studies, 1980.

Schwamm, H., and Germidis, D. *Codes of Conduct for Multinational Companies: Issues and Positions.* Brussels: European Centre for Study and Information on Multinational Corporations, 1977.

Seidman, A., and Seidman, N. *South Africa and U.S. Multinational Corporations.* Westport, Conn.: Lawrence Hill, 1978.

Tugendhat, C. *The Multinationals.* New York: Random House, 1972.

Turner, L. *Multinational Companies and the Third World.* New York: Hill and Wang, 1973.

United Nations Department of Economic and Social Affairs, *Multinational Corporations in World Development.* New York: United Nations, 1973.

Vernon, R. *Storm Over the Multinationals.* Cambridge, Mass.: Harvard University Press, 1977.